THE POTATO FACTORY

Bryce Courtenay is the bestselling author of *The Power of One*, *Tandia*, *April Fool's Day*, *The Potato Factory*, *Tommo & Hawk*, *Jessica*, *Solomon's Song*, *A Recipe for Dreaming*, *The Family Frying Pan*, *The Night Country*, *Smoky Joe's Café*, *Four Fires*, *Matthew Flinders' Cat*, *Brother Fish*, *Whitethorn*, *Sylvia*, *The Persimmon Tree* and *Fishing for Stars*.

The Power of One is also available in an edition for younger readers, and *Jessica* has been made into an award-winning television miniseries.

Bryce Courtenay lives in the Southern Highlands, New South Wales.

Further information about the
author may be found at
brycecourtenay.com

Bryce Courtenay

THE POTATO FACTORY

PENGUIN BOOKS

PENGUIN BOOKS

Published by the Penguin Group
Penguin Group (Australia)
250 Camberwell Road, Camberwell, Victoria 3124, Australia
(a division of Pearson Australia Group Pty Ltd)
Penguin Group (USA) Inc.
375 Hudson Street, New York, New York 10014, USA
Penguin Group (Canada)
90 Eglinton Avenue East, Suite 700, Toronto, ON M4P 2Y3, Canada
(a division of Pearson Penguin Canada Inc.)
Penguin Books Ltd
80 Strand, London WC2R 0RL, England
Penguin Ireland
25 St Stephen's Green, Dublin 2, Ireland
(a division of Penguin Books Ltd)
Penguin Books India Pvt Ltd
11 Community Centre, Panchsheel Park, New Delhi-110 017, India
Penguin Group (NZ)
67 Apollo Drive, Rosedale, North Shore 0632, New Zealand
(a division of Pearson New Zealand Ltd)
Penguin Books (South Africa) (Pty) Ltd
24 Sturdee Avenue, Rosebank, Johannesburg 2196, South Africa

Penguin Books Ltd, Registered Offices: 80 Strand, London, WC2R 0RL, England

First published by William Heinemann Australia, 1995
First published by Penguin Books Australia Ltd, 1997
This edition published by Penguin Group (Australia), 2006

5 7 9 8 6 4

Copyright © Bryce Courtenay 1995

The moral right of the author has been asserted

Cover design by Debra Billson © Penguin Group (Australia)
Cover photographs by Andrea Kuehn/Getty Images and Hulton Collection/Getty Images
Typeset in 10/12.5 pt Sabon by Midland Typesetters, Maryborough, Victoria
Printed and bound in Australia by McPherson's Printing Group, Maryborough, Victoria

National Library of Australia
Cataloguing-in-Publication data:

Courtenay, Bryce, 1933– .
The potato factory.
ISBN 978 0 14 300456 1.
1. Convicts – Tasmania – Fiction. 2. Criminals – England – London – Fiction.
3. London (England) – Social conditions – 19th century – Fiction.
4. Tasmania – Social conditions – 1803–1900 – Fiction. I. Title.

A823.3

penguin.com.au

For my beloved wife, Benita, who always
had absolute faith and never failed to
wrap it in abundant love.

ACKNOWLEDGMENTS

The first thing a writer learns is that real life contains far more coincidence than any he or she will ever be allowed to get away with in a fictional plot. Life is simply stranger than fiction. Almost at a glance any daily newspaper carries examples of character and plot well beyond the imagination of the boldest of fiction writers. Good, historical fiction may be said to be fact that went undiscovered at the time it happened and the historical novel is the writer's ability to dig deep enough to find some of the truth as it was at the time. To help me do this a lot of people gave generously of their knowledge, intelligence and time. Without them there could be no book. While they may appear below only as a list of names in alphabetical order, I count myself most fortunate to have known them all, for they are the fuel which fed the fire of my fiction.

Louise Adler, Jennifer Byrne, Adrian Collette, Benita Courtenay, David Daintree, Owen Denmeade, Margaret Gee, Alex Hamill, Jill Hickson, Elspeth Hope-Johnstone AM, Rabbi J.S. Levy, Dr Irwin Light, Larry Lyme, Essie Moses, Libby Mercer, Ross Penman, Roger Rigby, Jeff Rigby, Irene Shaffer, Michael Sprod, Paula Teague, Barbara and John Tooth. There are others who helped in smaller though no less important ways and I am grateful to you all.

There are always one or two people who need to be singled out for special mention, My editor Belinda Byrne qualifies as the star at the top of the tree, closely followed by Dr John Tooth and Paul Buddee AM. Also my publishers, Reed, who chewed their collective fingernails but kept their patience and their expletives to themselves when my manuscript was well past its promised deadline.

I thank you all.

I acknowledge and recommend Phillip Tardiff's book, *Notorious Strumpets* and *Dangerous Girls: Convict Women in Van Diemen's Land, 1903–1829*, as an important piece of scholarship and a valuable source of information on the transportation of female convicts to Tasmania.

Finally, I acknowledge my gratitude to all those writers and historians past and present who go before me; they are too numerous to mention and too wonderful for words.

PREFACE

Some people are bound to argue that this book is the truth thinly disguised as fiction and others will say I got it quite wrong. Both sides may well be correct.

That Ikey Solomon existed and was perhaps the most notorious English criminal of his day is not in dispute, and wherever possible I have observed the chronology of his life and that of his wife, Hannah, and their children. That Charles Dickens based the character Fagin in his novel *Oliver Twist* on Ikey Solomon is a romantic notion which I much prefer to believe. But the moment I allow him and all the characters in this book to speak for themselves I have created a fiction of the fact of their historical existence. By every definition this is therefore a work of fiction.

In reading it I ask you to take into account the time in which my story occurs, the first half of the nineteenth century. In these more enlightened times this book may be regarded as anti-Semitic; in the terms of the times in which it is written, it is an accurate account of the prevailing attitudes to the Jews of England.

These were dark times, bleak times, hard times, times where a poor man's life was regarded as less valuable than that of a pig, a poor Jew's far less valuable even than that. That Ikey Solomon's life could have happened as it did in fact, allows my fiction to exploit the ability of the human spirit to transcend the vile tyranny of which humankind has proved so consistently capable. In these terms Ikey Solomon was a real-life hero and my fiction cannot possibly do him justice.

In history there are no solitary dreams;
one dreamer breathes life into the next.

Sebastiao Salgado

Be This a Warning!

This little work is held up as a warning
beacon to keep the traveller from the
sands of a poisonous desert, or from
splitting upon the rocks of infamy.

It is necessary in such a case to point
out 'hells' and brothels, girls and bawds,
and rogues, by name and situation, not
as a direction for youth to steer towards
them, but that he may take the contrary
course – for no reasonable man would
enter a whirlpool, when he could pass
by it on the smooth surface o'
the reaches of a tranquil river crossing.

The life of Ikey Solomon is filled with
iniquitous adventure; he has acted with the
rope round his neck for twenty years,
but by his cunning always avoided being
drawn up to the beam, where he is
likely to end his infamous career.

We are duty bound to hold him up as a
depraved villain, whose conduct must
disgust, and whose miseries, with all his
wealth, will show how preferable a life
of honesty and poverty is to a guilty
conscience, and treasure gained by blood
and rapine.

From *Ikey Solomon, Swindler, Forger,*
Fencer & Brothel Keeper, 1829

BOOK ONE

London

Chapter One

Ikey Solomon was so entirely a Londoner that he was a human part of the great metropolis, a jigsawed brick that fitted into no other place. He was mixed into that mouldy mortar, an ingredient in the slime and smutch of its rat-infested dockside hovels and verminous netherkens. He was a part of its smogged countenance and the dark, cold mannerisms of the ancient city itself. He was contained within the clinging mud and the evil-smelling putrilage. Ikey was as natural a part of the chaffering, quarrelling humanity who lived in the rookeries among the slaughterhouses, cesspools and tanneries as anyone ever born in the square mile known to be the heartbeat of London Town.

Ikey was completely insensitive to his surroundings, his nose not affronted by the miasma which hung like a thin, dirty cloud at the level of the rooftops. This effluvian smog rose from the open sewers, known as the Venice of drains, which carried a thick soup of human excrement into the Thames. It mixed with the fumes produced by the fat-boilers, fell-mongers, glue-renderers, tripe-scrapers and dog-skinners, to mention but a few of the stench-makers, to make London's atmosphere the foulest-smelling place for the congregation of humans on earth.

The burial ground in Clare Market was full to the point where gravediggers would be up to their knees in rotting flesh as they crammed more bodies into graves. Corpses piled on top of each other often broke through the ground emitting noxious gases, so that the stench of rotting bodies was always present in nearby Drury Lane.

Since infanthood Ikey had grown accustomed to the bloated effluence of the river and the fetidity that pervaded St Giles, Whitechapel, Shoreditch, Spitalfields and the surrounding rookeries. His very nature was fired, hammered and hardened within this hell which was the part of London he called home.

Ikey Solomon was the worst kind of villain, though in respectable company and in the magistrates' courts and the assizes he passed himself off as a small-time jeweller, a maker of wedding rings and paste and garnet brooches for what was at that time described as the respectable poor. But the poor, in those areas of misery after Waterloo, had trouble enough scraping together the means to bring a plate of boiled potatoes or toasted herrings to the table. If Ikey had depended for his livelihood on their desire for knick-knackery, his family would have been poorly served indeed.

In reality he was a fence, a most notorious receiver of stolen goods, one known to every skilled thief and member of the dangerous classes in London. In Liverpool, Manchester and Birmingham young pickpockets, footpads, snakesmen and the like referred to him in awed and reverent tones as the Prince of Fences.

Ikey Solomon was not a man to love, there was too

much the natural cockroach about him, a creature to be found only in the dark and dirty corners of life. It might be said that Ikey's mistress loved him, though she, herself, may have found this conclusion difficult to formulate, love being a word not easily associated with Ikey. Mary wasn't Ikey's wife, nor yet his mistress, perhaps something in between, an attachment for which there is not yet a suitable name.

The doubtful honour of being Ikey's wife was reserved for Hannah, a woman of a most terrible disposition who did little to conceal her dislike for her husband. Such acrimonious sentiments as were commonly expressed by Hannah were usually forbidden to a woman, who was expected to accept with a high degree of stoicism her husband's peregrinations in life. A woman, after all, had no rights to carp or pout at the results of her partner's misfortunes. Nor decry his errors in judgment or his lack of moral rectitude but share the good, silently accept the bad and hope always for the best, which is the female's natural lot in life, though if this was ever made plain to Hannah, it had not sunk in too well.

Moreover, setting aside for a moment what might be considered formal filial duty, Hannah had a good case against Ikey. Their children also were on her side, both puzzled and somewhat ashamed of the curious man they took to be their father.

If Ikey understood the duties of a father he chose never to exercise them. To his children during the hours of daylight he was a dark, huddled, sleeping bundle wrapped in a large, extremely dirty coat from which protruded at one end strands of matted grey hair surrounding a mottled bald dome. Looking downwards, first there was a thick hedge of unkempt eyebrow and then a nose too long for the thin face from which it grew. Still further downwards in the area of the chin grew an untidy tangle of salt and pepper beard, thick in some parts and in others wispy, all of it most uneven and ratty in appearance.

From the other end of the greasy coat stuck a pair of long, narrow, yellow boots, their sharp snouts concertinaed inwards and pointed upwards. These boots were never seen to leave his feet and to the curious eyes of his children their dented snouts seemed to act as sniffing devices. With the first whiff of danger they would jerk Ikey from the horizontal into a wide-awake seated position, their snouted ends testing the air like truffle pigs, quickly establishing the direction from whence the danger came. Whereupon, Ikey's boots would become in appearance two yellow cockroaches, plant themselves firmly on the ground, then scuttle him away into some dark, safe corner.

Ikey was also a series of daylight noises to his children. A cumulation of slack-jawed snoring and wet spittle sounds issued constantly from a mouth clustered with large yellow and black teeth. Several appeared to be broken or missing, worn down by the gnashing and grinding of a torturous sleep which came to an end precisely at six-thirty of the clock in the evening.

At night Ikey's children, hugging each other for moral support, would watch wide-eyed from dark corners as he shuffled about the house, sniffing, snorting and whimpering as though expecting somehow to find it changed for the worse during his sleep. If Ikey should come across a clutch of children he would halt and stare momentarily as though curious to who they might be.

'Good!' he'd snort at them and shuffle away still sniffing and whimpering as he carried on with his inspection of the premises.

At seven of the clock precisely, the Irish woman who looked after the children in Hannah's absence would place in front of him a mutton and potato stew with a thick wedge of batter pudding. He'd eat alone in the skullery, his only implement a long, sharp pointed knife with which he'd stab a potato or a fatty piece of mutton and feed it into his mouth. Then, when the solid contents of the bowl were disposed of, he used the batter pudding to soak up the broth, polishing the bowl clean with the greasy crust.

Ikey's evening meal never varied. Neither beef nor fowl ever replaced the greasy mutton, and he would complete his repast with a bowl of curds swallowed in one long continuous gulp which made his Adam's apple bounce in an alarming fashion. Milk with meat was not kosher and Ikey, who had a regular seat in the Duke's Place synagogue, was a good Jew in all but this respect. With his hands, first the left and then the right, he'd wipe the remains of the frothy curd from his lips then run both greasy palms down either side of his coat, this action bringing scant improvement to either.

At this point the children listening at the door would strain their ears for the various oleaginous noises coming from his stomach. They'd hold their breath for the magnificence of the burp they knew must surely follow and the horrendous fart which would cap it, a single explosion which signalled the end of Ikey's repast.

His evening meal over, Ikey picked his teeth with a long, dirty fingernail. He would then take up Hannah's ledger and repair to his study. Before he unlocked the door he would pause and look furtively about him, then enter and immediately lock it, restoring the brass key to somewhere within the interior of his overcoat.

Ikey would light the two oil lamps in his study to reveal a smallish room thick with accumulated dust except within the precinct of his writing desk. This he kept pristine, the quill and blacking pot neatly lined up, a tablet of evenly stacked butcher's paper to the right.

Ikey would then take a cheap imitation hunter from the interior of his coat and lay the watch together with Hannah's ledger upon the desk. He then removed his coat and waistcoat, leaving him standing in his dirty woollen undershirt. The coat and waistcoat he hung upon the coat-stand, one peg of which already contained his flat-topped broad-brimmed hat. Then moving to one corner of the room, he sank to his knees and, in turn, pushed four knot-holes contained in the floorboards. These immediately sprang up an inch or so at one end, whereupon Ikey carefully removed the nails from the holes. He lifted the floorboards to reveal a small dry cellar no deeper than four feet and filled with ledgers. Ikey removed three and carefully clicked the sprung floorboards back into place, positioning the nails in the holes in which they belonged. He then crossed to his desk, placed the ledgers down, seated himself on the high stool and lit the lamp which hung directly above his head. Seated quiet as a mouse, he worked until midnight.

Precisely ten minutes later, the time it took to tidy his desk, return the ledgers to the cavity beneath the floorboards, get into his coat, fix his hat upon his head, douse the lamps, lock the door to the study, take Hannah's ledger back to the pantry and place it in the sack

containing potatoes and leave the house, he slid furtively from a half-closed front door into the passing
night.

Ikey wore his great coat buttoned tightly with the
collar pulled high so that it wrapped around his ears.
He pulled his hat down low across his brow and hardly
any part of him was visible as he moved along, the hem
of his thick woollen coat inches from the scuffed and
dented caps of his scuttling yellow boots.

The irony was that Ikey's entire identity was revealed
in his very self-concealment – his wrapping and scuttling, chin tucked in, head turned around at every half
a dozen steps, dark eyes darting, as though seen through
a brass letterbox slot; the crab-like sideways movement,
stopping, sniffing, arms deep into the pockets of his
great coat, instinctively seeking for a wall to sidle
against, so that the shoulders of the coat were worn
with scuffing against brick and rough stone.

These mannerisms clearly identified him to the street
urchins and general low-life who used their rapacious
eyes for observing the comings and goings of everyone
they might prey upon. If Ikey had completely disrobed
and walked, bold as a butcher's boy, in broad daylight,
whistling among the stalls in the Whitechapel markets,
this would have been a more complete disguise.

Perhaps the broad daylight aspect of such a disguise
would have been the most effective part of it, for light
in any form was repugnant to Ikey who, like Hannah,
was nocturnal. Both were involved in duties best completed well after sunset, and before sunrise.

Ikey would be out and about after midnight, sniffing
for business in the thieves' kitchens, netherkens and
chop houses in the surrounding rookeries, while

Hannah was the mistress of several bawdy houses which traded best as the night wore on.

Hannah had been born a beautiful child and lost none of her fine looks as she grew into a young woman, but then the pox had struck. Unable to restrain herself she had scratched at the scabs until the blood ran, leaving her pretty face and pubescent breasts badly and permanently pocked.

From childhood Hannah had imagined herself away from the hell of Whitechapel and occupying a small residence in Chelsea. She would be a courtesan, exquisitely perfumed and coiffured, dressed in fashionable gowns of shot silk. She would wear diamonds from Amsterdam and pearls from the South Seas which, naturally, were the grateful gifts of the young gentlemen officers of the Guards, the Blues and no other, or of the older, though equally handsome, titled members of the Tattersall Club. She would be seen at the opera and the theatre and remarked upon for her extraordinary beauty. Wherever Hannah went young swells and flash-men on the randy would evoke her name as one might a princess, knowing her to be beyond the reach of their impecunious pockets, dreaming of a windfall which might cause such unfortunate circumstances to be overturned.

Instead the dreadful scars had caused her to become a barmaid at the Blue Anchor in Petticoat Lane. Here her pretty figure and large blue eyes could have earned her a handsome enough living as a part-time prostitute, but the idea was repugnant to her. She was not prepared to deny her previous expectations to work on her back as a common whore.

Hannah's bitterness had left her moody and recalcitrant and the young men who paid her attention soon dwindled. Her tongue was too acerbic and her expectations too high for their aspirations or resources. Quite early in her pock-marked life she had conceived of the idea of owning a high-class brothel. She saw this as her only chance of resurrecting the original dream to associate with the better classes in dress and mannerisms, if not in respectability.

So she cast her eyes about for a likely patron. Perhaps an older man easily pleased with her generous hips and big breasts whose needs, after his nightly libation, were seldom onerous, satisfied after a half-dozen grunts and jerks whereupon he would fall back exhausted onto his duckdown pillow to snore and snort like the fat pig he undoubtedly was.

When Ikey, who at the age of twenty-one was already coming on as a notorious magsman and was thought not without spare silver jiggling in his pockets, came along, his very repulsiveness made him attractive to her. True, he was not elderly nor yet rich, but young, clever and careful, his dark eyes always darting. Appearing suddenly at the door of the Blue Anchor, he scanned the patrons, his eyes sucking in the human contents of the room before he entered. Hannah could sense that he was greedy, secretive, a coward and moreover he made no advances of a sexual nature during his pathetic attempt at courtship. What she had expected to find in an older man she now found in Ikey. Ikey would be her ticket to glory, the means by which she would achieve the remnants of her earlier ambition.

They were married in London in 1807 in the Great Synagogue at Duke's Place with all the trappings and regalia of the Jewish faith. It was a bitterly cold January morning, but it was well known that a morning ceremony was less costly and Hannah's father, a coachmaster, was not inclined to waste a farthing even on his family. If, by a little thought and negotiation, a small extra sum could be saved for ratting, the sport on which he chose to gamble most of his earnings, so much the better.

Hannah and Ikey were a well-suited couple in some respects and they shared a thousand crimes and ten thousand ill-gotten gains in their subsequent life together. As a consequence they became very wealthy, though Hannah had not achieved her ambition to mix with the male members of the best of society and be seen in the gilded boxes of the opera and theatre. Instead her bawdy houses were frequented by lascars and Chinese and black seamen from North Africa, the Indies and the Cape of Good Hope, and of course all the scum from the English dangerous classes. Panders, crimps, bullies, petty touts, bimbos, perverts, sharpers, catamites, sodomites and unspecified riff-raff, as well as the famine Irish with their emaciated looks and long thick swollen dicks. They were more in need of a feed than a broken-down tart, robbing their families of what little they had to boast of fornication with a poxy English whore.

Ikey counted himself fortunate to have found a wife as avaricious and morally corrupt as himself, yet one who could play the prim and proper lady when called upon to do so. Upon their marriage Hannah had adopted the demeanour in public of a woman of the highest moral rectitude with the strait-laced, scrubbed and honest appearance of a Methodist preacher's wife. This was only when she was in the presence of her betters and as practice for a time to come when, she told herself, she would run the most exclusive brothel in London Town.

Ikey's success as a fence had precluded such an establishment, designed, as it would be, to cater for the
amorous needs of the better classes. It would be too
public and draw too much attention. Hannah had reluctantly and temporarily put her ambitions aside. Instead,
by working at the lowest end of the sex market, she
often proved to be a useful adjunct to Ikey's fencing
business.

This subjugation to her husband's needs did not come
about from loyalty to him, but rather from simple
greed. Ikey had been successful beyond her wildest
expectations. Hannah began to see how she might one
day escape to America or Australia, where she could set
up as a woman of means and attain a position in society
befitting her role as a wealthy widow with two beautiful
daughters and four handsome sons, all eligible to be
married into the best local families. It had always been
quite clear in Hannah's mind that Ikey would not be a
witness to her eventual triumph over the ugly scars
which had so cruelly spoiled her face and with it, her
fortune.

In the intervening period, Hannah felt that she had
sound control of her husband. Her sharp and poisonous
tongue kept him defensive and it was as much in her
natural demeanour to act the bully as it was for Ikey to
be a coward. She prodded him with insults and stung
him with rude remarks as to his appearance. Ikey was
constantly shamed in her presence. He knew he possessed no useful outside disguise to fool his fellow man
and he greatly admired this propensity in her, who
added further to his infatuation by giving him six children and proving his miserable, worthless and reluctant
seed accountable.

Moreover, Hannah had gratified him still further, for none of his children had inherited any onerous part of his physiognomy and all took their looks strongly from her. She claimed that Ikey's puerile seed had been overwhelmed by her own splendid fecundity and, as he had no confident reason to doubt that this was true, he was grateful that she brought an end to his line of unfortunate looks. Hannah, who so clearly held Ikey in her thrall, had no cause whatsoever to suspect him capable of dalliance with another. The thought of a Mary or any other such female coming into Ikey's life was beyond even Hannah's considerable imagination or lack of trust in her husband.

Chapter Two

Temper and charm, it was these two contradictions in Mary's personality which were the cause of constant problems in her life. She showed the world a disarming and lovely smile until crossed. Then she could become a spitting tiger with anger enough to conquer any fear she might have or regard to her own prudent behaviour. In a servant girl, where mildness of manner and meek acceptance were the characteristics of a good domestic, Mary's often fiery disposition and sense of injustice were ill suited. However, without her temper – the pepper and vinegar in her soul – it is unlikely that she would have captured Ikey's unprepossessing heart.

Mary was the child of a silkweaver mother and a sometimes employed Dutch shipping clerk. She grew up in Spitalfields in pious poverty brought about by the decline in the silk and shipping trades in the years following Waterloo. Mary's consumptive mother was dying a slow death from overwork. Her despairing and defeated father sought solace in too frequent attention to the bottle. At the tender age of five Mary had learned to hawk her mother's meagre wares in nearby Rosemary Lane and to defend them from stock buzzers and the like. She quickly learned that a child faced with danger who screams, kicks, bites and scratches survives better than one given over to tears, though it should be noted that she was of a naturally sunny disposition and her temper was spent as quickly as it arrived.

Mary was also the possessor of a most curious gift. Although she could take to the task of reading and writing no better than a ten-year-old from the more tutored classes, she could calculate numbers and work columns of figures with a most astonishing rapidity and accuracy well beyond the ability of the most skilled bookkeeping clerk.

This ability had come about in a curious manner. Her father, Johannes Klerk, a name he'd amended simply to John Klerk when he'd come to England, had wanted Mary to be a boy and so instead of learning the art of silkweaving, as would have been the expected thing for a girl child to do, he had taught her the ways of figuring on an abacus. He learned this skill as a young man when he'd spent time as a shipping agent's clerk in the Dutch East Indies.

He had first come across the rapid clack-clack-clacking of beads sliding on elegant slender wire runners in Batavia. To his mortification, the framed contraption being used by the Chinee clerks in the spice warehouses soon proved superior in making calculations to his most ardent application by means of quill and blacking. Johannes Klerk soon learned that he could never hope to defeat the speed of their heathen calculations and so he determined to learn for himself the ancient art of the Chinese abacus. This curious skill, never developed to a very high aptitude in John Klerk, together with a few elementary lessons in reading and writing, was his sole inheritance to his daughter.

As an infant, the bright red and black beads had enchanted Mary and by the age of six she had grasped the true purpose of the colourful grid of wooden counters. By ten she had developed a propensity for calculation that left the shipping clerks at her father's sometime places of employment slack-jawed at her proficiency with numbers.

Alas, it was a skill which her family's poverty seldom required. But this did not discourage Mary, who practised until her fingers flew in a blur and her mind raced ahead of the brilliant lacquered beads. Despite her father's attempts to obtain a position for her as an apprentice clerk in one of the merchant warehouses on the docks, no such establishment would countenance a child who played with heathen beads. Added to this indignity, God had clearly indicated in his holy scriptures that those of her sex were not possessed of brain sufficient to work with numbers, and her ability to do so just as clearly indicated a madness within her.

When Mary was eleven, she was entered into domestic service by her father, her consumptive mother having died two years previously. John Klerk passed away not long after he'd secured employment for his daughter; he was a victim of a minor cholera epidemic which struck in the East India Docks.

Mary found herself quite alone in the world as a junior scullery maid in a large house where she was to begin what became a career, the outcome of which was determined more often by her fiery disposition than her maidenly demeanour.

Mary was popular among the below-stairs servants,

well liked for her cheery disposition and bold intelligence, but her quick temper at some injustice shown to those unable to come to their own defence got her into constant hot water. She would inevitably alienate the cook or under-butler or coachman, those most terrible senior snobs in most households, who would thereafter wait for an opportunity to bring her undone. As a consequence Mary's career as a domestic servant was always somewhat tenuous.

At fifteen Mary was promoted above stairs, where she was a bedroom maid who would sometimes assist as lady's maid to her mistress. Her lively intelligence made her popular with her mistress, who felt she showed great promise as a future lady's maid. That is, until an incident occurred with a lady of grand title from Dorset, a weekend guest to the London house of her mistress to whom Mary was assigned as lady's maid.

Mary was most surprised when the very large duchess took her by the wrist after she had delivered her breakfast tray to her bed.

'Come into bed with me, m'dear. You will be well rewarded, now there's a dear. Come, my little cherub, and I promise you will learn one or two useful little things in the process!'

Whereupon the duchess, visibly panting with excitement, had pulled Mary off her feet so that she fell onto the bed across her large bosom.

'Oh I do hope you are a virgin, a nice little virgin for mummy!' the duchess exclaimed, planting several kisses on top of Mary's head.

Mary, a product of the Spitalfields rookery, wasn't easily given over to panic. She simply attempted to pull away from the fat duchess. Whereupon the huge woman, thinking this most coquettish, locked her arms about her and smothered her in further wet kisses. At this point Mary lost her temper. 'Lemme go, you old cow!' she gasped, still not taken to panicking at the mixture of sweet-smelling rouge and foul, dyspeptic breath which assailed her senses.

The duchess, much larger and stronger than the young servant girl, clasped her tighter so that Mary found her face smothered in heaving breasts and thought she might at any moment suffocate. She was no match for the strength of the duchess even though she fought like a tiger to break free.

'Such a silver tongue! Oh, you are a fiery little maid-ikins! A plump little partridge and all of it for mummy!'

With one huge arm the duchess continued to pin Mary down and with the other attempted to remove her bodice.

'Come now, darling,' she panted, 'be nice to mummikins!'

Mary, pushing away with her arms, momentarily managed to get her head free from the giant canyon of heaving flesh.

'You fat bitch!' she yelled. 'You keep your soddin' 'ands off me!'

It was to this last remark that her mistress, hearing the commotion, had entered the room. As a consequence, Mary lost her job, though her mistress was careful to furnish her with a good reference. It was well known in all the better houses that the duchess preferred her own sex to the wizened Duke of Dorset. She had, after all, come from poor stock, an ex-Drury Lane actress who had married the elderly and heirless duke and given him two sons in an amazingly short time, whereupon she had converted her stylish figure and good looks into lard and her taste from male to her own sex, with a decided preference for plump young servant girls.

In those late-Georgian times there remained in some London households a little of an earlier tolerance for the sexual proclivities, preferments and foibles of the nobility, and Mary's mistress was not as scandalised over the incident as might have been the case a little further into the century when the young Victoria ascended to the throne. Her parting words to Mary had proved most instructive to the young maidservant.

'You are a good worker, Mary, and quite a bright little creature, though you really must learn to respect the wishes of your betters and to control your peppery tongue. Have you not been instructed in your childhood in the manners required of your kind? Were you not taught by Mr Bothwaite the butler by heart the verse of the noble Dr Watts when you came into our employment?'

'Yes, ma'am.'

'And what does it say? Repeat it, if you please!'

Mary scratched around in her mind for the words to the catechism which every young domestic was expected to know upon commencement of employment in a big house. In a voice barely above a whisper she now recited the words to the verse:

> *Though I am but poor and mean,*
> *I will move the rich to love me.*
> *If I'm modest, neat and clean,*
> *And submit when they reprove me.*

'There you are, so very neatly put in a single verse by the great hymnist, you would do well to remember it in the future.'

Whereupon Mary's mistress gave her a not unkindly smile.

'Now you will not mention this unfortunate incident at your next position, will you? I have given you an excellent reference,' she paused, 'though it can always be withdrawn if it comes to my ears that there has been some idle tittle-tattle below stairs.' She placed her hand on Mary's arm. 'You do understand what I'm saying, don't you, my dear?'

Mary understood perfectly well. From the incident with the duchess she had derived several lessons; the first being not to resist the advances made to her, but instead to profit from them. The next, that a scandal, should she be caught with a member of the family or guest, gave her power to negotiate and so to leave her place of employment with her reputation intact.

Mary also understood the different standards which prevailed for promiscuous behaviour below stairs. Similar comportment involving a male member of the household staff would leave her without references, on the street, without the least prospect of obtaining a job in any respectable London house.

Mary even understood that she could learn to keep her big mouth shut. Though in this last endeavour she was never to prove very successful and she would privately, and to the secret delight of the junior maids below stairs, declare the verse by the great Dr Watts to be a load of utter shit.

Before her ultimate undoing she had served in two further households. In the first, the master of the house had left her several gold sovereigns richer, and in the second she had been promoted to the position of abigail, that is, lady's maid, and the youngest son in the family had been inducted by her into the delights of Aphrodite in return for lessons in reading and writing.

When two years later this scion of the family went up to Oxford, Mary was promptly, though discreetly, dismissed, again with an excellent reference and, as a result of her lover's tuition, a small knowledge of Latin and a facility at writing which was contained in a good copperplate hand studiously learned from a copybook he had bought for her. On return from the Michaelmas term her boy lover was said to have wept openly at the discovery that his dearest mumsy was now attended by a flaccid and cheerless personal maid in her late forties.

Mary's next billet was to prove her final undoing. Appointed as upstairs maid she soon found herself at odds with the family nanny, a middle-aged lady of imperious manner known as Nanny Smith. Well established in the family, the old woman exercised considerable power over all the other servants. She soon took a dislike to the new young maid, who seemed much too forward and confident around the male servants in the house and was not in the least afraid to speak before she was spoken to.

For her part Mary accepted Nanny Smith's carping instructions and held her tongue. But one day the old girl accused her of poisoning her cat, an aged tabby named Waterloo Smith who coughed up fur balls on the Persian rugs and stumbled about with a constant wheeze and permanently dripping nose. Mary had made no attempt to conceal her dislike for this creature, who returned the compliment by arching its back and hissing at her whenever they met along a corridor or in one of the many upstairs rooms.

'You ought to be dead and buried, you miserable moggy!' Mary would hiss back. Her abhorrence for Nanny Smith's cat was soon the joke of the below stairs staff and no doubt her dislike was soon communicated to Waterloo Smith's ill-tempered owner.

Then one morning Waterloo Smith went missing. Nanny Smith had placed him as usual on a broad upstairs window ledge to catch the morning sun and upon her return an hour later he was nowhere to be seen.

Mary, together with the second upstairs maid, was made to search every cupboard, nook and cranny and under each bed and, in the unlikely event that the disabled creature had somehow managed to negotiate the stairs, each of the four levels of the downstairs area of the house.

Bishop, the butler, had ordered the footman, the stable boy and Old Jacob the gardener to inspect the lavender bushes which grew forty feet below the window ledge where Waterloo Smith had been sunning himself. When this yielded nothing the speculation that foul play was involved started to grow. While nothing was said, Mary's well-known dislike for the cat made her the prime suspect.

By evening it became apparent that Waterloo Smith had disappeared quite into thin air, and his distraught owner retired to her bedroom, where her unconstrained weeping could be heard by all who worked above stairs.

Mary was given the task of taking a supper tray to the old lady and upon knocking on Nanny Smith's door the weeping from the other side immediately increased in volume.

'Come in,' the old woman's tremulous voice cried.

'Cook 'as made you a nice bit 'o tea and 'opes you feels better,' Mary said, placing the tray down beside Nanny Smith, who lay on the bed with a silk scarf covering her head.

At the sound of Mary's voice Nanny Smith sat bolt upright, the scarf falling to the floor. 'You did it, didn't you! You killed him!' she screamed, pointing a trembling finger at Mary.

Mary's jaw dropped in astonishment at this pronouncement and as she bent to retrieve the scarf the old woman continued, 'You horrid, horrid girl, pushed my pussy! I shall see that you are dismissed at once!'

Mary should have immediately panicked at Nanny Smith's words, for this time she was in no position to negotiate. The old cow's word against her own left her in no doubt as to who would prevail. Then Nanny Smith snatched the scarf from Mary's hands in such a rude manner that Mary lost her temper and a deep flush overtook her face.

'I never laid a finger on your bloody cat! Though I must say it's good riddance to bad rubbish, if you ask me, with 'im hissin' and wheezin' and doin' 'is mess all over the place! I 'ope 'e broke 'is bloody neck!' The offending words were barely out before Mary regretted them.

The following morning, in the manner to which his breed had been trained for countless generations, Samuel the family spaniel politely presented Waterloo Smith, stiff as a board, to Mrs Hodge the cook at the kitchen door.

Waterloo Smith's fur was matted and covered in fresh dirt, suggesting that Samuel, finding the dead cat in the lavender bushes, had contrived a hasty burial in some remoter part of the kitchen garden, but that later his conscience got the better of him and he'd repented by laying the dead cat at the feet of the cook.

Later at the inquest held in the library, Mr Bishop, seeking to console Nanny Smith, opened the proceedings by suggesting that the unfortunate creature might have died from natural causes – a fit, or convulsions or similar which had by natural movement catapulted Waterloo Smith from the window ledge?

However, the dead cat's distraught owner, red-eyed from weeping, wouldn't countenance this suggestion and declared flatly that her darling had been brutally murdered.

Nanny Smith glared meaningfully at Mary, who had been summoned to the library together with the other upstairs servants. 'We all *know* who the murderer is, don't we?' she sniffed and then buried her head in her hands and wept copiously.

Turning to Mary, Mr Bishop enquired, 'Mary, the room in which Waterloo Smith was last seen is your responsibility to clean. Did you see the cat on the window ledge?'

'I saw 'im, Mr Bishop! But I swear to Gawd I never laid a finger on 'im! I swear it on me dead mother's grave!'

With no further evidence to go on, Mr Bishop terminated the proceedings and Waterloo Smith's murderer, if such a person existed, was never apprehended. In fact, Mr Bishop had been correct in the first place; Waterloo Smith had suffered a violent fit followed by a stroke, the contractions of which had thrown him from the sun-bathed window sill to a merciful death in the lavender bushes four storeys below.

However, Nanny Smith was not to be thwarted and she caused such a disturbance with the master and mistress of the house that the butler was summoned and Mary, despite her protestations of innocence and Mr Bishop himself believing her not guilty, was stripped of her starched pinny and mob cap and banished below stairs to the laundry.

The laundry was the most onerous task among the skilled domestic duties and therefore the most humble and disliked. But Mary, who had never been afraid of work, discovered that if she worked hard she had time for reading and for practising her handwriting. Besides, the laundry was the warmest place in the big cold house and, like most children from the rookeries, she suffered greatly from chilblains.

Mary remained in the laundry for three years, even taking pride in her work, in starching and ironing, removing stains by bleaching with the juice of lemons and in mending, so that she became a useful, though not excellent, seamstress. By this time her reading and writing skills were much enhanced and she had graduated from the penny papers that pandered to the taste of the lower classes for bloodthirsty plots and over-blown romances, to serious literature. Mr Bishop, feeling guilty for having politely complied with her demotion to the laundry without positive proof that she had pushed the cat from the window sill, negotiated for Mary to use the master's library. The master had agreed to this, providing the books were always taken from the shelves in his presence and after he had closely inspected the state of her hands.

It was in books that Mary discovered a world beyond any of her possible imaginings – Defoe's *Robinson*

Crusoe and Jonathan Swift's *Gulliver's Travels* which she especially liked and read many times, quoting often from it to Mr Bishop; Thackeray, Macaulay, an excellent English translation of Cervantes' wondrously mad *Don Quixote*, Jane Austen and Fanny Burney. All these and a host of others she devoured with a great thirst for knowledge.

While reading became her abiding passion, Mary did not connect the lives of the people she read about in books with her own. Her earlier life had been difficult and the people about her for the most part poverty-stricken, dulled and witless from lack of proper sustenance and the absence of any education. That is, apart from the kind needed to survive among thieves, scoundrels and villains. From a young age she knew the world to be a wicked place and had learned to defend the small space she occupied in it with her teeth and nails.

However, the human mind has the fortunate capacity to forget pain and misery. Mary had been in the protected environment of a domestic servant in a big house from the age of eleven, so by the age of twenty she had all but buried the turmoil of her younger years. The sheltered life she now led meant she had gained little additional experience of the adult world other than the hurriedly taken copulative embraces thrust upon her by two of her past masters and the infinitely more pleasant, though inexperienced, couplings with the young master of the last employer.

Mary did not regard these hasty assignations as the same act of fornication she had observed against the walls in alleys or on the dark stairwells of shared lodgings or in the nesting midnight rooms, occupied by three destitute families, in which she and her father had been

27

reduced to living in the years before she'd entered domestic service.

Some unknown affliction in childhood had rendered Mary sterile, not that she even equated the hasty love-making with her betters with the act of childbirth. Despite the presence of children in the houses in which she'd served, if she'd thought about it at all, she would perhaps have concluded that the idle rich had their children conveniently delivered by a stork, the evidence of this being ever present on the nursery wall. That the better classes should employ the same vile animal instincts which had been such a familiar aspect of her childhood would have seemed to her unthinkable.

In fact, Mary was both streetwise and naive all at once. While she longed for romance she knew in her heart that it was not intended for her kind, that *doing it* in some privacy with a clean and half-decent someone was the best she could hope for. Her body developed into a very desirable womanliness, and she would often feel the ache to use it other than by the deployment of her probing and urgent fingers.

Her moment came one morning at Shepherd Market in nearby Mayfair where she had been sent by Mrs Hodge to purchase the master's luncheon sole, Billingsgate being too far to walk and the coachman out with the mistress of the house all morning.

'Take the one wif the clearest eyes, lovey.' The young man pointed to a fish which lay upon a block of ice slightly to one side. 'That one! See the eyes, clear as a gypsy's crystal.'

Mary turned towards the voice and its owner smiled, showing two missing front teeth with the eye tooth on either side framing the gap and capped with gold. It was a smile devoid of any calculation, though mischievous enough.

Mary found herself smiling back, even though more prudent behaviour was called for from a servant girl in a nice house involved in a casual meeting with a strange man. She found herself immediately taken by the flash young man standing beside her and her heart beat in quite the strangest manner.

The possessor of these two astonishing gold teeth was flash in other ways too and wore a fancy corduroy waistcoat with a watch chain. His ankle boots, below a fashionable pair of breeches, were stitched with patterns of hearts and roses. His cloth coat with contrasting plush lapels was clean and carried large expensive pearl buttons and was cut to the back into heavily braided calf-clingers with an artful line of buttons at their extremity. On his head he wore a beaver-napped top hat that looked to be in excellent order, its nap neatly brushed and shining.

'Name o' Bob Marley, pleased to meetcha,' he'd said in a single breath, giving her another big grin which caused his incisor teeth to once more gleam and flash. 'Honoured to make yer acquaintance, Miss . . .?'

Mary had observed that he hadn't once taken his eyes away from her face and unlike most men with whom she had the slightest passing acquaintance, hadn't allowed his eyes to wander over those parts of her anatomy which usually brought a glazed look into their eyes and a gravel tone in their voices. His smile was ingenuous, quite open and impossible to resist.

'Mary,' she said simply. 'Them's lovely teeth,' she added, smiling.

Bob Marley jabbed a finger at his mouth, 'Like 'em

does ya? Eighteen carat, that is! Pure gold, can't get none better!'

Bob Marley cast his eyes over Mary's firm breasts and trim waist, and in an unabashed voiced declared, 'What a corker! Care for a drop o' ruin?' He indicated the public house with a toss of his head. 'Come on then, I'll buy ya a taste o' whatever's yer fancy, gin is it, or a pint o' best beer?'

Mary, though sorely tempted, could not accept his invitation for fear of upsetting Mrs Hodge by being late and returning to the house with the smell of strong spirits on her breath. She was not accustomed to drink, though on the rare occasions when, on a public holiday, she'd ventured out with Mrs Hodge, she'd found gin left her very excited in a physical sort of way.

'I'll not be seen with a costermonger,' she said tartly, this seeming the best way to end a relationship where she was already beginning to feel at a distinct disadvantage. She noted too that her breasts were heaving and she was finding it difficult to breathe.

Bob Marley drew back with an exaggerated expression of hurt. Cocking his head to one side, his mouth turned down at the corner, he looked down at his chest as though closely examining his apparel. 'Costermonger? Not bleedin' likely, lovey.' He patted a velvet lapel. 'This is me disguise. I'm what ya might call an hoperator, I do a bit o' this and a bit o' that, finding' a bit 'ere and disposin' of it over there, if ya knows what I mean?'

'Oh, a tout?' Mary shot back, bringing her fingers to her lips as she tried to contain her laughter.

'Well not exactly that neiver, jus' ... well ... er,' he smiled his golden smile, 'an hoperator!' He seemed disinclined to further discuss the subject of his occupation.

'Well, what 'bout yer place, then?' Bob Marley said cheekily tugging on his watch chain and taking Mary by the elbow.

'Who do you think I am? I ain't no dollymop! Shame on you, Bob Marley!' Mary pulled her arm away from him. But then she laughed, enchanted by the young rogue standing beside her. 'You can walk me 'ome and no touchin', that's all I'll promise for now.'

By the time they reached the house in Chelsea Mary was completely smitten by the young rogue. She kept him waiting in the lane at the back of the house while she unlocked the stout door set into the kitchen garden wall, whereupon she went directly into the kitchen to deliver the sole to Mrs Hodge, who, predictably, scolded her for the time she had taken on her errand.

Mary's heart pounded in her breast as she returned down the garden path to open the garden door and let Bob Marley within the precincts of the kitchen garden. Quickly locking the door behind him, she led him into the laundry.

Now, with less than half an hour having passed, fat Mrs Hodge stood over Mary's half-naked body having hysterics and crying out in alarm at the astonishing gymnastics taking place on a pile of dirty linen at her feet.

Bob Marley was the first to react. Frantically pulling on his breeches and snatching up his embroidered boots, he jumped to his feet and fled the scene, knocking aside the stout cook with his shoulder and escaping into the kitchen garden. Not bothering to test the door set into the garden wall, he threw his boots over the top into the lane beyond and, quick as a rat up a drainpipe, scrambled after them, stubbing his toe badly in the process, pausing only long enough on the other side to retrieve his boots before making good his escape down the lane and into the Kings Road beyond.

Mary found herself dismissed from her place of employment without references or even the wages due to her. Not an hour after her interrupted dalliance with Bob Marley she stood in the lane outside the rear of the large Chelsea house, her sole possessions the small wicker basket at her feet and her precious abacus under her arm. She glanced up at the big house and observed the odious Nanny Smith looking down at her from a top window. When the old woman realised Mary had seen her she leaned further out of the window and commenced to hiss in much the same manner as Waterloo Smith had done.

'The pox on you, you old cow!' Mary shouted up at her and then, picking up her basket, she proceeded to cross the lane. Then turning once again to look up at Nanny Smith, she yelled, 'I pushed your bloody cat off the window sill with me broom, it done two somersaults before it splattered on the ground!'

Then, head held high and without further ado, Mary proceeded in the direction of Hyde Park, not knowing why she'd bothered to lie to the old crone and not even sure why she had chosen this direction from any other, thinking only that she would find a quiet spot under one of the giant old beech trees and try to sort things out in her head.

Mary's future lay in tatters. She found a bench beside the Serpentine adjacent to a willow which hid her presence from passers-by. But no sooner was she seated than a dozen small brown ducks glided towards her, their webbed feet paddling frantically below the surface to give their smooth little bodies the look of effortless gliding. It was clear that they anticipated food from the wicker basket.

When Mary saw the ducks, quacking and fussing at the edge of the water, she realised Mrs Hodge hadn't even offered her a morsel to eat. A stern Mr Bishop had bid her pack her things and had shown her the door in the kitchen garden. Then, to Mary's enormous surprise, just as he was closing the door behind her, Mr Bishop pressed a small parcel upon her and announced in a deeply injured tone, 'You are ruined, my girl, utterly and completely ruined!' He paused and then added in the same melancholy voice, 'Now I simply cannot propose marriage to you.'

The door had closed behind her before Mary could fully comprehend this curious protestation. Mr Bishop had never entered the smallest part of her amorous ima-ginings, nor had he, perhaps with the exception of the obtaining of books from the master's library, shown any inclination to be especially kind to her. She placed the squarish parcel absently within her basket.

Now hungry and with nowhere to go, Mary started to weep softly. Although truthfully her tears were more for the warmth and security of Mrs Hodge's kitchen and the steaming plates of food so regularly placed in front of her than they were for love's labour lost with Bob Marley or, for that matter, Mr Bishop.

After a while Mary wiped her nose and dried her reddened eyes. 'C'mon, girl, cryin' never got a day's work done,' she said to herself, repeating a phrase she had heard so often as a little girl coming from her over-burdened and sad-faced mother. She thought then for the first time about the parcel the butler had handed to her. Removing it from her basket she removed the wrapping to reveal the book *Gulliver's Travels*, quite her favourite. She smiled, feeling somewhat better towards life and the clumsy man whose marriage prospects she had so inadvertently ruined. Picking up her abacus and wicker basket, she crossed the park in an easterly direction to St Giles, where she knew from bitter experience she could obtain cheap lodgings.

Chapter Three

It would be nice to report that Mary's literacy skills and excellent penmanship, together with her wizardry with numbers, led to a new and fortunate life. Alas, these were not skills required of a woman at that time and most certainly not of a woman of her class. In the next six months she wore out a pair of stout boots in an effort to obtain employment as a clerk. She was always the lone woman in a long queue of applicants for a position advertised, and she soon became the butt of their cruel male jokes.

Furthermore, her abacus was the cause of much hilarity among the prospective clerks. Mary's persistent presence in the line of men would soon lead to her being known to them by the nickname Bloody Mary. This came about after an incident when a tall, very thin young man with a pale pinched face and sharp rodent teeth, wearing a battered top hat that resembled a somewhat misshapen chimney stack, snatched Mary's abacus from her. He held it in front of her face announcing to the men in the line, 'See, gentlemen, a monkey, a lovely little monkey in a cage playin' at being a clerk with pretty beads!'

It was a feeble enough joke but one which neverthe-less brought some hilarity to the anxious line of unem-ployed men eager for any sort of distraction to alleviate the boredom. Mary snatched her abacus back from the ferret-faced clown and, lifting it, slammed it down upon the young comic's head, causing the top hat he wore to concertina over his eyes and halfway along his narrow snotty nose. This created a great deal more hilarity in all but the unfortunate owner of the hat who, upon removing the object of their mirth and pulling and bashing it back into some semblance of its original shape, placed it again upon his head, then delivered a vicious blow to Mary's nose before running from the scene.

Mary's nose had not yet stopped bleeding by the time it became her turn for an interview. The chief clerk, a coarsely corpulent man with a sanguine complexion and the remains of fiery red hair on the sides of a com-pletely bald pate, looked at her with disapproval, shaking his head in a most melodramatic manner. 'What's the name, girl?' he asked.

'Mary, sir, Mary Klerk.'

'Bloody Mary, more like!' The men in the queue laughed uproariously at this joke. 'G'warn scarper! Be off with you, girl. 'Aven't you been told, clerkin's a man's job!'

The men clapped and cheered him mightily and pleased with their response the chief clerk played further to the crowd, for he'd witnessed the earlier inci-dent with the clown in the top hat. 'What's to become of us if we allow a monkey on our backs?'

There is precious little charity in a queue of starving men, most of whom had a wife and young ones to feed, and soon upon Mary's arrival in any employment queue, a familiar chant would go up:

> Mary, Mary, Bloody Mary
> Who does her sums on bead and rack
> Go away, you're too contrary
> You're the monkey, the bloody monkey
> You're the monkey on our back!

The chant was to become such an aggravation that few prospective employers were prepared to even grant her an interview for fear of angering the men. The men, in turn, found it impossible to understand why a woman with a trim figure, of Mary's young age and class, could not make a perfectly good living on her back. More and more they came to regard it as entirely reprehensible that she should attempt to steal the bread from their mouths and allow their children to starve and, moreover, that she should attempt to do so with the help of a foreign and heathen contraption made of wood, wire and beads. They told themselves that a screen that quivered and rattled and ended up doing sums had a distinct smell of witchcraft about it.

As the weather turned colder and the queue more desperate, the resentment against Mary grew out of all proportion. In the fevered imaginations of the unemployed clerks Bloody Mary's presence in a job queue soon took on all the aspects of a bad omen. When they returned home empty-handed to their ragged and starving families they had come to believe that her presence had 'soured the queue', so the luck they all felt they needed to gain a position had gone elsewhere.

Mary's face had grown gaunt for lack of sufficient

nourishment and, in truth, there began to be a somewhat simian look about her. With her large green anxious eyes darting about and her head turning nervously this way and that, expecting danger from every corner, the men began to believe increasingly that she was an incarnation of some evil monkey spirit.

Her dress too began to be much the worse for wear and hung upon her thin frame to give Mary an altogether morbid appearance, her black cotton skirt and blouse, and modest bonnet and shawl, together with her worn boots peeping below the frayed edges of her skirt, all showed the wear and tear of the long hours spent standing patiently in every kind of inclement weather.

While there were tens of thousands of women in a similar state of dress, their own wives being of much the same appearance, they saw in Mary's forlorn and ragged clothing the black cloth of a witch's weeds. The monkey chant, as it became known, grew increasingly threatening in tone and it took the utmost stubbornness and will for Mary to present herself at an advertised location for a job interview.

Yet Mary persisted well beyond the dictates of commonsense and into the province of foolishness. The long hours spent at reading and writing and the childhood application she had demonstrated with the complexities of mathematics had somehow convinced her that within her capacity lay a destiny beyond her humble beginnings. Mary's father had told her almost from infancy that her abacus would be her salvation and she could not believe that she might end up like her consumptive silkweaver mother or the sad, destitute and drunken shipping clerk she knew as her father. She saw herself achieving something well beyond the modest expectations of a laundry maid, though quite what this could be was past anything she could imagine. She felt certain that this destiny would all begin, if only she could obtain a position as a clerk.

After six months Mary had used up most of her savings and had repeatedly changed her place of residence, on each occasion moving to a cheaper lodging house, until she ended up sharing a foul room with a family of five in the very cheapest of netherkens in Shoe Lane.

She would wake at dawn each morning and, with no more than a drink of water and without allowing herself to think, set out to seek employment, fearful that, should she pause to contemplate her increasingly desperate position, she would give up altogether and take herself to Waterloo Bridge and commit herself to the dark, foul river.

One bitterly cold morning she left her miserable lodgings at dawn to be the first in line for a clerk's position advertised in a warehouse on the south bank of the Thames at Saviour's Dock. This was one of the vilest slums in London, and the mist lay thick on the river, and the streets were dimmed to near blindness by the sulphurous-coloured smog from the first of the winter fires.

Huddled at the entrance of the gate and near frozen, Mary was thankful that her presence would be concealed by the thick fog. The misted air about her was filled with the groans of masts and cross stays. In her imagination, the dockside took on the shape of a jungle filled with the wild and fearsome growls of fantastical creatures, while the howl of the wind through a dozen mizzen masts and the slap of loose canvas became the spirits of the dead which had come to protect her from the living, the men who would soon be lined up behind her and who had the capacity to frighten her beyond any perceived ghosts.

She had not eaten for two days and in her state of weakness must have fallen asleep, for she was awakened by the toe of the gateman's boot placed against her buttocks.

'Be up now, the gov'nor will be on 'is way soon!' a gruff voice demanded. Mary stumbled to her feet, clutching her shawl about her thin shoulders. 'Blimey, if it ain't a female!' the voice exclaimed in surprise.

A large man dressed in a military great coat with a shako, polished like a mirror, upon his head stood towering over her. It was the shako cap, complete with its scarlet and white cockade and braid, otherwise devoid of any regimental insignia, that gave the man his fearsome authority. Mary had expected the customary gateman in cloth cap, woollen scarf, corduroy breeches and workman's boots, the advertisement having instructed simply that the queue would commence at the gate under the gateman's supervision.

'Yessir, I be enquirin' about the billet advertised. The one for a clerk?'

'Well then, I s'pose it ain't against the law now is it?' The gateman twisted the corner of his large moustache. 'It's a pretty rum turn, but I can't see that it be against the law. First is you? You shall 'ave your interview, miss.'

Glancing fearfully at the formless shapes of the men disappearing into the fog behind her, Mary felt suddenly safe and strangely hopeful. She told herself that such an unpropitious day must surely bring her luck. The first good omen had been that the men standing directly behind her were strangers and seemed not to recognise her. The ones behind them, pale shapes in the mist, would surely have among them a great many who were acquainted with her, but these had not yet become aware of her presence in the thick yellow fog.

The gateman turned away from her to address the vaguely defined line of men stretching away behind Mary.

'Now then, gentlemen, me name's Sergeant William Lawrence, late of the 40th regiment, veteran o' the Peninsular War, wounded in action at the Battle o' Waterloo. I am the gatekeeper 'ere and I'll brook no interference. It will be one at a time through the gate, no pushin' and shovin' and no idle chatter, if you please!'

There was a murmur in the crowd at the sound of a carriage rattling over distant cobblestones and then the rumble of its wheels as it drew onto the wooden dockside and shortly afterwards came to halt at the gate, the horse snuffling and shaking its head, blowing frosted air from its distended nostrils.

Mary, who stood close enough to see clearly, observed a small, very fat man alight. He was dressed in a heavy coat which swept to within an inch of the ground in the manner of a woman's skirt, his shoes being quite lost from sight. He wore a top hat which sat upon his head down almost to his eyes and rose alarmingly high into the air for a man so short. The remaining space between head and shoulders was wrapped in a woollen scarf so that in the uncertainty of the mist the whole of him took on the proportions of a very large perambulating bottle. The gatekeeper snapped to immediate attention and gave the bottle shape a rigid salute, his jowls and side-burns quivering with the momentum of it.

'Mornin', Mr Goldstein, sah!' Sergeant Lawrence shouted at the very top of his voice as though addressing the commander of a battalion of soldiers who was about to embark on a parade inspection.

'Goot mornink,' the bottle replied in a muffled voice. Then, without glancing at the line of men it entered the gate and waddled into the mist towards the unseen warehouse not twenty feet away.

The gatekeeper, pushing his hand between two brass buttons and into the interior of the great coat, pulled from within it a watch chain which soon enough produced a large, though not expensive-looking, watch. Glancing down at it from under his peaked cap he addressed the queue.

'I shall allow five minutes for Mr Goldstein to settle and then the first in the line will proceed through the gate to the door! You will oblige Mr Goldstein by knockin' on the outside door, whereupon you will remove your 'at and proceed in an inwardly direction and without waitin' for an answer! Mr Goldstein will be in the office to the left of the door upon which you shall again knock and then immediately enter! For them what is ambidextrous and 'asn't 'ad the misfortune to 'ave been trained in 'is Majesty's military forces, the left side is the side what's got the coat-stand!'

Anxious laughter came from the mist as men strained to catch every word, fearful of the consequences of making a mistake.

The imperious Sergeant Lawrence looked down at his watch again and then glanced sternly at Mary.

'Goldstein, you understand, miss? *Mr Goldstein!*'

Mary nodded, feeling herself beginning to tremble.

Mary knocked on the outer door of the warehouse and then, without waiting for a reply, did as she had been told and entered. To her left was a heavy, free-standing coat-stand on which hung the overgrown top hat together with its owner's coat and scarf. Behind it was a door with a frosted glass upper panel on which in gold relief lettering was the name *Jacob Goldstein, Prop.* The door seemed designed especially for Mr Goldstein, for it was not an inch higher than five feet though one and a half times as wide as one might normally expect an office door to be. Mary tapped nervously on the surface of the glass, her heart pounding in her ears, her knees feeling light, as though they might give at any moment, and the palms of her hands were wet.

'You must be here comink, please,' a voice answered in an accent which Mary immediately recognised. She had spent her childhood around Rosemary Lane and the Whitechapel markets and the accent was unmistakably that of a German Jew.

Mary entered and curtsied to the man, who sat well back from a large desk. He was dressed in a morning suit and his huge stomach, she felt certain, would not permit his very short arms to reach to the edge of the desk, the top of which contained a pot of blacking and a goose quill pen, a large writing tablet and a medium-sized brass bell of the kind a schoolmaster might use to summon his pupils from play.

'Good mornin', Mr Goldstein,' Mary said, summoning all her courage into a nervous smile.

Mr Goldstein seemed astonished to see her and commenced immediately to bluster.

'Ach! Vot is dis? A vooman? You are a vooman! Vot is vanting a vooman here? You are vanting to see me, ja?'

'I come about the job, sir. The assistant clerk ... the position what was advertised?'

Mr Goldstein's bewilderment persisted and Mary added desperately, 'It were advertised on the 'oardings, sir.'

'You are a vooman and you vant you can be a clerk?' Mr Goldstein was now somewhat recovered, though still plainly bemused.

'I'm most 'appy to do a test, anythin' you want, sir! Please, your 'onour, er, Mr Goldstein, don't send me away, give me a chance, I can do it, gov ... honest I can!'

Mary was suddenly conscious of Mr Goldstein staring at the region of her waist and that the merest semblance of a smile had appeared on his moon-round face.

'Abacus!' He pointed a fat finger at her midriff. 'You can use, ja?'

'Yes, sir, Mr Goldstein, your honour, since I was a brat ... er child, give me a sum, any sum you like, sir.'

'In Armenia, also ven I vos a *Kind! Das ist wunderbar!*' he chuckled. 'You are vonting I should give you some sums? Ja, I can do zis!'

Whereupon, to Mary's astonishment, he pushed his chair violently backwards. She now saw it to be on tiny wheels and possessed of a seat which could swivel. She observed that the points of his highly polished boots only just touched the floor. Using them to gain a purchase Mr Goldstein spun himself around so that the chair, with his fat dumpling body within it, flashed past

her astonished face fully four times, much like an egg
in an egg cup turned into a merry-go-round.

When it came to a halt Mary could see that Mr Goldstein now sat considerably closer to the ground and that
his boots were planted firmly upon it. Propelling himself
towards the desk his stomach now fitted neatly beneath
it, the desktop coming to just under his arms.

'A test? Ja, das is gut!' He pointed to the abacus.
'From vere are you learnink zis?'

'My father, sir. 'E were in the East Hindies.'

'He is Chinee man?'

'No, sir . . . er, Mr Goldstein, 'e were a Dutchie, from
'Olland.'

Mr Goldstein reached for his quill and dipping it into
the small pot of blacking he hastily scrawled an elaborate equation on the pad in front of him. Then he
pushed it over to Mary.

Mary examined the problem scrawled on the paper
tablet. Then, laying it down, she placed her abacus beside
it and began immediately to move the beads across the
thin wire rails, her long, slender fingers blurring with the
speed of her movements. She hesitated once or twice
before once again sending the bright beads flying. In a
short time she slapped the last bead into place and stood
back looking down at Mr Goldstein. There had never
been a more important moment in Mary's life.

She looked up to see that Mr Goldstein was smiling
and holding a gold hunter open in his hand. Mary
announced quietly, though her heart was once again
pounding furiously and she fought to keep her
breathing steady, 'Eight 'undred and sixty-two
pounds . . . at eleven pounds, fourteen shillin's and sixpence ha'penny a case, sir . . . er, Mr Goldstein.'

'Gut! Gut, young lady, in vun half minute! Now ve can see, ja?'

He placed the watch down on the desk and sliding open a drawer produced a large ledger which he opened and examined for a moment, running his fat index finger down several columns until it came to rest.

'Ja! Das is gut! And also *schnell*!'

'Beg pardon, sir?'

'Very fast!' he beamed. 'You can write also in ledger?'

He pointed to the pad on which he'd written previously and returning his quill into the blacking pot he handed it to Mary.

'Please . . . Numbers, also vords, let me see?'

Mr Bishop had not only provided books for Mary from the master's library but, upon her beseeching him, had on several occasions found old ledgers for her to copy out. Mary had studied these assiduously, emulating their neat columns and precise language a thousand times until she knew the contents of every page in her sleep. Now she wrote carefully in the well-formed and almost elegant copperplate she had studied so hard at the hands of her young Oxford lover, and later for countless hours on her own, to perfect.

34 cases @ a total of six hundred and twelve pounds no shillings and eightpence = seventeen pounds, one shilling and sevenpence halfpenny per case.

Then she repeated the sum in neat numerals directly below this sentence. She handed the quill and pad back to Mr Goldstein.

Mr Goldstein examined Mary's writing for a sufficient period of time for her to grow anxious that she might have made a mistake. Then he looked up, his expression stern and businesslike, shaking a fat finger with a large gold ring directly at her as in admonishment.

'I pay eight shillink for vun veek and Saturday only no verk. Half-past seven you are startink, eight o'clock you are finishink. Tomorrow half-past seven o'clock report, if you please, Mr Baskin, who is also here the senior clerk.'

Mr Goldstein pointed his stubby finger at the abacus, 'Gut!' he said.

Unclenching his remaining fingers he patted the air in front of him as though he were patting the abacus in approval, giving Mary the distinct impression that he had not employed her, but her frame of wooden beads.

Mary had to restrain herself from bursting into tears of joy.

'Thank you, sir, Mr Goldstein! You'll not regret it! Thank you and Gawd bless you, sir!'

Mr Goldstein grunted and taking up the bell on the desk he rang it loudly several times. Mary now became conscious that, in the short time she'd been in Mr Goldstein's office, the warehouse had filled with the hum of people going about their work. Now the buzz and clatter stopped as the bell rang out.

'Mr Baskin!' Mr Goldstein shouted into the sudden calm.

Presently a tall and very thin, Ichabod-Crane-looking man, stooping almost double, opened the wide door and entered the office. Mr Goldstein, writing in the ledger, ignored his presence for a full minute while the man stood with his hands clasped in the manner of a mendicant, his head downcast and his eyes avoiding contact with Mary.

Looking up from his ledger Mr Goldstein pointed directly at the abacus.

'Tomorrow Miss . . .' he suddenly realised that he had not enquired as to Mary's name, '. . . Miss Abacus!' he added suddenly and smiled at Mary. 'Ja! I can call you this!' He returned his gaze to Mr Baskin, 'Tomorrow she is startink vork. You show her varehouse, please!'

'Very well, sir, at once, show her the warehouse is it, Mr Goldstein? I shall attend to Miss Aba . . . Abacus?' He paused. 'For what purpose may I ask? A visit is it?'

Mr Goldstein looked up. 'Clerk, she is new clerk!' he said impatiently and then returned his attention to the ledger.

'The position? A woman? New clerk?' Mr Baskin was clearly confused as though the three bits of information couldn't somehow be joined together in his mind.

'Ja, of course, *Dummkopf*! Next veek she is maybe havink your job!'

Mr Baskin stiffened to attention as the three bits of previously disparate information, with an almost audible clang, shunted into place in his mind.

Once outside the office and well clear she turned to the unfortunate Mr Baskin. 'Me name ain't Abacus, sir, it's Klerk, spelt with a "K", it's a Dutchie name, me father was a Dutchman.'

Mr Baskin looked directly at her for the first time. 'If Mr Goldstein says its Abacus, then that's what it be!' Mr Baskin sniffed. 'No arguments will be entered into and the contract is legal and binding.'

He paused and seemed to be thinking and, indeed, his expression suddenly brightened. 'Unless . . .' he began looking directly down at Mary again.

'What?' Mary asked suspiciously.

'You don't turn up for work tomorrow!' Mr Baskin's

expression took on a most beseeching look and his voice carried a whining tone. 'It would be a most hon-ourable and decent thing to do, Miss . . . Miss?'

'Klerk!'

'Ah!' Mr Baskin said pleased. 'Ah, yes, well that's it, then isn't it? That is precisely the situation! We have no position here for a Miss Klerk! No such person is known to us here! Mr Goldstein knows of no such person! I know of no such person! No such person exists, I'm very much afraid to say you're a missing person! You will not be commencing tomorrow, we shall not be expecting a Miss Klerk!'

Mr Baskin announced this as though Mary were some impostor whom, just in the nick of time, he had cleverly exposed and quickly undone.

Mary bristled. 'Why, sir, you can call me Miss Spotted Chamber Pot if you like, but this billet is the most important thing to 'appen to me in me 'ole bleedin' life! If I 'as to crawl over broken glass all the way from Whitechapel, you may be sure, sir, I'll be standin' 'ere large as life tomorrow an' all!'

Her change of name was not of great concern to Mary, for she had never been christened and her own surname had not served her particularly well in the past. Her new one, compliments of the little bottle-shaped man in the glass office, at the very least identified her with an object she loved. She decided she would happily become Mary Abacus.

'Mr Goldstein said as you should show me the ware-'ouse, sir, Mr Baskin,' Mary now declared timorously.

Despite the sour reception she'd received from Mr Baskin, it was quite the happiest day of Mary's life. The large warehouse was stacked to the ceiling with goods of every description intended for America and the colonies and the chief clerk, despite his foul mood, seemed to take some pride in pointing out the extent of Mr Goldstein's venture into commerce and shipping.

Upon their leaving Mr Goldstein's office Mr Baskin had sent word to Sergeant Lawrence to disperse the waiting men and to announce that the very first candidate had been found suitable by the redoubtable Mr Goldstein.

At the end of the tour, Mr Baskin turned to Mary with a sniff. 'Right then. Half-past seven tomorrow and if you're so much as a minute late you'll not be starting here, miss!' Then he escorted Mary to the door, merely grunting as she bid him a polite and, in her heart, a most ecstatic farewell. All the chief clerks in the world couldn't have dampened Mary's elation – she'd turned the Klerk into a Clerk and fulfilled the dearest wish of her dead father. *Learn it well, my dearest child, for the beads, the beautiful Chinee beads, will set you free!*

To her surprise the sergeant seemed pleased to see her.

'Well then, miss, you could have blow'd me down with a fevva! Wonders will never cease, what a day an' age, eh?' He pointed to the abacus under Mary's arm. 'I mean 'is 'ebrew 'ighness takin' to your Chinee countin' machine contraption.' He seemed to know precisely what had taken place in the office with Mr Goldstein, though Mary couldn't imagine how this could possibly be.

''Ow did you know?' Mary asked happily, her eyes showing her surprise. 'The door was shut an' all!'

The old soldier patted her on the arm and then touched his forefinger to his nose.

'Never you mind that, miss! We 'ave ways an' means, ways an' means, there ain't much what escapes us!' He drew himself up to his full height. 'Mind, I can't say the gentlemen waitin' in line was too pleased, you getting the billet and being a woman an' all.'

He spread his hands and shrugged his shoulders. 'Don't suppose you can blame 'em, but it were curious, very curious, they 'ung about when I told 'em to scarper, then they done this chant, see, summink about a monkey. It were all very strange if you ask me, very queer indeed!'

Mary was only half listening, still feeling dizzy at her good fortune. 'I'm one now! Blimey! Fancy that, I'm a clerk!' Mary decided that she had never been quite as happy in her life.

And then the gatekeeper's words sunk in ... *then they done this most curious chant ... summink about a monkey* ... The fog had cleared a little, though it was still not possible to see beyond a few feet. The chill returned to Mary's bones and she felt terrified to leave the gateman's side and enter the ghostly gloom of the docks.

She was about to ask if she could remain in the sergeant's hut until the fog lifted when he said cheerily, 'Go on, then, orf you go, miss. See you tomorrow! Mind your step now, men workin', lots of rope lyin' about.'

Mary had hardly walked for more than a minute when she felt the presence of people about her, fleeting shadows darting in front and to the side of her, boots scuffing on the wooden surface of the dockside. In the distance she heard the deep bray of a steamer groping its way up the Thames and the rattle and screech of cranes and winches and chains as they lowered cargo into and brought it out of invisible hatches. She was afraid to call out, thinking that the shadows about her might be dock workers. No noise other than fog-muffled footsteps came from the darting shapes around her, each of which seemed to be consumed by the mist before she could properly focus upon it. Somewhere a whistle blew three short peep-peeps, its shrill sound fattened by the thick air. A suffocating fear rose up within her and she felt the need to flee, though the fog was much too thick for her to attempt to do so. Then, so low that she thought at first she might have imagined it, she heard the hum of male voices and as suddenly the dark shapes looming formed a circle about her and the hum rose and rose and the monkey chant began:

> *Mary, Mary, Bloody Mary*
> *Who does her sums on bead and rack*
> *Go away, you're too contrary*
> *You're the monkey, bloody monkey*
> *You're the monkey on our back!*

Mary froze, her throat constricted by terror. From within the thick fog strong hands grabbed at her and she was thrown to the ground.

She heard the clatter of her abacus as it landed somewhere near by. A scream rose within her, but a rough hand clamped down on her mouth. She felt a boot sink into her side, then another and immediately thereafter hands were everywhere as they tore at her bodice and skirt and grabbed at her legs, wrenching them apart. An excited, panting voice said into her ear, 'Scream and you die, Bloody Mary!' Then the hand was removed from her mouth and the weight of the first man thrusting between her legs pressed down upon her.

As each male completed and withdrew from her supine body he gave her a vicious kick or slapped her across the face with the back of his hand. Some loosened the phlegm in their throats and spat into her face.

Mary lay helpless, whimpering like a small wounded beast, her eyes wide open, though seeing nothing, the vile spittle running down her face and neck. She felt nothing, but the weight of the men pummelling her and the rasp of their foul breath was lost in the whirling confusion of shock. Even when they struck or kicked her, though she felt her body jar, no feeling followed.

She lay completely still while a dozen or more men mounted her. Then, with the chant continuing, they seemed to stop and her arms were torn roughly from where she held them stiffly to her sides. Strong hands stretched her arms out as though in a crucifixion, with the palms pressed flat against the wooden surface of the dockside. Two dark shapes pushed down on her, each with his knee pinning a shoulder and hand pressed down upon her wrists.

The shapes now stood in a dark circle, hovering over her, the yellow fog swirling about their heads. Two men stepped forward from the circle and stood to either side of her and as the chant rose, 'Mary, Mary, Bloody Mary . . .' they stamped down hard, crushing both her hands under the heels of their boots. The terrible pain cut through Mary's half-delirious state and a scream rose in her throat which was again cut short by the free hand of one of the men squatting to the side of her head. One after another the chanting men broke from the circle and stamped down upon her hands. Long before the last of the men had stamped and ground his heel into the broken and bloody flesh and bone, she had mercifully lost consciousness.

Despite her terror and revulsion, Mary would eventually overcome the physical invasion of her body. What broke her spirit was the wanton destruction of her beautiful hands. When the bones eventually knit she was left with blackened claws which more closely resembled those of an aged monkey.

For the remainder of her life, whenever Mary looked down upon her scarred and crooked hands, she would hear the monkey chant and see the dark shape of hate in the swirling, sulphur-coloured fog around her, on a day which had promised, upon leaving fat Mr Goldstein with his perambulating, merry-go-round chair, to be the happiest of her twenty-one years.

Chapter Four

Towards noon the fog had cleared sufficiently for two dock workers to discover Mary hunched in a dark corner, moaning. At first they thought her some drunken slut, her swollen face and broken lips the result of some gin brawl in the nearby and notorious public house, The Ship Aground, and so passed her by as they pushed their loaded barrow from a ship's hold to a nearby warehouse. Finally her continued and pitiful moans caused them to stop and examine her dark corner more closely. It was then that they observed that her skirt was wet with blood and saw her broken fingers pushed through the beads and bars of her abacus.

'Goldstein!' Mary groaned. 'Goldstein.'

The two men lifted her as gently as they could onto the barrow and wheeled her to Mr Goldstein's warehouse where they accosted the gatekeeper. 'She keeps callin' name o' Goldstein, ain't that yer gov, sergeant?'

Sergeant Lawrence nodded, then bending over Mary's body took in at once the nature of her injuries. 'Jesus Christ! The sharks, the bloody sharks got her!' He helped them lift Mary from the barrow and laid her down outside his hut.

Mary, who had long since given up any thought of God, would later in her life ponder on whether it had been divine guidance which had taken her to Mr Goldstein's gatekeeper. For at the great Battle of Waterloo he had been seconded as sergeant to a platoon of stretcher bearers.

The veteran soldier sent the yard boy to the warehouse and the lad soon returned with a large bottle of oil of tar and a length of used canvas. Whereupon the sergeant tore strips from an old canvas sail and soaked them in a solution of oil of tar. He bound Mary's hands in the Waterloo manner, as was done when a cannoneer had burnt or lost his hands from a breech explosion, binding the hands together in a single parcel of coarse cloth.

'She needs a bone-setter or 'er 'ands ain't gunna be no good no more,' the gatekeeper said to those gathered around, then he lifted his chin and pointed to the twisted abacus beside Mary, 'no more Chinee counting contraption for the likes of 'er, ain't a bone what's left straight in them fingers, nor one what ain't broke!'

'Bone-setter? Ja, zis is gut!'

Mr Goldstein in his coat and top hat suddenly stood bottle-shaped beside the gatekeeper. He opened his dumby and from it withdrew a five pound note. 'You must be fixink!' he said to the gateman. 'You get better this younk lady.'

Mr Goldstein bowed stiffly to where Mary lay whimpering on the dockside.

'Such a pity, so *schnell* for vorkink sums! Accht! Maybe she can be vun day chief clerk, now finish, ticht, ticht.' He bowed formally again. '*Aufwiedersehen*, Miss Abacus.' Then turning on a precise little heel he allowed the coachman to hand him up into the waiting carriage.

Mr Goldstein's five pound note paid for the bone-setter and ten days in hospital plus several bottles of physic of opium to kill the pain of her mutilated hands. This left Mary a pound over which would allow her to live for two months in one of the foul netherkens in Rosemary Lane, existing on a single tuppeny meal each day. Though the tar oil had prevented infection, for some reason Mary's hands remained a peculiar blackened colour. They had been too badly damaged for the bone-setter to repair properly and when some movement eventually returned to her fingers, they were twisted and bent, like the tines of a tin fork, and hideous in appearance.

As soon as she could stand the pain Mary began once again to practise on the abacus. She would work on it for six years before she would once again regain her old skills, although the beauty of her movements was gone forever.

The six years which passed were not good ones. It was not long before Mary was standing on a street corner as a lady of the night. But other prostitutes ganged up on her, chasing her away. Mary moved on to meaner and meaner streets until there was no pavement or doorway left on which she could safely ply her trade. Eventually she was forced into a brothel.

Mary had still not learned to hold her tongue. When she was intoxicated she had even more difficulty concealing her bitterness and controlling her temper. And so she moved ever lower down the whore's ladder, until six years later only the dockside brothels and opium dens were left open to her. She had formed an addiction for opium from the physic she had obtained from the hospital while her hands were mending and now she craved the dreams and oblivion the pipe would bring.

She caught the pox and the brothel mistress, a vile, toothless hag, sent her to a pox doctor who treated her successfully, though at some considerable expense. The money was advanced directly to him by the old woman who, in turn, advanced the debt to Mary at the rate of interest of fifty percent on the principal amount per week.

Mary knew herself to be enslaved for it was a debt she could never hope to pay. She was on her back eighteen hours a day, and in what time was left to her she sought the comfort of the dreams the opium pipe brought. She knew that should she attempt to escape, she would be cut. The 'Slasher' would be sent after her with his cut-throat razor and sulphuric acid, and her face would be disfigured forever.

Nevertheless, as might be expected, Mary reached a point where she could no longer tolerate the old hag's greed. One evening, having shared a pint of gin with a customer and having been continually chastised by the old hag to get back on her back, Mary finally lost her temper. In the furious battle which ensued, for the old woman was well bred to fighting, Mary lashed out blindly and her sharpened talons raked across the old crone's cheek. Her hands went up to cover her face and in a moment Mary could see blood running through her fingers. Mary took up her abacus and fled from the brothel, running wildly into the dockland night.

The acid slasher found her two days later in a dark alley in Spitalfields, led to her by two street urchins. Mary had collapsed from hunger, fatigue and the vicious cramps resulting from the withdrawal of opium and she lay propped against a wall, her chin resting upon her chest. After examining her by slapping her face several times with the knuckles of his hand and discovering that this did not have the desired effect of reviving her, the slasher hesitated, fearing that cutting her in such a state might lead to her bleeding to death. The earnings from a simple slashing with a drop of acid added did not warrant the risk of a murder charge being brought against him.

The police would make a light search for the culprit of a prostitute knifing, but the law required a full and exhaustive enquiry into a murder victim. Murder was a crime of an altogether more serious nature, even when done to a poxed up prostitute. Furthermore, the slasher knew himself to have been seen and heard enquiring after Mary in several public houses and netherkens and in all of the central London rookeries.

Paying the older of the two street urchins a farthing to watch over Mary in case she should revive and attempt to move, the slasher left and soon returned with a small toke and a quarter pint of rough brandy. He lifted Mary's inert body to a seated position and poured a measure of brandy down her throat. Handing what remained of the brandy to the older of the urchins to hold, the slasher slapped her hard several times until Mary, taken in a coughing fit from the sudden burning of the brandy on her empty stomach, returned to consciousness. Then he fed her small pieces of bread soaked in brandy until she had the strength to sit up on her own.

He handed a second farthing to the younger of the two urchins, though he knew the bigger boy would soon enough take the coin from him.

'She's me wife and ya saw nuffink, see? If you speak o' this to any geezer what may be interested, I'll come after ya and cut yer bloody throats, ear to bleedin' ear!'

The folded razor with its white ivory handle suddenly appeared as though by magic in his hands and the slasher slowly opened its bright blade. 'Now scat!' the slasher commanded and the two boys took flight and disappeared down the darkened alleyway.

The slasher now turned back to Mary, ready to complete his original purpose.

Mary, by now sufficiently out of her daze to understand what was about to happen, stared mesmerised by the razor in the man's hand. She was too weak to fight, too exhausted even to resist, yet the spirit within was not yet willing to die. 'Fuck me, kind sir,' she said, her voice hardly above a whisper.

The slasher leaned closer to her, carefully inspecting her face as if deciding where to make the slash. 'Ya can make it easy on y'self, lovey, jus' close yer eyes and think of summink beautiful.'

Mary fought back her fear and smiled in a coquettish manner, her hands concealed behind her back.

'I'm clean, I'm not with the pox, you have my Gawd's honour!' Her smile widened and her green eyes looked steadily at him, 'G'warn, just one more time with an 'andsome gentleman so I dies 'appy, please, sir.'

'Tut, tut, yer too pretty to die, lovey, it's just a little scratch and a bit of a burn. A bit o' punishment, a permanent reminder, 'cause you've been a naughty girl then, 'asn't ya?'

Mary kept her voice light, though inwardly her bowels twisted with fright.

'You'll fuck me to be remembered by and I promise

you, kind sir, you too will not quickly forget me lovin' ways!'

'No fanks, lovey, I don't mix business wif pleasure, know what I mean?' A slow grin spread upon his face, an evil grin but with some of the harm gone out of it. 'Yer game, I say that for ya, game as a good ratter and still a nice looker!'

'Game if you are?' Mary replied cheekily, knowing her life might depend on the next few moments. Though she had long since abandoned any faith in God she now made a silent prayer that, if she should survive, she would never again let strong drink or opium pass her lips.

'Tell ya what I can do,' the slasher said suddenly. 'I can give ya a bit of a kiss, ain't no harm in that is there?' He threw back his head and laughed. 'I'll not spoil yer gob, just a little slash, add a bit of character. It won't be the last time a man wants to kiss ya!'

For a fraction of a second Mary could not believe what she had seen. The slasher's laughter revealed that he was missing his two front teeth but to either side of the gap he sported gold incisors. Her heart leapt and started to beat furiously.

'If it ain't Bob Marley, last observed fleein' from the laundry of a certain Chelsea 'ouse, by means o' the garden wall with 'is breeches 'alf on and 'is boots carried, quick as a ferret down a rat 'ole you were, over the wall with your bum showin' where you 'adn't got your breeches fully up!'

Mary, though weakened by the effort this outburst required, held her smile. She had a good head for names and faces, though in the ensuing years both of them had changed greatly and for the worse.

' 'Ow d'ya know me name, then?' Marley demanded.

'The laundry maid? Remember? We met in Shepherd Market? Me buying fish, nigh eight year back! You 'ad a gold watch what had a brass chain. You was ever so posh! I took you back to me master's 'ouse. Remember, we done it on the linen pile. Well, not done it *really*. You see, before you'd 'ad your wicked way with me the bloody cook come in on us and you 'ad to scarper! Surely you must remember that, Bob Marley?' Mary, exhausted, lay back panting.

Bob Marley grinned broadly as he suddenly recalled the incident and the details of it flooded back to him. 'Blimey! That was you? You was the dollymop?'

He shook his head in wonderment. 'Well ain't that a turn up for the bleedin' books! I remember it now, I stubbed me big toe 'cause o' not 'avin' me boots on, all black an' blue it were, took bleedin' forever to come good so I could walk proper again. I've told that self same story a 'undred times or more. Oh, deary me, what a laugh, eh?'

Marley had closed the razor in his hand and now he slipped it into the pocket of his jacket.

They sat together in the alley and finished the brandy, talking of the things that had happened to them. Marley asked Mary about the abacus which lay beside her and she explained its use to him in accounting and numbers.

'Pity ya wasn't a man, lovey. I knows a gentleman, matter of fact I used to be 'is snakesman when I was a nipper, before I grow'd, I'd climb in an' out of 'ouses like a rat up a bleedin' drainpipe, thievin' stuff for 'im. This self same gentleman's got word out, very discreet mind, that 'e needs a clerk what 'e can *trust*. Someone wif a bit of form, if ya knows what I mean?'

Ikey Solomon, Marley explained, trusted no one and was loath to make such an appointment, but stolen goods were piling up unledgered and unaccounted for.

Bob Marley pointed to the abacus. 'Don't suppose 'e'd en'ertain a contraption like that,' he remarked gloomily, 'even if ya was a man. I think 'e's got more yer normal quill and blackin' pot in mind, some old lag what is a clerk and can be trusted never to talk to the filth and what can be suitably blackmailed into keepin' 'is gob shut.'

Mary explained to him that she could use a quill, ink and paper for clerking and that she knew how to write up a ledger. Bob Marley scratched his head, pushing his top hat further back in order to do so.

'If it were up to meself I'd give ya a go. "What's I got to lose?" I'd say. Nice lookin' tart like you, well worth a try, eh?' Marley mused for a moment. 'But then I got a kind 'eart and 'e ain't, 'e's an old bastard!' He looked up and smiled. 'I can give ya 'is address, confidential like, mind.'

He scowled suddenly. 'But if ya tells 'im who give it to ya, I won't take it kindly, know what I mean?'

Mary shook her head. 'Gawd's 'onour, Bob, I won't tell no one who it was what told me. I'm exceedin' obliged to you.'

Mary's hopes soared. Bob Marley was not going to kill her, or even mark her.

'It's Bell Alley, ya know, ring-a-ding-ding, bell, got it? Islington. I dunno the number, but it's got a green door wif a brass lion wif a loop through its nose, as a knocker, like. There's a lamp post in Winfield Street where ya turn into the alley, only light in the 'ole bleedin' street, but it don't work. Best time to catch 'im is dawn when 'e's coming 'ome. It's not 'is real 'ome, it's where 'e keeps 'is stuff and does 'is accounting like. Wait for 'im at the entrance o' the alley; 'e can't come no other way.'

Their conversation waned and then came to a complete silence. Bob Marley had shown no signs of producing the razor again, but the tension so overwhelmed Mary that she could not put the prospect of the razor aside and idle chatter between them became impossible for her.

'You ain't gunna cut me, then?' she asked finally, smiling disarmingly at the man squatting in front of her.

Marley coughed politely into his fist and looked up at Mary so that their eyes met again for the first time in a long while.

'I'm sorry, love, but I 'ave to.' He smiled in a sympathetic way, and his gold teeth flashed. 'I don't like doin' it in yer case, I sincerely don't!' Bob Marley shrugged and turned away.

Mary was flushed with the brandy, but with only a few mouthfuls of stale bread inside her stomach she felt it turn and she was sure she was going to be sick.

'Please don't cut me, Bob Marley,' she begged.

'I won't cut ya bad, lovey, just a straight slash what will 'eal quick, a slash and a little dab of acid to keep the scar permanent like and as witness that I done me job. Yer still a corker to look at an' all, I don't wanna spoil that, it don't say in the contract I gotta mutilate ya, I can make up me own mind 'bout that! Cut 'n acid, a slash 'n dab, that's all I gotta do accordin' to me code of efficks.'

Mary, attempting to hold back the bile rising in her throat, concentrated on looking into Bob Marley's eyes.

She didn't see the razor come out of his pocket and she barely saw the flash of its blade when she felt the sharp, sudden sting of it across her cheek.

'I'm truly sorry, lovey,' she heard Bob Marley whisper. 'If ya move now I'll splash the acid, stay still, very still, so I don't 'arm yer pretty mug too much.'

Mary wanted to scream and vomit at the same time but she clenched her teeth and held on and then there was a second blinding, unbearable sting as Bob Marley pushed back her head and poured acid into the cut. She could no longer keep her hands behind her back and now she clasped them to her face.

'Jesus Christ! What 'appened to yer 'ands?' Bob Marley exclaimed, then he rose quickly and was gone before the scream was fully out of Mary's mouth.

Mary could scarcely remember how she survived the next three weeks. Despite her pain and misery she had determined she would somehow fulfil her promise never to drink again. Denying herself gin and the opium pipe to which she'd become accustomed sent her into fearful spasms and cramps. She sweated profusely so that her clothes were soaked and she was only dimly aware of her surroundings.

By the time she had set out to meet Ikey Solomon, though still shaky, she was over the worst of her tremors. The scar on her cheek, though not entirely healed, was free of scab. Bob Marley had done his job skilfully and her face, despite the scar, was not in the least misshapen, the parts of it remaining as is normal on a woman's countenance, nose, lips and eyes where they ought to be and perfectly intact.

Mary waylaid Ikey at dawn, just as Bob Marley had

suggested. Standing in the shadows several feet into Bell Alley, she had seen him enter from Winfield Street and let him almost pass her before she stood suddenly in his path.

Ikey stiffened and gasped in fright, bringing his arms up to his face as Mary stepped out of the shadows, but then seeing it was a woman he lowered his hands, dug his chin deeper into his overcoat and proceeded on his way.

'Please, Mr Solomon, sir,' Mary called, 'can you spare just one minute of your time? I've waited 'ere all night with news that may be o' great benefit to you.'

'What is it, woman? 'Ave you got somethin' to sell?'

'Yes, sir, but I cannot speak of it here, you must grant me time to see you elsewhere. What I 'ave to offer is o' great value. You will wish to see a sample, I feel sure.'

'Where will I come? When? Be quick, it's late! I must be gorn. Where?' Ikey snapped, expecting to intimidate the woman who stood before him.

Mary had thought about this meeting too often to be thrown by Ikey's brusque manner. 'I shall come to you, sir,' she said calmly, though her heart was beating furiously. 'What I shall bring with me will be worth your while.'

'Bah, humbug!' It was unusual for a woman of Mary's standing to confront him unless she had some urgent business, probably of the stolen goods kind. Or she might be a spy of some sort, or a trap set by the runners.

'Who sent you? Who told you to wait 'ere?' Ikey asked.

'I cannot say, sir, I pledged to keep me gob shut, but it ain't no one what means you 'arm.'

'Hmmph! I cannot think that such a man exists,' Ikey sniffed, though his instinct in these things was usually sound and he could feel no malice of intent in the woman who stood before him. 'Very well, tonight, at seven o'clock precisely in Whitechapel. If you are late and not alone you will not be let in. You shall say one word, "Waterloo", to the woman what answers the door, "Waterloo" and no other, do you understand?'

Mary nodded, too nervous and overcome even to thank him as Ikey gave her the address of his home in Whitechapel.

'G'warn, be off with you now and don't you be late, you shall 'ave ten minutes tonight!' Ikey paused. 'That is, if you 'ave something of worth to show me, less, much less, I can assure you, if you doesn't!'

Without a word Mary moved past Ikey and into Winfield Street. She had succeeded in the first step, though she had done so with a trick, a deception, yes, but not a lie. Now she had given herself the chance to pick up the broken pieces of her miserable life and perhaps change it forever.

At seven o'clock precisely that evening Mary, carrying her abacus, tapped on the door of Ikey's Whitechapel home. It was not as big a house as any in which she had once worked, but imposing nevertheless and grand for where it stood one street from the Whitechapel markets. The door was answered by a raw-boned woman who appeared to be about forty and whose breath smelled of stale beer.

Mary, afraid even to offer the pleasantry of an evening greeting lest she betray Ikey's instructions, blurted out, 'Waterloo!'

'You're expected t' be sure,' the woman said in an Irish brogue. 'Will you be after followin' me then, miss?' The woman, taking a candle from a ledge in the hallway, then led Mary through the darkened house to the door of Ikey's study where she tapped three times and departed, leaving Mary waiting in the darkness. She had a sense of being watched and then she heard a sniff followed by the muffled giggle of a child, though she could see no one.

In a moment or so Mary heard the rattle of a key placed into the lock and the door opened, though only a crack. The light was behind Ikey's head and Mary could only just make out his long nose, a single beady eye and a scrag of beard in the space allowed by the opening. The door opened wider and Ikey silently stood aside for her to enter the small room beyond. The door closed behind her and she heard Ikey lock it once again.

Ikey brushed past where Mary stood, turned and surveyed her with his hands on his hips. He was wearing his great coat though he'd removed his hat and she now saw his face clearly for the first time. This she found the way she had imagined it to be. That was the point with Ikey's face – to those who saw it clearly it was exactly what you would expect his face to look like if you knew his vocation in life. Behind Ikey stood a coatstand and beside it a high desk above which a lamp burned brightly. Two further lamps lit the room to give it an almost cheerful look which contrasted markedly with the general darkness of the house.

Ikey did not bid her to be seated, though there was a small table and single chair some four feet from the desk. Mary moved past Ikey and placed her abacus flat upon the table and then returned to where she'd formerly stood.

'Well, what is it? Why 'ave you come? Show me, I 'ave no time to waste.' Had she been a man who might be carrying news of a rich haul, Ikey might have been more circumspect, he might have smiled at the very least, ingratiating himself, but such pleasantries were not necessary for a woman of Mary's sort.

'Please, sir, you 'ave granted me ten minutes, it will take some of this time to tell you me story.'

'Story? What story? I do not wish to hear your story, unless it is business, a story o' the business o' profit, some for who it is who sends you 'ere and some for yours truly! Be quick. I am most busy of mind and anxious to be about me work.'

Mary smiled, attempting to conceal her nervousness. 'You will assuredly profit from what I 'ave to say, kind sir, but I begs you first the small charity of your ears, no more, a few minutes to 'ear a poor widow's tale.'

Mary then told Ikey how she had been recently widowed from a merchant sailor who had been swept overboard in the Bay of Biscay. How she, penniless, had been forced with her darling infant twins to share a miserable room with a destitute family of five and pay each day from her meagre salary for an older child to mind her precious children while she worked as a laundry maid in a big house in Chelsea. How the husband of the mistress of the house took advantage of her desperate circumstances to use her body for his pleasure whenever he felt inclined and without any thought of payment. How one night a most frightful fire had swept through the netherken where she slept with her baby infants and she had been dragged from the flames but had rushed back to save her precious children.

'I bear the marks, good sir, the marks of that terrible tragedy!' She gave a little sob and withdrew the woollen mittens from her hands, holding them up to reveal her horribly blackened and mutilated claws. 'It were to no avail, me little ones was already perished when I pulled them from that ghastly inferno!'

'Ha! Burnt into two roast piglets, eh?' Ikey snorted.

Mary ignored this cruel remark. 'I lost me billet as a laundry maid 'cause of me 'ands and being burned an' all and not even a sovereign from the master of the 'ouse to send me on me way!'

At this point Ikey waved his hands, fluttering them above his head as though he wished to hear no more.

'Enough! I 'ave no need for a laundry maid 'ere, missus. Be off with you, at once, you will get no charity from me!'

'No, sir, you are mistaken,' Mary hastily exclaimed. 'I want no charity. I 'ave come to apply for the position as clerk, the same as what you was lettin' out you wanted, a clerk well acquainted with all manner of bookkeepin'.'

Ikey's face took on a look of bewildered amazement.

'A clerk? You come 'ere to offer your services as me clerk? A woman and a laundry maid is a clerk? 'Ave you gone completely barmy, missus?' Ikey thumped the side of his head with the butt of his hand. 'Bah! This is quite beyond knowing or supposing!' He made a dismissive gesture towards Mary. 'Go away, I'm a busy man. Be off with you at once, you 'ave already taken up too much of me time. Shoo, shoo, shoo!' He made as though to move towards the door.

Mary took the abacus from where she had placed it on the table. 'Please, a moment, sir, Mr Solomon! I 'ave a gift with the Chinee abacus, sir.' She held the abacus up in front of her. 'A most extraordinary gift what will make you very rich, sir!'

'Rich? That thing? A Chinee ... why, it be nothin' but a bit of wire and beads! Coloured beads! What manner o' trickery is this? Beads and laundry maids and 'anky panky, roasted twins and drownings, gifts and very rich! Bah! Go! Be off with you at once!'

'Please, sir, I beseech and implore you. I ask for no charity, not a brass razoo, only for a test.' Mary appealed to Ikey with her eyes. 'Me abacus, that is, me beads and wire, against your astonishin' and well-known and altogether marvellous way with numbers. Ways what people talk about in wonderment.' Mary gulped. 'While I know a poor clerk like me 'asn't got no chance against such as your good self, it's a fair chance I'm a better bet than most men who count themselves clerks.' Then she added, 'And I am trustworthy, most trustworthy and not known to the beaks, you 'ave me word on that, sir!'

'Ha!' Ikey barked. 'Trustworthy by your own word! I am the King o' Spain and the Chief Justice by my own word!'

'No, sir, but the Prince o' Fences and known chiefly for just dealin' by the admiring word o' others,' Mary said quickly.

Ikey, despite himself, was impressed with this quick wit. He knew himself to be a positive wizard with numbers and calculations, and enjoyed the flattery, though he knew it to be false. Ikey's heart had never so much as skipped a beat in the vaguest general consideration of charity or goodwill or justice, not ever, not even once since he'd been an urchin selling lemons on the streets of Whitechapel. Though he didn't believe a word of Mary's tale, even had it been true it would have drawn no emotion from him. Mutilation was so common in his experience that he hadn't even flinched at the sight of Mary's grotesque hands. Children being consumed by fire was a nightly occurrence as soon as the weather turned cold. The scar on her face told him all he needed to know about her. Moreover, it annoyed him that Mary had shown not the slightest sagacity in the concocting of the story she told. The least he would have expected from her was a letter from a screever, slightly worn and faded and perhaps even somewhat tearstained, purporting to come from the captain of the vessel from which her imagined husband had been swept overboard and to testify to this tragic event. Such a document would be readily available for a shilling or two from any forger, a fundamental requirement if the slightest degree of deception was to be practised. In Ikey's opinion Mary clearly lacked the most elementary criminal mind and he could waste no further time with her. The contest of numbers, an absurdity of course, was a quick way to be rid of her, to send her packing, for good and all.

'Bah! Beads and wire against me! Impossible, my dear, quite, quite absurd, ridiculous, improper and impossible!'

Mary sensed from this outburst that Ikey's curiosity had been roused and, besides, his voice was somewhat mollified. She smiled, a nice, demure smile.

'Announce me any five numbers in any number of digits in any combination of multiplication, division, addition and subtraction you please,' Mary challenged. 'If I best you in this purpose, then I pray you listen to me plea for a position as your clerk.'

'And what if I best you, me dear? What will you give me?' Ikey liked the idea of a challenge and the ferret grin appeared upon his face.

Mary smiled and her pale countenance was momentarily most pleasantly transformed, for she had an even smile that would light up her face and cause her lovely green eyes to dance, though this was beyond the ability of Ikey to notice. Po-faced once more, Mary stooped to lift the hems of her skirt and the two dirty calico petticoats beneath to just above her thighs. What Ikey witnessed was a pair of shapely legs quite unencumbered.

'It is all I 'ave to give, but I know meself clean, sir,' she said, trying to imagine herself a respectable though destitute widow so that her words carried sufficient pathos.

'Ha! Clean by your own word! Trustworthy by your own word! Bah! Not good enough for the master o' the 'ouse to pay for, but good enough for me, is that it, eh?'

Ikey, who had been standing in front of Mary now moved over to his clerk's desk. He removed the ledger from it and placed it on the ground, then reaching for a piece of paper from a small stack placed beside where the ledger had been he laid it squarely in the centre of the desk-top. Then he fumbled briefly within the recesses of his coat and produced a pair of spectacles which he took some time to arrange about his nose and hook behind his large hairy ears. Then he removed the coat and hung it upon the coat-stand.

The absence of his coat made Ikey look decidedly strange, as though he had been partly skinned or plucked. Mary was surprised at how tiny he appeared standing in his dirty embroidered waist-coat and coarse woollen undershirt beneath. It was almost as though

Ikey wore the heavily padded great coat, which stretched down to touch the uppers of his snouted boots giving the effect of a much larger man, to conceal from the world his diminutive size. That he should choose to remove it now so that he could more rapidly move his arms to write indicated to Mary that he had taken her challenge seriously. Or, otherwise thought so little of her presence that he cared nothing for her opinion of his physical stature or the rank, ripe cheesy odour which came from his tiny body as he climbed upon the stool and hunched over his desk.

Ikey glanced scornfully at Mary over his spectacles as he took up his quill.

'You shall 'ave your challenge, my dear, and if you win, which I very much doubt, I shall make enquiries as to your past.' Ikey paused and shrugged his shoulders. 'If you pass you shall 'ave your billet, you 'ave me word for it.'

Mary laughed. 'And *your* word, it is to be trusted and mine is not, sir?'

Ikey did not reply, nor even look up, but he liked the point and the boldness it took to make it. He turned away from Mary's direction and briefly rubbed the tip of the quill with his thumb and forefinger, testing its sharpness, whereupon he dipped it into an inkwell and dabbed its point on the blotter which lay beside it.

'But if you lose . . .' Ikey looked down at the area of her skirt, now once again concealing her legs, and pointed the tip of his goose quill at its hemline. 'Lift, my dear, lift, lift, a little 'igher if you please!'

As Mary's skirts rose slowly to her thighs, she tried desperately to remember some past incident of embarrassment so that she would appear to flush with modesty. Instead she felt herself growing angry and fought to contain her temper while her face remained impassive. 'Now turn around, my dear, right around, that's it! Now lift, 'igher . . . Ah!' Mary now stood with her back to Ikey. 'That will do very nicely, my dear,' his voice grown suddenly hoarse. 'You may turn around again, though keep your skirt raised if you please.'

Mary's face was a deep purple as she beat back her rising anger. The display of her buttocks and now her cunny did not dismay her, it was the feeling of complete powerlessness which angered her. She was at Ikey's mercy. The billet he was empowered to give her could mean the beginning of a new life for her, but if he summarily dismissed her, she felt certain that she would not survive. She dropped her hands from her skirts and did not look directly at Ikey for fear her eyes might betray her anger.

'Ah, you 'ave done well to flush, my dear. A touch of modesty is most becoming in a laundry woman, even in a poor widow what 'as lost 'er darlin' 'usband and precious little ones, the one in water, the terrible stormy briny and t'others in a roastin' pit, the crackle o' hell itself!' Ikey paused and smiled his ferret smile. 'Perhaps you will make a modest clerk, a *very* modest clerk, so modest as not to be a clerk at all but altogether something else, eh? What do you say, my dear?'

'I shall be most pleased if you would give me your calculation, sir,' Mary said quietly. She kept her eyes averted, fearing that should she glance up she might lose control and spoil her chance to take him on at calculations.

Ikey leaned backwards in the high chair showing a surprisingly large erection through his tightly pulled breeches. He was most gratified at this unexpected event. He could not remember when he'd been so encouraged by a woman's display of immodesty, especially a woman such as the one who stood before him. Women and sex seldom entered his mind. He had thought simply to humiliate Mary and to erode her confidence before the contest by showing her he knew her to be a whore, yet she had stirred a part in him so seldom stirred that he had almost forgotten that it was possessed of a secondary purpose beyond pissing.

Ikey looked down at his swelling breeches with some approval, then looked up at Mary with a mixture of pleasure and fear. If anything, this woman, with her ridiculous contraption of wire and beads, had gained the upper hand and he knew he must do something at once to regain the advantage. The thought of losing to her caused an immediate diminishing within his breeches, but upon his becoming aware of this, the perverse monster came alive again, pushing hard against the cotton of his breeches.

Ikey concentrated desperately and cast his thoughts to embrace his wife Hannah, an act of mental flagellation which was at once sufficient to damp down the unaccustomed fire that burned in the region of his crotch.

Waving the goose feather quill in an expansive gesture above his head, Ikey announced to Mary, 'If you should lose, do not despair, my dear. Mrs Solomon, a woman of a most benign nature and generous heart, who 'erself is an expert on,' Ikey coughed lightly, '. . . er, *figures* . . . is in need of someone capable of your very well-presented, ah, hum . . . *figurations*.'

Ikey moved forward, leaning both his elbows on the

desk so that the area of his loins was concealed. His bony shoulders were hunched up above his ears to make him look like an Indian vulture bird. 'You will do very nicely, my dear, very nicely indeed, my wife will be most pleased to make your acquaintance!' Ikey felt immediately better for knowing what Hannah might do to the woman who stood before him should she lose to him.

Mary remained silent nor did she change her expression, though she was acquainted with Hannah's vile reputation and Ikey's insidious suggestions were not lost on her.

'I shall need a surface upon which to place down me abacus,' was all she said in reply.

Ikey motioned her to a small table and chair and Mary seated herself, placing the brightly beaded abacus at the required distance in front of her. Her voice was hardly above a whisper. 'I am ready please, sir.'

'Mmph!' Ikey said in a tight voice. 'Ready you may be, but beat me you shan't, not now, not never and not likely!'

It is a matter of history how Ikey threw all sorts of mathematical computations at Mary and before he could properly ink his quill her flying fingers sped the coloured beads this way and that to find the answer. This she announced in a steady voice free of emotion, fearing to upset Ikey if she appeared too bold and forward with her triumph over him.

She need not have feared, for had she whispered the answers in a voice most demure and modest she would have upset Ikey no less. He soon grew furious and, it being in his nature to cheat, attempted to grab back the advantage by trying to think ahead the total of the sum before announcing it. Yet Mary bested him, beat him on every occasion, until finally he was forced to concede defeat. This he did with the utmost bad temper, claiming a headache, a blunt quill and the mix of blacking ink in his pot not to his usual liking.

'You 'ave won the first round, my dear,' he finally mumbled without grace. 'The second test remains.'

Mary held her gaze steady as Ikey continued. 'Now we shall 'ear of your past, my dear, for the position of my clerk is one requiring great trust and I shall want to know that your background is spotless, blameless and pure as churchyard snow.'

Mary knew the game was up. The hideous little man was playing with her. She now realised that he'd been playing with her from the beginning, though she felt sure she'd caught him by surprise with the abacus. Why, she now asked herself, had she not simply told him the circumstances of her life? Why would her feigning of respectability, a widow fallen upon hard times, have influenced this odious creature? Perchance he would have preferred the real story of her descent into debauchery and whoring. It was much more the world he knew and understood.

Mary could feel her temper rising, the heat of her anger suffusing her entire body. She rose without haste from where she was seated and, taking up her abacus from the table, moved in slow, deliberate steps towards where Ikey sat smiling triumphantly at the counting desk. She came to a halt in front of the desk and it seemed that she was about to beg him for his mercy, but instead she lifted the abacus above her head and swung it as hard as she might at the grinning little fence. The abacus caught him on the side of the head and sent him sprawling from the high chair onto the floor. Ikey's spectacles launched from his head and landed with a clatter in the corner behind him.

'You can keep your poxy job, you bastard!' she cried. 'Fuck you!'

'No, no! Please! Don't 'it me! Please, no violence! I beg you, missus! Anythin', take anythin', but don't beat me!' Whereupon he began to sob loudly.

'You shit!' she said disgusted, though the anger had already gone half out of her voice as she looked at the pathetic, whimpering weasel cowering at her feet.

Ikey, sensing the danger was over, let go of her leg. He scrambled frantically to his haunches and with his arms propelled himself backwards into a corner. He sat down hard upon his spectacles which promptly broke and pierced through his breeches and cut into his scrawny bum.

'Ouch! Fuck!' he yelled, then lifting his arse he felt frantically at the damaged area and his hand came away with blood on the tips of his fingers. He looked down at his bloody paw, his expression incredulous. 'Blood! Oh, oh, I shall faint! Blood!' he sobbed. 'I shall bleed to death!'

Mary moved towards him, the abacus raised above her shoulders ready to strike him again. Ikey, sobbing, pulled up his knees and covered his head with his arms.

'No, no! I'll pay you! Don't 'urt me! For Gawd's sake, I beg you! Don't 'it a poor man what's bleedin' to death!' Ikey, cringing in the corner with his arms about his head, waited for the blow to come.

'Get up, you gormless lump!' Mary snapped.

Ikey scrambled hurriedly to his feet, sniffing and sobbing, snot-nosed and flushed with fright. Mary grabbed him by his scrawny neck and steered him towards the counting desk, bending him over it so that his arms hung over the front and his head lay upon its writing surface. Then she placed the abacus on the floor beside the desk.

'Now be a man and don't cry while I remove the glass from your arse,' she laughed.

It was at that precise moment, crouched with his bleeding bum facing her and his miserable head face downwards on the desk that Ikey knew for certain he was deeply and profoundly in love for the first and only time in his life.

Chapter Five

Ikey found Mary to be a studious and diligent clerk, quick to learn even if somewhat lacking in experience. He also knew that working for him was Mary's only chance to make something of her life and that consequently she would work tirelessly to bring her change of fortune about. Ikey exploited the situation and he paid her little and worked her late with no thought of gratitude for her services, though, each week, he paid her the agreed sum without demurring.

Mary was content with such an arrangement. An amorous Ikey was only acceptable if the experience was infrequent and she soon realised that her skill at numbers made her indispensable to him and that she need no longer show her gratitude to him on her back. It did not take long for Mary's quick mind to grasp the peculiar language of Ikey's ledgers and to learn the ways of disposing stolen goods throughout Europe and America. She soon showed that her bookkeeping skills extended to a good head for business. Ikey found himself possessed of a clerk who managed his affairs exceedingly well, though it concerned him greatly that Mary had come in the process to know a disconcerting amount about his nefarious dealings.

It was time to put a little salt on the bread but he could not embrace the idea of raising her salary. Not only because he was exceedingly mean, but also because it involved the idea that he was pleased with her progress, or even that he admitted to himself that Mary had become indispensable to his wellbeing. To Ikey, who could flatter a penny out of a pauper's hand, the notion of openly caring for another human was the most dangerous idea he could conceive of, a weakness which would, he felt certain, lead inevitably to his demise.

As Mary's confidence grew her natural impetuosity returned and with it her lively temper which caused her to argue with Ikey, for she found him stuck in his ways and not readily open to new suggestions. She became convinced that Ikey's connections in Amsterdam and Brussels were cheating him in the melting down of silver and gold and the resetting and re-cutting of diamonds.

Ikey would say, 'It is appropriate that those who cheat should also be cheated. It is in the nature of thievin', my dear. There is a saying among my people, "Always put a little salt on the bread." It means, always leave a little something for the next man, leave a little extra, a little taste on the tongue, a reason to return. It is true in business and it is even more true in the business o' fencin'!'

How curious it was then that Ikey, who understood this principle so well, could not see how to bring it about with Mary, that is without perceiving himself as made impossibly vulnerable in his emotions.

Mary's mind lacked the subtlety of her opponent but she was not entirely without gall. She knew herself to be worked hard for very little remuneration and she expected no less. But by showing her concern for Ikey's interest in other matters, she was proving her loyalty to him.

Besides, she had a plan which concerned the house in Bell Alley and so she worked without complaint, becoming more and more indispensable to Ikey until she perceived his concern that he could no longer afford to be without her. Then she made the suggestion to Ikey that she work without salary at his bookkeeping and that, in addition, she be allowed to open a brothel in Bell Alley in partnership with him.

Ikey was delighted. It meant that she was fully compromised. She would do his bookkeeping and add even further to his gain and, at the same time, completely negate his fears. Mary, he told himself, knew decidedly more of whoring than of clerking, and as the mistress of a brothel as well as his bookkeeper she would be tied to him for ever. Greed was the only emotion Ikey trusted in himself as well as in others. An agreement was struck between them whereby Ikey would put up the capital for the brothel for which he would receive seventy percent and Mary thirty percent after the deduction of running expenses. Moreover, the house would still be a repository of stolen goods, it being possessed of a large attic, and the dry and commodious cellar would also be in Ikey's sole possession.

The last point was a master stroke on Ikey's part. Through Hannah he had met a notorious Belgian forger who had been forced to escape from the authorities in several European countries and had proposed a business deal. The forger, a man named Abraham Van Esselyn, was also a Jew. Moreover he was deaf and dumb and, if he was to make a living at his craft, needed a partner.

Ikey was ideally suited to this purpose, for he could procure all the materials needed for a sophisticated forgery operation through his various contacts and had an established network of fellow Jews in Europe and America through whom the fake banknotes could be laundered. He would set up a printing operation in the cellar at Bell Alley.

Ikey now had the premises in Bell Alley working to his complete satisfaction. He hated waste and now he had turned every inch of space to profit – the cellar turning out counterfeit notes and, in daylight hours, printing handbills and pamphlets; the centre of the house supplying the physical and fantastical needs of bankers, lawyers, judges, magistrates and toffs in general; the attic serving as a counting house and storage for the rich fruits of his nocturnal harvesting.

Ikey was well pleased with himself. There remained no chinks in his emotional armour and he had kept Mary at his side by involving her in two of these activities. The forgery he shared with his wife Hannah and not with Mary, who did none of the bookwork involved.

Ikey had also persuaded Hannah never to venture near the premises at Bell Alley as implication in the forging of high denomination banknotes led to the death penalty. Ikey pointed out, though unnecessarily, that if they should both go to the gallows, all their property confiscated, their children would be alone and destitute in a cruel and uncaring world. Hannah needed no further encouragement to stay away. In this way Hannah was completely unaware of the existence of a high-class brothel at the Bell Alley address nor was she aware of Mary, the second woman in Ikey's life.

Though Ikey hated Hannah, she owned half of his ready fortune. That is, his convertible wealth, the gold sovereigns and ingots, silver and precious stones, for Ikey believed in liquid assets of the kind you could pack into a smallish space when you beat a hasty retreat. They shared everything equally by means of each of them only knowing a half of the combination to the safe they kept under the floorboards in the pantry of the Whitechapel house, so both were required to be present to open it and neither could escape with the contents without the co-operation of the other.

This was an agreement Ikey had foolishly made in earlier years when he had first been released from a prison hulk and the money taken from Hannah's bawdy houses had supplied the cash he needed to start up in the fencing business. Hannah had insisted on the basis that if Ikey was arrested again he might, under duress, reveal the combination to the authorities or various villains. He now regarded it as the single most foolish thing he had ever done, but Hannah had been unrelenting in her insistence that the practice be continued. Ikey comforted himself that while this prevented him from stealing the contents some day and deserting his wife, Hannah was placed in the very same predicament.

Mary took to the standing upright part of her profession handsomely and developed clear ideas of how she would conduct her role as mistress of a whorehouse to the gentry. She successfully persuaded Ikey that they must go first class with no corners cut and create an establishment second to none in London.

She furnished the house much like the Chelsea one she'd been chased from after the aborted affair with Bob Marley, though with a distinctly oriental flavour she'd observed in a picture of a salon in the window of a printing shop and which she persuaded the proprietor to sell to her. Mary spared not a penny in making the premises in Bell Alley grandly ostentatious with a front parlour lavishly done out in silks and rare carpets as well as erotic statues showing every form of human copulation. Many of the statues were painted in gold and bedecked in coloured ostrich feathers to make a dazzling display of erotica.

Ikey was a rich man, a very rich man, but not one given to spending it upon others. But persuaded by Mary that the best of London's professional and commercial society would beat a path to her door, or more correctly between her expensive linen sheets, where they would be attended by the most skilled and beautiful young courtesans in return for large amounts of money, he opened his purse to the fullest. At the same time he allowed that Mary should owe him thirty percent of the total cost of refurbishing, to be paid off from her future brothel earnings.

Mary was delighted. For the first time she was in control of her own life and she did not regard Ikey's terms as onerous. On the contrary, she was aware that she owed him a great debt and was determined that she would repay it with the utmost loyalty. Ikey was the first person who had shown her the least charity and she would never forget this. A great deal would happen in the course of this strange partnership, some good and much bad, but Mary would never deny that Ikey had been the means of her salvation.

In Mary's bawdy house Ikey could take vicarious pleasure in observing the high and the mighty at work through a peephole in the ceiling. He found it ironic and immensely pleasing to think that one day he was bound to stand trial before a bewigged and scarlet-robed judge and have the image recalled of this same m'lord, without breeches, fat belly wobbling, rogering one of Mary's plump little pigeons.

Mary's establishment made Ikey feel clean and respectable and even somewhat superior for the first time in his life and he grandly imagined himself a member, if only by proxy and proximity, of London's professional classes. Indeed, it gave him the greatest possible satisfaction that it was lawyers, judges, magistrates and bankers who became Mary's regular clients, the very men who, throughout his life, had caused him so much anxiety.

For Ikey it was money well spent and soon it was money most easily earned as men of the bench and at the bar and in the city knocked discreetly at the scarlet door of Mary's Bell Alley brothel.

For the most part Mary's clients shared two characteristics: the sprightliness and easy randiness of youth had long passed, though the memory of it remained bright as a sunlit morning. They came to Egyptian Mary's, as it became known, to attempt to relive the past while indulging any current fantasies.

The story of Mary's missing hands, often told with great conviction, added greatly to her fame and customers believed that many of the sexual fantasticals available to them stemmed originally from her time spent in the mysterious orient. Mary took to wearing a turban of multi-coloured silks which did nothing to dispel the rumours and added greatly to her mystique.

Mary taught her girls the use of belladonna to lift their spirits and to enter with enthusiasm into the many bondages, recitations, titivations, dressing ups and stripping downs, spankings, pretendings, offendings, excitements, oral, anal, frontal and often curiously banal, which her ageing, mostly pot-bellied, clientele required. They learned to be extravagant in their compliments and the most inadequate sexual performance was built to high praise so that the ageing participant left Egyptian Mary's convinced of his renewed and awesome virility.

There were three things not on offer at Egyptian Mary's but which could be procured at any other London brothel. Mary did not trade in little boys or girls or in young men.

This was not because Ikey had any morality in regard to the exploitation of children or whoresons, but Mary did. She loved children and each day at noon the brats would be at the scullery door for soup and bread which she had cooked up in a steaming cauldron so that she would feed fifty or more. Though she took care not to show them more than a rough affection, she longed to take the smaller children into her arms and hug them. Street children, she knew from her own experience, were feral animals and must be treated as wild creatures that would always bite the hand that fed them. Mary expected nothing from them and somehow they knew she was their friend, and even perhaps that she loved them. She earned their loyalty slowly with food and some physic and an occasional dressing for a cut or yellow ointment for their eyes, and they repaid her with gossip. Should a constable appear to be snooping there was always a child at the back door to alert her.

Though a new client might occasionally demand the services of a child or a young boy, a common enough request in almost any London brothel, Mary would refuse him and often in the process offend some high-ranking toff. London Town was swarming with starving urchins who would go with anyone for twopence or a plate of toasted herrings. There was no class in that sort of rough trade which was more for the likes of Hannah to supply, which she did without compunction. Mary had no trouble convincing Ikey, who wanted no close attention from the law paid to the premises on Bell Alley and he knew, better than most, that children cause trouble when grown men of the middle and upper classes are involved.

Several hours past midnight, long after the customers had been gratified, satisfied, slumbered, sobered and finally put into carriages and sent on their way, when the clicking of Mary's abacus beads ceased and the accounting books were made up in straight lines and neatly squared columns, Ikey would arrive.

He would come in from his vile night abroad where he received and paid and argued and bartered for stolen property in dimly lit taverns and tap rooms, brothels, flash-houses, netherkens and thieves' kitchens and it was usual for him to drop into the Pig 'n Spit where he passed some time at the ratting. His life was populated by all manner of villains, thieves, swell mobsmen, flashmen, touts, pickpockets, pimps, itinerant criminals and scallywags. His last call before returning to Egyptian Mary's was always within the great St Giles rookery, known in the vernacular as the 'Holy Land', to a decaying building long vacated by its original occupants. Here he unlocked the door and in darkness crept up a set of rickety stairs to the very top where the damp and decay had not yet fully penetrated.

Within this building resided a gang of carefully chosen urchins, street children who had been trained to Ikey's ways and who did his bidding. The youngest of them were stock buzzers or smatter haulers, stealers of silk handkerchiefs known as kingsmen which, as was the fashion with toffs, were conveniently carried protruding from the coat tail. Ikey would pay ninepence each for these, though some were worth as much as three shillings when later sold in Rosemary Lane.

Ikey was always on the look-out for a talent, a boy with fingers light enough to make a tooler. A tooler was the most elite of the pickpockets, a planner and plotter, a boy with brains, daring and courage. At any one time Ikey hoped for four toolers in the making and two fully blown and working at the top of their trade. A great tooler could go on to be a swell mobsman, though most, even some of the best, got their hands to shaking from too frequent imbibement of gin or brandy or found their minds preoccupied and numbed to action by the fear of being caught and transported.

Tooling was where the real money lay in the art of pickpocketing and it required four boys, the tooler himself, a stickman and two stalls and, if available, up to four urchins to transport the goods from the scene of the crime as quickly as possible.

The first stall would go ahead, scanning the crowd for members of the law or even a group of workmen or a large shop boy who might give chase to a thief in return for the prospect of a reward. The second stall was on duty between the tooler and the stickman and was generally a larger boy who was required to impede the progress of any person in too hot pursuit of the stickman, who was the first to receive the article from the tooler and get the transportation of the lifted goods under way. The tactics followed were to set a pattern, a routine worked by Ikey until it became second nature to the boys.

Choosing a victim was a task not taken lightly, for the tooler was trained to observe human nature in the smallest detail, to watch the mannerisms of a chosen quarry, how each talked and walked and where they placed their hands, with whom they conversed and where they stopped. Ikey would demand patience and careful selection. A pogue taken from a dizzy shop-girl containing one silver shilling carried the same penalty at law as a dumby lifted from a rich toff stuffed with Bank of England longtails and jingling with gold sovereigns. A garnet brooch deftly unclipped from the bombasine blouse worn by a nanny earned a gaol term or transportion no different to the neatest unclipping of a diamond pin from the silk bodice of a duchess.

'It's quality we's after, lads. To be sent abroad for the lifting of a tin brooch is a sin of character what can't never be recovered from. A gentleman's gold 'unter or a diamond pin, now that's a lay worthy o' true respect!' Ikey would pause, taking in the eager faces around him. 'We does not sell ourselves cheaply, my dears. Tooling is a most ancient and noble art and we are artists. Our fingers play as lightly upon a purse or dumby, diamond clip or gold yack as the fingers o' the greatest virtuoso alight upon the ivories of a harp-sichord at a concert in 'onour of the King 'imself.'

Sometimes a promising quarry would be watched for days until the tooler knew precisely how and where to make the pull. A lady might be taken while shopping in the afternoon, this being regarded as light-fingered practice for the more meaningful tooling of toffs and gentlemen during the evening to come. ' 'Umans is all predictable, observe the pattern and you know the mark,' Ikey would repeat ad nauseam to his dirty-faced pupils.

Ikey seemed never to tire of the training of these small boys. He started with them very young, not older than six or seven, for it was his belief that the lad who had not mastered the grammar of his art by the time his voice broke seldom reached any high degree of competence. He even taught them to cheat skilfully at the game of cribbage, for he understood that they would naturally grow up to be gamblers and he hoped to give his boys a better chance than most of keeping their ill-gained money in their own pockets.

In this respect and in many others he was known as the best and most famous of all the kidsmen and his toolers became the élite on the streets and in the busy arcades. Urchins would implore him to be enrolled in what Ikey referred to as the 'Methodist Academy of Light Fingers', a spoof on the Methodist Academy of Light, a salvationist school for the honest poor, situated in an adjacent slum court in St Giles.

While there were a great many kidsmen to be found, men who trained street urchins for snakesmen, pickpockets and as beggars, they were generally most harsh in their methods, ignorant men with a too frequent hard, flat, impatient hand to the side of an urchin's head. Should a boy fail to exhibit the required amount of tact and ingenuity in dipping it was the custom for him to be given a severe beating from the other boys or by the kidsman himself. To this punishment was added no food to eat until the hapless child improved his pick-pocketing technique or simply starved to death.

Ikey, however, offered not harsh punishment but reward, a bright penny handed over, a large chop rimmed with fat added to a child's plate at supper, or even a glass of best beer given with a pat on the back. Ikey's thorough ways and his understanding of the competitive nature of small boys created the best toolers to be found in London, all most proud to be graduates of the Methodist Academy of Light Fingers, Proprietor, Isaac Solomon, Esq.

At practice Ikey would use a tailor's dummy set up in a pool of lamplight and dressed up with the garments most likely to be worn in the street. Sometimes these would emulate the attire of a toff, swell or country gentleman and at others, a grand lady, a doxy or, for the smallest of the children, a nanny or shop assistant. Into these clothes were sewn tiny bells that tinkled at the slightest vibration.

At the conclusion of each week it was the custom among Ikey's boys to take a vote decided by the acclamation of all. The most proficient boy at the practice of dipping was voted the title of Capt'n Bells, whereas the least competent was christened Tinkle Bell. The former was a title much prized among his young apprentice thieves, while the latter was worn with a fierce resolve to be 'unchristened' as speedily as possible.

Bob Marley had come from among these children and there were a number of talented magsmen, swell mobsmen and flash-men who could claim 'a proper education' by the redoubtable Ikey in the ways of thieving and disposing and the general nature of surviving in the trade of taking what rightfully belonged to others. It was this foundation, laid early and trained carefully, which later supplied much of the goods which Ikey would receive as a fence.

Ikey would arrive at the boys' squalid quarters around three in the morning, whereupon lectures and demonstrations on the art of light fingers and the brightening of minds took place. Afterwards those boys with goods to dispose of, such items as they might have taken on the street since the previous night's visit, would wait back while the remaining urchins would repair to a nearby chop house where a private room was held for them. Ikey would carefully examine the prize each offered, explaining its composition in stones or judging its value in precious metal or as an article alone.

'Know what you takes, my dear. A bit o' glass set in lead and gold dipped ain't worthy o' your knowledge, emeralds or diamonds set in gold is what your fingers is trained to lift. Watch the light, see it play, diamonds shoot, emeralds pulse, rubies burn, pearls glow. Judge the wearer, not the glory o' the gown, the toss o' the head, the modesty of eye. Fake pearls is more common than real and when worn on a bosom young, temptin' and firm, is most likely to be that of a tart playin' at courtesan than a lady o' quality. Judge the laughter – too shrill and too often is the 'abit o' the badly bred. Details, my dears, everythin' is in the details. Sniff the perfume, examine the nap o' the boots and the 'em o' the skirt for old dirt or much mending. If the gentleman's 'ands is too familiar with 'is escort then the lady is too cheaply bought. It's all there waiting for your eyes to measure and your mind to equate before you decides to make the vamp.'

Ikey would then pay them, naturally at a much

reduced price to the street value of the goods, though never were the articles so cheaply purchased as to encourage a young lad to take the merchandise elsewhere.

The business of the night completed, Ikey would join the dozen or so boys who ranged in age from six to sixteen for a meal in the nearby chop house. Here they would all be fed from Ikey's purse, though in the order and quality of their performances. Those who had not done well at practice or failed to bring in any merchandise taken on the street would be denied a plate of chops or steak, meat being the reward for performance, though all were equally given a thick wedge of bread and a large bowl of thick steaming broth, enough to keep body and soul together. Ikey himself partook of a bowl of mutton and potato stew, followed by a dish of curds.

Some of the smaller boys, their bellies replete, would leave the chop house to crawl back into their squalid quarters and sleep until noon in a bed of dirty rags. Those who had money or friends who would share what they'd won would stay to grow drunk on a pint of gin or brandy.

During the progress of one night Ikey might be seen, his hands working in the gestures of unctuous trading, in the reeking hubbub of Rosemary Lane doing business among the festoons of second-hand clothes. Or if the tide was in and to run before dawn, he might be seen working his way to the river to the regions of Jacob's Island and those parts known as the Venice of Drains in Bermondsey, which he reached by traversing the impenetrable alleys, dives and runways round Leicester Square and the Haymarket, this part of the great rookery being the convenient asylum for the thieves, flash-men, touts and prostitutes working the rich fields of the West End. Here could be found the rakish members of the upper classes with their courtesans, their ears and necks and decolletage awash with diamonds and pearls, the starched young swells, toffs and codgers on the randy, the gamblers and cashed-up jockeys and the furtive old perverts from the privileged classes who mixed vicariously with the low-life. This place, too, was an essential nightly visitation for a fence of Ikey's status in the underworld.

Ikey could come upon these places from Whitechapel or Spitalfields along dark, fetid lanes, and through vile netherkens crowded to suffocation with thieves and beggars and the desparate, starving poor sleeping and copulating on straw-filled billets and bundles of rags.

Sometimes he moved along well-established paths formed over rooftops or through cellars and dark alleys, sliding past the stagnant open gutters which ran down the centre of these narrow filth-choked runways. Even in the dark he knew the whereabouts of the numerous cesspools which would trap many a gin-soaked hag, or drunkard who'd lost his way and having slipped on the surrounding excrement could not regain a foothold and would be sucked into the shit to drown.

Ikey knew with intimacy this great rookery of St Giles and many others, and was as much at home in them as the rats scurrying ahead of him along the soot-stained walls. He could reach the destination of his choosing without once crossing an honest thoroughfare or appearing within the light of a single street lamp, seen along the way only by the incurious eyes of beggars, thieves, night-stand prostitutes, petty touts, sharpers and the broken and desperate humanity who lived in these festering parts. Those who saw nothing unless they were paid to do so and who, upon being questioned by a magistrates' runner, knew nothing of a person's whereabouts, even if they had glimpsed them, bold as brass, not a moment beforehand.

On a rising tide Ikey might be seen furtively moving close to a wall or along a pier in the dock areas before disappearing below the malodorous deck of a boat. Before dawn's light it would slip its moorings and on the morning tide move silently down the river, its progress concealed by the sulphurous mist and smog that sat upon the Thames.

By sunrise this vessel, which outwardly carried hemp or tiles or any of the other miscellanea which made up the maritime drudgery of commerce between England and the continental ports, would be safely into the Channel. It carried about Ikey's consignments of stolen jewellery to be reworked in Amsterdam and Antwerp; parcels of Bank of England notes in every denomination to be laundered in Hamburg and Prague banks; silver and gold bound for Bohemia and Poland to be sold or melted down in the shops and workshops of various foreign Jews.

Ikey would arrive at Egyptian Mary's not a minute beyond five in the morning. He would greet Mary upon his return from the foulness of his peripatetic night and before anything else he would look at the house takings, always wheedling and quarrelling, as if the bitter bargaining of the night must be run down and unwound before he could be brought to a state of calm.

He would carp at the cost of a haunch of ham, or

measure the level of the claret cask, as much to bring himself to an emotional repose as to attempt to gain more than his fair share of the night's profit. Thereafter he would unload the takings of his fencing business for that night, valuing each item expertly and suggesting what might become of them; a melting or resetting or re-cutting, what could be disposed of in London, what must needs be sent abroad.

Mary entered all this into her receivals ledger. Ikey also acquainted her of the whereabouts of heavier merchandise: bolts of cloth, linen and brocade, a handsome pair of Louis XIV chairs or a valuable tapestry. Mary would arrange to have these picked up and delivered at a time when they would arrive unobserved. In this last regard she would often use Bob Marley, the slash man, whom she trusted and who proved to be a careful and reliable go-between.

Ikey had a passion for order in his affairs and this had made him extremely rich. When this final task for the night was completed, Mary would place the books in a secret place, this task always overseen by Ikey. Then, at last, often just before dawn, they would pause to share a glass of chilled champagne in her little private parlour at the rear of the establishment.

This was the happiest time of Ikey's life and he composed an epigram which he would pronounce to Mary and which encapsulated the satisfaction he took from being the joint proprietor of Egyptian Mary's. Holding his glass of champagne to the light and watching the tiny beaded bubbles rise in straight and orderly lines to the surface he would announce, 'My dear, I 'ave a theory fantastic for the success of our enterprise. Shall I say it for you?'

'You certainly may, sir! You certainly may!' Mary
would rise and top up his glass and then do the same
to her own, whereupon she would seat herself again
holding her glass and wait. Ikey would lower his glass
and take a polite sip of champagne, then in a preacher-
like manner, intone:

> *If the angle of the dangle*
> *is equal to the heat of the meat,*
> *then the price of the rise,*
> *is decided by the art of the tart.*

'There it be, my dear, the entire business of brothel
keepin' contained in a simple rhyme.'

Simple as he claimed it to be, Ikey thought it exceedingly clever and never tired of the reciting of it. At the
conclusion of the rhyme they would clink glasses and
entwine arms, each taking a sip of champagne, whereupon Mary would say, 'May our bubbles keep risin'.
Amen!'

It was as close as the two of them ever came to sentimentality of the kind which might be described as
love.

For Mary the bawdy house on Bell Alley was a daily
confirmation that she could be a woman of enterprise
and that by her own wit and skill she could gain a security in life she had never known. Ikey was proving to
be her way out of poverty, misery and an almost certain
slow crippling death from syphilis, or a quicker one at
the hands of some madman with a shiv in need of the
means for an opium pipe. There were a thousand ways
a prostitute could meet her death, but very few ways in

which she could expect to remain alive much beyond her mid-twenties.

In gratitude Mary showed Ikey more tolerance than ill temper. She was often sorely tempted to screw his scrawny neck, but for the most part refrained from violence, boxing his ears only when provoked to the extreme. She knew him to be a coward, a cheat, a liar and, of course, a notorious thief, though this last characteristic she regarded simply as Ikey's profession.

Without the thief there would be no magistrate or judge or lawyer or half the regular clientele of her bawdy house. And so she had no reason to place Ikey's choice of vocation in any poorer light than that of her clients. When the poor embrace the tenets of morality it comes ready-made with misery as its constant companion. Mary counted herself fortunate to have Ikey in her life and very occasionally in her bed, which was as close as anyone had ever come to loving him, or she to feeling affection for any other person since her mother and father died.

But it is not in the nature of things to remain calm. Contentment is always a summer to be counted in brief snatches of sunlight, while unhappiness is an endless winter season of dark and stormy weather. The cold wind of Ikey's and Mary's discontent was beginning to howl through the rat-infested rookeries, sniffing at the mud and shit of the dark alleys and stirring the slime of the river into a foment of disaster which was about to wash over them both.

Chapter Six

At the end of a miserable night in December with the wind roaring and the snow swirling, Ikey was just turning into Bell Alley from Winfield Street when a figure leapt from the shadows directly into his path. Ikey jumped in fright as the dark shape presented itself through a sudden flurry of snow.

'It be friend!' Bob Marley shouted into the driving wind. 'A word is needed in yer ear, Ikey, an urgent word!'

Ikey relaxed. Bob Marley was to be trusted. As a young 'un he'd been a chimney sweep whom Ikey had plucked from his miserable trade to work for him as a snakesman. He recalled how he hadn't cheated the boy particularly and so had no reason to fear him. He was a likely lad in his day who seemed to be double jointed in all his connected parts, and could squirm and slide through apertures too small for a dock rat to enter. While he had remained small Ikey had profited well from his talent for entering property.

As a boy Marley had been intelligent and naturally cunning and would have made a good leader if he had not always been a loner. Though it was this very characteristic which meant he could be trusted not to open his gob or boast of his conquests to the other street urchins. With money in his purse for frequent visits to a chop house, the pocket-sized lad had grown quickly and was soon too big to be a snakesman. Ikey had trained him as a pickpocket but he never amounted to greatness for he refused to work in a team. He'd grown into a villain, dangerous if crossed, but known to work only for himself and only for gold. In the terms of the times and the kind with whom Ikey naturally mixed, Bob Marley was reliable as a new-minted sovereign. Ikey stepped deeper into the alley where the noise of the wind was less intense.

'I 'ave information important to ya, Ikey, most important, most important indeed! Yes! If I say so meself, information o' the kind a person doesn't come upon every day.' Marley paused and then added in an ominous voice, 'Thank Gawd!'

Ikey removed his hands from the pockets of his great coat and slipped off the filthy fur-lined glove of his right hand, then he re-entered the coat through an entirely different part of its anatomy and opened his dumby secretly. He allowed his fingers to slip through the coins in the leather purse until he sensed the warmer touch of a gold sovereign, whereupon his nimble fingers worked until they touched six sovereigns which he carefully pushed to one corner of the purse, then he took three. These he produced held between thumb and forefinger as though they were a single coin conjured from the air. He had already gauged the worth of Marley's information, which he'd set in his mind at six gold sovereigns. He knew from the tone of his informer's voice that the information was kosher. He'd think less of Marley if he didn't manage to extract another three sovereigns from him for its deliverance. He held the three gold coins out to the man in front of him.

'Three sov? Three bleedin' sov!' Marley removed the scarf that covered all but his eyes, looked at Ikey in disgust and then spat onto the snow at his feet. 'This ain't no bleedin' social call!'

But Ikey held the gold sovereigns in front of Marley until his fingers began to tingle with the cold and finally Marley, shrugging his shoulders, removed the woollen mitten from one hand and took them without a word, testing their weight in the palm of his hand before biting each in turn with a gold eye tooth. He grunted and placed them into his vest-pocket. Though he'd hoped for more, he'd been standing around in the bitter night for more than an hour, and he needed a large steak with relish and a pint of hot gin or he was sure he would perish from the cold.

'You've been shopped!' Marley said finally.

'Who done it?' Ikey asked.

'It come up from Rosemary Lane. No names. Just a good friend what's got an ear connected.'

'When?' Ikey asked.

'Termorra, early mornin', sparrow fart!' Marley paused, then added, 'After all the toffs 'ave scarpered from yer 'ouse of ill repute!'

'This mornin'! Oh Jesus! Oh me Gawd! Oh shit! This mornin'? This very mornin'?'

Bob Marley nodded and dug into the interior of his coat to produce a gold hunter at the end of a brass chain. Clicking it open, he examined its face.

'I'd say 'bout three 'ours, tosh!' He closed the lid of the watch with a flick of his thumb. 'Reckon they gotcha this time, me lovely!'

'Where?' Ikey asked tremulously. It was an important question, for if it was the house he and his wife Hannah shared he would be less concerned. The house in Whitechapel had been raided several times, but the trapdoor under Hannah's bed, which led to a large false ceiling in which his stolen property was stored, was so cunningly contrived as to be invisible to the naked eye. But the house at the end of the alley in which he stood was less well accommodated to the concealment of stolen goods. A raid on Mary's bawdy house, even if he could clear it of contraband in time, which hardly seemed possible, would be a disaster. Its basement contained the heavy mechanicals of the printing press which had been brought in, one piece at a time, over several months, to make up a press of a very peculiar kind, and such as would be of great interest to the law if examined with the printing of banknotes in mind. There could be no thought of its removal, which would take several days.

Bob Marley's hand went out and he rubbed his forefinger and thumb together. Ikey returned to the interior of the great coat and produced another gold sovereign. Marley pocketed it and simply jerked his thumb down towards the interior of Bell Alley. 'Right 'ere, me lovely.'

It was not possible for Ikey's sallow skin to grow more pale. ''Ere? Oh me Gawd! Not 'ere, not tomorrow!' He looked up at Marley in despair. 'Who? Who will it be?' Ikey produced a gold coin without Marley encouraging him.

Bob Marley took it with a grin. He'd hoped for five sov and he'd got it. He was not to know that Ikey had reserved another but, given the nature of the news, would have paid five times as much for his information.

'Is it a question of *feeing* the officers, my dear?' Ikey's lips trembled as he asked. ''Ave they sent you? Is that why you've come? Do we 'ave any time? No, o' course not, no time, no time whatsoever and at all!'

Bob Marley shook his head slowly and replaced the woollen mitten, rubbing his hands together to restore the circulation in his recently exposed limb.

'No set up, Ikey. City!'

'City!' Ikey howled. 'Oh Gawd, oh mercy, oh no!'

''Fraid so, me lovely, it's them machines you got in the basement what's got you in this awful pre*dicta*ment!'

Ikey drew back alarmed. 'What's you know about that then?'

Marley chuckled. 'It's me business to know fings, ain't it? Just like I knows it's City what's comin' after yer!'

The single word 'City' had struck mortal terror into Ikey's heart. 'City' was simply another word for the Bank of England. For the private police force they ran who were said to be as remorseless as a pack of blood-hounds when they set upon a case.

Ikey's worst nightmare was taking place. He had been tempted into dealing with queer screens, the making of forged Bank of England notes, knowing it to be the most dangerous criminal vocation of them all. It was also as good a business as a villain could think about, providing you had the capital and the skill to set it up and the courage and wit not to be caught.

Forged English notes were laundered in Europe, mostly in Russia, Poland and Bohemia, where frequent enough commercial travel took place from England through the Hanseatic Ports. These countries, unlike France, Holland,

Austria and Italy, were not sufficiently traversed for the smaller banks to be totally familiar with the larger denominations of English notes, so that a good forgery would more easily deceive their bank officials.

Ikey was making an enormous profit all round, paying for the European remodelling work on stolen jewellery with forged long-tails, this being a splendid way to launder the counterfeit English banknotes. It was also why he allowed Mary to chastise him for being cheated in his over-seas transactions. Ikey was cleaning up at both ends.

Forgery was nevertheless an exceedingly dangerous endeavour. Ikey knew that no feeing or bribing of a Bank of England officer was possible and that once on his tail, the City police would not give up until they had him safely in the dock at the Old Bailey or, better still, posted for a hanging and locked in a condemned man's cell at Newgate.

Ikey had broken the first rule of a good fence, this being that a criminal endeavour in which bribery is not possible is the most dangerous of all possible pursuits and not, under any circumstances, to be undertaken. Ikey was not given to self-recrimination but now he cas-tigated himself for the fool he had been. There were fine pickings elsewhere and he was already a rich man. Forgery carried the death penalty and no crime under English law was considered more heinous, for it attacked the very basis of property, the oak heart of the English upper classes.

Ikey mumbled his thanks to Bob Marley, who had started to move away.

'It's nuffink, me pleasure,' Marley called back laugh-ing. 'I'll visit you in Newgate, me lovely, bring ya summink tasty, wotcha say then, jellied eels?'

''Ave you told Mistress Mary?' Ikey shouted at the retreating Marley.

'Nah!' His dark shape disappeared into Winfield Street.

Ikey waited a few moments before he too traced his steps out of the alley back into the gusting snow storm. In less than fifteen minutes he'd arrived at the netherken where his boys slept. Here he found two likely lads and sent them to Covent Garden to borrow a coster's cart narrow enough to move down the alley. Ikey arranged to meet the two boys at the Bell Alley brothel half an hour hence.

It was fortunate that it was Christmas and much of the goods, usually kept in the attic above the brothel, had been 'doctored'. That is, the monogram and other forms of identification removed and the goods sent back into the marketplace or to the continent, this time of the year being most expedient for the disposal of expensive merchandise. If Ikey could get the two lads back in time and the load of contraband away, at the very least, they would not be able to charge him for receiving.

Ikey was a deeply frightened man as he turned his key in the lock of the rear door of the Bell Alley premises and slipped quietly into the scullery. The house was still. The last customers had long since been sent home by carriage, and the girls put to bed with a hot brandy toddy into which Mary always mixed a sleeping draught.

He decided not to tell Mary of the events to occur but simply to say that he was unwell with a stomach ache and wished to take her ledger home with him so that he might go over it later. This had occurred once or twice before and she would not be overly suspicious at such a request. He would explain the removal of the stolen goods from the attic as goods sold in a bumper Christmas season.

However luck was on Ikey's side in the event that he discovered Mary asleep in her chair as he crept silently into her parlour. She was still seated in an over-stuffed chair wrapped about in a comforter with her chin resting on her chest. On the small table beside her was her ledger and to the side of it stood two pewter tankards and an open bottle of good claret wine. Ikey moved to the wall and turned the gaslight lower, then quietly lifted the ledger and one of the tankards together with its doily from the table and stuffed them into a pocket in his great coat.

Ikey worked quickly, using a bull's eye lamp he'd trimmed in the scullery, to move the stolen goods from the attic down to the small back room leading into the alley. He left a large square parcel carefully wrapped in oilcloth until last. Ikey was forced to rest several times as he struggled with it down to the scullery and, despite the cold, he was perspiring profusely by the time he heard the low pre-arranged whistle of one of the lads. The cart, the noise of its wheels padded by the six inch fall of snow, had arrived silently at the rear of the house. The two boys stood rubbing their hands and blowing into their mittens as Ikey opened the scullery door.

With the help of the boys the goods were quickly loaded, placing the square oilcloth parcel into the cart last before covering the whole load with a blood-stained canvas, the cart having been obtained from a mutton butcher at the Garden. Ikey gave each lad a shilling, with the promise of another to come, and asked them to await him at the Pig 'n Spit.

Ikey then let himself into the basement quarters down a short flight of stairs and through a door within the house to which only he had a key. Upon entering he became aware of a deep and resonant snoring coming from behind a curtained partition at the far end of the large room which his partner kept as his own quarters. He had no need to concern himself with careful movement since Van Esselyn, the deaf and dumb master forger, would not awaken unless shaken.

Ikey knew the room off by heart, having often enough visited it before dawn. The remainder of the room contained the engraver's bench with etching tools, a large lock-up cupboard for storing the special paper and precious inks procured from a source in Birmingham, a general work bench, hand press, guillotine, and finally the splendid Austrian-manufactured printing press.

Ikey quickly crossed over to the beautiful press and, kneeling beside it, he pushed down hard on what appeared to be a knot-hole in the floorboard. The board immediately snapped open an inch. Ikey repeated this with similar knot-holes in adjacent and parallel boards until the ends of four short boards stood raised an inch above those surrounding them. Ikey then removed the loose nails and lifted the boards to reveal a steel safe set into the floor, its door facing uppermost.

Ikey quickly worked the combination and removed five copper plates etched with the markings of Bank of England notes of various denominations. The etching for the Bank of England five pound note he immediately placed back in the safe. Then he removed all the counterfeit notes from the safe, save for a small bundle of five pound notes. He locked the safe again and carefully replaced the floor boards, clicking the knots back into place and pushing all but one of the nails back into their slots, so that it was once again firm underfoot. The nail he placed not quite beside the empty hole into which it belonged so that even the most careless searchers might eventually become suspicious.

Ikey spent several minutes more looking about the room and then quietly left, carrying the etching plates and counterfeit notes under his arm. He collected a hemp bag, into which he placed the copper plates and the larger denomination forged notes taken from the safe. Dipping into the interior of his coat he added Mary's ledger, the pewter tankard and the doily, and killing the wick of the bull's eye lamp, he returned it to the scullery, whereupon he let himself out into Bell Alley and back onto Winfield Street. He had less than an hour left before dawn, when the raid was due to take place.

The snow storm seemed to have abated, the wind had dropped and now everything lay quiet, covered in a blanket of fresh snow. But Ikey, his yellow boots crunching on the carpet of white, saw none of the new innocence of his surroundings. Nor did he appreciate the crispness of the clean air which the wind had punched through the rookeries, replacing the foulness which lingered all year, trapped within vile-smelling yellow smog, until the first big snowfall froze the stench, covered the filth and banished the smog. Ikey's mind was otherwise occupied with the problems which lay ahead. In his entire life he had never faced a more difficult situation. If he were to be arrested and convicted on a conspiracy to defraud the Bank of England through forgery, he would be fortunate to escape the hangman's noose. But should this misfortune be avoided it would most certainly be replaced with 'The Boat'. He was sure to get life and be transported to Botany Bay or the new prison island of Van Diemen's Land.

It had been Hannah who had persuaded Ikey to deal in counterfeit money. Ikey recalled how he had at first been most reluctant, but eventually became pleased with the suggestion for all the wrong reasons, the major one used by a nagging Hannah being that the notorious Van Esselyn was deaf and dumb. This, to someone of Ikey's cautious nature, had been what had finally persuaded him.

At first Ikey had insisted on the most basic equipment for the forger, such as could be quickly disposed of in an emergency, but the Liverpool contact grew too greedy and demanded too great a share of the resultant notes. The decision to add the latest in printing machinery finally came about when Ikey discovered a method of obtaining the very paper used by the Bank of England. Furthermore, he had also located a source of inks from Birmingham which closely matched those needed for all the denominations of Bank of England banknotes. The temptation to print on his own had simply been too great and Ikey set about obtaining, mostly from Austria, the machine parts needed for a highly sophisticated press. The only drawback was that such specialised and large equipment could not be easily dismantled, or moved, nor could it be passed off as a press used for printing works of the usual everyday kind.

Ikey cursed his carelessness and his vanity. The location of his forgery business was another of his exquisite ironies. Often a rich banker would be in the process of dalliance, his fat bum pumping up and down, while directly under his squeaking mattress, separated only by a wooden floor, was a sophisticated printing press in the hands of one of Europe's most skilful engravers and designed to rob the very institution to which this pompous and randified gentleman belonged.

Ikey once confided in Mary that he had invented the three 'f' system of profit: 'A modern economic marvel, my dear, fencin', fuckin' and forgery. We take profits from the bottom, the middle and the top, an excellent arrangement, do you not agree? In the basement we make money, in the house proper we employ your plump little pigeons to make riches from downed breeches and at the very top, we store plate, silver and gold taken from the rich by the bold!'

Ikey, although in shit deeper than that which flowed from the two hundred sewerage outlets which spilled into the River Thames, was far from witless in this matter facing him. For example, he had all the documents of rent and receipts for the printing machinery made out in Van Esselyn's assumed name, this being Thomas Thompson. These were all signed by Van Esselyn. Nor did Ikey's name appear, other than as landlord, on any other documents of a formal nature. In the event of a raid, Abraham Van Esselyn, alias Thomas Thompson, would take the blame and Ikey would assume the unlikely role of a rather stupid absentee landlord, hugely astonished to find his premises, hired innocently to a simple printer, so ill-used by this rapacious and untrustworthy foreigner. The fact that the printing press was of such a specialised nature that it immediately condemned its owner as a high-class printer of banknotes he would claim was beyond his limited knowledge of mechanicals and machinery.

Ikey's genius for avoiding disaster was revealed in his arrangements to have the bank's people find Van Esselyn not only with the machinery to print forged notes but with a plate for a five pound note, the mixing inks and some of the notes themselves, though no paper. Van Esselyn was known to the Bank of England, and should he be found with the printing press but with no other evidence of forgery such as engraving tools, at least one etched copper printing plate and some samples of the completed notes they would be forced to conclude that Van Esselyn was not acting alone. That he was being supplied from elsewhere with the further materials needed to create forged banknotes.

This would immediately cast suspicion on his landlord as a known fence and receiver. But if they found the complete means of achieving a forged banknote under the one roof, and evidence that the process was undertaken alone by a known master forger, any barrister defending Ikey could argue that no proof of a conspiracy between the two men existed and that Van Esselyn had acted on his own accord.

Furthermore, while forgery of high denomination notes, those above five pounds, carried the death sentence, this especially for foreigners, the making of notes up to five pounds in value only carried a protracted prison sentence. Ikey had saved Van Esselyn's neck from the hangman's noose and at the same time probably his own.

It was nice planning, for in the eyes of the law and the officers of the Bank of England who wished to be seen accountable to their depositors, Van Esselyn's

arrest would effectively put an end to the forgery operation and conveniently supply both a foreign victim and
a successful prosecution. A foreign villain was always
better news, and one who could be construed as French
even more so. With a bit of luck the City might, in time,
give up the quest to get Ikey arrested and even if not,
once again, in the hands of a good barrister (Ikey could
afford the very best), his prosecution in the Old Bailey
could be made to look like blatant victimisation.

Ikey's relationship with Van Esselyn had, as far as he
knew, never been witnessed by any other person.
Though Mary knew of it, she had never actually seen
the two men together. So only Van Esselyn and Mary
could testify to the connection and both could, if the
need arose, be declared hostile witnesses and have their
evidence discounted.

Ikey knew full well that no judge would possibly
believe this, nor any jury for that matter, but he knew
also that the letter of the law was often in direct contrast to its spirit. In the hands of a talented King's
Counsel, all the evidence could point to his being the
innocent landlord. The paper submitted for scrutiny by
his defence, the leases, receipts and ledgers would show
clearly that he'd acted only as a property owner hiring
his premises for commercial purposes. In fact, it was
essential that Van Esselyn do all in his power to implicate Ikey as his partner in crime. In this way counsel
could demand evidence to support this assertion, a
receipt, note, possibly a witness who had seen them
together. Even if the jury convicted Ikey, he would take
his case to the Court of Appeal where his 'technical'
innocence would be almost certainly upheld by a judge.
Ikey's cool head and knowledge of the law had on more

than one occasion saved his skin. But he had never before been up against the Bank of England.

Though he was most hopeful that he could make a case for his innocence regarding the printing press and Van Esselyn's forgery practice, the same was not true with Mary's occupation of the premises. While she too carried documents testifying that she rented the premises from him and that she was the sole owner of the business which she conducted within the house, it would be almost impossible to prove himself unaware of the nature of her vocation.

However, Ikey was almost certain that the City police would not be interested in arresting Mary as a brothel keeper. The premises were outside the City area and they were unlikely to stoop to such menial policing matters as the arrest of the mistress of a brothel. Besides, in the case of this particular house of ill fame, there was no knowing on whose potentially awkward toes they might be treading.

All things considered it was a neat enough arrangement, but by no means a plan without obvious flaws. Several occurred to Ikey's untrusting nature at once. For instance, who had shopped him? Would they appear as witness for the prosecution? Was Bob Marley reliable, or a part of the conspiracy? How drastically would Hannah react when she heard about the goings on in the house in Bell Alley and the existence of Mary? Ikey grew pale at the thought of her anger, for he feared Hannah almost as much as he did the law.

Ikey determined that he would secure the contents in the cart at his Whitechapel house and leave on the early morning coach for Birmingham, waking Hannah only to inform her that he would be gone for some time.

In Ikey's experience, a little seeking and finding always cooled matters down. The hullabaloo which the capture of a notorious international forger would make in both *The Times* and the penny papers would be sufficient initial glory for the bank, and he hoped they might keep his name out of it until they had more concrete evidence of his involvement, by which time he felt sure he would have constructed a web of outrageous circumstances to meet every question, legal or filial. But everything depended on the Bank of England police being forced to accept that Abraham Van Esselyn, alias Thomas Thompson, was a lone operator free of Ikey's influence.

He then ran a second scenario through his head, this being the possibility that he and Mary would be arrested and convicted as brothel owners. Ikey soon saw that there might be some advantage in this occurrence. He could readily admit to his partnership in Egyptian Mary's and would then be able to claim that the presence of a sample printing business on the premises was a ploy to conceal the existence of a brothel at the same address. It was a common enough occurrence, concealing an illegitimate business behind a legitimate one.

Being the silent partner in a whorehouse was a minor crime when compared to the crime of forgery of Bank of England notes. Again, with a good barrister, he might escape with a heavy fine and a couple of months in Newgate. Mary, alas, would almost certainly be transported. The female wickedness of running a brothel far transcended the loan of the finance to set up such a business, or even the crime of enjoying the profits resulting from such a loan. Many a magistrate or member of parliament was a slum landlord, investing his money for profit and not overly concerned about the purpose for which his premises were used, whether for a Sunday school or a brothel. Profit enjoys the divine blessing of the Church and was to be worshipped without question.

In England money and property were thought to be the business of God and both received His absolute sanction. But the corrupting of the young and the innocent by a madam in a bawdy house was a crime against the Almighty and His angels of the most heinous nature. Mary, Ikey knew, would be severely punished if she was convicted.

For the first time in his life Ikey found himself at odds with a conscience which he had hitherto not known to exist. His love for Mary was directly opposed to his greed and his greed was entirely tied up with Hannah and her children.

Ikey was well used to walking the thin line between safety and disaster, but he was getting older and was very much richer and, for the first time, happy with much of his life. It was a pity that Mary might need to be sacrificed, for she was in large part the cause of his contentment. But kind regard was such a recent experience in Ikey's narrow universe of feelings that he neither trusted it nor appreciated its worth. It was a sentiment he had never once felt directed towards himself, and even his children had shown him none, their mother careful, on the rare occasions they were together, not to allow him the slightest influence over them.

Ikey's low regard for himself meant it was impossible to contemplate that Mary might care for him in the least. His nature and the world he lived in allowed for neither sentiment nor pity. Survival was the only rule to which there was no exception. And so he felt some sadness at the possibility of losing Mary, an entirely new and alien experience, but in no sense did he feel remorse. In the most unlikely event of the brothel being included in the raid Mary must be sacrificed if he was to survive.

Besides, Ikey told his recently discovered conscience, it was far better for him to be on the outside so that he could secretly pay Mary's counsel and other legal fees and, if she was convicted, to fee the turnkeys and officials at Newgate prison in order to make her incarceration tolerable. Should she be sentenced to transportation and accommodated first, as was the custom, for several months in a prison at Chatham, Bristol or Plymouth or with luck on the Thames, the many bribes, remunerations and emoluments she would require to survive this experience would need to come from his unfortunate purse. Although the thought of parting with money, even in so noble a cause, filled him with an unhappy sense of himself being the victim, he decided he would accept this sacrifice as some sort of repayment for the time he had spent with Mary.

Ikey arrived at the Pig 'n Spit where the boys waited for him, jumping up and down in one spot and hugging themselves against the bitter cold. He lifted the canvas cover and removed the parcel wrapped in oilcloth, then sent the boys on their way, agreeing to meet them at his Whitechapel home in less than half an hour.

Struggling with the heavy parcel, Ikey walked down a small alley to the side of the building and into the skittle yard at the rear of the public house. He placed the parcel at the back door and walked over to the cellar chute, where he bent down and lifted the heavy wooden cover with some difficulty to reveal a further barrier, a set of iron bars which were locked down from within the cellar. Removing his boot, he rapped loudly on a single steel bar with its heel, at the same time calling out to the cellar boy to wake up and open the back door of the public house. In a few moments a lantern appeared at the base of the chute, though it was too dark in the cellar below to see the face behind it.

'Let me in, lad, it be Ikey Solomon,' he called, keeping his voice as low as possible. 'I 'ave most urgent business with your mistress. 'Urry now, I've no time to waste!'

Ikey left the public house less than ten minutes later. The streets and alleys were white with snow though a few early-morning market carts, and a small herd of scraggy-looking sheep being driven to a slaughter house were already beginning to turn it into slush. It was six o'clock in the morning and not yet light when he reached his house in Whitechapel and waited for several minutes in the freezing cold for the boys to arrive with the cart.

Ikey and the boys, their breath frosting from the effort, unloaded the contents of the cart and placed the load in the front parlour. Then Ikey paid the young lads a second shilling and sent them, well pleased, on their way.

Mary's ledger he took straightaways to his study and added it to those already concealed in the cavity below the floorboards. Then removing the counterfeit notes and copper etching plates from his bag he put each of the plates carefully aside. He then took up the notes, several thousand pounds of counterfeit longtails, which he placed in the grate and set alight, setting fire to the pile three times in all to make certain that there was nothing left but a handful of ashes. Whereupon he carefully swept the ash onto a piece of butcher's paper and put them into a small pewter tankard which he half filled with water, stirred well and swallowed.

Destroying the counterfeit banknotes was the most difficult thing Ikey could remember ever having to do – the notes were almost perfect and he might quite easily have allowed them into the London markets without fear of immediate discovery. But he was a consummate professional and in Ikey's mind releasing the notes in London was the equivalent of shitting on your own doorstep, in effect asking to be caught. Laundering the false notes through foreign banks was an example of the finesse which had earned him his title as the Prince of Fences. Though, having finally swallowed the contents of the mug, he allowed two silent tears to run down his cheeks and permitted himself the luxury of a single-knuckled sniff.

Ikey then took a needle and thread from the drawer of his desk and sewed the copper engraving plates into the hem of his great coat, first wrapping them carefully in four sheets of strong white paper. Each sheet was taken from separate books in a collection of several dozen handsome leather-bound volumes contained within a breakfront bookcase. Had any person been observing him they would have been curious at the manner of obtaining these squares of paper. Ikey removed the four volumes seemingly at random and opened them to the back cover where he carefully peeled back the endpaper. This revealed a second sheet of paper which Ikey now used as wrapping for the plates, first binding them with twine before sewing them into the hem of his coat.

All this activity took longer than he had intended and Ikey was anxious to make good his escape. He climbed the stairs and shook Hannah awake so that she might help him carry the stuff from the parlour, to be hidden within the false ceiling. Hannah, naturally cantankerous and more so by having been awakened after less than two hours of sleep, cursed Ikey, though she was not unaccustomed to this sort of disturbance. Ikey was known to use several places to store goods at this time of year and sometimes they needed to be hastily moved. Neither was she surprised when after the task was completed Ikey grunted a brusque farewell, explaining only that he had decided to travel to Birmingham. News of a rich haul had come to him and seeking to amuse her so as not to arouse the least suspicion he added a sentiment she loved so much to hear: 'Ah, my dear, the gentile scriptures are *not* correct. Even at Christmas time it is *never* better to give than to *receive*!'

Chapter Seven

Ikey arrived at the coaching post at Whitechapel markets just as the coachman's call to climb aboard was heard, and he seated himself beside the far window so that he could look outwards with his back turned to the other passengers. He pulled his head deeply into the lapels of his great coat so that his hat appeared to be resting upon its upturned collar. Thus, cut off from the attentions of his fellow passengers, he fell into deep cogitation on the matters which had unfolded in Bell Alley in the earlier hours of that morning.

It was not long before his ruminations allowed him to see the entire affair in an altogether different light, and Ikey suddenly felt himself ennobled by his sacrifice on Mary's behalf.

As he sat hunched in the coach, with its rattle and bump and clippity-clop, the general rush and rumble of wheels on flinted stone, rutted road and hard white gravel, and watched the country racing past, from deep within his great coat Ikey felt the warm glow of goodness enveloping him.

This sense of saintly satisfaction was not one Ikey could previously remember experiencing, for it is an emotion which comes to a man who has sacrificed his own needs for those of another. It contained a strange feeling of light-headedness and was an experience Ikey was not entirely sure he would like to repeat. While he knew himself very fond of Mary, he was quite inexperienced in matters of the heart, and was therefore unable to recognise that strange emotion which sentimental women referred to so knowingly as true love.

He had once, as a boy of eight selling oranges and lemons on the street, bought a secondhand halfpenny card from a barrow in Petticoat Lane. The card was braided along its edges with pink ribbon and showed a circle formed of tiny red roses at its centre, and within the circle two blue doves perched side by side upon a silver branch, their heads touching. Above the circle and below the braided ribbon was the legend, *To my one and only true love*. Ikey had carried the card with him until he was twenty-two years old, convinced that one day he too would find his one and only true love.

At twenty-two, and quite soon after he had married Hannah, he was convicted of stealing a gentleman's purse. He was sentenced at the Old Bailey to transportation for life and removed to the hulks at Chatham. Here he was to remain for six years, avoiding transportation to Australia through the influence of an uncle who was a slops dealer at the port, and who pleaded directly and successfully to the naval authorities for him to remain in England.

While on the hulks Ikey made the aquaintance of a convicted forger named Jeremiah Smiles, who had taken to being a tattoo artist and proved to have an exceedingly fine hand at the matter of ink rubbed into human flesh. Ikey had paid him to tattoo the design on the card onto his upper arm. The card, by this time much faded and worn, had lost, by means of a missing portion, the last two words of the legend and it now read, *To my one and only . . .*

Ikey explained that the two missing words were *blue dove*. Smiles, like all forgers, was not a man of great imagination. His aptitude being for detail and accurate copying of the known rather than depicting in fantasy the unknown. 'Humph!' he snorted. 'Them's birds, doves most likely. Birds don't love and doves ain't blue!'

Ikey was never lost for an explanation. 'It be a well-known curiosity that doves o' this particular and brilliant hue takes only one partner in their life,' he lied. 'Should one dove die then the other will remain faithful to its memory, takin' no other partner to itself ever again.'

'Blue doves? Bah! Ain't no such creatures, doves is grey and piebald and brown, speckled and pure white if they be fan-tails, but they ain't blue. There never was, nor ever will be, blue doves!'

'Ah, but you're wrong my dear!' Ikey announced. 'Quite wrong and emphatically incorrect and absolutely misinformed! In Van Diemen's Land there is a great wilderness which begins at the edge o' the clearing to a prison garrison place name o' Cascades.' Ikey sighed heavily. 'Gawd forbid, we may yet see it in our lives. It is to the edge o' this clearin' that the blue doves come at mornin's light, each paired and seated with their 'eads together. They sit and coo softly in the 'igh branches o' the blue gum trees and should they witness a convict fellow at work on the ground below, it is reliably told that they cry human tears for the misery they sees and the compassion they feels for the injustice done to all of us who suffer in the name o' the unjust and 'einous laws o' Mother England.'

Ikey paused, for he could see the beginning of contrite tears in his listener's eyes.

'When a convict dies from an act o' violence, such as a floggin' with the cat o' nine, or a beatin' by an officer or by means of a hangin' or starvation or from a charge o' shot while attemptin' to escape, then a blue dove dies with 'im, dies of a broken 'eart.'

By this time Smiles, seated on his haunches on the deck in front of Ikey, was sobbing unashamedly.

'There is told of a tree at this vile place,' Ikey continued soulfully, milking the moment to its extreme, 'an old tree without leaf, its bark peeled and its branches pure silver, where at sunrise the blue doves come in such numerosity that they become the very leaves o' the tree. The tree becomes a shinin' blue thing in the antipodean sunlight. But, if you should observe with careful eyes, you will see no two doves are perched with 'eads together. No dove is partner to another, for each o' these doves is the partner of a blue dove who 'as died when a convict 'as violently perished.'

Ikey lowered his voice to a whisper. 'It is said that the blue doves that sit upon that great silver tree are too numerous for any man to count!'

Much taken with this story, Jeremiah Smiles had faithfully rendered onto Ikey's upper arm the circle of roses and within it the two blue doves, whereupon he had inscribed above the heart the words: *To my one and only blue dove.*

Now, nearly twenty years later, on his way to Birmingham, the thought crossed Ikey's mind that Mary was his one and only blue dove and he grew suddenly greatly sentimental at this thought.

Ikey told himself he would take good care of his little blue dove, and that no violence would come to her, as she would not lack the means to bribe and pay her way. Should she be arrested, convicted in due course and, as was most likely, transported to New South Wales, he would pay for her continued good treatment in prison and upon her eventual transportation she would lack for nothing.

It was at this point in his rumination that an idea of startling magnitude came to him, one so bold that it caused his head to pop completely up and out of his great coat to see whether the nature of things had changed so entirely that he was not, as he supposed, on the coach to Birmingham, but on some celestial flight of fancy – a voyage of the imagination which had taken himself out of himself and transformed him into another creature of an altogether different nature and disposition.

But all he could see upon his tortoise-like emergence was a line of stringy winter willows tracing the path of a stream, the familiar dotting of black-faced sheep upon the rise, and a solitary crow high on a winter-stripped branch of a sycamore tree. Upon the road, wrapped in rags and skins, their breath clouding in the cold, trudged the usual conglomeration of feckless wanderers, gypsies, tinkers, navvies, moochers, beggars and tradesfolk.

Moreover, the people within the coach seemed the same as those with whom he had embarked at White-chapel markets. There was a fat woman in mourning, her poke-bonnet festooned in black dobbin and upon her lap a very large wicker basket. Beside her sat two gentlemen from the city, Tweedledum and Tweedledee, square-rigged in black with coloured waistcoats, their top hats pulled over their eyes, bearded chins upon their breasts asleep.

On the same side as Ikey, but at the opposite window, occupying fully the space for two passengers, sat an enormously stout red-bearded countryman. He wore a rough tweed jacket and breeches, and a pair of enormous countryman's boots. The colour of his clothes was matched by his wildly gingered chin, upon which the stem of a curved pipe was gently cushioned, the tobacco of his choice being particularly acrid and rank smelling.

At the ginger man's feet lay a large hound with one eye missing, its head upon its paws, its single cyclops eye fixed balefully upon its master, who being a jolly fellow had purchased a ticket for the dog which entitled it to human passage, but then, in a gesture of goodwill, had invited the other passengers to place their feet upon its large, furry carcass. This the woman and two city gentlemen had promptly done as there was no possible alternative, the great lolling dog having filled most of the floor space available.

On a warm summer's day the foul pipe and the presence of the large panting creature who undoubtedly carried a host of fleas upon its back would have proved most onerous for a person delicate of stomach, but on this bitterly cold December afternoon it made for a certain snugness, even an unspoken friendly fugginess within the coach.

Ikey was now much alarmed, for he was sure some mental aberration had struck his febrile brain, and now the banal scene about him seemed to contradict this very supposition.

There had risen up in Ikey's fevered mind the idea that he would reform, take on the mantle of respectability and the strictures of moral rectitude, forsake his born ways and take ship to Australia where he would establish himself as a gentleman and tend to Mary's needs until she received her ticket of leave and was able to join him. Her head and his touching, blue doves together again.

It may cause surprise that Ikey could think in such a mawkish manner, but even in the foulest heart there lies a benign seed of softness. It may long lie dormant, but if given the slightest chance will swell to fecundity and surprise all who have previously known its owner. Was this not the very point made by the salvationists who despair for no man and follow their hopes for redemption to the gates of Tyburn and to the knotted cord and final trapdoor itself?

It must also be remembered that Ikey's potential metamorphosis did not include his wife Hannah or his children. The milk of human kindness had not entirely washed away the stains of his known and expected character and he felt no compunction about deserting his wife and children providing he could contrive to take his money with him. This Ikey knew to be an unlikely circumstance as he was made to account to Hannah for almost all the transactions which passed through his hands. Besides, she held the second half of the combination safe under the pantry floor.

Ikey's obsession with bookkeeping was his downfall. He had trained Hannah to keep books on her five brothels and these he inspected every evening before leaving home, entering the profits in a ledger of his own. Hannah, who pretended to the outside world that she was illiterate, demanded the right to see Ikey's ledgers, which she understood to a degree which often frustrated him.

Ikey could not bear for anyone to know his business and the ledgers Mary kept so diligently for him consisted only of the merchandise coming in, a stocktaking list and first evaluation of stolen and fenced articles, not a final accounting. So she never entirely knew the state of his affairs.

Ikey's ledgers were of the final reckoning of profits cross-referenced in astonishing detail; the what, why, when and where of every stolen article, so that no two articles from the same source would appear for sale in the same market. These great books were an extension of his mind, a beautiful reckoning of the results of his every business endeavour. Each ledger was a tangible proof that he existed, the strong vellum pages, the stoutly bound cover of softest calf leather with his name embossed in gold upon it, the squareness of the corners and the beautiful marbled endpapers. These all spoke of strength, respectability and an ordered and handsome masculinity.

Ikey's ledgers were everything he couldn't be and when he wrote within them in his neat copperplate hand, each entry adding to the sum of his wealth, in his mind the ledger became himself, brave, strong, valuable, clean, permanent, respectable and accepted. Ikey's ledger was an addiction as necessary to him as an opium pipe is to the captain of a China clipper.

For a man whose every instinct was to conceal his affairs, his compulsion to record everything was a terrible weakness which Hannah had exploited to the fullest. His year-end ledgers, which contained all the profits made from both his work and his wife's, were kept in a large safe built into the floor of a small basement chamber. Its casual appearance resembled a cold storeroom for provisions, being without windows and fitted with a stout iron door to resist rats, and it was referred to as the pantry.

Indeed, Hannah kept potatoes, flour and apples within it and from the ceiling hung the papery white carcasses of dried cod and a large bunch of Spanish onions. The safe was concealed in exactly the same manner as the one in Van Esselyn's printing shop and in Ikey's own study. Along with the ledgers, it contained a vast amount of paper money as well as gold, mostly in sovereigns, though some melted down bars, and several small velvet bags of precious stones worth a king's ransom. So cunningly was the safe hidden that several raids on the house had not come even close to discovering its whereabouts.

Alas for Ikey, Hannah's insistence on them each knowing only half the combination meant that neither could open the safe without the presence of the other. Thus the bulk of their fortune could never be removed from the safe without their mutual agreement.

It was against this background that Ikey found himself lost in the imaginings of escaping to New South Wales with the eventual prospect of uniting with Mary. Now, as the coach drew to a halt at a staging post to allow its passengers to take refreshment, he realised that he must have momentarily lost his sanity.

Ikey's wealth was irrevocably tied up with Hannah's, and though he surprised himself by still determining secretly to help Mary should she be arrested, there was no reconciliation possible between them. Mary would forever remain the sweetest passage in Ikey's life, but if it came to a choice between riches and sentiment then, Ikey reasoned, the short journey they'd taken together in life was already concluded.

Mary had spent an eventful day. She had been awakened, considerably confused by the noise in the basement and, lighting a candle, hurried downstairs to investigate, only to be met by a stout policeman shining a torch into her eyes. He promptly ordered her back upstairs, though in a remarkably polite tone.

'We'll be up shortly, madam, to search your premises, but we'll not be making any arrests of your good self or your girls. Would you be so kind as to wait upon our attentions and make a large pot of strong black tea with sugar added.'

'Tea be too expensive for the likes of you lot,' Mary retorted, 'you will 'ave to be satisfied with beer!'

Mary had hurriedly retraced her steps to her little parlour. She thought only of the concealment of the ledger and was struck with panic when she entered the room to see that it no longer rested on the table beside the bottle of claret. Then she noticed the absence of the second tankard, and with a grateful sigh concluded that Ikey had been and had removed the ledger.

But after a moment she became bewildered. Why had Ikey not wakened her? Had he known of the raid and betrayed her? Mary, her head filled with the anxiety of the moment, made her way to the kitchen where she filled a large jug with beer and set it upon the table. Then she took half a dozen pewter mugs from a cupboard and placed them around the jug. She walked into the scullery and noticed the bull's eye lamp lying on the stone sink. She picked it up – it was still slightly warm to the touch. Ikey had most assuredly been, but why would he need the lamp? A gas light was kept burning low in all the passages except the attic and he would need only to have turned these up to see his way perfectly. Besides, Ikey seemed to see like a cat in the dark while others would tread fearfully with their arms stretched out in front of them.

'Jesus! The attic!' Mary exclaimed aloud.

The police were about to search the house and they would find the attic filled with stolen articles. Mary, now fully awake, raced up the stairs leading into the attic when she realised that only Ikey kept a key to the door. Then she saw that the door was slightly ajar. She opened it and sufficient pale light filtered through the barred dormer window to reveal that the attic was empty. Not a bolt of linen or brocade, no silver candelabra or plate, or fancy clocks, nothing remained.

Mary felt suddenly completely betrayed. She was not the kind to sob, but a great hollowness filled her being. Why had Ikey not alerted her? She sat heavily upon a step on the narrow stairway leading up to the attic door. Then she recalled the officer's words of a few minutes previously, *'We'll not be making any arrests of your good self or your girls!'*

Mary felt herself filling up with joyous relief. He'd fee'd the law. Ikey had bribed the officers not to arrest her! Mary felt a great warmth go out towards him. He loved her! The miserable sod *actually* loved her! Mary was suddenly as happy as she had been in her entire life, as happy even as she had been on the morning Mr Goldstein had hired her as a clerk. She hurried downstairs to stoke the embers and add coal to the stove, and then to make a large pot of sweet tea for the law. Her head whirled with the discovery that someone cared about her, that Ikey had escaped before being arrested for forgery, but first he had seen to it that she was safe! Mary vowed that she would never forget his loving act towards her.

The arrest of notorious forger Abraham Van Esselyn, alias Thomas Thompson, was a triumph for the bank officers. Though they had found no evidence in the form of large denomination forged banknotes, the discovery of an etching plate for the five pound denomination, together with a small stack of freshly minted counterfeit five pound notes taken together with the implements of forgery, the Austrian printing press, inks, though no paper, was sufficient to incarcerate him for the term of his natural life. Nonetheless, the City police were bitterly disappointed. They wanted Ikey Solomon, and they knew he had escaped.

The search of Egyptian Mary's had revealed nothing, though it had been thorough in the extreme. The beds and closets of the startled girls were overturned, mattresses ripped open, floorboards removed, false walls looked for and ceilings holed and tapped. The tiniest apertures were poked into and closely examined, even the coal had been removed from the scuttle, and the peephole Ikey used to spy upon Mary's clients was examined in the hope that it might reveal some secret hideaway. But at the end of a full morning's search, accompanied by Mary's repeated protests that Ikey was simply her landlord and that she knew the business in the basement to be a printing press and no more, nothing was found in the brothel part of the premises, nothing which could connect Ikey Solomon to forgery or, for that matter, to any other crime beyond that of allowing the premises he owned to be used as a brothel and his basement as a printing press.

Under normal circumstances Ikey's landlord activities might still have been sufficient to arrest him on a charge of conspiracy to defraud the Bank of England by allowing the printing of forged notes on property he owned. But the bank's officials knew Ikey could afford the best King's Counsel London could furnish and nowhere in the world was there better to be found. They needed much more than a possible charge of complicity. They needed traceable, verifiable stolen goods and banknotes which proved to be forgeries and which were found to be in his possession or concealed on premises where he was known to live.

Furthermore, Van Esselyn seemed not in the least inclined to bear witness against his landlord, though he had yet to be thoroughly worked upon. A deaf mute who purported to write only in the French language was, at best, a dubious witness. But even if his confession proved compelling, evidence taken from a forger of Van Esselyn's reputation could, they knew, be easily negated in cross-examination by any half-competent barrister with half a wig on his head.

Late that afternoon, as Ikey's coach was rumbling across the countryside, a meeting took place at the Bank of England on Threadneedle Street between its directors and various officers and in the presence of the Upper Marshal of the City of London. It was here a decision was quietly taken that Ikey Solomon must, by all means available, be apprehended and permanently removed from London's criminal society. A decision was also passed with a show of hands, and therefore not entered in the minutes, that should any emoluments be incurred in this endeavour, they would be met by the bank and dispensed through the services of a reliable go-between, so that these 'expenses' were not traceable back to the officers of the bank nor to any person acting on their behalf.

The task of apprehending Ikey and building a watertight case against him was made the personal responsibility of the Upper Marshal of London, Sir Jasper Waterlow. Sir Jasper was a member of the Select Committee on Police which was about to look into the whole question of policing in London. There was already a great deal of speculation about the formation of a Metropolitan Police Force to replace the corrupt and inadequate magistrates' runners and Sir Jasper could see himself as the head of such a body, a position which must inevitably lead to a peerage and a seat in the House of Lords. The additional responsibility for apprehending the notorious receiver and now head of a conspiracy to defraud the Bank of England was an unexpected turn of good fortune, and he was well pleased with the bank's nomination.

With this decision to persist in the hunt, Ikey Solomon became, at once, the most wanted man throughout the length and breadth of Britain, even though no actual warrant existed for his arrest.

Chapter Eight

It did not take long for Hannah to learn of the arrest of Abraham Van Esselyn and the reason for Ikey's hasty departure to Birmingham. Not more than an hour after Ikey had departed an officer from the City police had knocked loudly on the front door of their Whitechapel home. 'Name o' Ikey Solomon. Is this 'is 'ouse?' he demanded.

Hannah, who was accustomed to both rudeness and crisis, nodded calmly and invited the officer into her front parlour. 'Shall I take yer coat and mittens, officer?'

'Gloves, they's gloves,' the policeman corrected her. 'Thank 'e kindly, I'll stay put.'

Hannah smiled. 'And what brings ya out at the crack o' dawn, officer? Bit early to come callin', ain't it?' Without waiting for the policeman's reply, she rubbed her hands together against the cold, ''Ave a pew, officer, make y'self at 'ome, don't blame ya for stayin' with yer coat and mittens, cold as charity in 'ere, 'ang on a mo, good idea, I'll light the grate.' She said all of this with such rapidity that the policeman hadn't yet mustered sufficient wit to reply to her original question.

He cleared his throat, preparing finally to answer, but Hannah turned her back on him and kneeling in front of the fire-place struck a lucifer to the kindling in the grate.

'Sit, sit, officer,' Hannah said. A tiny curl of yellow flame licked between the dark lumps of coal and a wisp of smoke followed it up the chimney.

The policeman, a stout, heavily jowled man with a bushy black moustache, lowered himself slowly into the chair. 'Your 'usband, madam, we should like to talk to 'im on a matter 'o some urgency.'

Hannah rose from the fireplace and turned towards him, her expression most conciliatory. 'What a bloomin' shame, you've come all this way for nuffink! 'E's gorn, sir, 'fraid 'e's not 'ere.'

'Gorn?' The policeman looked quizzical. 'Madam, I must inform you, we 'ave the 'ouse surrounded.'

'That won't 'elp none, you could 'ave the bloomin' 'ousehold cavalry outside, 'e still ain't 'ere. 'E left three days ago on business.'

'And where might 'e 'ave gorn, madam?' the police officer demanded. He was aware of Hannah's reputation and would not normally have appended the word 'madam' to his questions, the criminal classes being best addressed in the bluntest possible way. But such is the regard of the English for property that he was in truth paying his respects to the imposing three-storey residence and the expensive furnishings, in particular the magnificent Persian carpet upon which his large feet rested. He hadn't expected anything like this, and they demanded a courtesy which he knew the frumpy whore in curling papers, who hadn't even bothered to wear a mob cap, should be emphatically and officially denied.

Hannah's face puckered into a frown. 'I beg ya to understand, sir. I cannot tell ya the whereabouts of me 'usband. These are 'ard times and 'e is on the road seekin' customers for 'is bright little bits!'

The officer now leaned forward feigning exasperation, raising his voice and speaking in an imperious manner.

'Come now, we all know your 'usband's vocation, don't we! 'E ain't no jeweller sellin' 'is wares at country fairs an' the like, now is 'e, madam?'

Hannah shrugged her shoulders, wondering briefly why they'd sent this clumsy man to interview Ikey. She felt vaguely insulted – they deserved better, a more senior man who spoke proper and who would be a fair match in the wits department for Ikey or herself. She could almost see the cogs turning in the big policeman's head.

'I dunno what ya can possibly mean, sir! 'Onest to Gawd, officer, I swear I dunno where 'e is.' She folded her arms across her chest and pouted, 'He scarpered three days ago, that's all I can tell ya.' She gave the police officer a brief smile. 'Shall I tell 'im ya called when 'e returns?' Hannah raised her eyebrows slightly. 'Whenever, from wherever? What shall I tell 'im it's in connection with? Shall I tell 'im you've a warrant out?'

The policeman ignored Hannah's questions. 'Scarpered? You mean 'e's left you, done a runner on you and the kids?'

Hannah smiled, inwardly relieved. She knew from the policeman's reply that Ikey wasn't yet under arrest, they hadn't taken out a warrant nor had they a search warrant for the house. 'Nah! I mean 'e's just gorn. 'E'll be back. Sellin's 'is trade, ain't it? When 'e's sold 'is stock 'e'll be back orright, grumblin' and cantankerous,' she sighed, 'just like 'e never left.'

The policeman sniffed. 'Receivin', more like! Gorn to Birmingham or Manchester then, 'as 'e?'

Hannah shrugged again, though she was slightly more impressed. At least the officer had done some homework. 'What you take me for, a bleedin' clairvoyant? I told you, I dunno nuffink about where me 'usband's gorn, for all I knows 'e's gorn to Windsor Great Park to see the giraffe what the Mohammedan from Egypt give to the King!' Hannah's expression brightened at this bizarre thought and she added, 'Perhaps 'e's stayed to play a game of battledore and shuttlecock with 'Is Majesty? Wouldn't put it past 'im.'

The policeman sighed heavily and rose from the chair, pointing a stubby finger at Hannah. 'We've got the Froggie and we'll get Ikey! You can quite be sure o' that! This ain't no normal enquiry from the magistrates' runners, this is City, Bank o' England!' He sniffed again and turned towards the front door. 'We'll be back with a warrant, you may be sure o' that!'

'Always welcome, I'm sure,' Hannah said, smiling brightly at the officer. 'Next time, stay for a cuppa.' She arched an eyebrow and sniffed. ' 'Ardly worth lightin' the fire, that was, the price of a lump o' coal bein' what it is!'

Despite her outward calm, Hannah was far from in possession of her wits. The single word 'City' followed by the three others 'Bank of England' had struck terror into her heart, for they told her all she needed to know. They'd arrested Van Esselyn, and now they were after Ikey. The house in Bell Alley must have been raided and Ikey had somehow been informed just in time to make good his escape.

Hannah knew the seriousness of the situation, but she also knew her man and unlike Mary she did not for a single moment think he'd either betrayed or deserted her. Not when all their wealth was still sitting in the basement safe. Ikey had made no attempt to take a large sum of money with him, therefore he was not planning to escape to America as he'd often speculated they would do if there was no hope of either of them beating a rap.

Hannah would have liked to go to Australia where John and Moses, their two oldest sons, had been sent, well capitalised, to establish themselves in respectable vocations in Sydney Town. But she knew that New South Wales was not beyond the reach of the law or, even more so, the wrath of the Bank of England.

Hannah wanted her children to have a better life than her own. For them to be accepted as respectable members of society, even if it was only colonial society, was uppermost to her ambitions. The idea that they should follow in the path of their loathsome father was unthinkable. Curiously, Hannah did not see herself as an example of moral degeneration. She was, in her own eyes, a good girl turned temporarily aside by the events which Ikey had caused to happen to their family. Hannah saw her immorality as an expedient to be discarded as easily as a petticoat when the time came to lead a respectable middle-class life.

Left destitute as a young wife with two small children by a husband imprisoned on a hulk as a common thief awaiting transportation to Australia, Hannah had been forced to survive on her wits. The brothels she now owned were simply the end result of her determination not to be destroyed. She had even come to think upon herself as a necessary component in a complex but pre-destined society. The gin-soaked whores, starving brats, the deformed, witless, the whoresons, freaks, cripples, catamites and opium addicts, they all came to her and, if she thought she could convert their tortured minds and broken bodies into a cash flow, she employed them. Hannah took a secret pride in the fact that she was called '*Mother Sin, The Queen of the Drunken Blasphemers*', in a popular Wesleyan tract widely issued by the salvationists. To her this inglorious title meant she had earned her place in life's rich tapestry, that she had triumphed within a social structure not of her making, and had overcome obstacles which would have defeated most other young women saddled with two infant mouths to feed.

Hannah saw herself as a good mother who worked hard and selflessly so that her children might grow up to have both the trappings and the virtues of respectability. She told herself it was all for them, John and Moses, who were already on their way in life, and David, Ann, Sarah and baby Mark. She was convinced that while they remained in England they would be regarded as the bottom of the social heap, the criminal poor. She was quite unable to recognise that she was already in possession of a grand fortune, that her children would never starve again.

The capacity to delude herself had been a part of Hannah's personality from a very young age, and her subsequent social disintegration had become so complete that she felt not a morsel of shame for her actions. Her life, she told herself, had been a bitter disappointment, meaningful only in the fact that she had been blessed with children, so she extracted, and continued to extract, her revenge upon it. Hannah was a woman who was possessed by hatred which had long since consumed her conscience. The only purity in her life was her offspring, the precious fruit of her loins, and the major object of her hate was their father.

It was quite clear to Hannah that Ikey would be returning and that he must have already evolved a plan to beat any indictment against himself for forgery. Although she loathed him, she respected his brains and his ability to make money and even, in a perverse sort of way, she enjoyed the 'respectability' he gave her as a criminal of international repute who carried the undisputed title of Prince of Fences.

Long after the departure of the police officer, Hannah continued to sit with her hands cupping her chin, staring into the fireplace which now filled the little parlour with its warmth. Her first task, she told herself, was to determine precisely what had happened earlier that morning. She could not go around to what she now thought of as the deserted house in Bell Alley, though she would need to ensure that it was securely bolted against intruders. She had often witnessed how the desperate poor could strip a deserted house of its contents, then occupy it in a matter of hours and destroy its worth in a matter of days. Of course, she knew nothing of Mary and imagined the property completely vulnerable, doors left off their hinges by an uncaring City police, windows thrown open to create a deliberate deadlurk. Hannah determined to send a dozen street brats immediately to scatter throughout the surrounding rookeries to find Bob Marley who she knew, given sufficient incentive, could be relied upon to see that the house was made safe against intruders.

To put this thought into action Hannah simply walked down the hall, opened the front door, put two fingers to her mouth and let out a piercing whistle. It was a trick she'd been taught by her coachman father as a child and was a well-known signal to any children in the neighbourhood. In a matter of moments two ragged urchins appeared and Hannah instructed them to gather ten of their mates. The boys soon returned with well in excess of this number.

Hannah explained what she wanted. Marley was well known in the Whitechapel markets and in Rosemary Lane where the local urchins looked up to him as a flash macer and both feared and greatly admired his reputation as the acid slasher.

'Me, missus, me!' they shouted, jostling each other. 'Please, missus, I'm yer man, I knows 'im, I knows 'im well! This Bob Marley cove, I knows where 'e lives, missus, 'onest I does! Please, me, me!' they yelled, clamouring around the front step, their skinny arms protruding from the tattered rags they wore.

Hannah selected ten helpers. Then she went into her kitchen and put a dozen apples into her pinny together with a sharp knife. From each apple she cut a single wedge a different size and handed the smaller piece, one to each of the selected boys, returning the apple to her pinafore pocket.

'I must 'ave Mister Marley 'ere on me doorstep in one 'our, no more, mind!' she instructed, then added, 'The boy what Mister Marley 'imself declares found 'im, gets a silver shillin'!' The urchins around her gasped and Hannah continued, 'The rest gets tuppence for yer 'ard work 'o lookin', can't be fairer'n that now, lads, can I?'

'No, missus, that's fair!' they chorused.

Hannah waved her forefinger and admonished the children standing directly below her. 'Don't no one eat the piece o' apple what 'e got, not even a tiny bite, if the piece ya brings back don't fit what I got in me pinny, ya don't get bugger all!'

'Does we get to eat the 'ole apple too, missus?' one of the urchins asked hopefully, his breath frosting in the air about his dirty little face as he pointed at Hannah's bulging pinny.

Hannah laughed. 'Cheeky bugger!' she looked down at the tiny, malnourished child standing below her with his arms folded across the dirty rags covering his chest. Cold sores festered around his mouth and his nose ran so that he was constantly sniffing. Hannah saw none of the collective misery contained in the urchins crowded at her steps, they were all the same to her, dirty, ugly, starving, cruel, thieving and drunken and to pity them was a waste of time and sentiment. 'I'll 'ave to think about that,' she said at last. 'Make a nice apple pie these apples would.'

'Can we 'ave a penny now, missus? In advance, like?' the urchin tried again.

Hannah looked down at him in horror.

'You again! Well I never 'eard o' such a cheek! Think I was born under a cabbage leaf, does ya? Give ya a penny and 'ave ya all go out an' get a tightener or a mug o' gin and yours truly never sees 'ide nor 'air of any of ya brats again. Think I'm bleedin' barmy or summink?' Hannah looked down scornfully at the hungry, eager faces looking up at her. 'Righto, you lot! Tuppence and ya all gets the 'ole apple thrown in, that's the deal! Now scarper, before I changes me bleedin' mind!'

With the immediate details taken care of Hannah returned to the parlour to think, though moments later she was called to the front door by the arrival of the wet nurse to feed and care for baby Mark.

Hannah stood at the door and made the woman bare her breasts and squeeze them with both hands so that she might see her lactate. She wasn't paying for a wet nurse who was short of milk. Then she made the woman open her mouth and she smelt her breath to see if it carried the fumes of brandy or gin. The woman's teeth were rotten and her breath was foul, further burdened with the sour smell of the ale she'd had for breakfast, though nothing else. She allowed her to enter.

The children hadn't risen yet, though she knew the nurse would tend to them when they did. She instructed the woman not to disturb her or allow the children to do so and returned to the parlour, asking only that the woman bring her a cup of tea before she fed the baby.

The wet nurse was one of two selected for their milk. One stayed with the children at night while Hannah was at work and the other took care of the baby during the day and also tended to the house. This one, as well as breast feeding Mark, was employed for the rough work. Both women, Hannah knew, ate her out of house and home, but short of catching them stealing food for their own young 'uns, she didn't mind. The food they consumed, she told herself, went into making milk for baby Mark.

Hannah, only slightly comforted by the fact that no warrant existed for Ikey's arrest, was nevertheless fearful of what the future might hold and she knew she would need to make plans. She had endured one six-year period with almost no means when Ikey had been imprisoned. Now they were rich and they should think about going to live in America or, if Ikey should escape the forgery charge, Sydney Town, though she was realistic enough to know that this was unlikely.

On the rare occasions Hannah had discussed the consequences of crime with Ikey, he had pointed out to her that the crime of forgery carried the hangman's noose, the death penalty. Hannah dared not think further on that matter.

However, she was not above thinking that the ideal situation was to see Ikey transported for life to Botany Bay, leaving her to settle in America with their total assets in her sole possession, though she could think of no way to bring this about. If Ikey avoided being indicted for forgery but was arrested as a fence and proved unable to fee the arresting officers, then she too could be implicated and would receive a similar sentence of transportation. In the unlikely event that she was able to prove her innocence, Ikey knew she could easily live off the proceeds of her six bawdy houses and, while the hope of completing his sentence existed, would never agree to giving her control of their combined resources.

Even if she should contemplate divorce, by definition of law the wealth they'd accumulated together remained the property of the husband. Hannah was quite unable to contemplate such an outcome. In the event of a separation, she would be rendered virtually penniless. Yet in Hannah's mind, all the money rightfully belonged to her. Ikey was no more than a retriever is to a hunter, the dog that brings in the bird and who has no subsequent rights to the spoils from the day's shooting.

In this Ikey seemed to support Hannah's expectations, for he had no apparent need for money. He spent none on himself – even his watch and chain were of very little value lest he be robbed for it. He had only one small personal indulgence, this being the sport of ratting. He kept three of the best rat-killing terriers in England, cared for by a trainer, a butcher in the village of Guildford. But even in the ratting pit he would bet modestly.

Ratting was a sport which involved every grade of society, the ordinary poor, criminals, shop assistants, servants, toffs and even occasionally some of the nobility on the slum, each gambling according to his own means. Or, as Ikey hoped, beyond his means. Ikey saw the rat-pit as another opportunity to make money. There were very few seasoned gamblers at the rat-pits on Great St Andrews Street who, at some time or another, were not in debt to him.

With little taste for the sport of gambling itself, but with a fondness for the game little terriers, ratting was the closest Ikey ever came to being of a charitable nature, for should a client owe him a considerable sum of money, he would extend him a further loan against the odds given on one of his own terriers. This was considered most generous in the circles of ratting, for should his terrier win the bout then Ikey accepted the winnings as part or full payment of the loan.

However, if Ikey's terrier lost, then the money loaned would be added to the gambler's outstanding debt. Ikey's charity was limited to a single attempt to wipe out a gambling debt and, as often happened, if the debt was a large one and the gambler, being as gamblers are, bet sufficient on one of Ikey's terriers to eliminate the money owed, and the terrier lost, then the debt naturally doubled. When this happened it was generally agreed that the offender should forfeit goods or services to cover the outstanding money. Many a toff or member of the moneyed classes lost an item of value from his household in this manner, the convenience and advantage that Ikey was a fence and the article could be handed straight over to pay the debt without first being converted to cash.

Common criminals who had given their marker to Ikey undertook many a burglary and handed the contents of their night's work over to him, whereupon their marker was returned so they would remain in good standing for a future loan.

It was generally conceded in ratting circles that Ikey's terriers, which came from the Forest of Dean on the Welsh border, were exceedingly well bred and highly trained for courage and of the very best disposition for the rat-pit. The little black and brown terriers, usually the smallest dogs brought to the rat-pits, more often than not took the prize from bigger and more naturally brutal animals. Ikey's sparing use of his terriers to regain money lost by his clients was well regarded in the sport, and it was the only endeavour in Ikey's life where those about him did not look upon him as a rapacious and vile member of the Christ-killing race.

However, Ikey's reluctance to let his little terriers into the pit too often had nothing whatsoever to do with his desire to be well regarded, but was in a great part due to a sentimental consideration for them. Sewer rats give dogs canker, which is eventually the death of them. After each killing in the rat-pit Ikey would rinse the pretty pink mouths of his tiny terriers with peppermint and water and return them to their trainer with instructions to carefully tend the rat bites they had sustained.

It was a tenderness he had never shown his children or any other living person, not even Mary, whom he would have been quite unable to stroke or touch as he did the little dogs he owned.

Ikey, like every other dog owner in England, dreamed of one day owning another Lord Nelson, a legendary ratter. Lord Nelson was so small he used to wear a lady's jewelled bracelet as a collar, weighed but five pounds and a half and had once killed two hundred rats in a single evening. It was said that, at times, some of the sewer rats pitted against him were his equal in size. But there was never a one or even a dozen together in the rat-pit who could bring the little terrier to a halt or bail him up. Ikey dreamed of owning a dog such as Lord Nelson though, for once, not for the money it could wring from the rat-pit. It was because he was so small, the smallest ratter ever to win in the pits, yet this miniature terrier, like Lord Nelson himself, who stood at only four feet and ten inches, contained a courage greater per pound of weight than any dog that had ever lived to kill a rat.

Ikey, too, was small and thought of himself as weak and a coward. A dog such as Lord Nelson proved the exception to the rule that the small and the weak must always eat shit. Had another such as Lord Nelson presented itself for sale, then Ikey might for the first time have understood a reason for money beyond avarice. He would be prepared to pay a king's ransom for a dog like-proportioned to Lord Nelson and as well proven in the pits.

Even the sport of ratting could not claim to involve Ikey in the need for money, since the costs of keeping the dogs fit for ratting constituted only a small part of his total earnings from the sport. Ikey didn't need or use money for the material things it could buy, he simply accumulated it. When he required clothes or boots, he bought them secondhand in the markets around the corner or in Rosemary Lane, bargaining fiercely for an embroidered, long-sleeved waistcoat, or a pair of well-worn boots from a secondhand shoe dealer in Dudley Street. Ikey couldn't abide new shoes or even new hose and preferred his stockings to be well darned at the heels and knees. Only his great coat was purchased new, made bespoke of the finest wool to his own precise instructions with a hundred concealed pockets, the whereabouts of which required an exacting layout memorised in his mind.

In fact, this coat represented the very nature of Ikey Solomon. He, himself, was a hundred pockets, each concealing hurt: some contained past abuse, some inadequacies and some were stuffed with deformities of thought. In others past injustices rattled, yet other pockets contained abnormalities and social obscenities. A host of pockets were filled with past woundings which rubbed raw against insults, hatreds and peculiar malice. Ikey carried all the sins and bitter blows, pocks and pits of his wandering kind in the pockets of his mind. They became the total of who he was, the whole, concealed by a cloak of indifference to the outside world.

The sole importance of money to Ikey was protection. Money bought sycophancy and this passed well enough for respect. Money kept those who would destroy him at a proper arm's length. Money was the lining of the protective coat which concealed him from a dangerously cold and malevolent world.

For Hannah no such problem of concealment with a metaphorical garment existed. Her loathing of Ikey was the centre of her everyday preoccupation, and his accumulation of wealth her single reason for their coupling. Hannah saw Ikey as a servant to her ambition, and his wealth the means to purchase the social aspirations she so earnestly desired for herself, and for the futures of her six children. She had invested in Ikey as one might in the cargo of an opium clipper, and her expectation was for a handsome end profit.

Chapter Nine

Two days later Hannah received a very discreet messenger sent by the Upper Marshal of the City of London, Sir Jasper Waterlow. The messenger, a small, polite man in a frock-coat and top hat, somewhat too big for his head, stated that Sir Jasper wished to see her on a matter to her great advantage. She was naturally filled with apprehension though it did not occur to her to refuse his request, especially as the messenger had gone to great pains to assure her that she was not under arrest. She was to present herself at the Blue Wren coffee house in Haymarket on the following day, at precisely two o'clock.

Dressed in her Sabbath finery and having purchased a new best bonnet in the latest style, she pulled up at the Blue Wren, her barouche, hired by her father for the occasion, arriving at the coffee house door at precisely the appointed hour.

She announced herself to the surly proprietor, who took her cloak and ushered her to a small room to the rear of the premises where Britain's senior policeman, Sir Jasper Waterlow, waited for her. He neither rose from his chair nor took her hand at her entry. His expression was most acidic, as though the task at hand caused a sour taste in his mouth. Hannah thought this appropriate enough, expecting no different from the law.

Sir Jasper pointed to the remaining chair, there being but two upright chairs and a small table in the room. 'Sit, Mrs Solomons. I know you are aware of who I am, so I shan't introduce myself. Ceilings in such places have ears and the walls act as veritable trumpets for the deaf.' Then he added, 'It is not one's custom to be seen *or* heard in such an establishment and so I shall come directly to the point.'

The Upper Marshal of London was a small man though with a markedly large egg-shaped head. Its surface, including his chin, was quite free of hair but for three separate places: a very handsome black moustache curled and waxed at the ends, his eyebrows, equally dark and shaggy to the extreme and a pair of elaborate side whiskers which appeared to have been hot tonged and curled to resemble two dark tubes. They rested upon his jowls as though convenient handles to lift his over-sized head from his exceedingly narrow shoulders. His eyes were tiny, almost slits and his lips so narrow and straight that they suggested themselves as a single bluish stripe under his moustache. Indeed, had it not been for the large unlit cigar clamped between them, his mouth might have gone unnoticed. The only feature not yet remarked upon was his nose. It seemed a creature of independent life, large, bulb-shaped and wart-textured, and all together of a purplish hue. It sat upon his smooth, pink face like a conglomerate of several noses, where it twitched and snorted and seemed to wiggle continuously as though in great disagreement with the circumstances in which it now found itself.

This large head with its impatient, alienated nose was attached to a small, thin, short-legged body not more than five feet one inch in height. However, seated as he was with the cloth of his breeches pulled tight at the front, Hannah's practised eye observed that he carried the bulge of a surprisingly large engine for so small a man.

Sir Jasper was dressed in a dark cutaway coat above pale trousers and elegant boots, the heels of which were higher by a good two inches than might be normally supposed to be correct for the fashion of the day. A white silk choker finished off what Hannah knew to be the street uniform mostly favoured by men of the upper classes. Finally, Sir Jasper's very tall top hat had been placed with its brim uppermost on the small table between Hannah and himself, so that to observe the Upper Marshal she was forced to slightly crane her neck and look past the black hat's brim.

'So, madam, you are the spouse of the notorious criminal, Ikey Solomons?'

'Solomon, sir, it don't 'ave an "s",' Hannah corrected him, her heart fluttering at the presumption. Then she looked slightly bemused. 'Married yes, but as to criminal, not that I knows of, sir.' She drew a breath and then continued, 'Me 'usband, Ikey, 'as served 'is time, one year in Newgate and then on a hulk at Chatham. After six years 'e received the King's pardon.' Hannah paused again. 'Since then one or two small offences in the petty sessions, but nuffink what you might call *notorious* or *criminal*, if ya knows what I mean, sir?'

The officer sighed, 'Mrs Solomons, do not treat me

like a simple-minded Bow Street runner or you could find yourself implicated in this unfortunate business.'

'And what unfortunate business is that?' Hannah asked politely, maintaining her calm.

'Forgery, madam! Defrauding the Bank of England by the printing of large denomination counterfeit notes of astonishing artistry to be passed through European banks and exchanged for foreign currency, and then re-converted to English currency again, though this time as the absolutely genuine article!'

'Me 'usband can do that?' Hannah asked, incredu-lously. 'Me 'usband can make money out o' scraps o' paper?' She shook her head. 'You 'ave the wrong man, sir, me 'usband is but a poor jeweller what makes a small and 'onest profit from sellin' o' betrothal and weddin' rings and bright little brooches for servant girls, shop assistants, country folks and the likes!'

'Ha! And how, pray tell, does he come to own the salubrious premises in Bell Alley?'

'Salubrious? 'Ardly that, sir, modest 'ouse to say the least. An uncle in Chatham, a slops dealer by trade, who passed away, Gawd rest 'is soul, a good man, sir, who left me 'usband a small legacy what we used to buy the 'ouse for rentin' purposes to decent folk. Our own little nest egg against 'ard times.'

'A modest house? Decent folk? A bawdy house in partnership with a well-known madam. A high-class establishment fitted out at great cost and with a printing press of the latest design in the basement, a nest all right, a nest of vipers!'

He pointed his unlit cigar at Hannah. 'Mark you carefully, we have arrested . . . ' He hesitated and then removed and unfolded a small slip of paper from a pocket in his waistcoat. 'Damned silly names these Froggies ... ah yes, Van Esselyn ... Abraham Van Esselyn, a notorious forger whose services do *not* come cheaply, and who is *not* paid in the currency his nimble hands create, but with the *real* thing!'

The nose on Sir Jasper's face looked at Hannah in a decidedly smug manner. Then, without so much as a moment's warning, Sir Jasper pushed back his chair, rose and banged his fist down on the table, causing the top hat upon it to jump and wobble, then fall to its side.

'Damn you, woman! Do you take me for a complete fool? I will have the truth, do you hear me!'

At first Hannah thought it must all be a mistake. They had somehow confused her own brothels with an imaginary one in Bell Alley. After all, Bob Marley, whom she had commissioned to report on the aftermath of the raid, had said nothing of a brothel at Bell Alley. But the information on Abraham Van Esselyn was perfectly correct. And who was the woman who ran the fashionable brothel which now seemed to exist at the Bell Alley premises?

Hannah needed time to gather her wits and to conceal her surprise at Sir Jasper's astonishing news. There was more going on at Bell Alley than she knew about. She told herself that if some other woman, with an eye to her husband's considerable fortune, was trying to gain his good favour, both this whore and Ikey would be made to suffer a consequence far worse than the noose at Tyburn.

'Yes, sir, no, sir, but I dunno what it is ya want me to say, sir,' Hannah blustered as she set about gathering her inward composure. 'You seems to want me to say me 'usband's guilty, is that it? A wife turnin' against 'er innocent 'usband and the law makin' up all sorts o' lies about brothels and mistresses to make 'er do so. Me a faithful wife and lovin' mother what cannot tell a lie without blushin' summink awful.'

'Mrs Solomons, I'm sure you are aware that a wife cannot testify against her husband. Only those frightful frogs across the Channel have such a damned stupid law, which, I'm led to believe, leads to all manner of female revenge, not at all in the interest of male justice! Sanctity of marriage, my dear, it's the foundation of British justice!'

Hannah's lips started to tremble and a muscle on her left cheek to twitch. She brought her hands up to cover her eyes so that the absence of tears could not be seen, although, when needed, they would come soon enough.

'I dunno what it is ya want from me, sir. Me what's got four little mouths to feed, you wants to take me darlin' 'usband away! 'Im what's done no 'arm to no one! Where's the British justice in that?' Hannah choked out the words and then began to sob miserably. 'When I come 'ere it was to a promise o' reward! But when I gets 'ere, all I 'ears is talk o' brothels and mistresses and takin' away me poor 'usband what's done nuffink to deserve no punishment!' Hannah commenced to howl loudly for some time, real tears now running down her cheeks, judging the Upper Marshal's patience carefully.

'For God's sake woman, stop your damned caterwauling!' Sir Jasper demanded, banging his tiny fist once more down upon the table. 'I want your co-operation! I'm willing to pay a very handsome price for it!'

Perhaps it was the words 'pay' and 'very handsome

price' that Hannah's ears, always alert to a matter of profit, picked up. Her distress died down to a whimper and her head lifted, her large, tearful eyes peeping through her fingers. ''Ow much?' she asked in a broken, tiny voice, throwing in a loud sob for good measure.

Sir Jasper immediately relaxed and digging into the pocket of his coat produced a box of matches and commenced at last to light his cigar. Then he leaned back so that his chair rested against the wall balanced on its rear legs, the front ones being raised from the floor. Blowing a most satisfactory cloud of cigar smoke to the ceiling, he addressed Hannah in a calm voice.

'Mrs Solomons, we have the luxury of a choice – we can either offer your husband's mistress an incentive to co-operate with our enquiries or you may, with some little encouragement, decide to . . . er . . . help.'

'Beg pardon, sir, me 'usband ain't got no mistress! 'E ain't the sort. All along I been thinkin' you must 'ave the wrong man, now I'm certain in me own mind.' She smiled ingenuously, her eyes bright from recent tears. 'Maybe the person what yer looking for is *Solomons*. Common as dirt, they is, everywhere! We is *Solomon*, no "s". Me darlin' 'usband is very particular on that point, you see it means summink entirely different, it's not so kosher with an "s". Cohen is priests, Levy also, but Solomon, that's yer actual royalty, that is! That's yer Royal 'Ighness, yer genuine King Solomon, ya know the geezer what met the Queen o' Sheba? 'E wasn't called King Solomons, was 'e now? Nobody ain't never 'eard o' the wisdom o' *Solomons*, 'as they?'

'What on earth are you talking about, woman?' Sir Jasper leaned forward so that the front legs of his chair clunked to the floor. 'Whatever you're called, does it really matter?' He waved his cigar in the air. 'You are from the criminal classes and so your name, whatever it happens to be, spells thief, villain, ruffian, rascal! Solomons, Cohen, Levy, they all spell damned Israelite!

'Now, where was I? Oh yes, indeed! There is no possibility of a mistaken identity, I assure you, Mrs Solomons, and as to the other matter, I cannot vouchsafe that your husband is paramour to Egyptian Mary. But that she is his tenant we have from the woman's own lips. She has confessed, in a signed statement, that she rents the premises in Bell Alley from Isaac Solomons. Three of her strumpets have also made statements to the effect that your husband is a part owner, quite sufficient evidence to get him apprehended for allowing a bawdy house on the premises he owns or, even more compelling, being in partnership with another in this tawdry business.'

Hannah knew now with certainty that Ikey had betrayed her. She knew that Ikey would never simply rent out premises for a brothel without owning the larger part of the enterprise. Her first impulse was to feel an absolute fool, but then a darker anger rose within her. With great effort she fought it down and forced herself to concentrate on what the policeman was saying, though she was unable to control her rising voice, her venom turned to scorn.

'What? Do me a favour? On the evidence o' three tarts?' Hannah threw back her head and laughed. 'Even if me 'usband was convicted, which ain't likely, with a sharp counsellor 'e'd get no more than a drag. What good's a three month sentence gunna do ya? Ya must be jokin', sir?'

'Joking? Well no, not really,' Sir Jasper blew smoke towards the ceiling. 'Keeping a bawdy house is a perfectly indictable crime. But I'll grant you, madam, you do have a point, prostitutes make poor witnesses.' He glanced irritably at Hannah, suddenly deciding to take her into his confidence. 'It's damned messy really, not the sort of stuff the bank goes in for as a rule.'

'If it's a 'igh-class establishment, never know who comes and goes, does ya?' Hannah said cheekily, then added, 'Could be dodgy, knows what I mean?' She paused, once again in control of her emotions. Her anger, now well bedded down, would keep for another time. 'So what's ya want from me? Can't rightly see 'ow I can 'elp ya.'

'Yes, well, frankly you're right, it's not much to take before the bench.' He looked up at her and seemed for a moment to hesitate, then added, 'We also have a problem with the damned frog forger chappie we arrested in the basement of your husband's premises.'

'Oh, the geezer what's got the printer? What's the problem?'

Sir Jasper drew on his cigar and threw Hannah a dark look. He appeared to be thinking, his eyes narrowed, his head only half visible in a miasma of cigar smoke. 'Unfortunately he's deaf and dumb!'

The Upper Marshal batted away the smoke from his eyes, looked at Hannah and smiled, seeming for a moment genuinely amused. 'Ideal for a man of his occupation, eh? Most decidedly nimble of hand and eye, though deaf and dumb. Not much chop in the witness box, though.'

'Three tarts and a madam in the Old Bailey and a bludger what's deaf an' dumb, it ain't much to go with, is it then? I'll bet ya London to a brick that in ten minutes I can find you four tarts who'll swear on the 'Oly Bible, even swear on their dyin' muvver's 'ead, that yer forger geezer just recited the ten commandments personal to 'em, forwards and then backwards and finished it orf with a rendition of 'Andel's 'Allelujah Chorus, and this Van Summink's a Jew as well!'

'Well, yes, you might be right! What we need is *someone* or *something* else.'

' 'Ere, wait a mo!' Hannah, astonished, exclaimed. 'Yer not askin' me to invent evidence against me 'usband, is ya?'

'Well, no, not precisely.' He arched one of his magnificent eyebrows. 'That would simply be making five witnesses of a kind!' Sir Jasper's nose suddenly came alive again, delighted at the tartness of this last remark. 'As you so wisely observed, women of your vocation will swear to anything on the heads of their dying loved ones.' He pulled at his cigar, satisfied that he had once again achieved the upper hand.

Hannah's hidden frustration at the news of Ikey's betrayal suddenly overwhelmed her sense of caution. She wanted to bite back and Sir Jasper was available. 'It takes a whore to know one! Whore's ain't only of one sex!'

Sir Jasper shot upright, the legs of the chair hitting the floor with a crack. 'Madam!'

To Hannah's surprise, after this single admonishment, Sir Jasper returned his chair to its former two-legged position and smiled, a small secret smile. With the sharpness quite gone from his voice he said, 'I'm grateful we've reached common ground at last, madam. Down to brass tacks, eh? I was hoping we might not have to raise the matter of the five, or is it six brothels *you* own?' His voice grew suddenly sharper again. 'Correctly prosecuted, you should receive more than a drag or even a stretch, transportation, fourteen years at the very least, Botany Bay or perhaps Van Diemen's Land.'

He waited for a reaction from Hannah and when none was forthcoming he cleared his throat and continued, 'Why, madam, such would seem the only possible sentence. You shall have fourteen years to regret your lack of co-operation! Do you not think you ought to think upon this? Or is your loyalty and affection to Mr Solomons of such a purity that you would protect him at the cost of a dark, rat-infested prison at the other end of the world for much of the remainder of your miserable life?'

Sir Jasper waited, removed the cigar from his mouth and examined it at arm's length. Hannah saw that it had become dark stained with his spittle at the sucking end, while it carried a full inch of spent ash at the other. She observed his cigar, not from any personal interest, but because her wits had temporarily forsaken her, and she knew herself to be hopelessly trapped and entirely at the mercy of the small, cigar-toting policeman.

Curiously, it did not occur to her to blame the smug little knight for her predicament. Nor did she recall that it was she who had persuaded a reluctant Ikey to employ Abraham Van Esselyn. All she could think was that it was Ikey who had once again caused her downfall. He had absconded and left her as his hostage. He had betrayed her with a whore and robbed her of a prize which was rightfully hers. Come what may, she would make him pay! She would not take a moment's punishment for the miserable, sodding shit.

'I should remind you that you will never see your

darling children again,' Sir Jasper added. 'What do you say to that, Mrs Solomons?'

Hannah inhaled sharply and then in a low voice asked, 'Now, sir, what was it ya jus' said about it 'aving to be, ya know, *someone* or *summink else* what is needed for the case at 'and?'

Sir Jasper, now also smiling, leaned a little closer and placed his hand on her knee.

'Well done, my dear, how very sensible of you. I feel sure we can come to some satisfactory arrangement, what?'

Hannah looked up suddenly. 'Could we not leave England, scarper, never come back no more?'

'Why, madam, that's preposterous! Simply unthinkable!'

'Why?' Hannah asked simply.

'Justice, there must be justice! Good God, woman, where would we be if we simply let our hardened criminals escape to other societies. What would *they* think of the English?'

'They probably don't think all that much of 'em as it is,' Hannah said laconically.

'Balderdash! There's not a civilised man on earth who doesn't wish he was an Englishman! An arranged escape? Unthinkable and positively unpatriotic!'

Hannah cleared her throat, averted her eyes and spoke in a small, almost girlish voice. 'We could probably leave a little bequest, a little summink to remember us by, a little personal summink what we could leave to yer discretion to use for whatsoever good you might consider in yer wisdom can be done for Mother England?' She paused and looked furtively up at the policeman. 'If you knows what I mean, sir?'

The cigar fell from Sir Jasper's lips, 'Good God, woman! Are you attempting to bri– '

At this point Sir Jasper leapt from his chair with a terrible yowl, upsetting the table and sending his top hat flying across the room as he frantically beat at the front of his trousers. The cigar, nowhere to be seen, must have fallen through his waistcoat and down into the interior of his trousers, for Sir Jasper continued to beat at his crotch, while turning in small agitated circles, his legs pumping up and down as though dancing on the spot. Then his foot caught the leg of the upturned table and, losing his balance, he landed in Hannah's voluminous lap. His head fell upon her breast and his now panicked nose was inches from her own. But for the fact of the room being so small, and that the back of her chair was placed almost against the wall, Hannah, together with Sir Jasper, would have turned topsy-turvy, landing on the floor in a heap of kicking legs, petticoats, pantaloons and flailing arms.

Hannah was the quicker of the two to recover. She looked down at the hapless Sir Jasper, who was flapping, whimpering and snorting, and observed the smoke rising from that area of his trousers which is known to be most delicate when assaulted. With one arm she pinned him to her breast and with her free hand hastily undid the last two buttons of his waistcoat, shot into the front of his trousers, and plucked the offending cigar from within.

Hannah's shameless sense of humour overcame her as she held up the still smouldering cigar. 'There were two of them little devils down there, sir. I chose the bigger one!' she cackled. Then, the gravity of the situation reasserted itself and she released him, and clamped her hand over her mouth to smother any possibility of a further outburst.

If Sir Jasper was conscious of this coarse attempt at humour he gave no sign of it. As though caught within a collapsed tent he was struggling wildly to find his way out of the folds of Hannah's commodious skirts. He regained his feet finally and, clutching his singed and painful scrotum in both hands, he roared at Hannah, 'You have not heard the last of this, madam! By God! I shall see you and your husband hanged at Tyburn yet!'

He removed a hand from his crotch and grabbed the cigar from Hannah, throwing it to the floor and stamping on it several times until it became a soggy, pulpy mess. Removing his hands he glanced down upon his recently violated area and observed a hole in the light coloured material not larger than a sixpenny bit, but in a strategically awkward area. Again clasping both his hands over it he backed away from Hannah.

'Damnation and blast! I have an appointment at four of the clock and cannot first go home!' Sir Jasper cried.

'Why, sir, it is not much of a mend,' Hannah remarked calmly, 'an 'ole no larger than the tip o' me tongue, and what might come about if a gentleman could 'ave took forty winks in his club chair with 'is pipe or cigar in 'is mouth. You must let me attend to it at once – I am a clever seamstress who will soon repair it invisible.'

'Keep your filthy harlot's hands off me!' Sir Jasper said fearfully, backing still further away from Hannah, so that he now stood in the corner with his back against the wall like some miscreant schoolboy who has failed at spelling.

'Tut, tut!' Hannah clucked. She was accustomed to

crisis and mostly took immediate possession of the situation. 'Come now, sir, it ain't that bad!' She rose from her chair. 'See I shall move yer chair and sit upon it and you shall stand behind me back, remove yer trousers and pass 'em to me across me shoulder. I 'ave needle and thread with me and I am trained as a seamstress.' She smiled brightly, acting quite unconcerned and natural in her manner.

Sir Jasper looked at Hannah suspiciously, then he turned slightly away and uncupped his hands briefly to observe the damage once again. 'Very well, madam,' he said, the sulkiness still contained in his voice, 'but this service rendered does not alter your predicament! Attempting to fee an officer of the law is a very serious offence!'

Hannah chose, for the moment, to ignore this remark. A man without his breeches, she reasoned, is much more amenable to compromise. She rose and placed the table upright, then crossed to his chair and turned it so that when seated her back was towards him. She sat down and arranged her skirts.

'Come now, sir, it is to mendin' we must now pay our attention.' She waited with her hand placed on her shoulder ready to receive the recently damaged garment.

Sir Jasper found it impossible to be in opposition to Hannah's calmly stated demands. His imagination took flight and he was once again a small boy intimidated by his nanny. Standing with only a woollen vest above his waist as she chided him for some small misdemeanour, running her hands down his thighs and massaging his buttocks as she threatened him with the back of her hairbrush, then kissing and fondling his tiny waterworks, which, now in its adult proportion, was growing at a quite alarming rate.

Sir Jasper, quite breathless, seated himself upon Hannah's recently vacated chair and hurriedly removed his boots and then his trousers, releasing his engine with a spring as the restraining cloth passed beyond it. Whereupon he replaced his high-heeled boots upon his feet.

'Quickly! We must 'urry to mendin', or you'll catch yer death,' Hannah said solicitously, her fingers fluttering impatiently upon her shoulder.

She had already prepared the needle and thread from her bag. Now she took the trousers from Sir Jasper, and quickly turning them inside out blew the cigar ash from the surface of the cloth, and commenced to work upon the hole, gathering its edges together and stitching it in the manner of a sutured wound, this being much the quickest and neatest way under the prevailing circumstances.

From the corner of her eye she now observed that Sir Jasper had come to stand close to her shoulder and was breathing heavily. She turned slightly towards him and was confronted by his stiffened prod almost touching the edge of her bonnet.

'Well, well, what 'ave we 'ere?' Hannah's vast experience of men made her summation almost instinctive. 'A little boy what's 'urt 'imself? A little boy who wants nanny to kiss 'im better?'

'Yes, yes, please, nanny, it hurts a lot, please can you kiss it better!' Sir Jasper gasped urgently, his voice a mixture of fear and anticipation.

Hannah laid down her needlework, took the pins from her best bonnet and removed it, placing it on the table, whereupon she unpinned her hair and shook her head, so that her hair fell to her shoulders in a cascade of brilliant titian-coloured curls. Her movements were deliberate and calculated to excite him even more. Then, with Sir Jasper wincing and groaning at her shoulder, she took his manly pride between her thumb and forefinger. Moving her head closer, she ran the point of her clever tongue around the underside of its purpled cap at the point where it joined the manly thrusting stem.

'Ooh! Oooh! Oh, God! Oooh!' Sir Jasper moaned.

Then she withdrew her tongue. 'We'll not be 'earing any more of bribery charges, will we now, ya naughty boy?' Hannah cooed.

'No, nanny! I promise! Please, please, I beg of you, suck upon me! Oooh!'

Hannah smiled and licked her lips, and took him once again and brought him to the ultimate point before she withdrew her tongue again. 'And no more of 'anging?'

'Oh, Jesus! No! No more of hanging!' Sir Jasper whimpered. 'I beseech yooooou!'

'Swear it as an English gentleman, upon the 'ead o' the King 'imself!' Her tongue flicked out and licked invitingly at her lips then, darting further, playing mischievously with the tip of her nose.

'I swear as a gentleman, upon His Majesty's head,' Sir Jasper gasped. 'Please, nanny, do me! Do me now, I beg of you. I cannot bear it a moment longer, suck me dry, ooooh!'

Whereupon Hannah took Sir Jasper into her mouth and, with the help of her lascivious tongue, proceeded to satisfy him beyond his wildest fantasies. Completely exhausted, he reeled back and collapsed, gasping and panting. Half sprawled upon the chair, his pot belly was an incongruous helmet placed upon his otherwise skinny frame, his naked, hairless legs, encased at their ends with high-heeled boots. Hannah noted with satisfaction that his nose, now flat and pale as a badly risen scone, cowered against his florid, sweating face.

'Yer trousers,' Hannah said, rising and covering his nakedness by placing the garment across Sir Jasper's lap. 'I apologise most 'umbly,' she said, grinning wickedly, 'I made much too light of yer other cigar, it is a most worthy smoke, sir!'

Sir Jasper looked up at Hannah and gave her a small smile, his tiny obsidian eyes expressing a much becalmed disposition.

'If we are to be *friends*, m'dear,' he panted, 'it is best that I state the terms right off.' He sat up, clutching his trousers to his crotch, attempting to sound businesslike in his manner. 'I can do nothing for your husband other than attempt to forestall his march to the gallows. We can enter a plea that no long-tailed notes were found in his possession, only those of five pound value, though these are of exceptional quality and most numerous. The judge may, with a little persuasion, come eventually to see that transportation rather than hanging is in order.'

Sir Jasper grunted, and bent down to remove his boots. Arising, he proceeded without shame to reappoint his trousers to his skinny frame, and then, seated once more, returned his boots to his small stockinged feet.

'We shall, of course, need your co-operation in the matter of the counterfeit fivers,' he said, looking up at Hannah for her confirmation.

'An' me?' Hannah asked. 'What's to 'appen to me?'

Sir Jasper rose from the chair and stood once more trousered and confident. His recent intimacy and claims of friendship seemingly quite forgotten, and with his thumbs hooked into the lapels of his cutaway coat, he declared, 'Ah, yes, the sewing woman! We must reward the sewing woman.'

He glanced down at his front, admiring the tiny, almost invisible finger pluck seam where the cigar hole had previously been.

'A capital job, m'dear, and most skilfully completed!'

He glanced slyly at Hannah, so that his double meaning would not be lost to her.

'Yer most welcome, I'm sure, sir,' Hannah said, returning his knowing look. 'Yer always welcome to me 'umble mouth!'

Sir Jasper pulled himself up to his full height, which was by no means impressive. 'Mrs Solomons, I must remind you, each of us has our place and you would do well to remember yours! Let me be quite clear, we shall have no blackmail here, do you hear?'

Hannah had half expected his return to pomposity, for she was well aware that the masculine mind is directed largely from below the waist, and that there is nothing so restoring to the male ego as the return of his trousers. Even so, she was not of a mind to apologise. She knew enough of these matters to be certain that the priggish policeman would be back for more in due course. The next time she would tempt him further with a good spanking. The back of the hairbrush on his noble little botty. Hannah felt confident that her relationship with the Upper Marshal was far from over.

Hannah answered sweetly, 'Blackmail, sir? I can't

rightly say that I knows what ya is talkin' about.' Then abruptly changing the subject Hannah looked ingenuously at Sir Jasper. 'Ya ain't answered me question sir. What shall become of our 'umble family? If me 'usband should be transported, 'ow shall we live?' She lowered her voice and its tearful character returned. 'With 'im gorn yer condemning us to the work'ouse!'

'Why, Mrs Solomons, you are by all accounts a resourceful woman. I feel sure your, er ... dockside establishments bring you a handsome return?'

Hannah feigned surprise. 'I'm sure I don't knows what ya mean, sir. If what ya said was goin' on, but what I said wasn't, but could be, that is, if a person was forced into supportin' 'er four starving kids without an 'usband, if such establishments were to 'appen to be about to ... open?'

'Yes, well, I dare say if you are prepared to co-operate fully, the bank isn't too interested in your, er ... *other* businesses.'

Hannah sniffed, reaching into her handbag for a dainty handkerchief and touching it to each eye in what she supposed was a genteel gesture, she looked imploringly up at Sir Jasper. 'Am I so bold as to believe, sir, that ya would turn the self-same blind eye to the establishment what is at me poor 'usband's 'ouse in Bell Alley?'

'The printing shop or the brothel?'

'No, sir, not the printin', definitely not the printin'. Me, what can't read nor write 'as no use for a printin' shop.'

'Ah! You are sprung, madam!' Sir Jasper laughed. 'So you *do* know Egyptian Mary? You wish to continue your husband's partnership? Two sows in the same trough, eh?' Sir Jasper chuckled at his own joke. 'Well, well, well, well! I would be surprised if Egyptian Mary would countenance such an arrangement, she is a woman of some pepper. Still, I guess you would know, eh?'

'No, sir, I does *not*!' Hannah snorted. 'Ya quite mistake me meanin'. I want me 'usband's so *called* partner arrested! It were *'er* what turned 'im to queer screenin' and printin' unlawful paper, if such a thing 'as been done by 'im! It ain't fair if she goes free! That's a blatant miscarriage o' justice, that is!'

'But there is no evidence to implicate her in his forgery,' Sir Jasper said frowning. 'We can't let you continue to run six bawdy houses and arrest her for running but one! Why, madam, we'd be the laughing stock of the City!'

'It ain't the same!' Hannah countered. 'I takes me earnin's from the criminal classes, the filth! Them what don't know, and never can know any better! What I does is as natural to them as stealin', they's born to it, it's a social 'abit, normal as breathin', I cater for them what doesn't 'ave no 'ope of risin' up from a life o' crime and grog!'

'I can't possibly entertain such a preposterous idea, Mrs Solomons!' In point of fact, though, Sir Jasper, who shared the contemporary social views that the criminal poor were born and not created by environment or circumstances, was not unimpressed with Hannah's argument. 'I must remind you, justice is blind. Running a bawdy house of whatever kind is an equal crime against the law. If we are to overlook the one kind, *your* kind, we must do the same for *her* kind, what?' Sir Jasper lifted his chin and looked down at

Hannah across his florid nose. 'British justice must prevail, there's an end to it now, the matter bears no further discussion!'

Hannah was not prepared to concede. 'Yer actual law, yes! That I'll grant ya is the same! But what about yer lot, the upper classes? What about *yer* morals? What about *yer* standards o' society? Me 'umble customers can't get no better. They ain't got no morals and they ain't got no standards what can be upheld. But what o' *yer* lot? What this Egyptian whore is runnin' is causin' the destruction of the moral standards o' the better classes! Them what's born to morals and standards and must set an example for the 'onest poor!'

'Clever argument, as a matter of fact, dashed clever!' Sir Jasper seemed genuinely impressed. 'Madam, I commend you for your reasoning, but . . . '

Hannah's interruption was of perfect timing. 'I really don't think I could give me complete co-operation, me absolute best o' information and 'elp in the matter o' me 'usband and the printin' press, if ya was to turn a blind eye to this den of iniquity and sinfulness what 'as caught me darlin' Ikey in a web spun by this 'orrible, 'eathen, Egyptian whore!'

Sir Jasper, taken aback by this sudden change of attack from Hannah, seemed momentarily lost for words. He paced the few steps left to him in the tiny room. 'Hmm! Very awkward.' He glanced at Hannah. 'I don't suppose it would make any great difference if I told you Egyptian Mary is English? Her name is Mary Abacus. Not her real name, carries an abacus see, damned clever at calculations, London as the bells of St Clements, not a drop of wog in her, born in Rosemary Lane, tough as a brigade boot, lots of ginger, hands deformed, some sort of bizarre accident down at the docks on Jacob's Island.'

Hannah was now breathing heavily. The Mary she knew, who carried the Chinee contraption wherever she went, was a drunken whore who had also taken to the opium pipe, usually the end of the road for her kind. Hannah was an expert in such women. Their last stop was a brothel such as hers, thereafter they would be soon dragged from the river with a boatman's hook, or found with their ears and nose and fingertips eaten by rats, their body submerged in some putrid cesspool or rotting in a dark, evil smelling alley. It was almost beyond believing that this Egyptian whore might be the same Mary. That bastard Marley knew all the time – the miserable sod owed her two sov! Ikey had chosen this *nemmo* scumbag above his own wife to partner him in the high-class brothel of *her* dreams. The humiliation was too impossible to bear!

Now Hannah, visibly shaking, glared at Sir Jasper. 'If that filthy whore don't *get the boat* then ya can stick yer threats up yer arse! I'll take me chances with the law. This very night all six o' me places shall become netherkens where the desperate poor can stay for tuppence a night, you'll 'ave to prove otherwise and all I can say is you'll 'ave a bleedin' 'ard time doin' it!'

Sir Jasper, much taken aback by Hannah's fury, brought his hands up to his chest as though to protect himself from the battery of words she hurled at him.

'Hush, hush, m'dear, you'll do yourself a harm,' he cried in alarm. 'I shall see what we can do!'

'Not good enough, sir!'

'Hell hath no fury, eh?'

Sir Jasper was sufficiently sensitive to realise with

some delight that Hannah's venom was largely directed towards her husband. Now she confirmed this, her scorn evident as she spoke. 'Ya can 'ave 'im, 'e ain't no good to me no more, I 'ope the bastard rots in 'ell!'

Sir Jasper smiled. 'Mary Abacus will be arrested, I promise.'

'And transported?'

'I can't influence the judge, m'dear.'

'Ya can 'ave a word in the ear o' the judge, like you said ya could in the matter of Ikey's 'anging!' Hannah said tartly.

The little man sighed heavily. 'That being a civil crime, this, madam, would be a social one!' As though to explain he shrugged and added, 'A crime against the people.'

'Swear it!' Hannah demanded.

'You strike a hard bargain, Mrs Solomons.' Sir Jasper paused. 'Very well, I swear I shall arrest Mary Abacus and cause her to be transported, though it will not be a popular idea in the City.'

Hannah, vastly relieved, sighed heavily. She had been angry, but now she found herself excited at the prospect of the demise of the whore with the beads and, even more thrilling, her nicely contrived revenge on Ikey. She loved the feeling of power it gave her. It was more than simply revenge on two people who'd dared to cross her, it was a portion of repayment for the bitter disappointment of her life.

But then, like a thunderbolt, it struck her that she had once again been denied. Hannah realised that she must forgo the sweetest part of her vengeance. She could not let Ikey know it had been she who had brought about his downfall. If Ikey knew she had betrayed him he would never agree to give her his half of the combination to the safe. He would rather rot in hell than see her benefit a single penny from his plight.

Hannah looked up knowingly and smiled indulgently at Sir Jasper. 'Men got weaknesses what they can't rightly be blamed for. I implore ya, sir! For the sake o' me young 'uns, I don't want me 'usband to know it was me who shopped 'im!'

Sir Jasper took a gold hunter from his waistcoat and clicked it open. He was anxious to conclude the business at hand. 'No, of course, Mrs Solomons, there is absolutely no need for your husband to know of your co-operation with the authorities.' He returned his watch to his waistcoat. 'Under the circumstances it is most honourable of you to spare his feelings.'

'Kindness 'as always been me great downfall,' Hannah, her eyes cast downwards, said modestly.

Sir Jasper cleared his thoat. 'Now, this is what we want and, I must warn you, I shall brook no altercation on the matter. We shall raid your premises in White-chapel and we shall expect to find a number of counterfeit five pound notes well concealed. The money we find will be some portion of the counterfeit notes we discovered in the basement premises at Bell Alley.'

'The money? In me 'ouse? You must be completely barmy, that makes *me* guilty too, don't it?' Hannah cried. 'Complicity in 'elping to conceal stolen goods? I ain't as *meshuggah* as I may look, ya know!'

'I have already given you our assurance as an officer of the law and a gentleman on that matter, madam.'

Hannah laughed. 'With the greatest respect, sir, what 'appens if ya drop dead? When I'm standin' in the dock in the Old Bailey and the judge passes sentence on me, what am I goin' to say? Oi! That's not fair, yer worship! Him, what's the Upper Whatsit, told me I 'ad 'is personal guarantee as a gentleman and officer o' the law that I can't be nicked!' Hannah rose indignantly from her chair and placed her hands on her hips. 'Ha! The bleedin' judge will think I've gorn soft in the bloomin' 'ead, *and* 'e'd be right too, allowin' counterfeit money to be found in me own 'ouse.'

Hannah sat down again, huffing and snorting. She needed a moment to think, for she had a secondary reason for not wanting the police to raid her White-chapel home. Though well concealed in the false ceiling under the floor of her bedroom, the house contained goods of great value. There was also the matter of the safe. The City police were an entirely different kettle of fish to the usual, dim-witted magistrates' runners. Hannah didn't want to take the chance that in the bogus search for the counterfeit banknotes, this too might be discovered.

Sir Jasper was visibly growing impatient. 'You will have to trust me, madam!' he said sharply.

'It ain't a matter o' trust, sir. It's a matter o' natural caution, a matter of survival. I wouldn't trust me own rabbi from shoppin' me if 'e was to find counterfeit money in me 'ouse! Stands to reason, don't it? In the eyes o' the law, Ikey and me, we'd both be guilty!' She paused and smiled at the police officer. 'May I suggest summink more appropriate?'

The Upper Marshal banged his fist down hard upon the table. 'No, madam, you may not! I hardly think a woman of your background could improve on our methodicals! This plan is the work of experienced officers, it requires no alteration, being quite perfect as it is!' He folded his arms across his chest and glowered at Hannah in a most imperious manner.

Hannah remained silent until she gauged that Sir Jasper's exasperation had somewhat calmed, then she persisted. ' 'Is coat. Sew the money in the linin' o' his coat, then nick 'im on the street, away from 'ome, away from me and the young 'uns!'

The police officer, despite his irritability, looked up at her in surprise. 'I say, do you think you could do that?' Then he rested his chin on his chest and mused, as though to himself, 'Lining of his coat? Caught red-handed with the money on his person, in his possession?' He looked up and smiled at Hannah. 'By, Jove, that's perfectly splendid! No way of wriggling out of that, eh?' Sir Jasper rubbed his hands gleefully together, completely mollified. 'Perfect! Why, it's quite, quite perfect, m'dear!'

'Not so perfect, already!' Hannah scowled. ' 'E don't ever take 'is coat orf, not never and not particular never at this time, when the weather is inclement and comin' up to Christmas.' She cocked her head and thought for a moment, 'On the other 'and, if 'e don't ever take orf 'is coat ... ' she paused, thinking again, 'then the only person what would 'ave put the money there is 'isself, ain't that right, then?'

Sir Jasper clapped his hands in delight. 'I say, that's damn clever, m'dear! Capital, how very wise of you!'

Hannah knew the task of apprehending Ikey away from home would be a most difficult one. Ikey's mode of travel through the rookeries was nocturnal and shadowy, never tiring in the task of concealment. No magistrates' runner or Bank of England law officer could ever hope to follow him, or even dare to enter those parts where his crepuscular fellow creatures engaged in business with him.

Ikey's coat was a very elusive target and the more she thought about it the less confident she was that such a scheme could be made to work. But with the knowledge that all the stolen property concealed in her White-chapel home would come into her possession while she was, so to speak, under the protection of the law, Hannah possessed a powerful additional incentive to succeed.

'When will ya let me 'ave the false finnies, sir? I needs no more than two.'

'Finnies? Oh, you mean the five pound notes? You shall have them promptly on the morrow.'

'In the afternoon, if ya please. I needs me beauty sleep!' Hannah smiled and then, with one eyebrow slightly arched and her head cocked to one side, her expression coquettish, 'Perhaps you would like to bring 'em y'self, sir?'

Sir Jasper Waterlow's complexion turned a sudden deep purple and his nose began to twitch alarmingly. Avoiding Hannah's eyes he gathered up his top hat from the table and moved towards the door where he paused, and slid the slender fingers of his left hand into a bright yellow leather glove. He was quite exhausted and in urgent need of a stiff brandy.

His expression now somewhat composed, he looked directly at Hannah. 'I shall require you to wait five minutes before leaving,' he grunted, then added, 'I should also be very careful not to *lose* the five pound notes I shall send you. It would be most difficult to convince me that such a calamity was honestly come about.' He pulled the second glove on and glanced briefly at Hannah from under the rim of his top hat. 'Though, of course, in such an event, we do have others.' Then he touched the brim of his hat. 'Good day to you, Mrs Solomons,' Sir Jasper said and, passing through the doorway, closed the door behind him.

Hannah smiled. She could hear the clatter of his mincing high-heeled steps in the hallway and then the silence as he stopped to retrieve his cloak from the proprietor, then a few more steps as he departed the Blue Wren. 'That's gratitude for ya,' she said to herself. 'But that one will be back soon enough for a good spankin' from 'is adorable nanny, nothin' surer.'

Not long after this meeting, Hannah once again summoned Bob Marley. He was surprised to be contacted by Hannah so soon after it would have been apparent that he had duped her in the matter of the raid on the premises in Bell Alley. Hannah was not known for her forgiving nature. Marley was therefore understandably suspicious at her openly friendly manner. She sat him in the parlour where a bright fire blazed and where she had laid out a single glass and fresh bottle of brandy with a plate of oat cakes.

Apart from his initial greeting Bob Marley remained silent, pouring himself a large glass of brandy and helping himself to a couple of the cakes.

'It weren't nice what ya done, Bob Marley,' Hannah began. 'Takin' advantage of a poor woman what was 'elpless.'

Marley, with a mouth full of cake, stopped chewing and rose from his chair as though to leave. 'No, don't go!' Hannah added hastily, smiling. 'We got things to talk about what could be to yer advantage.'

Bob Marley swallowed the cake in his mouth and took a gulp of brandy to wash it down. 'It were you who called me, remember? All I done was take advantage of a situation what was not o' me makin'!' He was still holding the glass and, bringing it up to his lips, paused. 'It would 'ave been unprofessional not to 'ave done what I did. People might 'ave thought I was losin' me grip o' things!'

Hannah refrained from reminding him that there was only herself involved. When she thought about it, she supposed she too would have thought less of him if he hadn't exploited such an opportunity to benefit from her predicament. It was this very self-serving aspect of Bob Marley's nature which she now wished to use to her advantage.

'I needs a job done, no questions asked,' Hannah said finally.

Marley gave her a bemused look. 'There's always questions, lovey.'

'What I means is, I don't want to talk about me motives, I wants ya to accept 'em, no questions asked.'

'No questions costs more money, it means I can't measure the exact amount o' risk involved.'

'No more risk than if ya knew everyfink, you 'ave my word on that.'

Marley waited, saying nothing, and Hannah continued. 'Ikey will come back to London, reasons that don't matter to ya, but 'e'll be back. He can't come 'ome, too dangerous. 'E'll need a place to 'ide and somebody 'e can trust to find it for 'im and act,' she paused and looked at Bob Marley, 'sort of as a go-between 'tween me and 'im.'

Marley took a long swig at the brandy in his glass, prolonging his lips on the rim of the glass longer than would have seemed necessary, as though he was thinking carefully on the proposition. Finally he looked up at Hannah. 'There's a big reward out – I'd 'ave to be paid 'least that, and expenses, mind. Findin' a deadlurk what will keep 'im safe wif 'arf the bleedin' world keepin' a greedy eye out for 'im ain't goin' to be easy!'

Hannah had already taken herself through the process of having to pay Marley the equivalent of the reward on Ikey's head, but she was nonetheless shocked at the prospect when she heard it coming from Marley's own mouth. She swallowed hard, 'For that sort o' money I'd want more,' she said, her gaze steady.

'More? What's ya mean?'

'I wants ya to plant some fake stiff on Ikey.'

Marley brought his palms up in front of his face. 'Hey now, Hannah, we's family people! Ya going to shop Ikey by plantin' snide on 'im, that ain't nice. That ain't nice at all?'

Hannah stiffened. 'Remember, I said no questions. I 'as me reasons, Bob Marley.'

Marley whistled. 'I bet ya 'as, lovey.' He sighed and looked directly at Hannah, 'Sorry, I don't do domestics.'

'I'm not askin' ya to take sides! Jus' to plant some fake soft.'

'I'll not shop 'im, Hannah. I'm no copper's nark.'

'I didn't ask ya, did I? Just to do a plant, that's all.'

Marley looked up. 'Jus' the plant?' He seemed to think for a moment. 'It'll cost extra.'

Hannah laughed and then shook her head. 'Sorry, love, when ya asked for the reward, that be the limit. There's 'undred pound on Ikey's 'ead and I'll pay that, but not a farthin' more.'

Chapter Ten

Since time out of mind, long before the coming of the great belted engines with their hiss and suck of steam and whirr of wheels and pistons, before the city provided warmongery to the world with its mountains of iron ore, furnaced, hot rolled, steam hammered, pressed, poured and moulded into the fiery spit and spite of small arms, Birmingham had always been the Babylon of baubles. It was here that goldsmiths and silversmiths, in a thousand tiny workshops, made jewellery so wickedly extravagant as to turn many a fine lady into a whore, and many a whore into a fine lady.

As may be expected, where there is gold, silver, plate and wicked little stones with nimble fingers to shape and polish them, there are gentlemen with even lighter fingers to fleece them from their rightful owners into the greedy hands of the unctuous fence.

Ikey arrived in Birmingham at eight o'clock in the morning of his second day out from London, not stopping to pass the night in a comfortable tavern, though several of these establishments existed for this sole purpose – inns where a weary traveller could expect a crackling fire, a sizzling pot roast, a pewter mug of good mulled claret and, upon a quiet word into the landlord's ear, a bed warmed by a ploughman's daughter, a wench with ivory skin and thighs as creamy to the sight as fresh churned butter. It was common enough talk among those who often travelled these ways that the yokel's daughter, so lasciviously described, had indeed been much ploughed and so often seeded as to sprout half the snot-nosed bumpkins in the parish.

It was most surprising that Ikey chose to continue on the smaller, faster night coach to Birmingham. He was, after all, a natural coward and it being the Christmas season the danger of meeting a highwayman or footpad on the road was greatly increased. Only a fool or a traveller with most urgent business would think to travel with a mail-coach running hard through the night. But Ikey, a creature of the dark hours, felt most vulnerable when exposed to the brightness of sun-pierced light and, in particular, within a restricted location such as a coach. He had sat miserably all day trapped and huddled in the corner of the day coach from London, the collar of his coat pulled high and his hat placed deep-browed upon his head, with his face turned outwards to the passing countryside. Should his fellow passengers have wished to observe him they would have seen only the collar of his coat and the broad-brimmed hat which appeared to rest upon it.

To all appearances these aforementioned fellow passengers looked innocent enough: the ginger-bearded horse dealer with his shaggy one-eyed dog, the two long-fenced clerical types in dark cloth, only the colour of their waistcoats telling them apart, and of course the monstrously fat woman in widow's weeds, a human personage so big she could easily turn a living in the grand freak show at Southwark Fair. But Ikey was taking no chances and said not a single word all day, not even allowing the most banal of courtesies.

When evening came and his fellow passengers left the coach for the comforts of a night spent in a village tavern, the opportunity to continue on alone was presented to Ikey by the departure of a lighter and faster mail-coach travelling through to Birmingham. It contained sufficient room for four passengers, though he seemed to be the only one to purchase a ticket from the coachman.

It was a most bitter disappointment to Ikey when Tweedledum, the red-waistcoated clerk, climbed unsteadily into the coach. He smelled strongly of cider and barely nodded as he found his seat at the window opposite but on the same side as Ikey, so that their eyes could not meet. Now they both faced in the direction in which the coach was travelling. Ikey had not thought of him as separate, but as one component of a two-part presence in red and yellow, and it disturbed him to think that he'd made such an unthinking assumption based simply on their attire.

Ikey's first instinct was to become immediately suspicious of the man's presence. But if Tweedle was an officer of the law sent to keep an eye on him, his recent intake of the local cider had rendered him ineffective, for Tweedle was becoming increasingly cross-eyed, his head lolling with the delayed effects of the local scrumpy.

The ostler had all but completed checking the harnessing and the coachman was already aboard, whip in hand, when the fat widow, clutching her large hamper to her bosom, emerged panting from the tavern and came towards them.

The coach was delayed ten minutes as the ostler and the coachman pushed and squeezed, panted and shoved to fit the giant woman through the door of the smaller carriage. Once contained within its interior it would have been quite impossible for any further souls to occupy the remaining space, of which there was now very little. The lighter mail coach, though harnessed with a full team of horses, was built for speed and not for the comfortable accommodation of passengers. The gargantuan woman filled one entire side of its interior, her fat knees occupying the corridor between them, and her hamper taking up the centre of the opposite seat with the silently drunken Tweedle at one side, and Ikey huddled tightly into the corner at the other.

It was snowing quite hard, though the road was still clear and the post-chaise set off at a brisk pace into the night. The widow completely ignored Ikey's presence and shortly after they reached the first toll-gate she reached over for the hamper, placed it on her lap and clamped her fat arms around its lid. Then she fell into an immediate and seemingly deep slumber.

Ikey hoped to do the same, for he was desperately tired and had been awake more than twenty-four hours, and with the absence of the hamper the seat beside him promised to make an excellent bed. But Tweedle, as if struck by a blow from an invisible hand, collapsed into the space left between them. The cider had finally rendered him senseless.

Ikey turned up the collar of his coat and, pulling its lapels around his chest, settled down to sleep. Alas, the widow soon put this prospect from his mind, for she caused a great deal more trouble for Ikey asleep than ever she'd done in a state of wakefulness.

During the day Ikey had observed from the corner of his eye and by a direct assault on his nostrils, that the widow had partaken of several large meals, the fare coming out of the seemingly inexhaustible larder on her lap.

Now, as she snored, her tightly compact innards fought back with a series of combustible noises. From her vast interior oleaginous gases rumbled in ferment. After a period of time all these internally combusted sounds combined to reach a climax. It seemed that at any moment the pressure within her would become so great that a cork must surely pop from her navel, cause a huge efflux and send coach and horses, Ikey and the unconscious Tweedle all the way to kingdom come.

Ikey sat huddled in his corner with the collar of his coat and the brim of his hat tightly pushed against his ears, though the sounds prevailed, penetrating the protection of his cupped hands. Just as he supposed he could stand it no longer, when the noises and fumes of regurgitated gases and thunderous farts became too noxious even for his seasoned nose, with a soft sigh the widow quietly awakened and proceeded to open the hamper on her lap.

A small lantern swinging from the coach roof cast a to-and-fro shadow across the interior of the cabin, so that the widow would disappear into the complete darkness and then a moment later appear again, lit by the dim light of the swaying lamp.

Ikey watched from the inside of his coat as food began to appear. First was the smaller part of a haunch of ham, one side showing white to the bone and the other plump with pink meat. From it the widow carved, at the very least, a pound of pig flesh and proceeded to layer it upon a thick crust of bread. This she sprinkled with a generous pinch of salt, swiped with a blade of yellow mustard and garnished with pickle forked from a large jar. Finally she added to the conglomeration several thumps of thick, dark, treacle-like sauce.

Each meal was taken precisely on the hour, each different; a mutton pie large enough to feed a hungry family, a plump chicken and a raisin tart, a turkey leg and a pound of white breast meat, a large cold sausage and apple pie, a slab of cold roast beef and several boiled potatoes. A large pork and leek pie was the last but final means of satisfying the giant woman's voracious appetite.

Ikey, thoroughly miserable, watched as a cold blue dawn appeared over the gently rolling countryside, the tops of the low rounded hills blanketed with snow. He was desperate for sleep and his small belly, so seldom demanding of food and having observed so much of it during the night, now rumbled with the need for sustenance, though even now food was not his greatest need and he would willingly have remained hungry for another day in exchange for two hours of uninterrupted sleep. He envied Tweedle who seemed not to have stirred on the seat beside him.

With no further food to consume, the widow settled down to finish off the demijohn of gin. She seemed unaware of the sleeping shape of Tweedle, whose face lay only inches from her plump white knees, but fixed Ikey with a stern and disapproving eye, or rather, she fixed her disapproval on the dark, silent upright bundle in the corner. Holding the neck of the demijohn in her fat fist, she brought it to her lips, and with a tolerable level of sucking and lip smacking and occasional bilious burps the widow proceeded to get very drunk. Ikey, at last, was able to fall into an exhausted sleep.

He was awakened three hours later by the sound of giggling accompanied by several sharp prods in the region of his chest and stomach. 'Wake up! We be in (hic!) Brummagen soon.' The widow was jabbing at him with the stick and giggling, her fat head wobbly with her mirth and she drooled like a well-fed infant. 'Wakey-wakey!'

Ikey sat up quickly, dazed from insufficient sleep. It was by no means the first time in his life that he'd been prodded awake with the point of a stick, and he immediately imagined himself to be in a prison cell, for the smell was much the same and the ride had become unaccountably smooth, so much so that, to his blunted senses, the coach appeared not to be moving at all.

In fact, the coach was completing the last mile into the centre of Birmingham by way of the new road composed of a material known as macadam. This was a tar-like substance as used for caulking vessels. It was heated until it was treacle-like and ran easily, whereupon it was poured upon a bed of small stones (the men who mixed it might use no stone larger than one they could roll on their tongue and still repeat: 'God save the King!'). The substance was soaked into the stony surface and while steaming was compressed with a large steamroller and allowed to dry smooth and hard. The result was a surface impervious to the most inclement weather and upon which any manner of wagon or coach wheel could travel. All was made without the need for skilled labour and at a fraction of the cost of the quarrying, shaping and laying of cobblestones.

Ikey's mind was not tuned to dullness and he was soon aware of his surroundings. The widow, satisfied that she'd done her Christian duty and wakened him, did the same for Tweedle. He sat up groaning and holding his head in both hands, eyes bloodshot and his hair standing up in untidy tufts. 'Oh my Gawd!' he moaned.

Ikey stared out of the coach window at the houses, some with chimneys already smoking in the early light, growing more and more numerous and close-built as they approached the city centre and the coach terminus. Staging posts, particularly at the terminus from one great metropolis to another, were much inhabited by the watchful eyes of the law as well as those of informers hoping to earn a few shillings for spotting a known villain. Ikey's fondest hope was that he would be allowed to skulk unnoticed from the scene into the nearest darkened lane, and thereafter to a nearby rookery where he would be free from the ever curious attentions of any members of the law or the underworld.

He now became concerned with the presence of Tweedle. His earlier anxiety returned and Ikey imagined him to be a law man who would elicit the aid of a waiting law officer from the Birmingham constabulary to arrest him, his task while on the coach simply being to keep a watchful eye on him lest he take his departure before reaching the city.

Ikey was tired and his senses somewhat blunted. He told himself one moment that he was imagining the danger, and the next that he should have reasoned it out long before this and left the coach when they'd stopped to change horses at a village during the night.

Caution, with its partner suspicion, being his more natural instinct, Ikey decided he would make a dash for it the moment the coach drew to a complete standstill.

Ikey carried no personal baggage. In fact, Ikey's taking a chance that a highwayman might waylay the coach during the night journey was not as courageous as it might have outwardly seemed. Highwaymen seldom shoot their victims and Ikey had no fear of robbery, for he'd carried in his purse coin sufficient only to purchase the coach ticket and to eat frugally and pay for his accommodation for a day or two upon his arrival, with a little left over for miscellaneous expenses. A secret pocket under the armpit of his coat contained fifty pounds, though a highwayman would need to remove the coat and most carefully dissect its lining to find this. To be robbed of what he superficially possessed would have been no serious matter. He carried only a cheap watch and chain and a small cut-throat razor and the deeds to the house in Bell Alley, a paper which would make no sense to a common robber. Also resting in a pocket was the key to his home in Whitechapel.

It being so close to Christmas, this absence of serious cash on Ikey would have been somewhat surprising. Anyone who knew him was aware that he would often carry a thousand pounds on his person, for the season's pickings would be exceedingly good and ready cash was what was needed to make the most of the many opportunities certain to come his way. But, this time in Birmingham, Ikey was playing for much bigger stakes than the fencing of a few bright baubles taken in the Christmas crowds.

The coach drew at last to a standstill, the coachman

laying aside his horn and shouting, 'Whooa! Whooa!' to the wild-eyed beasts in the time-honoured way. The horses thus brought to a stop shook their heads in a jingle of brasses, champed at the bit and stamped their feet on the hard surface of the road. Their coats were lathered with sweat from their final gallop and their nostrils snorted smoky air.

The coach official opened the door on the widow's side. 'Oh me Gawd!' he exclaimed fanning his nose. He immediately turned to the waiting crowd. 'Anyone come for a show freak?' he yelled. 'If 'e is, she be blind, 'opeless drunk! Need ter fetch cart and oxen, or special sprung carriage. She'll not be walkin', I can tell 'e that for sure and absolute certain!'

The widow reached out and took the unfortunate official by the collar of his coat and pulled the top half of him backwards into the coach so that his head lay upon her lap. ' 'Ullo, dearie, fancy a kiss?' she said, then burped loudly into the man's astonished face.

Ikey glanced quickly at Tweedle, who sat frozen upright looking directly out of the window, trying to ignore the bizarre antics of the drunken woman and the wildly struggling and whimpering official.

Taking advantage of the confusion, Ikey quietly unlatched the coach door on his side, leaving it ajar. Then he rose and lifted the still surprisingly heavy hamper and placed it down upon an astonished Tweedle's lap, quite preventing him from rising in pursuit should he take it in his mind to do so, whereupon he pushed the door open and stepped through it. But alas, his coat caught on the sharp corner of the small door and pulled him back. Ikey pulled desperately at the coat and a six-inch tear appeared in the thick wool as he wrenched it free, and then dashed into the dark shadow cast by the terminus building. In a few moments he had escaped up a narrow alleyway which ran between the stage coach terminal and the building beside it.

Ikey's immediate destination in Birmingham was not, as might normally have been the case, one of the more notorious flash-houses nor thieves' kitchens where he might be expected to take up temporary residence, but to a stabling property on the outskirts of the city.

This large, unprepossessing building of rough-hewn stone had all the appearances of a farmhouse. It was set on the road to the village of Coleshill, with stables on the ground level for several horses and above it two additional storeys, which a visitor might naturally suppose was the owner's residence. However, in this instance, the large building was much, much more than a simple farmhouse and might even have been called a kind of factory, a paper and ink factory to give this most improper and anonymous business a proper name.

The property belonged to Silas Browne Esq., outwardly a respected horse dealer but to those in the know, one of the greatest forgers of soft in the land. He was a man of great ingenuity and reputation known to all who dealt in a serious manner in good forged banknotes throughout England and continental Europe.

Birmingham was the chief centre of the production of good hard, this being the name for counterfeit coin. Since it had always been a place where fine jewellery, watches and military medals were made, it was easy enough for Birmingham craftsmen to turn to this illicit trade. The same was not necessarily true for the forging of banknotes, and had it not been for the remarkable talents of Silas Browne and his wife Maggie the Colour, the city might not have become a recognised centre for banknote forgery.

While the city supported a great many clandestine coining workshops it contained only a handful of talented engravers. These mostly derived from men who had been decorators of gold and silver plate. Though these few very skilled men together gave it an acknowledged presence in banknotes and forged letters of credit, and even some work on share certificates, their efforts were no greater than other major English cities.

Etching was an exacting task and a superior engraver might take a year or more to perfect the plates required for a single banknote, so that these men needed to be financed and carefully safeguarded by those who profited most from their skills. Silas Browne and Maggie the Colour were known to employ the very best engravers. But to the engraver's skill they added two ingredients which gave Birmingham an advantage in the forged banknote trade. The house to which Ikey now hurriedly set out was used for making this paper and ink.

Silas Browne, though seeming a ponderous and somewhat befuddled man, made the best counterfeit paper in England and his wife, Maggie the Colour, the best inks. This combination, together with the fact that Silas financed most of the more skilled engravers and so came into possession of the best engraved plates, made them very wealthy. It was claimed they had a share in every forgery printing operation in Birmingham and, as well, sold ink to Manchester printers and even to some of the better London operators.

Maggie the Colour was the daughter of a Manchester dyemaker and possessed a talent for mixing inks and

dyes and an eye for subtle colour, shading and gradations, which was truly remarkable. She was known to
use mostly local tinctures, some from plants and herbs
she collected in the surrounding countryside, the juice
of mulberry and pomegranate imported from Spain, as
well as tannins from various types of wood. These she
mixed with the exotic pigments and dyes available on
the English market, but which came from India, China
and from Dutch Batavia used by the silk makers in
Macclesfield and the cotton spinners of Manchester.
Any forger worthy of his name would use no other ink,
the powdered galls mixed with camphor supplied by
Maggie the Colour were so good that even the officials
at the Bank of England could find no major fault with
her product.

Given the very best engraver's plates, expertly prepared paper, perfect ink matching and superior printing, the work done by Silas Browne and Maggie the
Colour was among the finest in England. But it fell
short of perfection because the paper used for bills
simply could not be reproduced, and the plates used for
banknotes above the ten pound denomination were
thought to be too complicated for a single engraver, and
could never hope to deceive even the most casual banker's eye.

Abraham Van Esselyn's forged plates were near to
being the exception. They were the very finest of their
kind available, perhaps in the entire world of forgery, so
perfect that they might have been prepared by the Bank
of England's own engravers. These plates, now about to
be offered by Ikey to Silas Browne, were the work of a
single man of undoubted genius and moreover, each was
perfect to the point of almost any magnification. This

made them of the greatest possible value to a team like Browne and his wife, Maggie, though, of course, it was not concerning these alone that Ikey had come to see them.

Ikey, having walked for almost an hour, came at last to the end of the city's sprawling slums, and soon found himself in more open ground where cottages rested separately, some with small gardens to the front or back. Ikey disliked space of any sort and his eyes darted hither and thither. He shied away from a barking dog, and jumped wildly at the sudden crow of a cockerel or the hissing of a goose. Some of the lanes along which he passed contained hedges on either side which provided some concealment, though nature's walls of hawthorn thicket did very little for Ikey's peace of mind. Strange things went click and buzz and chirp within them, and none of these noises equated to the myriad sounds to which Ikey's highly particular ear was tuned.

It was coming up mid-morning when he finally reached the open field in the centre of which stood the house of Silas Browne. Ikey was in a state of high nervous tension. The daylight hour, though some snow had started to fall, coupled with the open terrain through which he had been forced to travel on this final part of his journey, had brought him very close to complete panic. He was hungry but so single-minded in his mission that he hadn't even thought to enter a chop house for a meal. Now he stopped and rested at the gate leading into the field and, removing his neckcloth, wiped the nervous perspiration from his brow and the back of his neck.

The large treeless field appeared to be flat and, but for a dozen or so horses grazing about it, completely empty. Ikey expected that the moment he entered the gate someone would appear from the house to meet him. In fact, this is what he hoped might happen before he'd intruded too far into the large field, and so was unable to retreat back to the gate should a savage hound, designated for this very purpose, be set upon him. An envoy sent from the house would give him an opportunity to explain his reason for coming, and to send ahead of him a sample of his credentials for perusal by the redoubtable Silas Browne and his wife.

Ikey entered the field, his eyes darting everywhere, forwards and backwards and to either side. To his dismay no one came from the distant house and he was forced to move ever closer to it. Therefore it came as a fearful surprise to him when his hat was tipped over his eyes from behind, and a voice declared.

'Don't turn around, sir!'

Ikey, despite the fright he'd received, was of course an expert on young boys, and this voice was no more than ten or eleven years of age. This didn't do a great deal for his confidence, however, as street children of this age were as tough as grown men. Besides, they were sometimes larger than himself. He removed his hat and replaced it squarely back on his head.

'A penny for a word then, my dear,' Ikey said slowly, digging into his coat to find a copper coin which he held between finger and thumb and proffered behind his back.

His unseen assailant snatched the coin from Ikey's hand.

'Where does you think you're goin' then?' the boy enquired.

'Silas Browne! I begs to see Mr Silas Browne. That

is, with your permission o' course, your very esteemed permission, my dear.'

'Mr Silas Browne, is it? 'Ow does you know such a name, then?'

'Business! We is in the exact line o' business. Mr Browne is what you might call a colleague, though, I'll freely admit, I 'aven't exactly 'ad the pleasure of 'is personal acquaintance.' Ikey shrugged his shoulders. 'You see, we share what you might call a vocation. Yes, that's it, precisely and nicely and most specifically put, my dear, an exact and precise and similar vocation!'

'Oh, a voca . . .' the voice gave up trying to pronounce the word, 'and what line o' business does you share, then?'

Ikey was surprised at the sharpness of the boy. He'd come across similar boys before, but these were few enough to be an exception. Most street lads this age were already dulled from gin and the lack of proper nourishment, and would not have the wit to become involved in a conversation the likes of which the two of them were now conducting. This one would have made an excellent addition to his Methodist Academy of Light Fingers.

Now that he'd properly gathered his wits Ikey was impressed at the boy's sudden appearance behind him, seemingly rising out of nowhere. Ikey's eyes missed very little and even though he was unfamiliar with open terrain and the lack of shadow in daylight to reveal the bumps and undulations in the grassy field, it was no simple task to deceive him. The boy who crept up could not have followed him for any distance, for Ikey was in the constant habit of glancing over his shoulder. He must have walked right past the boy without seeing him, and this Ikey found both admirable and very disconcerting.

'The copper business … copper plates that is.' Ikey paused, 'Also, you could say, also the paper and inks business. I can say no more, from this moment me lips is sealed and can only be opened by Mr Silas Browne 'imself!'

'Does you 'ave an affy davy to say who you is, then?'

'Affidavit?' Ikey held an additional penny behind his back, wiggling it invitingly, but the boy did not take it this time. 'Most certainly and o' course absolutely right and correct to ask, my dear! An affy davy you shall 'ave, right away and immediately, for 'ow would your master know the manner o' person who 'as come so far and taken so many risks to talk with 'im? 'Ow indeed? All the way from London, that is, with barely a wink o' sleep and not a morsel o' nourishment from sunrise to sunset. I asks you, 'ow is 'e to know the 'umiliations and vicissitudes inflicted or the extreme importance o' the mission? Quite right of you to ask, quite right and proper.'

'Your affy davy,' the boy repeated bluntly, seemingly unimpressed by Ikey's verbosity and still not taking the proffered coin. 'Give't me, sir, or you get nowt more from us!'

Ikey carried no personal identification whatsoever, and even if he had papers to prove himself, he would not have willingly let them into the boy's hands, especially without having first seen his face. He was on the run, and young likely lads like this one schooled in the rookeries learned early the value of informing, of keeping their eyes peeled for the opportunity of a little crude blackmail.

The engraved plates he carried concealed in the lining of his coat would be instantly recognised as masterpieces by any competent forger and a glimpse at one of them, Ikey knew, would be likely to have Silas Browne scurrying out to meet him, his voice a bluster of apology and his hands all apatter. But if he let the boy have only one plate as a proof of his integrity, and if his master should choose not to see him nor to return it, the single engraved plate in the right hands was still worth a considerable fortune.

'I shall give you a piece o' paper, a small piece o' paper you must promise to take to your master, to Mister Silas Browne 'imself and to no other. Do you understand, my dear?'

'It'll cost,' the boy added cheekily.

Ikey sighed and retrieving the copper coin he held it once more behind his back.

'A sprat! Cost you a sprat or nowt 'appens.'

'Sixpence!' Ikey howled, though he did so more for the form of it than anything else. The boy was good, very, very good and he wished he could have him under his tuition. The boy reminded Ikey of the young Bob Marley, same cheek and quickness of mind. He smiled to himself, for he knew he could now trust him to take the paper directly to Silas Browne. Ikey returned the copper coin to his dumby and found a silver sixpence which he handed backwards to the boy.

'This paper what I want you to take to Mr Silas Browne, it is concealed upon me person. I shall need to stoop down to reach it and to cut open the 'emline o' me coat to remove it. I 'ave a small razor to do so, but my dear, do not be in the least alarmed, we, that's yours truly, is not at all a creature o' violence and disputation.'

'Don't turn about now!' the boy said threateningly, trying to put a deeper tone into his voice.

'No need, absolutely no need! No need in the least, you have my guarantee upon that, my dear.'

Ikey reached for the cut-throat razor in his pocket and opening it he stooped down and cut quickly at the line of the hem, though above the hidden plates, and only a cut wide enough to ease one of the plates sideways through the slit. He untied the twine and removed the wrapping from around the engraving. With the razor he sliced a small triangular corner from the square of paper, which he handed backwards to the boy.

'Take the paper to Mr Silas Browne, my dear, it's me affy davy.'

Ikey waited.

'Hey, mister, 't ain't say nowt onnit!' the boy exclaimed. 'It be blank paper what's got nowt writ onnit!'

Ikey chuckled. 'On the contrary, my dear, it speaks most eloquent to those what knows 'ow to read its message.'

There was silence behind him and Ikey imagined the confusion the boy was feeling. Seeking to put the lad out of his agony, he added, 'It's invisible like, but to such as Mr Silas Browne Esquire who knows the trick o' reading it, it's a magical paper.' Ikey spread his hands. 'Trust me, my dear.'

'You'll stay 'ere, see! You'll not be doing nowt 'til I returns!' The boy added threateningly, 'There's dogs, big bastids what can be let loose and sent after you in a twinklin', you'll not get t'gate before they's torn you t' bits!'

'Not a muscle, my dear, not a single twitch, not a

cat's whisker, not a scintilla o' movement until you gets back. Quiet as a mouse, silent as a ferret in a chicken coop, that's yours truly, Ikey Solomon, late of London Town. Tell your master there's more, much more where that come from, 'eaps and 'eaps more! 'E'll be most pleased, most pleased indeed to know that.'

The boy ran past Ikey and towards the house, laughing, not caring now whether Ikey saw him. He carried a long stick which he waved in the air. He was tiny, small enough even for Ikey to box his ears or place a sharp-toed boot into his scrawny little arse.

The boy, at first delighted to have made sevenpence so easily, grew anxious at his own reception as he drew nearer to the house. Silas Browne and the half dozen men and boys who worked with him stood waiting at the head of the ladder for him to climb into the room above. The lad, afraid he might lose the paper, held it between his lips as he climbed the ladder.

'Wotcha got then, Josh lad?' Silas Browne asked as the boy stepped from the ladder into the room.

Together with the others he'd stood watching from the windows at Ikey's original approach. They'd seen the boy Joshua, who'd been earlier sent on an errand, waylay Ikey from behind, before they could send an adult out to accost the stranger. Josh, though only ten years old, was known to be bright enough to make a judgement, yet young enough not to arouse any suspicion if the stranger was thought to be from the law. Silas knew that if the lad decided the man was up to no good he would drop his stick on the ground and then pick it up again. Whereupon he'd send one of the other lads down and set the dogs after the intruder to see him off their land.

One of the men pulled the ladder up after the lad had

climbed clear and closed the trap door behind him, bolting it firmly back into place. The boy Joshua looked somewhat sheepish at the greeting given by his master and, removing the tiny slip of paper from between his lips, handed it to Silas Browne.

' 'Tain't much, sir, but 'e sayed it was magical like, that you'd understand immediate like?' The boy, a most concerned expression upon his face, looked up at Silas Browne. 'Did I do wrong, sir?'

Silas Browne took the paper and rubbed it for a moment between his forefinger and thumb, whereupon he jerked back in surprise.

'No, lad, methinks you done good!'

He moved immediately to the window, where he held the paper up to the light.

'Jaysus!' he exclaimed.

' 'E says there's more, lot's more where't come from, Mr Browne, sir,' Josh shouted across the room, much relieved at this reception.

'Bring sponge, lad ... a wet sponge!' Silas Browne shouted at one of the boys nearest to him. ' 'Urry!'

In a few moments the boy returned and handed Silas Browne a damp sponge. Placing the scrap of paper again against the window glass, Silas wiped carefully over it several times. Then he lifted it from the window with the edge of his thumbnail and called for a pair of tweezers. Holding the paper at one corner with the tweezers, he walked over to a hearth where several cast-iron pots of blacking plopped slowly on the open coals. He held the pincers and paper to the heat of the embers, and the tiny scrap of damp paper took only moments to dry. Silas Browne returned to the window and held the paper once again to the light.

'Jaysus, Mary and Joseph!' he shouted, ' 'Tain't possible, watermark's stayed! Bloody watermark's stayed put right 'ere on paper! Quick! Call Maggie!'

Another young lad dashed off while the rest of the men gathered around, astonished to see that the faked Bank of England watermark had remained undamaged, as though it was woven within the very substance of the paper.

'What's 'is name, Josh?' Silas demanded.

'Ikey . . . Ikey Sausageman, sir . . .' Josh looked uncertain. 'Sonomins, summit like that, sir.'

'Ikey Solomons! Jaysus Christ!' Silas pointed to one of the men. 'Go with the lad, Jim, bring 'im along, 'e be famous like in London!' He looked around impatiently. 'Where's bloody Maggie?'

Not twenty minutes later Silas and Maggie looked on in amazement as Ikey produced the first of the engravings. Ikey unwrapped the watermarked Bank of England paper covering the copper rectangle, and leaving it lying in the centre of the paper he straightened out the sheet, smoothing its sides with the edges of his palm without touching the shining copper plate, so that the rectangular etching lay pristine, a precious slab of polished metal catching the light. Then Ikey tried to lift the etched copper plate from the centre of the paper but his hands were too cold and his fingers were quite unable to function. Maggie, seeing his distress, bid him warm himself at the hearth while she brought him a plate of bread and a deep bowl of beef and potato broth.

'There you be, then, Mr Solomons, a bowl of broth will soon warm you proper well!'

While Ikey greedily slurped the creamy broth, thick

almost as a good Irish stew, Silas and his wife, who, in her wooden clogs, stood as tall as her husband, examined the etching but did not touch it or the bill paper on which it lay. Halfway through the large bowl Ikey stopped and pointed to the sheet of paper with its corner missing, and nodded to Maggie the Colour. 'Take a good look then, my dear! Never was there a better drop o' paper for your marvellous colours and tinctures, and never a plate etched more perfect!'

Maggie picked up the etched copper plate while Silas examined the paper, neither saying a word, as Ikey went back to slurping his soup. Maggie the Colour handed the copper plate to Silas, holding it carefully between her fingers at each end and took the paper Silas had placed back on the table and walked over to the nearest window. She carefully flattened a portion of it against the window pane.

After a few moments she turned to Silas. 'What you think, then?'

'Never seen nothin' the likes o' this engravin' before! Never ... and that's Gawd's truth!' exclaimed Silas, examining the plate through an eyeglass.

'The paper?' Maggie asked, turning now to Ikey. ''Ow'd you do it, Mr Solomons?'

'Solomon, it don't 'ave no "s",' Ikey said, placing down his spoon, the bowl close to empty. He was suddenly aware that hunger and cold had driven him to show too much without the attendant patter required to work them up to the first unveiling. He had neglected the basic tenet of business, to reveal only a little at a time, enough to whet the appetite, so to speak, while holding sufficient back to feed the urgency of the bargaining that must inevitably follow. Now he attempted to recover somewhat from this poorly managed beginning.

'I've 'ad the pleasure o' being a regular customer for your work, my dear. Marvellous! Ain't no personage in England, perhaps even the world, what can mix tinctures, colours and gradations as subtle as you. Work o' pure genius, madam! Pure and simple and undisputed genius, no less.'

Maggie the Colour smiled thinly and looked down, embarrassed. 'Now, Mr Solomons, 'tain't *that* good!'

'Not a scrap less praise and 'onour is due to you!' Ikey declared. 'Them colours is o' the 'ighest possible magnitude, the work of a genius!' Ikey cleared his throat and grinned at Maggie. 'Now supposin' I was to ask you 'ow you come about them colours, asked Maggie the Colour the secret o' her dyes and tinctures and the mixtures for your ink galls? What say you then, my dear?'

'Quite right!' Silas Browne laughed and with the eyeglass still clamped in his eye, clapped his hands. 'You'd be gettin' nowt from our Maggie! Them inks and dyes, tinctures and juices, they be 'er secret to 'er final dyin' breath, till grave an' beyond!'

'Ah, you see?' Ikey exclaimed. 'A secret is only a secret when it remains in the 'ead of one person. Share it with another and it ain't a secret no more. You can kiss it goodbye, my dear, it's gorn forever. It's like a bloomin' swallow what's left England for warmer climes when winter approaches. Next thing you know it's on the other side o' the bloomin' world, darkest Africa or wilds o' South America! Good secrets all 'ave a price and the tellin' o' them is never cheap!' Ikey resumed slurping his soup, satisfied that he'd somewhat recovered the initiative.

'Do we take it you 'as a proposition to make, like?' Silas Browne asked, carefully placing the plate he'd been examining back on the square of paper which Maggie had returned to the table.

Ikey's untidy eyebrows lifted halfway up his brow and his eyes widened in pleasant surprise, his spoon poised in mid-air.

'A proposition? Why sir, that is exactly and precisely and unequivocally what I 'ave! A proposition, a business proposition, a remarkable opportunity, a proposition the likes o' which may never come your way again. A truly great conjunction of opportunities, of copper and paper and ink, an opportunity not never to be matched in its potential for wealth! A proposition you say! Why, I couldn't 'ave put it no better meself.'

Ikey went back to the remainder of his soup, and when the scraping and rattling of his spoon had ceased he further stalled the opportunity for an answer from his hosts by wiping the interior of the bowl clean with the last of the bread. 'A proposition as delicious, madam, as this bowl of excellent broth!' he finally concluded.

Maggie the Colour smiled at the compliment, knowing it to be the first thrust in the bargaining to come. 'Where shall we begin, then ... paper or plate? I can see the plate but paper be but one sheet and cut at corner like?'

'Paper's good, but 'ow much? 'Ow much 'as you got?' said Silas Browne, repeating his wife's question.

Silas was not a man inclined to much subtlety nor one to beat about the bush, and he'd already spent as much good humour as he was known to offer anyone. Ikey, seeing him for the more clumsy of the two, had hoped that he might be the mouth. But it took him only moments to realise that Maggie the Colour's smile was a clear indication of where the brains in their partnership lay.

'Depends o' course what denominations you want to print, my dears.'

'Denominations?' Maggie the Colour looked at Ikey curiously. 'This plate is for ten pounds.'

Ikey jabbed a finger at her. 'That it is, my dear, but it could be supposed that there might be others if an interest is shown in what 'as already been revealed and remarked upon? There could be a plate to the astonishin' denomination of one 'undred pounds!'

'One 'undred pounds? You say engravin' be for one 'undred!' Silas said scornfully. 'Bullshit! 'Undred pound engravin' be too 'ard for single engraver, too 'ard by 'arf and then some! 'Undred pound engravin' take four scratchers, maybe five. 'Tain't humanly possible!'

Ikey shrugged. Things were beginning to go to plan; show the top and the bottom of a proposition, the extremities of the deal, and the middle. The details, could usually be relied upon to take care of themselves.

He reached into his coat pocket and withdrew the small cut-throat razor and opening it slowly, he stooped down, lifted the hem of his great coat and laid it with the dirty lining facing upwards on the table. Then he carefully extended the previous slit he'd made by perhaps three further inches. His thumb and forefinger acting as pincers entered the slit and soon withdrew a second wrapped plate. How Ikey knew this to be the hundred pound plate is a tribute to his very tidy brain, and an indication that he'd secured the four etchings in the lining of his coat before leaving London.

Now he handed it to Maggie the Colour, who carefully opened up the neat little parcel to reveal the plate for a one hundred pound Bank of England note. Ikey let the hem of his coat drop back to the floor as Silas Browne swept up the copper rectangle, this time making no pretence at care, so that Ikey was seen to wince. He twisted the eyeglass back into his head and commenced to examine the plate. As he did so, his breathing increased until he was positively panting in surprise. 'Jaysus! Jaysus Christ!' he said.

He laid down the plate, this time with care. ' 'Tain't possible,' he turned to his wife, 'but it be there and it be nigh perfect!'

'Does we take it the paper and the plates go together, like?' Maggie asked, 'the ten pound and 'undred pound plates and you ain't said 'ow much paper you got?'

Ikey chuckled and spread his hands wide. 'And I ain't told you 'ow many o' these little copper darlin's we've got, my dear!'

'Four,' Maggie said calmly. 'You 'ave four.'

Ikey's eyebrows shot up. 'Well done, my dear, you 'ave turned my supposin' into proposin'. Indeed I 'ave four.' Ikey pulled the hem of his coat back onto the table, and his long dirty nails disappeared within the slit he'd previously made and withdrew each of the remaining parcels.

'Twenty and fifty, I do declare!' Ikey announced triumphantly and laid the two parcels on the table. Maggie the Colour sucked at her upper lip and commenced to untie each of the small parcels, not opening either until the twine had been removed from both. Then she revealed the etchings, leaving each on its own square of bill paper.

Ikey took a corner of each sheet and pulled them together then added the wrapping from the hundred pound plate, and the original piece with the corner removed, so that the four pieces of paper formed a rectangle two feet wide and three square.

'There you are, one complete sheet? Big enough, if I may say so, to make three dozen banknotes of any denomination you likes, my dears.' He paused and then added, pointing to the square made from the four separate sheets of paper, 'We 'as the pleasure o' makin' available to your good selves one 'undred and ten sheets o' the very same watermarked and quite perfect paper!'

Maggie the Colour snorted. 'And at what sort o' risk do these one 'undred and ten sheets come to us? Too 'ot to touch, I should think!'

'I shall sell you one 'undred and ten pristine sheets o' this bill paper without any risks o' the source becomin' known, this bein' me available stockpile. Then, if the paper proves to your likin', I could offer you a continuin' supply at the rate of one 'undred sheets per annum, the delivery to be made at eight sheets per month and paid in gold sovs on delivery.' Ikey was not sure how he would bring this about, but as the business opportunity presented itself so neatly he found it impossible not to capitalise on it.

'Eight sheets per month, that be only ninety-six sheets, not one 'undred!' Maggie snapped.

Ikey laughed, impressed at her quick calculation. 'Madam, we 'ave a sayin': "Always leave a little salt on the bread!" You gets the extra four sheets as a Christmas gift, compliments o' the 'ouse o' Solomon!'

'The paper, it's too good, you didn't make it did you, it's the real thing, ain't it?' Maggie said pointedly.

Ikey touched his finger to his nose and sniffed. 'Well I must most reluctantly confess, my dear, you've hit the nail on the 'ead. It's the same what the Bank of England uses, not a scintilla different, not a smidgin, not one jot or tittle different from what they uses to print their own longtails.'

'And the watermark?'

'The same! Woven in, my dear, the very innermost part o' the bill itself. Can't be removed no matter what you does, stamp, wash, bite, tear, while the paper remains, the mark is there!'

'And you've got one 'undred and ten sheets o' same?' Silas Browne asked again.

Ikey picked up the plate for the hundred pound Bank of England note and cackled, showing his yellow teeth. 'Or three 'undred and sixty thousand pound worth o' paper if you've a mind to use only this little beauty, my dear!'

'Why 'ave you come to us, Mr Solomons?' Maggie asked. 'Why 'as you not gorn into business y'self like?'

Ikey shrugged his thin shoulders and spread his palms and smiled.

'I only works with the best. It ain't me line of business, see. Ain't me expertise, ain't what I knows best. A man must stick to what 'e knows, the cobbler to 'is last, the butcher to 'is block, the poacher to 'is traps. These,' he pointed to the copper plates, 'they come about in the business o' receivin'. Receivin' and disposin' is me business, my dear, I received these and now I am disposin' o' them. Simple arithmetic, if you knows what I mean?'

'Aye, 'e be the prince of all the London fences,' Silas Browne agreed, glad to find a way back into the conversation. 'I knows him for that reputation.' He looked directly at his wife. 'That be the truth Maggie m'dear, Mr Solomons 'ere is a well-regarded London fence, also known and trusted in these Midland parts.'

Maggie the Colour sniffed. 'And the paper? That be fencin' business too?'

Ikey looked amused. 'If you 'as the right connections, my dear, everything Gawd made on this earth is fencin' business! All it takes is a little cash and a mind for makin' a connection 'ere, another there. Innovation is what some modern folks calls it. Let me give you an example. A lovely little silver candlestick goes missing from Mrs A's 'ouse and is brought to Mr B, what is me, yours truly. I knows Mr C, who will melt it down and sell the silver content to Mr D, a most excellent silversmith who is innocent of all guile. He will craft it into a fish server what might then be bought again by Mrs A to console 'erself over the tragic loss of 'er lovely little silver candlestick!'

Ikey clasped his hands together and dry rubbed them. 'All because o' the noble art o' ready cash and steady connections the world o' trade goes round and round, and we all profits nicely on that particular merry-go-round. What say you, my dear?'

'You may speak for y'self,' Maggie sniffed. 'We are not accustomed to the ways o' stealin'.'

Ikey smiled. 'Quite right, my dear, only from the banks who can afford it, ain't that so? Forgery ain't fencin', that's the truth, forgin' is the veritable Robin Hood profession, almost Christian, a perfect example o' robbin' the rich to pay the poor, an honourable profession it is to be sure.' He paused to take a breath. 'But one what also requires from time to time a connection or two? Maybe a paper connection what come from A

to B, what's me, and then goes on to C, what's thee!'
Ikey clapped his hands, pleased with his neat little
summary.

'Aye, it be good paper, the best, that I admit,' Silas
Browne said, 'though we'd be more friendly disposed if
we knew more about where it come from.' He pointed
at the bill paper. 'Paper the quality of your'n, tha' be
mill, tha' be special!'

Chapter Eleven

It had all begun when a carpenter and works mechanic named George Betteridge, who was much taken by the game of ratting, fell into debt to Ikey. Despite two separate attempts with Ikey's own little terriers to get back his promissory notes, he still owed a considerable sum. Ikey, as was the custom, requested that he pay up by the following week, either in cash or in kind to the value of what he owed, a debt of nearly ten pounds. The hapless Betteridge confessed that he was penniless. He had a wife and seven children, lived in a single rented room in a village in Hampshire, and possessed nothing of sufficient value to match the debt. Furthermore, he saw no prospect of obtaining goods to the required value as a petty thief. Nor was he placed in a position to steal from a rich master, being employed as a carpenter doing general maintenance work for a paper mill in the village of Whitechurch.

'Paper is it? What sort o' paper?'

It was a routine question. Ikey was accustomed to probing into the unused corners of the minds of men who lack imagination, and who are unable to see the opportunities for profit right under their bumpkin noses.

'All sorts o' paper, all special,' the carpenter replied.
'Special is it? What's its name then?'

'Name o' Laverstoke Paper Mill, very reputable, been
making particular papers for nigh sixty years, they 'as.'

'Laverstoke eh? By particular, does you mean
expensive?'

'No, no, it ain't paper you can buy, like!' Betteridge
corrected then lowered his voice and cupped his hand
to the side of his mouth. 'Paper for bills, banknotes,
very secret it is, very 'ush-'ush!'

Ikey concealed his excitement. 'May I ask you a question, Mr Betteridge? Does you know, or could you
make the acquaintance, o' someone what works in this
section what you says is strictly private. That is, the
particular section what makes your actual paper for
these . . . er, bills?'

The carpenter scratched his head, thinking. After a
moment he volunteered, 'Me wife 'as a second cousin,
a young cove what goes by name o' Thomas Tooth.
Methinks 'e works in one o' the sections by front office,
though I can't say for sure, 'e being a clerk an' all and
me only 'umble carpenter and mechanic.'

'This second cousin o' your dear wife, this Mr
Thomas Tooth, do you think 'e might be partial to a
night o' rattin' and a good tightener at a chop 'ouse
after? Or even two tickets to the Adelphi Theatre in the
Strand, compliments o' yours truly with a nice little
doxy thrown in for 'is particular amusement?' Ikey
looked at Betteridge slyly and spread his hands. 'We'd
be most honoured, my dear, and 'ighly complimented
to 'ave 'im as our esteemed guest!'

The young Thomas Tooth proved to be everything
Ikey had hoped for, naive but not without a certain

arrogance, married with two children and another in the oven. He was also ambitious to improve his lot in life, resentful that he was being held up by a doddery chief clerk by the name of Seth Robinson, a Quaker, and entirely trusted by his masters at the Laverstoke Mill.

Ikey was careful to build up his confidence in the game of ratting and to guide him in the ways of the sport, even teaching him a few of the finer points, until the young Thomas Tooth felt compelled, through Ikey's generosity and good spirits towards him, to trust him completely as a friend and confidant. The first requirement of the sharper, the confidence man, is complete trust from the dupe, and it did not take Ikey long to have this condition firmly in place in the mind of the young clerk.

The more serious sharping now began and Ikey elicited the help of Marybelle Firkin, the mot of the Pig 'n Spit, the public house where the ratting took place in St Giles. With her went the aid of George Titmus the rat master.

Ikey was therefore absent on the earlier part of the night when Thomas Tooth was finally netted, this action being almost entirely left to the enormous lady publican and her diminutive rat master.

Marybelle Firkin was a very large woman, said to consume an entire saddle of the roast beef of old England at one sitting, whereas George Titmus, her rat master, was four feet eight inches tall and weighed eighty-five pounds wringing wet, though this did not happen very often as he had not taken up the habit of cleanliness. Working with rats and blood made him stink to high heaven, but he sensibly reasoned that should he wash it would occur all over again at the very next evening's fights. His skill with rats was such that his stench was tolerated among the punters, most of whom were themselves none too keen on the deadly touch of water from the Thames.

Both Marybelle and George worked well together on the magging of Mr Thomas Tooth of Laverstoke Mill, Whitechurch, Hampshire, chubbing him along and building his self-esteem the entire evening until there was only one more contest to come, and young Tooth was twenty pounds behind.

This last contest was between a little black and white terrier named Valiant, a good fighter who wore the champion's silver collar around his tiny neck. The young terrier was known to possess an excellent ratting technique and could usually be depended on to make a kill of thirty to thirty-five rats in a timed spell. The odds were called very short so that there were no punters save Thomas Tooth interested in betting.

The young country clerk, though too drunk for his own good, and heedless of the peril he faced should he lose, nevertheless knew the odds to be wrong and asked for better, for an evens bet.

'Gentlemen there is no sport in you!' Tooth cried. 'Will you not take a chance? Thirty pounds on an *evens* bet!'

Thirty pounds was a very big bet, and the crowd grew silent and waited to see if a bookmaker would accept the offer. Instead one of them laughed and waved Thomas Tooth away with the back of his hand. 'G'warn, be orf with you, lad, go on 'ome and kip it orf!'

Thomas Tooth, swaying slightly, took out his dumby

and made as though he was looking into the depths of his wallet at a fortune lying at its bottom. 'My credit is good, I swear it!' Tooth cried, persisting with the lie. 'Who will take my marker?' He turned to look at the four bookmakers. 'If I should lose I swear I shall settle before the midnight hour.'

The young clerk looked desperately over at George Titmus the ratting master who had earlier been so free with his compliments. 'Who'll take evens, thirty pounds on Valiant to kill thirty rats, small rats ... no sewers, cess or docks?'

Titmus nodded, seeming to take the young gambler seriously. 'Small it is, sir. I've a nice sack o' small 'ouse and country, just right for the little fella 'ere.' He glanced in the direction of the dog Valiant held in his owner's arms. 'Should do 'is thirty rodents easy enough, strong little fella, known to be most game!'

The punters around the ring grew silent, looking towards the bookmakers to see what would happen next. Tooth had called for small rats, house and country, which was a fair enough call as some sewer, cesspool and dockside rats were almost as large as the little terrier himself. The rat master had accepted, the contest was fair game.

From the darkness of the stairway leading to the ratting room and to the backs of most of the punters a booming voice rang out. 'Aye, I'll take it! I'll take ye marker evens on thirty rodents killed! Settlement afore midnight, did ye say?'

'Ah, a sporting man, at last!' the young gambler cried, turning to face the darkened stairway. 'Certainly, midnight! Payment you shall have precisely at the striking of the hour, my good sir!'

'Aye! May the devil hisself help ye if ye doesnae pay, laddie!'

There was a surprised gasp as the owner of the voice stepped out of the gloom into the room. The brutish, broken face which moved into the light was well known to be Dan Figgins, ex-heavyweight boxing champion of Glasgow and London, now a bookmaker with a reputation for very rough and unfavourable handling should his clients fail to settle on time.

Dan Figgins was not a regular at the ratting ring, being a horse man and well known, even by the aristocracy, at his betting box at Newmarket and Ladbroke Grove. Thomas Tooth, almost alone in the room, was unaware of this infamous pugilistic personage and besides, was now too desperate and too drunk to care. He scribbled his marker for thirty pounds and handed it to Figgins. Whereupon the rat master called for the rat boy to bring the ratsack, shouting: 'Mixed smalls, country and 'ouse, bring out the ratsack!'

This was where the final phase of the sharping began. The rat boy, a tiny, ragged lad of about ten years old, his dirty face and mucoid nose not having felt the touch of soap for a year or more, had prepared a bag of thirty-five large sewer rats to earlier instructions.

The rat master, cupping his hands to his mouth called again to the rat boy. 'Ring in the rats and shake out the tails!'

The boy, dragging the rat bag, which was tied with twine about its neck, brought it over to the outside edge of the ring. He hopped nimbly over the three-foot wall of the small circular enclosure and the bag of rats was handed to him by Titmus. The boy dropped the sack in the ring and placed his boot onto the centre of the jumping sack, which immediately calmed the rats within. The boots he wore were greatly oversized and the property of the house and were crusted with the dried blood of the night's previous bouts.

'Slap, shake and pat a rat!' George Titmus called. 'Step up the gentleman what's makin' the touch! All's fair what finds no sneaks or squeaks!'

Thomas Tooth, being the only punter, stepped into the ring to do the honours. Puffed with drunken self-importance, he commenced to beat solidly at the boy's threadbare coat, slapping hard into his skinny ribs and pummelling his shoulders and thighs in such an enthusiastic manner as to cause the lad to wince at his careless blows. Finally he required the urchin to hold his arms downwards and away from his body and, first feeling down the length of each arm by squeezing tightly across the bicep and forearm along the greasy sleeve towards the boy's wrists, he then demanded that the lad shake both sleeves vigorously. This deployment was intended to remove any rats which might miraculously have escaped the previous rigorous inspection.

Tooth, now finally satisfied, gave a nod to the rat master, who pronounced on the punters, 'All's clean what feels clean, nothin' squeaked, nothin' seen!' He turned to the rat boy. 'Sample the show, three in a row!'

The boy bent over and taking up the bag at his feet, began to untie the twine, though mid-way through this task he appeared to have acquired an itchy nose. He held the top of the bag with his left hand and scratched his nose with the other, finally wiping the copious snot from under it into his open palm and appearing to wipe his hand on his matted and greasy hair. His hand disappeared completely beneath his very large cap seemingly for this very purpose.

His sniffing and scratching finally over, the rat boy returned his attention to opening the bag and without as much as a glance inwards plunged his arm into the bag of squeaking rats and brought up the first 'show', a rat selected blind to show that the bag had been called correct, and selected as specified, 'small, house and country'.

'One-o!' he shouted holding a small house rat up above his head and then dropping it into the ring at his feet before plunging his arm back into the bag and withdrawing it again. 'Two-o!' The second rat was almost identical in size to the first. Once again his arm entered the rat bag, which was now jumping and bumping around his boots 'Three-o!' the boy finally yelled, holding a third rat above his head.

'All's fair what's shown fair! Ring the rats and free the tails!' the rat master shouted.

Whereupon the boy upended the entire bag of rats into the ring and they fell in a large tail-twisted and squirming clump. The rat boy commenced to sort them out, untying their tails and scattering them helter-skelter about the ring. Free to sniff and scratch while their eyes grew accustomed to the bright light, they seemed now to be quite calm. The rat boy climbed out of the enclosure as George Titmus rang the starting bell and the terrier, Valiant, straining in his master's arms and yapping in great excitement, was dropped in among the rodents.

What Thomas Tooth hadn't witnessed was that the three sampling rats the boy appeared to have pulled at random out of the rat bag, in fact came from under his

large cap. These three small house rats, so ceremoniously shown, had been nestling quietly in his hair. They
had been trained to the smell of mucus on his hand,
and upon it entering his cap they had slipped down his
coat sleeve where he'd concealed a crust of bread. So
that he now only had to put his hand inside the bag
and let a rat drop down his sleeve into it, whereupon
he would withdraw it again to show that the rats in the
bag had been selected small. He repeated this twice
more to show three small rats in what was seen to be
an honest call.

The rats which were upended into the ring from the
bag stank of the river and the sewers, a particular smell
no person experienced in the game of ratting could possibly mistake. Their bite was most infectious and often
quite deadly, and they were larger by as much weight
again as the three smaller house rats the boy had
'shown', though a direct comparison was no longer possible as all the rats in the ring now appeared to be of
similar size.

This was achieved by a second clever ploy, though it
would take a more sober man than Thomas Tooth to
see the trick. The rat boy, having emptied the rats from
the bag, scattered them about the ring, though a
moment before doing so he had again wiped his nose.
The three smaller house rats in the ring, trained to the
smell of the mucus on the boy's hand, once again darted
up his sleeve, leaving only the larger rats behind.

Moreover, while Thomas Tooth was busy patting and
slapping at the boy in the ring, behind his back the silver
collar was taken from the dog Valiant's neck and placed
around the neck of a second terrier of similar markings.
This second ratter, a bitch named Rose, cankered from

rat bites, was a sister to Valiant from an older litter. Enfeebled from the gnawing of the canker, she could no longer fight well, even though her canine instinct and eagerness to fight remained, and to all appearances she was equal to the task.

Rose worked briskly, picking up a rat and shaking it, biting deep behind its head to snap its neck and then drop it, immediately grabbing at another. Blood dripped to the floor and the little canine was soon slipping as she scrambled to snatch at the now panicky rats. The terrier lunged at a very large rodent, slipped in the blood on the ring and missed. The rat, panic stricken, bit deeply into the little bitch's nose and hung on. Rose, who had already killed twelve rats, was beginning to tire. She tried to shake the large rat off, but it held fast and soon the little bitch's slender neck started to drop. As though by some primeval instinct, the remaining rats rushed at the weakened ratter and pulled her down. She tried to rise but the rats smothered her, tearing at her tiny black and white pelt.

The bell sounded and the rat master shouted: 'Rats high, dog low! Take yer dog or let it go!'

The rats had won and the rat boy, wearing a thick leather mitten, for the rats were now maddened by the taste of blood and would bite at anything, jumped into the ring and pulled a frenzied rat from the still alive terrier's body and threw it back into the ratbag. Some of the rats held on so tenaciously that the boy had to grab about their blood-matted stomachs, lifting the terrier's body with the rat still attached to it. With a twist of the wrist he removed the rat, leaving its teeth embedded in the pelt, as the little bitch fell back into the ring to be smothered again by the feeding rodents.

With the rats finally safely in the bag, the boy tied the top and lifted it out of the ring. The blood-crazed rats would continue to attack each other inside the bag in a squeaking feeding frenzy until only one was left alive. Such a rat was tagged and much prized as a symbol of luck and, should it recover from the numerous bites to its body, was eagerly sought by a keen ratter as a pet.

The rat boy climbed from the ring, the ragged ends of his trousers and the toes of his boots soaked with fresh blood. The stench of death was everywhere and the punters, the fun over for the night, began to leave. As was the custom, most of them repaired downstairs to Marybelle Firkin's public house where the gin whores would be carousing and the fiddler would be playing a merry jig on a gypsy fiddle.

Marybelle Firkin's inglorious establishment was well known for both ratting and whores and was well frequented by gonophs and macers and magsmen, and all manner of thieves and villains. Towards the latter part of the evening, when the ratting was over, the Pig 'n Spit became a place of great merriment and fornication with every dark corner as well as the skittle court behind the public house taken up with thrusting bodies and much loud groaning. Lust and loving was bought here for the price of three drams of gin. Hence the people in the surrounding rookery took much amusement by referring to both Marybelle Firkin and the Pig 'n Spit as 'Merry Hell Fucking at the Pig 'n Shit'.

George Titmus, the last to leave the ratting ring, turned the lamps down low. Rose, the little terrier, tried to rise, but slipped on the blood-stained floor. She tried again and this time got shakily to her feet, whimpering and looking up with trusting eyes to see if she could find her master. But she lacked the strength to hold herself up and collapsed back among the dead rats. She was dead before her owner sneaked back up the stairs to retrieve the silver collar about her neck.

With the contest declared in favour of the rats, Thomas Tooth owed thirty pounds to Dan Figgins to be paid by midnight. The fish was landed.

Dan Figgins' small, cold, agate-blue eyes, only just visible within the multiple folds of scar tissue surrounding them, grew sharp as pin-points as he heard Tooth explain his inability to pay up at the appointed hour.

'There's naeone t' blame for tha' except yourself, laddie,' Figgins growled.

Thomas Tooth grinned foolishly and with some courage from the brandy yet within him said, 'I cannot pay you, sir, you will simply have to wait!'

'Nay, laddie, ye doesnae understand, ye'll nae be breathin' God's breath beyond the midnight hour!'

Thomas Tooth shrugged. 'Methinks you cannot get blood from a stone now, sir, can you?'

The crowd gasped at his temerity.

'Aye, that I can, laddie!' He turned to the crowd. 'You cannae blame us for givin' him a doing, it wasnae our fault he couldnae pay, was it?'

The drunken crowd murmured their approval and someone shouted, 'Drub 'im, Danny boy!' Then added in a dismissive tone, 'Cheeky bastard!'

'Ye shouldnae have said tha', Mr Tooth. I'm a patient mon, but tha's gone a wee bit too far, I cannae let ye get away wi' it!' Dan Figgins smashed his huge fist into the young clerk's face, breaking his nose in a gush of blood and sending the hapless Tooth sprawling across the room. He knocked into a whore, who careened backwards screaming as she bumped against the far wall, and slid to the floor with the young gambler's bloody head imprisoned between her thighs.

This created uproarious laughter from the crowd who quickly gathered around the huge fighter, who was now standing with his fists balled above the young drunk.

Dan Figgins reached down, preparing to jerk the sniffing and whimpering Thomas Tooth to his feet, when he felt himself propelled backwards and then turned completely around by an arm the size of a doxy's leg.

As if by some peculiar magic the huge shape of Marybelle Firkin was suddenly seen to stand in front of him. Her great ham-like arms were now folded across her huge bosom. The congregation of drunks and whores grew silent as the giant mot and the fierce Figgins locked eyes, hers bigger and even more blue than his own.

The fiddler leaped upon a table beside the huge woman and pulled a long melancholy note from his fiddle, then he tapped her lightly on the shoulder with his bow. Marybelle sighed at his touch then smiled a most beatific smile at Dan Figgins, dropped her arms to her side, and in a voice astonishingly sweet and pure started to sing.

Fine Ladies and Gents
come hear my sad tale
The sun is long down and
the moon has grown pale
So drink up your gin
and toss down your ale
Come and rest your tired heads
on my pussy ... cat's tail!

The crowd, delighted and immediately distracted, took up the merry ditty and started to sing it over and over again as they cavorted around the tables and the fiddler sawed his bow across the gut, raising his knees high, prancing nimbly on the table top. The gin whores and the younger doxies danced with the drunks and the place was soon grown most merry again. Even Figgins was taken up by two whores, who whirled him across the room and planted copious kisses upon his broken face.

Ikey arrived back at the Pig 'n Spit shortly before midnight to find the miserable young Tooth seated in a corner sniffing and blubbing, now rapidly come to realise that he would not see another sunrise. Just when he thought he might try to bolt, hoping to escape into the darkness, Ikey tapped him on the shoulder.

Thomas Tooth, reduced to tears of drunken self-pity, clutched at the sleeve of Ikey's great coat and begged him to save his life by making good his debt to the awesomely ferocious Dan Figgins, who was threatening to take his life on the stroke of midnight.

'O' course, my dear.' Ikey spread his hands. 'What are friends for? A friend in need is a friend indeed! Do not fret, all's well what ends well!'

The arrangements which followed over the next couple of weeks between Ikey Solomon, the contrite young gambler and the carpenter George Betteridge, would prove to be one of the best investments Ikey was to make in his entire life of crime and punishment.

In the testing laboratory at the Laverstoke Mill, Thomas Tooth explained to Ikey, some thirty sheets of the bill paper used for banknotes were brought twice weekly to be submitted for testing and verification of their quality.

It was Thomas Tooth's task to count the sheets against the number which originally arrived for testing. Then he had to enter his count into the receivals and exit ledger before taking them across a large quadrangle and through a maze of buildings to where the furnace was located, at the opposite end of the mill from the laboratory.

Ikey had George Betteridge build a false floor into a cupboard under a stairway which Thomas Tooth had to pass on his way to the furnace. A single floorboard was hinged so that it lifted neatly up at one end if correctly touched. In a matter of moments Thomas Tooth could conceal two sheets of rolled paper under the floorboard as he passed.

Later, Betteridge, on the pretence of going about some small maintenance task, would retrieve the paper, conceal it in his tool box and take it out of the mill gates under a pile of wood shavings and off-cuts. As a mill carpenter, he was entitled to sell or take these home for his own use as kindling.

The Laverstoke Mill was a quietly run business where standards of workmanship were the preoccupation of the partners. The familiar and trusted local employees were often represented by three generations working at the mill, and not subject to the slightest suspicion. Security measures in this country backwater plainly left something to be desired, but any systems beyond the ones which had existed for more than sixty years seemed entirely unnecessary.

This scam soon proved so successful that Thomas Tooth repaid his gambling debt to Ikey, and agreed to be paid in gold sovereigns for each sheet subsequently delivered. Five sovereigns to himself and two to George Betteridge, whose anxiety that his good fortune might come to an end caused by some impropriety from Thomas Tooth caused him to watch carefully over the younger man so that no errant bragging should bring about their mutual downfall.

The method by which the paper came to Ikey was simple enough. The money would be left with George Titmus at the Pig 'n Spit, and the paper delivered to him concealed within one of the two similarly constructed long thin wooden boxes and tightly sealed so that the rat master did not know its contents. An empty box would then be returned with the receipt of the one containing paper, whereupon both men would repair to the rat ring where the young Thomas Tooth, for the most part, would be fleeced of the greater portion of his payment while his carpenter cousin kept a steady eye upon his drinking.

It was late into the evening when Silas Browne and Maggie the Colour finally concluded a deal for the paper and plates of twenty thousand pounds and agreed to a cash deposit of five hundred pounds. While Ikey knew this to be but a fraction of the true value of the merchandise, it was better than he'd expected.

Five hundred pounds was sufficient for Ikey to purchase a passage to New York and allow him to live for a few weeks while he learned the layout of the new city and made acquaintance, by means of some lavish entertainment, with the right connections.

The remainder of the money for the remaining bill paper Ikey requested to be in the form of a letter of credit from a thoroughly reputable Birmingham bank, one acceptable to Coutts & Company, 59 the Strand, London, so that when Ikey presented it to the great

London bank they would transfer the money into an account in his name to a bank in New York, without questioning the credit of the bank of original issue.

Maggie left the parlour and shortly after returned with five hundred pounds in Bank of England notes. Ikey examined each of these using Silas's eyeglass. When he was satisfied to their authenticity, he handed over the four sheets of billpaper, requesting only the return of the small corner he'd cut away for the boy Josh to deliver earlier.

'And now for ongoin' paper supply, how will 'e do it?' Maggie asked.

Ikey hesitated. 'It's late, my dear, perhaps we can talk about that at some other time?'

Maggie the Colour was adamant. 'Now is as good as any other. We likes to know where we stands in business o' money, Mr Solomons.'

Ikey felt immediately frustrated; his presence in America would not allow him to negotiate a further supply of bill paper from Thomas Tooth and personally gain from such a transaction. But he also knew that life has a way of twisting and turning back to bite its own tail, and he was reluctant to close the door on the prospect of a future sale, so he proceeded to negotiate as though his life should depend on the outcome.

Finally, after a great deal of bargaining, an agreement was reached whereby Silas and Maggie would pay one hundred and fifty pounds a sheet for any future paper supplies. This was a much lower price than they'd paid for the stockpiled paper, but Maggie insisted that it involved them in a far greater risk of being caught.

Ikey requested a needle and cotton and a pair of scissors, and when Maggie brought these he removed a large silk scarf from somewhere within the interior of his coat and cut it into four similar sized pieces. Then using the twine from the previous wrapping he rewrapped the plates, each in a square of silk, and returned them to the hem of his coat, making a fair hand at sewing them back within the lining.

Then, thinking to avail himself of the means of sewing, he attempted to stitch together the rip made in his coat when he'd caught it in the door of the coach earlier that morning. The needle proved too small for the heavy felt and would not easily pass through the thick, greasy material, the thread breaking each time and rendering his efforts fruitless. Ikey could feel Maggie's mounting impatience and finally she remarked curtly, 'Will you be long, Mr Solomons? It is late and well past time we were abed.'

Ikey finally gave up the task of mending the tear and placed the needle and cotton down on the table. Rising, he walked over to the window and put his nose to a pane, looking out into the darkness where the winter wind howled and buffeted, rattling the stout window frame.

'I needs to sew them plates in the hem o' me coat to 'old me down against the blast o' the bitter wind what's blowin' in the dark and stormy night outside!' He turned and looked at Silas Browne and pointed to the fire. 'O' course, a night's lodgin's spent in a warm chair beside your hearth could leave these 'ere plates on the premises where you'd know they'd be safe from robbery?' He looked querulously at Silas. 'I could be gorn before the sparrows wake, my dear, one o' your likely lads paid a 'andsome sum to deliver me to me lodgin's?'

Maggie the Colour shook her head and spoke sharply. 'No offence, Mr Solomons, we be glad to do business with you, but we'll not 'ave a Jew sleepin' under our roof!' She cast a meaningful glance at Silas. 'That be bad luck brought upon our 'eads by our own stupidity!'

'Aye, we'll not be doin' that!' Silas Browne confirmed.

Ikey was aware of the common country superstition that a Jew sleeping under a Christian roof brought the devil into the house. It even existed in some of the smaller country taverns where he'd been turned away in the past. Nevertheless he was greatly in need of sleep and very wearied. The prospect of returning on foot, in the dark, along the way he'd earlier come was a daunting, if not to say, dangerous one.

'No offence taken to be sure, my dear!' Ikey said hastily. 'We all 'as our own little ways, but I caution you to think upon the matter a moment longer. If I should use shank's pony to get back to me lodgin's, it could turn out most dangerous at this time o' night.' He flapped the lapel of his coat meaningfully.

'We'll 'ave a boy take you in 'orse and trap,' Maggie snapped. 'You'll be back 'ere day after tomorrow, at night if you please, with remainder of paper and plates, one 'undred and ten sheets by the count, then we'll do further letter o'credit business, right?'

'No! No, my dear, beg pardon for abusin' your sensibilities on that question. You 'ave all day tomorrow and all night and part o' the following' mornin'. Then if you'll be so kind to send young Josh to the coach terminus to be there at ten o'clock in the mornin' with a note what contains the name o' the bank, which must be of excellent standing, and the time o' the appointment and such other details as what I'll need. The appointment is to be made the afternoon o' the day after tomorrow, the paper and the plates to be 'anded over in the bank after you 'as 'anded over the irrevocable letter o' credit made out in me name to Coutts & Company, the Strand, London.'

''And over plates and paper in bank? Are you daft?' Silas exclaimed.

'What better place, my dear? We simply asks the bank official for a private room to view the merchandise. It be none of 'is business what the package contains.'

Maggie the Colour sniffed. 'Don't you trust us to do it 'ere, then, Mr Solomons?'

Ikey laughed. 'You 'as your bad luck what you just described as a Jew spendin' a night under your roof, this you claims is *deliberate stupidity*. We also 'as a similar superstition, my dear. We believes that to practise *deliberate stupidity* is worse than witchcraft, and superstition and, most decidedly and emphatically, brings about a great deal o' bad luck to the person what is stupid!'

'The coach terminus, ten o'clock, mornin' day after tomorrow then,' Maggie the Colour snapped.

'That be quite right, my dear. Young Josh will give the letter of instructions to someone what might come up to him and say politely, "Dick Whittington's 'ungry cat 'as come to fetch a juicy rat".'

Maggie's head jerked in surprise. 'Beg pardon?'

'The passwords, my dear, 'case I can't make it meself, other pressin' business intervenin'.'

Maggie the Colour sighed, her patience close to

ending. 'Password? Bah, what rubbish! Anyway, what's wrong with a single word, like "copper" or " 'orse" or if you must, "cat"? Them words about Dick Whittington's cat, that be proper nonsense!'

Ikey smiled. 'You're quite right, my dear, rubbish it is, but it be more excitin' for a small lad what's intelligent! Much more excitin' to carry more than one word in 'is little 'ead as he sets out upon such a grand adventure. It is properly suitable to an occasion such as what we've been discussin', and what is worthy o' much more than a single word like "copper" or " 'orse" or "cat"!'

Ikey was tired and a little testy but he'd deliberately created the nonsense about the cat to frustrate Maggie the Colour's desire to see him depart. It was a small revenge for her rudeness, but sweet enough at that for the lateness of the hour. Now, with the prospect of being taken into the city in a pony trap, he was as anxious to depart as she was to see him go.

Chapter Twelve

It was just past midnight when Ikey fought his way against the buffeting wind and sudden flurries of snow to a Birmingham netherken where he was well enough known. It was as foul a place as you could expect for a shilling a night, but by no means at the bottom of the rung. The wind howled about the eaves and the windows rattled as Ikey hammered on the door to be allowed to enter.

The landlord, carrying a candle cupped with his hand against the wind, welcomed him with a scowl, which changed into a sycophantic smile when Ikey stepped out of the dark into the dim candlelight.

'Oh it's you! Welcome back to our ever so 'umble abode, Mr Solomon. We 'ave much improvement since your last stay. New straw stuffed only last week, like goose down them beds is, and the room I have selected for you is near empty with only two other fine gentlemen sharin'!' He sucked air through his rotten teeth. 'Two shillin' a night and summit to eat in mornin'! There, couldn't be fairer than that now, could there, sir?'

Ikey handed him a shilling. 'Master Brodie, your

straw's damp with piss and alive with all manner o' vermin, and it ain't been changed in three months. A bowl o' cold gruel in the mornin' ain't what you calls "summit to eat" and I'll wager the two villains what's sharing the room 'as paid no more'n sixpence apiece for the privilege!'

Brodie tested the coin Ikey had given by biting down on it, then he shrugged, placed it in the pocket of his filthy waistcoat and beckoned for Ikey to follow him. They made their way through the dark shapes which seemed to be lying in every available space, some penny-a-nighters asleep seated, while tied about the neck with heavy twine to the banisters of the rickety stairs.

Panting with the effort, Brodie halted as they came to the upper reaches of the house and stopped outside a door no more than four feet in height.

'It be top room and there be no grate in there, so you'll be wantin' a blanket. That'll be sixpence extra.' Brodie pulled open the door to reveal a tiny attic with a dirty dormer window through which a pale slice of moon was shining across a window ledge crusted with snow. The window rattled loudly, and Ikey felt the freezing draught as the wind forced its way through the cracks in the frame. One of the men at his feet ceased snoring and moaned, then commenced to snoring again. The rhythm of the two men's rough breathing filled the space around them, so that there seemed not an inch left for another person to occupy. Ikey, observing the moon, sensed that time was running out for him, that before it reached its fullness he should be safely on a ship to America.

Ikey declined Brodie's offer of a blanket, knowing it would be infested with vermin. He stepped over the two sleeping bodies to reach the straw pallet nearest the window where the cold seemed at once to be at its greatest. His nocturnal perambulations had been thrown into disarray for a second day running as Ikey lay down on the filthy straw. Wrapping his coat tightly about his aching body, he fell into an exhausted sleep.

The following day Ikey went out early and purchased quill, blacking, paper and sealing wax, whereupon he hired the landlord Brodie's tiny private parlour for a further shilling, with sixpence added for a fire in the hearth to burn all day.

Ikey had also arranged with a small jeweller's workshop to make him a copper cylinder nine inches long by an inch and a quarter wide in its interior, with a cap to fit over one end rounded in exactly the same manner as the end of a cigar cylinder. Ikey stressed that the cap should screw on and when tightened fit so snugly that it had the appearance of being one object with no separation, that should a finger be run over the point where the cap fitted to the body it would barely discern the join. Ikey instructed that the cylinder be ready late in the afternoon of the following day.

Despite his outward appearance of complete disarray, Ikey was possessed of an exceedingly tidy mind. He liked his affairs to be well ordered, and the fact that he'd been forced to leave London at a moment's notice left him with a great deal undone, the most important being the fortune which lay beyond his grasp within the safe in his Whitechapel home.

For almost the entire coach journey to Birmingham his mind had been preoccupied with thoughts of how he might get his hands on all of the money he and Hannah jointly owned, leaving only the house and the stolen goods stored within it for her and the children.

Ikey's greatest fear was that she would send him packing without divulging her half of the combination of the safe, and then later have it drilled and tapped so that she might possess its entire contents. Genuine tears of frustration ran down his cheeks as he contemplated this ghastly possibility.

Ikey sat down to the task of tidying up his affairs before leaving Britain. There would be no time in London, which he might be forced to leave after only a few hours. There were the little ratting terriers he kept, he must take care of their welfare; instructions for Mary should he not see her again; and letters to his contacts in London and on the continent. On and on he worked in his arachnoid hand, and it was quite late in the afternoon when Ikey had finally completed these business matters. He placed the letters in his great coat and went looking for the landlord. Ikey found him over the communal hearth stirring a large cauldron of cabbage soup, and carrying a steaming kettle in his free hand.

'Ah, there you are,' Ikey exclaimed. 'It might be most profitable for you to step into your own little parlour, if you please, Mister Brodie.'

'What? Right now? This very moment?' Brodie answered, without looking up. 'Can't now! This soup what is blessed with 'erbs and spices and all manner of tasty ingredients is about to come to the simmer. Then I must add a fine shank o' veal and extra onions and potatoes to gift 'er with a most delicate degustation.'

Ikey laughed. 'All you've ever added to your cabbage soup is the water what's in that kettle! Come quickly, Mr Brodie, or you may be poorer to the tune of five shillings!'

Brodie almost dropped the kettle in his haste to place it back on the hob and follow Ikey into the parlour.

'Master Brodie can you repeat: "Dick Whittington's 'ungry cat 'as come to fetch a juicy rat!"'? Can you say that?'

'Dick Whittington's angry cat come to fetch a Jewish rat!' Brodie repeated, then looked bemused at Ikey. 'That's daft, that is! Rats is rats, ain't no Jewish rats, leastways not in Brum, that I can assure you! Rats 'ere is Christian or not at all!'

Ikey corrected Brodie and repeated the phrase, making the landlord say it over several times before asking him to go to the coach terminus the following morning at precisely ten o'clock, to spend the password he'd just rehearsed on Josh and to receive a note from the boy to be returned to him.

Brodie scratched his head, bemused. 'When I done this you'll give me five shillin's?' He was plainly waiting for some catch.

'If you takes a most round-about route 'ome and makes sure you ain't followed there'll be two shillin's additional comin' to you, Master Brodie!'

'You've found yer man, 'ave no fear o' that – I can disappear in a single blinkin' and you wouldn't even know I was gorn. Ain't no lad on Gawd's earth could 'ave the cunnin' to follow me,' Brodie bragged.

Ikey left soon afterwards to visit an eating establishment in an adjoining rookery only slightly less notorious than the one in which he was staying. Here Ikey had often done deals with thieves and villains and the landlord welcomed his custom and willingly allowed him credit, his bills to be paid at the end of each visit.

This time, though, as Ikey greeted him he seemed less

239

sure, and asked if he might have some money on account as the debt for food supplied to Ikey's guest was mounting by the hour.

The small room to which the landlord escorted him was almost completely occupied by the corpulence of Marybelle Firkin who sat at a table strewn with bones and crusts and empty dishes, as well as the half-eaten carcass of a yellow-skinned goose. She welcomed Ikey with a chop rimmed with a layer of shining white fat held in one hand, and a roasted potato in the other. Ikey looked around anxiously and was most relieved to see the hamper occupying one corner of the room. Marybelle pointed the chop directly at Ikey and spoke with her mouth crammed, a half masticated potato dropping into her lap.

'It was marvellous, eh, Ikey? If I says so meself, that performance on the coach were fit to be seen by the bleedin' Prince o' bleedin' Wales!' She cackled loudly, more food tumbling from her mouth. 'Better than any I performed on the stage in me 'ole career. What say ya, lovey? Was it the best ya seen?'

Ikey smiled thinly, his hands expanded trying to match her enthusiasm. 'What can I say, Marybelle? You was magnificent, my dear, the performance of a lifetime by a thespian o' rare and astonishin' talent!'

Marybelle blushed at the compliment and swallowed, her mouth empty and her voice suddenly soft and low. 'Ah, that's nice, Ikey. 'Ere, 'ave a pork chop, do ya the world, skin 'n bone you is, there ain't nuffink to ya!'

Ikey winced and drew back. 'No thanks, it ain't kosher!'

'Suit yerself, lovey, there's a lot o' nourishment in a pork chop and very little in religion!' Then, pointing to the hamper, she declared, 'All be safe. Paper's come to no 'arm.'

Ikey nodded. 'Thank you, my dear, I am most obliged, most obligin'ly obliged.'

Ikey appeared to hesitate, then continued, 'Marybelle, I needs a favour done and in return I shall put you in the way o' a nice little earner.'

'That's nice, lovey. What is it ya want, then?' She pointed at his coat. 'Sew up the tear in yer coat? I ain't much of a dab 'and at sewin' I warns ya.'

Ikey grinned, though in a feeble way. 'A bigger favour, my dear.'

'Bringin' yer paper, that *weren't* favour enough?'

'Yes, my dear, and you shall be paid the fifty pounds I promised you.'

'And this favour, it's worth more'n fifty pounds?'

'Much more, if you plays your cards right!'

It is only necessary briefly to describe the scene which took place in the bank, and the look of consternation on the faces of Silas and Maggie the Colour when Marybelle Firkin arrived in Ikey's place. She carried a letter from Ikey stipulating that she should act as his negotiating agent for the business at hand and the letter further asked that the banker, Mr David Daintree, sign the letter and return it to Marybelle as proof that she had been present. The letter also required the signatures of Silas and Maggie Browne.

Indeed, Ikey was wise to seek proof that the meeting had taken place, for the husband and wife team had conspired to rob him. They had concluded that he had no ongoing supply of paper, but only what he would bring to the bank. If they could rob him of the letter of

241

credit and the money on his way back to London, or even at his place of residence in Birmingham – after all, he was not the sort who could go to the police – then they would possess the plates and the paper without having paid for them.

Mr Daintree, impressed with the handling of so great a sum of money, conducted the proceedings with the utmost rectitude, carefully pointing to where Marybelle should sign her name. When Marybelle handed the hamper over to Silas and Maggie he retired, as had been arranged, to a small inner chamber, while the two of them closely examined the hamper's contents.

Maggie then took a sheet of paper from the banker's desk and using his quill filled nearly half a page in her neat handwriting. Then she dusted the paper and allowed it to dry, whereupon she handed it to Silas. He read it, smiled, nodded and returned it to her, whereupon she indicated that he call the bank officer to return. Neither Silas nor Maggie passed so much as a single word in Marybelle's direction. Marybelle sat patiently, thinking about Ikey's promise of a fortune and trying to imagine how much nourishment it might buy. How many roast beef sides, fat geese, plump partridges, chops and pies and every manner of sweet dish known to the human species.

With the return of Mr Daintree the couple allowed that the credit note be duly signed in her presence by the bank officer. But before handing it to Marybelle, Maggie placed the page of writing on the desk in front of her.

'This be the document we wish to 'ave Mrs Firkin sign before we 'ands over letter o' credit,' she said bluntly, her eyes challenging the banker.

The letter simply stated that as Ikey had not arrived at the bank himself to collect the letter of credit and as Silas and Maggie the Colour had no way of knowing whether Marybelle was not an impostor, the letter of credit could only be presented in London by Ikey himself. If the Coutts & Company Bank in London did not inform Mr David Daintree of the Birmingham City and County Bank that Mr Ikey Solomon had himself presented the letter of credit within one week of the date which appeared on it, then the money should be returned to Silas and Maggie Browne and the goods returned. But Mr Ikey Solomon himself and no other.

'Is what they done against the laws of England?' Marybelle asked the bank officer.

Daintree frowned, pinching the brow of his nose. 'No, not strictly. A credit note issued in a contract involving two specific parties and identifying one specific party to another specific party and not redeemable by a third party is not uncommon,' he replied, though he was clearly bemused.

Marybelle shrugged. The implications were not lost on her. The husband and wife team would attempt to rob Ikey of the letter before he arrived back in London. She well recalled the look of consternation on their faces when she'd entered the banker's personal chambers. Any plans to retrieve the money and letter of credit, or to harm Ikey, would be based on someone identifying him as he came out of the bank. She, on the other hand, was unknown to any potential robbers.

Marybelle was a brave and tough woman not accustomed to being threatened and she set great trust in Ikey's cunning, so she comforted herself with the thought: *Since when is two clumsy bloody country bumpkins a match for two London Jews, fuck their goyim eyes!*

'Where does I sign?' Marybelle asked smiling.

'Really, Mrs Firkin, I should caution you, this may not be in Mr Solomon's interest!' the banker exclaimed.

Maggie the Colour jumped from her chair and accosted the man from the bank. 'Really, sir! We don't know *who* this woman be! We've never laid eyes on 'er before today! We 'ave no specimen o' Mr Solomons' signature, not the least identification, maybe the letter what introduced 'er is a trick? Maybe she stole the merchandise what we just paid for? We'd be plain daft if we took chance with letter o' credit!' Maggie the Colour's brittle tone suddenly softened and she smiled. 'You see, sir, Mr Solomons is much respected by me 'usband and me. If this woman is an impostor and 'as done him wrong, then, at great personal expense to ourselves, we 'ave protected 'is interests with the letter what I just wrote?'

'What about the small scrap o' paper what was in yer letter? Ikey said it were 'is affy davy, what made everyfink kosher?'

'Paper?' Maggie held up Ikey's letter. 'This be no proof 'e wrote it. It could be plain and simple forgery!'

'Not that! The small piece o' paper what was a triangle shape come wif that?'

Maggie the Colour looked at Mr Daintree and then at Silas, her expression plainly bemused. She shook her head slowly. 'Paper? What was triangle shape? That be plain daft for letter writin'. Small piece you say, triangle shape?' she repeated and held up Ikey's letter again. 'This be the only paper Mr Solomon sent and it be rectangle, not triangle and not small neither. I doesn't know what you can possibly mean, Mrs Firkin.'

Mary sighed, her huge bosoms quivering. 'Give us the quill then. Yer a right pair o' villains, you two!' She reached out for the paper which now lay on the desk in front of the banker. 'Be so kind as to show us the exact place where I puts me mauley, Mr Daintree, sir.' Then she looked up and asked, 'Is the address of 'er and 'er 'usband on this 'ere letter?'

Mr Daintree glanced at the letter and pointed to the left-hand corner. 'It's right there where it should be,' he confirmed.

'Will ya read it out loud, lovey? We don't want them two doin' a runner if they's up to some monkey trick!'

The banker, somewhat bemused, read the address out aloud.

Marybelle looked at Silas and Maggie Browne. 'I'll remember that I will, make no mistake!' Whereupon, her pink tongue protruding from the corner of her mouth, she tediously applied her signature to the letter. 'There you are, missus,' she said at last, and then cast a second malevolent glance at the husband and wife. 'Be that good faith enough for the likes o' you lot?'

Maggie the Colour sniffed, and gave the letter to the banker to apply his signature, and thereafter she made Silas do the same. Marybelle recognised in him the same tedious effort in signing his name and concluded that he too had difficulty with writing.

Marybelle then addressed the banker. 'Now, if ya please, sir, I requests the pleasure o' the monickers o' them two on the letter what Mr Solomon gave me what states my position as negotiator on 'is be'arf!'

Daintree attempted to conceal his grin. 'Of course, Mrs Firkin, it is completely in order for you to do so.'

He picked up the letter from where it lay on the desk and handed it to Maggie the Colour who read it with her lips pursed and an altogether sour expression upon her face.

'Humph!' she said finally and took the quill up again, signing the letter, as did Silas and Daintree, who blotted it carefully, before handing it back to Marybelle.

Maggie the Colour then asked the banker if he would be so good as to have a clerk make two fair copies of the letter she had written, this to be on bank stationery. When these arrived back she read both carefully, they were duly signed again by all four people present and the original given to the banker for safekeeping. A fair copy was handed to both Marybelle and the Brownes.

With this seemingly watertight agreement in their possession, Maggie and her husband could now set about the task of preventing Ikey from ever presenting their letter of credit. The total cost to them of the paper and plates would be five hundred pounds, though, if they could apprehend him soon enough, the larger part of this too might be recovered.

Marybelle Firkin was helped to her feet by a triumphant Silas Browne and a smiling Maggie the Colour. A concerned David Daintree placed the letter of agreement, Ikey's returned letter and the letter of credit in a heavy linen envelope, sealed it and pressed the bank's insignia into the hot wax. Then he rose and took Marybelle by the arm and guided her to the doorway. Marybelle paused at the door and turned to face the smug-looking couple. She smiled sweetly. 'I wish ya both *meesa meschina*!' she said, a Yiddish expression meaning, 'I wish you sudden death'.

Mr Daintree handed Marybelle the envelope, first

cautioning Maggie the Colour and Silas Browne to remain seated in his chambers until he returned, then he walked Marybelle across the marble foyer of the bank chambers to the front door.

'Ten minutes it says in the letter? You'll not let them two miserable bastards out o' yer chambers for ten minutes, will ya?' Marybelle paused. 'Mind, I'd be right obliged if you'd make that a bit more, wotcha say, lovey?'

Mr David Daintree, member of the board of Birmingham City and County Bank, smiled. 'My pleasure, Mrs Firkin, fifteen minutes at the least, what?' He turned and instructed the guard at the door to see Marybelle safely to her carriage where two footmen with red rosettes on their top hats waited to work her enormous frame through the carriage door and safely into the interior.

Before pulling away the coachman reported quietly to Marybelle that four horsemen of rough looks and a young lad of about ten were waiting under a group of elm trees not fifty feet from the bank, and that he'd taken the trouble to make a casual enquiry to the doorman who'd indicated that they'd arrived shortly after two in the afternoon.

'Watch to see if they follow us,' Marybelle instructed.

After an hour the coachman stopped at a village inn and Marybelle was helped from the carriage into the hostelry, and taken immediately to a small room which contained only a table and two chairs. The room was fuggy with the steam of dishes covering the table. The landlord bid Marybelle *bon appetit* and bowing, backed out of the door, locking it behind him. A few minutes later she heard the rattle of a key again and Ikey stepped into the room and locked the door behind him.

'Loverly grub! I got to 'and it to ya, Ikey, ya knows a good nosh 'ouse when ya sees one.' Marybelle pointed to the envelope which sat on the only corner of the table not covered in dishes. 'There you are, lovey, signed, sealed and delivered by yers truly!'

Ikey snatched at the envelope and tore it open. 'You wasn't followed, was you, my dear?'

Marybelle's mouth was already full with a bite from a large chicken pie, and she shook her head unable to answer. Ikey waited until she could speak. 'Nobody followed us, but in the bank, there was complications.' She pointed to the envelope in Ikey's hand. 'Inside is a letter what I didn't know what to do about, so I signed.' Marybelle looked concerned. 'I only 'opes I done right?'

Ikey opened the sealed envelope and examined the letters within. He shook his head and grinned in admiration as he read Maggie the Colour's letter. Ikey looked up at Marybelle, who once again had her mouth full. 'You done good to sign, my dear.'

Marybelle swallowed, and with her mouth now empty she reached for a chicken leg and waved it in Ikey's direction. 'They be after ya, Ikey Solomon.' Still holding the chicken leg, she took up a roasted potato, popped it into her mouth and continued talking, with her mouth full. 'We wasn't followed 'cause the people they sent didn't know to follow me.' She frowned. 'But they'll be lookin' for ya, mark me words, they's a right pair o' villains them two!' She giggled. 'I wished them *meesa meschina*!'

Ikey laughed. 'More like they wished me!' he said.

Marybelle sucked the flesh of the entire chicken leg from the bone with a soft plop and commenced to chew. Ikey's hand went into his coat, and he withdrew it holding the copper tube he'd ordered in the shape of a cigar container, though somewhat thicker and longer. He placed it on the table beside the letter of credit.

'They aim to do ya in before ya gets 'ome wif that there letter o' credit. That's what 'er letter was all about, weren't it, Ikey? Do ya in, steal yer letter and then claim the contract's been broken!' Marybelle cocked her pretty head to one side and gave Ikey an ingenuous look. 'What's an irrevocable letter o' credit? What's all the fuss about, any'ow?' She pointed to the letter on the table. 'That don't look like no paper what's worth dying for!'

'It's money promised what can't be unpromised once it's been presented from one bank t'other,' Ikey said, trying to stay vague. 'You're perfectly right, my dear, they'll be after trying to stop me gettin' to a bank in London.' Ikey shrugged. 'It's only natural ain't it? You did good not to be followed, my dear. I 'ave made plans, we will make good our escape.'

Marybelle smiled, shrugged her shoulders and looked expectantly at Ikey. 'Ya said I done good, we wasn't followed, so where's me fortune what ya promised?'

Ikey dry-soaped his hands, his shoulders hunched. 'You've done special good you 'ave, my dear, you've done it perfect and exact and splendid. I couldn't 'ave asked for no more, 'cept one small thing?'

'What?' Marybelle asked suspiciously, holding another large piece of chicken poised in front of her greasy mouth.

Ikey reached across the small table, picked up the copper cylinder and unscrewed the smoothly fitting top. He carefully rolled the letter of credit into a tight cylinder itself, which he then neatly slipped into the copper container and screwed the top back on.

'Will you take this letter o' credit back with you to London tonight, my dear?'

Ikey placed the cylinder in front of Marybelle, then he announced he was giving her the rights to future instalments of paper from Thomas Tooth and George Betteridge. 'Until I returns to London to live, my dear, though I daresay that be never.'

'This bill paper to come, is it still kosher? I knows yer doin' a runner, Ikey. The law ain't on to it is they?'

Ikey cleared his thoat and answered truthfully. 'They is and they isn't, I expects. O' course now, at this very moment, I suppose the Bank o' England will be goin' over the mill at Laverstoke with a fine-toothed comb, though I'll vouch if them two, Tooth and Betteridge, 'ave the good sense to lie low for a while, they'll find nothin'. Give it two months, maybe three or even four to be completely on the safe side, and the scam can be brought back intact. Clean as a whistle, free as a bird, kosher as the Beth Din! The bill paper be worth a king's ransom, keep you in nosh for the rest of your life!'

'Only if you knows 'ow to get rid of it, Ikey. I ain't got no contacts what wants bill paper.'

Ikey raised his eyebrows in surprise, 'Why, my dear, you sells it to them two you met in the bank today!'

'What? Do business wif that filth?'

Ikey shrugged. 'They's villains, but the best, my dear. We're all villains, given 'arf a chance, everyone in the whole world is villains. But in me experience there be two kinds o' villain, them what's got a bit o' class and them what ain't.' Ikey's dark eyes shone. 'That letter Maggie wrote today, that be most excellent. That be topnotch thinkin', nacherly nasty nogginin', my dear!' Ikey spread his hands wide. 'That's a rare combination

250

what you doesn't find too often in the business o' villainy, brains and the stomach to act.' He paused, scratching the tip of his nose. 'You take my word for it, they be your natural customers, my dear! All you does is wait a year, then come down here with the bill paper what you 'as accumulated, startin' again in four months.' Ikey leaned back. 'You'll make thousands, my dear, thousands and thousands. Your table will be the envy o' dukes and duchesses. The King himself, I dare say, will come to 'ear o' your fine banquets.'

Marybelle picked up the cylinder and waved it at Ikey. 'And what if some villain they send catches me wif this on me way to London?' She drew the cylinder across her throat. 'That's what 'appens.'

'They won't find it will they?' Ikey said puckering his lips. He pointed to the cylinder. 'It be made to be put in a place what a man 'asn't got and a lady 'as. A place where your average villain ain't likely to go pokin' about without your express permission, if you knows what I mean, my dear?'

Marybelle's pretty blue eyes grew large and then shone with delighted surprise. She gave a little squeal, running her fat, greasy fingers along the cylinder's smooth surface.

'Jesus, Ikey! You bleedin' thinks o' everyfink.' In between her laughter she managed to gasp. 'Methinks it will be a tight fit ... *ha-ha-ha-ha!* But wif all the bumpin' o' the coach to London ... *ha-ha-ha-hee-hee!* ... I daresay it will bring a lady o' me proportions, oh, goodness lummy, oh, oh ... a good deal o' pleasure on the ... *ha-ha-hee-hee!* ... journey 'ome!'

Chapter Thirteen

Ikey returned to London three days after he had left Marybelle Firkin at the inn with a pork pie stuck in her gob and his precious cylinder safely tucked away elsewhere on her large person. Waiting in the back room of a chop house in Houndsditch until well after dark when a light snow storm, churned with frequent wind flurries, began to fall and which he judged would further conceal his passage, Ikey slipped into the rookery of St Giles and soon thereafter let himself into the seemingly abandoned building which housed the Methodist Academy of Light Fingers.

Creeping up the rickety staircase, he appeared suddenly and to the utmost surprise of half a dozen boys who were playing a game of cribbage by the light of a solitary candle. Huddled beside the hearth directly behind them were as many boys again wrapped in rags and old blankets against the bitter cold.

'Now 'ow many times 'as I told you, keep a sharp eye!' Ikey admonished. 'The lad what's supposed to be watchin' out is asleep on the landin', lushed out and smellin' o' gin!' Ikey sucked at his teeth and wagged a mittened finger at the urchins seated crosslegged around a box. 'Gentlemen, gentlemen! Cribbage in this kind o' light ain't no good for the senses. You'll lose your touch, the light of a candle dulls the mind and makes it too easy to palm a card or deal a crooked 'and. Brightness be what's called for, where everything can be seen, clear as daylight, open and negotiable as a whore's cunny.'

The boys laughed loudly at this last remark but Ikey held up his hand for silence. 'A cardsharp to be warranted any good must make 'is play in the best o' conditions. We'll 'ave no second-rate broadsman spreadin' the flats in darkness in my school o' learnin'! A trade ain't worth 'avin' if you're not the best there is at it.'

His young pupils crowded about him. 'There's a people what's lookin' for ya, Ikey, is ya in lavender then?' a young tooler named Sweetface Mulligan enquired.

'Perhaps I is and perhaps I ain't, it all depends on who is lookin' and whether it be opportunity knockin' or disadvantage breakin' down the door.'

'It's Bow Street! Some say it be City police! All about Petticoat Lane they is! Anyone seen ya, they asks! Rewards is offered! Never seen so much law about, 'as we lads? Wotcha do, Ikey? Murder was it? There's talk o' forgery! Millions o' pounds! There be a poster o' yer gob pasted everywhere! We's proud to know ya, Ikey!' All this and more they chorused crowding around Ikey, the smaller ones hopping up and down and jumping on the backs of the larger boys to get a closer look in the semi-darkened room.

'And Mistress Hannah!' a boy they called Onion, whose birth name was Pickles, shouted. 'She been lookin' for ya an' all!'

Ikey shrugged his shoulders. 'It's true, my dears, the constabulary 'as a sharp eye peeled for me.' He looked around slowly, spread his hands and his face took on a look of regret. 'O' course I apologises for scarperin' without informin' you, gentlemen. A matter of urgent expediency, you understand? No offence intended and I 'opes none is taken. No time to pay me respects or bid you all adieu.'

They nodded, happy at the compliment he'd paid their mutual fraternity. Ikey rolled his eyes and seemed to look at each of them in turn. 'Now we 'asn't seen me, 'as we, lads? I means, no seein' to the degree o' not seein' nothin' at all!'

Ikey's fingers flicked heavenwards as though to expel the memory of having seen him completely from their minds. He stopped and lifted the candle from the box, the hot glass warming his mittened fingers. Holding the lighted jar before him, he inspected each boy's dirty face, watching as they solemnly nodded acquiescence. 'We doesn't want no pigs sniffin' round askin' awkward questions now does we, my dears?'

It was not Ikey's intention to stay long at the Academy of Light Fingers, although he did not indicate this to the urchins around him. While they were well trained in all matters of villainy and each had a healthy disregard for the constabulary, he knew he could ill afford to trust them. They were 'street Arabs' seldom allowed the importance of being noticed and any one of them with three or four noggins of gin to loosen his tongue would not be able to resist the urge to boast of his knowledge of Ikey's return. Ikey needed them now for only one purpose, to find Bob Marley as quickly as possible.

Under normal circumstances there were half a hundred places in the surrounding rookeries where Ikey might indefinitely conceal his presence, though he was not foolish enough to suppose that these would now apply. As a Jew in trouble with the law he was fair prey for all but his own kind. Even though his standing as the Prince of Fences was considerable, they would come snarling in for the kill, the promise of a large reward sufficient to overcome their normal tendency to remain stum. Ikey was aware the criminal code of honour was a fragile thing and would always buckle with the opportunity for a quick profit or a favour returned. He knew this as a certainty, for he was himself no different.

With the promise of a good tightener washed down with a pint of best beer at the nearby chop house, and with the further inducement of a shilling for all and a gold sovereign for the boy who turned out to be the fortunate finder, Ikey sent his young associates off into the winter streets. He directed them to the Haymarket at the popular West End to find and bring Bob Marley back to him.

'When you finds 'im, ask for 'is ear, very quiet mind, say that Ikey Solomon requests the pleasure of 'is company.'

It was not an hour later when Ikey, drowsing at the hearth, was awakened in a great start by a small urchin named Sparrer Fart, a tiny lad of ten with an open angelic face which, together with his size, gave him the appearance of being much younger. He showed all the makings of becoming an expert tooler, with fingers light and sticky as cobwebs and the fearless disposition of the young.

'I brung 'im, Ikey. I found Mr Marley. Can I 'ave the sov what's mine?' Sparrer Fart stuck out his dirty hand and grinned. 'Much obliged, I'm sure!'

'Where?' Ikey cried, shocked at the sudden awakening and alarmed that he hadn't heard the boy ascend the stairs, though the howl of the winter wind and the natural creaking and groaning of the ancient building would have masked Sparrer's light footfall.

' 'E won't come up them stairs.' Sparrer grinned. 'Too dane-gis, 'e reckons.'

Ikey, by now fully recovered of his senses, removed a gold sovereign from the interior of his coat and held it out to the youngster, pulling it out of the reach as the urchin snatched at it. Ikey shook his head. 'Tut, tut! First principle o' business, Master Sparrer Fart! Seein' is believin', always inspect the merchandise before you pays fer it, my dear.' Bending to retrieve the candle, he rose from where he was seated on the cribbage box and proceeded carefully down the stairs.

Bob Marley was waiting in the darkness of the tiny downstairs hallway which was now clearly lit by the light of Ikey's candle. He wore a heavy dark coat which fell almost to his ankles with a pair of stout boots protruding from trousers of rough corduroy. A tartan scarf was wrapped about his face so that only his eyes showed between the scarf and the rim of his battered top hat. He removed the scarf at Ikey's approach and stuffed it into the pocket of his coat.

This form of attire was unusual for Marley, who liked to be seen about the town as a proper swell, dressed in the latest fashion. Ikey's keen eye noted this disparity in his dress and concluded that Marley had not been found by Sparrer Fart in the Haymarket, where a man of his reputation would not venture dressed in so poor a manner.

Ikey turned to look sternly at Sparrer Fart. 'We went

off to spend our shillin' on a tightener and a noggin o' gin then, did we? We went local and not to the Haymarket did we? We didn't do no lookin' at all!' Ikey glanced at Bob Marley and winked. 'Methinks, we chanced upon Mr Marley 'ere by sheer luck and great good fortune and because we 'as a greedy guts!'

The boy shuffled, looking down at his feet. 'I found 'im di'nt I? I done good!' He moved up to Ikey and began to clutch imploringly at his coat. 'It were a fair find an' all!' he whimpered into the folds of Ikey's greasy coat.

Ikey clucked, wrapping his free arm around the boy's shoulder. 'We all needs a bit o' luck, my dear. Gawd knows yours truly could use a speck o' good fortune right now.' He pushed the young lad gently away and his hand went into his coat and a moment later appeared with half a sovereign held between forefinger and thumb. 'I tell you what I'll do, we'll keep 'arf a sov back on account of 'ow you disobeyed instructions and I'll give you 'arf a sov for deliverin' the goods. Punishment and reward both at the same time, now what could be fairer than that, my dear?'

The small boy looked doubtful. 'It ain't fair, I done what ya asked! Ya said a sov for 'im what found 'im!' He moved close to Ikey plucking at his coat. 'It ain't fair, I done what ya asked, I found 'im.'

This time Ikey pushed him away roughly, but the boy grabbed onto the coat and Ikey smacked him across the ear. 'Disobedience! Discipline! 'Arf a sov and you're lucky to be keepin' it, boy!'

Marley's hand shot out and snatched the coin from Ikey's fingers. ''Arf a mo, Ikey, one sov was promised the lad, one sov must be given!'

'Lessons! Boys must learn lessons! Obedience, discipline,' Ikey whinged.

Marley laughed. 'Promises! Boys must 'ave promises kept.' He tossed the half sovereign into the air and caught it. 'This'll pay for the inconvenience o' crossing the lane,' he said, pocketing the coin. 'Ya owe the brat a sov, so pay up, Ikey Solomon!'

Ikey's eyes widened in surprise. 'You was in the Hare and Hounds?' he exclaimed, naming the flash-house across the lane.

Marley nodded. 'Ya was due back 'bout now, ya couldn't 'ave gone to too many places what wouldn't 'ave shopped ya, this were one,' he explained simply, giving Ikey a slow smile. 'How may I be o' service to ya?'

Ikey turned to Sparrer Fart and handed him a sovereign. ' 'Ang about and you might learn something, me boy! See what we just seen demonstrated?' He turned and gave Bob Marley an oily smile, returned his gaze to the small boy and stooping low he pushed the candle close to his dirty little face. 'See? Discipline!' He tapped the side of his forehead with his forefinger. 'Use o' the noggin, thinkin'! That's trainin', my dear, that's discipline, that be what makes a great tooler into a swell mobsman, an aristocrat o' the art o' pickin' pockets!' Ikey straightened up, satisfied that he'd recovered his dignity by making his original point and at the same time had sufficiently softened Bob Marley with his flattery. Patting Sparrer Fart on the head, he said, 'You 'as just 'ad the benefit o' the wisdom o' Solomon, my dear!'

Sparrer Fart looked up and pointed to Bob Marley and then to Ikey. 'Oh yeah, 'ow come Mr Marley's got 'arf a sov what's yours and I've got a sov? Be that the wisdom o' Solomon?'

The boy ducked as Ikey swatted at his head with his free hand.

Marley laughed, delighted at the boy's quick mind. 'You've not lost yer touch, Ikey, yer still the best o' the kidsmen, there ain't no one knows better 'ow to pick the fly ones!' He too patted the top of Sparrer Fart's greasy cap. 'Stay away from the gin, you've got all the makin's, son.'

Sparrer hadn't moved. 'What about t'other lads, Ikey? You promised them a shillin' fer lookin' and a good tightener wif a pint o' best beer to follow.'

Marley looked suspiciously over at Ikey. 'That true?'

Ikey gave him a sheepish grin and a reluctant hand went into the interior of his coat and shortly returned with two sovereigns which he handed to Sparrer. 'Mind you give this to Sweetface Mulligan to share out. He's the kidsman when I'm away. Now scarper! Bugger orf!' He turned to Marley. 'Shall we go upstairs, there's a fire in the 'earth.' Then remembering Marley's reluctance he added, 'It ain't dangerous, only a tad rickety but the stairs be solid enough.'

'What, up them?' Marley said in alarm and pointed above to the dark shape of the stairs where Sparrer Fart had disappeared as though swallowed into a deep black hole. 'Not bleedin' likely! We'll talk down 'ere if ya don't mind.'

Ikey clasped his hands together in front of his chest. 'I needs a lair, a place where somebody what's lookin' 'ard and knows what they's lookin' for, can never 'ope to discover who it is they wants to find.'

'Hmm, a good 'iding place o' that nature, cost ya 'eaps,' Marley said speculatively. 'Big reward out, Ikey, 'arf London Town's lookin' for . . . ' grinning he quoted

The Times, 'the Jew what's financially undermined England!' Marley shook his head in a melodramatic way. ''Fraid ya ain't got no friends no more. City police is spreadin' five pounds notes about just for keepin' a sharp eye out. There's a fortune on yer 'ead.' Marley paused and gave Ikey an evil grin. 'Matter o' fact, I could be interested meself!'

Ikey reeled back in horror, his eyes large with fright. 'Don't talk like that, Bob Marley! I taught you everythin' you knows. Was I not your kidsman?' Ikey smiled, his voice somewhat calmer as he remembered. 'You was a good snakesman though, that I'll freely admit. In and out o' the smallest openin's, a natural eye for good stuff too!' Ikey spread his arms and smiled disarmingly. 'Look at you, my dear! Not a copper's dirty great 'and on your shoulder in all these years. Never stood in front o' the bench, never seen the judge's dreaded gavel come down pronouncing a sentence, nor 'as you 'ad the misfortune to look out from the inside o' the bars o' a Newgate cell.'

Ikey paused to emphasise his point, jabbing his fore-finger at Bob Marley. 'That don't come natural, my dear! That's trainin', expert trainin', what you got young from a certain someone what is present and is beseechin' you to offer an 'elping hand in 'is hour o' most urgent need!'

Ikey cleared his throat and his tone became unctuous. 'I'm a bit short at the moment, unforeseen expenses and the like, but you knows me credit to be good. Me lovin' wife Hannah will pay you when she comes to see me.'

Marley shook his head. 'Don't know 'bout lovin' wife, Ikey. Yer missus weren't none too pleased findin' out 'bout Mary and yer high-class brothel in Bell Alley an' all!'

260

'Oh shit, she knows about Mary? 'Ow'd she know about Bell Alley then?'

Marley laughed. 'S'pect she read it in *The Times*. The 'ole of London's talkin' 'bout you, Ikey. What ya done an' all, inta-nash-nil forgery ring, plots to send the 'ole country broke wif fake English longtails floodin' the European market. Britain's credit in question by the Frenchy parley-ment! Austry-'Ungarian empire financially embarrassed and undermined! Yer a right notorious bastard, you is. If ya wasn't in so much shit you'd be the bloomin' toast o' the London criminal class. You is the biggest thing what's 'appened since Queen Caroline's trial!'

Ikey ignored Marley's exaggerated banter. 'Well, you may be sure Mary will pay you, then,' Ikey whined.

'Mary? Mary's in Newgate! She's been in front o' the beak and is awaitin' sentencin' at the Old Bailey. She's Botany Bay bound for sure.' Marley sniffed and looked ominously at Ikey. 'City arrested 'er three days after ya scarpered, charged 'er wif runnin' a bawdy 'ouse, but that were only the excuse.'

'Oh Jesus!' Ikey cried. 'Mary get the boat for runnin' a bawdy house? It ain't possible, runnin' a respectable brothel ain't no crime what merits transportation!'

'That's what folks is sayin' in the Lane. There's talk she'll get the full fourteen years.' Then Marley added darkly, 'On account of you, ya bastard. City ain't convinced she don't know nuffink 'bout that printin' press and what you've been up to wif the deaf and dumb Frenchy.'

Ikey looked up astonished. 'She kept stum? She didn't bleat?' If Mary had turned King's evidence and Ikey were caught there wasn't a judge in England who wouldn't find her information damning.

'She didn't say nuffink to nobody! That's a bloody good *nemmo* that is.' Marley jabbed a finger into Ikey's scrawny chest. 'Better'n what the likes o' you deserves, Ikey Solomon.'

Marley paused and shook his head. ''Fraid I can't give ya no credit, Ikey. I can't take no chances.' He shrugged. 'So that's it, it's all a matter o' business, knows what I mean? Pay up and I 'elps you to escape, don't and I marches ya straight to the City constabulary and collects me considerable reward for the heroic happrehension of England's number one notorious villain.'

Ikey examined the tops of his mittened hands, shook his head slowly, then looked up at Bob Marley accusingly. 'You got a bet each way, is that it!' In a broken whisper he added, 'Shame on you, Bob Marley!'

Bob Marley shrugged. ''Fraid so, me old matey. Business is business!' He paused, grinning. 'Now who was it taught me that?'

''Ow much?'

'Twenty sovs down.'

'Twenty sovs!' Ikey wailed. 'That be pure daylight robbery!'

Marley, not bothering to reply, shrugged and held out his hand.

'Fifteen? Fifteen sovs!'

Marley shook his head slowly. 'I'd like to, Ikey, but this ain't no ordinary deadlurk what's needed. I got expenses. Twenty sovs now and ten fer every week what I keeps ya safe in 'iding.'

Ikey made one final attempt. 'Twenty and five!'

'Twenty and ten, take it or leave it. I 'asn't got all night.'

Ikey sighed and, turning his back to Bob Marley, he foraged deep within his great coat and fished into a bag of coins which he knew contained two hundred and seventeen gold sovereigns, the last of the money Silas Browne and Maggie the Colour had paid him in cash for the Bank of England watermarked paper.

Getting back from Birmingham had proved an expensive business. Twice he'd had to pay heavy bribes when he'd been recognised from his picture on posters which seemed to be sprouting like crocuses in April on the walls of every village or town through which he passed on his circuitous route to London.

Ikey slowly counted the twenty sovereigns into the slasher's hand. Marley counted the coins for himself, biting every second one as a test. Satisfied, he placed them in the pit pocket of his vest, then held his palm out to Ikey, wiggling the ends of his fingers.

'What?' Ikey asked, his eyes large and innocent.

Marley wiggled his fingers again. 'The ten sovs what's the first week's rent in advance,' he said quietly.

Ikey seemed at the point of tears as he counted ten more coins into Marley's outstretched maw.

'Cheers, Ikey!' Marley said, acknowledging the payment, then added, 'I got a nice little place, a dead-lurk on Jacob's Island what is perfect for the purpose o' bein' in lavender. Lots o' bolt holes. Mind, 'iding a man o' yer extreme notoriety what everyone's lookin' for ain't easy and is very dangerous to me own safety.'

Bob Marley, now all business, placed his hands on his hips and looked quizzically at Ikey. 'You'll not be goin' out wif me dressed like that. Ain't a magistrates' runner or nark in London wouldn't recognise ya in an instant in that *schemata*. Buggered if I know 'ow ya got this far. Ya stick out like a bloomin' whore at a christening, ya does!'

Ikey opened his arms wide, palms outwards, and looked down at his chest in surprise. He had always assumed himself totally disguised in his long coat with his wide-brimmed hat pulled low over his forehead. 'I'm as invisible as the very night itself, my dear,' he said, clearly bemused at Bob Marley's uncharitable remark.

'Quite right! Invisible as the bleedin' 'arvest moon on Chatham Common.' Bob Marley pointed at Ikey's coat. 'Take your'n orf and put mine on.' Then removing his battered top hat he retrieved a cloth cap from within it and placed this upon his own head. Removing Ikey's hat, he dropped it gingerly to the floor, replacing it with the top hat which he set firmly on to Ikey's head, giving its crown a solid thump. The brim immediately dropped over Ikey's eyes and kept sliding until it stopped, trapped halfway down Ikey's nose.

Ikey gave a small squeak of alarm. 'Not me coat, I can't take leave o' me coat, not now, not never!' he pleaded.

'Christ, Ikey. I'll wear it! Ya won't lose it!' Marley said impatiently. 'Ya can 'ave it again when we gets to the isle.'

Ikey now pushed the top hat furiously off his head so that it tumbled backwards bouncing on the floor and rolling. 'Never, not ever, no, no no, not me coat!' he moaned.

Marley watched in amazement as Ikey clasped his arms about his chest hugging his coat, whimpering and rocking as though his life depended on it remaining on his back.

Which, of course, in Ikey's eyes was most certainly

LONDON

the case. Without his coat Ikey considered himself
skinned and in no way different to an animal being led
to the slaughteryard. Once skinned of his coat he
believed he'd soon enough be hooked and hanging like
some freshly peeled beast.

Marley appeared to be thinking, his hand cupped to
his chin, 'I tell ya what . . . ' He was about to say something, then changed his mind, paused and looked at
Ikey. 'But it will cost ya another two sov.'

'What?' Ikey asked tremulously, backing away.
'You'll not have me coat, Bob Marley!'

'It be cold enough outside to freeze ya balls orf, but
ya can wear me coat over your'n.' Bob Marley gave
Ikey a fierce look. 'Mind, if I catches me death of this
act o' extreme generosity, I'll cut yer bleedin' throat,
Ikey Solomon!' He began once more to remove his coat,
though first he removed the woollen scarf from its
pocket and placed it about his neck.

For once, at the mention of money, there was no hesitation from Ikey. Almost before Bob Marley had
ceased speaking, and long before he'd removed his coat,
Ikey held out the two extra gold coins. 'Not me coat,'
he whimpered. 'Not never me coat!'

Marley's coat proved sufficiently voluminous to
accommodate Ikey within his own, but when it was
fitted to his tiny body it dragged nearly ten inches on
the ground. Furthermore, the sleeves extended six
inches beyond Ikey's mittened fingers. Though this was
of little consequence, the hemline of the coat dragging
on the floor made it almost impossible for Ikey to walk
at anything but a snail's pace.

Bob Marley looked puzzled, then suddenly he
grabbed the back of the collar of the outer coat and

265

lifted the entire garment so that the collar dropped over the top of Ikey's head in the manner of a monk's cowl. With his whiskers mostly concealed behind the lapels of the borrowed coat, Ikey now looked like an old crone.

Marley then produced a large silk handkerchief and, twirling it from corner to corner, tied it about Ikey's neck so that the hoisted top of the coat would not slip from his charge's head. This gave Ikey an even greater likeness to the shape of an old woman who, if casually observed in the darkness of the street, might be thought to be wearing a shawl about her head. Furthermore, with the lifting of the coat over Ikey's head, the sleeves now almost fitted, the tips of Ikey's mittened fingers protruding from the ends. It was an altogether admirable arrangement and Bob Marley stood back and felt well pleased with himself.

'Perfect! Even if I says so meself. If we're stopped by a crusher, you is me dear old muvver what's come up from the country. 'Ere, wrap this around yer gob so they won't see no whiskers if the law wants to take a closer gander at ya.' Marley handed Ikey the woollen scarf which hung from his neck.

Ikey reached out for the scarf. But with two coats on his back he could barely move his arms, much less wrap the scarf about his already tightly cowled head. Bob Marley grabbed the scarf and wound it around the bottom half of Ikey's face so that all that showed were the bright points of Ikey's bloodshot eyes.

' 'Ullo, old darlin',' Marley said and blew a kiss in Ikey's direction. His expression became suddenly impatient. 'C'mon, then, let's scarper. I'm ready so chilled me arse'ole thinks it's suckin' on a lemon!'

'What about me 'at? You've left me 'at!' Ikey cried in a muffled voice, pointing at his hat discarded on the floor.

Marley walked over to the banister and retrieved the candle. 'Fuck yer 'at, Ikey!' he said, kicking the hat into a dark corner. 'Fer Gawd's sake let's be rid o' this place before the law adds two and two and comes up wif a very popular arrest!' He rolled the jar containing the smoking candle back into the hallway and closed the door behind them.

Outside the wind howled and a sudden flurry of snow beat down on them, so that neither man heard the door open and then close again, or noticed the small shape of Sparrer Fart as he too left the Academy of Light Fingers. Under his arm, its broad brim almost touching the ground, the urchin carried Ikey's hat. He watched carefully as the two men turned towards Rosemary Lane and then he began to follow them into the bitter London night.

Hannah was woken to the loud knocking at the door of her Whitechapel home. The knocking seemed to have been going on for some time for she remembered it in her sleeping as she struggled to emerge from her laudanum-induced stupor. She'd returned home from the last of her brothels in the dock area just hours before dawn and had expected to sleep until midday.

She was too bleary-eyed to think why the Irish maid-of-all-work who slept with the two younger children hadn't responded to the knock. Wrapping herself in a blanket and thinking only that the slut had probably been at the gin again, having first fed it to the children to quieten them for the night, Hannah made her way down the stairs. She opened the front door to see Sparrer Fart standing on the snow-covered bottom step clutching what appeared to be a large hat.

At first the small urchin holding the hat made no sense. The street about her was transformed from its usual greyness and was white and clean from a fresh snowfall. It was still too early for people to be making their way to the Whitechapel markets around the corner, so that the street had the quality of a dream, enhanced further by the residual effects of laudanum. Hannah's face screwed up in vexation at the sight of the small boy who had the temerity to hammer at her door. She was about to send him packing with an oath when he stammered, 'Itttt's 'bbbout Ikkkey Ssssolmon, mmmissus!' Then slowly, her confused mind focused on the shape of Ikey's hat clutched under the urchin's arm.

Hannah rubbed her eyes, now suddenly fully awake, though the vestiges of the drug caused her words to slur when she spoke. 'Ikey? Ya got news?'

'Iiiit's urrrrgent, mmmmissus!' the small boy managed to say through half-frozen lips, his breath smoking in the freezing air.

'Come in, boy!' Hannah opened the door wider to let Sparrer Fart pass into the hallway. 'Keep walkin' to the kitchen in the back, I'll not 'ave such as you in me parlour.' Her head was surprisingly clear as she directed the urchin to the rear of the house.

'We ggggot 'immmmm missus!' Sparrer said, turning to her as they reached the kitchen.

'Got 'im, who's got 'im? Who's we?'

But the boy now seemed in a state too frozen to communicate further. He silently held up the hat for Hannah to see. He was shivering violently, his teeth chattering so furiously that it was plainly impossible for him to talk. Ikey's hat jerked and shook as though it might jump of its own accord from his tiny fist.

Hannah took a key from around her neck and opened a cupboard from which she took a quart bottle of brandy. She unhooked two small pewter mugs from the dresser, poured a small splash into one and handed it to Sparrer Fart. ' 'Ere, get that down yer gob, do ya the world.'

Sparrer dropped Ikey's hat and grabbed the mug with both hands, gulping greedily at the raw liquor. He began to choke and cough as the fiery liquid hit his stomach and chest, though he showed that he was well enough accustomed to such a reaction. Soon enough he took a second, more cautious, sip from the mug.

Hannah, clutching the blanket around her with one hand, poured a dash of brandy into the second mug and seated herself at the table.

'Well, what 'as ya to say for y'self, boy?' she demanded, pointing to Ikey's hat. 'No way Ikey would o' parted with 'is 'at.' She looked suspiciously at Sparrer, who was still shaking and clapping at himself. 'Ya ain't done Ikey no 'arm now, 'ave ya?' she demanded.

Sparrer shook his head and lifted the mug to his still chattering teeth for another sip.

Hannah sighed and reluctantly took the blanket from around her and handed it to the urchin who grabbed it gratefully, wrapping his diminutive body into its warmth. Hannah wore a thick red woollen nightdress which reached down to her ankles which, in turn, were encased in bedsocks and a pair of fleece-lined slippers. Warmed by a second sip of the brandy, she rose and went to the kindling box and laid a fire in the hearth, adding a few lumps of coal to the twigs before lighting it.

'Can I 'ave some more, missus?' Sparrer held out the pewter mug.

The tiny boy had consumed a good half inch of brandy which, apart from having restored his voice and stopped his shivering, appeared to have had no measurable effect on him. 'Got yer tongue back 'as ya, boy? Sorry, no more, not 'til after you've said what ya come for. What's yer name?'

'Sparrer, missus, Sparrer Fart, but they jus' calls me Sparrer.' He put the mug down on the table, licking the brandy taste from his lips. 'I'm 'ungry, missus, I ain't et since yesterday mornin'.'

Hannah sighed. She was growing impatient. 'What ya think this is, a bleedin' chop 'ouse? I ain't givin' you nuffink to eat until ya tells me what ya come for!' She pointed to the hat on the table. 'Ya can start with that!'

'It be Ikey's. Ikey Solomon! Honest, missus, I wouldn't tell you a lie!'

'I know that, but where'd you get it, boy?'

Sparrer, sensing Hannah's anxiety for an answer, looked suddenly forlorn. 'I'm 'ungry, missus, real 'ungry I is.'

Hannah realised she'd get no more from the urchin until she'd fed him, so she fetched a plate of cold salt beef from the cupboard and cut two large hunks from a loaf of yesterday's bread. Then she filled a bowl with curds and placed the offering in front of the small boy, who immediately began to devour the food.

In between mouthfuls Hannah got the story from Sparrer. Hannah listened as he told her how, a day or two back, he'd attempted to lift a kerchief from Bob Marley's pocket in the Hare and Hounds. How Marley had caught him at it and after boxing his ears for being clumsy had found that Sparrer was one of Ikey's brats.

'Maybe I could use ya, 'e says. 'Ow good are ya as a tooler, boy? I just caught ya, that ain't a good sign. I'll give ya a test, fail and ya gets yer arse kicked!' Sparrer cleverly mimicked Bob Marley's voice.

Bob Marley had watched as Sparrer demonstrated his skill on several of the patrons of the house, returning with a cheap watch, two snot rags and no value except as a demonstration of Sparrer's light fingers and a fob chain, also of little value, as it was made of brass. Marley had been sufficiently impressed to recruit Sparrer for what the urchin, imitating Bob Marley again, described as, 'A little job what may or may not 'appen, but is the very opposite to what you 'as been trained to do.' He had not said anything more except to instruct Sparrer to check into the Hare and Hounds late every afternoon to see if Marley had left a message for him.

'Then Ikey comes back. One moment 'e's not nowhere and the next there 'e is standing in the Academy in front o' all the lads. Then 'e says 'e wants us to find Bob Marley.' Sparrer stopped and thought for a moment. 'No 'e don't, first 'e starts puckering 'bout cribbage, 'ow we mustn't 'andle flats in the dark. Then 'e asks us to find this cove Bob Marley. Ikey says to us there's a sov for 'im what finds this cove, and a shilling and a tightener for all what goes lookin'. 'Cept he says Bob Marley will be in the Haymarket when I knows perfectly well that's where 'e ain't!' Sparrer, feeling very pleased with himself, looked up at Hannah.

'So they all scarpers, pushin' and shovin' to get down the stairway first so it nearly come down!'

'Yes, yes, go on,' Hannah said impatiently.

'So I goes back to where I seen me friend, Mr Marley, a couple o' hours before. To me surprise, 'e were still there an' all! I taps 'im on the back. Mr Marley, I says, Ikey Solomon asks for the pleasure of yer company.'

Sparrer laughed. ' " 'Ow'd you know I was lookin' for him?" Mr Marley says.' Sparrer looked pleased with himself. 'I didn't know 'e was lookin' for Ikey, but I ain't gonna tell 'im that, am I? I stays stum, don't I?' Sparrer paused and Hannah nodded her approval. ' "Ikey, what's picture is on all the posters, ya means 'im?" Mr Marley asks again. I nods, the very same person, 'e's our kidsman. "Blimey!" 'e says. "Miracles will never cease!" '

Sparrer could see Hannah was intrigued. 'Mind if I 'as another drop o' brandy, missus?'

'No more mecks, ya ain't no use to me drunk!' Hannah said, her lips tight.

Sparrer picked up the mug and looked into it disappointed, but then continued to talk. ' "Want to make 'arf a sov, Sparrer?" Mister Marley asks me. "Nacherly," I says. "Righto, Mister Sparrer Fart, let's see 'ow good a tooler ya is!" An' 'e 'olds up these two five pound notes.'

'Two?' Hannah interjected. 'Two five pound notes?'

'Yeah, that's right, then 'e give me instructions like, he says, "When we goes back and meets wif Ikey Solomon I wants you to plant these on 'im, Sparrer." Now I finks to meself, queer, even queerer than queer, all me life I 'as been practising to lift stuff, now this cove wants me to plant perfectly good soft on Ikey

Solomon, the same person what's done all me trainin' in toolin'. It don't make no sense if ya asks me.'

Hannah was breathing fast. 'Well? Did ya do it?'

Sparrer, grown more loquacious with the brandy and enjoying his own story, continued without replying. ' "I'll try, Mr Marley, sir," I says. 'E grabs me by me coat. "No! Just don't fail! If it don't look like ya can do it, don't take no chances, ya hear me boy?" ' Sparrer's imitation of Bob Marley was near perfect. ' 'E 'ands me 'arf a sov. "Money in advance, win or lose, do it right or not at all! Ya understand?" ' Sparrer straightened up in his chair and unconsciously stuck out his chest. 'Blimey, missus, 'e's paid me before I done the job. Win or lose I wins! "I'll do me best," I says. "Seein' 'ow you trusts me an' all." '

Hannah grabbed the mug out of Sparrer's hand and banged it down onto the table. 'For Gawd sakes stop muckin' about, did ya or didn't ya?'

Sparrer jumped and pulled his head back instinctively, expecting to be hit. 'What did I do?' he exclaimed in alarm.

Hannah felt suddenly foolish but, unable to explain her agitation, attacked further. 'Yer lyin'!' she shouted, trying to recover her composure. 'Ain't nobody could plant nuffink on Ikey Solomon. Leastways, no tooler what's just a brat!'

Sparrer rose to the bait. 'I did so! It were easy, missus!'

Hannah laughed. 'Easy was it? You think Ikey is some moocher what's just come in town from Shropshire?'

Sparrer explained how Ikey had tried to welsh on the sovereign he'd promised, offering him half a sovereign instead. Hannah nodded. This part was familiar enough.

'So I starts to blub, see. "It ain't fair!" I says and goes up and 'angs onto Ikey's coat, cos I seen this tear in the front what 'asn't been mended yet, so I keeps blubbin' and pluckin' on 'is coat which he thinks is me beggin' for the other 'arf sov what he owes me. So I tucks the soft what Mr Marley give me inside the tear and right-away it falls down into the lining.' Sparrer grinned. 'It were easy as pie!'

'So, tell me,' Hannah asked, 'Bob Marley gets ya to plant the soft on Ikey's person, real money what's valuable. Why would 'e do that? It don't make no sense now do it?'

Sparrer scratched his head. 'Buggered if I knows, missus.' He thought for a moment. 'Maybe it were a trick an' all. A joke or summink.'

Hannah said nothing until the boy grew uncomfortable under her steady gaze. Sparrer looked up and shrugged. 'I don't know why 'e done it, missus,' he said, ashamed that he could come up with no adequate explanation.

Hannah began, her voice soft at first, then building in volume, 'Let me tell ya summink for nuffink, Mr Sparrer Fart!' She pointed at the hat on the table. 'I think ya found Ikey's 'at, I dunno 'ow and I dunno where.' She reached over and picked up the hat. 'Look! It's got dust on it, 'ere look, on the brim, where it's been lyin' somewhere what's dusty! Ya found Ikey's 'at and ya thinks, " 'Ullo, 'ullo, this be worth summink", so ya comes round 'ere and makes up some cock 'n' bull story about fivers what ya planted on me 'usband's person, stories what is ridiculous and stupid even for a brat the likes of you!' Hannah's voice rose even higher.

'I don't think you've seen Ikey Solomon. I think you've only seen 'is 'at!'

'It ain't true! It ain't true what ya says, missus! I knows where Ikey is, where 'e be 'iding. I can show ya!' Sparrer protested.

'I suppose Bob Marley showed ya?' Hannah sneered.

'No! I followed them two. When they left the Academy last night. I followed them to the Isle! It were snowing, they didn't see me.'

'The Isle?'

'Jacob's Isle, Ikey's got a deadlurk there.'

'Ha! Jacob's Island! Fat chance! That be docks and 'ouses what's mostly condemned!'

'C'mon, then, I'll show ya, missus!' Sparrer challenged, caught up in the argument and forgetting that his purpose for coming was to try for a couple of sovs in exchange for Ikey's whereabouts.

Hannah's expression changed suddenly and she smiled disarmingly then gave Sparrer a supplicating look. 'Please, Sparrer, don't fool with me poor broken 'eart. I loves me 'usband. I know 'e ain't much, but I loves 'im. If ya knows where Ikey is, I must go to 'im, 'e needs me.' She leaned forward and took Sparrer's dirty little hand in both her own. 'Look at me, a poor woman what's 'usband is in mortal danger. Please Sparrer, if ya 'as any loyalty to Ikey what's taught ya all ya knows, you'll let 'is poor, miserable wife visit 'im.'

Hannah's change of mood quite took Sparrer by surprise. The fact that she appeared suddenly to believe him, combined with the feel of his hand cradled in the warmth of her own, caused his eyes to fill with tears of relief.

'I can show ya, missus, the exact place,' he said.

Hannah went to the cupboard and returned with the plate of salt beef and what remained of the bread. She placed a knife beside Sparrer. ' 'Elp y'self, love, I won't be long.' She took the bottle of brandy and locked it in the cupboard, replacing the key around her neck and tucking it into the bodice of her nightdress. Then she took Ikey's hat. 'I'll be back in two shakes of a duck's tail. Be me guest, make y'self completely at 'ome.'

By the time Hannah had dressed for the street and returned to the kitchen, Sparrer was asleep, his arms on the table with his head cradled within them. It took a considerable amount of prodding and shaking to wake him. Hannah was anxious to be away before the early morning market crowd began to fill the streets. At last she got the urchin to his feet and escorted him to the front door.

'Ya go first, Sparrer, to the Pig 'n Spit and wait for me outside. I'll be along shortly in a hackney. We'll ride most o' the way, then, when we gets near the Isle, we'll walk.' Hannah gripped Sparrer's shoulder at the door. 'Be sure ya isn't followed, pigs in any number could be watchin' the 'ouse.'

Sparrer, after running most of the way to keep warm, had not long been waiting at the Pig 'n Spit when Hannah called to him from the interior of the hackney. The driver slowed down and Sparrer jumped into the small cabin and sat beside Hannah.

'When we gets close, but not too close, give me a nudge and we'll get out and walk. 'Ere, sit up close to me so I feels ya,' Hannah whispered. Sparrer moved up against Hannah's heavy woollen coat. Warmth and comfort seemed to emanate from her plump person. It stirred long forgotten memories in the child so that the tears began to run down his dirty cheeks and he became momentarily lost in the past. Consequently they found themselves closer to Ikey's deadlurk than was perhaps prudent before Sparrer finally nudged Hannah.

They walked onto the Isle and Sparrer led Hannah by a circuitous route to an area where the houses seemed deserted and were so closely packed that they appeared to be leaning on each other for support. They walked down an alley, wide enough to take a wagon, which was strewn with debris and foul with mud and evil-smelling puddles some of which appeared to carry a thin veneer of ice. Hannah had cause to lift her skirt and, despite the care she took, her boots sank into the stinking ooze, often almost to their tops. Sparrer, who walked ahead, came to the end of the alley and put his hand up to signal Hannah to stop. Then he called her forward with a flick of his fingers, indicating that she should move slowly and without making a sound. Hannah came towards him more carefully than ever, though the squelch and sucking of the mud, and crunching of thin ice under her feet seemed to be announcing her every step.

When she reached the far end of the alley Hannah discovered that it led to a small loading yard in the form of a quadrangle. It appeared to have once been paved with flagstones, though most of these had been removed and were piled high into one corner and partly covered with snow. The building which occupied three sides of the quadrangle had once been a fairly large warehouse backing on to the river. The warehouse seemed to have been deserted for a long time and its few windows and the main doors, big enough to take a horse and cart, were boarded up. The urchin put his finger to his lips and pointed to the pile of snow-covered flagstones.

'Entrance be there, missus,' Sparrer whispered. 'Be'ind them stones.'

Hannah's heart pounded furiously. She stood a few feet back from the entrance and deep within the shadows so that she could not possibly be seen, but she nevertheless imagined she could feel Ikey's eyes boring into her from a gap between two planks which boarded up the hoist door, set high up into the roof of the three-storey stone building. Hannah could sense Ikey crouching on his knees, wild strands of greasy hair flying from the sides of his head, his shiny bald pate vulnerable for want of the security afforded by his broad-brimmed hat. She could almost feel his eyes glued to the gap between the boards, willing her to come to him, though too fearful to call out lest her presence be some sort of trap.

She waited until she felt her breathing grow calmer then placed her hand on Sparrer's shoulder and gave it a tiny squeeze. Sparrer turned his head and looked up at her.

'Come!' she whispered and, turning about, began to retreat down the muddy alley. She walked ahead of Sparrer until they were well clear of the buildings. Not a soul had appeared in all the while they had been in the vicinity of the derelict row of houses. The part of the island they were on seemed to be totally desolate and their footsteps showed clearly in the snow, but it had begun to snow lightly again and they would soon be concealed. A low pewter-coloured sky added to the sense of isolation and misery of the broken-down surroundings. Hannah let out a discernible sigh of relief once she considered they had retreated sufficiently far

278

from the deserted houses to communicate.

'Ya sure that be it, Sparrer? Gawd's truth, that old ware'ouse be Ikey's deadlurk?'

Sparrer looked hurt. 'Yes, missus, 'course I is. I knows these parts like the back o' me 'and. Before I growed up, Jacob's be where I come from.'

Hannah walked with Sparrer to the small causeway connecting Jacob's Island to the city side of the Thames. Here she opened her purse and took out two single pound notes and held them up in front of Sparrer.

'Ya never seen me, ever, ya understand? If ya tells a single livin' soul about Ikey's deadlurk I'll tell Bob Marley ya followed 'im and 'e'll come after ya with 'is razor and cut yer bleedin' throat from ear to ear!' Hannah ran a mittened hand across her throat for emphasis. 'You 'as never seen me, we's never met, ya understand, Sparrer?' Sparrer nodded, his eyes fixed on the money she held in her hand. 'Good!' She handed him the one pound notes. ' 'Ere, for yer trouble. Now disappear, scarper, I never seen ya, whoever you are.'

Sparrer placed one of the pound notes between his lips which were beginning to tremble from the cold again, then using both hands, he held either end of the second note and brought his fists together then snapped them suddenly apart pulling the banknote taut to test its strength. Satisfied as to the quality of the bank paper he held the note up to the sky to examine the Bank of England watermark. He seemed pleased with what he saw, but opened his mouth, the remaining note sticking to his bottom lip as he wet his fingers with spittle and rubbed the watermark on the note with his wet fingers to see if it would disappear. Sparrer then tried to remove the remaining note from his bottom lip, but it had frosted to the skin and he pulled gingerly until it finally came away, leaving a bright smear of blood where the paper had removed the skin. He folded both notes together and pushed them somewhere deep within the interior of his tattered coat.

Then, his breath making smoke in the cold air, Sparrer scanned the desolate surroundings at some length, then brought his gaze back to Hannah's face, his eyes showing no recognition.

'I must 'o been dreamin',' he declared in an exaggerated voice, ' 'cause I could o' sweared there was a woman standing right 'ere in front o' me not a moment ago!' He turned and began walking away from Hannah, not once looking back.

Hannah crossed the causeway and stopped at a hoarding where a man was busy pasting up a poster for Madame Tussaud's Travelling Waxworks. She purchased a handful of torn poster paper for a halfpenny and, seated on a low stone wall, she commenced to clean her muddy boots. Soon thereafter she hailed a hackney. 'Take me to Threadneedle Street, Bank o' England,' she instructed the driver.

Chapter Fourteen

Ikey was arrested by the City police in the early after-noon of the day Hannah visited Jacob's Island with Sparrer Fart. He was taken to Lambeth Street Police Office and bound over. After a thorough search of the inner parts of his body and clothes the two counterfeit five pound notes were discovered in the lining of his overcoat. Thereafter he was taken to Newgate, where he was lodged in a single cell reserved for prisoners thought to be dangerous.

'Oh shit! I 'as been shopped!' was all he was heard to cry when the fake soft was found. The senior con-stable, who went by the unpropitious name of George Smith and who had searched him, looked disgusted. A notorious old hand at the searching of suspects, he was known to any who had 'passed through his hands', as 'The Reamer', for he would delight in prodding his victims. Two great sausage-like fingers with fingernails grown long and filed sharp as a mandolin player's thumb entered their rear passage with a jabbing and stabbing that left them bleeding for days.

'Yer full o' shit, Ikey! But clean o' contraband!' he'd exclaimed in a booming voice, much to the delight of the constables who were holding down the screaming, blubbing Ikey with his breeches pulled down below his skinny white thighs. Then, after first having gone through the amazing configurations of pockets, slots, tubes and hiding places within Ikey's coat and eventually finding the two offending notes secreted within the innocuous tear on its outside, the senior constable held up the counterfeit notes and, shaking his head, declared, 'It ain't worthy o' you, Ikey, me boy, I expects much better from the likes o' you! Summink more ingenious, a hiding place what could challenge yours truly! A glorious adumbration to bedazzle the mind!' The Reamer waved the two notes in the air above his head and grinned. 'You'll be the laughin' stock o' Newgate Gaol, me boy!'

Ikey immediately concluded that Bob Marley had betrayed him and by means of half a sovereign placed into the hand of a turnkey sent urgent word for Hannah to come to Newgate. Here he had been placed in a cell on the third floor of the central block where, if he stood on the stone bed, he could catch a glimpse through the small barred window of the great dome of St Paul's. Though the stench was no better at the top of the building, some natural light penetrated into the cell. Moreover, the floor and walls, while of stone, were not covered with faeces, urine and the evacuation of drunken stomachs as in the dungeon cages. Nor were they especially damp, so that the fear of gaol fever, now known as typhoid, and which was said to be carried by the appalling fumes into every cell, was less likely to strike.

Ikey's more private incarceration was not intended to indicate his superior status but rather his notoriety. It was designed to keep him from being murdered in a public cell where drunkenness, fornication, starvation and every form of despair and degradation did not preclude a peculiar loyalty to the King of England.

It is an English paradox that prisoners who are flogged and starved in the name of the Crown and treated far worse than a barnyard pig by the society in which they live, remain loyal subjects to the King. The scurrilous and exaggerated stories of Ikey's attempt to bring financial ruin to the Bank of England were as well known in the dark public cages of Newgate as elsewhere, and should he have been thrown among these poor wretches it was feared that he would not live to face the full force of British justice.

Ikey, always the perfectionist, was as much dismayed as the senior Bow Street constable had pretended to be that someone had managed to plant the two five pound notes within the tear on his coat. He cursed himself bitterly for neglecting, after escaping from the coach in Birmingham, to immediately sew up the offending rip. It was just such lack of attention to detail which leads to downfall and, Ikey told himself, if a mistake of the same magnitude of neglect had occurred with one of his urchins, the young tooler would have been most severely punished.

Ikey's disappointment in himself was therefore profound. He prided himself on being alert to the lightest of fiddling fingers. So how had Bob Marley managed to plant the fake soft on him? Ikey knew Marley was no tooler. The slasher's fists were ham-like and would not have had the skill required to plant the notes within the coat.

Finally, after a process of elimination in which his

careful mind examined every detail of his escapades over the past two days, Ikey arrived at the correct solution. Sparrer Fart had been the perpetrator. Ikey recalled how the young pickpocket had moved close, begging for the half sovereign he withheld from him. Such was the curious nature of Ikey Solomon's mind that he congratulated himself for having trained both Marley and Sparrer Fart – Marley for the foresight he showed in recruiting the urchin and young Sparrer for the way he had executed the plant.

Ikey was aware that he had finally come to the end of the line, which, in this event, was dangerously close to the end of a rope. All of England was braying for the noose to be placed around his scrawny neck, the public having believed the scurrilous twaddle in the penny sheets. Ikey's nefarious plans to undermine the very throne of England itself with fake currency, its distribution undertaken by a gang of international Jews and spread across all the capitals of Europe, was discussed in even the poorest netherkens. All of London wanted the case dealt with in a summary manner and damn the due process of the law. 'Hang the Jew bastard now!' was the popular call of the day. There were even some among the better classes who paid a reserve price for a window overlooking the scaffold erected in Newgate Street outside that notorious gaol. The only question which remained was the date on which Ikey's execution would be celebrated.

In Ikey's mind, though, there was a more urgent need in his life than the business of avoiding the hangman. He must, at all costs, contact Marybelle Firkin and retrieve the letter of credit for delivery to the bankers Coutts & Company before the seven days for its presentation expired. Ikey faced what appeared to be an impossible task. He had just three days to lodge the note in person and found himself trapped, a prisoner of His Majesty, locked in a guarded cell.

Moreover, and to Ikey's enormous chagrin, if he failed to present the letter of credit and lost the money he would not even be permitted to enjoy the satisfaction of shopping Silas and Maggie the Colour. To inform on them would be to indict himself as surely as if he had been caught with the bill paper in his possession. Ikey, for once in his miserable life, had been simply and elegantly foiled by a man with a mind like a suet pudding and a woman who wore wooden clogs.

However, having paid much for it in a lifetime outside the law, Ikey was possessed of a good mind for legal procedure. He knew that in England a man could be sentenced in a magistrate's court to be transported for stealing half a crown or a fat goose. But should he be able to afford the costs involved in a rigorous defence in a higher court, he had a much greater chance of avoiding transportation even though the crime committed be a hundred times more extravagant in its nature.

Ikey comforted himself that it could be argued by a good barrister that the two fake five pound notes found in the lining of his coat might well have been planted, the offending and obvious tear in his coat being the evidence to show how simply this might have been done without his knowledge.

This argument, if successful in casting some doubt in the mind of the judge, could be further supported by a timely stroke of great good fortune. Abraham Van Esselyn, who had taken full advantage of his twin afflictions and admitted nothing in his trial, had been sentenced to fourteen years transportation and had hanged himself in Cold Bath Fields Gaol just three days previously. The deaf mute, never able to share the joy of social intercourse with his fellow man, had finally decided to take his leave of the silent world around him. Ikey's defence could therefore proceed unencumbered by evidence of collaboration with his erstwhile partner.

Ikey's case could be built around the premise that he, a simple man, inexpert in the ways of machinery, was merely the landlord of the premises, unaware that amazing works of counterfeiting longtails were being created by the Frenchy foreigner, a deaf mute unable to communicate in the English language. Ikey had merely knocked on the door of the basement premises, accepting the rent due to him in an incurious and routine manner early each Friday morning.

Similarly, Mary Abacus had declared Ikey to be her landlord and her testimony had implicated him in no other way. It was on this issue of being the duped landlord for both prisoners that Ikey's case would depend. In this way the burden of proof lay with the prosecution and, as always in such cases, the silver tongue of an expensive advocate could be used to its greatest effect.

It was a neat enough argument, though as an initial defence Ikey knew it had little chance of working at his first trial in the magistrate's court. Here he would almost certainly be indicted. The scuttlebutt in the penny papers would have long since pronounced him guilty.

However, in the Court of Appeal at the Old Bailey where a fair trial could be guaranteed, and in the hands of a good barrister, this argument could be made to seem most compelling, or, at the very least, it would cast some doubt on the serious nature of the case against Ikey.

Ikey had just three days to contact Marybelle Firkin and lodge the letter of credit. To a man of less fortitude this might have seemed somewhat of a forlorn hope. But Ikey had been in more than one tight spot in his life and, in his mind, formulated a plan which, with Bob Marley no longer his go-between, depended almost entirely on Hannah, her coachman father, Moses Julian, and two carefully selected members of Ikey's own family. The first was an uncle who happened to be of similar age to Ikey, with a striking family resemblance around the eyes and nose. He possessed a small reputation as an actor and a slightly larger one as a broadsman, a card sharp, cheating at cribbage being what he did during the frequent 'resting' periods of his capricious career. His name was Reuban Reuban, a moniker which would have been better suited to a more illustrious thespian. Though he affected the manners of an actor, he was clean shaven and dressed sharp. The second was Ikey's cousin, a young tailor by the name of Abraham Reuban. Actor father and tailor son both had cause in the past to be grateful to Ikey and resided near the Theatre Royal in the Haymarket, this being in close enough proximity to No. 59, the Strand, the home of the bankers Coutts & Company.

To bring to fruition his plan to lodge the credit note on time Ikey was obliged to tell Hannah of its existence. She would therefore know soon enough the extent of the funds Ikey was proposing to transfer to New York. This was a major concern to Ikey. If Hannah suspected that he had been funding his escape without her knowledge she would not reveal her part of the combination to the Whitechapel safe, which, of course, amounted to a great deal more in value than the nineteen thousand, four hundred pounds he was sending to New York.

Ikey would therefore need to concoct a story which convinced Hannah that the credit note was to their mutual benefit. He would have to persuade her that he had gone to Birmingham at great danger to himself, when he could just as easily have escaped to America immediately he knew of the raid. He would express in most compelling terms his reason for not so doing, his only thought having been to add to the funds they would have when she joined him with the children in New York.

Alas, his escape had been thwarted by his betrayal and premature arrest and it was Hannah who was now free to act in the matter of their mutual fortune. He would convince her that he must escape in order to lodge the letter of credit with Coutts & Company and so ensure the money would be transferred to New York.

Hannah, Ikey felt confident, would co-operate. Her greed would convince her as well as the knowledge that Ikey, should his escape prove successful, would not leave her without the prospect of his share of the Whitechapel safe. Their mutual assurance lay in each keeping their part of the combination secret from the other.

On her arrival at Newgate, Hannah was escorted by the keeper himself to Ikey's cell, being quite puffed by the steep stairs. Outside the door of the cell sat a turnkey, a large, slack-jawed, vacant looking man with very few teeth, chosen no doubt for his strength and not the wit at his command. Hannah waited for the gaol officer who had acted as her guide to depart before she fee'd Ikey's guard a fushme.

'I begs ya to stand well clear o' the grille, mister. I 'as things to do what a wife is obliged to do for 'er 'usband and what ain't respectable to be within the 'earin' or seein' of.' She looked boldly at the turnkey. 'If you knows what I mean?'

The man nodded and grinned, showing the stumps of four yellow and black teeth. Pocketing the five shillings she'd given him with obvious delight, the usual fee for 'showing a blind eye' being sixpence, he fumbled with a set of keys hanging from a large ring, which, in turn, was attached to a stout brass chain affixed to his belt.

'I'll be down the corridor a bit, missus,' he said, then making a small ceremony of unlocking the cell door, he added, 'Take yer time, now, I ain't goin' orf for two 'ours yet.' He let Hannah pass through into the cell, then locked the door behind her, making no attempt to search her hamper or, as was the usual case, to extract the larger share of its contents for himself.

Ikey was seated on his stone bed and did not rise when Hannah entered. She placed the basket down and immediately fell upon him, her demeanour most sorrowful and sympathetic.

'My poor Ikey, they 'ave caught ya and locked ya up!' she moaned. She grabbed Ikey and held his head clasped to her breast. 'My poor, poor darlin'!' she exclaimed, rocking his head in her arms.

Ikey grew much alarmed at this unexpected attack. Hannah had not placed a loving hand on him for years. Even their coupling had been completely without emotion, she taking him while he was piss-erect and half asleep, her single purpose to become impregnated with the minimum of time and effort. Before coming to visit him in gaol she had splashed some vile-smelling potion between her breasts and Ikey felt sure he must suffocate with the effect of this noxious perfume. He struggled frantically and managed after a few moments to extricate himself from Hannah's smothering grasp.

'For Gawd sakes, woman, leave orf!' he exclaimed as he backed away from his wife, adjusting the bandana he wore in the manner of a seaman's scarf and which had slipped to the back of his head from Hannah's embrace.

'Oh, Ikey, what shall we do? We are destitute! I am a poor woman with four small children, now deserted! Oh, oh, woe is me! What shall become of us?' Hannah cried, this time so loud that the turnkey, now seated at the opposite end of the corridor, could plainly hear her.

Then, as sudden as this surprising outburst, her voice dropped to a loud whisper. 'Ya bastard, ya piece of crud, who is this Mary, this whore ya give a 'igh-class brothel to?' Her expression had changed to a snarl. Then, stepping back, she slapped the seated Ikey so hard across the face that his head was thrown against the wall of the cell, and for a few moments he thought he would lose his wits completely. 'Ya shit, you will pay for this!' Hannah spat, though none of her furious invective carried much above a hoarse whisper.

Ikey pulled his legs up onto the stone shelf that served as his bed and backed himself into the furthermost corner, his hands protecting his face. After a few moments he parted his fingers and peeked at Hannah, who stood with her arms folded, nostrils flared, snorting like a bull halted at a turnstile.

'Please my dear, don't 'it me!' he whimpered. 'It were business, that be all it were! Business to our mutual benefit, my dear,' Ikey wailed plaintively.

'Ya fucked her, didn't ya? Ya fucked that *shiksa* bitch!'

Ikey looked genuinely alarmed. 'Shhsssh! No, no, my dear, not ever, not once, not possible, you knows me, it were business, it were no more,' he lied.

'Humph!' Hannah snorted, then added, once again in a rasping voice, 'Well the whore got what she 'ad coming to 'er, at least there be some justice in this world!'

'We's in *shtunk*, my dear. I've been blowed and planted,' Ikey said, hoping to change the subject.

'What! Who blowed ya? Planted? What with?'

'Soft, two fives.' Ikey reached down and pulled at his coat and pointed to the tear eighteen inches up from the hem. 'Young tooler planted 'em in there, Bob Marley were the blow!'

'Marley?' Hannah, feigning surprise, shook her head. 'Nah! Not 'im, not Bob Marley, 'e's family!'

''E done it, couldn't 'ave been no one else.' Ikey shrugged. ''E were the only one what got close enough and knowed about the longtails, 'im with the kid what did the plant.'

''E wouldn't 'ave told no kid, not Bob Marley! Too careful. It must o' been someone else.'

'No, my dear, it were 'im. Kid would 'ave thought the bills were genuine.'

Hannah was, of course, thrilled. Ikey did not in the least suspect her. It had turned out exactly the way she had hoped. She took a kugel cake from her basket and handed it to Ikey who absent-mindedly broke a piece off and handed the remainder back to Hannah.

Ikey then told Hannah about the case he thought he could mount with a good barrister and her heart immediately sank. Although Hannah despised her husband, she had never underestimated his cunning. If Ikey should prove himself innocent of no more than being the negligent landlord of the premises in Bell Alley, he would receive only a short sentence, at most a stretch. In twelve months he would be out and her plans for the future of herself and her children would be in tatters.

'I must escape, it be a matter o' the utmost importance, I must get out of 'ere!' Ikey suddenly declared.

'Get out? Escape?' Hannah looked puzzled. 'But ya jus' said – ya jus' told me yer a good chance to beat the rap?'

Ikey then proceeded to tell Hannah about the letter of credit and asked her to visit Marybelle Firkin at the Pig 'n Spit and retrieve it. He also asked her to have Reuban Reuban and his son Abraham come to visit him. Then he carefully outlined the plan for his escape. As he spoke he pushed tiny lumps of the cake into his mouth, so that by the end of his lengthy instructions the piece of cake he'd broken off seemed to be much the same size as when he'd started.

'Whatsamatter? You ain't 'ungry?' she said, trying to collect her thoughts.

Ikey shook his head. 'Your father must be standin' exactly where I said, on the exact spot what I told you outside the Pig 'n Spit. A hackney what can take four, doors both sides o' the cabin.'

Hannah nodded, though her head was in a whirl. She thought Ikey's plan too far-fetched to succeed, but on the other hand she wanted him to lodge the letter of credit. It represented a great deal of money, enough in itself to set her up in America even without the contents of the Whitechapel safe, though it was unthinkable that she would not have this as well. In her mind she too began to formulate a plan.

Ikey's plan was based on the writ of *habeas corpus*, that is, the right of every Englishman to apply for bail to be granted until his case came up for hearing. In order for this to happen he would need to appear before a judge at the King's Bench court at Westminster, where he would be granted a hearing. This would entail being escorted by two turnkeys to the court and would allow him to travel outside the confines of the gaol.

It was standard procedure for two turnkeys to escort a prisoner by foot to the Court of King's Bench, which was situated not more than a mile from the gates of Newgate, though it was not unusual for a prisoner with funds, wishing to keep his identity and his shame from the passing crowd, to offer to pay for a carriage to be escorted in privacy to the courts.

Ikey had applied for bail the moment he had been bound over at Lambeth Street and the hearing was set for two days after Hannah had visited him. Reuban Reuban and his son Abraham, alerted by Hannah, had arrived during that afternoon. Ikey had spoken to them at length and Abraham had taken several measurements of Ikey's person.

At half-past nine on the morning of the hearing two turnkeys marched Ikey through the gates of Newgate. It was the custom for turnkeys who had been on duty to take the extra duty of escort to court hearings so that the day staffing would not be disrupted. This was an unpopular rule, as it attracted no extra stipend for working, at the least, half of the day shift, or even more if the court was delayed. The two men who escorted Ikey were therefore tired and somewhat dulled from the frequent tots of cheap gin and Spanish brandy they had received from prisoners during the night and were not inclined to treat him with respect.

The King's Bench in Westminster was a steady half an hour's walk from Newgate and was scheduled to commence at half-past the hour of ten o'clock. It was a week before Christmas and while no snow had fallen during the night a chill wind blew in from the North Sea. It brought with it a light fog which, added to the smog caused by the winter fires, made the streets as dark as the night itself. Moreover they were packed with Christmas shopping crowds and the smoking flares carried by the coaches and brandished by messenger boys dodging through the crush of people and between carriages added to the general annoyance and difficulty of conditions on foot.

It seemed almost a miracle when a hackney coach appeared through the gloom and appeared to be empty.

'Shall I 'ave the pleasure, gentlemen, of offerin' you a ride?' Ikey asked. He silently congratulated Hannah's father, Moses Julian, for his expertise in having the coach so 'fortuitously' available. Ikey's two escorts needed no further persuasion and he hailed the hackney with a sharp whistle.

'Where to, guv?' the coachman called down to them.

'Westminster!' Ikey called back. 'King's Bench!'

'We'll 'ave to go 'round back way, guv, through Petticoat Lane. Coaches jammed tight as fiddlesticks from 'ere to Westminster. It be the bleedin' fog,' he pointed his whip into the barely visible crowd milling along the pavement, 'and them bleedin' Christmas shoppers.'

Ikey glanced questioningly at the senior of his two escorts, a coarse looking man with a bulbous nose to rival that of Sir Jasper Waterlow, upon the tip of which resided a large wart not unlike a woman's nipple in appearance. It was therefore truly astonishing that his name was Titty Smart, though it may be supposed that this was a sobriquet and not his christian name. He was also the senior of the two men, much experienced and seventeen years in the prison service, and he now grunted and frowned saying gruffly, 'Mr Popjoy and I accepts.'

Ikey, with both his hands shackled, one to a wrist of each man, was held steady at the rear by the younger Popjoy as he climbed with difficulty into the interior of the hackney. The coach turned off the Strand at the first convenience and into a lane which despite its narrowness immediately seemed to improve their progress. The lighted flares stuck to each side of the hackney momentarily turned the drab grey walls of the smog-shrouded buildings into a bright mustard-coloured burst of light as they passed, giving the effect of magic lantern slides changing with rapidity. This flickering effect and the rocking of the coach soon began to have an effect on the weary turnkeys. Ikey watched as their chins sank to their chests and their eyelids rolled shut, only to jerk open every once in a while until the effort became too great and they could no longer stay awake.

The coach turned into Petticoat Lane and then into Rosemary Lane and, as they were about to pass the Pig 'n Spit, Ikey called loudly to the coachman to halt. The two turnkeys wakened with a start and their free hands went immediately to their truncheons.

'Gentlemen, you are wearied from your duties as good men should be what have spent the long night in the service o' the King.'

Ikey dragged the arm of Albert Popjoy with him as

he took his watch from his fob pocket and clicked it open, examining its face briefly. 'We are makin' excellent progress and will arrive at the King's Bench well before the time we are to be called before 'is worship.' He nodded towards the window. 'This 'ostelry, a tavern o' most excellent reputation, be closed to all at this hour, though I assure you it is open to us at any hour. 'Ere be a supply o' brandy the likes o' which may not be found anywhere in the kingdom. A veritable elixir of a miraculous nature what is said to heal the sick and cause the lame to walk again! A tonic extracted from the finest Frenchy vines, matured in English oak for twenty year or more, to render it now more British in its character than ever it were French. It can be mulled in old pewter and be used with great purpose to warm the cockles and keep the eyes brightly open! What say you, gentlemen?'

The thought of a pewter of mulled French brandy, expensive at the best of times, was too much for an old soak such as Titty Smart to refuse. 'The one. We'll have the one and then be off.' He looked at his partner, the younger Albert Popjoy, whose expression seemed doubtful. 'The one, it can't hurt to have the one, lad, now can it?' Smart sniffed, snorted and then rubbed his nose furiously with the edge of his forefinger, as though awakening it to the delicious prospect of the delectable brandy fumes.

'Pull in around the back,' Ikey instructed the coachman.

The coachman touched his whip to the horses and the hackney moved into the small lane which led to the courtyard behind the Pig 'n Spit, drawing up beside the back door. Smart opened the door on his side of the coach to see the head of the cellarman's boy suddenly appear through the open barrel chute at ground level. 'We be closed, sir, we opens again four o'clock. Four o'clock 'til four o'clock o' the mornin',' he yelled, squinting up at the turnkey.

Ikey stood up and leaning over the lap of the still-seated Smart stuck his head out of the coach door. 'Open, my dear, it be urgent business with your mistress!'

The boy's head disappeared underground again and a couple of minutes passed before he opened the back door. He wore a leather apron and carried a cooper's hammer and, judging from his height, appeared to be about fourteen years old. 'Who be it what's come callin'?' he asked.

'Call your mistress, my dear. Tell 'er, Ikey Solomon.'

The boy stood his ground. 'She won't take kindly, sir, she ain't been aslumber more'n two hour.'

'There'll be a shillin', lad,' Ikey said, then repeated, 'Call Mistress Marybelle, tell 'er Ikey Solomon and friends 'as come 'round to pay their respects.'

The expression on the boy's face remained dubious but finally he nodded his head and closed the door. The three men climbed from the coach and the coachman moved the hackney to a tethering post. Several minutes later, which they spent waiting, with their breath smoking the air around their heads and their feet stamping the frosted ground, the door was once again flung open. Filling its entire frame was the giant shape of Marybelle Firkin. She was clad in a bright red woollen dressing gown which gave the immediate effect of a giant tea cosy with a pretty porcelain head in curling papers sewn upon its top as an ornament of decoration.

'My Gawd, bless me if it ain't you! Ikey Solomon! What a bloomin' pleasure!' There was no hint of annoyance in Marybelle's voice at the early hour. Had the turnkeys been more alert they might have wondered why this was so. A woman who has been up all the night to the boisterous demands of her drunken customers is not usually wakened as easily or in a mood of such pleasant alacrity. They might also have questioned why, when the tavern had been closed to patrons a good five and some hours, a hearty fire blazed in the private parlour with the mulling tongs in place between the coals.

'Come in, come in gentlemen,' Marybelle invited, turning and waddling down a passage, leading the way into a bright, warm room. 'Welcome to me 'umble parlour, make y'selfs comfortable.' Then, seeing the three men standing huddled close together at the door, she pointed to the leather chairs beside the fire. 'Sit, make yourselves at 'ome. Ikey sit 'ere, love.' She patted the back of a comfortable leather club chair nearest to where she stood.

Ikey lifted his arms, at the same time lifting the arms belonging to each of his gaolers, displaying the manacles for Marybelle to see. He looked at her sheepishly, raised his eyebrows and shrugged his shoulders in a mute explanation of the predicament in which he now found himself.

'Blimey, o' course! The pigs, they's nabbed ya!' Marybelle folded her great arms across her bosom and glared at Titty Smart and Albert Popjoy.

'Now listen to me, gents, this be me private parlour.' She pointed to the panelled walls. 'See it ain't got no windows for boltin', and there be a key in the door what ya can use to lock it!' She walked over to where they stood and removed the large brass key from the stout oak door and handed it to Titty Smart. 'Yer welcome to me best brandy and the warmth o' me 'earth, but ya ain't welcome wif yer manacles in me tavern!' She pointed at Ikey. 'Mr Solomon 'ere be me right good friend what's me guest. I'll thank ya kindly to remove them pig's bangles from 'is wrists or ya can fuck orf right now!'

As she spoke the boy who'd earlier been sent to waken Marybelle came to the door followed by the coachman. The lad carried a cask of brandy and waited as Ikey and company moved further into the small room before he pushed past them and seated the small barrel of brandy carefully in a cradle placed on a carved oak dresser. On the shelf above the barrel were several rows of pewter mugs.

'Well?' Marybelle asked. 'What's it to be?' She moved over to the cask and taking a pewter tankard from the shelf above it placed it under the spout and allowed just a splash of the golden brown liquid into the tankard. Then she walked over to the fire and removed the mulling iron which she plunged into the interior of the tankard. Immediately a ribbon of flame leapt from the tankard almost to the height of the heavy oaken man-telpiece and the room was filled with the inviting fumes of good French cognac.

The effect on Titty Smart's nose was too much to bear and he reached into his pocket and quickly unlocked the manacle attached to Ikey's wrist and thereafter his own. His partner, perhaps not quite as taken with the need of strong drink and pyrotechnics, hesitated a little longer.

'Just the one, lad!' Smart grunted. 'Just the one for keeping us alert an' all.'

'It ain't regular,' Popjoy muttered, though in an undertone. 'There's regulations.'

Titty Smart glared at his partner. 'We ain't be paid for this escort, this ain't our shift, we be nights, not day, this be our own time what the bastards 'ave robbed from us, you can stuff yer regulations up yer arse, lad!'

Before his young partner could protest further Ikey interjected, clucking the two men to silence. 'What the 'ead keeper don't see 'e don't 'ave to grieve about, now does 'e?' He rubbed his left wrist with his right hand, deliberately pulling Popjoy's arm across with him in order to do so. Then he pointed to the parlour door which still stood ajar and grinned. 'Better lock the door 'case I takes a runner!'

Albert Popjoy, shaking his head in silent disapproval, unlocked the manacle on Ikey's wrist while leaving the one on his wrist. Titty Smart walked over to the parlour door, locked it, and placed the key in his pocket.

Marybelle pointed to the manacles dangling from the wrist of Albert Popjoy and laughed. 'Don't look cosy, knows what I mean? Official. We don't go much on duty 'ere.' She cocked her head to one side and grinned at the younger turnkey. Albert Popjoy, embarrassed at the attention, took the key from his pocket and unlocked the manacle around his wrist, placing the set within his coat pocket. 'That's it, lads, nice 'n cosy, take a pew, make y'selfs at 'ome.' She looked at the coachman. 'You too,' then she took up four pewter tankards and turned again to the now seated men, arched her eyebrows and nodded her head in the direction of the cask. 'A drop o' me very best brandy for all, is it then, gentlemen?'

It came as some surprise when no more than twenty minutes later, the mulled brandy having warmed, refreshed and lighted that small, bright flame that sputters in the stomach until temporarily doused with a second drink, Ikey suggested that they must depart and offered his wrists to the two turnkeys so that they might manacle them once more.

Titty Smart nodded to his partner. 'I told you, just the one and that will do for the manacle too.' The younger man fished into his pocket and produced his set of manacles and attached them once more to Ikey's and then his own wrist.

Ikey felt momentarily triumphant. 'One down, one to go!' he thought. He felt almost free with only one wrist attached to Albert Popjoy.

Marybelle Firkin saw them to the back door and placed her hands on Ikey's shoulders. 'Cheerio, lovey,' she said and Ikey was surprised to see the brightness of moisture in her large blue eyes. She paused and grinned, though when she spoke her voice was serious. 'Yer wife told me everyfink, good luck, Ikey.' Then she turned to Smart and Popjoy, ignoring the coachman who had taken his brandy but had said no single word except to nod his thanks while he had been in the parlour. 'Always welcome, I'm sure,' she said to the two turnkeys.

She stood at the door, her red dressing gown once again filling its entire space, her pretty head almost touching the lintel. 'Come back soon, gents!' she called at the departing hackney.

To Ikey's surprise, Titty Smart licked his lips and rolled his eyes. 'Ooh, ah! I'd like to be up to a bit o' fancy 'anky panky with the likes of 'er, I would an' all!'

He turned to Ikey and added, 'That be damned good Frenchy brandy, just like what you said.'

Albert Popjoy looked out of the window of the carriage and smiled in a supercilious manner, which Smart must have observed, for he turned to his partner and barked, 'Wipe that smile orf yer gob, lad. Lady like that be much too good for the likes o' yer poxy little prick!'

They arrived at the courts in Westminster with a good twenty minutes to spare. 'Would you wish me to wait, guv?' the coachman asked. 'It ain't much point in this weather toutin' for a fare. I could drive you back afterwards, no trouble and no extra fare charged, 'cept o' course for the run back and a sixpenny bag of oats for me 'orse while we's waiting.'

Ikey nodded his agreement and the three men entered the precincts of the court to be met at the steps leading into the Westminster courts by Hannah and several of Ikey's associates, most of whom were Jews from the Whitechapel markets, Petticoat and Rosemary Lanes. Their attendance was less a show of loyalty than a favour returned for a similar attendance by Ikey and Hannah at some past occasion when each of those present had faced an indictment. This was because of the well-established fact that, should a Jew be in the dock, the likelihood of a conviction was near five times that of any other Londoner. It became therefore the custom to try to fill the court with 'sympathetic voices' so that the mood of the rabble in the gallery would not influence the judgment.

In Ikey's present predicament this was of overwhelming importance, the fear being, that if news of his application for bail should spread, the court would soon be filled with the rabble from the streets howling for his blood and the judge, sensitive to the animosity of the public at large, might think it safer for all concerned for Ikey to remain behind bars until his trial came up.

But when the time came for Ikey's hearing to be called the clerk of the court informed Titty Smart that the judge was in his chambers. He said there would be a delay of at least an hour, taking the hearing almost to the noon hour. The man, his lips pursed, had consulted his watch, whereupon he had shaken his head. 'No time, gentlemen, at noon his worship takes luncheon at the Athenaeum Club, he'll not return until two o'clock at best!' This meant that Ikey's writ of *habeas corpus* would therefore not be served until the early part of that afternoon.

Ikey suggested that he stand his two keepers a good tightener at a local chop house and requested that his friends be allowed to accompany them.

'I could go a good tightener and a jug o' best ale,' Titty Smart agreed, patting his large stomach without his mandatory show of reluctance. His attitude to Ikey had considerably softened following the time spent at the Pig 'n Spit and now he turned to Albert Popjoy. 'Drop o' fodder can't 'urt, now can it, lad?'

Popjoy nodded. He too was hungry and the idea of a plate of meat – mutton chops surrounded by a generous collar of yellow fat – was a most enticing prospect. It was difficult for him to maintain his official demeanour and not show his pleasure at the anticipation of such an unexpected treat.

'That be fine,' he said in a brusque voice, though he was salivating at the thought of the tightener to come at Ikey's expense.

'My pleasure, entirely, gents,' Ikey said with great alacrity.

Hannah, who stood close to her husband, shook her head. ''Ang on a mo'! We go into a chop 'ouse round these parts, in fact, any parts, there's plenty what will want to do Ikey an 'arm!'

A look of mutual disappointment crossed the faces of the two turnkeys, although Ikey could scarcely believe his luck. 'Gentlemen, what's to worry? Mistress Marybelle will welcome us back to the Pig! There be a dozen chop 'ouses in Rosemary Lane what can send in a banquet to suit the fancy o' the most particular appetite.' He spread his arms wide. 'What it is my great pleasure to satisfy.'

The matter was quickly settled and fifteen minutes later the three men arrived back at the Pig 'n Spit followed shortly afterwards by two hackney coaches containing the six others eager to avail themselves of Ikey's generosity. Hannah, though, protested to Ikey that she would follow a little later as young Mark had a bad cough and she must fetch some physic for him before joining them.

The fog had lifted somewhat, but the ever present miasma at rooftop level and the winter smog kept the day sombre and the visibility low. Therefore none but Ikey noted the outline of a gentleman's coach with four horses which had followed them and now passed them as they turned into the rear of the Pig 'n Spit. Nor would they have seen that it too came to a halt only a few yards further along the road.

Marybelle, now dressed, welcomed them with the same equanimity as on the earlier occasion. Upon entering the parlour Titty Smart, observing Marybelle's previous demand, had unmanacled Ikey and Popjoy had done likewise. Waiting for the other guests to enter the room, the older of the turnkeys once again locked the door and dropped the key into his coat pocket.

The parlour, if they should stand in a rather close-packed manner, was only just large enough to accommodate them all. In fact, the near proximity of Ikey's guests to each other, the warmth of the excellent fire in the hearth and the dispensing of generous quantities of Marybelle Firkin's best brandy coupled with her friendly banter added greatly to the jollity of the occasion. Ikey's two keepers were soon as loquacious as any in the room as they continued to imbibe the excellent brandy. But their stomachs were empty of food as Marybelle had delayed, by an hour, its delivery from a nearby chop house.

At last the food arrived and at the same time Hannah appeared. Titty Smart, Ikey noted, had with some difficulty inserted the key into the lock, to allow the trays to be brought into the room. Two large trays of chops, aproned with deliciously crisped fat and at least a dozen plump whole carcases of spatchcock stuffed with chestnuts together with mounds of golden roasted potatoes were hoisted above the heads of the guests and placed upon the dresser. Ikey watched again as the older turnkey made several unsuccessful thrusts at the lock before pausing to carefully place his tankard of brandy on the floor between his legs. Then with the key held in both hands, and squinting fiercely at the key hole, he finally managed to lock the door.

The smell of the roasted meat appeared to have much the same effect on Titty Smart as had been the case earlier with the flaming brandy fumes. Forgetting the half-filled tankard on the floor between his legs he kicked it over as he rudely pushed his way through the throng towards the trays of steaming food. As he passed, Ikey simply dipped his hand into the turnkey's coat pocket, and in a foolishly simple example of the art of tooling retrieved the key to the door.

While a mood of genial drunkenness overtook the room, Ikey retained a completely sober disposition. Marybelle pretended to frequently fill his pewter but, instead, merely splashed a lick of cognac into the bottom of his tankard, which was not sufficient to cause a comfortable night's sleep to a teething infant.

Ikey measured the cacophony of the room. It was, after all, filled with people who were easily inclined towards talking over each other in a manner seldom confidential, and when it seemed all were shouting and none were listening, he prepared to make his move. First he checked the whereabouts of Albert Popjoy and found him pinned to the wall by two *shmatter* traders from the Lane both battering him with expostulating words too mixed in the general banter to hear. Popjoy's eyelids seemed heavy with fatigue and he appeared to find it difficult to focus on the two men. Ikey moved towards the door and carefully unlocked it, whereupon he slipped quickly through to the other side, closed the door quietly and locked it again, placing the key above the lintel.

He made his way down the passage to the back of the Pig 'n Spit and was about to step into the courtyard when the cellarman's apprentice made an appearance.

'Me shillin'? You promised us a shillin', Mr Ikey.'

Ikey looked behind him in a panic, but he and the boy were alone. He fished into his coat for his dumby and from the purse produced two single shillings. Ikey dropped one of the shillings into the lad's hand and held the other up between forefinger and thumb and whispered urgently, 'There, a deuce hog, one for the promise and t'other for not seein' nothin' what's happenin' in front of your eyes at this very moment. Does you understand, my boy?'

The boy nodded and Ikey dropped the second shilling into his dirty hand and scuttled across the yard to the street entrance. In a matter of moments he was beside the coach where Moses Julian, who had followed them from the courts, had been waiting for him.

'Quick, Moses, be orf!' he said in a loud whisper, clambering into the carriage. 'To the 'ouse o' Reuban Reuban.'

Chapter Fifteen

On Ikey's arrival at the lodgings of the actor and his tailor son there was soon a frenzy of activity as Reuban Reuban clipped and trimmed Ikey's hair until it was short and much to the latest fashion, brushed close and forward to the forehead. Then he trimmed the sideburns in the shorter vogue allowing an inch or more between the side whiskers and the commencement of the beard, which he then clipped short and close to the face. With expert hands he shaved the remaining whiskers from Ikey's face and completely removed his moustache. The result was such a transformation of appearance that Hannah herself would have had great difficulty recognising her husband. Ikey had shed fifteen years in age and his appearance was of a man of handsome demeanour. His looks, occasioned by the wildness of his hair, scraggy beard and length of the nose which rose from his hirsute face like a mountain peak above the forest line, now looked well proportioned and passed well for that of an upper-class English gentleman.

It was Abraham who was next to work upon the transformation of Ikey. He stripped him quickly, though Ikey whimpered at the removal of his beloved coat, until Ikey stood stark naked, his only adornment a chain to which was attached a small medallion of gold which hung about his neck. Commencing with woollen long johns, piece by piece Abraham refurbished him from his under garments to a fine frock coat until his subject stood before him square rigged and every inch the prosperous City gentleman. Ikey, shown his new visage in a mirror, came near to fainting from the shock of witnessing the remarkable re-creation of his personage. Abraham's final act of sartorial brilliance was to produce a top hat and silver-topped malacca cane. Carefully brushing the nap of beaver fur with the elbow of his coat, he placed the hat upon Ikey's head, whereupon he handed him an elegant pair of pigskin gloves and the cane.

'Blimey! You looks a proper toff, Uncle Isaac!' Abraham exclaimed, well pleased with his work. 'You could pass for the Guv'ner o' the Bank o' England, walk right through the door, you could, no questions asked!' He turned and shouted to Reuban Reuban who, shortly after having trimmed and shaved Ikey, had departed to another room. 'Come see, father!'

'Me coat, where's me coat?' Ikey called out in alarm.

'Your coat? Why it be upon your back, Uncle Isaac!' Abraham's expression changed and showed sudden consternation. 'You'll not be wearing *that* coat?' He pointed to the greasy heap upon the floor. 'That'd be dead give away, that would an' all!'

' 'Ang it up! 'Ang it up!' Ikey commanded in an agitated voice, dancing from one foot to the other in his shiny black gentleman's boots.

Abraham looked momentarily confused, but then hastily took the coat hanger from which had hung the frock coat Ikey now wore, fitted the collar of Ikey's coat about it and suspended it from a hook behind the door.

'Now leave us, if you please!' Ikey said, his composure regained.

Abraham, in somewhat of a sulk, left the room. He was disappointed at Ikey's complete lack of interest in his clever tailoring and the remarkable change he'd brought about to such an unpropitious subject.

Ikey quickly rummaged through his overcoat, putting the contents of all its secret places into the few available pockets in the frock coat. All the bits and pieces that had a known and accustomed place. Cards, promissory notes, pencils of red and blue, string, wire, keys of innumerable configurations, money in small denominations, purses of various sorts containing various amounts, some filled with sixpences, others with shillings. Money in soft and hard, betting slips and receipts for the care of his two little ratters, the terriers he would so sorely miss, a magnifying glass and an eye piece for the assessment of jewellery, spectacles, pincers, pliers, tongs and probes. Each piece filed in its own place was now removed and flung onto a horrendous junk pile within his frock coat pockets, as though they were to be discarded willy-nilly as fuel to a bonfire of Ikey's past.

Finally Ikey took the long cigar-like cylinder containing the letter of credit from the breast pocket of his coat. He folded the letter neatly, added it to several other documents which Reuban Reuban had obtained and placed them in a leather wallet stamped with his monogram in gold on the outside cover. This was yet another small detail prepared by the actor, who had already put a small silver card container beside the wallet which carried the precise cards Ikey had instructed him to print. This too carried the letters I S inscribed upon it.

Whimpering like a newborn puppy, Ikey took leave of his coat. The loss of his beloved coat seemed almost more than Ikey could bear, for his new outfit felt altogether alien to him. It stiffened his joints and rubbed in strange places, so much so that he thought of himself as being not just transformed but as if somehow he had sloughed his old body, and mysteriously come upon a new one. One moment he was Ikey Solomon and then, with a little trimming, shaving and the application of new linen and half a bolt of suiting, he had been created into some curious unknown personage.

The smell and touch of the new cloth enveloped Ikey's bony body and added to this strange feeling of otherness. He wondered for a moment whether it all might drive him mad, his urgent mission with Coutts & Company quite forgotten as his newly tonsured head was utterly confused.

It was at this precise moment that Ikey saw himself in his old personage walking into the room, with wildly flying grey and gingered hair, scraggly beard and untidy, shaggy brows, his nose rising majestic between two small obsidian eyes looking directly at him. He saw old Ikey reach behind the door and take his beloved coat from its hook and place it upon his thin, angular body. He observed himself at once become stooped, his neck lowering itself tortoise-like into the shiny collar of the coat. His chin came to rest upon his breast, and, most remarkably, how, with all this doing, a sly, furtive expression had crept upon his former face.

Suddenly his nephew appeared in the doorway, a rude intrusion standing directly behind the vision.

Abraham placed a flat-topped, broad-brimmed hat upon the apparition's head identical to the one Bob Marley had discarded at the Academy of Light Fingers. Ikey now observed himself standing in front of himself so completely that he pushed the fingers of both hands deep into his mouth. The astonishing manifestation before him was a more perfect likeness of himself than he knew himself to be.

'Not the fingers, Uncle Ikey! No gentleman swallows 'is fingers,' Abraham cried.

'What say you, Ikey?' Reuban Reuban asked. 'Do I well fit your personage? Is the likeness true, my dear?' His voice was thin and carping in the exact timbre of Ikey's own and his hands imitated perfectly the other's mannerisms.

It was not a moment more than half an hour later when Moses Julian, dressed in the expensive livery of a private house and accompanied by Abraham, similarly dressed as a footman, drew their carriage to a halt in a lane leading directly into the Strand. Inside sat Ikey and his remarkable likeness to his former self, Reuban Reuban, who touched Ikey's knee in a quick salute and slipped out of the coach even before it had completely come to a halt. Whereupon Moses urged the horses on and the coach moved away and soon enough came to the end of the lane and turned into the Strand.

The afternoon was already beginning to darken from the smog and the general effects of the fog so that the thronging humanity who moved along the crowded sidewalk were of a mind much occupied with their own progress in the failing light, so took no interest in the Jew as he made his way among them.

Nor, within a moment of turning into the Strand,

could the coach have been recognised in the numerousness of similar carriages and coaches and hackneys that jammed and pushed their way along the great choked thoroughfare where they were yet further hidden by the smoke from the flares that ostensibly guided their way.

Abraham had the previous morning posted himself outside the bank to observe the protocol of a gentleman's manner of entering the premises. Thus he observed that, alighting from his coach, a person of quality would be greeted by the doorman, who would summon an usher from the interior of the bank. This bank officer, in all appearance a man of some mature age and authority, dressed in a frock coat and square rigged in the best of form, would immediately appear armed with a small silver salver which he would proffer in an obsequious manner while requesting the gentleman's personal card be placed upon it. At this point, of course, the doors were once again closed and Abraham had no way of knowing the manner of the client's further progress within the august establishment.

Abraham had returned home by way of Newgate Gaol, where he had informed Ikey of the manner of obtaining entry to the bank and Ikey had instructed him in the exact manner of the cards he required Reuban Reuban to have printed for the occasion.

It was just before the hour of two o'clock in the afternoon and the more important officers of the bank were returning to work from luncheon at their club when Ikey's carriage approached Coutts & Company on the Strand.

Abraham looked to see whether Reuban Reuban had arrived on foot. When he spotted him standing close to the wall of the bank, half concealed behind a Doric column, he tapped the roof of the carriage to tell Ikey that all was in order, and waited for Ikey's return tap to tell him to signal to Reuban Reuban to proceed. The two return taps came promptly and Abraham signalled to his father to proceed by appearing to rub an itchy nose and then smacking his gloved hands together as though against the cold.

Reuban Reuban commenced to walk boldly up the steps of the bank to where the doorman waited. Though boldly is perhaps an exaggerated description for he walked in the manner of Ikey, which none could even in their wildest imagination call bold. Ikey, watching from the interior of the carriage, saw the doorman stiffen slightly as Reuban Reuban drew nearer. Ikey, his instincts sharpened by a lifetime of experience with the mannerisms of a policeman, knew at once that he was a member of the constabulary. In as much as it was possible from the interior of the carriage he looked about to see if there were others, but could see no suspicious characters who might be miltonians, that is to say, policemen out of their official uniform.

Reuban Reuban halted beside the doorman and while Ikey could not hear what he said the doorman allowed that he should enter without apparently requesting his personal card or summoning an usher or in any manner following the form which Abraham had so carefully observed the previous morning. The door opened and Reuban Reuban disappeared into the interior of the building followed closely by the doorman. A few moments passed and a new doorman was seen to take the place of the old one, a man who stood more easily and assumed more naturally the accustomed nature of his task.

The interior of the bank comprised a large central hallway which at first seemed entirely composed of marble, with huge pillars of the same material supporting two storeys of gallery above which the offices of the partners were located and where the clerks worked at their ledgers. At one end of the impressive hallway were a set of brass tellers' cages and a stairway leading downwards, presumably to the underground vaults. At the other end was a similar stairway, though this one led upstairs to the galleries and carried a heavy banister of gleaming brass and was carpeted in brilliant red. Brass rods secured the carpet to the hinge of each step and they too shone with a brightness which gave the effect of a pathway leading heavenwards to untold wealth.

Reuban Reuban barely had time to take all of this in when he was accosted by an officer of the bank whose quick, sharp steps tapped out on the marble floor showed him to be most purposeful in his confrontation. Reuban Reuban was also aware that the doorman had remained and stood directly behind him as though to block any retreat he might contemplate. Several other men seemed now to have mysteriously emerged from behind the marble columns and were seen to be pacing the polished marble floor, although no work of banking seemed to be taking place in his immediate vicinity.

'Good day to you, sir,' the bank officer greeted Reuban Reuban. 'May I be of service?'

Reuban Reuban smiled unctuously and shrugged his shoulders in an admirable imitation of Ikey. 'Some other time maybe. I 'ave just remembered, uh . . . all of a sudden, if you knows what I mean. With the greatest respect to yourself, sir, I 'ave urgent business I must complete elsewhere!' Reuban Reuban turned towards the door again, only to see several of the men who had but a moment ago been contemplating their own business converge on him. He started to run towards the door but in a moment was grabbed from behind. It took only a few moments longer for several of the men to reach him and he was thrown roughly to the floor where he was quickly manacled by the doorman.

Reuban Reuban was pulled to his feet and immediately observed a small man with a very large red nose wearing a top hat exceedingly tall for the remainder of his size, approaching him.

'Ikey Solomons, in the name of the law, I arrest you,' Sir Jasper Waterlow shouted, so that his voice echoed through the hall and up into the galleries.

As they led Reuban Reuban away the galleries overlooking the entrance hall were soon filled with clerks and bankers observing the dramatic arrest. Even the partners had emerged from their offices to share in the excitement.

Sir Jasper Waterlow, not wishing to let the auspicious moment pass without some show on behalf of the Bank of England and his own future prospects, had deliberately shouted his orders of arrest at the uppermost tone of his voice so that all within the Coutts & Company bank might witness his triumph over Britain's most notorious villain and know that the Bank of England, like God, is not mocked.

Indeed, Sir Jasper Waterlow had just reason to congratulate himself. He had only a matter of some two hours to prepare his entrapment of Ikey. Hannah had informed him of the possibility of Ikey's escape that very morning, after Ikey had left the King's Bench courts upon the postponement of his hearing. By pre-arrangement she had met Sir Jasper in a coffee house on the Strand and acquainted him of Ikey's intended escape and his need to visit the premises of a certain bank, though she did not inform him of the name of the establishment until she had extracted in writing from Sir Jasper certain assurances and conditions. The first of these was that Ikey should be allowed to visit the bank and transact his business and that he would be arrested only on his way out. The second was that regardless of the outcome of Ikey's trial for forgery, he receive a sentence of transportation for his attempt to escape from custody.

Sir Jasper had no choice but to accept. The sentence Hannah had asked for was more or less a foregone conclusion and so presented no barriers. Furthermore, an arrest made after they had Ikey trapped within the confines of a building which could be easily surrounded, with additional men also placed within its interior, seemed much the better method of operation. Therefore, he issued Hannah with the written assurances she required. He told himself that she had previously delivered Ikey, as she had promised, with the counterfeit notes planted on his person. Now, when he might well have successfully escaped, she was once again informing on her husband. He therefore had no reason but to accept her information as genuine.

Sir Jasper told himself that whatever Ikey's business with Coutts & Company, it could hardly be the concern of the Bank of England. He had therefore given the chairman of Coutts & Company permission to process the transaction. This had occurred in a hastily contrived briefing when he had arrived at the bank with twenty City policemen in plain clothes. The senior bank officers were to allow Ikey to enter the premises and to afford him the normal protocol involved in making a transaction. Sir Jasper insisted that refusal by the bank to comply with this instruction would only be permitted if the transaction Ikey Solomon required was not a legitimate request for the bank's services, or would in some way threaten or undermine the safety or finances of Coutts & Company or of the Bank of England itself.

To ensure that the staff would go about their business in a normal manner Sir Jasper requested that one of his policemen, dressed in the uniform of a doorman of the bank, should replace the doorman on duty and that the doorman, along with the remainder of the bank's staff, be told nothing, other than that he should resume his normal duty when the policeman at the door was seen to escort Ikey into the interior of the bank.

The arrangements had all been finalised in great haste and Sir Jasper had no opportunity to consult the directors of the Bank of England. He was well aware that his instructions to Coutts & Company might have been beyond his authority as chief City policeman and Upper Marshal of London. With Ikey's sudden and most fortuitous panic and resultant attempt to escape the premises of the bank, Sir Jasper had even more reason to be pleased with himself. There would now be no awkward official enquiries as to why Ikey, upon visiting the illustrious private bank, had been allowed to make a transaction which, in every likelihood, resulted in remuneration to him as a consequence of a crime against the people. He had fully met Hannah's requirements, both as a gentleman and a police officer, and it had cost him no compromise with the law.

Moreover, there was much talk in parliament by the supporters of Sir Robert Peel of the organisation of a new police force, and Sir Jasper could see his candidacy for the position of its head much improved by both the first and second arrests of Ikey Solomon.

Ikey watched from the carriage as Reuban Reuban was led out of the bank manacled and surrounded by a dozen police officers out of uniform. A black maria, that is to say, a horse van drawn by two well-conditioned horses and built in the manner of a closed box with a door at the rear and no windows excepting narrow ventilation slits, appeared from the alley beside the building. Reuban Reuban was unceremoniously bundled into the back of it, whereupon the door was locked and three of the policemen mounted the platform protruding from the back of the van to further guard the villain residing within.

The crowd had halted and immediately formed around the van and on the steps of the bank and someone shouted, 'It be 'im, Ikey Solomon, the Jew forger!'

Almost at once the crowd grew angry and converged on the black maria. Despite the plain-clothes policemen who attempted to protect the van, part of the crowd pushed past and beat their fists against and commenced to rock the black maria, threatening to overturn it, so that the horses grew restless and began to stamp upon the ground and throw their heads up in alarm. The three men on the platform at its rear were forced to use their truncheons with fierce abandon, raining blows down upon the shoulders and heads of the angry attackers. The crowd had commenced to chant, 'Ikey! Ikey! Ikey!' and the coachman, working his police rattler so that the other coaches in the vicinity might move clear, finally managed to get the horses underway and direct the van into the stream of passing traffic. Though several urchins, skilled in the ways of dodging the traffic, followed the police van, they were quickly discouraged by the three policemen protecting the artful Reuban Reuban within.

Ikey watched until the crowd began to disperse, but with the sidewalk still somewhat crowded, Moses Julian moved Ikey's carriage forward to come to a halt directly outside the bank, whereupon Abraham alighted from the rear of the carriage, opened the door and with some ceremony, took Ikey's elbow in his white-gloved hand and guided him with care to the surface of the cobbled pavement.

Ikey moved quickly up the steps to the doorman, who, as is the nature of his profession, had been alert to his arrival at the moment his coach had pulled up. He had tugged at the lapels of his overcoat and adjusted his gold-braided top hat, conscious of the well-polished carriage and the livery of its retainers, and was therefore hardly surprised at the conservative, well-dressed gentleman who stepped from it onto the sidewalk.

'Good afternoon, sir!' he had offered in a manner akin to the military and which suggested both efficiency and respect, saluting Ikey.

Ikey grunted, though it was a well-modulated and upper-class grunt. 'Foreign transactions?' he asked, in a clipped and imperious voice.

'I shall call you an usher at once, sir.' The doorman opened the door, lifted his hand and crooked a finger to denote a requirement from someone within, where-upon he further opened it for Ikey to pass through.

It had all occurred just as Abraham had suggested and was quite unlike the reception Reuban Reuban had

320

received. Ikey breathed a silent sigh of relief; the bank, it seemed, had assumed its normal routine. It felt like his lucky day.

Nathaniel Wilson, Coutts & Company's foreign transactions officer, had spent the morning with the ambassador from Chile, who had wanted to discuss the final interest rate for the public issue of a loan for his government, a part of which was being underwritten by the bank. The ambassador had plied him with glasses of an atrocious sherry he claimed was the pride and joy of the pampas and Wilson, who had finally departed to take luncheon alone at his club, in an attempt to be rid of the taste of bad sherry had imbibed rather too generously of a bottle of excellent burgundy, and followed it with two glasses of vintage port. The wine had left him thoroughly disgruntled and a little inebriated. The ambassador had demanded a shaving of one-tenth of one per cent of interest off the loan and towards the end had stamped his feet and brought his fist down several times hard upon the table and behaved in an altogether inappropriate manner. Wilson did not find foreigners in the least agreeable. Furthermore, he was not looking forward to facing the bank's senior partners with the Chilean ambassador's demand. He had returned only a few minutes after Reuban Reuban had been taken away in the police van and, as was his usual custom, entered the building through a private entrance to the side of the bank. He had repaired directly to his office on the first gallery, taking the back stairs used by the staff, and was therefore quite unaware of the excitement which had taken place in the bank before his return.

The usher knocked on Nathaniel Wilson's door, the two rapid knocks required to indicate a bank employee of inferior status to the occupant.

'Come!' the banker called.

Wilson looked up as the elderly usher opened the door and observed that he was carrying a salver.

'What is it, Coote?' he said with annoyance. 'I was not aware of any appointment at this hour.'

'No, sir, gentleman says he's from Germany.' Coote placed the salver containing Ikey's card on the desk. 'He requests an urgent interview, sir.'

Wilson reached for the card with obvious distaste. Ikey's card was well printed on expensive board and, in the manner of a man confident of his position in life, it contained no detail other than a name and address.

Herr Isak Solomon
114 Bunders Kerk Strasse, Hambourg

Nathaniel Wilson looked up at Coote. 'German Jew?'

'No, sir, English. Well spoken, proper gentleman.'

Nathaniel Wilson threw Ikey's card back into the tray. 'You will inform Mr Isak Solomon that I shall see him, but that I regret it must be a short interview as his appointment comes as an unexpected but not entirely convenient pleasure.'

Coote returned shortly with Ikey and Nathaniel Wilson rose from behind his desk to greet him. 'Ah, Mr Solomon, are you aware that the name Solomon has much been in the news lately?' He offered his hand to Ikey. 'Indeed a coincidence, what?'

Ikey removed his pigskin gloves, then his top hat and placed the gloves within the interior of the hat and gave it to Coote together with his cane, deliberately keeping the banker waiting. 'Oh? And why is that, Mr Wilson?' he replied in an incurious voice as he moved forward and finally took Wilson's hand, barely touching it before releasing it again.

'Ikey Solomon, or is it Solomons? Notorious forger chap. Arrested several days ago for counterfeiting, it seems he got away with a fortune in sham Bank of England notes, devil of a mess, what?' Wilson concluded.

'Really?' said Ikey in bored tones. 'I've been abroad, you see. Now, I am aware you do not have much time, so I shall be brief. I wish to lodge a letter of credit with you from the Birmingham City and Country Bank and require you to transfer these funds to the First Manhattan Bank on New York Island.' Ikey withdrew an expensive leather folder from the interior pocket of his frock coat and placed it on the desk in front of him.

Nathaniel Wilson opened the leather folder and quickly examined the documentation, his eyes seeking the letter of credit. He was immediately struck by the large amount of money involved. His time would not be wasted, as the bank's commission from the transfer transaction would be considerable. It was therefore in a much more respectful manner that he conducted the remainder of the negotiations and verifications.

Not more than twenty minutes later, with the Coutts & Company certificate of deposit safely in the folder, and with effusive assurances from the banker of the utmost of service available at any future occasion, Ikey was escorted by Coote down the red-carpeted stairway with its brass banister, across the hall of polished marble, through the imposing doors and down the steps to where Abraham and Moses Julian waited beside the carriage. Ikey paused as Abraham held open the carriage door for him and handed Coote a sovereign.

'Good day to you, Coote,' he said in his newly acquired accent.

'Bless you, sir,' the old man replied warmly. 'It's been a pleasure.'

The notorious luck of Ikey Solomon had once again held. With a pinch more, a *soupçon* of the same, he was on his way to America.

In his mind there formed yet another conclusion which he was most hard put to ignore any longer.

It was Hannah who, on both occasions, had betrayed him.

The thought of Hannah's betrayal brought Mary to Ikey's mind, Mary who had not betrayed him when she could have turned King's evidence and given witness most damaging to his case and, by so doing, spared herself the boat.

Ikey now felt a rare and genuine pang of conscience within his breast. Mary was in Newgate, incarcerated in a dungeon cage with a dozen other foul wretches and he had made no attempt to acknowledge her presence. This sharp stab of guilt almost immediately transformed itself into a surprising softness of feeling for Mary. It was an emotion not altogether different to the crisis of feeling which had overcome him in the coach to Birmingham. Ikey wondered in some panic whether there was a connection between the interior of coaches and his soft-headedness, for he was possessed suddenly by a compelling need to send fifty pounds to Mary so she might ameliorate the rigours of her transportation and be supplied with the necessities required on the troublesome and dangerous voyage to Van Diemen's Land. He would urge Abraham to seek her out in Newgate, acquaint her of his good wishes and give her the money as a token of his great esteem.

Ikey was uncertain as to whether this generosity came about because of the tender feeling for Mary which had come so overwhelmingly and unexpectedly upon him, or whether he wished only to ensure the continuance of his luck by putting right his bad conscience towards her. He knew only that he felt compelled to comply with this strange dictate which otherwise made no sense to his head and yet seemed so powerful to his heart. He told himself, though to no avail, that he was being foolishly generous with a gesture which could show him no future profit as he would not, in the further course of this life, see Mary again.

This last thought left Ikey in a surprisingly melancholy mood, for he realised how the routine of his life had been brought undone and how much a sustaining and pleasant part of it Mary had become.

This further onrush of sentiment led to an even more surprising gesture than the money Ikey told himself he had effectively thrown away. In fact, so foolish was the new thought that he feared some mischievous *golem* had possessed him. Around his neck he wore a gold chain from which was suspended, in the exact size and weight of gold in a sovereign, a medallion which commemorated the battle of Waterloo, and which carried a likeness of the Duke of Wellington on one side and a crescent of laurel leaves on the other. Nestled in the centre of this leafy tribute, fashioned in a small pyramid of words, was inscribed:

I
Shall
Never
Surrender

Ikey, shortly after his release from the hulk in Chatham and while working with his uncle, a slops dealer, that is to say a dealer in workmen's and sailor's clothes, had won the gold medallion at a game of cribbage from a sergeant in the Marines. It had been won fair and square and also while Ikey was legitimately employed, a conjunction of events which was never to occur again in his life, and so the medallion was a significant memento and had come to assume an importance to him. He always wore it under his woollen vest, where the warmth of its gold lay against his scrawny chest unseen by any other. Like the tattoo of the two blue doves on his arm, which, as a young man, had signified his secret and now entirely forsaken hope that one day he might find his one and only true love, the Wellington medallion was his special talisman.

At each narrow escape from the law or at the hands of the various people who would harm him, he had come to think of it more and more as the reason for his luck. Now he decided that if his luck should hold to the point when later that very night he would slip aboard a cargo vessel bound on the rising tide for Denmark, Mary should have his Wellington medallion.

Ikey, having determined this course of action, tapped on the roof for the coach to come to a halt, whereupon he bade Abraham come and sit beside him in the interior. As the coach moved on towards the docks he told Abraham in great detail what he was to do and say to Mary, his speech punctuated with a sentimentality Abraham had not thought possible in the man he knew Ikey to be. Ikey then took the medallion from about his neck and handed it, together with fifty pounds, to the young tailor to deliver to Mary.

In truth, it must be supposed that the concerns of the past few hours had greatly affected Ikey's mental state, for at the moment of this decision, if he had paused to consult his head and not pandered to the susceptibility of his heart, it would have declared him insane.

Ikey was giving Mary his luck.

Chapter Sixteen

Mary had been cast into a communal cell in Newgate to await her sentencing. Charged before a magistrate for running a bawdy house and with moral corruption, she was bound over in Newgate to await trial at the Old Bailey.

She had good reason to hope that her sentence might be a lenient one. Prostitution and earning a living off prostitutes did not generally earn the penalty of transportation. Indeed one might venture to say that 'moral corruption' was a fair description of the institution of the State itself.

The hard times which followed the Peninsular War against Napoleon, the effects of factory-produced cotton from Manchester on the wool and silkweaving cottage industries, and the migration of the Irish to England during the famines, created untold misery in the rural population. Their desperate migration in search of work caused calamity in the cities and, in particular, London, where among the poor prostitution, though not officially stated as such, was looked upon as a legitimate occupation for women who would otherwise be destitute, reduced to the workhouse or left to starve.

Mary had every reason to feel confident that she would receive perhaps as little as three months and no more than twelve months. Prior to her trial she had been approached by a City police officer to turn King's evidence against Ikey. But she had not implicated him, insisting that their relationship had been one of great circumspection and that he was merely her landlord.

Mary had invested ten pounds of her limited resources on a lawyer and hoped that the judge would see through the hypocrisy of her arrest, or, in any event, judge her most leniently. The lawyer, too, was confident and assured her of a speedy trial with, at most, a short sentence.

'Why, my dear, there is every chance that the judge has himself enjoyed the tender ministrations of your young ladies and behind his worship's wig and po-faced visage he bears you nothing but goodwill!' He was pleased that so simple a case to plead had earned him so generous a fee, for had Mary claimed hardship, he would happily have taken a case so free of conjecture for half the amount she had paid him.

It was therefore a shock beyond any imagining when Mary, arraigned before a judge she did not recognise at the Old Bailey, listened in increasing consternation to the clerk of the court. He, having read the original indictment, paused and informed the judge that the prosecution wished to add a further two charges, requesting the court's permission to do so. The judge agreed to add a further two counts and issued the warrant returnable immediately.

Mary listened in horror while the new charges were read out: 'That the accused had wilfully and maliciously killed the pet cat of Miss Maude Smith, nanny to the house of Sir James Barker of the King's Road, Chelsea. Furthermore, and in the second indictment, that she did steal a book, to wit, *Gulliver's Travels*, loaned to her through the negotiations of Thomas Bishop, the butler to Sir James, who had sought the co-operation of his master to make his private library available to the accused.'

Mary's lawyer immediately entered a plea asking that the two additional charges be set aside for a later hearing, pointing out that his client had not been apprehended for either supposed crime.

The prosecution then presented a warrant for Mary's arrest and the judge agreed that it be served on her within his court, whereupon he ruled that both new charges could be included with the original indictments and that they could be heard concurrently.

In discovering the details of Mary's background Sir Jasper Waterlow had proved himself a clever detective. At the same time he had met Hannah's conditions without the need for complicity with a member of the bench. While the charge of running a bawdy house was unlikely to receive a sentence of transportation, this was not the case with the new charges.

It was during the hearing of the second set of indictments that Mary's life came suddenly and irrevocably unstuck. Despite her desperate pleas from the dock that she had not put a hand on the ageing, nose dripping, fur shedding, pissing, fur ball vomiting Waterloo Smith and, furthermore, that the book, *Gulliver's Travels*, had been a parting gift from Thomas Bishop himself, it soon became obvious that she had no hope of being believed by the court. Both Nanny Smith and Thomas Bishop appeared as witnesses for the Crown, and while Nanny

Smith was triumphant in her testimony, Bishop spoke quietly with downcast eyes throughout the hearing.

Whether the judge was a cat lover or a bibliophile, or both, is not known, but he seemed to be strangely agitated by the evidence he had heard. Before pronouncing sentence he saw fit to deliver, to the increasing delight of a cackling Nanny Smith, a lengthy address on Mary's moral turpitude.

'I find myself unwilling to grant leniency in this case before me, as it strikes at the very heart of civilised behaviour. It is common enough in the assizes to confront a person, a yokel who may have stolen a sheep, or pig or poached game, a fat pheasant or a clutch of partridge eggs, from his master's estate. Heinous as these crimes may be, it can be argued that the poor wretch may have had need of the flesh of these beasts or birds to feed a hungry family. While his be no less a crime in the eyes of the law, it is one which, in some instances, is worthy of our compassion, if not our mercy.'

The judge sniffed and looked about the court, finally allowing his eyes to rest again upon Mary. 'A sheep or a pig or a game bird, though valuable to its owner, is seldom an object of great love unless it be a champion.' He paused and looked about him as though he were delivering his message at the Lord Mayor's Banquet. 'But a cat? A cat is another matter. A cat to its owner can be an unquestioning and loyal friend when no other may exist. That the cat in question, so brutally disposed of in this case, was an object of great love and comfort to its owner is not, for one moment, to be doubted.' He looked across at Mary again. 'You did cold heartedly and with malice aforethought do away with one Waterloo Smith,

331

a cat owned by the plaintiff, Miss Maude Smith.' He wagged an admonishing finger at Mary. 'This court cannot take lightly such a callous and deliberate action to bring about the death of one of God's innocent creatures.' The judge paused and glared at the jury, who had previously found Mary guilty. It was as if he felt that guilty was probably not sufficient, that perhaps they should have pronounced her 'Very guilty' or 'Guilty beyond normal guilt'. He turned again to Mary. 'You have been found guilty and I choose therefore to sentence you in exactly the same way as if you had stolen and killed a prize sheep, or bull, or pig, or poached a brace of pheasants from the country estate of an honest gentleman.'

The judge brought his gavel down as though he were about to pronounce sentence, but, in fact, the judicial hammer was intended to serve only as a punctuation. Warmed to the task of castigation, he now continued:

'As to the second charge against you. You found yourself in a position of great privilege in the home of Sir James Barker who, due to the kind interceding on your behalf of his butler . . . ' The judge paused to look at his notes, 'er . . . Thomas Bishop, it was agreed by Sir James that you should have the full use of his considerable library. In this one magnanimous gesture he was, in effect, opening up to a mere servant girl, if I should not be mistaken a laundry maid, the whole sublime world of literature and learning. It appears that you did not with honesty and a full heart, mindful of the great privilege accorded you, take advantage of this opportunity. On the contrary, in the face of such remarkable generosity, you chose instead . . . ' he paused, searching for the correct words. 'You who have shown intelligence enough to have mastered reading and writing, to plunder this depository of knowledge by stealing from it one of its most precious jewels!'

The judge now brought his gavel down three times and in an even more sonorous voice than he had previously employed picked up his written judgment and commenced to read it.

'Mary Klerk, also known as Mary Abacus, it be therefore ordered and adjudged by this Court, that after having served three months in Newgate Gaol in accordance with the previous judgment of this court, you be transported upon the seas, beyond the seas, to such as His Majesty King George IV, by the advice of his Privy Council, shall see fit to direct and appoint, for the term of seven years!'

The judge's gavel rose up and went down upon its block one last time. The sound of it reverberated around the dusty, close-smelling and largely empty courtroom, and Mary's life was once again plunged into the darkest despair as she was manacled and led from the dock to the public cells, the 'bird cages' in the dungeons of Newgate Gaol. For Mary it was a descent back into hell.

It was her companions, those women with her in the cage, against whom she knew she must needs take the greatest care. There were few who would not tear her eyes out for the promise of a tot of gin and, in their drunken state, when the candles burned down, she would need to constantly defend herself against the groping hands that would possess her. At night, the grunting, panting cries of the fornicating women intensified when the younger women were seduced or raped by the larger 'bull whores' who owned the darkness.

Mary attempted to keep to herself, occupying one small corner of the large cell which contained eleven others. She had been placed with prostitutes who had been caught at various crimes – thieving, drunkenness and destroying public or private property. At the approach of a drunken woman Mary would reveal her blackened talons and snarl. But it soon became apparent that she could not remain separate. In a gaol cell it is the strong who rule and the weak who must be made to submit. The time would come, Mary knew, when she would be subjected to the needs of the strongest in the cage. Mary waited until her fellow inmates were drunk and distracted and then she bribed a turnkey to have a tinsmith visit her.

She instructed him to make four brass rings half an inch in breadth which fitted tightly to the topmost knuckle of the second and third fingers of each hand. Mary then told the tinsmith to fashion from each band a metal talon, sharpened to a point and arched, an inch beyond the extremity of each finger, to give the effect of four vicious nails. The tinsmith delivered them the next day, demanding an extortionate price in return for his speedy workmanship. But he had created weapons for her hands most fearsome to behold and Mary was happy to pay.

Mary attached the lethal hooks to her fingers and saw that they fitted well, then she placed them in the pocket of her pinny. The final meeting with the tinsmith had taken place in the morning before eight of the clock while her cell mates still slept, snoring and blubbering and often shouting in some nightmarish dream, unaware of her newfound protection. She knew that they would soon awaken and scream for water to quench their parched tongues and cool their throbbing brows. She was now ready to make her presence felt.

Mary paid the turnkey twopence for a large bucket of water and a ladle which she placed in the corner beside her. The water was their daily entitlement, an allowance of three gallons for each communal cell. The turnkeys demanded payment for it, although it was intended that it should be free. There was very little that came free in Newgate, and starvation was as much a cause of death within its walls as was gaol fever or brutality. If the twopence was not paid the turnkey would sell the bucket of precious water for a penny to an adjacent cage or, if there was no hope of gain, place it at his feet and piss into it before handing it into the cell.

Mary waited for the first of the women to wake up. It was Ann Gower, who couldn't remember when she hadn't been on the streets. She was probably still in her thirties but the effects of gin and her brutal life had left her looking twenty years older. Two of her front teeth were missing and matted brown hair hung over her eyes, which she was now in the process of knuckling in an attempt to clear her head of the gin she'd swallowed the previous night.

'Water, where's water?' she mumbled, as she stumbled over to the bars of the bird cage. Grabbing them she shouted, 'Bring the fuckin' water!' The shrill sound of her own raised voice caused her to hold her head and groan in agony.

' 'Ere,' Mary said, 'Over 'ere, love.'

Ann Gower turned slowly and looked at Mary through bloodshot eyes. 'You? Little Miss 'Orner what sits in a corner?'

Mary laughed, surprised at the woman's wit considering the state of her health.

'Wotcha fuckin' laughin' at?' the other woman snarled.

Mary, still with a smile on her face, dipped the ladle into the bucket and held it up towards Ann Gower. 'Drink.'

Ann Gower's hands were shaking as she took the large wooden spoon. She brought it unsteadily up to her lips and managed to spill a good portion of it down the front of her dirty pinny and upon the floor. The remainder she drank, slurping greedily. 'More!' she demanded, handing the ladle back to Mary.

'Sorry, love, that be it, there ain't no more.' Mary calmly put the ladle back into the bucket and stood up with one hand behind her back.

'Who says?' Ann Gower advanced menacingly towards Mary.

'I says,' Mary said, keeping her voice calm. 'That be your lot, Ann Gower.'

'I spilled 'arf of it!' Ann shouted.

'That be your problem, love. Next time be more careful.' Mary's voice remained steady and betrayed none of the fear she felt in the pit of her stomach. She was ready when Ann Gower lashed out at her and her hand came swiftly from behind her back, the two brass hooks at the end of her fingers cutting a double streak of crimson straight across the line of Ann Gower's jaw.

'Jesus!' she gasped, clutching at her face in surprise. 'The fuckin' bitch cut me!'

'Don't fuck with me, Ann Gower,' Mary said defiantly.

Ann Gower took one of her hands from her cheek

and saw that it was covered with blood. 'Jesus! I'm bleedin'!'

'Next time it be your eyes.'

'I only wanted some water, wotcha do that for?' Ann Gower whined.

Mary forced a grin. 'Teach you some manners, darlin'.'

Mary was only five feet and two inches and carried no lard and Ann Gower was half as heavy again and at least three inches taller. But the larger woman, her head pulsating, and her cheek burning from the savage cut to her cheek, knew the ways of the street and realised she must make her move now or be beaten. The look in Mary's clear, cold green eyes told her that she had met a formidable opponent.

'You takin' charge, then?' Ann Gower said in a much mollified voice, one hand still clutched on her bleeding face.

'Somethin' like that,' Mary said.

Ann Gower smiled, the gaps in her teeth showing as she appeared to accept. 'Can I 'ave some water then?' she said, looking directly at Mary.

'No!'

Mary's eyes held the other woman's gaze and Ann Gower took two involuntary steps backwards. The fight was over, Mary had won. She had shown she was strong enough, hard enough to win the other woman's respect, or whatever passed for respect among the dispossessed.

Mary had also proved to herself that she had not forgotten the harsh lessons of the street and now indicated the sleeping women in the cell with a jerk of her chin. 'Wake them lot up, will you, tell 'em there's water, show 'em your face, tell 'em there's more where that come from if any should want it.'

Though Mary now controlled the cell she did not try to convert it to better ways. The women became drunk at any opportunity they could get their hands on a quart of gin and the nocturnal couplings continued. But the bullying stopped, the water was equally shared among all, and the cell was cleaned.

She was challenged on several occasions by older women, emboldened by a pint of gin in their bellies. But they stood little chance against her ferocious claws, and soon the rumour grew in Newgate Gaol of Mother Mary Merciless, who sat like a vulture in a corner of the whore cage cleaned of shit and dirt. It was said that she possessed the blackened talons of a great bird of prey and, if one should venture near, great slabs of flesh would be torn off in a single terrible swipe to feed her need for fresh blood and live human flesh.

A report which appeared in the *Newgate Calendar*, itself treated with gross exaggeration, was turned into a scurrilous and wholly lurid pamphlet sold in the streets and at fairs and in the Vauxhall Gardens and which was entitled: *'Mother Mary Merciless, the flesh eating demon of Newgate Gaol!'* It sold ten thousand copies at the full price of a penny ha'penny.

Though her infamous name did nothing but good for her reputation, increasingly Mary came to impress her cell mates with her tongue, sharp eyes and the agility of her mind. They marvelled at the rapidity with which she worked the beads and boasted to the other inmates that she could do any calculation which might come into their minds. The number of days Methuselah had lived, and then the hours and minutes. Or if an ounce of dried peas should contain one hundred peas, how many peas would there be in a two-hundred-pound sack? Though they had no hope of verifying the answers, it was the speed of Mary's fingers as they flew across the wire slides to push the blurring beads this way and that which confounded and fascinated them. With such skill, they reasoned, the answers she gave must be correct. Furthermore, if any should have any unseemly ideas, hands so cruelly tortured which could move so fast were a reminder to them all that the dreaded claws could strike before they had a chance to blink.

They became like small children, enchanted and silent when Mary read to them by the light of the candle from *Gulliver's Travels*. For the much-worn volume, which, in the end, cost her so dear, like her precious abacus had seldom left her side.

Mary also read to them from the Bible. But they were stories of conquests and the persecution of the Israelites and the wonders of the land of Canaan. She did not read to them of Christ's love and salvation, sharing with them the lack of enthusiasm for this particular God of love, and much preferring the one of wrath who practised revenge and waged war in the hurly-burly of the Old Testament.

Mary took to writing petitions for prisoners and preparing their pleas to be read in court, for few could afford the fees of even the most down-at-heel lawyer or screever. She would write letters to the authorities about husbands and the welfare of children of inmates carted off to orphanages. Or she would write to loved ones, this latter in particular for the Irish, who placed great store in the mystical properties of the written word.

While they, and those who received their letters, could neither read nor write, the priest in their parish could, and so the entire parish would know of their love and tenderness. They fervently believed that writing a letter was a divine affair which would bestow good fortune and protection upon those they loved who still lived in the sad and broken places they had fled from in Ireland. A letter of love, they most fervently believed, had the spiritual substance to prevent these same loved ones from suffering the sad fate to befall its sender.

Mary would always begin an Irish letter with the same words, for it was this single opening sentence which inevitably brought those on whose behalf she wrote to swoon with the ecstasy of its poetry.

My dearest beloved,
The prayers of a sincere heart are as acceptable to
God from the dreary Gaol as from the splendid
Palace. The love of a prisoner as pure and sweet
as that of a prince ...

The cost in delivering such a letter to Ireland was prohibitive and would often mean that the sender must sell all that she possessed. But for the comfort it brought her, and the gift of love it was thought to bestow on the receiver, it was thought among the Irish women to be but a pittance to pay.

The inmates, usually the women, would often bring their squabbles to Mary to settle. Her judgments, using the peculiar logic of the criminal, left each with a portion of self-respect, and neither party's guilt confirmed. This would indubitably stop further trouble in the bird cages. When Mary was forced to judge one or another to be guilty this was seen as an exception, and her verdict, with the penalty she imposed, accepted by all and duly carried out.

This did not stop the drunkenness and lechery, the fighting and the cruelty, for these things were as much a part of Newgate as the bricks, and damp, the excremental filth and the gaol fever. But there was observed to be some small measure of calm about the bird cages. Mary was tough and her talons fierce and she was one of their own kind. Hers was a light which had not been dimmed and was a great source of courage to them all.

The most cherished moment of Mary's life came the day Abraham Reuban arrived at Newgate to visit her.

The excitement of Ikey's escape from custody was on everyone's lips that day, the story of his escape having spread like gaol fever among the inmates. The tale of how he had persuaded the two turnkeys to take a coach which had been 'conveniently upon the spot' when it was needed, and how he had persuaded both turnkeys to unlock his manacles and be his guest at the Pig 'n Spit was the cause of great laughter in Newgate. The simple device of picking the pocket of Titty Smart, the fat turnkey, and letting himself out of the door of Marybelle's parlour, leaving the key on the lintel, was told with glee and constantly repeated with not a little admiration for his brazenness.

Ikey Solomon had, after all, escaped from the most notorious gaol in Britain without resort to violence and had been gone a full hour or more before the dunderheads realised anything was amiss. Moreover, the cunning of Ikey had seen to it that Popjoy, the more diligent turnkey, with the help of a strong potion, was locked in the arms of Morpheus, slumped in the corner of Marybelle Firkin's parlour, while his older partner was too drunk to take two steps in pursuit of a quarry without falling full upon his own face. By the time the constabulary was alerted, as one of the penny papers reported:

Ikey Solomon was allowed time enough to row himself to France with sufficient over to fish mid-stream for a rack of herring to sell in Paris to the Frenchies!

Moreover, when the police had been alerted, they had immediately contacted the City division who had informed them, somewhat pompously, of the Bank of England's recapture of the villain. It had been a full eight hours later before Reuban Reuban revealed his true identity, and at least nine or ten since Ikey's initial escape from the Pig 'n Spit. By the time the hunt for him was under way again, Ikey had already slipped down the Thames, his ship long buried in the coastal mist as it headed for the North Sea and the kingdom of the Danes.

In fact, even at the point when Reuban Reuban had revealed his true identity, the City police officials on duty that night had not believed him, thinking that Ikey had merely shaved his head in some clever ruse. But no amount of logic applied to the conundrum could reveal what intention this clever ruse might serve. Ikey had, after all, presented himself as himself at the premises of Coutts & Company, and if this be a ruse it was a most mysterious one. It was only then that Sir Jasper Waterlow had been visited at his home in Kensington and aroused from his bed to be informed of the presence in the cells of the duplicate Ikey.

Ikey's double had been duly charged with complicity but this was small consolation for Sir Jasper who knew that, unless he brought the true Ikey Solomon to trial, his hopes for an illustrious future as Britain's foremost police officer, and ultimately a seat in the House of Lords, had been completely dashed.

He swore silently that Hannah, whom he immediately believed responsible for his humiliation, would pay dearly for her husband's escape, though, on further thought, this conclusion made little sense, for his detective's mind reasoned that if she *had not* told him of Ikey's intended escape she would have been thought by him to have been equally guilty of complicity. Sir Jasper was therefore reluctantly forced to conclude that Hannah had been telling the truth and that the cunning Ikey had outsmarted them both.

The curious thing was that neither *The Times* nor any of the penny papers made mention of Ikey's subsequent visit to Coutts & Company in the guise of a gentleman of means returned that very day from abroad.

It may only be supposed that the directors of the bank, not wishing to be the laughing stock of all England, had remained silent about the presence in the bank of the real Ikey and the transaction he had made. In fact they had suggested to *The Times* that the abortive ruse by Reuban Reuban was merely an attempt to gain notoriety. He was not to know at the time that the real escape of the notorious fence was taking place. A difficult coincidence to believe, but a coincidence nonetheless, life itself being so often stranger than fiction.

In actual fact, the Bank of England had deliberately conspired with Coutts & Company not to release the story of the real Ikey's visit in the supposed interest of national safety, thus making the story of the hapless actor's attempt at publicity necessary to explain the arrest of Reuban Reuban. In any event, Ikey's transaction was allowed to go through without hindrance to New York and the banker, Nathaniel Wilson, found himself somewhat of a hero for the manner in which he had conducted himself.

Furthermore, Sir Jasper Waterlow, conscious that royalty itself made use of the great private bank, was not in the least keen that the notorious Ikey Solomon's patronage of the same facility be known to the public at large. He had therefore dropped the conspiracy charges against Reuban Reuban, merely holding him in solitary confinement for a week, charged with being a public nuisance. When the greater part of the public furore over Ikey's escape had died down, he was sentenced to twenty-five lashes and released on the condition that he would say nothing more to the newspapers than was already known.

This was thought by Reuban Reuban to be the mildest of sentences. He had received the sum of one hundred pounds for his role as a thespian, the highest salary he would ever be paid for plying his craft. Realising that he had just completed the greatest performance of his life in a real life drama, Reuban Reuban hit upon the idea of using the money Ikey had paid him to mount a grand theatrical production in which he starred and was titled: *'The Jew who Bankrupted England!'*

Though this, when the sensibilities of the times changed under the new young queen, would be altered on the poster hoardings and outside the theatre to read:

'The Man who Bankrupted England'

* * * *

Presenting, in the title role:
The great Reuban Reuban himself!
The original and real life impersonator
in the escape of the notorious Ikey Solomon!

His role playing Ikey Solomon, Prince of Fences, in his own production was to earn the previously struggling actor a handsome living for the remainder of his career.

When Abraham announced his visit the day after Ikey's escape, Mary withdrew with him to a dark corner of the dungeons, taking a candle so that she might see the truth in his face. It was here that he told her the entire story, though the young tailor omitted the details of Ikey's passage on a Danish ship carrying ballast back to Denmark. Instead, he suggested that Ikey had left their coach on the road to Southampton and had been met by another, which was presumably to take him to a ship bound for America.

He told Mary of Ikey's most earnest resolve that she should have money to facilitate her voyage to Australia and that it was Ikey's fondest hope and desire she should lack nothing in order to extract the maximum comfort from so arduous and unpleasant an experience upon the high seas.

Abraham stressed Ikey's most heartfelt regrets at what had happened to Mary, and then took great pains to explain Ikey's reasons for making no attempt to contact Mary while they had both been incarcerated in this very same gaol – the explanation being that Ikey, thinking only of Mary's personal welfare, was mindful that their past association might reflect badly upon her and cause needless suffering and humiliation.

It was a succinct enough explanation and Abraham, who had watched his father at rehearsal since he had been a small boy, delivered Ikey's message with sufficient ardour to suggest that he might himself have enjoyed a career upon the stage.

Mary became at once so bemused with Abraham's message containing Ikey's solicitude that she could scarcely believe her ears. It was with great difficulty that she forced into her mind the true picture of the rapacious, greedy, whingeing, entirely selfish and self-serving Ikey she knew as her erstwhile partner.

'What does 'e want?' she demanded sternly, pushing the candle close to Abraham's face.

'In truth, I swear, he seeks only your high regard, Mistress Mary,' the young tailor protested, much enjoying the sound of such highminded phrasing. 'Those are the words from his own dear lips,' he added.

'Ha!' Mary replied. 'Ikey never done nothin' in 'is whole life what wasn't for profit! 'Igh regard, you says? Where's the profit to be found in that?'

'His sentiments were most soft in your regard, most spontaneous soft, Miss,' Abraham protested again. '"Abraham, my dear," he says to me, "you must convince Mistress Mary of my high regard, my most 'umble 'igh regard!" He said it three times, I swear it, Mistress Mary. There was tears in his eyes when he spoke them words and then he handed me the soft. "You must give 'er this fifty pounds, for she 'as been done a great wrong and it is I who is responsible!" That's what he says to me, Gawd's truth!' Abraham concluded.

Mary looked genuinely startled. 'Ikey said that? Ikey said it were 'im what was responsible?'

Abraham nodded. 'He was most sad, most very sad indeed at the inconvenience he'd caused your fair self.'

'Gawd 'elp us! Miracles will never cease!'

Despite her deep suspicion, Mary could think of no way that Ikey, at the moment of his escape, could possibly profit from her by a further penny. So why, she asked herself, had he parted with a small fortune? Could it possibly be for the reasons Abraham had given? Had Ikey grown a conscience? She could not imagine a repentant Ikey, nor one who was capable of feeling the slightest remorse for a fellow human. We all want to feel the love of another and Mary had not been loved since she had been a small child, when she had briefly known the tenderness of a consumptive mother. Did Ikey really love her, not simply regard her as a profitable partner, as she had always quite contentedly supposed? It seemed too bizarre for words that he might do so, or for that matter, that she could harbour in her breast, unbeknownst to her, a love for him in return.

Love was not a word in the vocabulary which had existed between Mary and Ikey. Even on those rare occasions when she had taken him to her bed, there had been no thought of love. Mary had long since packed that hope away, concealing it in the darkest corner of her soul. Love was not for such as her. And so she simply shook her head, silently forcing back a tear, truly not knowing what to think of the whole matter of Ikey's amorous protestations brought on the importuning lips of a young man with a strong sense of melodrama.

At that moment Abraham Reuban produced Ikey's Duke of Wellington medal.

'Ikey wishes you to have this as a further token of his

most remarkable esteem, Mistress Mary,' he said, holding the medallion and chain against the light of the candle. 'It be pure gold an' all!'

'So, where'd 'e steal it, then?' Mary asked tartly, though her heart thumped within her breast at the sight of the medallion.

'No, no, missus, it be his luck, what be called his talisman!' Abraham then told Mary the story of the medallion as Ikey had related it to him in the coach.

Mary had a dim recollection of having once observed a gold chain about Ikey's neck. Stripped down to his vest and long johns, the gold chain had disappeared into the top of his tightly clinging woollen upper garment so that she had no knowledge of what might be contained at its extremity. Now the thought that it might be his medallion, Ikey's talisman, opened her heart like a summer rose. She took the Wellington medallion from Abraham and, turning it over, read the inscription nestled between the garland of laurel leaves. Whereupon Mary's broken hands pressed Ikey's talisman to her bosom and she knew with a fierce certainty that she would survive, that she would never surrender and that somehow she had inherited Ikey's uncanny luck.

At that moment, despite his innumerable faults and thinking him no more than she knew him to be, Mary loved Ikey Solomon.

Chapter Seventeen

Mary was to spend five months in Newgate Gaol, two months longer than her original sentence, this to await a convict ship bound for Van Diemen's Land. On the 15th of May 1827, with eighteen other female convicts, she was placed in light irons and transported by open cart to Woolwich, where the convict ship *Destiny II* was berthed to await its full complement of female convicts.

The weather was grand, the winter frost well past, the elm and larch and sycamore, the bright green oak, in new leaf all. The orchards showed a bedazzlement of white and pink, the fancy dress of pear, apple, cherry and of summer's blood-red plum to come. The woods through which the cart rumbled were carpeted with bluebells and the yellow splash of daffodil, in an England ablaze with bud and blossom and the joyous fecundity of spring.

Several of the convicts were heard to sigh that this was a poor time to leave the shores of England, their most ardent wish being to make their last farewell in the fiercest needle sleet and howl of north wind. This, so their memories might be consumed by the bitter gales and so send them, half cheerful, on their way to the hell of Van Diemen's shores.

This sky of clear blue with the high call of larks and the singing of thrush in the hedgerows was too much a bittersweet parting. This single memory of the darling buds of May would linger with them for the remainder of their lives. They would hold their grandchildren in their laps under a different sky, and tell of the soft shining of the English countryside. They would remember these two days, when they had rocked and bumped in shackles along a rutted road, as if, for this short space in time, they had been transported through the gates of paradise itself.

It was an unbearable wrench for several of the younger women, who wept piteously for the time it took to arrive at Woolwich, where *Destiny II* creaked and groaned to the slap of the tide. They came upon it suddenly at the turn of a large warehouse and they immediately forsook the rattle and rumble of the cobblestones and turned into the quay, where the wheels of the cart squeaked and lurched along the uneven dockside timbers. Only then, with the cart drawn to a halt beside the squat vessel and with the sudden silence, into which dropped the call of a gull and a soft *phlurrr* from the nostrils of one of the cart horses, did the finality of the sentence of transportation come to each of them.

Standing on the dockside next to the gangway was a diminutive male in frock coat, dirty shirt with a sweat-soiled neckerchief, breeches, hose and tiny brass-buckled shoes much in need of repair. His hair was cropped, though not evenly or in the convict style, and stuck up in raggedy bits an inch or so all about his skull, with whiskers, once dark and now densely speckled with grey. These also stuck out and framed his face from sideburns to the circumference of his chin. Heavy tufted eyebrows, black as pitch, seemed to entirely encase his small bright eyes. Jutting at right angles to this furry visage were two large thin-skinned ears to which the light from the sun behind him gave a bright crimson glow. The total effect was of a remarkable likeness to a simian creature, a monkey dressed in a frock coat, breeches and hose.

'Gawd, look at that!' Mary exclaimed.

The tiny man chuckled and threw an arm upwards pointing to the sky. ' "Gawd", now that be a partickler name what Mr Smiles don't like folks to take in vain! That be three punishments all at once!' He tapped the first finger of his left hand with the forefinger of the right. 'Short rations and no port wine for the father!' He tapped the finger beside it. 'Two days' bread and water in the coal hole, for the son!' He tapped the third. 'Attendance to Bible study for a month, that be for the Holy Ghost!' He looked up at Mary. 'Swear away, me dear, help yourselfs, last chance afore comin' on board to be rid of all that bile! What's your name then?'

'Mary Abacus. What's it to you if I swear?' Mary challenged.

'Ah, yes! For me? Well it be a delightful hopportunity, Mary Habacus. A most pleasant task to do you ...' He paused in mid-sentence and pointed to the abacus under Mary's arm. 'What be that? A contraption is it? Them black and red beads, it ain't witchcraft is it?'

'Abacus. It be an abacus.'

'A habacus, eh? An' pray tell us, what be an habacus if it ain't your name what is also Habacus?'

Before Mary could reply Ann Gower asked, 'What day o' the month and year ya born in, then, mister?'

The small, hairy creature thought for a moment, then decided to co-operate. 'April seven in the year o' our Lord, seventeen seventy-six or near enough, I reckons.' His voice had a cackle to it, his words sharp and fast and somewhat high-pitched like Chinese crackers going off in a bunch.

Ann Gower turned to Mary and whispered from the side of her mouth, 'Show lover boy, darlin'.'

'Lover boy, is it?' The little man had the most astonishing acuteness of hearing, for Mary had barely heard Ann's whisper herself.

Mary shrugged. She was manacled but the clamps were on either end of a good twelve inches of chain so that her hands were more or less free to work the abacus. She rested it on the side of the cart and instructed Ann to hold the abacus firmly. A moment later her twisted fingers began to fly in a clicking and clacking so rapid that the red and black beads slid across their wire runners faster than the eye could possibly follow them. After what seemed only a few minutes she stopped and read the beads.

'You been alive eighteen thousand, six 'undred and sixty-four days. You was borned on a Sunday.' Tapping the abacus, Mary added, 'That be what me abacus does, it counts things.'

'Ho, ho! We's got us a smart one 'as we? A Jack 'n a box what springs out above others! Well, Mary Habacus what's got an habacus what counts, pleased to meetcha, me name's Potbottom, Mister Tiberias Potbottom, that be the full complement o' me cartouches.' He spread his hands and grinned disarmingly. 'They

352

calls me, "The Scrapins"! Now can you imagine why that could possibly be, eh?' His head jerked enquiringly from one woman to another, waiting for the women in the cart to acknowledge him with a laugh or some sign of acquiescence. But no laughter or even a nod was forthcoming, for Mary sensed a trap and the others had held back, waiting for her reaction. She remained stony faced looking down at the diminutive creature on the dock.

All at once the bright eager to-and-fro of Potbottom's head ceased and he looked down at his scuffed and worn shoes. His head began to nod slowly as though it were coming to some sort of conclusion. His dark eyes moved to each of the women above him, lingering as though taking in all their details, as if, in his observance, he had suddenly learned much about them and what he found was of the utmost disappointment. His eyes came last to Mary and held her gaze as he spoke.

'Ha! What about leap years, then? Your habacus didn't count no leap years, now did it?' He pointed a sharp finger at Mary and jumped from one foot to the other. 'Ho, ho, habacus ain't such a clever Dick now is it?'

The female convicts all looked questioningly at Mary.

'What you takes me for, an idjit?' Mary sniffed. 'There be eleven in all, they's all counted, leap years and even this mornin's included in.'

The women in the cart clapped and yelled their approval and there was much rattling of chains and laughter at Mary's sharp rejoinder.

'Well, well, we'll soon see about this mornin' included in, won't we?' Potbottom said, his lips drawn to a tight line. 'Welcome aboard His Majesty's convict ship, *Destiny II*. Destiny be a good name,' he jerked his thumb over his shoulder at the boat, 'for her gracious ladyship. You see, if you be o' the kind what trusts to destiny to supply yer needs, I is most pleased to inform you that you has got it exactly right! On board we supplies all the misery yer heart could desire, lashin's and lashin's o' the stuff, and, as well, we tops it up with despair, more of it than what you could possibly digest in one plain sailin'!'

Mary laughed nervously and the others followed, a titter ran through the cart.

'Oh, *now* we laughs, does we?' Potbottom's eyes narrowed. 'I knows not how many days you has been alive on Gawd's sweet earth, Mary Habacus, but I makes you this most solemn promise.' Potbottom's eyes held Mary's. 'The worse ones hasn't yet come for you!' He paused and gave her a malevolent smile. 'But they will. Oh deary me, yes! They will, they will!'

Tiberias Potbottom turned his back on them and hurried up the gangway, his short bandy legs making his shoulders jump from side to side, his long arms hanging loose, so that he lurched along very much like the monkey creature he so closely resembled. It was only then that they noticed that one shoulder was higher than the other, that there was a hump, though not overly large, resting behind it. Tiberias Potbottom was a hunchback.

'Blimey! Who'll be touchin' that one's hump for luck,' Mary exclaimed softly.

The women in the cart giggled and watched as Potbottom disappeared on to the deck above them. 'Jesus!' Ann Gower said in a loud whisper. 'Talk about 'ot an' cold! What were that all about?'

'Whatever it were, it ain't good news for me,' Mary sighed. She turned to one of the two turnkeys who'd escorted them on the trip down and who had just that moment returned from reporting to the ship's surgeon-superintendent, the already infamous Joshua Smiles. Neither of their guards had witnessed the exchange between the convict women and Potbottom, who'd brushed past them just as they'd reached the top of the gangway.

'Can you take off our irons now, Mr Burke, we be exceeding tired o' standin'?' Mary asked politely.

'Not till you 'as been counted and numbers taken,' Burke said. 'Sorry, that be regulations.'

A murmur of dissatisfaction came from the cart which caused the second of their guards to raise both hands and pat the air in front of him. 'Now, now, girls, you been good so far, don't you go spoilin' things now!' He smiled up at the women in the cart, 'Besides, Mr Potbottom, what be assistant to ship's surgeon, be 'ere soon enough to count and take your numbers.'

An hour later with the spring sunshine turned unseasonably hot and uncomfortable they still remained standing in the cart. The female convicts had no protection but for their mob caps, their ankles were swollen and painful from standing and their throats were parched for want of water. Many of the older women were close to swooning in the heat. They commenced to shouting, demanding and begging from all who mounted the gangway to release them from their chains and allow them to step down from the cart and into the shade cast by the ship's side. When they were ignored by the coming and going throng they cussed loudly, calling out obscenities. Finally two jack tars appeared at the top of the gangway, the one carrying a small table and the other a chair. They walked down and placed them in the shade on the dock.

'Call the bleedin' baboon what's meant to count us!' Mary shouted angrily at the two tars, her temper quite lost. 'There's some near dyin' for want of a drop o' bloody water!'

'Baboon, is I? Well thank you very much!' Potbottom said, appearing at the top of the gangway. 'A baboon what can count and take numbers, an extraordinary baboon what is blessed with a very long memory for the slightest slight and insults what injure!'

'Oh shit!' Mary said in a loud whisper.

Tiberias Potbottom, a small smile on his face, walked down the gangway and skipped lightly on to the dockside where he continued on to the table and chair.

'Shit it be, but not for me! Shit it be for such as thee!' He smirked.

He was carrying a large ledger under his arm which seemed to raise his hunched shoulder even higher and now he took it and opened it on the table to show one of its two opened pages half filled with writing. From the side pocket of his worn frock coat he produced a pot of blacking and, undoing its cap carefully, placed it beside the ledger. Then he took a goose feather quill from an inside pocket and this too he laid beside the book. Having completed this task he stepped to the front of the table and placed his hands behind his back, whereupon he commenced to rock on the back of his heels looking up at the women in the cart.

'Has we had enough, then? Enough profanity to last us all the ways to Hobart Town?' He did not wait for their response, but continued. 'Or does we stay another

hour and get the rest o' the bile out of our vile hearts?'
He paused and this time waited. 'Well?' he finally
asked.

'Enough, sir,' Mary said, her eyes suitably downcast
and her hands clasped in humility in front of her. The
others nodded eagerly. 'We's 'ad enough o' cussin', sir,'
Mary repeated. 'Can we step down now, if you please,
sir, Mr Potbottom?'

Potbottom squinted up at Mary and, shaking his
head slowly, said, 'Oh, I very much hopes so, Mary
Habacus, I very much hopes so! You see, Mr Smiles
don't take kindly to profanity and me,' he shrugged, 'I
is his sharp eyes and his large ears and I must warn
you!' He paused and chuckled. 'Me eyes is exceedin'
good and . . .' he touched one of his ears lightly, '. . . me
ears is even much better'n that!'

From his back pocket he produced a large red silk
handkerchief and held it open in front of him, the silk
hanging limp from one corner. 'Sailing is Gawd's
breath,' he began, as though he were about to give a
lecture, which indeed was his intention. 'When the sails
lay limp that means Gawd has taken away his breath
and we is becalmed.' He glanced at them as though to
assure himself of their attention. 'Becalmed, that be an
awesome thing. To be upon the ocean without Gawd's
breath, to be forsaken by the Almighty.' Potbottom's
small body seemed to shudder at the very prospect.
'That be a time for the devil to skip across the flat sea
and come aboard.' He waited for the effect of his words
to sink in and then, with his free hand, he took up a
second corner of the scarf so that it hung square in front
of his face, whereupon he blew upon it so that the silk
billowed away from him. 'Gawd's gentle and steady

breath be everythin' to them what sails upon the oceans wide. It be His gift to us for observin' His ways, ways you lot has long since forsaken!' Potbottom suddenly flapped the scarf furiously and his voice rose in pitch. 'You makes Gawd angry! Terrible angry! And when He be angry, His breath be angry! His angry breath be a storm at sea, a hurricane what takes small ships and drives 'em up high onto the furious waves and dashes them down, and breaks their backs and smashes 'em to tinder, and sends 'em to the bottom o' the ocean!' His voice lowered. 'Planks and carcases and barrels and bilge, spat up later on some distant and forsaken shore!'

Tiberias Potbottom, breathing heavily through his nostrils, crumpled the cloth into his hand and stuffed it angrily back into the pocket of his breeches. He appeared quite overcome, struggling to contain himself.

The women in the cart watched silently. Potbottom swallowed twice, his Adam's apple jumping along his scrawny neck, then he spoke slowly and quietly. 'That's why we talks to Gawd in prayer and meditation, we asks Him for His fair and lovely breath upon our voyage. When we uses profanity, when we take His name in vain, He will take His breath away, or, if He be angry, sufficient enough angry, if the blasphemy be too great, He will blow and blow until we is doomed upon the calamitous waves!'

Potbottom, his hands now once again clasped behind his back and his demeanour recovered, walked around the cart so that the prisoners within it were forced to follow him with their eyes and turn as he moved. The chains of their manacles rattled and clinked. Finally the tiny man came to stand directly in front of Mary.

'Me remarkable ears, Gawd's special gift, can hear a

whisper o' profanity in the full face o' the Roarin' Forties! I am Gawd's watchman! When you's spewin' yer heart out in the sea sickness what's soon to come, if one of you so much as moans, "Oh Gawd!" I'll have you on bread 'n water in leg irons.' He looked at each of them in turn and then suddenly shouted, 'We only have Gawd's sweet breath to save us! And with your kind on board we places our lives in great jeopardy! Mr Smiles will not have no whore language, no profanity, no blasphemy on board, does you understand?' His voice lowered and spitting each word out as though it caused a bad taste in his mouth he added, 'Does-I-make-me-self-per-fekly-clear?'

Potbottom did not wait for any of the female convicts to nod but turned and moved around the table to sit down on the chair. Seated, he looked up again and addressed himself to the two turnkeys, who had been standing, eyes downcast, more or less at attention, beside the cart.

'Unshackle!' he instructed, taking up his quill and dipping it into the pot of blacking in front of him. Then he looked back up at the women and jabbed the quill at Mary and then at Ann Gower. 'Them two shall be last!'

Mary brought her hands up and placed them over Ikey's medallion until she felt the comfort of the small gold object in the centre of her flattened palm. The long hard voyage to Van Diemen's Land had begun. Ikey's medallion, his luck, she suddenly knew, was intended for the second great passage of her life. She must survive.

It was three weeks before all the female convicts had arrived from gaols as far away as Scotland, Ireland and

Wales. The bright spring weather had turned into a wet, miserable early summer. Many of the convicts arrived with coughs, colds and bronchial infections, and a number of the older women suffered profoundly with the added affliction of rheumatism which often bent them double and made them seem like old crones twice their age. The children's dirty faces were pinched and wet with a constant flow of mucus leaking from their nostrils, and many were consumed by high fevers.

As each cartload, or coach, unloaded, Mary watched from the deck as Tiberias Potbottom met them, hopping and jumping about and, in general, making their arrival as difficult and fearful a prospect as he possibly could.

Upon coming aboard the *Destiny II* they had been taken directly to Joshua Smiles and his assistant, who had given them a medical examination of a most cursory nature, but carefully documented down as though of the utmost importance. A lifting of the bottom and top eyelids, a probing in the ears, an inspection of the tongue and a tapping of the chest for the almost certain signs of bronchial infections. This was followed with a more thorough inspection a week later which became known on shipboard as 'Bloody Pusover'.

Each week prisoners were examined for blood and pus in the ears, in the mucus, in the eyes, in the nose and mouth, and finally in the cunny for the glim or syphilis. There was little notice taken when an infection was discovered, though, apart from it being written in the surgeon's book with details of a most generously prescribed medication. This medication, though well conceived according to the contemporary dictates of treatment, was never administered.

Upon completion of the very first medical examination Joshua Smiles, in a burst of volubility not to be repeated outside of his prayers, explained the rules to be followed during the voyage. He then launched into a lengthy dissertation which included much comment about the dangers of immoral behaviour, the need for cleanliness and the benefits and rewards of a religious life. He left until last his admonition that profanity and blasphemy would earn the harshest of punishments and warned any female prisoner to bring the name of the Almighty God upon her lips in no other manner but in prayerfulness.

Mary and her intake were divided into two groups, each of which was termed a mess. From each mess a monitor was chosen to speak for all. Mary was elected monitor by the insistence of all in her group. Ann Gower was also selected as monitor in the second mess, which contained six convicts who were from Dublin, they being whores and thus thought to be most compatible to the other members.

The prison uniform consisted of a coarse particoloured cotton shift, two petticoats and two sets of ill-fitting undergarments, a pinny, with a spare, and two mob caps. The women's own clothes were washed by three members of each mess, hung out on the deck to dry then dry packed away in boxes with camphor balls. The idea behind imposing uniformity of dress was to eliminate a natural pecking order derived from the status of possessions – rags or fine gowns, tortoise shell brushes or combs of ox bone, bottles of perfumes or tincture of lavender water, a fine brooch or merely a few bright buttons or a single trinket. These were all placed on the mess inventory and packed away, so that those wearing a silver brooch and fancy outfit could not earn precedence over rags and a simple garnet pin. Upon arriving in Van Diemen's Land their belongings would be handed to the matron of the Female Factory in the presence of their owners to be kept until their release.

The money they had brought with them in gold, silver, copper and soft was ordered to be handed to the surgeon-superintendent, who entered the amounts into his cash book and, upon arrival, lodged these funds with the authorities in Van Diemen's Land. They were to be returned to the owners at the completion of their sentences.

This inventory of cash was undertaken by Tiberias Potbottom and such became Mary's fear that she would never again see what rightfully belonged to her, that at the risk of the most severe punishment if she should be discovered, she elected to keep her small personal horde of gold coins. Fifteen gold sovereigns remained from Ikey's gift and this she kept in her 'prisoner's purse' along with Ikey's medallion.

The prisoner's purse, readily obtained for a few shillings in any English gaol, consisted of a small metal tube of brass with a fitted cap and rounded end. It was fashioned in much the same manner as the cigar-shaped container Ikey had caused to be made and which had carried his letter of credit, so comfortably worn by Marybelle Firkin when she had travelled from Birmingham to London. Only, the prisoner's purse of the kind Mary wore was much smaller and made to fit, without too much discomfort, in either of the 'treasure caves' that is to say, the rear or front orifice, convenient places to bury contraband on a female person.

On bloody pusover days Mary would transfer the brass container to within the rear cave, which although uncomfortable was safe from Potbottom's supervision, and the probing fingers of the convict matron who would examine that other part of her anatomy and report it free of infection to the surgeon's assistant. He hovered behind her with quill and ledger in the hope that he might be able to record a finding of pus to transform into profit.

From the time the prisoners began to arrive the Ladies' Committee commenced to visit the ship. Mary, suspicious by nature of charity, was at first wary of these high-minded women, but she soon grew to respect them. Though pious in their ways they earnestly sought to alleviate the discomfort of the voyage and could, on occasion, become quite cantankerous if they found a facility in the prison which did not adhere to the prescribed regulations.

Potbottom did his unctuous best to earn their approval, dancing attendance like some small simian creature trained especially for the task of serving, assuring them with much dry-soaping of hands and nodding of head and frequent obsequious expression of his utmost co-operation. He insisted that any complaint they might make would be his personal pleasure to attend to in the time it took to snap his greedy fingers.

Nevertheless the formidable Mrs Fry and her Ladies' Committee were not easily deceived and they soon earned the approbation of all but the hardest and most recalcitrant female convicts. Though the world of the two classes of women was divided by a chasm too wide to leap, or even for one to imagine the life of the other, these committee women were not from the authorities, nor were they easily intimidated by them. Furthermore, they laboured trenchantly and with goodwill on behalf of the female convicts. They showed themselves as women who cared greatly for their unfortunate sisters. By notable contrast, with the exception of many of the surgeon-superintendents who often took the utmost care of their convicts (Joshua Smiles and some few others being the exception), the male administrators were, for the most part, totally indifferent to their welfare. In fact, most went to great pains to indicate that they cared not a rat's tail for the wellbeing of their charges but, instead, regarded every female prisoner as a whore transported to keep the men, both convict and free, sated.

Mary's misshapen hands did not allow for needle-work but to her great delight, along with cloth and thread, the resourceful Quaker ladies had supplied a small library. While there were no novels, plays or other improper books, the single box contained, as well as religious works, travel, biographies and history books and poetry. This last gave Mary a new-found pleasure, and was to bring her considerable joy for the remainder of her life.

Most of the convicts on board adapted to the order and routine the Ladies' Committee established at the commencement of the voyage, and those within Mary's mess, though all of them prostitutes, encouraged by her, soon proved eager to take up needlework. They were frequently rewarded for their diligence by Mary with readings while they worked, but this was not true of Ann Gower's mess.

These were the women who were branded by the authorities within the surgeon-superintendent's report at the conclusion of each voyage with words such as, 'notoriously bad', 'disorderly', 'profligate wretches', 'quarrelsome', and for those with a flair for invective and a good, well-inked goose feather quill, 'the basest and most abominable wretch of a woman', or 'scheming, blasphemous vixen and prostitute' – this last description being appended to Mary's name by Tiberias Potbottom on the very first evening of her coming on board. When the ship arrived in Hobart, this single entry in the surgeon's report resulted in her being incarcerated in the Female Factory instead of being assigned as a servant to a settler. In truth, with the exception of theft and blasphemy, fighting and the urgent couplings which took place at night, most of the offences committed on board were minor breaches of discipline such as insolence and refusal to obey orders, howling and singing a hymn or prayer to the tune of a well-known bawdy and sentimental song.

In the week before the departure of the vessel the relatives of those convicts on board began to arrive to farewell their wives and daughters. Mary, having no family of her own, witnessed the piteous sight of parents parting from their daughters with no likelihood of ever seeing them in this life again. The deck of the *Destiny II* was washed with the tears of country folk who had seen their dear daughters leave home to find work as servants or some form of livelihood in the city only to end up, unbeknown to them, selling their bodies on the streets of London, Dublin, Glasgow or Liverpool or resorting to petty crime in order to stay alive. These were good, honest people, who, for the most part, worked at backbreaking labour to earn barely enough to put bread and broth upon the table. They brought what they could as gifts, though frequently this was no more than the tears they shed and the love they bestowed for the last time upon their unfortunate and wretched offspring.

The *Destiny II*, flying the red and white pennant, 'the whip' which denoted a convict ship, sailed with the evening tide on the 14th of June amid the dreadful cries of distress from both those on board and the ones they'd left behind forever. The wind was from the nor'west, the temperature 68 degrees Fahrenheit and the sailing down channel was steady and most pleasant until about midnight when the winds changed to the west. This brought choppy seas and frequent squalls and the weather billowed into gales and huge seas by the time they entered the Bay of Biscay.

By midnight, when the prisoners had long since been confined below decks, almost the entire complement of convicts became sick to the point of frequent vomiting and nausea. They commenced to howling and blaspheming until no strength existed for these bitter emotions, whereupon they lay in their own vomit and moaned, willing themselves to die in the insufferable atmosphere of the water-logged prison.

The *Destiny II* was a 'wet' ship, that is to say, when the huge waves washed over the decks the water poured down into the prison quarters so that not a single flock mattress, pillow or blanket or anything contained within the female prison, including the convicts themselves, remained dry. The swinging stoves were hung in the prison to help dry the prison quarters but to no effect. The constant downpour of water rushing in from the deck above caused the contents of their stomachs to somewhat dilute, and with the hatches tightly closed, by the time dawn's light came the stench and the mess from the swill at their feet was beyond any possible description.

Sea sickness has no medication other than a tranquil sea and the weather remained inclement for the following week and then continued foul with intermittent calm of no more than, at most, a day, until they reached Tenerife, twenty days after departing from Woolwich.

At almost the moment they made the harbour at Santa Cruz at seven of the clock on a Sunday morning with the church bells summoning worshippers to early mass, the wind died and the sun blazed up to chase away all signs of the threatening cumulus cloud gathered above the high conical peaks above the town. While there was no thought that the convicts might be allowed to go ashore, they rested for several days while the ship took on new provisions. The women were allowed fresh fruit bought from the various boats which pulled to the side of the vessel and all were kept occupied at cleaning-out below decks and drying their bedding, clothes and personal effects.

As each cloudless day passed, the women became more hysterical at the prospect of leaving. On the third day, as they up-anchored in preparation to depart, the convicts went berserk and were confined to below decks with the hatches of the prison quarters securely locked. This was for fear that they might riot at the expectation of atrocious weather such as they'd endured during their first month at sea.

Only Tiberias Potbottom and Joshua Smiles seemed content to be on their way again. God had blessed the voyage with gale force winds and stormy seas, though not sufficient of either to cause harm to the *Destiny II*, and this was seen by both men as a blessing breathed upon their journey to the other side of the world.

Soon the routine on board ship assumed a semblance of normalcy. Most of the women were allocated jobs on board which helped somewhat to alleviate the long empty hours. Some of these positions carried the promise of a small reward while others were reward enough by helping to pass the hours between six o'clock muster when they rose and the time, roughly twelve hours later at dusk, when they were confined below decks. Most, being experienced in domestic service, adjusted easily enough to the routines on board and took readily to the added pleasures of sewing and needlework. They were not averse to working as servants in the kitchens and hospital or in other menial tasks of cleaning and labouring. Mary asked that she might teach those who wished to learn to read and write. She was the only one among the female convicts with sufficient learning to impart this knowledge to others and the Ladies' Committee had encouraged the formation of a school. But this was refused as a duty, in Joshua Smiles' name, by Potbottom and so Mary was obliged to run her school during the afternoon. Potbottom saw to it that she was on constant duty cleaning out the prison each morning, dry scrubbing the deck with holystone and sand and washing down and refilling the water closets, these being the most menial and hated tasks on board ship.

Moreover, at every opportunity, Potbottom would try to humiliate Mary and at each bloody pusover he would make cruel jokes about her hands or comment on the scar upon her face, or make her linger longer before the matron with her skirts held above her waist and her flannel undergarment removed. On two occasions, when he had caught her in utterance of bad language, he had caused Mary to be placed in a scold's bridle, a strap worn tightly over the mouth, tied at the back of the neck and which made it quite impossible to speak, nor, for the space of one week, was she allowed to read from a book, a punishment she found far more onerous than the silence the bridle enforced.

The increasing tropical heat did not help the disposition of the convicts or that of the officials and crew who, increasingly, tormented them. Each passing day the breeze seemed to slacken a little more and the sun to grow hotter as it beat down on deck from a sky too high and blue for anything in their previous comprehension.

The women wakened each morning in a lather of perspiration with no breeze at all coming in from the hatches and the portholes, which were thrown wide open. Even the scuttles were opened, the sea being calm enough to allow it, but this too was to no avail. Nor was there a breath of air from the supposed 'ventilation shafts' in which the ship's officers had shown no trust. These wind sails and shafts were designed to blow cool air below decks, but such was their scorn for this new-fangled idea that the crew purposely neglected to adjust them according to instructions.

Soon it made no difference whether they had it right or wrong, for the ship had entered the equatorial doldrums in the Atlantic Narrows and the sails, whatever their purpose, lay limp and useless. Joshua Smiles watched the topgallant with increasing fear, for even this tiny sail trapped not the slightest breath of wind and the red and white 'whip' hung flat against the topmast.

With the sea totally calm and the heat each day

climbing, a hellish invasion overtook the vessel. Hordes of vermin, once snug within the cracks and crannies in the woodwork and the bilges – cockroaches, bedbugs, lice and fleas and whole colonies of rats – emerged from the crevices and dark holes to attack the human inhabitants of the *Destiny II*.

The crew and officers were not spared in this, for if the vermin knew not convict from free man and spared not the one in preference to another, nor did the incredible stench, which pervaded the prison and the apartments of crew and officers alike.

For Mary the real hell of the outward journey to Van Diemen's Land was about to begin at the hands of Tiberias Potbottom. The assistant to the surgeon-superintendent, whether at the behest of his master or by his own decision, came to conclude that the becalming of the vessel and the invasion of the pestilence from the cracks and the bilges, which had in itself a biblical connotation as if one of the plagues upon Egypt, had come about because of the blasphemy of the whores on board. That God, in His righteous wrath, had withdrawn His breath, demanding that those who mocked Him should be punished.

With the extraordinary heat it was decided that the convict women might bring their bedding and sleep on deck, occupying the poop and quarter decks which could be safely enough guarded from the crew. Though the nights were exceedingly hot and and the air still, this was a most pleasant experience compared with the furnace of the prison quarters below decks, and the prisoners received this concession to their comfort with great joy.

'All may sleep on deck except the whores!' Potbottom

had declared. 'These be the orders o' the surgeon-superintendent!'

There was a howl of consternation from Ann Gower's and Mary's groups.

'All what's declared whores on ship's manifest will take their beddin' down below after evening muster,' Tiberias Potbottom continued. Then he grinned. 'This be a little taste o' hell, a sample o' what's comin' to them what mocks the Lord Jesus Christ or takes His name in vain! Gawd is not mocked!' he repeated.

'We ain't done nothin'!' Mary shouted. 'Why pick on us, then? We ain't taken nobody's name in vain!' She turned to her group and then to Ann Gower's group. ''As we, ladies?'

'Oh, be that so?' Potbottom exclaimed. 'And I says different and surgeon thinks different and ...' he pointed upwards to the limp sails, 'evidence says different!'

Mary showed her indignation, bringing her hand to her hip and throwing her shoulder forward. 'It ain't *our* fault there be no bleedin' wind!'

'Ah! That be a matter of opinion, Mary Habacus, Gawd's opinion, surgeon's opinion and me own opinion, we all be against your single opinion!'

'Not single, mine too!' Ann Gower shouted. 'It ain't fair! We done no 'arm, we done nuffink wrong! It weren't Gawd what made them sails still, it be 'em doll drums!'

'That's right, it be the doldrums!' Mary shouted in support. 'They be perfectly natural, a phenomenon what sometimes happens near the equator!'

'Oh it be clever Miss Jack 'n a Box again! Phenomenon is it?' Potbottom paused. 'And Gawd! Is He not a phenomenon? Is He not the creator o' the heavens and the earth? The rain and the glorious clouds what is His billowin' breath!' Tiberias Potbottom stopped again and looked about him at the women assembled for muster. He finally fixed his eyes on Ann Gower and then again on Mary, and began to speak, this time most rapidly and in a high-pitched voice. 'Without His breath to drive the clouds there be no rain, without the rain there be starvation upon the face o' the earth! Gawd's breath be the breath of all life itself and when Gawd takes His breath from us it be a sign o' His anger!' He pointed upwards to the limp sails above his head and spoke more slowly. 'Gawd has taken His breath away from us! Doldrums just be another name for Gawd's anger!' Then Potbottom brought his hand down again and pointed to the group of convict women gathered around Mary. 'And we all knows the reason for it, don't we!'

'That be a whole 'eap o' bilge water!' Mary shouted angrily.

'Ha! And that be blasphemin'! Callin' Gawd's breath bilge now, is we?' Potbottom shouted triumphantly. 'You'll all go below right now, all the whores and blasphemers! We'll put the lid o' hell on the Jack 'n a Box and all her consorts, in the name o' Jesus Christ our Lord and Saviour!'

Ann Gower's group and Mary's group were sentenced to be locked in the prison below decks for three days on half rations, but with the full daily allowance of two pints of water, this ration not halved, for it would likely have caused them to perish.

The heat below decks was so intense and the vermin so prolific that the women were soon forced to remove their clothes and after several hours below they could think of nothing but the need for water. Many were so overcome that they fainted away, these faintings frequently terminating in fits. At night the portholes as well as the hatches were closed and by morning the following day many of them were delirious, wandering about unable to recall their own names.

By midday, when the sun was at its zenith, the heat upon the blazing deck would cause the pitch between the deckboards to melt. This molten hell would drop onto them in the prison below where it would bubble upon their flesh, the fiery pitch sticking long enough to arm or leg or back or head to burn savagely through the skin or scalp and deep into the flesh, so that they were permanently scarred from its effect.

On the afternoon of the second day Ann Gower, maddened by the circumstances below decks, attacked Mary, accusing her of causing the calamitous situation they found themselves in. Mary had been sitting alone in a corner against the bulkhead, clasping her legs together with her head resting on her knees when Ann Gower approached and stood over her.

'It were you, not us! It were you the sod wanted!' Ann began. 'All along it be you givin' 'im lip! In the wagon 'an all, when we first come. Then on an' on an' on, always makin' it 'ard for us. You what thinks you is better than a whore. Ya think 'cause ya can read that ya be clever, that ya knows everyfink! Well let me tell ya, all ya knows is 'ow to make trouble for all of us wif that fuckin' gob o' yers! Now Potbottom's gettin' 'is own back and it's us what's sufferin'! It were you, Mary Abacus, what done this to us and I reckons you 'as to pay!' Ann Gower turned and faced the others.

'What do ya say, girls, the bitch 'as gotta pay for our misery!' She indicated the prison around them. 'For this!'

As Ann Gower spoke Mary's hands were under her skirt, for she was one of the very few who had not removed her clothes, which hung soaking from her body. Suspended from a string about her waist was a small bundle of cloth concealed in her flannel undergarment which contained her brass talons. Mary's twisted fingers worked frantically at the knot, but it was too tightly bound to open without some persistent plucking and pulling. Long before it had yielded Ann Gower's right hand swept down and knocked Mary's mob cap from her head. She gripped a fistful of hair in her left hand and pulled Mary squealing to her feet. Balling her hand into a fist, she struck Mary a violent blow which broke her nose.

At the sight of the blood spurting from Mary's nose the other women seemed to go berserk. Howling, they rushed at her, tearing and pulling and pushing her to the deck. They kicked and jumped on Mary and drove their fists into her face and body, raking her with their nails in a furious frenzy of fighting.

So intense were the screams and caterwauling and hysteria that the hatches were hurriedly opened and three guards and Potbottom rushed below. At the sight of Potbottom the women turned like a pack of howling wolves and made towards him. The two prison guards were barely able to retreat and hold them off sufficiently long for Potbottom to beat a hasty retreat, his tiny bow legs propelling him as fast as they could carry him back on to the deck.

More guards arrived together with the prison matron

and two of her assistants, and it took fully ten minutes before any order was restored and they were able to gain control of the hysterical women.

When the matron came upon Mary she lay unconscious, one of her purpled and twisted hands clasped tightly into a ball and resting on her bloodstained breast. She was carried to the hospital where she was washed and her wounds dressed, though every attempt to open her left hand failed. Her fingers seemed to have clamped shut with the shock of the beating she had taken, and had the appearance of the claws of a great bird of prey pulled tightly inwards as though in death.

Mary regained consciousness an hour later and took water from the matron which she drank greedily, asking for more in a hoarse whisper affected by her cut and swollen lips. She was still groggy and not fully possessed of her wits, unsure where she was and with both her eyes closed unable to see the woman who nursed her.

Mary was awakened by someone shaking her roughly and then she heard the cackle of Potbottom's voice, 'Wake her, matron, she has slumbered enough! Wake her at once, this be no inn for gentlefolks!'

Mary attempted to open her eyes and while the right eye still remained tightly closed the left had improved somewhat and she could see with a measure of clarity. Potbottom sat beside her bunk, perched on a stool with his hands clasped to his breast. He seemed to be positively shaking with excitement. One hand suddenly jerked out and a finger prodded into the side of Mary's ribs. A sharp pain shot into her lungs where the ribs had been broken. Potbottom's hand shot back to be clasped again by the other in their former position. 'Wake up! Wake up at once! Say somethin'!'

'Mornin'' Mary said through her cracked and bulbous lips, and then added, 'Miszer Pobothum, sir,' in a voice slurred and hardly above a whisper.

'That's better, much better, you'll soon be well again, me dear.' He dry-soaped his hands. 'Well enough for bread 'n water and a bit o' loverly solitude in the coal hole!' he cackled. 'Guilty o' startin' a riot we is.' He clucked his tongue several times. 'Now that be most wicked. Mr Smiles don't like that, no he don't, indeed we don't tolerate no riot on Gawd's ship.'

Mary groaned and lifted the hand which was still fisted shut and Tiberias Potbottom gasped and reeled back, thinking she might hit him, though she barely had strength sufficient to lift her arm. 'No!' Mary rasped and tried to lift and shake her head. But the pain of it was too much to bear, and she winced and her head fell back and her hand fell limply by her side.

'No, says you! Yes, says I! Startin' a riot, now that be a most serious offence what will earn a floggin' if I be not mistaken. Surgeon-superintendent don't like that, no he don't, I'll vouch for that, not like it, not one little bit!'

Mary tried once again to move her head. 'No!' she managed again. She was suddenly aware of a strange sound and at the same time the vessel shuddered and then rolled slightly. 'Wind?' Mary whispered.

'Oh yes, wind! Glorious wind! Gawd's breath is back with us, Mary Habacus!' Tiberias Potbottom said triumphantly then pushed his ugly little monkey face close to Mary's. 'Gawd is not mocked!' he said, spraying her face with his fierce spittle. 'You have been punished and He has restored His precious breath to us!'

Tears ran from Mary's swollen eyes and she drew

blood as she bit her top lip in an attempt to stop them. She did not want to show her physical pain, nor her confusion and agony of mind to the creature perched on the stool beside her.

'What's this then?' Potbottom asked suddenly.

Mary made no attempt to look, thinking him to be making comment over her distress. Instead she kept her lumpy eyes closed fighting back the tears that threatened to grow into a desperate sobbing. They were stupid tears, tears that showed Potbottom that he'd won, that he'd broken her spirit, tears for the past and the present and the future, tears that washed over her awful life.

'What be this I'm holdin', eh!' Potbottom asked again, and this time his demanding impatient tone caused Mary to open her one good eye. Tiberias Potbottom held up a prisoner's purse. 'Never know what you'll find when you looks, does you, me dear?'

Mary's hand went instinctively to her cunny but she knew before she reached it that her prisoner's purse was no longer hidden there. The brass tube Tiberias Potbottom held contained her fifteen sovereigns and Ikey's precious Waterloo medallion and chain and Mary began to sob uncontrollably.

'Shall we see what we's got, then?' Potbottom said gleefully. His small hands twisted the brass cap, removed and upended it, tapping it into the centre of his palm. 'Very curious,' he said, 'it don't have nothin' in it!' He tapped the tube once more in the same manner then held it with the open end facing Mary. Potbottom raised his dark, bushy eyebrows, his tiny black eyes shining. 'A pleasurin' device is it? A poor convict woman's comfort for the dark lonely nights at sea?'

Potbottom shook his head and clucked his tongue several times. 'I don't think Mr Smiles will take kindly to such a device. Not kindly at all!' He replaced the cap and, leaning over Mary, he placed the small metal tube on her chest. As he did so, Ikey's medallion fell from within his linen shirt and dangled on its chain directly above Mary's breasts. Then, without a further glance at the hapless, sobbing Mary, he scuttled out of the hospital, leaving her to contemplate the loss of everything she possessed in the world.

Mary had secretly dared to hope that her life might change, that despite the hell of Van Diemen's Land she would survive and that something good, no matter how small, might come of it. Now she knew that she had been deluding herself all her life, in truth, the flame of her existence had been blown out the very moment she had been born. As she lay in the prison hospital Mary craved emptiness, to feel nothing, to walk upon the earth as a shadow until death came as yet another misadventure upon her senseless life. Her past filled her up, taking possession of every corner of her soul to make her life a dark, repugnant experience. Where others might have craved Christian salvation, Mary asked only for emptiness, for all feeling to be taken from her. She wanted neither God nor the devil, but what lay between. Without feeling, she told herself, she could continue to exist; with it, she wanted only to die.

Soon her tears dried up. They were pointless. To cry was to mourn and to mourn was to care and caring was what had always destroyed her. She cursed her mouth and its ability to find trouble; others knew their place and remained silent with their heads bowed in obsequious obedience. It was her big mouth which had

378

destroyed her life. If she could empty out all that had happened to her, she would grow silent forever, not be seen or heard, or be there at all, her lips frozen forever.

But instead of emptiness, as Mary lay perfectly still, there grew slowly within her a great anger and then through the anger came pain, a sharp throbbing in her left hand. She tried to ignore it, but it was too alive and demanding, and soon the pain within the centre of her hand burned as though it were a fire kindled there, a furnace of white heat expanding and filling her, roaring at the very centre of her being. She could no longer ignore it. Mary lifted her hand to within the line of her vision and perceived for the first time that it was held tightly in a claw-like grip, its dark twisted fingers resembling, not a human hand, but an ugly, twisted knot. Within the knot a searing, leaping, roaring flame called out to her for revenge.

Mary attempted to open her hand but the fingers would not respond to her will and the pain caused by the effort brought her close to fainting. But she persisted, and after several minutes, her stiffened and contorted fingers broke loose sufficiently to reveal within them the small knotted rag bundle containing her brass talons. Mary started to weep again, but this time with a sense of great relief, for she knew instinctively that she would recover, and that the odious little monkey creature had not broken her spirit. She knew that the hatred in her would restore her health, though to be God's or the devil's child she knew not, and cared even less.

Chapter Eighteen

Mary's punishment was not completed with her beating and admission to hospital. A week after being released she was paraded on the prisoners' deck and charged with causing a riot within the prison. This was too grave an offence for Tiberias Potbottom to resolve by the usual proxy of his prayerful master, and Joshua Smiles himself was required to preside. With a charge of inciting a riot, the safety of the ship had been placed in jeopardy and the ship's master and those officers not on duty were required to be in attendance.

A muster of all the prisoners was called mid-morning with Mary standing with her head erect before the pale and mournful Smiles. The surgeon-superintendent, as was his usual habit, was dressed completely in black. This colour included both his blouse and neckerchief and a top hat of unusual height. The total effect gave him the appearance of being perhaps on stilts. He towered over the remainder of the prisoners, matrons, guards and even the tallest of the ship's officers present, and Mary was seen to come not much above the waist of his frock coat.

In a tone incurious to the consequence of his words

he read out the charges against Mary and then, without raising his voice or heightening the inflections placed upon his words, he pronounced sentence. It was a noticeable contradiction to the blandness of his voice that throughout his reading the surgeon-superintendent, on no single occasion looked up or at the prisoner, and his hands shook as though in a tremor as they held the paper from which he read.

'. . . Mary Abacus, I, Joshua Jeremiah Smiles, under the authority given to me by the Admiralty and further, under the provisions of the Home Department and in the name of His Majesty King George IV, sentence you to twenty-five strokes of the lash to be administered at one time. Whereupon you shall have your hair shaved and be placed in solitary confinement within the coal hole and shall remain there for one week, this to exclude the Sabbath. During this time you shall be given bread and water as your only sustenance. I further order that the sentence be carried out immediately by Mr Tiberias Potbottom and that all prisoners and those who be in charge of them, and therefore under my authority, shall bear witness to these proceedings.'

There was a gasp from the prisoners, for even the whores felt great remorse at what they'd done to Mary.

'Ya bloody bastard!' a voice shouted from the centre of the crowd.

'Who said that?' Tiberias Potbottom called out, jumping up and down to try to see into the lines of assembled women.

'I did, ya fuckin' ape!' Ann Gower called as two guards moved into the crowd of suddenly thronging and excited women and grabbed her. 'You murderers!' she shouted again as she was pulled away and led from the deck. 'May ya rot in 'ell!' A guard struck her on the side of the head with his truncheon, so that she fell to her knees and was dragged down the hatchway.

Mary was placed over an empty barrel, her arms and legs held by the wrists and ankles, each limb by a separate male prison guard. The matron of the hospital, who had so recently nursed her back to health, was then required to fully expose her back. Mary was given a small square of folded cloth to place between her teeth.

The sky above was brilliant blue with no cloud to interrupt its surface, a storm having come up during the night so that the ocean and the sky seemed to shine in a world washed clean. The ship sailed steadily at eight knots to a breeze from the south-west, its prow cutting majestically through the waves. Even the sun, though warm, was not torturous, the breeze cooling the deck where Mary lay sprawled over a barrel in preparation for 'the Botany Bay dozen' – that is, twenty-five strokes of the lash. Potbottom stood over her wielding the dreaded cat. He was so tiny that the lash, with its three knotted leather straps attached to a wooden handle, seemed too big in his hand.

That he should have been allocated such a task was unusual in the extreme. Had such a need befallen a male convict ship there would have been some person skilled in the use of the whip. But flogging was exceptionally rare on female convict ships, and no such expert existed on the *Destiny II*.

While Potbottom gleefully held on to the whip handle with both hands, he was not himself sure quite how it should be used for maximum effect, so he slapped it down upon the deck at his feet to get the hang and angle of its correct use.

Meanwhile Joshua Smiles produced from the pockets of his top coat the two small knee cushions, 'Jesus' and 'Saves', which he had carefully strapped to his legs so that the two words embroidered in red against a white canvas background might be clearly seen by all. With his back turned to Mary and his eyes fastened upon the topgallant sail, he kneeled upon the deck, having first respectfully removed his top hat and placed it beside him.

Potbottom, the awkward whip in hand, observing the surgeon-superintendent to clasp his hands in prayer and then, no doubt by pre-arrangement, to briefly nod, brought the lash up above his shoulders and hard down upon Mary's back.

'Oh merciful God forgive this poor wretch her transgressions,' Joshua Smiles loudly intoned, his voice directed upwards at the topgallant sail.

He paused after delivering this single sentiment, then once more nodded. Whereupon Potbottom again wielded the lash.

'Oh Lord Jesus may she repent her sins and accept your merciful forgiveness!'

Pause, nod and Potbottom's lash came down a third time. Thin welts like the beginnings of a spider's web now began to rise on Mary's back.

Thus the prayers, the nods and the whipping continued until the twenty-five strokes were completed. Mary's back was now bleeding profusely and covered with ugly welts, much to the satisfaction of Potbottom.

Many of the convict women were weeping as Mary was lifted to her feet and the gag removed from her lips. Sobbing and sniffing, both her eyes still ringed purple from the beating she'd taken, her clawed and withered hands clasped to her trembling breast, Mary was in all appearance a most forlorn and heart-rending sight.

Witnessing her misery and dejection the convicts increased the volume of their weeping. Mary was pushed back on to her knees and the prison matron stepped up to her and commenced to crop Mary's hair close to her scalp. The soft, pale hair fell to the deck, where a sudden zephyr blew it about and then carried it out to sea.

When this initial cropping was completed a bowl of soapy water was produced by one of the prison assistants, who proceeded to lather the hair remaining on Mary's head. The matron then exchanged her scissors for a cut-throat razor and shaved Mary's head, the uncaring blade removing the crusted scabs where her hair had been previously yanked out from her scalp, so that the blood, turned pink with the foamy lather, ran down Mary's face and neck.

The howling of the convict women increased in intensity and, while prison guards drew closer with their truncheons at the ready, Potbottom jumped and skipped beside them, bringing the lash down upon the deck as a gleeful warning to any who would promote a further mischief.

Mary was taken to the hospital and made to wash. Her uniform was stripped from her and she was given an old and tattered garment to wear. It had been washed soft, ready to be used as a rag, and so brought some comfort to her burning back. When her blood-stained uniform was returned to the mess a quarrel broke out among the whores, each of whom wanted to wash and repair it. Mary was then taken to the coal hole, the darkest and gloomiest part of the ship, where she was locked up with the supply of coal used in the vessel's kitchens.

There is nothing as destructive to the mind as complete darkness and silence. If there be a hell then eternal fire would come but a poor second to an eternity filled with complete solitude, for humans are gregarious creatures, in the main, and not designed to be alone. Soon the will to live breaks down and the mind ceases to see things rational and coherent; instead, nightmares grow out of a darkness populated with beasts and demons and hob-goblins with sharpened teeth and long treacherous claws.

It was most fortunate therefore that a prison guard, bringing Mary's ration of water and ship's biscuit, took pity on her and agreed to bring her abacus to her. Had it not been for this, the week spent in the coal hole might well have robbed Mary of her sanity. In the pitch darkness she would work the beads until her fingers were raw. Her mind grew to memorise the numbers of red and black upon the wire rails, and she spent hours making the most bizarre calculations to keep her mental condition sharp. She knew the height and width and circumference of the dome of St Paul's, and worked out the number of bricks it would have taken to build it. She knew the width and the length of the Mall and estimated the size of a single cobblestone, whereupon she worked out the number of these contained in the entirety of this regal way. It was with this kind of foolishness that she remained fully possessed of her wits in the darkness and silence of the dreadful hole into which she had been cast.

Sometimes Mary's hands became too painful and she was forced to leave her abacus alone. When she did so,

her mind became filled with the spectre of Tiberias Potbottom, who now possessed her luck.

Mary was philosophical about the fifteen gold sovereigns he had stolen from her, but this was not the case
with the medal. Potbottom's wearing of Ikey's talisman
was an abomination. The usurping of her future luck
was not a robbery but a snatching of her very soul. The
legend inscribed upon it, '*I shall never surrender*', was
a determination she now regarded as endowed to her
along with the luck it possessed. Mary told herself that
without this talisman, her life upon the Fatal Shore was
most surely doomed. She had convinced herself that
without the determination it engendered and the luck it
brought as a consequence she would be helpless. It also
concerned her that in wearing the medal, Potbottom's
own determination, the very power and potency of his
evil, was greatly enhanced.

Mary truly believed that what had befallen her on
board ship was simply a continuation of her previous
life. The *Destiny II* was still in her mind English terri-
tory, thus resulting in English circumstance. The luck
Ikey's talisman contained was hers for a foreign land
and remained Ikey's until she reached her destination.
Lying in the darkness of the coal hole, Mary became
obsessed with the urgency of retrieving the medal, for
while Potbottom wore it about his neck, Ikey, wherever
he might be, went unprotected. Furthermore, if she
arrived in Hobart without the blessing of the golden
charm, she would have no reason to live, her dreadful
fate having been already sealed.

Mary had a naturally observant nature and now as
she lay in the dark she tried to think of all the daily
movements of Potbottom about the ship. She earnestly

contemplated his habits, those small things which appeared consistent in his daily routine. Alas, she found that, in contrast to his master, he was most gregarious, seldom alone or still for one minute at a time and not at all consistent. At muster, in the hospital or during bloody pusover he was always amidst a group and the centre of attention. Into this daily routine Mary silently followed Potbottom in her mind, but never could she discover a time when he was on his own.

And then she remembered that during her two days in the prison hospital the hatch was unlocked an hour earlier than that of the prison itself to allow Potbottom to enter. It was his habit to send the convict night assistant and the hospital assistant up on board while, on behalf of the surgeon-superintendent, he made an inventory of the medication in the small dispensary.

In fact, although this could not be known to Mary, what he was occupied in doing each morning was removing and packing the physic and medication prescribed and written in the ledger at the previous day's sick call or at the weekly bloody pusover. He would carefully remove from the dispensary the amounts prescribed for each treatment in the surgeon's ledger, packing the unused medicine into a small leather portmanteau. Then he would repair to his cabin where the contents of the case would be added, each medication to its own type, to the stock already accumulated on the voyage.

This contraband medicine, intended for the sick on board, would eventually be sold for a most handsome profit when the ship berthed in Rio de Janeiro. Potbottom also saw to it that some small part of the profit was paid to the hospital matron, a professed Christian, who had a most remarkable propensity to see no evil when to be blind was to her benefit.

It was a foolproof method, for when the medical supplies remaining were checked by the authorities in Hobart Town against the surgeon-superintendent's prescription ledger and subtracted from the amount placed on board at the port of embarkation, the amounts would tally perfectly. If any convict should complain to the authorities that she had not received medication for an illness, the hospital matron would swear that this was a lie. Furthermore, if a member of the crew or prison staff required attention while on board they would be treated most generously with whatever physic was required, so that they would readily testify to the probity of the ship's surgeon and the diligence of its hospital matron.

The dispensary was situated in a small cabin behind a bulkhead at the end of the hospital and Mary, while recovering from the attack on her in the prison, had observed that Potbottom entered it alone each morning, leaving the door slightly ajar. He worked there unobserved and, at the same time, allowed sufficient air into the tiny room which lacked a porthole of its own.

Mary tried to recall every detail of Potbottom's early morning entry. He had never spoken, which was unusual, for his busy cackle was as much a part of him as his quick, nervous movements. He was a prattler of exceptional talent. Yet he would enter the hospital silently and, Mary now realised, in a most agitated state fumble the key into the lock of the dispensary as though he were on a most urgent mission.

However, when some time later he emerged he would be his usual vile self, cackling and quick-tongued, small cruel eyes sparkling as he stood at her berth to say something unpleasant. He would leave the hospital in a fine mood, delighted with himself, eager to embrace the task of making those around him afraid of the consequences of doing anything which might displease him.

Mary's berth had been almost beside the door of the dispensary and on the second morning in hospital Potbottom had entered in an even more agitated state than usual. His arms were clasped tightly across his chest and he shivered as though he were very cold. His tiny claws scratched with great irritation at the topmost part of his arms. Mary observed that his lips were cracked and without colour, a thin line of white spit bubbles stretching the length of his mouth. Feigning sleep, she watched as his hands fumbled to unlock the door to the dispensary. In his haste to enter he left the door somewhat more ajar than usual, and by craning her neck Mary could see into the tiny cupboard-sized cabin.

Potbottom, his hands trembling, quickly mixed an amount of raw opium in a small glass container into which he poured what looked to be a syrup from its distinctive blue bottle. Mary was most familiar with opium, it having come close in the past to taking her life. The syrup she took to be laudanum, a mixture of opium dissolved in alcohol, used by prostitutes on the way down. Only those most heavily addicted would think to use more opium in their laudanum, as she herself had done in that darkest time of her life.

Mary watched as the surgeon's assistant hastily swallowed the liquid and then waited, with eyes closed, for it to hit. She knew exactly how he felt. The jangled nerves suddenly straightened, the tension relaxed and his mind and thoughts once more collected. The muscles of his arms and legs no longer jumped and as his craving body received the devil's tonic the dreadful itching under his skin mercifully melted away.

Mary knew at once that Tiberias Potbottom was a helpless victim of the oriental poppy and, judging from the amount of opium grains he'd mixed with the laudanum, he was greatly dependent upon its effects and well accustomed to its constant use.

As Mary lay in the darkness of the coal hole a plan slowly began to emerge in her mind. She prayed that some small part of all her future luck, the golden luck which now dangled around the little monkey's scrawny neck, might be granted to her on credit. Her prayers were directed at whomsoever cared to hear them, whether God or the devil, she didn't much care.

After her flogging and the week spent in isolation, Mary became the subject of great admiration among the convict women. They had greatly missed Mary reading to them in the hot afternoons and the wry and cryptic comments she made about many of the morally uplifting books the Quakers had so generously supplied. Mary's readings of faraway places and of great journeys undertaken allowed for pictures to grow in their minds. And when she read of the lives of great men, for there were no biographies of women, the prisoners felt as though they too were a part of the grand story of the human race and not merely the scum and sweepings of a society which had rejected them. The children on board would clamour around her the moment she was free from her work, plucking at her skirt. 'Please, Mistress Mary, a story!' they would beg, pestering her until she would relent and gather them around her in a corner of the deck and read to them from *Gulliver's Travels* or from the books left for children by the Quakers.

Mary would also sometimes talk of the great journey they were themselves making. She would recount it, not as though it were themselves taking part, but as if it had happened to a group of intrepid adventurers cast adrift and sailing at the merciless whim of the winds to the outer reaches of the universe. Mary's story filled them with pride and hope at their own resolve, and told how the women in this strange and magnificent adventure would one day tame a wild land. Their eyes would shine as she envisaged how they would make this wild frontier a safe place for their sons and daughters, who would be free men and women possessed of handsome looks, sturdy of body and mind, prosperous in every circumstance.

Mary had also taken on the task of running the school for those who wished to learn to read and write, and her pupils, including the eleven children on board, had missed her greatly. For while Mary was a strict task mistress, they had almost all progressed and took great confidence from the new light which was beginning to shine within their minds.

Potbottom insisted that Mary still be allocated the most menial of tasks for her morning duties. She persuaded the matron of the prison hospital to allow her to be a cleaner, this being in return for reading religious tracts to the patients for half an hour each day. The matron, Mrs Barnett, readily agreed, as Mary had been prepared to accept the most onerous of tasks, to clean out the water closets and to act as the laundry maid.

Mrs Barnett had no cause to be suspicious as Mary's

request was a common one, given that rations for the sick were greatly superior to the food served to the other prisoners and included preserved tinned vegetables and rice. Those prisoners who were fortunate enough to work in the prison hospital would sometimes benefit from the scraps and scrapings left in the pots or on the plates. Or, on a propitious day they might come upon half a mug of beefy broth with golden gobbets of fat swimming on its surface, or a portion of food left by a patient who was too poorly disposed to eat. In contrast to their usual fare, which consisted of salted beef or pork, or a helping of plum pudding, all of which was served with a portion of weevily ship's biscuit, the heavenly taste of an ounce of tender preserved beef, a mouthful of peas or a spoonful of rice gathered a few grains at a time from several plates, was well worth the lowliest task required in the hospital.

Mary soon ingratiated herself with Mrs Barnett, who mistook her beautiful readings of the religious tracts to mean that Mary had seen the light and had herself embraced the Lord. Such was the tenderness of her rendering of the gospel that often those who lay sick in the hospital would weep openly for their sins and beg to be granted God's forgiveness. Mary, who could see no harm in it, would happily grant salvation to those who so earnestly sought it. But when one of her redeemed souls passed away from bronchial pneumonia she worried that her credentials as a Salvationist might not be acceptable at the heavenly portals, and that the poor woman might be sent elsewhere.

Matron Barnett, impressed with Mary's sanctity and often enough herself brought to tears by the readings, soon came to see her in an entirely new light. Mary was taken off cleaning the hospital closets, excused from laundry duties and made a convict assistant to the matron. It required only one small step for Mary to be allowed to be the convict assistant who slept in the prison hospital at night, and this privilege was soon enough granted her by the redoubtable Mrs Barnett. Mary had managed, in the space of four weeks and on the eve of the ship's arrival at the port of Rio, to find herself exactly where she needed to be when Potbottom entered the prison hospital each morning. All she now needed was a few moments access to the dispensary.

The ship lay anchored at sea and then sailed into Rio harbour with the evening tide as the sun set over the magnificent mountains that rose above the bay. The prisoners were allowed a brief glimpse of this paradise before they were sent below, the hatches closed while the jack tars stood with the hawsers and the capstans.

They would stay a week to make repairs and take fresh supplies on board. Of this land of church bells and beautiful dark-skinned people, of bright parrots and macaws and baskets laden with exotic fruit, the hapless convict women would see nothing. They would spend the entire time in the convict prison with the hatches closed.

Fortunately they benefited from excellent beef and fresh vegetables and fruit, in fact all the fruit they could eat, so that Rio became for them a place of fruit. They tasted the exotic mango and the pink-fleshed guava, supped on melons with tiny jet-black pips set into blood-red meat and gorged on papaya, a fruit with a soft, sweet orange flesh that proved most calming and efficacious to constipation and agreeable to the digestion.

At night, across the water, they could hear the drums

beating out a rhythm that sent the blood racing and sometimes, if they lay awake late at night, a lone troubadour would come to the dockside and with an instrument resembling a mandolin play love songs in the strange, haunting language of the Portuguese. Playing to the silent ship, his brown naked chest, dark hair and seductive smile, all glimpsed in the moonlight by those who were fortunate enough to have a porthole facing the dockside above their berth, invited them to indulge with him in hot, tropical lovemaking. The convict women allowed that Mary should take her position at the porthole closest to the singer so that she might tell of him in future days, and weave his songs, laughter and the soft, sensuous swinging of his hips into her stories as they journeyed onwards to the hell of Van Diemen's Land. Rio would always remain in Mary's mind as a place of exotic fruit, love songs and of a young man of giant stature and ebony beauty.

On the evening of the final night in Rio, for the *Destiny II* would sail on the morning tide, the captain and surgeon-superintendent were dining ashore with the British consul when the police brought to the ship a cartload of seven sailors who had been gathered from the premises of a notorious brothel on the Rua do Ouvidor. They had been in a fight and from all appearances had received the worst part of it. Their blouses were red with blood from multiple lacerations to their bodies. Potbottom had also gone ashore, ostensibly to sell the prisoners' quilts and handiwork, and was not yet returned to the ship. The only medical authority on board was Mrs Barnett, who was summoned by the officer of the watch and instructed to make the hospital ready. Mrs Barnett called at once for all assistance, which included the convicts who worked in the hospital, and so Mary was called to duty.

The men were in an advanced state of drunkenness having consumed greatly of the local firewater, the deadly *aguardiente*, and had not yet come to their senses or seen how badly lacerated and beaten they were. Great confusion reigned in the hospital as the matron tried to clean away the blood and stitch and dress the stab wounds. Mary too was kept busy as several of the jack tars started to vomit. She was on her hands and knees cleaning up beside the dispensary door when she observed it to be open. Mrs Barnett had rushed in to fetch medication, and in her haste to get back to the injured sailors had left the door ajar.

Mary glanced quickly around to see the whereabouts of the matron and her assistants and, observing that they all had their backs to her, she hurriedly entered the dispensary. The candle the matron had earlier lit was still glowing so she lifted it and quickly found what she wanted, the blue bottle she'd seen Potbottom use. She sniffed it and established immediately that it was laudanum. Mary soon found the pewter box from which the surgeon's assistant had obtained the opium, and she transferred a sufficient quantity into the bottle of laudanum to make a most powerful mixture, in fact twice the strength she'd observed Potbottom make for himself. No more than a minute had elapsed before she was back on her knees cleaning the hospital decking some distance from the dispensary door, only to see Mrs Barnett enter the dispensary, blow out the candle and lock the door. Should the matron's life depend on it, she would have sworn that no person but herself had entered the dispensary.

It took several hours to attend to the wounded men before they were dispatched back to their own apartments on the ship. Mrs Barnett and her hospital assistants were in a state of extreme fatigue and when Mary had made them a cup of tea she bade them goodnight and returned to the prison. The hospital contained no prisoners at that time, as none had been poorly disposed with the ship's arrival in Rio. This meant Mary could not sleep in the hospital, and she dared not ask Mrs Barnett for fear that she might refuse or, worse still, agree and then remember later that Mary had been the only one within the hospital when Potbottom arrived in the morning.

Mary wondered desperately how she might be at hand when Potbottom arrived without causing any suspicion, but could think of no way to bring this about as the prison hatches were opened a full hour after those of the hospital. The solution she chose was simple enough, but fraught with the danger of discovery. She climbed the stairs leading to the hatchway, making sure that the sound of her footsteps on the ladder was clearly audible. At the open hatchway she sat upon the topmost step and quickly removed her boots, whereupon she climbed silently downwards again and into the hospital, concealing herself under one of the berths adjacent to the stairway. After a short while Mary saw the feet of the weary women pass and heard them climb towards the hatchway. Shortly afterward she heard the bolt slide behind them. In the dark she removed her prisoner's purse from its snug hiding place and took from it the four brass talons which she now fitted, two to each hand. It was nearly dawn and she would have less than two hours to wait until Potbottom arrived at seven to attend to his urgent need for the fruit of the Chinese poppy.

Mary must have dozed off for she awoke to the sound of the bolt being pulled back, and then she heard the slight creak of the hinges as the hatch was pulled upwards. Her heart was suddenly beating so hard that she felt sure Potbottom must hear it as one might a drum on the dockside at Rio de Janeiro. His tiny feet soon scuttled past where she lay and she could hear though not see him fumbling with the key as he unlocked the door to the dispensary. She hadn't long to wait, perhaps no more than two or three minutes, when she heard what sounded like a loud gasp followed shortly thereafter by a dull thud as Potbottom hit the deck.

Mary crawled out from under the berth and crept silently to the dispensary door. Potbottom lay with the top half of his body outside the small room, as though he had turned to leave just as the effects of the opium hit. Mary bent over him and peeled back his eyelids, observing that his pupils had constricted and his dark eyes showed no movement. She shook him several times but he was as limp as a wet mop. Potbottom was unconscious.

Mary rolled Potbottom onto his stomach, being careful to place his head to the side so that he could continue to breathe. Then she removed the talons from her left hand and, lifting his head slightly, she took the chain and medallion from around his neck and clasped it to her bosom. The feel of the precious medallion in her hand was too much to bear, and tears ran from Mary's eyes.

There is something perverse in the nature of humans,

stubborn and quite nonsensical to the intelligence, where we will do something impulsive which may culminate in the most dire consequences, but which, at the time, we cannot seem to prevent. It is an action of the heart which temporarily overpowers any recourse to the head.

Mary, her luck restored to her in the form of the Waterloo medallion, had need only to make her escape. Should Potbottom regain consciousness he would have no cause to be suspicious, or even, in the unlikely circumstances that he should be, would have no way of proving that the dosage had been tampered with, without revealing his own addiction. Mary had committed the perfect crime, providing she could escape from the prison hospital unobserved, and conceal herself until morning muster where she could simply join the other women prisoners on deck.

She wiped the tears from her eyes and was about to remove the brass talons from her right hand when she looked down again at Potbottom's unconscious form. All the anger and humiliation he had caused her suddenly coalesced within her breast as though it were a great fist which squeezed her heart. Mary took the remaining talons from her right hand and placed them on the deck beside the body where she'd left the others. Now she rolled Potbottom onto his back, quickly unbuttoned the front of his worn and greasy frock coat and opened it wide, whereupon she rolled him back onto his stomach. She then stripped the sleeves from his limp arms and pulled off the jacket. Mary was panting loudly, both from the effort of manhandling him and from her tremendous fury. She laid the coat aside and pulled the dirty blouse he wore from the top of his breeches and lifted it high over his back and the back of his head. This action completely exposed his back and with it the hump which now seemed larger than when it was concealed beneath his coat. Mary was whimpering as she replaced the talons onto her left hand, and with them she drew a long deep stroke across Potbottom's back, weeping afresh with a volatile mixture of anger, spite and despair. She was doing to someone else what had been so often done to her. Coldly, precisely, she carved twenty-five lines across the surgeon-assistant's hairy back, in a random criss-cross fashion, sparing not even the ugly hump.

'That be your twenty-five lashes back, Tiberias Potbottom! Gawd is not mocked, you 'ear?' Mary laughed, though somewhat hysterically, for she felt no humour in it. 'That be one stroke for every whore aboard and one for me, you cruel bastard! That be *our* Botany Bay dozen!' Panting with the emotional effort, Mary began to weep softly as the anger left, completely spent by her revenge.

After a few moments Mary ceased crying, sensing her own imminent danger. She sniffed and wiped her nose on the sleeve of her smock. She now felt strangely calm and pulled Potbottom's blouse down over his back, tucking the ends neatly into his broad leather belt. Bright crimson designs of a random pattern seeped through the dirty cloth.

Mary could feel the ship moving as she lifted Potbottom to a seated position so that he was propped against a berth. She then calmly returned his jacket to his person, buttoning it up as before and adjusting his neckerchief, whereupon she laid him back with his broken little buckled boots placed within the door of the dispensary. The remainder of his body was lying within the main cabin of the hospital. Then she took the bottle in which she'd mixed the opium and the laudanum and emptied what remained of its contents in the slop bucket and, stepping over her victim, returned it to the shelf in the dispensary. Mary then quickly checked that Potbottom was still breathing and, gathering up the two remaining talons, left by climbing up through the open hatchway onto the deck, where she threw the vicious brass claws over the side.

The rising sun caught the small brass objects and for a moment the wicked claws winked and then fell into the trough of a wave. It was a small enough thing to do and some might say Mary was simply destroying the evidence of her perfidy, but this was not the case. With the dreaded hooks went the past, that hard dark passage of time which was not of Mary's making. Ahead lay another life. And though Mary would enter her new land in captivity, she felt herself to be free at last.

The *Destiny II* had reached the entrance to the harbour between Fort San Juan and Fort Santa Cruz, so that the crew's attention was to the foredeck looking out to sea. With the prisoners still below decks, there was no one to observe her as she moved aft.

Mary moved rapidly to the stern of the vessel and up onto the poop deck where, as soon as the vessel was safely out to sea, morning muster would take place. She squeezed behind two barrels lashed to the deck and crouched there. High above her a flock of macaw parrots flew across from the headland, their brilliant plumage flashing in the early morning sun. Mary could see the high peak of the Sugar Loaf above the sweep of the bay and the dark green jungle which grew upon its slopes and almost to the pinnacle of the great mountain. She would always remember the immense height of the tropical sky and its infinite blueness so much sharper, brighter, fiercer than the English sky.

Potbottom was not missed at morning muster, for it was not unknown for him to be absent. But he would always surface later when sick call was made directly after muster, and those prisoners hoping to escape for a few days of improved rations remained behind on the poop deck endeavouring to persuade Mrs Barnett, or even the ship's surgeon, that they were right poorly disposed.

On the morning of sailing from Rio, Joshua Smiles had himself attended the sick call, and it had been assumed that Potbottom must have returned from ashore in the early hours of the morning and was still abed. But when the surgeon-superintendent asked for him a guard was sent to rouse him from his cabin.

However, before the guard could return one of the hospital assistants came up to the poop deck and from her demeanour she was seen to be most distressed. She went directly to Mrs Barnett, but because the surgeon was busy with his ear to the chest of one of the convict women the matron hushed her attempt to talk by placing a finger to her lips. When Joshua Smiles withdrew his ear the assistant, a rather fat young girl with an ugly pock-marked face, was wringing her hands and blurted out.

'Mr Smiles, excuse I, sir, Mr Potbottom be dead on 'ospital floor!'

It took several hours before Tiberias Potbottom regained consciousness. In truth he had been conscious a full hour before he allowed that this be known. By which time he was aware both from the pain and from the talk about him, of the mutilated condition of his back.

Joshua Smiles, more pale than usual and in a state of considerable distress, sat beside him praying, imploring the Lord Jesus to save his precious and diligent servant. By the time Potbottom was prepared to squeeze the hand of his mentor, to indicate his return to life, he had well grasped the nature of his own dilemma, and had concocted a story which explained his situation in the dispensary. This took several hours to emerge and came out in half-coherent snatches, whether due to his latent condition or a deliberate ploy is not known. By the end of that day he told a story of having been given some strange draught. 'In one o' them *bodegas* what they's got and where I stopped to partake o' a bowl o' the strong black coffee what they serves with the juice o' the cane plant.'

'Mescaline!' Joshua Smiles announced triumphantly. 'The juice from cacti, a most stupefying narcotic. They put mescaline in your coffee!'

'That be dead right, Mr Smiles, sir!' Potbottom exclaimed, delighted to have a name to add to his plot. 'Mescaleen eh? That be for sure as I were not aware o' what befell me after, save to know that me purse be stolen and a valuable gold chain and medal were taken from about me neck. Though how this came about I truly cannot say, I awoke in me own cabin in the early part o' the mornin' not knowing how I got to the ship and with me head poundin' something horrible and feelin' in every part a great discomfort.'

'And the lacerations to your back, can you perchance

venture as to how they happened?' the surgeon asked.

'That I can't, sir. How it come about I haven't the slightest knowledge of,' Potbottom replied and then continued where he'd left off. 'But I looks at me watch what I had the good sense to leave aboard and sees it be time for me to attend dispensary.' Potbottom looked up beguilingly. 'As is o' course me daily duty and one which I takes most conscientiously.'

'Indeed, we are all most grateful for your diligence, Mr Potbottom,' Mrs Barnett said.

Potbottom ignored her remark and continued. 'I makes me way to the hospital when I perceived me back were hurtin' somethin' horrible, so I goes to make a physic of anodyne for the pain, like.' He looked soulful. 'That be all I remembers, nothin' more till I feels your blessed hand in mine,' Potbottom choked back a tear, 'and hears your generous prayers to the Almighty for me safe recovery, sir.'

'God has been good, Mr Potbottom. He has restored you to us to continue your good works among the heathen and the rapscallions.' Joshua Smiles paused and slowly shook his head and a small smile played upon his lips. 'We are all mightily blessed by His glory and compassion.'

He clasped his hands together and, looking up at the bulkhead as though the Almighty could be clearly seen seated upon its heavy cross beam, commenced to pray loudly and fervently, giving thanks for the recovery of God's most precious child, Tiberias Potbottom.

Mary's luck had held. Potbottom, whatever he thought, could make no open enquiries as to his misadventure for fear that his addiction to opium be discovered. While he subjected Mary to a great deal more persecution, confiscating her twice weekly ration of port and sending her back to work in the prison closets and to scrubbing and holystoning the interior of the prison and the decks, he could find no way of proving that she was the one who had brought about his undoing.

At each subsequent bloody pusover he had subjected Mary to the indignity of a front and rear inspection, though he was unable to discover the whereabouts of the chain and medallion. Once, when he had undertaken a surprise medical inspection, he had found her prisoner's purse and confiscated it only to find it disappointingly empty.

In fact, Mary had removed the sole of her boot, hollowed it out and placed her precious luck within it. She wore her boots all day and at night, as was the habit of the prisoners, she tied them about her neck so that they would not be stolen.

Weeks of great tedium passed as the *Destiny II* neared her destination, the tiny ship often climbing to the crest of waves that saw it half a hundred feet above the level of the ocean, and then sinking into the trough of a great wave where the ocean rose to the height of the topmast. The great swells of the Indian Ocean caused many to return to their previous sea sickness, but they were fortunate that they did not encounter a great storm at sea.

Of the trip, it can be said that it was not remarkable but typical of any other transport carrying female convicts. Two prisoners had died, an aged woman who was said to have a condition of the heart and an infant only just weaned, who had come aboard with bronchial pneumonia. They were most ceremoniously buried at sea with a consideration they had not known in their mortal lives.

Perhaps the one thing that might be said to have been remarkable about the voyage was the schooling Mary had given during the hot afternoons. Though schooling was encouraged on convict ships, it was usually conducted by an educated free passenger or the surgeon-superintendent. It achieved good, though often somewhat dubious, results, for the art of reading was often construed as having been achieved when a prisoner could recite a psalm while holding the Bible and appearing to be reading from it.

Mary's teaching was different, for she taught the rudiments of writing as well as reading, insisting on phonetics until her pupils could identify each letter with a sound and connect them with another to make a word. By the time they had reached their destination, fifty-five of the one hundred and twenty-six female prisoners who had come on board without a knowledge of reading would disembark with an ability to read individual words from a page and connect them aloud and continuously to make sense. Though this was done slowly and often with great movement of their lips and expostulations of breath, it was nevertheless the precious gift of the printed word.

Thus Mary, though the surgeon's report would place her in a most reprehensible light, was regarded by the female prisoners as a person of goodness, the best most of them had encountered in all of their unfortunate lives, while the children openly loved her. She was not the sort of pious personage they had been accustomed to regard as a saint, some creature whom they might have seen within the configurations of a stained glass window, with an aura about her head, clad in a diaphanous gown with her feet floating above the ground. Or some curate's daughter who saw her cunny only as an affliction and a shame and not as a delight. Nor did she resemble, in the least, the Quakers of the Ladies' Committee.

Mary was like themselves, hardened by the vicissitudes of a poverty-stricken life, though unlike themselves, not beaten by it. She was a woman who spoke her mind, had a tongue as harsh and foul as many, but who could not be easily led and who intuitively knew her own mind at all times. She could laugh and cry with the best of them and, most importantly of all, she showed that she believed in them.

Mary had demanded their attention at learning and had done so with a mixture of patience, encouragement, mockery, harsh words and foul language. The stories she read to them over the long, hot afternoons had opened their minds. And her great spoken story of their own voyage across the seas to the furthest ends of the earth had given them hope for the future. The women would be eternally grateful to Mary for bringing light into their lives where before there was only ignorance and darkness.

On their last night at sea Ann Gower called all to attention in the prison. 'We 'as one last duty to perform afore we goes ashore termorra, ladies!' Ann Gower shouted. 'Would ya be kind enough to be upstandin', then!' The women climbed from their berths and stood jam packed within the corridor, smiling and nudging each other for what they knew was about to happen.

'Afore we goes to Gawd knows where in the mornin' we 'as a crownin' to do!' Ann Gower then produced a crown made from paper mashed with flour, covered most decorously in cloth sewn about with small, diamond-shaped patches for the rich jewels. It was embroidered with tiny flowers, bluebells and crocus, daisy and honeysuckle, garlands of cottage roses and all the flowers of England. Many loving hands had worked on the crown in secrecy and with great skill to fashion it quite perfectly.

Ann Gower held the beautiful crown high above her head for all to see and they sighed with the pleasure of their own creation.

'Mary Abacus, we crowns ya 'er Royal 'Ighness, Queen Mary, Queen o' Van Diemen's Land!'

There was much clapping and laughter as Ann Gower placed the crown upon Mary's head. 'Blimey, it don't 'arf grow fast do it?' she said, pointing to Mary's scraggy fair hair, now two inches grown about her head and a most unsightly thing to behold. 'Soon be able to braid that ya will, honest!'

She looked about her and shouted once again, 'Never were a crown what was better deserved to an 'ead!' There was a roar of approval from the prisoners and Ann Gower waited for it to die down before addressing Mary.

'One question please, yer most gracious majesty! 'Ow come Potbottom got twenty-five beautiful, deep an' permanent stripes upon 'is back? Be it a coincidence that it be the same number as there is whores on board plus countin' yer good self?'

There was a loud gasp from the surrounding women, and then an excited murmur.

'Shush!' Ann Gower called and waited for the excitement of this new speculation to die down. 'Be it also a coincidence that you was called from the prison to do duty in the 'ospital that very night and that we knows about yer talons o' brass?'

There was a hush as everyone waited for Mary to answer. She was silent for a good while, the beautiful crown resting on her head. Then she looked up and her lovely green eyes seemed to dance with the mischief of her thoughts. 'I can't say as I knows and I can't say as I doesn't know, it be a secret, Ann Gower.' She paused and then gave a little laugh. 'A royal secret what's treason to tell about!'

There was much laughter and banter at this reply and Mary had never felt as loved or wanted. She knew herself to be a leader and now she also knew she had the courage to demand from life more than she had hitherto been given. She looked at the women surrounding her; like them, she was going into a new life and fate would play its hand, but she was different from them too. She would make her own luck, for she had seen the distant shore not as a place of servitude, but as a conquest, a place to be taken with a full heart, where the shadows of the past were leached out by a brighter sun. She would live under a higher sky washed a more brilliant blue, a heaven against which green parrots flashed like emeralds. She could make something of this place. Tomorrow, when the *Destiny II* sailed the last leg of the voyage up the Derwent River and she went ashore in irons with Ann Gower, she would wear Ikey's Waterloo medallion about her neck. For she knew, whatever happened to her, she would survive, the words '*I shall never surrender*' inscribed not only on Ikey's medal, but forever on her heart. They would bring Mary Abacus to a new and astonishing beginning upon the Fatal Shore.

BOOK TWO

Van Diemen's Land

Chapter Nineteen

The *Destiny II* lay at anchor in the D'Entrecasteaux Channel waiting for the morning tide to take it up river to Hobart Town. They had lain at anchor during the night, for the often shallow and treacherous channel waters, even though they appeared calm under the bright moon, were not to be embarked upon beyond sunset.

The morning was a smoky colour with a thin mist shrouding the surface of the water, and the prisoners, gathered on deck for muster, clasped their arms about their chests against the cold. They had been roused at dawn with the familiar 'Rouse out there! Turn out! Turn out! Huzza huzza!' and the words new to their ears resounded through the boat: 'Goin' ashore, huzza for the shore!' This was the last muster of the voyage and the cold could do nothing to conceal their excitement.

On the starboard side the Black Rocks and the cliffs of Bruny Island appeared most forbidding and their un-inviting nature seemed to pervade the leaden-coloured landscape on either side of the ship. But when the sun came up not much past the hour of six, the sky was soon a clean high blue, somewhat darker than the tropical skies they'd grown accustomed to, and colder, a touch of ice in its high dome. The incoming tide was beginning to slap at the stern of the *Destiny II* when Joshua Smiles, with the ever-present Potbottom at his side, stood to address the female prisoners.

Smiles constantly rubbed his palms down the front of his frock coat, avoiding direct eye contact with any of the prisoners. From his coat he produced a tiny square of paper folded many times upon itself, which he commenced to unfold in a slow and tentative manner, each corner lifted as if he expected the words to leap off the paper and harm him. The women in the front row observing him at this silly task began to giggle. Finally, with the page fully opened, he began to read in a most lugubrious voice.

'I, Joshua Templeton Smiles, surgeon-superintendent of the prisoner ship *Destiny II*, do on this 18th day of October in the year of our Lord 1827 declare . . .' He glanced up from the page, his height enabling him to look over the heads of the assembled convicts towards an unseen Hobart thirty miles away. Then he slowly brought his eyes back to the pages held in his fist. '. . . that with the notable exception of a handful of refractory and turbulent spirits you have behaved well and I have marked your reports accordingly.' He paused again and cleared his throat. 'But for two prisoners who have shown themselves to be profligate wretches and designing blasphemous whores throughout this voyage.' Pleased to have surmounted this last statement he continued more slowly. 'I have therefore made recommendation to His Excellency Colonel Arthur, lieutenant governor of Van Diemen's Land, that with the exception of these two prisoners, you all be placed into service with the families of settlers as soon as this may be conveniently arranged.'

There was a collective gasp and then a swelling murmur of excitement among the female convicts, who had not known what to expect upon arrival but who had, as is usually the case, feared the worst rumours circulated on board during the voyage. Many of the convicts had worked as domestic servants in England and saw this arrangement as ideal, their immediate hope being that they might attract a considerate and kind master.

'Those two prisoners who will not be granted this privilege will be conveyed in light irons to the Female Factory where their vile natures and ardour of their blasphemous utterances might be cooled to a more silent, pleasing and obedient temperature. These two wretches, who Mr Potbottom informs me are well acquainted to you all as trouble makers, will *not* be granted the privilege of remaining on deck to witness our arrival, nor allowed to be present at the governor's inspection, but will be placed instead in the coal hole as a final gesture of our Christian contempt!'

'I am not mocked saith the Lord,' Potbottom shouted gleefully, 'Mary Habacus and Ann Gower now step you forward at once!'

A flock of bright green parrots flew over the ship calling raucously as though in a mocking welcome. Mary, determined to show no emotion, watched as the rising sun caught the gloss on the wings of the beautiful birds as they drew away from the ship.

She had seen a flock of parrots fly overhead as they sailed out of Rio de Janeiro. Now here they were again.

Mary smiled as Ann Gower came up to her. Then she opened her arms and embraced her, the smaller woman holding the much larger one clasped to her thin chest.

Mary looked over Ann Gower's shoulder at Joshua Smiles and to her own surprise she heard herself say, 'Hear you, Joshua Smiles, we are the women o' this new land! You cannot defeat us, because we will never again surrender to the sanctimonious tyranny o' your kind!' She paused momentarily and pointed her crooked finger at the surgeon-superintendent. 'Gawd is not mocked!'

It was late into the afternoon when the hatch to the coal hole was opened and Mary and Ann Gower were allowed to emerge onto the deck. Their eyes, grown accustomed to the pitch darkness, were at first blinded by the brightness of the afternoon light.

The *Destiny II* had anchored late in the morning in Sullivan's Cove and the last of the prisoners were being cleared to disembark. Now as Mary and Ann Gower stood on the deck they observed a town of quite harmonious appearance. Built on the water's edge and rising steeply back from the Government Wharf, Hobart contained many well constructed buildings of stone and brick, and its streets were straight and broad. Several large native trees, saved from the builder's axe, gave the town an appearance of permanence which belied its recent development.

It was then that Mary, her eyes adjusted to the spring sunshine, glanced well beyond the waterfront to where Hobart Town climbed upon an even steeper slope, and saw the mountain. It rose into the ice-blue sky fully four thousand feet above her, its great rounded dome covered in late snow.

Mary gasped, bringing her hand to her chest, her heart pounding. This morning she had seen the parrots fly over her head and now, as in Rio de Janeiro, she had been given the gift of the great mountain. 'It all begins now, with the green birds and the magic mountain,' she whispered to herself. 'The luck begins for me. Whatever may follow, I swear I shall never knowingly surrender it again.' As if it was a catechism, she repeated the words on the Waterloo medal, 'I shall never surrender'.

What followed was a most tedious induction by the muster master, who sat at a table further along the deck, a canvas canopy having been built above his bald head to keep the sun at bay. He was in a most churlish mood, having been at his task several hours, and snapped at the two convicts to step forward.

Each in turn was made to stand before him while he completed their records. They were fortunate to have missed the visit on board by the lieutenant-governor, for it proved a tedious and longwinded occasion. The prisoners had been paraded on board and made to stand a full hour on deck before the great man, seated on a handsome black stallion, arrived at the Government Wharf. Colonel George Arthur dismounted to a short, sharp roll from a kettle drum and a salute by a platoon of troopers in scarlet jackets. Ignoring the large crowd, he stepped into a longboat where he stood upright in a stiff military manner as he was rowed to the vessel.

Once on board he lost no time with pleasantries, nodding brusquely at the master and officers and grunting, 'Well done!' Then turning to Joshua Smiles he shook his hand in a cursory manner, acknowledging him with the single word, 'Surgeon!' This may well have been a deliberate attempt to exert his authority for Colonel George Arthur was short in stature and came not much beyond the belt of the surgeon-superintendent. Although his exceedingly short legs did not hinder him in a frock coat, whenever he appeared in full vice-regal uniform or in a military deck-out his sword would drag along the ground as he walked. He was a man of rigid formality who would not entertain the possibility of a sword trimmed to less than regulation size, and so he always inspected his troops on horseback, selecting a large and fiery stallion for this purpose.

The governor tucked his small hands beneath the tail of his deep blue frock coat and commenced to stride up and down the assembled ranks of convicts.

'The hearts of every man and woman are desperately wicked and there is but one means of salvation, this be to have faith in the Lord and in Christ's crucifixion! You will attend church regularly and twice on Sunday, that is an order!'

All his entreaties and warnings were completed crisply and without prevarication, enumerating in exact detail what he regarded as both good and bad behaviour and giving a dozen examples of each. The ultimate result of good behaviour was the prospect of an early ticket of leave; of bad, the certain demise of the repeatedly offending prisoner.

Suddenly, Arthur stopped pacing and pointed across the narrow strip of water separating the ship from the shore, to beyond the crowds waiting on the wharf, and further still to some point imagined on the steep road leading up the hill.

'As you come ashore on the way to the Female

Factory you will pass a gibbet. There you will observe that the two corpses which hang from it are male. We have not yet on this island hanged a woman by the neck, but that is not to say we cannot.' The governor paused for the effects of his words to sink in. 'I implore you all to look well how they hang and to take great care to ensure that your destiny upon this island does not converge with that of these two unfortunate wretches.' Colonel Arthur pulled himself to his full stature. 'I will have you know that since I assumed this office, fully one hundred and fifty prisoners have been capitally convicted and executed! I tell you now, I am a fair man, but there is no mercy for those who will not observe the spirit and the letter of the law in its most infinite detail!' Colonel Arthur cast a cold eye over the prisoners. 'Do not disappoint me, for I warn you, I am not a man who takes well to disappointment!'

Now, several hours after the governor had departed, Mary and Ann Gower were subjected to a most thorough interrogation by the muster master, no doubt occasioned by his fear of the governor himself. He was a small, balding, bespectacled man of a most pernickety clerical appearance with an abundance of grey hair sprouting from his ears, who scratched the answers to his sharp and practised questions in a large black book which bore upon its gold-embossed cover the title: *Conduct Register*.

It was this book which ruled the lives of every prisoner on the island and from whence came the expression, *'I am in his black books'*, to mean that things do not go well for someone.

Colonel Arthur fervently believed that every convict should be strictly accounted for and that the course of

417

THE POTATO FACTORY

their lives, from the day of a prisoner's landing to that of their emancipation or death, should be written down. It was necessary therefore that every particular concerning a convict should be registered on their day of arrival and before they were taken ashore.

Mary's description was accordingly written down: *Light straw coloured hair, green eyes – placed wide apart, scar on left cheek, brow high, hands badly deformed – black/blue in colour, height 5 feet and 2 inches, skin fair, face clear – no pox pitting, comely in appearance.*

Next followed details on her crime and the events surrounding it, her non-marital status, date and place of birth, trade, next of kin and religion. Mary's literacy and numeracy were noted and both these tested and a sample of her handwriting added to the records. At the conclusion of her writing and numeracy test the muster master had said not unkindly, 'I 'ope you be'aves yourself, Prisoner Abacus. Orphans' school be most pleased to 'ave you, they would.'

'Orphan school?' Mary said, suddenly alert. 'There be a school 'ere for brats what's not owned?'

'Wesleyans, not Church of England. Don't know that much teachin' be done, though. I could put in a word?' He paused and then added, 'Got any,' he coughed lightly and grinned, 'gold ... a sovereign perhaps?'

Mary sighed, 'Blimey! For a moment there I thought you was all 'eart, sir!'

The muster master shook his head, 'No 'eart to be found in these parts, only money! All the 'eart you wants if you can pay for it!' He cleared his throat and pursed his lips, suddenly conscious of his position, then he resumed writing.

'Be there a library, sir?' Mary asked.

The muster master looked up over the top of his spectacles. 'Mrs Deane runs the Circulating Library, books to hire. There's no books for convicts though, Mrs Deane don't 'ave no dealings with convicts.'

At the conclusion of the interrogation Mary was allocated a police number. Being kindly disposed to numbers she was delighted to find hers was No. 7752. In her mind she immediately converted this to three 7s which she knew to be astonishingly good luck. Abacus, Mary – Female Convict, No. 7752 became, together with the name of her ship, as affixed as her surname for the entire period of Mary's sentence.

Once these preliminaries were completed, Mary and Ann Gower were issued with new clothing. This consisted of a cotton gown of cheap, coarse material, a petticoat, jacket and apron, and a straw bonnet. Large yellow Cs were marked in a prominent place upon each article of clothing, though this was not necessary, the outfit itself bespoke a prisoner as surely as if it had been patterned with arrows. Those possessions they still had on board were taken from them though Mary was careful to conceal Ikey's medal in her prisoner's purse safely tucked away in its usual place. She was able to persuade the prisoner matron to allow her to retain her beloved abacus and her papier mâché crown, but her precious copy of *Gulliver's Travels* was taken from her.

The two women were then placed in light irons and ferried ashore. Here they were met by a lone trooper and marched under guard up Macquarie Street to the Female Factory. On the way they passed the two men hanging from a gibbet, though Mary did not look. Her mind was filled with anticipation of a new land and she did not need so ready a reminder of where she had come from.

'Poor bastards!' Ann Gower spat. 'Looks like nothin' 'as changed.'

'No, Ann, you must see it differently. Everythin' 'as changed for us, everythin'!' Mary said.

The Female Factory was abutted to the male gaol forming a part of it and separated by a twelve foot wall. In all, it consisted of only four rooms. Two sleeping rooms had a total capacity of fifty women, thirty in one and twenty in the other, the sick room could accommodate another nine bodies and the work room another forty. At this point, the Factory was fully accommodated in terms most onerous to the comfortable accommodation of the inmates. With the addition of the women and children from the *Destiny II*, it was crowded almost to the point of suffocation. The prison yard could hold forty prisoners at one time, but could not be used at night for the cold and, besides, was at all times most dreadfully befouled.

Mary and Ann Gower soon found themselves placed without ceremony or further processing, beyond their names being registered, in the larger of the two sleeping rooms which contained fifty of their shipmates, all of whom, it became immediately apparent, were in a high state of excitement. They had been told that they would be assigned and collected the very next day, each to the family of a married settler, where they would work their sentences out as domestic servants, cooks, dairymaids or nursemaids.

As these vocations were to be readily found among their numbers, they had cause to entertain great hopes for a good future. Even those not previously exposed to the particularities of domestic work were confident that they would soon learn the tricks of the trade, having been put to scrubbing, cleaning, sewing and laundry work on board ship.

The women loudly cheered Mary and Ann Gower as they entered, crowding around them and offering their sincerest condolences for the severity of their sentences. But it was apparent that, while both women were greatly admired for their courage, each convict thought herself fortunate not to be sentenced to remain as a refractory prisoner in the Female Factory.

On that first overwhelmingly happy evening ashore, despite the insalubrious environment, the prospect of a good, clean life seemed very possible. Each silently marvelled at the good fortune that had landed her upon the Fatal Shore. They did not yet comprehend that the settler became their absolute master and they his official slaves, a system which openly encouraged the most shocking abuse. The masters of Van Diemen's Land counted few among them who contained a tincture of compassion in their callous and self-serving natures.

The penal system was designed from the beginning to work in three ways, all of which were intended to place the least expense upon the government. The first was to put the responsibility for the care and maintenance of convicts into private hands. This saved money and provided the second advantage, a source of cheap labour for the free settlers who were largely responsible for opening up the land. Finally it was intended to be a useful tool of reform by removing the convict from others of her own kind, separating her from the temptations, bad influences and vices which inevitably flowed from close confinement with her sisters.

In this way it was argued that the convict woman would be given the opportunity to gain self-respect, mend the error of her ways and re-enter society as a sober, God-fearing and useful citizen.

The convict prisoner had no set working hours, was not allowed out at night, must reside in her master's house, could not labour for herself in her free time, if ever such were granted to her, and could not move off the master's property without a pass. She must wear at all times a convict's uniform, though most seemed to find a way around this.

To all this was added the single concession, that a master could not punish his convict servant but had recourse to a magistrate should he have cause for complaint. The prisoner had little redress of her own. Though permitted to give evidence against her master, she was seldom believed unless a free settler was prepared to bear witness for her cause. This was a situation which rarely prevailed, while its converse, brutality and exploitation, was a daily occurrence.

But here too lay a paradox. While *only* magistrates could punish, most officers of the law were in a quandary to know what to do with females who required punishment. Constant and severe punishment as might have been the case in England would have defeated the unwritten reason why women were sent to Van Diemen's Land – to stabilise the colony through marriage and concubinage. It was silently held that the crimes a female committed brought little permanent harm and posed no danger to society, consisting mostly of absconding, being drunk and disorderly, insolence, fighting, refusing to work, being out without a pass after hours, immoral conduct and minor pilfering.

Whereas a male convict might be given two hundred lashes of the cat o' nine until his flesh was flayed from his back for minor offences, a female convict could not be flogged. Under Governor Arthur's rigid system of order, punishment for a crime other than stealing the property of another was seldom physical. Instead, confinement to gaol and hard labour were imposed. This largely consisted of working at the male prisoners' wash tub, or cleaning the prison slop buckets and water closets. If harsher punishment were deemed necessary, a female convict would receive solitary confinement on bread and water for a week, the cropping of her hair, and be placed in the public stocks for an hour or two. For the truly incorrigible, when all of these remedies had failed, an Iron Collar, a device which fitted about the prisoner's neck and weighed seven pounds, was worn for two days to publicly point to the infamy of the wretch who carried it.

These remedies, when compared to the treatment of convict men, were undoubtedly exceedingly mild, especially as it was generally held that the female convict was far more difficult to reform than the male, her general characteristics being immodesty, drunkenness and foul language, though, of course, this was a male assertion and not to be entirely trusted.

While official leniency may have existed for the female of the species, no such thing was true of the unofficial behaviour of men towards women. Van Diemen's Land was a brutal society and violence towards women was so common as to place a female convict, who was thought to be of little worth, in constant jeopardy. Rapes were frequent and brutal bashings of females were as commonplace as a Saturday night tavern fight. Settlers, returning home drunk, would beat their female servants, sometimes crippling or even killing them. The body was usually dumped on the outskirts of Hobart Town and the murder would then simply be explained by reporting the prisoner as missing.

It is doubtful that the less stringent laws Arthur imposed on females were very successful in reforming them. But there was danger enough abroad for any convict woman, and fear of the law was the least of her concerns, nor observance of it likely to make her life any easier. Only the threat of being sent to the interior seemed to have any real effect. No greater fear existed in these city-bred women than that they should find themselves in the wilderness of the interior, where the cruelty of the men who lived as woodcutters in the forests was the subject of many fearful and gruesome tales told in the taverns and the disorderly houses of Hobart Town.

In short then, although Mary's confinement to the Female Factory might have seemed the harsher sentence, assignment to a settler was not the easy ride so fondly imagined by Mary's shipmates.

The moment Mary had heard of the existence of the orphans' school she had determined to gain a post within it as a teacher. The orphans' school housed the children who, shortly after birth, had been separated from their mothers. They were, for the most part, the children of assigned convicts. The women were routinely returned to the Female Factory by their masters, always with the story that the prisoner had been absent without a pass and had become pregnant while whoring. Hobart was full of orphan brats who bore a remarkable resemblance to many a settler's family.

The child would be born at the Factory, which also acted as a maternity hospital, and taken from its mother the moment it was weaned. Arthur considered the female convicts the very last persons to whom children ought to be entrusted. The mother would then be detained in the Female Factory to be punished for her licentious and drunken ways, and after serving her additional sentence either returned to her original master or assigned to another.

The children who had come to the island with their convict mothers and who were not convicts themselves were simply allowed to stay in the Factory with their mothers, as few settlers would entertain the prospect of another mouth to feed. They became wild creatures who wandered about the town and learned to pick pockets, bring in contraband, mostly tobacco and grog, and soon became rapscallions and petty thieves of the worst possible kind. Many of them were hardened criminals before they had reached the age of ten.

Mary would capture the hearts of these prison children with her stories and teach those who would submit to learning to read and write. She would also use them in quite another way, which was to earn her great power and respect among the other female inmates.

Mary was put to work in the prison bakery. This was not brought about by her intelligence or any skill she possessed, but because of her hands. They were thought to be too mutilated to be useful at any of the other tasks, while kneading dough was considered within her limited capacity.

It was a decision which, together with the requirement that Mary work two afternoons a week in the prison allotment, would give the direction to her future life. The allotment, an acre on the slopes of Mount Wellington, was used to grow potatoes, cabbages and some Indian corn, two of these, most fortuitously, being vegetables with a use beyond the platter, though a use not in the least contemplated by the prison officials.

Chapter Twenty

Ikey had eight hundred and thirteen pounds on him. Some of this was the remainder of the money paid to him in Birmingham by Maggie the Colour and Silas Browne, and some furnished by Hannah as a ploy to convince him of her sincerity in aiding his intended escape. It was sufficient to pay his fare to America from Denmark, as well as allowing him to stock up on merchandise likely to be in short supply in the New World.

Ikey, always a dreamer and schemer, saw America as a land of rich pickings for a man of his character and talent. It was his intention to land with a portmanteau stuffed with merchandise to confound the locals.

Alas, this was not to be, the prices for these articles in Denmark being too high at the shopfront and, besides, it was against Ikey's principles to purchase goods which afforded only a small margin of profit. It had not occurred to him that the Danish Jews might not speak Yiddish or contain a Jewish criminal class who would furnish the merchandise he required direct from the fob pockets of the unsuspecting citizenry, and therefore at prices a lot more competitive than those obtainable in wholesale jewellery emporiums.

So Ikey took the first ship he could find bound for New York. Though his hands were empty his head was full of plans for a life lived on the straight and narrow path as a merchant jeweller.

The crossing was rough and utterly miserable. In late February the Atlantic swells were large and frequent gales whipped the tops of the steel-coloured waves into a fury of howling white spray. The small three-masted packet was tossed like a cork seemingly all the way to the mouth of the Hudson River.

On a cold March morning, with dirty islands of late ice still floating on the river, the ship anchored at the immigration wharf at Castle Gardens. By early afternoon Ikey had paid his entry fee, been subjected to a smallpox vaccination and was allowed to step onto the streets of New York as free as an English lark.

It is a part of the human imagination to carry in our minds pictures of places we have heard or read about, pictures which have no substance other than the bricks and mortar of pure speculation. Ikey had expected New York to be a city not unlike London, though perhaps more primitive, for New York too lay on a great river and spoke the English tongue with a strange half-Irish intonation.

As an English Jew Ikey had assumed that he would fit in snugly enough. After all, the Jews of his world were street traders and merchants and of a naturally talkative and friendly disposition with the inclination to congregate together, marry among themselves, and on those several pious occasions such as Passover, Rosh Hashanah and Yom Kippur to share their faith. They would also attend synagogue on the Sabbath as brothers according to the ancient laws of Abraham, the prophets and the rabbinical creed.

Being a Jew, while being a matter of religion and orthodoxy, was also one of temperament. A Jew does not expect any but his own kind to understand him. Being Jewish is not something you wear outwardly like a badge, rather it is something you feel inwardly. It is as if your heart beats to a different cadence. This is as true of the Jew who is a villain as it is of one who is a rabbi. The smell of a chicken soup fart with noodles is absolutely one hundred per cent unmistakably Jewish. If you should be making chicken soup, delicious chicken soup, and you wish to make it Jewish, maybe you could try making these noodles.

Beat two eggs with a bit of pepper and salt. Add flour until it is a stiff paste. Flour a cutting board, then roll out the paste until it is very thin. Allow to dry for two hours. Now cut the dough into strips about three inches long by one inch wide. Stack and cut again into matchlike strips. Separate them by tossing, and spread them out to dry. Then toss them with boiling chicken soup and boil for ten minutes. Guaranteed to produce first-class farts when added to chicken soup!

New York, Ikey told himself, would have its own Rosemary and Petticoat Lanes, its rookeries with noxious smells and a low-life similar to St Giles, Whitechapel and Shoreditch, and a population composed from rags to riches which seemed to live the one on top of the other. This was the situation in London, Amsterdam and Hamburg and, in fact, wherever European urban Jews could be found. A Jew was not a part-time Jew or a sometime Jew or a non-observing Jew, he was Jewish for the duration of his life. This gave a wandering Jew a strength and unity he could depend on wherever he found a congregation of his own people.

Ikey had not stopped to think that being a Jew also made him accountable to the dictates and rituals of his community. In the matter of being Jewish he was expected to act in a prescribed manner, but not necessarily as a good man. In the good man business, the ritualised and formal nature of the English and European Jewish code of behaviour had allowed the form to become more important than the function, Jewishness being more important than goodness.

Ikey never missed going to the synagogue, where he gained a reputation for being a devout man and an Israelite without guile. In the synagogue each has a separate seat with a box where he deposits his holy books and locks them up until he returns to worship. Ikey frequently made use of his box for the most unhallowed of purposes, concealing within it items which if discovered would have sent him 'across the water' several times over.

Yet Ikey was an excellent example of a pious, if not strictly orthodox, Jew. While he did not observe the dietary laws, mutton stew followed by a dish of curds being his most frequent repast, he never worked on the Sabbath. He paid his tithes, contributed to Jewish charity, took his seat in the synagogue and observed with a full heart Rosh Hashanah, Passover and Yom Kippur.

Therefore it came as a great surprise to him to find that what he had always taken for granted was no longer the case in New York. Being a Jew was none, or very few, of the mystical things he'd always supposed it to be, nor was it any longer the secret satisfaction, despite the eternal suffering of the Jews, to be gained from being one of the chosen people.

The New York Jews neglected the Sabbath and many of them were now taking their rest on Sundays without the slightest show of guilt. The lighting of Sabbath candles and the singing of the Sabbath song was seldom practised. Secular learning of a pragmatic nature was regarded as more important than the study of the Torah. Moreover, philosophical thinking, based on the precepts of freedom and emancipation, was being given precedence over rabbinical discussion. The rebbe was not the centre of the universe nor did he settle all the arguments on behalf of Jehovah. The new *Bnai Jeshurun* synagogue on Elm Street contained only a handful of worshippers on any given Sabbath morning.

However, if the loss of the rituals and strictures of orthodoxy defined the American Jews, it did not lead to a corresponding loss of ideals, moral misconduct and social irresponsibility. In all this secular speculation, they had not given up a belief in Jehovah or the responsibility of God's chosen people to behave in a moral and honest way. Instead they rejected meaningless ritual and accepted natural goodness as the central tenet of their faith.

To be a good Jew meant to be a good man. What all this amounted to was that Ikey could no longer hide behind his observance of Jewish ritual while continuing to behave in an altogether reprehensible manner. While he had determined to turn over a new leaf in America, this realisation nevertheless came as a profound shock to him.

Ikey was also astonished to find that New York had

few poor Jews and that the Jewish community lived openly in the mid-town area spread on both sides of Broadway. New York contained only five hundred Jewish families. Most were American-born and had formed into a community over the past one hundred and fifty years. There was none of the frantic struggle to gain a foothold in a new society or the clash of contradictory cultures between the immigrant and native-born children. The Jews of New York were an established, sober, moral and well-integrated minority population, most of whom had been in America before the War of Independence. They all seemed to know or be on nodding terms with each other, and had excellent business and social relations with their gentile neighbours.

Ikey had timed his arrival badly, for if he had landed in New York ten years later he would have found some forty thousand European Jews in New York, and their numbers would continue to grow hugely for the remainder of the century. The dreadful slums, starvation, poverty and crime of the Lower East Side would come to exist as poor Jewish immigrants came to *Goldeneh medina*, 'The Golden country'. Alas, in Yiddish *Goldeneh medina* had a second meaning and was the name also given to a 'fool's paradise', a false gold, bright but worthless.

In this fool's paradise Ikey would have been completely at home. But he was totally at odds with the calm and ordered society he now found himself in, despite his determination to lead a sober and respectable life. Ikey's notoriety had not escaped the notice of the Jews of New York and the tight-knit community immediately closed ranks against him. England's most notorious Jewish criminal was not given a warm welcome. Ikey, despite his apparent wealth and appropriate philanthropy, found himself largely ostracised by his own kind.

Even those contacts to whom he had previously shipped stolen watches and silver objects had conveniently come to see these consignments as having been legitimised by the fact of arriving on American soil. They saw themselves as moral men, albeit practical, who had asked no questions of the origin of the merchandise and so heard no lies, their guilt assuaged.

But while they chose to believe that the stolen merchandise Ikey had sent them had somehow been 'washed' in the Atlantic crossing and thus transformed into honest goods, they were unwilling to accept that, by the act of the same crossing, Ikey had converted from being a criminal to an honest man. They felt morally obliged not to encourage a notorious criminal to establish himself in business in their own city or neighbourhood.

They would not recommend Ikey to wholesalers or to jewellery craftsmen, the greatest majority of whom were Jewish. Diamond merchants would not trade with him and the gold and silversmiths found themselves regrettably short of supplies or lamented that their consignment books were filled with orders beyond their expectations to complete. Despite his offer to pay them in cash, even in gold, their doors were closed to him. The few goods Ikey managed to assemble he sold only to gentiles. His poor selection, together with the used nature of his merchandise, attracted little attention and earned him a reputation not much beyond that of an enterprising pawnbroker.

The only respect Ikey commanded was from the First Manhattan Bank of New York where the manager, wreathed in unctuous smiles, would come out of his office to greet him personally. On the Sabbath, Ikey sat, a stranger in a strange land, alone in the bright new synagogue on Elm Street. The psalms the cantor sung were old, but the feeling of complete and abject loneliness was new.

Ikey had always thought of himself as a loner, a solitary soul who kept his own counsel. In his own eyes, but for his money, he was a worthless person. But now he began to realise that he had lost the human infrastructure, the supporting cast of thieves and shofulmen, card sharps, pimps, whores, actors, street urchins, his Academy of Light Fingers. How he missed the coarse company around a ratting circle, the hustle of Rosemary Lane, the rank humanity of the poor and hopeless, the tinsel and despair of the West End, the pickpockets and swells, beggars and noblemen who made up the street community of his native London.

America was proving completely alien to his past, his talents and to his very demeanour. Ikey's fortune and life had been developed on the mean dark streets and in the chop houses, taverns and thief dens of the grandest and most woebegone city on earth. He was by nature a creature of the night, wrapped in his familiar coat of secret pockets and accustomed to skulking within the dark shadow cast by a flat-topped, wide-brimmed hat.

Now all that had been forsaken for shopkeeping in daylight on Broadway, dressed in a suit of good American broadcloth which constantly scratched and itched. Ikey was a deeply unhappy man, but one determined to redeem himself in the eyes of his fellow Jews in his new country. Ikey was in search of personal redemption, but first he had to save himself from himself. He must separate from Hannah without losing the fortune contained in the Whitechapel safe. Four months after arriving in New York, he sat down to write to his wife in London.

My dear Wife,

America has proved a most pleasant place and the prospects for the advancement of our ambition is most encouraging. With the early summer come to us, at last the climate is most salubrious. You will take kindly to the air and space and the houses are of a solid brown stone and well proportioned. There is a spacious central park with room enough for children to play to their hearts content in safety. It is as though they should find themselves in some country dell. I have opened a jewellery establishment with excellent fittings on Broadway, a location which shows the promise of good trading if goods to the liking of the population can be offered at a price to be afforded. The craftsmen here are not of a sufficient standard to be desired, or of the same quality to be found in London, there being a notable shortage of finely made fashionable jewellery, the Americans being behind in what is of the latest mode in London and Paris. There is here also a great shortage of good watches of the medium quality variety and I beseech you to obtain quantities of the same. I have reason enough to believe I can turn these to good account, though I charge you to send me none but 'righteous' watches and not to touch even one what has been gained 'on

the cross'. I shall require these to be of an assort-
ment of nickel plate, sterling silver and gold. I
believe these will here obtain up to six times the
price of the watches purchased by you on the
straight. My greetings to your children.
   I am, as ever, your humble husband,
   Isaac Solomon.

Ikey took care to be cheerful in his letter, though not
overly so, for he knew that Hannah might smell a
trap, the discussion of cheerful subjects and outcomes
not being the usual nature of their conversation
together. His mention of children and the park was
sufficient to alert her to his desire to have her join
him. He also deliberately refrained from sending a
money order for the goods, giving her to understand
that she should finance the purchase herself for their
future mutual benefit. This thought being conveyed
with the single sentiment '... *for the advancement of*
our ambition ...' She would receive the letter and see
it clearly as a test of her intention to follow him to
America, in which case, provided she co-operated with
him, he would eventually send her his part of the safe
combination.

By using Hannah as his purchasing agent Ikey was
putting into place yet another plan. If the wholesale
merchants and jewellers in New York would not take
his custom then he would import all his merchandise
from London. The passage across the Atlantic had been
reduced to a little less than a month and the superior
craftsmanship of the London and Paris workshops and
their lead in the fashions would soon establish him in
the forefront of Broadway jewellery establishments. He

would deal in only the best merchandise, all of it initially honestly purchased. An evaluation and certificate of authentication would be issued with the more valuable pieces.

Ikey was determined to continue to obtain his merchandise through Hannah and always without payment, forcing her to finance the orders he placed by enclosing a signed I.O.U. for the amount against the time she would arrive in America. He intended this debt to accumulate until it matched half the amount of cash in gold sovereigns which Hannah knew to be contained in the safe of their Whitechapel home. Ikey knew full well that Hannah would not accept his I.O.U.s without knowing them to be covered by his share of the gold coin.

The deposit of thirty thousand pounds in sovereigns was by no means the most valuable part of their joint fortune. Within the safe lay precious stones: diamonds, rubies and emeralds contained within beautiful brooches, pins, necklaces and rings, and a double strand of exquisite South Seas pearls taken from the home of the Duke of Devonshire. There were also several hundred heavy fob chains of eighteen carat gold, a quantity of silver and gold plate and a dozen exquisite jewelled watches with rare movements. Finally, encased within a velvet-lined box and further protected by a chamois leather pouch, a jewelled and enamelled French carriage clock said to have belonged to Louis XIV. These objects, collected over fifteen years of fencing, represented much the greater part of Ikey and Hannah's personal fortune.

However, almost all the pieces were marked goods so particular in character that they dared not be presented in the London market where they would be instantly recognised. Even on the Continent they would need to be most carefully arranged within the world of the demi-monde if they were to escape detection. The best chance by far lay in the American market where new wealth was eager to acquire the trappings of an old culture and families such as the Astors and the Vander-bilts possessed the money to purchase it without asking too many awkward questions.

Hannah did not have the experience to value cor-rectly this merchandise, nor did she have the knowledge to dispose of it discreetly. The precious stones could be removed from their casings and sold separately and the gold chains melted down, but not without a thorough knowledge of how this should be done to prevent the attention of both the underground and the police.

No middleman in the thief kingdom of London had the resources to pay or the foolhardiness to dispose of such a haul in under a year at the least. And even then each stone, if it were not cut into smaller specimens, would need to be entered onto the market with the greatest possible discretion. Therefore the chances of a gem stone of note being discovered and traced back to Hannah was exceedingly great. Indeed, even in America, it would take all of Ikey's considerable skill and the shopfront presented by a thriving and out-wardly respectable jewellery establishment on Broad-way with a reputation for straight dealing to judiciously dispose of the contents of the safe to the richest of the American gentiles.

In his subsequent letters Ikey decided he would increase his caution to Hannah to always buy 'right-eous' goods, emphasising the great risk that she would be caught if she attempted to do otherwise. He knew that she would take this warning to include the disposal of the contents of the safe, this risk being even greater than the purchase of stolen merchandise should Hannah be foolish enough to try to act as a fence. Ikey was conscious that Hannah cared about her children more than anything else and the prospect of being transported and losing them was the one great fear he had to exploit in her.

Ikey also knew that if he should give Hannah the combination to the safe she might be tempted to abscond with only the money, the value of the gold chains and the proceeds obtained from the sale of their two London properties. The rest of the hugely valuable haul she might wait to dispose of at another time in some foreign country of her choice.

He had therefore determined on a ploy which, over a series of letters, would let her know that he was negotiating the sale of the pearl necklace to an American of great wealth. When he came close to the limit of his credit with her he would reveal this personage to be the redoubtable John Astor, said to be the richest man in America, 'American Royalty' as the saying went. The pearls were worth one hundred thousand pounds and Ikey was confident that Hannah's greed would persuade her to come to America with the contents of the safe.

Of the two of them, Ikey was the more vulnerable. Hannah would continue to exist whatever might happen, for Hannah hated not herself, only everyone else, and Ikey was simply the incarnation of everything she despised. Ikey, despite the fact that he might yet make a new and separate wealth in America, saw Hannah's determination to rob him of his fortune as an action more hellish in its nature than if she had plotted to murder him. If she were to succeed in stealing his fortune she would have won, not just his wealth, but his very existence. Her victory, and the hate contained within it, would destroy him completely. Victory over Hannah and therefore over himself lay in his retaining the contents of the safe. Hannah was playing a game with her husband for his money and because he was the perfect focus for her extraordinary resentment against the world. Ikey was playing a game with his wife for his very life.

Alas, the best laid plans . . . ! Ikey was not to know that his luck was on its way to Van Diemen's Land and, at the moment of Hannah's receiving his letter in London, it was dangling freely on its gold chain about the scrawny neck of Tiberias Potbottom.

Chapter Twenty-one

The London police records of the time show that a large consignment of watches, said to be more than one hundred, were stolen from the premises of a wholesale merchant in Cheapside. This coincidence was to completely change the lives and luck of Hannah and Ikey Solomon.

A theft of such proportion would soon be known in the Whitechapel markets and in Rosemary and Petticoat Lanes and around the Haymarket, where there would be much discussion as to who might have brought it about and who might be capable of fencing such a 'delicate' haul.

It might at first be supposed that it would be simple enough to bring a consignment of new watches back onto the market, but such was not the case. The numbers and markings of the watches were all furnished to the police, being available from the manufacturer, and so each watch would need to be carefully 'christened', that is, the number altered and the name upon the face carefully removed or the face itself replaced. This was a task which took some skill and, moreover, time and was not often worthy of completion on a fob watch that was not of

gold or silver. The watches taken were of a varying assortment, but mostly at the cheaper end of the quality market.
This meant that such merchandise, while cheaply procured by a fence, was difficult to place into circulation –
a trickle placed here and there in market towns and
country fairs and all of this over a lengthy period of time,
so that the risk of discovering the source of the trickle
was greatly decreased.

Hannah, hearing of the theft, was quick to realise
that it matched almost precisely the consignment Ikey
had commanded her to obtain. Accordingly, and contrary to Ikey's instructions that ' ... *none but "righteous" watches be sent and not to touch even one what
has been gained "on the cross"* ', Hannah sent for Bob
Marley.

It was late afternoon when Marley knocked on the
door of Hannah's Whitechapel home. He was dressed
as a regular toff, ready for an evening of jollifications
in Drury Lane and the Haymarket, and did not even
bother to remove his top hat as he entered the house.
This was an intended insult, designed to go along with
his failure to greet Hannah as he brushed past her into
the familiar parlour. Here he appropriated a glass of
the good brandy Hannah had got in and took a bagel
from the plate. He commenced to chew with his mouth
open; his two gold eye teeth showed clearly as he stared
blankly at Hannah, who had followed him silently into
the parlour.

'Long time no see, eh, Bob?'

Marley took a gulp of brandy then pushed what
remained of the bagel into his mouth. He did not
acknowledge her greeting, sucking the crumbs from his
fingers as he continued to stare at Hannah.

Hannah smiled ingratiatingly. 'Now, don't be like that, Bob, it were only business.'

'Humph!' Marley grunted.

'Ya done me one in the eye when they made the raid on Bell Alley, ya took me money under false pretences!' Hannah shrugged. 'So I got me revenge.' She grinned. 'That's all, it were tit f' tat!'

Marley swallowed, his Adam's apple bouncing. 'Ya made me look like a copper's nark! That's not the same thing! Me, a man o' me word, I gave Ikey me word, I took his contract!' He paused and took a slug of the brandy. 'Ya done in me fuckin' reputation!'

Hannah laughed uneasily, but then brightened. 'Well Ikey escaped anyway, no 'arm done, in the end ya done 'im a big favour, know what I mean?'

Marley jumped suddenly from the chair and grabbed Hannah by the throat with one large hand. 'Fuck Ikey! It were me reputation ya destroyed! Me a copper's nark, a fuckin' informer!' He shook Hannah, almost lifting her feet from the ground. 'Ain't nobody what trusts me no more!' His fingers tightened about her neck and Hannah's face grew purple, her eyes almost popping from their sockets. 'Don't never try that again, ya 'ear? You'll be dead meat!' Bob Marley released Hannah, who sank to her knees clutching her neck with both hands, forcing herself not to sob. Bob Marley held an open razor in his right hand.

Marley flicked the razor closed and placed it in the pocket of his coat, then threw back his head and swallowed the rest of his brandy. He thumped the glass down upon the table and started towards the door.

'I trusts ya, Bob,' Hannah said in a hoarse voice, rising slowly to her feet. 'Please wait.'

Bob Marley turned at the door and gave a short laugh. 'Ya trusts me! Well ain't that a fuckin' caution!'

Hannah moved up to him and touched him on the sleeve. 'Please?' she smiled again, her throat aching. 'G'warn, 'ave another brandy, a nice bagel, do ya good. I can explain everyfink, honest.'

Marley, eyeing the bottle of excellent brandy, hesitated. 'Explain what?' He crossed back to the bottle. 'Ain't nuffink to explain, ya fucked me reputation, that's all!'

'It ain't true, Bob. You is the best. Ya always was, ya still is. The best there be. Ikey always says, " 'E's the best, 'e is, always use the best, Hannah". I says so too, the best o' the best!'

Bob Marley looked up at Hannah, his expression slightly mollified. 'What's ya want?'

'Watches!' Hannah removed Ikey's letter from within her bodice and waved it. 'Ikey wants watches in America.'

Despite himself Bob Marley was impressed. 'Jesus! 'E made it, eh? Cunnin' bastard!' He poured more brandy into his glass and glanced up at Hannah. 'Fencin' then is 'e?'

Hannah was reluctant to explain. 'Yeah, sorta.' She replaced the letter. 'Them watches what's been lifted from Cheapside, know anyfink?'

Marley shook his head. 'Too 'ot, 'Annah, they's got to cool down first, ain't nobody goin' to handle them yet. They's numbered and all, mostly cheap shit, not worth christenin'.'

'Could ya find 'em?' Hannah asked. 'Make a good buy? I'll take the lot if the askin' price be right.'

Marley shook his head. 'Too dangerous. I told ya, watches be too 'ot to touch!'

'I'll pay fifty per cent o' the shop price,' Hannah said quickly, knowing this to be a generous offer, also knowing that she would charge Ikey the full retail price for the watches.

'Sixty! Sixty per cent o' the retail, take it or leave it. And I'll need twenty sovs down payment,' Marley said emphatically. 'There's expenses, ya understand?'

Hannah nodded but inwardly she was concerned that Marley was losing his grip, that perhaps he *had* lost his reputation and therefore his old, greedy confidence. His sudden attack on her had left her frightened, but in the peculiar way of villains, it had also given her confidence in him. You knew where you stood. She'd fully expected to pay sixty per cent of the full price of the watches, but she'd also set aside fifty gold sovereigns as the down payment.

'Sure, I understand,' she said. 'Gimme a mo', I'll fetch it fer ya.'

'Mind, I can't take no chances,' Marley said. 'It may take a while to get to them yacks.' This was said almost as an aside.

Hannah turned at the door. 'Not too long, Bob. Ikey 'as great expectations.'

Marley frowned and shook his head slowly. 'If I 'as to take chances, make indiscreet enquiries like, that's no good fer me 'ealth! Pigs is everywhere, the Lane's tight as a duck's arse!' He looked over to where Hannah was standing and sighed. ' 'Fraid that kind o' haste is gunna cost you forty sovs extra on the down.'

Hannah smiled inwardly, her mind put at rest. She was dealing with the same dead cunning Bob Marley. She was anxious to get the watches and so impress Ikey with her diligence and continuing goodwill towards him. She was not foolish enough to imagine that he would send her his half of the combination after only one such consignment, but her heart had lifted at the opportunity his letter presented. She had high hopes that Ikey must eventually send her the combination to the safe when she pleaded impecuniosity, his debts incurred by his orders having become too large for her to carry any further on her own. Whereupon she would be rid of him forever.

But Hannah had completely underestimated Bob Marley. She'd quickly come to see his attack on her as a show, a token effort to assert his male pride, give her a fright, as he had well succeeded in doing. She didn't think for a moment he would have used the razor. Marley, Hannah felt certain, could always be bought with gold.

She was wrong, however. Marley would have used the razor on her as lightly as he would have smiled. Hannah was unable to see the proud man who despised his fellow villains and thought himself quite different. She did not comprehend that, in his own eyes (and no others counted), she had damaged his reputation and done him irreparable harm. When she'd shifted the blame for betraying Ikey to the police onto him, she had delivered a blow to his pride which could entertain no possible forgiveness. Marley did business only for solid gold, for that is how he saw his reputation. And he always delivered. Hannah had compromised him, and because he always delivered, she would be no exception. The wolf would tear her flesh as well as any other.

Bob Marley made no attempt to locate the whereabouts of the watches stolen from Cheapside, this being much too dangerous. Instead he made directly for a jeweller of his acquaintance in the Haymarket, a Polish Jew by the name of Isaac Isaacson whom Ikey had used regularly when Marley had been his snakesman as a child. It was Isaacson who had moulded and created Marley's two gold teeth and so it came as somewhat of a surprise when his visitor bid him find one hundred mixed watches of brand new quality and all righteously purchased. They haggled at great length to finally reach an agreement of a thirty per cent reduction off the retail price of the proposed consignment.

Bob Marley was about to leave the premises reasonably well satisfied with the negotiations when Isaac Isaacson beckoned him to come closer. He explained in an urgent whisper that he was long owed a certain sum of money for a gold and diamond bracelet sold to a Miss Myrtle Manners, the governess of a well-known brothel in the Strand known appropriately enough as 'Girls with good Manners'. This 'Governess o' whores', he claimed, had flatly refused to pay him the final two instalments, a sum of three hundred pounds, claiming he had overcharged her and pointing out, with the least amount of subtlety, that she enjoyed the special patronage and protection of a senior police officer in the Haymarket watchhouse.

'You can cut, maybe a little, this person, ja?' Isaacson enquired of Bob Marley.

'Most certainly!' Marley replied. 'It'd be me pleasure to be o' service, Mr Isaacson.' He paused and scratched his eyebrow with the tip of his forefinger. 'Though it'll cost ya anuvver ten percent orf the cost o' the yacks. O' course, if ya wants a really nasty acid job, right down a cheekbone, and includin' a little turn o' the blade to slice away the corner o' the gob so it don't fit proper no more, it could be a little extra.'

Isaac Isaacson grew suddenly pale and threw his hands up in alarm. 'No, no! Ten per cent, no more, please, I beg you! A small violence only, if you please!'

Bob Marley grinned. 'Fer ten percent I can do ya a nice little job, Mr Isaacson. Gimme two days. Reckon you'll 'ave the yacks ready by then?'

The jeweller nodded, hunched his shoulders and spread his hands. 'A little cut, no more!' he begged again.

Bob Marley left the Haymarket and made his way to the Hare and Hounds in Rosemary Lane almost directly opposite the Methodist Academy of Light Fingers. He had not long to wait before he observed a boy leave the Academy in an old coat that fell to beyond his knees, the sleeves rolled up to fit his scrawny arms, bare feet showing below ragged trousers. The brat crossed the street to enter the tavern and Marley observed him to be snotnosed, dirty and small, with the pinched, rodent-like features of a street urchin. He appeared to be about ten years old as he placed two pennies down on the counter and ordered a daffy of gin.

'Make that a shant, m'dear!' Marley called to the barmaid.

The barmaid and the urchin both looked up at Marley. 'Suit yerself,' she said, picking up a bigger glass.

'And a double o' yer best brandy, love. I'll pay fer the lad's.'

The boy looked up at Bob Marley. 'You a turd burglar, mister?' he asked, swiftly taking up the two pennies on the counter and dropping them into the pocket of his coat.

Bob Marley enquired if the urchin knew Sparrer Fart.

'Maybe I does and then maybe I doesn't,' the boy replied cheekily.

'Tell 'im I wants to see 'im, two o' the clock termorra, in 'ere. Tell 'im no 'ard feelin's, I wants a job done, Bob Marley wants a job done. Got it?'

The boy nodded.

Marley lifted his head and called to the barmaid. 'Another gin fer the lad, love!' Then he placed a shilling on the counter and without a further glance at the boy he left the tavern.

Sparrer Fart was waiting for Marley when he entered the Hare and Hounds the following day. He was wearing a slightly battered top hat, coat and breeches all of which fitted him surprisingly well, though his entire outfit, including his shirt, neckerchief and scuffed boots, bore the signs of having been placed upon his tiny body some months previously and not having since been removed for the purposes of laundering. His face seemed also to have missed this opportunity to wash. Sparrer looked somewhat apprehensive as Bob Marley approached, backing into the safety of a group of men standing at the bar and glancing quickly over his shoulder to ascertain the shortest escape route should he have to make a sudden dash for it.

Bob Marley pushed into the group and extended his hand, smiling. 'I oughta beat the livin' shit out of ya, Sparrer!' Sparrer Fart backed away, ready to make a run for it. The barmaid looked at Marley questioningly. 'Brandy, love, the best o' the 'ouse!' Marley turned back to Sparrer, who now stood alone. 'What's your poison, gin is it?' The urchin nodded.

'C'mere, I'm not gunna 'arm ya,' Marley said, walking over to where Sparrer stood. The barmaid brought their drinks over. ''Ow's the fingers?' Marley enquired. 'Not drinkin' too much is ya? 'Aven't lost yer touch, I most sincerely 'opes?'

Sparrer Fart took the gin the barmaid placed in front of him, then he looked up at Bob Marley, his eyes large, his expression most contrite. 'I'm sorry what I done, Mr Marley,' he said tentatively.

Bob Marley lifted his drink and held it up. 'Cheers! Never say you is sorry, boy! Sorry be the sign o' a weak man!' He up-ended the glass and swallowed its contents in one gulp. 'Ahh! Same again, love!' he shouted to the barmaid.

'I wouldn't 'ave! I swear I didn't know she was gunna shop Ikey!' Sparrer said.

''Course ya didn't! 'Ow much she give ya?'

'Four quid,' Sparrer lied.

'Ya was robbed! Sovs or what?'

Sparrer shook his head. 'Soft. It were good paper though, not fake.'

Marley clucked his tongue. 'Never take no paper money, boy! Gold! Don't never take nuffink else, that is, if ya wants respect.'

'I don't think as I can afford respect what's always gold,' Sparrer said softly, taking a tiny sip from his gin.

'Lemme see yer 'ands. 'Old 'em out, spread yer fingers.'

Sparrer held his hands out and spread his fingers. They were tiny, dirty and beautiful, and they remained perfectly steady.

'Nerves! 'Ow's yer nerves?'

'I'm still the goodest, still the best o' everyone!' Sparrer boasted.

450

'Oh yeah? 'Ow does I know that?' Bob Marley challenged, amused at Sparrer's confidence.

Sparrer Fart dipped into the side pocket of his jacket and produced Bob Marley's gold hunter, handing the watch back to him.

'Jesus!' Marley exclaimed. He shook his head admiringly. 'Didn't never feel ya touchin' me! You're good, Sparrer, I'll give ya that!'

Sparrer shook his head. 'Nah! If ya was Ikey, he'd o' caught me. We don't get 'nuff trainin' since 'e's gorn away.' He took a sip from his gin and looked up at Bob Marley with big eyes. 'Academy's fucked!'

'You'll do nicely, lad,' Marley said, giving Sparrer's shoulder a comforting squeeze. 'Very nicely.' He explained what he required. 'There's three sovs in it fer ya, plus the worf o' the lift, three sovs in gold, what's got the King's 'ead on it,' he emphasised. He stabbed a finger at Sparrer Fart. 'But mind ya bring me silver, a good 'un!'

Marley met Sparrer in the Hare and Hounds at ten the following evening. In a leather satchel he carried the one hundred fob watches Isaac Isaacson had obtained for him.

'Well then, lad, 'ow'd ya go?'

Sparrer dug into his pocket and produced a silver hunter which he handed to Bob Marley.

'Like ya said, Mr Marley, not too cheap not too 'spensive, sterlin' silver, worf fifteen sovs new!' Sparrer declared expertly.

Bob Marley examined the watch. 'Jesus, Sparrer, it be monogrammed! Look, J.R., that be the 'nitials o' the cove ya nicked it from!'

Sparrer shrugged. 'Ya didn't say nuffink 'bout that. Do I still get me five sovs then?' he asked hopefully.

Bob Marley counted five gold sovereigns into Sparrer's tiny hand, then added three more.

'Ya done good, lad. I didn't say nuffink 'bout no 'nitials.'

Sparrer looked pleased. He was rich enough to eat and get drunk for a week and sit in on an endless game of cribbage. 'Thanks, Mr Marley, I done me best, sorry I fucked up.'

'Got a yack o' yer own, then?' Bob Marley asked suddenly.

Sparrer shook his head in alarm. 'Too dangerous in me profession! Pigs might find the cove I nicked it from, it'd be the boat fer me, fer sure!'

Bob Marley's hand went into his pocket and produced a handsome nickel-plated fob watch which he placed on the bar counter. Then he pulled out a watch chain and dropped it beside the watch.

'Take it, it be your'n.'

Sparrer looked confused. 'Huh?'

Marley laughed. 'A present, fer yer birfday!'

'I don't 'ave no birfday,' Sparrer said quietly, still bemused. 'Ya didn't nick it, did ya? Cos, if ya nicked it I can't 'ave it.'

'Nah, it were a bonus for doin' a job, a little favour fer a friend like.' He pushed the watch over to Sparrer. 'G'warn, take it, everybody's got a birfday even if they don't know when it be.'

Sparrer picked up the watch in one hand and the chain in the other, appearing to weigh both in his hands. 'I ain't never before seen a new one what's not nicked.'

'Guaranteed, honest to Gawd nab proof that is. Pig come up to ya, ask ya where ya got it, tell 'im it's kosher, Isaac Isaacson o' Drury Lane, "Jeweller to Thespians and Gentlemen, Established 1792"!'

Sparrer's eyes shone as he realised that the watch was safe for him to own. 'Thanks, Mr Marley, thanks a lot!' he said clicking open the lid and looking at the pristine face of the watch. Then he closed it and clipping the watch onto the chain placed it into his fob pocket, looped the chain over his tiny belly and fitted the cross-bar at its other end into its appropriate buttonhole. The chain was much too long for his narrow torso and dangled in an arc to below his crutch. 'I never 'ad a watch o' me very own,' Sparrer said excitedly.

'Mazeltov!' Bob Marley said, patting him lightly on the shoulder. 'One good turn deserves anuvver!' He pointed to Sparrer's fob pocket. 'What's the time then?'

Sparrer took the watch from its pocket and expertly clicked it open again. ' 'Arf past ten o' the clock,' he said proudly.

'Read what it says,' Marley demanded.

The boy looked up at Bob Marley, then down at the inscription inside the watch cover as though he had seen it for the first time. He touched it lightly with his forefinger tracing the words inscribed into the metal as though by feeling them they might reveal their meaning to him. Bob Marley cleared his throat.

'No, don't read it, Sparrer! Lemme tell ya what it says,' he said quickly, rescuing the urchin. 'I sort o' composed it meself, see. So it be better said than read, knows what I mean?' Bob Marley leaned back as though thinking for a moment. 'It says: "To S.F. – A man's repitashin be more valiable than gold! B.M."'

'What's S.F. and B.M. mean?' Sparrer asked.

'S.F. stands fer Sparrer Fart, that bein' you ... and B.M., why that's yers truly, the same what's talkin' to ya and whose repitashin be more valiable than gold!'

'Thanks, Mr Marley.' Sparrer touched the inscription again with his forefinger. 'S.F., eh? Blimey, that be me!'

Marley laughed and pointed to the watch. '*Tempus fugit*, that means "Time flies", I gotta scarper.' He threw down what remained of his brandy. 'Ya done good, Sparrer, cheer'o then.'

Sparrer didn't quite know why, but as he watched Bob Marley's back retreat out of the tavern door he wanted to bawl.

At near enough to ten o'clock the following morning, Bob Marley knocked on Hannah's door. Hannah's expression was at once anxious when she saw who it was.

'Bob!' Then she added quickly, but in a whisper, 'You 'asn't got 'em, 'as ya?'

Marley grunted and held up the bag.

Hannah, unable to conceal her excitement, invited him into the parlour. 'Wait, I'll get brandy! 'Ere, sit. 'As ya eaten?' She didn't wait for Marley's reply but left the parlour and moments later appeared with a large biscuit tin, a glass and a bottle of brandy. ' 'Elp yerself, love, I'll fetch yer money,' she said, leaving the room once more.

Half an hour after Marley had left the police arrived at Hannah's house with a search warrant, discovered the watches and arrested her on suspicion of obtaining stolen property. She arrived at the watchhouse where she was to be retained overnight to hear that Bob Marley was also being held by the police.

Both of them were arraigned before a magistrate the following morning, Hannah being the first to stand in the prisoner's dock, where she pleaded not guilty. She asked for the clerk of the court to bring her Ikey's letter which she'd caused to be held in evidence. 'See 'ere, yer worship, where it says in me 'usband's letter,' she commenced to read the lines ' . . . *"I charge you to send me none but 'righteous' watches and not to touch even one what has been gained 'on the cross'. I shall require these to be of an assortment of nickel plate, sterling silver and gold. I believe these will here obtain up to six times the price of the watches purchased by you on the straight."'*

The magistrate read Ikey's letter for himself and then looked up at Hannah. 'Hmm, I see that we shall not have the privilege of supplying your husband with accommodation in one of His Majesty's antipodean hostelries. We can only hope that the Americans may prove more successful at this task, eh, madam?'

Hannah smiled weakly at the judge. 'Yer worship, I 'as always been a good and obedient wife and I would not think to go against me 'usband's wishes and commands.' She dropped her gaze, wringing her hands piteously. 'I's a poor woman with four brats to feed and 'ousework to do.' She looked appealingly at the magistrate. 'What does I know about findin' one 'undred watches what's been nicked?'

'And how do you suppose these watches came into your possession then, madam?' the magistrate asked sternly.

Hannah pointed to Bob Marley, manacled and seated between two constables in the court. ' 'Im! I asks 'im to purchase on be'arf o' me 'usband one 'undred watches what's kosher, what's not nicked, but what's bran' new. 'E said 'e done it, but 'e didn't, did 'e? 'E gorn and got 'em on the cross!' Hannah suddenly clasped her hands together in front of her breasts and burst into tears. 'Oh, what shall become o' me children?' she wailed.

'You may stand down, Mrs Solomon.' The magistrate was not in the least affected by Hannah's tears. 'I shall presently call you to stand before me again.' He nodded at the clerk of the court, who rose from his seat and proclaimed.

'Robert Matthew Marley will take the stand!'

Hannah listened with increasing bemusement as Marley proved conclusively that the watches he'd obtained for her were unencumbered and purchased legitimately. To further support his case the respectable Haymarket jeweller, Isaac Isaacson, appeared as a witness for Marley, showing the number and names of the watches purchased by the accused as matching exactly the wholesaler's invoice. Bob Marley then produced in evidence Isaac Isaacson's own receipt to him. Furthermore, the Crown now admitted that none of the watches matched the serial numbers of those taken in the notorious Cheapside robbery.

The charges against Marley were summarily dismissed and the magistrate called for Hannah to appear before him again, whereupon he commenced to remonstrate severely with her for accusing the said Robert Matthew Marley, a man who had never been before the courts and whose reputation she had needlessly and maliciously impugned.

Hannah protested vehemently. 'Yer worship it were the police! They said them watches was stolen! I 'mediately supposed they was! I supposed that Mr Marley'd gorn an' nicked 'em, 'oping to profit from chargin' me the full price while 'avin' got 'em at a thief's rate!'

'And you did not think to ask Mr Marley for a receipt as proof that he'd made a legitimate purchase as you requested?'

'Yer worship, I were most pleased what Mr Marley 'ad done, knowin' as 'ow I 'ad served me 'usband's request wif promptness and exactitude. I am not accustomed to the ways o' doin' business, bein' a poor woman what knows nuffink about such things as bills and receipts and the general goin's on o' commerce!'

The magistrate snorted loudly. Hannah's reputation as a businesswoman was well known to the court.

Hannah, though appearing distraught, was delighted with the altogether surprising outcome. She had considered herself already bound for Botany Bay, but now Bob Marley's innocence conclusively proved her own. She waited impatiently for the miserable beak to conclude his tirade and to dismiss the case.

Finally the magistrate picked up a document and began to read.

'Hannah Margaret Solomon and Robert Matthew Marley you have been jointly charged with having obtained and, or, being found in possession of, a consignment of one hundred watches thought to have been stolen from an establishment in Cheapside. This has subsequently been proved to be incorrect and you, Mr Marley, have been cleared by this court of any charges relating to that robbery.' He looked up at Hannah, who smiled back at him. 'You too, madam, are free of this charge.'

'Thank you, yer worship,' Hannah said primly, preparing to step down from the dock.

But the magistrate held up his hand to stay her. 'If you please ... ' He picked up another document and began to read again. 'Hannah Margaret Solomon, you are further charged with being in possession of a sterling silver watch known to be the property of Joseph Ridley, the said watch being discovered concealed in a biscuit tin in the pantry of your home.' The magistrate looked up sternly. 'How plead you to this charge, guilty or not guilty?'

Hannah's mouth opened in astonishment and she glanced quickly to where Bob Marley sat, but all she could later remember seeing was the dark gap between his two shining gold teeth as he grinned at her.

'Not guilty, yer worship,' she said, then added in a whisper, 'Oh, me Gawd!'

Chapter Twenty-two

The first of the autumn leaves were starting to turn in Hyde Park and the geese on the Serpentine, plump with summer feeding, were increasingly feeling the primal urge to migrate to a warmer clime. On the 13th of September 1827, Hannah, a bird of a quite different feather, was sentenced to a less voluntary migration, though also to a warmer climate.

If her sentence at the Old Bailey to fourteen years' transportation appears rather too harsh for a crime so small, it may be supposed that much frustration had gone before it in the many unsuccessful attempts to trap both Hannah and Ikey. The law has a duty to be both parent and teacher and sometimes, in order to wipe the slate clean, a recalcitrant child must be dealt with more harshly than a particular crime seems to merit, in order to compensate for successful crimes which have gone unpunished. Hannah's conviction may well have rendered an opportunity to balance the scales of justice.

Ikey's escape to New York, as proved by the evidence of his letter to his wife, was reported in *The Times* and was blown up to exaggerated proportions in the penny dailies, where it created much merriment in the rookeries and even some grudging admiration among the lower classes. The law is blind only when it does not wish to see and the embarrassment to the City police and directors of the Bank of England caused by Ikey's gaolbreak may well have condemned Hannah to a harsher sentence.

To Hannah's fourteen years' transportation was added the condition that she never be permitted to return to her native land.

On hearing her sentence Hannah brought her hands up to her face and wailed, 'Oh! Oh! What shall become o' me precious mites?'

Whereupon the judge, to prove that the severity of the law may be tempered by compassion, gave permission for her children to accompany her to Australia so as to be under her fostering care.

The *Mermaid*, carrying Hannah and her four children together with ninety other female convicts, some also with children, sailed from Woolwich on the 10th of February 1828.

The voyage proved no better or worse than most. There was the usual sea sickness, bouts of catarrh and rheumatism brought about by the dampness between decks on the voyage to Tenerife. These ailments soon yielded with the coming of the sun, though an obstinate form of constipation remained. This was thought to be due to the fact that the Irish women on board, as was the custom in Irish prisons, received only gruel and milk. Now the introduction of salt and beef and pork to their shipboard diet proved most deleterious to their unaccustomed stomachs.

As is always the case, bickering, fights, bad behaviour and thieving among the women prisoners were much in evidence. In the matter of whoring, though, which was known to plague even the most watchful of voyages, Hannah was to play a part so skilful that the surgeon-superintendent would state in his report that the prisoners had co-operated well and had shown little pernicious disruption and almost none of the moral turpitude so commonly experienced on a convict ship carrying female prisoners.

This 'co-operation' had come about when Hannah, soon determining the nature of the voyage, grew fearful for the health of her children and concluded that the only advantage to them could be brought about by the chief steward.

Other than in matters of punishment, there are only two other aspects of life on board a convict ship which it is in the power of someone to improve, these being the daily tasks allocated to the prisoners and the nature of the food. Hannah soon ascertained that by greatly increasing the 'comfort' of the officers and certain members of the crew, and by enriching the chief steward in the process, both these rewards could be enjoyed by herself and her children.

It was a relatively easy matter for her to be appointed a monitor in charge of the more profligate and wayward of the female prisoners. The next step was one to which she was most accustomed as a whore mistress and governess of a brothel. She quickly organised a discreet service in which the chief steward acted as go-between and which both the co-operating prisoners and crew soon found to be greatly advantageous. The officers and crew received sexual favours which were arranged with a simple payment to the steward, and the prisoner-prostitutes were allocated pleasant duties and extra rations of food and beverages.

Hannah needed the surgeon-superintendent to turn a blind eye, so she set about the task of satisfying his desire while allowing him to maintain the utmost celibacy demanded of him in his position as disciplinarian, surgeon, superintendent and as His Majesty's representative on board ship.

This Hannah did not with her hips, but with the same 'Sir Jasper-like' employment of her skilful lips. In this way the surgeon-superintendent could not be accused of indulging in fornication or of the slightest neglect of his moral duty.

Hannah had found the key to a more comfortable voyage for herself and her children and was rewarded with special food and a plentiful supply of liquid refreshment. The importance of this arrangement cannot be stressed enough. While the food was monotonous it was deemed to be adequate to the prisoners' needs. It was liquid refreshment which was especially craved, particularly when the *Mermaid* lay becalmed on a shining tin-flat sea and the prisoners were possessed of a tropical torpor as they lay gasping below decks.

It was then that they would implore the steward for a drop of water to cool their parched tongues. But he would answer with an aggrieved shake of the head.

'Can't do it, allowances have been had.'

Hannah entered into business with the steward, who saw to it that 'hospital extras' were given to her and her four children. Indeed, it must be said, due to the importuning talents of their mother, these brats enjoyed every advantage to be obtained on the voyage. When Ann, Hannah's daughter, went down with the fever for a period of two weeks she was favoured with the most delicious diet and the tender ministrations of the surgeon-superintendent. She was also given a berth directly below a porthole to catch the clement breezes. Baby Mark, on the sick list for five days with diarrhoea (no doubt from an excess of rich rations), received the same conscientious attention and hospital food, served each day in an adult portion so that it might be shared by his brother and sisters.

Hannah was the matriarch of the first contingent of her tribe of Solomon to arrive in Van Diemen's Land on the 27th of June 1828, where they were to prove to possess stubborn and hardy roots. They would do much of both good and evil to shape the destiny of this new land, and would add their ancient faith to a burgeoning new culture.

A pause is necessary to contemplate a singular phenomenon. In every convict ship which carried Britons, from the First Fleet onwards, there were Jews to share their fate. In this haphazard way Australia was to become the only community of European people in which Jews were present from the moment of inception. For nearly nineteen centuries the Jews had not enjoyed a permanent welcome in European lands. Now, though only a tiny contingent, they were nevertheless a noticeable part of the convict community. Here they were regarded no differently from their fellows, a condition which has continued to exist in this the most egalitarian country on earth, where Jack is thought to be as good as his master, though it should in fairness be added that, at the time Hannah arrived in Van Diemen's Land, neither Jack nor his master were thought to be much good. Furthermore, the contention still persists, though noticeably among the English, that in the intervening years, nothing much has changed.

The new Female Factory was not yet fully constructed and Governor Arthur had allowed that a prisoner who had shown exemplary behaviour on the way
out should be processed on board ship and then permitted to go directly to the home of a settler as an
indentured servant.

Hannah and her children were consigned immediately to the home of Mr Richard Newman, a police
officer of Hobart Town, who greeted her on the dock
with the utmost civility as though she were of equal
status and not a convict wretch with the additional
burden of four extra mouths to feed.

This was thought most surprising, for Newman was
said to be a happily married man of small means, so
there could be no thought of concubinage, nor was
there any profit to be gained from the labours of the
two older children, David and Ann, as they were not
convicts and so not obliged to work under his roof.

It soon became apparent that Hannah did not intend
to be burdened with the duties of a servant or suffer
the instructions of a master. She did nothing except loll
about the cottage, dawdling through the most unde-
manding tasks. Her quarrelsome ways soon alienated
all who came in contact with her. It was often observed
that Mrs Newman, a quiet soul, was the real servant
and Hannah the mistress of the house. It was never suggested that this had come about because the convict had
ensnared her master with her feminine guile, as Mrs
Newman was both pretty and of a most cheerful nature
and Hannah was not burdened with either of these
pleasant characteristics.

The truth of the matter was rather more simple. Ikey
had made arrangements ahead of Hannah's arrival, and

Richard Newman was most handsomely recompensed for the accommodation of Hannah and her children.

This convenient arrangement may well have been beyond the talents of a man less enterprising than Ikey Solomon, who had heard about Hannah's arrest in a letter from Abraham Reuban, the son of the actor Reuban Reuban who had been a part of the great bank scam.

Abraham Reuban's letter, sent on the first packet bound for New York, arrived in Ikey's hands not more than twenty-six days after the conclusion of Hannah's trial. Furthermore, Ikey was kept abreast of the court case in *The Times*, news of the arrest and subsequent trial of the wife of the notorious Ikey Solomon being much in demand.

Ikey's most immediate concern was for the safe in the Whitechapel home. He hastily dispatched a letter to young Reuban by the next ship bound for London and enclosed with it sufficient money for the windows of the Whitechapel house to be bricked up and the doors to be boarded up.

Ikey was so certain that Hannah had been compromised in the matter of the watch that he was under no illusion that she might be acquitted. He knew she was capable of disobeying his instructions in the matter of purchasing the consignment of watches. But, when it transpired that the one hundred watches had been honestly purchased by Bob Marley, he knew immediately that she would not, under any circumstances, include a watch gained on the cross in the same shipment. Hannah was greedy and wilful but never stupid. She had been set up, either by Bob Marley, or the Law itself, of that much he was entirely convinced. It remained only for him to know whether she would be transported to Van Diemen's Land or to New South Wales for him to spring into action.

With the news that Hannah was to be transported to Van Diemen's Land, Ikey sent a letter by means of a certain Captain Barkman, master of a whaler sailing out of Boston and bound for Sydney, and then directly to Hobart where it would commence upon a whaling expedition in Antarctic waters. In his letter Ikey instructed his eldest son John to take passage with the captain to Hobart Town, and there to negotiate whatever comforts or conditions would be to the benefit of his mother and his brothers and sisters.

John Solomon arrived in Hobart Town not two weeks prior to Hannah's arrival on the *Mermaid*, and was quickly acquainted with Governor Arthur's desire to place female prisoners with settlers or emancipists in a manner most favourable to the containment of government expenses. Arthur ran the colony like a small-town grocer, aware of the cost of every tin, jar and package on his colonial shelves. Even a single night's detainment in the Female Factory meant a debit in the government books.

Richard Newman, an emancipist and police officer, with a third child on the way, was easily enough convinced by John Solomon that he should apply for Hannah to be assigned as his servant. The formalities were arranged with the authorities, who sought to look no further than sparing the government the responsibility and expense of accommodating and feeding not one, but five additional mouths.

John Solomon arranged for a monthly stipend to be paid a year in advance to Richard Newman, and thereafter to be subject to renewal only if Hannah found the arrangements to her personal satisfaction. In paying the money to the policeman he had demanded a receipt, which had been foolishly supplied without thought for what this might mean at a future time.

It was an unfortunate arrangement from the very first, and the policeman and his long-suffering wife were often to contemplate that all the riches in the world could not make up for the presence of Hannah Solomon and her children under their roof.

Without Hannah in London, Ikey's plans for his Broadway business had to be severely curtailed, and he decided that he had but one card left to play. He must immediately go to Van Diemen's Land and convince Hannah to let him have her half of the combination to the safe. If he could assure her of his constant concern for her welfare while supplying her with every creature comfort, he was confident of an early success. He told himself that his wife would soon come to see the utmost sense in his retrieving their now securely bricked-up fortune so that he might establish a prosperous platform against the time of her release. Perhaps in Canada, the West Coast of America or even the Cape of Good Hope where the English were beginnning to settle in some numbers.

Ikey had made several speculative purchases of land in New York, most of these on the island of Manhattan and in the Bronx. He now set about feverishly turning these back into liquid assets, accepting far less for a quick sale than the true worth of the property.

Ikey managed finally to sell all his interests with the exception of one half-acre corner block in Manhattan which in a moment of weakness he had leased to the

Council of American Jews for the Land of Ararat. This was in order that they might build a hostel and reception centre for Jews fleeing from persecution in Europe and the Orient. The buildings were to be of impressive proportions and would be known as the Mordecai Manuel Noah, Ararat Foundation.

Mordecai Noah was a prominent American Jew who had been the consul to Tunis. During his travels he had discovered the plight of the homeless Jews in the Orient and Europe. He dreamed of seeing Palestine returned as a homeland for the Jews, but as a diplomat he was conscious of the impossibility of achieving this mission among the Arab rulers. His thoughts then turned to the great open spaces of America and upon his return from Algiers in 1825 he purchased a tract of seventeen thousand acres on Grand Island on the Niagara River near the city of Buffalo. This he nominated as the site for the temporary Land of Israel and declared himself Governor and Judge of Israel, issuing a manifesto to Jews all over the world to come and settle in the new land which would guarantee them freedom under the protection of the constitution and laws of the United States of America.

Whether the Jews of New York saw this new and temporary Israel as a holy mission worthy of their support, or simply regarded it as an effective way to keep the immigration of undesirable European and Oriental Jews out of their city is not known, but they determined to build an impressive reception centre for the 'New Israelites' so that they could be expedited as speedily as possible to the Land of Ararat. It was the real estate for this centre which Ikey had agreed to lease to the council for a period of fifty years.

This was the most generous gesture Ikey had made in his entire life but it gained him no favour in the eyes of his American co-religionists. They felt that it showed his true criminal rapacity, for they maintained that a good Jew would have donated the land to them free of all encumbrances and conditions.

However, for a man of Ikey's background and temperament this was simply not possible. He could not bring himself to give away something he owned, despite the fact that he did not give a fig for his heirs and was quite aware that he would be long dead before the land reverted to them. Perhaps, had they agreed to call it The Isaac Solomon Welcoming Centre for the Land of Ararat, or some such fancy name to honour his donation, he might well have relented. Men do strange things to perpetuate their importance. However, this too is unlikely given Ikey's nature and the fact that his instincts told him the great Mordecai Noah was a dreamer of dreams and not a creator of schemes. In this he proved to be entirely correct for not a sod was ever turned in the Land of Ararat, nor a brick placed upon its welcoming gate.

Ikey was well supplied with funds, despite having lost considerably on the resale of his land, and he spent a short time stocking up on goods to sell in Hobart Town. He also purchased a large quantity of tobacco from Virginia and cigars from the Cuban Islands. He planned to sell the hard goods as quickly as possible upon his arrival on the island and thereafter to open a tobacconist shop so that he might pose as a legitimate merchant.

Ikey reasoned that tobacco, like grog, was a commodity which would always be in demand in a society where men greatly outnumbered women. For this reason he did not venture to take with him a quantity of jewellery. He quickly surmised that trinkets and rings and bright shining things would not be so much sought after on an island consisting largely of convicts, emancipists and troopers. Furthermore, those free settlers who had made Van Diemen's Land their home had done so because their limited resources precluded the purchase of land and influence in the more civilised climes of the West Indies, Canada, America or the Cape of Good Hope.

Ikey took a ship in New York bound for Rio, where he hoped to join a vessel from England bound for New South Wales. In later years he would talk of this voyage as a moment when he thought the end was nigh. The ship had no sooner passed the island of Trinidad, in the temperate latitudes of the Caribbean, than the mercury in the barometer dropped alarmingly and the vessel became becalmed. Ikey would recall how there was a complete stillness as though the silence impregnated and thickened the air. There was no breath of wind and the sea grew flat as a sheet of rolled metal until not even the single slap of a wave upon the prow of the ship could be heard.

The captain, no stranger to conditions in these parts, ordered the portholes to be shut, hatches battened down and new rope was brought to secure what cargo remained on deck. Then he furled canvas and waited for the tropical cyclone to hit.

Slowly a sound, as though the sea itself had given off a soft sigh, grew into an ear-splitting whistle and soon became a ferocious howling. It was as though the forces of chaos had gathered above the ship to plan its total destruction.

The flat sea rose suddenly to mountainous proportions. An aft stay snapped like a twig though no responding crack was heard to penetrate the wail of the wind. The ship, a cork upon the sea, plunged deep into each troughed wave and then rode towards its crest seventy feet above the prow.

Huge seas smashed over the vessel so that below decks the wash came up to the waist and all felt they must surely perish, though sickness forbade them contemplating their lives. Besides, they knew with desperate certainty that no God existed with power sufficient to hear their repentant cries above the raging gale.

On the morning of the third day the cyclone left them and, once again, a benign sun twinkled on the calm blue waters of the South Atlantic. While no single pieces of cargo lashed to the deck remained, the damage to the vessel was surprisingly slight. The repair of several broken stays and rigging was all that was necessary to allow them to continue the voyage. Ikey arrived in Rio much shaken by the experience though none the worse for wear.

Of Rio we have spoken before and Ikey, ever active in 'turning a penny', spent his time selling the trinkets he had been unable to dispose of before closing his Broadway shop.

He thought little of the Latinos and even less of the mosquitoes which swarmed in from the surrounding mangrove swamps at night. Ikey had no eye for the watery plumes of splashing fountains, and even the dirt and squalor to be found in the wide avenues was not to his familiar taste. It was therefore with alacrity that he accepted passage, despite some inconvenience of arrangement, on the *Coronet*, an English ship bound most fortuitously for Van Diemen's Land.

471

Ikey boarded the ship under the name of Sloman, and it must be assumed that he crossed the palm of the captain most generously, for no berth remained on board. Dr William Henry Browne, LL.D., soon to be Hobart's colonial chaplain, was on deck taking morning prayers when his tiny cabin was forced open on the captain's orders and a berth added to accommodate the generous Mr Sloman.

Dr Browne arrived back to find his books and baggage piled in a most haphazard manner to one side of the tiny cabin, and a Hebrew personage ensconced where they had once lain in a well-ordered convenience. The clergyman, who was of a naturally choleric disposition, demanded that Ikey be removed, though without success, whereupon he took great umbrage and showed no grace or charity whatsoever towards his fellow passenger, who meanwhile remained quietly seated with his arms folded and said not a syllable to offend during the cleric's entire conniption.

However, Ikey's mute tolerance was not to last. While he was well accustomed to the slings and arrows of outrageous fortune, a long and tedious voyage is best peppered with an ongoing debate, whether this be an acrimonious or a pleasant one. Therefore Ikey, unable to win his cabin partner with affable conversation, amused himself by baiting the learned Dr Browne with matters of the Anglican religion, of which Ikey knew a surprising amount. This vexatious debate, in which Ikey did not fail to score some telling points on the resurrection and the Holy Trinity, did nothing to improve the temper of God's representative on board. No sooner had the clergyman landed in Hobart than he hastened to Colonel George

Arthur with a burden of bitter complaint against the vile Mr Sloman.

This proved an altogether disastrous beginning for Ikey, as it brought the full attention of the governor to his presence on the island. Colonel Arthur, himself a devout believer, accepted Dr Browne's version of the voyage without question and promised that the blasphemous newcomer would be watched with an eagle eye.

Nor did it take long for Ikey to be discovered for his true self. He foolishly moved in with the Newmans as a lodger, where his very presence with Hannah in the tiny cottage caused jocular speculation about the nature of the bed he occupied. As soon as he walked the streets there were people who were quick to recognise him, Hobart Town being the enforced home of many of his old colleagues and not a few of his former customers.

'Oh, Ikey me boy, me boy! How are ya? Blow me down, but I'm glad to see ya! What a cursed lucky fellow yerv been, escapin' the rope and thereafter the boat. How are ya, m'boy?'

Other remarks were not as well intended. 'I say, there goes Ikey Solomon – he used to fence me swag, the cursed rogue! Were it not for him I should not be here now!'

Ikey, though his intelligence must have warned him otherwise, chose to ignore these remarks, walking on without appearing to recognise his verbal assailant or, if forced to respond, he would look upon the speaker with incurious eyes.

'You're quite mistaken, my dear, very much and entirely mistaken. I am not him whom you suppose I am, though I am pleased enough to make your acquaintance.'

He would extend a long, thin hand. 'Sloman, recently off the *Coronet*, tobacconist by way of trade. A fine display of Cuban cigars and other inhalatory delights await your pleasure in my Liverpool Street establishment.'

Ikey had lost no time opening up as a tobacconist and all at once he became the best of his kind in town, his American stock being far superior to the leaf grown on the mainland of Australia, or imported from Dutch Batavia or the Cape of Good Hope. When complimented over his cigars he'd roll his eyes and grin knowingly. 'Ah, the secret be they roll 'em on the sweat of a nigger girl's thighs!'

However much Arthur might fume, his solicitor-general advised him that there were no grounds available for Ikey's arrest unless he committed a felony on the island. Until Colonel Arthur had written to England and acquainted the under-secretary of the colonial office of Ikey's whereabouts so that a warrant could be issued for his arrest in the colony, his iniquitous quarry was as free as a lark.

Ikey, most eager to show Hannah that he had turned over a new leaf and was determined to become a devoted family man, bid his two elder sons leave New South Wales and join their mother in Hobart Town. He then set up John, the eldest, as a general merchant, with Moses his brother as his junior partner. Their establishment was stocked mostly with the hard goods Ikey had transported from America.

John and Moses Solomon would soon prosper, though gratitude would not be Ikey's reward for so swiftly reuniting his family and increasing their material well-being. Their indifference to their father is not impossible to understand, as they had no opportunity in their childhood to know Ikey, nor were they ever given a single reason to love him. They had, however, been instructed in every possible vilification of their father by their much beloved mother.

Almost from Ikey's arrival, Hannah commenced to quarrel with her husband, drawing her family into the arguments on her side. She had become convinced, and soon convinced them, that she had been made a scapegoat and was carrying Ikey's sentence.

With that peculiar logic of which women are sometimes capable, Hannah had also convinced herself that Ikey had somehow bribed Bob Marley to plant the stolen watch in the biscuit tin. Though no possible logic could explain such a bizarre scheme, Hannah was nevertheless quite blind to reason on this issue, and saw it as part of Ikey's grand plan to get her to part with her half of the combination to the safe. Thereafter, she knew with certainty, he would abscond with the contents, leaving her, whether free or convict, as a destitute prisoner on this God-forsaken island.

Affairs in the Newman household soon reached a point where Hannah's disagreeable manner even overcame the patience of the mild-mannered Mrs Newman, who demanded of her husband that he ask Ikey to leave and that he send Hannah back to the Female Factory. Richard Newman was, it must be supposed, either a weak or an honest man, the latter being so unusual in a police officer as to make it reasonable to suggest that the first quality formed a large part of his nature. If he returned Hannah to the authorities he would be obliged to return an amount of twenty pounds in lieu of the remaining three months of the accommodation agreement he had struck with John Solomon. If he should return Hannah, he found himself open to blackmail as he had been foolish enough to issue Ikey's eldest son with a receipt which would now prove his complicity.

Newman begged his wife to allow the Solomon family to remain for the three months. He pointed out that he had already spent the whole amount of the year's stipend on extensions to their cottage, and had no way of paying back the twenty pounds. In addition, he observed that Ikey's contribution of rent was paying for furnishings which they could otherwise not contemplate owning. Mrs Newman, a good and faithful woman, agreed that they should honour the agreement until it expired, whereupon, she made her husband promise, Hannah and her children would be returned to the authorities and Ikey asked to leave.

Hannah heard of Mrs Newman's plans and in a state of intoxication she confronted her, shouting wildly and accusing her of ingratitude while, at the same time, threatening to tell the authorities of the unlawful financial arrangement her husband had entered into with Hannah's son.

As with many mild-mannered people who are finally provoked, this was the straw that broke the camel's back. Mrs Newman flew into a fit of fury such as had never occurred in her life and she struck Hannah repeatedly with a broomstick and drove her screaming from the cottage.

This was the moment for which the officials had been waiting. Under the governor's instructions they had been watching the goings-on in the Newman household and, at the first reasonable opportunity, had been instructed to move against the Solomons in the hope of ensnaring Ikey in some public misdemeanour. Hannah was arrested and taken to the Female Factory and her children, as they were still assigned to her care and therefore the responsibility of the authorities, taken to the orphanage.

An official investigation followed where it was convincingly shown that Hannah had never been treated as an assigned servant and that Newman, a constable and guardian of the law, had not reported as living under his roof a 'suspected' criminal who, though not positively confirmed, was thought to be the runagate Ikey Solomon.

While this was a slender enough accusation and one which would scarcely have withstood the scrutiny of even a colonial magistrate, it was sufficient to frighten Newman. In order to avoid possible censure, he claimed that Hannah's behaviour had greatly changed since the arrival of Ikey, who had on several occasions boasted to him that he had plans to take her out of the colony at the first opportunity. Newman completed his statement with the words: 'He told me that even should she be placed in the Female Factory he would use sufficient influence to free her again'.

This attempt to implicate Ikey in a conspiracy failed, but the colonial secretary, hearing of this boast by Ikey to bring about the escape of his wife, ordered that Hannah be closely confined within the Factory and never assigned as a family servant again.

Hannah once again took this to be Ikey's work, her reasoning being that, despite his constant supplications, her continued refusal to give him the combination to the safe had caused him to punish her further. Though she truly dreaded the prospect of the Female Factory, it was the loss of her children which caused her to hate Ikey even more,

477

and she swore she would rather die than allow him the use of a single penny of their combined fortune.

Ikey, who still went officially under the name of Sloman and so was not permitted to attend the hearing, was greatly distressed at the outcome. Hannah was slipping further and further from his grasp. Though they had quarrelled incessantly since his arrival, he was certain she would eventually be persuaded to his cause. Now, with her incarceration in the Female Factory after nearly a year of freedom, her children taken from her, he knew the likelihood of his gaining her co-operation in the matter of the numbers to be severely diminished.

Ikey decided to throw all caution to the wind and appeal to the English weakness for an act of selfless nobility, and Arthur's strong desire not to waste the financial resources of the colony. He wrote directly to Arthur, dropping the name of Sloman and admitting to his real identity.

Hobart
His Excellency Colonel George Arthur
Lt. Governor of Van Diemen's Land

Sir, I beg to State the following for Which I most Humbly hope that Your Excellency will be pleased to take into Your Consideration.

While in America I have read of my wife's unfortunate situation and, acting solely from those natural causes, feeling and affections unnecessary, I trusts, to explain to Your Excellency, I have travelled 30,000 miles, expressly to settle and pass the remainder of my life in the bosom of my family. I therefore beseech Your Excellency most humbly that You may allow my beloved wife to be assigned to me as servant as I am certain that a woman of her refined nature and frail disposition will not long survive the place of oblivion in which she is now confined to the utter discomfiture and bereavement of your memorialist.

I wish to explain to Your Excellency that in the matter of Mr R. Newman of which You are well acquainted, were it not for his constant demands for money there would be no such trumped up complaint as was brought before You. With the result that my beloved wife has been torn from the arms of her precious children and sent to that dreadful confinement which is worse than death.

I further promise Your Excellency that should You release my wife to my care I shall be happy to enter into a bond of indemnity to prove my utmost good faith on this matter.

I have the honour to Subscribe – Your Excellency's Most Humble Servant
Isaac Solomon.

Arthur's reply was a blunt and unequivocal refusal: ' . . . *the ends of justice would be entirely defeated, if his wife, so soon after her transportation to this colony, should be assigned to her husband.*'

Meanwhile, Ikey, all his life a cautious man who seldom made mistakes of judgement concerning the law, seemed so entirely obsessed with the desire to get the information he needed from Hannah that he did not appear to realise he had come to the end of his efforts and ought to be making a hurried departure from Van Diemen's Land.

Caution, and the knowledge that opportunities are seldom singular and that another occasion will always arise to gain your purpose, had always been Ikey's favoured philosophy. This patience and trust in his luck had served him well in the past. Now it seemed as if, by giving his Waterloo medal to Mary, he had sacrificed his sound judgement and good sense. It was almost as though he was under a delusion that even the determined arm of the law was not long enough to stretch across the twelve thousand miles separating London from Hobart Town.

But stretch it did and its fingers began to close around Ikey with the necessary documents relating to the issue of a warrant for his arrest arriving in Hobart.

Time has warped the facts of Ikey's arrest and different versions have come to exist to satisfy the appetites of amateur historians bent on intellectual booty. The Sydney *Monitor* of 17th March 1830 reported Ikey's arrest thus:

At about 2 p.m. two constables, in the disguise of out-settlers, came into the shop, one of whom said he wanted some tobacco and the other a pipe. On coming in they asked for the old gentleman, as they preferred dealing with him to the young ones. Ikey, who was behind the counter, started up and said: 'I am the person,' and instantly one of the men seized him and said: 'You are the person we want.' On this apprehension, Ikey turned as pale as death, and after recovering from the stupor of a few moments exclaimed: 'So help me Heaven! I am a done man now; it's all over for me; I am done for!' He made a rush towards a desk at the upper end of the counter, on which there was lying a pen-knife, which he endeavoured to seize hold of, no doubt for the purpose of committing suicide, but was prevented in the attempt by the constables, to whose assistance four of the military, who were stationed outside, came with drawn bayonets and fire arms. Having rendered him powerless, they handcuffed him, and brought him before the Police Magistrate of the Colony. After identification as Isaac Solomon, he was committed to gaol, where to guard against the possibility of escape, he was heavily ironed.

It is on such dull documentation that history must build its case.

Mary would come to tell of it differently, for she had it from one of the prison urchins she taught in the Female Factory who was in the shop at the time.

Children have a better ear for the truth and can repeat quite clearly what they have seen and heard. This is particularly true of the street urchin, who must depend on his ears and his eyes to avoid trouble from shopkeepers, officials, grown-ups in general and, of course, the law. The boy, who stood in the corner of Ikey's shop unnoticed while the arrest took place, told it as an amusing piece in which two bumble-mouthed constables made a proper mess of the arrest procedure.

The young lad had barely entered the door when he was brushed aside by two settlers dressed in the rough manner of workmen from the bush. Ikey, who was trimming a split thumb nail with a small penknife, looked up and seeing the two men approach immediately placed the knife down upon the counter to give his two out-of-town

481

customers his attention. His shopkeeper's smile appeared and his hands spread wide to welcome them.

'Gentlemen, a pinch of snuff, compliments o' the 'ouse, American, Kentucky blend and not to be sneezed at!' Ikey cackled at his own tired joke, expecting his grateful customers to do the same.

The two men became confused and then looked the one at the other.

'Go on, 'elp yourselves, lads, it be a custom o' the 'ouse when strangers comes to town.' Ikey pushed the yellow snuff tin along the counter towards the two men, one of whom gave a small shrug and took a useful pinch, first to one nostril and then the other. His partner did the same and almost at once their nostrils were seen to dilate, their mouths to open, eyes to close and their heads to draw back, whereupon the sneeze arrived at almost the identical moment for each. Their heads were thrown forward so that they were taken to bending quite involuntarily at the waist, so mighty was the report from their nostrils.

After a few moments they looked up at Ikey through watery eyes and the larger of the two men sniffed and wiped the mucus from his nose with the back of his hand. Ikey now stood most casually with both hands placed flat upon the counter.

'A king o' sneezes, say you not, my dears? A prime example o' the veritable art o' the most honourable Chinese emperor, Ah-Tishoo! That sniff o' snuff be the best in the colony, though a humble enough sample o' me wares and quite nothing compared with the Cuban cigars or blends o' baccy we 'as for pleasing those who come from out o' town. What say you, gentlemen, how may I serve you?'

'Ikey Solomon?' the second bushman said.

'To whom does I 'ave the pleasure?' Ikey asked pushing his long thin fingers across the counter.

'We 'as come to arrest thee, sir!' the man with the snotty hand said, not shaking Ikey's extended hand.

Ikey pulled back and clasped both his hands to his chest in a show of horror, his eyes rolled and his expression was most comic afraid, then he picked up the penknife and held it with the tiny blade pointed towards his heart. 'Oh, woe is me, so help me heaven,' he said looking towards the ceiling, 'I am a done man now!' He grabbed at his throat with his free hand and made a strangling sound, his tongue protruding. 'Aargh! I shall take me own life rather than be taken alive!'

It was a most amusing display and Ikey, seeing the urchin standing at the door, winked broadly at him. Children, he understood, were much more intelligent of wit than those who have lost the enchantment of pantomime.

'Arrest is it? How very amusing, gentlemen, shall you chain me now?' Ikey extended his wrists to beyond the counter, his hands clasped together. Then, as though suddenly grown tired of the childish game, he withdrew them and clasped the edge of the counter. 'What is it I can get for you, gentlemen? I have much to do in this pretty day.'

'A clay pipe!' one of the men shouted, and Ikey jumped at the boldness of his voice.

'An ounce o' shag!' the other shouted equally loudly, causing Ikey to throw up his hands in consternation at the manner of their delivery which, curiously, had not been directed at him but in the direction of the door.

Almost at once four troopers with drawn bayonets

affixed to their firearms elbowed their way through the door in a clatter and banging of barrels and butts, the clinking of metal and thump of heavy boots. They wore their red coats and had polished their brasses in anticipation of the grand occasion.

'You are under arrest, Ikey Solomon!' the constable who'd earlier wiped his nose shouted, and this time produced a pair of police manacles from the pocket of his jacket.

'Ikey's luck 'as finally run out,' Mary said solemnly, after the boy returned in great excitement to the Female Factory to tell his story. She clasped the Waterloo medal to her bosom, the gold metal warm in her twisted hand. 'He should 'ave tried to see me, if only just to greet me!' Then she turned away so that the boy could not see her tears and in a voice too soft for him to hear she said, 'Stupid old sod! Maybe he could've shared some o' me luck.'

Chapter Twenty-three

Mary moved from the old Female Factory where she had spent the past eighteen months to the new one where, for a short period, she returned to work in the bakery. If new meant a larger factory it did not mean a better one. The new female house of correction was a remodelled distillery, secured cheaply by the government, and its site in the damp valley of the Hobart Town rivulet, under the shadow of a large hill which blocked almost all direct sunlight for a large part of the year, was most unsuitable. It was damp and dark and so unhealthy that during the first winter in the new Factory eighteen inmates and twenty-seven newborn babies died from bronchial illnesses.

While the kneading of dough was hard work, Mary found it pleasant enough. The ovens were warm on the cold days of drizzle and sharp, cutting winds which blew up the wide Derwent River from the coast in winter. Van Diemen's Land has a contrary climate and lies sufficiently close to the Antarctic Circle to have at least one of its toes permanently in ice. No local would be brave enough to pronounce a part of any day of the year safe from sudden bone-chilling cold, when summer's blue brilliance is turned, with a malevolent growl from atop the great mountain, into the misery of a winter gale.

The year and a half spent in the old Female Factory had not, at first, been easy for Mary. The overcrowded conditions, the constant fighting among the prisoners and the fact that the Factory was as much a brothel as a prison, made the day-to-day effort to survive most onerous. But Mary, convinced that her luck in life had changed the moment she had set foot in Van Diemen's Land, set about the task of surviving until she was granted her ticket of leave.

Life in a female gaol is no different from that of a male one – dominance and strength are usually all that matter. With Ann Gower at her side, Mary set about the conquest of her fellow inmates. She grew her nails until her twisted hands had the appearance of wicked claws. Ann Gower let the stories of Mary in Newgate and the raking of Potbottom's back be known. She also conveyed the fact that Mary had been crowned queen of the prisoners on the voyage because she had defied the authorities, earned a flogging and won the day. This was sufficient to make Mary Abacus greatly feared and respected among the prisoners without ever having to fight any of the inmates.

The prisoners at the Female Factory soon came to realise that Mary was on their side and was not a leader simply so that she might benefit herself or her cronies at their expense. The authorities also accepted that Mary's leadership was not necessarily to their disadvantage. She did not directly challenge their authority but, instead, organised the prostitution and the distribution of grog and tobacco in the Factory. Mary's past experience of running a brothel and organising the lives

of the girls within it made life in gaol a great deal more
bearable for all.

It was the custom of the Factory to elect female overseers and task mistresses from the prisoners and the
superintendent of the Factory begged Mary to take such
a position but she refused. They were obliged to accept
that Mary carried more unsanctioned authority than
those prisoners they had trusted with such a position.
They also knew that those convicts appointed overseers
would answer to Mary before them.

Payment by the troopers for services from the prison
whores was now, as it had been at Egyptian Mary's,
made not to the individual whore, but directly to Mary.
She in turn negotiated the price of tobacco and grog
among the corrupt turnkeys and, provided they did not
become too greedy, paid them what they demanded.
Mary retained a small percentage of the capital earned
and paid the remainder to the prisoners who were owed
it. This she did in money or in kind.

The clicking of her abacus could often be heard late
into the night as she reconciled her ledgers. Mary's calculations were scrupulously correct and, while there are
always those in a mutual society who whisper that the
bookkeeper is a cheat, the ten percent she took from
each transaction was considered by most to be fair for
the task she undertook.

In fact, it had been an attempt by the prison officials
to squeeze too great a profit from the prisoners which
had consolidated Mary's position and proved the value
of the ten percent levy. Those who profited dishonour-
ably from the poor wretches under their care demanded
an even higher price for their tobacco and grog. Mary
refused and at the same time withheld the services of

the prostitutes to the government troopers.

The Female Factory was unofficially endorsed by the military command as a soldier's brothel, and when it ceased to work the prison officials were forced to admit, in answer to the discreet though annoyed enquiries from the military command, that they could not alleviate the situation. This was the cause of much private embarrassment although, publicly, Governor Arthur had used it to his benefit. In fact, with much pomp and ceremony he had presided over an official commendation to the chief gaoler for having successfully put down prostitution in the Female Factory. In the same hour of the governor's departure the barracks commander had demanded, supposedly with the blessing of the governor, that 'the good work on behalf of my troopers be resumed at once!'

During the two-week strike Mary used the funds she had accumulated from taking her ten percent cut to purchase grog and tobacco which she dispensed to the workers while they were unemployed.

By organising the prison urchins, who could come and go as they pleased and, besides, had no problems evading the porter at the gate, Mary showed the corrupt officials that she had the means of bringing in adequate supplies of the commodities they had fondly imagined they exclusively controlled. Pressure continued to mount from the troopers who had come to see the Female Factory as their rightful source of recreation and so it was not long before commonsense prevailed. The turnkeys asked that the former prices should be maintained.

But Mary demanded the prices come down. She was sentenced to solitary confinement on bread and water on a trumped-up charge, but this manoeuvre was an abject failure. The prisoner whores refused to co-operate, although in all other things their behaviour was exemplary. In a pact which they named 'Legs crossed for Mary' they refused to lie on their backs on behalf of the Crown, and the authorities, fearing a public outcry, could not be seen to punish them.

Mary was released from solitary after only two days and a fair deal was struck with the turnkeys. Nothing like this had ever happened before. The fact that Mary had been prepared to be punished for their ultimate benefit deeply impressed the prisoners, and she now possessed their loyalty.

Mary also concerned herself with the prison urchins, and conducted a school for them for an hour each day in which they were taught to read and write. This ragged school was a great pride to the mothers of the children and also to many of the other prisoners, who were generally illiterate. They took comfort in the fact that ignorance was not, as they had been so often told, a permanent curse placed upon their kind by a malev-olent God. Even the whores looked with satisfaction upon the slates the children carried and regarded these as a positive proof that their work was not unworthy.

However, it should not be construed that Mary's presence in the Female Factory had turned it into a place of calm and order. Prison is still an institution where the back is broken with hard labour and the soul is destroyed by despair. Despite Mary's efforts, this vile degradation had not changed in Van Diemen's Land. Sadness and despair are ingredients without which the recipe of prison cannot be made acceptable to society. If the old Female Factory had never worked better than under Mary's leadership, this was only that it was a lesser kind of hell on earth. One of the most palpable examples of this misery was the inevitable consequence of institutionalised prostitution, the illegitimately born child.

A great many of the children did not survive long. The poor diet in the Female Factory resulted in serious malnutrition and many mothers could not produce sufficient breast milk to feed their babies. Those infants which did survive were removed from their mothers as soon as possible after birth and sent to the orphanage, which was known as 'the nursery'. One of the most commonly heard sounds in the Factory was of a mother wailing at the enforced loss of her child, for it cannot be supposed that the whore has less love for the miracle within her womb than does the wife of a preacher.

However, this was not thought to be the case by the authorities and many of the population and proof thereof was rendered when a female convict, Mary McLaughlan, was executed for killing her newborn baby. Though children died like flies from the lack of food, hygiene and warmth in the Factory, this was thought to be quite in order, whereas the act of a mother putting her tiny infant out of misery, so that it should not suffer longer than its day of birth, was regarded as a crime so gross that the whole island was deeply shocked at this example of the brutalised convict mind. When Mary had gently asked her namesake why she had taken the life of her infant the little Scots woman had wept bitter tears. 'Acht, I couldnae bear the bairn t' suffer. I had nae milk in me teets nor ought t' save its wee life.'

The Reverend William Bedford, the drunken chaplain

to the convicts who, in God's name, had been among the large concourse assembled to witness the last moments of Mary McLaughlan, preached a sermon while almost sober in the prison chapel on the Sunday following the hanging.

'She stood dressed in a snow-white garment with a black ribbon tied about her waist and a certain hope of forgiveness supported her in her final hour and, it is my belief, she died contrite and resigned.' Bedford looked about his congregation. Not all were prisoners and the townsfolk sat separated from the lewd looks of the male convicts by a curtain. 'On the falling of the drop, the instant before her mortal scene was closed, she did utter but three words of penitence, "Oh! my God!" though this may well have been a curse, I have chosen to see it as a plea to heaven for forgiveness! Hers was the dreadful crime of murder, the cold-blooded killing of the little innocent offspring of her own bosom.' He paused again, for he was in good form and had for once the complete attention of his congregation. 'Well has this first step to error been compared to the burning spark which, when lighted, may carry destruction to inconceivable bounds. But will mankind take a lesson from this?' He shook his head slowly then banged his fist upon the pulpit. 'Cannot the horrible tenacity be broken with which the Devil keeps his hold, when once he has put his finger on his victim?' The Reverend Bedford let this last sentiment reach the minds of his congregation before he added in a voice both sorrowful and low, 'I think not'.

And so the act committed by a desperate woman was entered into the history of the island as the most heinous of all crimes committed in that place of infamy.

Mary had always had a great love for children, though she would never be able to bear one of her own. She came to look upon the children in the orphanage as belonging to the women in the prison and therefore as her responsibility. Her heart seemed torn asunder when each newly weaned infant was taken away from its mother. On many occasions she had begged the prison authorities to allow the infants to stay, or even that the mothers might be allowed to visit their children at the orphanage on the Sabbath.

The reply had always been the same. The prisoner mother had no rights to a child born out of wedlock, nor could the prison authorities accept responsibility for its care. The best interests of the newborn infant were served away from the malignant pollutants of the prison atmosphere, where under the supervision of a benign government, a child would benefit from a Christian upbringing in the Reverend Thomas Smedley's Wesleyan Orphanage.

And so Mary had passed the first year and a half of her sentence in Van Diemen's Land, though one more aspect should be added which was to be of paramount importance to her future. She was naturally inclined to gardening, though she couldn't think why this should be, as her life had been spent almost entirely on cobblestones in decaying courts and alleys devoid of even a blade of grass. The names of flowers were quite unknown to her, but for the daffodil, rose and violet, and these three only because urchins sold them on the streets of London.

She loved to work in the potato patch and never failed to be surprised when, upon pulling up a dark green, hairy-leafed plant she would find attached to its slender roots great creamy orbs fit for the plate of a king. A little further digging would reveal more of the wonderful tubers and her hands, buried in the rich, damp soil, would for a moment seem whole, her long, slender fingers restored and beautiful.

In the new Female Factory her knowledge and disposition for gardening were recognised, and she was allowed to leave the bakery and spend all her prison working hours at this task. Mary talked to the Irish women in the Factory about the manner of growing potatoes, and learned much from them which improved the crop grown in the prison gardens. This, in particular, from Margaret Keating, who added further to her knowledge with information on the making of poteen, sometimes known as 'Irish whisky'. This is usually made from barley, but potatoes may be used instead. Though each kind has an altogether different taste, both are most astonishingly intoxicating.

Mary soon showed that her proficiency with potatoes carried over to Indian corn, cabbage, carrots and other vegetables. She asked that Ann Gower be allowed to work with her as well as several of the Irish women accustomed to working the soil, including Margaret Keating. She also asked that a good-sized shed be built so that the garden implements could be safely stored and the seeding potatoes successfully propagated. Behind this shed she proposed to build a hothouse for propagating seeds. This, she convinced the prison authorities, was because of the unpredictable weather, where frosts and cold snaps late into spring and early summer could destroy half an acre of vegetable seedlings overnight. This second project was considered to be outside the authority of the prison as it involved the purchase of glass, and was referred to the chief clerk of the colonial secretary's department, Mr Emmett.

Mary had greatly impressed Mr Emmett, who saw her use her abacus to calculate the cost of losing two crops as they had done the previous year to sudden cold snaps. She had offset this against the price of the materials, all of which, but for the glass used in the construction, were made by the male prisoners with only the smallest cost to the treasury.

For the hothouse Mary proposed a clever modification. She planned to build into one of the brick end walls a kiln which could be worked from the outside of the building. Ann explained to the authorities that one of the Irish women, skilled in the making of pots, had discovered a clay pit near the rivulet. The clay there was thought to be of excellent quality for pots. Mary proposed that they would produce water and plant pots for sale to the townsfolk and, with the advent of the hothouse, ornamental plants could be grown. The profits from this enterprise would go directly to the coffers of the colony. The chief clerk now took a keen interest in the hothouse as if the idea had been his own. He accepted the proposal and agreed that the hothouse should be built, together with the abutting kiln, a pottery drying shed and two wheels for turning the clay.

Mary had yet another modification in mind, though not one she thought to mention to the chief clerk. She requested of the prisoner bricklayer to construct a wide hearth on the inside of the end wall of the hothouse, which contained the kiln on its outside. This would be back-to-back with the kiln, so that there would be a fireplace with a good platform, wide working mouth and a double chimney flue shared by both hearth and kiln.

When, to Margaret Keating's precise instructions, the structure was complete, they had the basis of a first-class poteen still. The kiln could be fired separately from the outside and the hearth, if needs be, made to carry a fire of its own on the inside. Mary had a carpenter construct a door to the opening of the hearth, which had four stout wooden shelves built into its outside surface. If the authorities should arrive unexpectedly when the still was in progress the fire could be quickly doused, and the door closed to conceal it. Numerous pots containing plants could be hastily placed upon the shelves as though this was their permanent resting place. Smoke from the recently doused fire would carry up the chimney, where it could always be explained as being caused by the operation of the outside kiln.

All that was now required was the equipment needed to place within the hearth. This consisted of the numerous thin copper pipes which would be fed through the back wall of the hearth into the kiln so that they would be further heated by it, as well as the two chambers needed for the condensation and distillation of the spirit. These copper chambers would reside within the mouth of the hearth, where only a very small fire was needed to keep the water within the main cylinder producing the steam required for the distillation of the potatoes which had been set to ferment.

Ann Gower, who had not the slightest inclination to use a hoe or break her back in a potato patch, was nevertheless perfectly willing to work in a trade she knew best. Whoring in prison gained only a sixpence at a time, whereas in the private enterprise of the prison gardens she could command a quick shilling. She was given the task of procuring the pipes, cylinders and other equipment required for the still.

Ann took up permanent residence in the newly completed shed, where she soon attracted a regular clientele. She quickly discovered those among her clients who had the means to steal, or the skill to fashion and install what Mary required in pipes and cylinders, valves and taps.

They had been most fortunate to chance upon a randy mechanic who was masterful in his knowledge of pipes and pressures. By employing his considerable engineering skill Mary constructed a still which, with the turning of no more than half a dozen nuts, could be disassembled and quickly hidden in a specially constructed cavity, which was revealed by lifting one of the large flagstones which comprised the floor of the hothouse.

In return for their services, those few men who had been involved in supply and construction of the still were happy enough to be repaid in a free weekly fulfilment from Ann Gower for the period of 'snow to snow'. This was the time from the last snowfall on Mount Wellington to the first of the following winter, or, if they were exceedingly unlucky, to a summer fall, which was not unknown in these parts.

Mary Abacus and Ann Gower, with the help of Margaret Keating, had created the two things most in demand on the island, strong drink and lewd women, and both at a price most attractive to the customer.

Governor Arthur was determined to stamp out drunkenness within the female prison, and his orders were that any turnkey caught selling grog was to be instantly dismissed and severely punished with three hundred strokes of the lash. While it had been comparatively easy to use the children to smuggle tobacco and liquor into the old Factory, it was considerably harder in the new, where they were regularly searched by the guards at the gates.

Now Mary and her partners could not only sell grog to the free population but they could also bring into prison significant quantities of the fiery poteen concealed in the loads of vegetables delivered to the kitchen each evening.

The three women worked well together, Ann Gower being utterly loyal to Mary and Margaret Keating being a quietly spoken and sensible woman who was a political prisoner. Within six months of the completion of the still, having served three years in prison, she was assigned to an emancipist of good repute who offered at the same time to take her as his wife.

To her husband's surprise she brought with her a small but much-needed cash dowry, the source of which he was sufficiently prudent not to enquire about. And so Margaret Keating left her two erstwhile partners to enjoy a life of hard work and the utmost respectability, where she would lose one child and raise four others in the happiest of family circumstances. Mary took over the working of the poteen still.

Both Mary and Ann Gower knew well enough that whoring and strong drink taken together spelled trouble, so they were careful not to create a convivial atmosphere about the running of their business. Hobart Town abounded in sly-grog shops where all manner of homemade liquor could be obtained. This was a most potent and dangerous concoction and often laced with laudanum. When the revellers became too drunk and noisy they were given a finishing glass which consisted of a strong poison and was designed to render the drinker unconscious so that he might more easily be thrown out onto the street or, if he was a whaler with a pocketful of silver American dollars, robbed of all he possessed.

Men were not permitted to congregate or drink on Mary's prison vegetable plot, but only to use Ann's services or make a purchase of grog. A single transaction, the purchase of a 'pot', as a small container of poteen became known, took two minutes. A double transaction, a 'pot 'n pant', took no more than ten, a shilling being paid for each service, after which the recipient was required promptly to scarper from the premises.

Mary's poteen soon earned a reputation for its excellent quality and as men must always put names to things, this being especially true for things clandestine, where a wink and a nod may be involved, or a euphemism employed, some began to call the enterprise 'The Potato Patch'.

'Where are you going, mate?' a man might enquire of another.

'To the Potato Patch,' would be the reply.

However, late one winter's afternoon a trooper, not a usual customer, after obtaining his two shillings worth demanded company to go with his proposed drinking. When promptly ordered to leave he grew most cantankerous and, stumbling away, he turned and yelled at Mary.

'This place be shit! It be nothing but a damned potato factory!'

The name stuck and Mary's still became known as

'The Potato Factory'. It was a name thought most excellent to those who used its services, for it contained some character and style, which is an essential ingredient in any decent man's drinking habits, the Potato Patch always having had about it a somewhat base and primitive feel.

Now it might be supposed that an operation such as this would soon enough be the subject of the tattle tongues to be found in great numbers in a women's prison, and that the prison officials would soon come to know about it. But Mary and Ann Gower saw to it that the prisoners had drink sufficient to keep them happy, and that their children had clothes and physic when they had colic or were otherwise taken with sickness. Mary reigned as Queen no differently in the new Female Factory than she had done in the old.

Similarly, it must be expected that a customer of the Potato Factory would at some time reveal its whereabouts to such as an undercover plainclothes constable set about gathering useful information within the premises of a brothel or a tavern. Gossips and narks are among the most virulent forces at work in any convict community, but no sooner had one sly-grog outlet closed down than another would spring up in its place.

Even if human weakness is more often exercised than human strength, a community such as was to be found in Hobart Town could keep its secrets well. Most of the people who walked the streets were either emancipists, ticket of leavers or active prisoners, and all felt they had just cause to resent authority and to keep some things secret from the free settlers whom they disliked almost as much.

Mary saw to it that the troopers connected with the

Female Factory were kept silent with a regular supply of poteen. Furthermore, several key members of the local constabulary would receive a pint-sized 'pot' with a tight wooden cork, brought in by a street urchin each week. And, at least one magistrate was known to consider Mary's poteen 'The purest water o' life itself!' and took pains not to ask his clerk, who declined to take payment for it, where he habitually obtained it.

Mary's vegetable garden and pottery continued to prosper and the prison authorities had no cause to complain. Abundant vegetables and sacks of splendid potatoes arrived at the Female Factory kitchen and, while much of this fresh produce never found its way onto the prison tables, being appropriated by those in charge, this did not concern Mary. She well understood that those in charge had even further reason not to look too closely behind the cabbage leaves.

From time to time, the chief clerk, Mr Emmett, would receive a reasonable sum of money, being the proceeds for the sale of plant and water pots. He would receive the funds together with a summary of what had been sold, to whom and at what price. A clerk sent about the town confirmed Mary's reconciliation correct to the penny – all this in Mary's neat hand, the columns precisely drawn and the addition and subtraction without error. The payment would always come together with a handsomely turned pot which contained some exotic forest bloom, Mr Emmett being famous for his garden and his cottage, Beauly Lodge, was considered the most beautiful in Hobart Town. Once, for his daughter Millicent on her tenth birthday, Mary sent a standard rose, a veritable pin cushion of tiny, perfectly formed pink blooms.

Mr Emmett, observing the honesty and integrity of Mary Abacus, called on the Female Factory to offer her the position of a clerk with the colonial secretary's department. But, though Mary had declared herself most flattered, she declined the offer.

'Do you not understand, Mary, that there are no women in my department or, I dare say, in any other? You should perceive this as a great honour.' Mr Emmett smiled and then resumed. 'No woman, I'll wager, and *never* a convict woman has been placed in so great and fortunate a position of trust on this island, my dear!'

Mary wondered how she could possibly think to refuse. Then she looked down at her twisted hands and her eyes filled with bitter tears at the memory of the cold winter morning in London's docklands, when she had left Mr Goldstein's warehouse with her heart singing. How in the swirling yellow mist the male voices had risen to envelop and crush her . . .

> *Mary, Mary, Bloody Mary*
> *Who does her sums on bead and rack*
> *Go away, you're too contrary*
> *You're the monkey, the bloody monkey*
> *You're the monkey on our back!*

The harsh memories flooded back and Mary was most hard put to restrain herself from weeping.

'I'm sorry, sir, I may not accept. There be reasons I cannot say to you, though me gratitude be most profound and I thank you from the bottom o' me 'eart.' Then she looked up at Mr Emmett, her eyes still wet with her held back tears. 'I prefers the gardens, sir. The air be clean and the work well disposed to me ability.'

Mr Emmett made one last effort to persuade her. It was apparent that he did not like being refused and now spoke with some annoyance. 'There are few enough on this cursed island who can read or write, let alone reconcile a column of figures! Good God, woman, will you not listen to me? You are ...' he took a moment to search for words, '... wasted in this ... this damned potato patch of yours!'

'Then let me teach, sir!' Mary pleaded urgently. 'So that we may make more of our children to read and write and meet with your 'ighest demands!'

'Teach? Where? Teach who?'

'The orphanage, sir. The prison brats. If I could teach three mornings a week I could still manage the gardens.'

Mr Emmett looked bewildered. 'Your suggestion is too base to be regarded with proper amusement, Mary. These are misbegotten children, the spawn of convicts and drunken wretches!' It was apparent that he had become most alarmed at the thought. 'They cannot be made to learn as you and I may. Have you no commonsense about you, woman?' He shook his head and screwed up his eyes as though he were trying to rid his mind of the thought Mary had planted therein. 'First you refuse my offer, now this urchin-teaching poppy-cock! These children cannot possibly be made to count or write! Surely you know this as well as I do? Have you not observed them for yourself? They are creatures damned by nature, slack of jaw and vacant of expression, the cursed offspring of the criminal class. I assure you, they do not have minds which can be made to grasp the process of formal learning!' He smiled at a sudden thought. 'Will you have them to do Latin?'

'*Ergo sum*, "I am one",' Mary said quietly. 'I were

born a urchin same as them, slack-jawed and vacant o' face the way you looks when you be starvin'!' She cocked her head to one side and attempted to smile, though all the muscles of her lips could manage was a quiver at the corners of her mouth. She reached up to her bosom and clasped the Waterloo medal in her hand. 'Only three mornings?' she pleaded. 'I begs you to ask them folk at the orphanage, sir.'

The chief clerk seemed too profoundly shocked to continue and for some time he remained silent. 'Hmmph!' he growled at last. 'I shall see what I can make of it.' He shook his head slowly, clucking his tongue. 'Clerks out of street urchins, eh? I'll wager, it will be as easy to turn toads into handsome princes!'

A week later Mary received a message to see the Reverend Thomas Smedley, the Wesleyan principal at the orphanage in New Town which had been given the surprising name of the King's Orphan School, though no teaching whatsoever took place in the cold, damp and cheerless converted distillery which served as a home for destitute and deserted children. With this invitation came a pass to leave the prison garden so that she might attend the meeting scheduled for the latter part of the afternoon.

The Reverend Smedley was a short, stout man, not much past his fortieth year, who wore a frock coat and dark trousers, both considerably stained. Neither was his linen too clean, the dog collar he wore being much in need of a scrub and a douse of starch. He wore small gold-rimmed spectacles on a nose which seemed no more than a plump button, and the thick lenses exaggerated the size of his dark eyes. Though it was a face which seemed disposed to be jolly, it was not. Any jollity it may have once possessed was defeated by a most profoundly sour expression. The Reverend Smedley was clean shaven and his cheeks much crossed with a multiplicity of tiny scarlet veins, a curious sanguinity in one so young and not a drinking man. He was a follower of Charles Wesley and, unlike his Anglican counterparts, was sure to be a teetotaller. Instead of adding a rosy blush, these scrambled veins upon his fat cheeks exacerbated further his saturnine expression. It seemed as though he might be ill with a tropical fever, for apart from his roseate jowls, his skin was yellow, while a thin veneer of perspiration covered his podgy face. To Mary he looked a man much beset by life who was in need of the attentions of a good wife or a sound doctor.

'What is your religion, Miss ... er, Abacus?' Mary had been left to stand while Thomas Smedley had flipped the tails of his frock coat, and sat upon the lone chair behind a large desk in the front office of the children's orphanage.

'I can't rightly say, sir. I don't know that I 'as one.' Mary paused and shrugged. 'I be nothin' much o' nothin'.'

'A satanist then? Or is it an atheist?'

'Neither, sir, if you mean I believes in the opposite or not at all.'

The Reverend Thomas Smedley looked exceedingly sour and snapped at Mary in a sharp, hard voice which contrasted with his flaccid appearance.

'Do you, or do you not, have the love of the Lord Jesus Christ in your heart? Have you or have you not, been washed in the Blood of the Lamb? Are you, or are you not, saved of your sins? If not, you *may* not!' These three questions had been too rapid to answer each at a time and his voice had risen fully an octave with each question so that the last part was almost shrill, shouted at Mary in a spray of spittle.

However, at their completion he seemed at once exhausted, as though he had rehearsed well the questions and they had come out unbroken and, to his surprise, much as he had intended them to sound. Now he sat slumped in his chair and his head hung low, with his chin tucked into the folds of his neck, while his chubby hands grasped the side of the desk and his magnified eyes looked obliquely up at Mary as he waited for her reply.

'May not what, sir?' Mary asked politely.

'Teach! Teach! Teach!' Smedley yelled.

'I do not understand, sir? I shall not teach them either of lambs or washing of blood, or sins and least of all of God, but of the salvation of numbers and letters, sir.'

The clergyman looked up and pointed a stubby finger at Mary. 'I am not mocked saith the Lord!' he shouted.

Oh, Gawd, not another one! Mary thought, casting her mind to the dreadful Potbottom, though outwardly she smiled modestly at the Reverend Smedley. 'I had not meant to mock, sir, my only desire is to teach the word o' man and leave the business o' Gawd to the pulpit men, like yourself.'

'God is not business! God is love! I am the way, the truth and the light saith the Lord! Unthinkable! Quite, quite, unthinkable!' His eyes appeared to narrow and his fat fist banged down upon the desk. 'Unless you are born again we cannot allow you to teach children! How will you show them the way, the truth and the light? How will you example the love of Jesus Christ?'

'Who is teaching them now?' Mary asked, hoping to change the subject.

'They have religious instruction twice each day,' the principal shot back angrily. 'That is quite sufficient for their need.'

'Oh, you have used the Bible to teach them to read and write,' Mary said, remembering this was how the Quaker women had suggested they perform this task on board ship.

'We teach salvation! The love of the Lord Jesus and the redemption of our sins so that we may be washed clean, we do not teach reading and writing here!' the preacher barked. 'These children shall grow up to be hewers of wood and drawers of water, that is the place for which they are destined in the Scriptures. They are no less the sons of Ham than the blacks who hide in the hills and steal our sheep. These orphan children are loved by the Lord, for He loves the sparrow as well as the eagle, the less fortunate as well as the gifted child.'

'Then, with Gawd's permission and your own, I will teach them to be more fortunate, sir. Surely Gawd will see no 'arm in such tinkering?'

Reverend Smedley looked up at Mary who stood with her back directly to the open window so that the light from behind flooded into the tiny room to give her body a halo effect, though, at the same time, it caused her features to darken, so that, to the short-sighted clergyman, she seemed to be a dark, hovering satanic form.

'Tinkering? Permission? God's permission or mine, you shall have neither. You shall have no such thing! You are *not* saved, you are *not* clean, you are *not* born again, you are an unrepentant and dastardly sinner whom I have every right to drive from this temple of the Lord!'

Mary sighed. The worst that could happen to her was that she be sent back to the Female Factory and to the prison gardens and this was no great matter. She was not in the least afraid of the silly little man who yapped at her like an overfed lap dog. Her fear was for the orphan children, for the child she had been herself, for the fact that had it not been for the Chinee contraption of wire and beads she would have remained in darkness. Her fear was that if she were not permitted to teach these orphan children they would grow up to perpetuate the myth that her kind were a lower form of human life, one which was beyond all salvation of the mind and therefore of the spirit.

'What must I do to be saved?' she asked suddenly.

The clergyman looked up surprisd. 'Why, you must repent, of course!'

Mary shrugged and raised her eyebrows. 'Then I repent,' she announced simply.

Smedley sat up, suddenly alert. 'That's not proper repenting. You have to be sorry!'

'So, I'm sorry, sir,' Mary sighed. 'Most sorry.'

'Not me! Not sorry to me, to the Lord Jesus! You have to go down on your knees before Him and repent!'

'Repent or say I'm sorry? Which is it to be?' Mary asked.

'It's the same thing!' Thomas Smedley shouted. Then abruptly he stood up and pointed to the floor at Mary's feet, where he obviously expected her to kneel.

'No it ain't! It ain't the same at all,' Mary said, crossing her arms. 'I could be sorry and not repent, but I couldn't repent and not be sorry, know what I mean?'

'On your knees at once. The glory of the Lord is upon us!' the Reverend Smedley demanded and again jabbed a fat, urgent finger towards the bare boards at Mary's feet.

Mary looked about and indeed glory had entered the tiny room. A shaft of pale late afternoon sunlight lit the entire space, turning it to a brilliant gold, and small dust motes danced in the fiery light.

Mary looked directly at the clergyman. 'If I repent, can I teach?' she asked.

'Yes, yes!' Smedley screeched urgently. 'Kneel down! Kneel down at once! His glory be upon us!'

Mary knelt down in front of the desk and the Reverend Smedley came around from his side and placed his fat fist upon her head. 'Shut your eyes and bow your head!' he instructed. Then he began to pray in a loud and sonorous preacher's voice which Mary had not heard before.

'Lord I have brought this poor lost lamb to Thee to ask Thee to forgive her sins, for she wishes to repent and accept Your Glorious salvation and receive life eternal so that she may be clasped to Your glorious bosom and receive Your everlasting love.' There was a silence although it was punctuated several times with a loud sucking of the clergyman's lips as though he were undergoing some mysterious ecstasy. Then suddenly his preacher's voice resumed. 'Thank you precious Jesus. Hallelujah! Praise His precious name!'

Mary felt his hand lift from her head and in a tone of voice somewhat triumphant but more or less returned to its former timbre the Reverend Smedley announced calmly, 'Hallelujah, sister Mary, welcome to the bosom of the Lord Jesus Christ, you are saved, washed in the blood of the Lamb! You may rise now.'

Mary rose to her feet. 'That was quick,' she said brightly. 'When can I start, then?'

The Reverend Smedley smiled benignly. 'You have already started on the journey of your *new* life. God has forgiven you your sins, you are a born again Christian now, Mary!'

'No, no, not that,' Mary said impatiently. 'When does I start with the brats?'

For a moment the Reverend Thomas Smedley looked deeply hurt, but then decided not to turn this expression into words. He had scored a direct hit with the Lord and saved another sinner from hellfire and he was not about to cruel his satisfaction.

'Why, tomorrow morning. You will be here by eight o'clock and will have fifty pupils.' The Reverend Smedley paused and looked at Mary. 'Though we have no slates, or bell, or even board or chalk and nor shall we get them if I know anything of the government stores!' The irritable edge had returned to his voice.

Mary turned to leave. 'Thank you, sir!' she pronounced carefully. But she could barely contain her excitement and took a deep breath, though she was unable to conceal her delight. 'Thank you, I'm much obliged, sir.' She held her hand out and the Reverend Smedley shuddered and involuntarily drew back, so that Mary's crippled paw was left dangling in the air. Then he scuttled to the safety of his side of the desk and opened the ledger to reveal a letter which had been placed between its covers. He spoke in a brusque voice, attempting to conceal his terror at the sight of Mary's hands.

'It says here in your letter of appointment from the governor that you are to take the noon meal with myself and my sister. Have you learned proper table manners, Miss Abacus?' It was obvious to Mary that the image of her hands at his table was the focus of Smedley's question.

Mary suddenly realised that her appointment to the school was not the decision of the irritable little clergyman at all, but that Mr Emmett had independently secured her position from Colonel Arthur himself. The interview with the Reverend Smedley was simply a formality.

'Blimey, sir, I ain't been born again no more'n two flamin' minutes, I ain't 'ad no time to learn proper christian manners!' She held up her hands. 'They ain't pretty but they works well enough with a knife and fork and I knows what spoon to use for puddin'.' She turned and took the two steps to the door then turned again and grinned at the preacher. 'See you tomorrow, then!'

Mary had no sooner escaped through the front door than she reached for the Waterloo medal and, clutching it tightly, rushed down the path away from the orphanage. She should have told the fat little bastard to sod off, but her heart wasn't in it. A little way down the road she turned and looked up at the great mountain towering above the town.

'Thank you,' she said quietly to the huge, round-shouldered mountain, then she threw caution to the winds. 'Thanks a million, rocks and trees and blue skies and Mister oh-so-magic Mountain!' she shouted at the top of her voice. Mary remembered suddenly that yesterday had been her birthday and that she was twenty-nine years old, though for a moment she felt not much older than the children she would begin to teach in the morning.

'Go on, then, send us a nice bright day tomorrow, will you, love?' she shouted again at the mountain. To

Mary's left, high above the massive swamp gums, a flock of brilliant green parakeets flew screeching upwards towards the summit of Mount Wellington. 'Tell 'im I want a real beauty! A day to remember!' she yelled at the departing birds. 'Thanks for the luck!'

Chapter Twenty-four

Ikey arrived back in London on the *Prince Regent* on the 27th of June 1830. He was accompanied on the voyage by the chief constable of Van Diemen's Land who was under instructions from Governor Arthur not to let Ikey out of his sight, even to attend to his needs at the water closet.

On board ship Ikey had set about the task of starving himself and no manner of coaxing could bring him to eat a sufficient amount to sustain normal health. He would go for days on end sipping water alone and then he would add a few spoonfuls of gruel to his diet in order that his frail heart should continue to pump. He seldom spoke to anyone and allowed his hair and beard to grow again so that the former fell to his shoulders and the latter almost to his chest.

If this was intended to make the citizenry of the great metropolis sympathetic towards him, the ploy did not work. In every tavern, dance emporium, club and home London celebrated his capture and the City police took on the mantle of the heroes. It was as if they had hunted their quarry to the ends of the earth and brought him back in chains to face the full retribution of British justice. At no time was any credit accorded to Colonel Arthur. The governor of an obscure convict colony was simply not grand enough for such a prominent capture.

Though retired, Sir Jasper Waterlow travelled up to London to ascertain that it was indeed Ikey Solomon who had been returned, and he was rumoured to have visited him in Newgate to shake his hand.

This time Ikey was placed in a cell in the very centre of Newgate Prison. He was guarded twenty-four hours a day and allowed no visitors except for the barrister, Mr Phillips, whom he had briefed to represent him. He was arraigned at the Old Bailey and charged with seven additional counts of theft on top of the original charge of forging Bank of England five pound notes.

These additional charges had come about when, following Hannah's sentence, the police had observed that Ikey's home in Whitechapel was in the process of being bricked up. They had immediately served a search warrant on Abraham Reuban and thoroughly ran-sacked every room. They found the trapdoor under Hannah's bed and within it the false ceiling which contained a small fortune in stolen goods. When Abraham Reuban was finally permitted to brick up the windows and doors, only the safe under the pantry floor remained undiscovered.

Eleven days can make a marked difference in the appearance of a man and Ikey still had a sufficient sum to treat himself well in prison and pay for the best legal advice in England. He abandoned his hang dog demean-our and hirsute looks and ordered a new suit of clothes and linen from a tailor, though not from Abraham Reuban, who was not permitted to see him. A gentle-man's barber from the Haymarket was brought in to cut his hair and to trim and shape his ragged beard. With ten days of good food in his belly Ikey was much improved in every circumstance but that of hope. When he stood in the dock at the Old Bailey to hear the reading of the indictments against him he was thought by many to be a man of handsome appearance.

The scene of the day of the trial, consequently much exaggerated by Grub Street hacks, is best described by reading from the eminently respectable *Morning Post* of the following day.

. . . shortly, after the opening of the Courts, every avenue leading to the New Court, in which the case was appointed for trial, was thronged almost to suffocation. The decided majority of the crowd seeking admittance was evidently the descendants of the patriarchs. As was but naturally expected the utmost anxiety was evidenced on the part of all those of the Jewish persuasion to catch a glimpse of the person and the features of the prisoner. At 8 a.m. the Common Sergeant took his seat on the bench and shortly afterwards Ikey was placed at the bar. In the Newgate Calendar he was described as a dealer and the age given as 45. He did not, however, appear nearly so old. During the time the indictments were read, he frequently and piercingly surveyed the persons in the body of the Court as if he were prepared to find an accuser in everyone his eyes rested upon.

Five of the eight indictments read out in court carried with them capital offences and Ikey, it was supposed, could not bring himself to hope that he might escape them all and so save his neck from the gallows. It was often enough reported that since his arrival in this country he had suffered considerable dejection of the mind, but there was no sign of this in court. When the indictments were completed and the prisoner allowed to answer them he spoke calmly and in a voice devoid of despair.

'Your honour, it is my modest hope that the jury will find me innocent and that under all circumstances His Majesty's Government will be induced to spare my life, and permit me to join my wife and family who are still residing in Van Diemen's Land.'

This little speech, short and sweet, when picked apart seems somewhat confused. It claims his innocence, then asks to be spared the rope *under all circumstances* so that he be allowed to go free to join his wife and family. It is most doubtful that there existed in court, or any-where in England, a person unaware of the notorious Hannah Solomon. Yet Ikey spoke of his wife as if she were some contented colonial settler's spouse waiting patiently for her loving husband to return home having been exonerated of all crimes by a just and benign English legal system.

The overcrowded court and the mayhem in the streets outside had delayed proceedings, but Mr Phillips, Ikey's barrister, was crisp on the uptake and the first two charges, neither of which were capital offences, were dealt with in a summary manner. Ikey, who naturally denied everything, was found not guilty by the jury.

Then three of the capital charges were heard and dis-posed of with equal speed. Thus in the process of one morning five of the charges against Ikey were dismissed. Mr Phillips had proved himself an able defender of his celebrated client and Ikey, standing in the dock, appeared almost nonchalant. He did not evince the slightest pleasure at the 'not guilty' verdict. It was as if he had not been possessed of the smallest doubt as to the outcome of each hearing. Though it was always allowed that the first five cases were weak in point of proof, three of them were also invalidated by the ruling that a person could not be called upon to account for the possession of goods found in his custody three months after they had been stolen.

However, the noose was not yet removed from Ikey's scrawny neck. The court was adjourned to the 12th of July, when the remaining three indictments would be heard. Two of these were capital charges and the evidence available for the prosecution was most compelling. All of London was ablaze with gossip and every tavern and chop house produced any amount of boisterous speculation. Customers with not a scintilla of knowledge of the law turned into street lawyers who waxed more wise with each jug of ale or snifter of brandy. A great deal of money was laid in bets as to whether the eventual outcome would be the rope or the boat. Only the most foolishly optimistic accepted the odds of a hundred to one on Ikey's ability to beat the rap entirely.

When Ikey returned to the Old Bailey the crush of people wishing to get in was even greater than on the first occasion. A near riot occurred when the court attendants attempted to close the doors to the New Court, there being not room enough for a dormouse to squeeze into the public gallery. Ikey was brought back to the bar of the court to face the final three charges against him.

The first charge to be heard, the only one of the three that was not a capital offence, was the one brought against him by the Bank of England and involved the forgery of banknotes of five pounds denomination. Sir Reginald Cunningham, a Scot and a barrister of the highest repute, led the prosecution. He proceeded to lay out in chapter and verse the story of Abraham Van Esselyn who was in partnership and under the influence of the notorious Ikey Solomon. Finally he had shown in evidence the result produced by Ikey and his Belgian partner. Sir Reginald then asked that he might present the two fake five pound notes to the judge together with two of legitimate currency, with the further request that the jury might be allowed to examine them thereafter.

In a dramatic gesture Sir Reginald handed the judge a large magnifying glass and begged him to choose the fake from the real. While the judge examined the banknotes Sir Reginald, in a further dramatic thrust, asked the judge to examine the watermarks on all of the notes, pointing out that they were all identical in nature, the paper used being the very same as was employed by the Treasury. The great barrister paused and waited for complete silence, then he added in a stentorian voice, 'I need hardly remind this court that the theft of paper used in the manufacture of banknotes is a crime against the Crown and the Treasury and therefore punishable by death!'

There was a murmur of astonishment from the public gallery, for in one stroke the Bank of England's case had been turned into a capital crime and Ikey seemed certain to hang.

'I should remind the prosecution that the decision as to whether a crime is a capital offence most fortunately does not rest with the prosecution but with this bench.

If it did not I fear that the least of crimes would earn the ultimate sentence!' It was plain that the judge was not pleased with Sir Reginald's final remark. He then caused the notes to be handed to the jury, and it might have been supposed that Ikey had, in the truest sense of the words, finally met his Waterloo. With the exception of his last statement, Sir Reginald appeared not to have put a foot wrong.

The noose was drawn tight and it seemed the trap door had all but sprung as Sir Reginald Cunningham retrieved the banknotes from the jury and held up two of them.

'These are the five pound notes on the person of the accused! They were printed from a five pound etched copper plate discovered in the Bell Alley basement premises owned by the accused.' He paused and then ended with a flourish. 'They were printed on the *very* same printing press also lodged at that address!'

Ikey's barrister, Mr Phillips, now rose to his feet. 'Can my learned friend please tell us how these two particular notes were discovered and by whom?'

'Your honour, we request permission to call up a witness, Mr George Smith, senior constable at the Lambeth Street watchhouse who will answer my learned friend's question.' Sir Reginald was well pleased with himself and his tone was most accommodating.

The clerk of the court stood up and called upon Senior Constable George Smith to take his place in the witness box.

'Mr Smith, is it not true that you go by another even more familiar name?' asked Mr Phillips.

The senior constable looked confused. 'Beg pardon, sir? I don't rightly know what you mean.'

'Let me put the question another way then. Is it true that you are referred to with the sobriquet, "The Reamer", in criminal circles?'

George Smith cleared his throat. 'I can't rightly say what the criminal classes calls me.' There was a buzz of amusement from the court and the policeman seemed to gain confidence from this for he grinned and added, 'And I don't think I cares that much neither.'

There was further laughter and the judge banged his gavel.

'Then let us suppose that the name "The Reamer", which you state is of no consequence to you, is in fact the name used by what you refer to as "*the criminal classes*". Can you venture to guess how this name came about?' His hand rose to prevent George Smith from answering. 'Before you answer, would you agree that a reamer is a sharp object placed into a narrow aperture which is used to scrape it clean of impediment?'

George Smith shrugged. 'If you say so, sir.'

'Mr Smith, would you kindly hold up the forefinger of your right hand.'

The policeman looked at the judge. 'Must I do this, your honour?'

'Is this request important to your line of enquiry, Mr Phillips?' the judge asked. 'I must say it doesn't seem to be leading anywhere.'

'Your honour, I intend to show that this witness is not accustomed to acting within the rules of the law and cannot be relied upon to act in the best interest of the truth.'

'That is a serious accusation to make against an officer of the law, Mr Phillips. You will need to be most careful how you proceed further.' He turned to the policeman in the witness box. 'You will hold your right forefinger up to the jury, Mr Smith.'

George Smith held up his forefinger which appeared normal in all aspects and there was a bemused titter from the crowded court.

'Whatever can you have in mind, Mr Phillips?' the judge asked frowning at Ikey's barrister.

A high-pitched voice suddenly sounded from the public gallery and an urchin in a top hat jumped up from his seat. ' 'E bit it orf. I seen 'im! 'E bit 'is nail orf while the judge were talkin'. 'E bit it orf and spat it out!' Sparrer Fart jumped to his feet in the public gallery and yelled at the top of his voice.

'Yeah, yeah we seen it!' several other urchins, seated around Sparrer, nodded their heads violently, confirming his outburst. Other members of the public gallery now shouted in agreement, so that the court was filled with their protestations.

The judge banged his gavel. 'Silence! I will have silence in my court!' he demanded. 'You will remove that small personage please, constable!' He pointed to the policeman nearest Sparrer Fart.

Sparrer was led out of the gallery, where the police constable cuffed him behind the ear before roughly throwing him out onto the street on his arse, though the other members of the Methodist Academy of Light Fingers were permitted to remain.

Sparrer had barely landed when he felt a strong hand grab him by the collar and lift him to his feet. All he could see was the man's waistcoat and fob chain as he frantically struggled to free himself.

'Steady on, lad, I mean you no harm,' a calm voice directly above him announced.

'Lemme go!' Sparrer yelled.

To his surprise the hand holding him released its grip. 'That was a brave thing you did in there,' the voice added.

Sparrer was about to run but then recognised the man as someone who had been seated near him in court. Sparrer dusted his coat and the seat of his pants. 'Stupid, more like!'

'What's your name, boy?' the man asked.

'I ain't done nuffink, mister,' Sparrer whined.

'On the contrary, you may have saved a man from the gallows.'

'You a detective then?' Sparrer asked, still suspicious of the stranger.

'No, no, a reporter.' He stuck out his hand. 'Charles Dickens. I thought I might do a small piece on you in the paper.'

'Blimey! In a newspaper?' Sparrer wiped his hand on his greasy lapel before taking the reporter's hand. 'Pleased to meetcha, Mr Dickens.'

'Well yes, likewise lad. What you did took real gumption. Would you *like* to be in the newspaper?'

'No thanks. Ikey says incognito be best, you don't want no name in the papers.'

'Incognito eh, that's a big word. Do you know Ikey Solomon?'

Sparrer squinted up at the reporter. 'Maybe I does and maybe I doesn't.' His confidence restored, he now stood with one foot placed on the boot cap of the other and with both his hands jammed into the pockets of his coat.

Charles Dickens took out his purse and offered a shilling to Sparrer.

Sparrer sniffed. 'Bloody 'ell, fer a shillin' I never seen 'im afore in me life, mister!'

Charles Dickens smiled and dropped the shilling back in his purse.

'Fer a shillin' ya gets me name,' Sparrer added quickly, realising he'd overplayed his hand.

'Your name? Is that all?' Charles Dickens laughed.

'For the newspaper! Ya can put me name in yer newspaper.'

The reporter took the shilling out of his purse again and handed it to Sparrer Fart. 'What's your name then, lad?'

Sparrer thought desperately. When he performed well at the Academy of Light Fingers Ikey would turn to the other lads and say, 'Look at Sparrer, a veritable dodger, nimble as a ferret!' Then he would pat him on the head and say, 'Well done, dodger, a most artful dodgin' performance, my dear!'

'They calls me the Artful Dodger,' Sparrer replied.

'And you know Ikey Solomon, Mr Artful Dodger?'

'That's fer me to know and you to find out,' Sparrer said cheekily, the shilling now safely deposited in his pocket.

Charles Dickens sighed. 'And how much will it take to find out?'

'It be a long and fascinatin' story what can't be told straight orf, it'll cost ya a daffy and a sov.'

'I'm not sure I have a sovereign on me.' Dickens reached again into his coat for his purse.

'What's the time then?' Sparrer said, pointing to the reporter's waistcoat.

With his free hand the reporter reached down to his fob chain and then more frenetically patted the lower part of his waistcoat.

'This yers then, mister?' Sparrer asked. The hint of a smile played on his pinched little face as he held up a gold hunter by its chain. 'Worth a lot more than a gold sov, now, don't ya think?'

'How the devil!' Dickens expostulated.

'Gotta be careful who ya picks up when they's fallen down on the pavement, mister. Grab a boy by 'is collar and 'e's got both 'ands free, ain't 'e now?'

Charles Dickens grinned sheepishly as Sparrer returned his watch to him. 'A daffy and a sovereign it is then. I do hope it's a good story, Mr Artful Dodger.'

'Best ya ever 'eard, mister,' Sparrer Fart shot back as he dodged into the oncoming traffic in Newgate Street to cross to a tavern on the far side.

Meanwhile in the New Court of the Old Bailey, Mr Phillips addressed the judge on the matter of Sergeant George Smith's missing fingernail.

'Your Honour, I request that the witness box be searched for a fingernail belonging to the witness.'

There was much laughter from the gallery at this notion, for most of the public had not understood the meaning of Sparrer's shouted accusation.

Sir Reginald rose quickly to his feet. 'With the greatest respect, your honour, the defence is both confused and confusing?' He glared at Mr Phillips. 'My learned colleague had first requested that the witness accept a new name, that of "The Reamer" and then asks that Mr Smith thrust his forefinger in the air. A most curious request to say the least! But then, when he perceives it to be a perfectly normal finger with a perfectly normal fingernail upon it, he demands that we all go on our hands and knees and look for a missing and imaginary finger part!'

523

There was a roar of laughter from the court and this time the judge threatened to remove all from the public gallery if the misbehaviour continued. Then he looked impatiently at Mr Phillips.

'Is that not substantially correct, Mr Phillips? Or do you have some motive which is beyond us in this court? Already you try my patience to a most precipitous point.'

'Your honour, it will take but a moment. I crave your indulgence. What I hope to find is of the greatest significance to this case. It is my intention to show that the word of Senior Constable George Smith is not to be relied upon.'

The judge looked stern. 'I have already cautioned you against this sort of imputation and warn you that you will be charged before the bench with misconduct if you do not satisfactorily resolve the accusation you are making against Mr Smith. You may search the witness box with an officer of this court in attendance.'

Ikey's barrister leaned over and spoke quietly to his instructing solicitor who, accompanied by a constable, entered the witness box. It took only a moment for the police officer to find the torn part of a fingernail which had fallen to the floor at the feet of George Smith. The piece of nail was filed to a point and appeared to be almost an inch and a half long. He handed it to the solicitor, who then took it across to the clerk of the court.

'Your honour, I suggest that the portion of fingernail which I now submit as evidence can be shown to have been formerly attached to the forefinger of the witness. I have several witnesses, including my client, who are willing to testify that the offending forefinger, with nail attached, was used for the purposes of searching the back passage of prisoners for contraband. It was intended that this action of reaming would render grievous bodily harm to the victims of this odious search. It is for this reason that the witness has been christened "The Reamer"!'

'I object, your honour. This matter of nicknames has nothing whatsoever to do with the case at hand. I refer to my learned colleague's original question which, if I recall correctly, was how the notes were discovered on the person of the accused!'

'Your objection is sustained, Sir Reginald,' the judge said and turned to the jury. 'You will ignore the imputation made by Mr Phillips as to the usage of the fingernail, and reference to it will be struck from the record.' He looked at Ikey's barrister. 'You will restrict yourself to asking direct questions, Mr Phillips. I shall not warn you again!'

'Yes, thank you, your honour, you are most gracious,' Mr Phillips said, appearing not the least chastened by the judge's warning. 'Mr Smith, can you tell this court whether the man you searched, known as Ikey Solomon, is in this court?'

The senior constable nodded and pointed to Ikey. 'That be him, sir.'

'Thank you. And you conducted a thorough ... er ... *body* search upon this person?' There was a roar of laughter in the court and the judge banged his gavel again.

'It were the normal search, sir, for what we calls routine contraband.'

'Where did you find the two counterfeit notes? Can you tell me precisely their location, Mr Smith?'

'They were in the lining o' the coat, sir.'

'In the lining? In the lining of whose coat?'

'The accused, sir, he wore a coat on the night 'e were brought in.'

'An expensive coat? Sewn into the lining?'

'Yes, sir it were a good coat but no, not sewn, there were a tear in it. The notes were pushed down the tear into the lining, like.'

'Isn't that a little obvious, constable? Would you concede that a large tear which had not been repaired on an expensive coat was a rather too obvious place to hide the notes?'

'That's not for the likes o' me to say, sir. That be where them notes were found and I did not say it were a large tear, sir,' George Smith said tartly.

Mr Phillips wheeled around and pointed directly at George Smith. 'No, sir, with the greatest respect, I submit to you that the two five pound notes were *planted*!' Mr Phillips turned towards the jury. 'How very convenient to make a tear in his coat, the coat which the accused was *forced to remove* while he was undergoing a thorough *body* search! A tear into which, *abracadabra*, the two five pound notes suddenly appeared, politely stuffed within the lining of the coat to make the evidence your masters requested appear in the most convenient manner! Is this not a much more reasonable explanation of what happened, Mr Smith?'

'No sir, it is not! The notes be found just like I said.'

'Then you will demonstrate how you found these two notes please, Mr Smith.' Ikey's barrister turned to the clerk of the court. 'We have asked that the accused's coat be brought in evidence. Would you please identify it and hand it to the witness?'

The clerk of the court stood up and turned to the judge. 'Your honour, the coat in question was not taken in evidence from the prisoner at the time of his arrest.'

The judge looked astonished and then addressed George Smith. 'Mr Smith, did you not say that the counterfeit notes were found in the lining of the coat and that they had been so placed by means of a tear in the outer material?'

'Yes, your honour.'

'Am I to believe that the coat was then allowed to remain with the accused and was not confiscated as evidence?'

George Smith looked decidedly sheepish. 'We forgot, your honour, it were a cold night.' Then he pointed at Ikey in the dock. 'He were wearin' it when he made his escape.'

'Thank you, Mr Smith, you may step down,' Mr Phillips said.

In his summary of the evidence the judge pointed out that the absence of the coat and the subsequent denial of the accused that a tear had ever existed in it constituted 'reasonable doubt' as to whether the banknotes had been placed in the lining by the accused or by the actions of some other person or persons unknown. Furthermore, without the evidence of the two notes there appeared to be nothing which linked Ikey with the crime of forgery. The etched plate and printing press found in the basement premises proved nothing beyond the fact that Ikey was the landlord and the forger Abraham Van Esselyn his tenant. He noted that all the receipts for the printing press and subsequent forgery materials were in the name or pseudonym of Abraham Van Esselyn whom, he reminded the jury, had been previously tried and found guilty.

Finally, there existed not a shred of evidence to show how Ikey might have procured the Treasury paper on which the forged notes were printed.

The jury took less than an hour to dismiss the charges of forgery against Ikey and the judge pronounced him not guilty for lack of evidence. Ikey's coat of many pockets had saved his life.

Only two more charges remained, those involving the purchase of goods known to have been stolen, and both were capital offences. Alas, with these Ikey's luck finally ran out and he was found guilty on both charges. The hangman had secured his man at last. But the judge did not place the black hood upon his head; instead he sentenced Ikey to fourteen years' transportation. This amelioration of Ikey's sentence may well have come about to prove to the barrister that the judge was independent of the pressure which might be placed upon him by those fronting the bench, though to this sentence of transportation was added the clause that Ikey was not permitted to return to England after he had served out his time in Van Diemen's Land.

But the redoubtable Mr Phillips had not entirely given up. Ikey's barrister instituted several legal quibbles on his client's behalf, the majority of which concerned the disposition of stolen property, and challenged the various Acts of Parliament involved in Ikey's conviction. This legal nitpicking served the purpose of postponing Ikey's transportation for nearly a year, though during this period Ikey was not, as was the usual custom, sent to a hulk on the Thames estuary but remained under close guard in Newgate.

The final outcome of this delay was that Ikey's prison expenses for food and drink and other luxuries, namely

The Times and reading matter on a variety of subjects, coupled with the exorbitant fees Mr Phillips imposed for his services, finally exhausted the funds Ikey had brought with him from Van Diemen's Land. For the first time since he had been a young flash-man, Ikey had not a penny to his name.

On the 31st of May 1831, Ikey Solomon, his spirit broken and his body in chains, set sail for Van Diemen's Land on the *William Glen Anderson*.

Chapter Twenty-five

A large crowd gathered at Sullivan's Cove to witness Ikey's arrival on the 1st of November 1831, but Hannah was not among them. She thought of herself as very badly done by, and she blamed Ikey for necessitating her departure from the Newman household and for her present incarceration.

In fact, she had been rather fortunate, for she was not sent to the Female Factory but to the Cotton Factory, this second institution being somewhat better in its treatment of prisoners. Hannah was employed as a seamstress to make prison garments. Thus she was able to avoid meeting Mary Abacus. But this did not prevent her from constantly speaking of Mary as the person who had seduced her husband, and brought about the present and calamitous destruction of her entire family. She vowed loudly and often that she would wreak revenge on Ikey's erstwhile mistress, whatever the price.

For Mary, Hannah's existence on the island hardly mattered. She heard from time to time of Hannah's threats, but she expected no less from Ikey's wife and thought little of them. She was unaware that Hannah had a new and powerful reason for hating her, one which had nothing to do with their shared past. Hannah's children – her ten-year-old son David, Ann, who had just turned eight, Sarah six, and Mark four – were placed in the Reverend Smedley's orphanage. David, Ann and Sarah found themselves in Mary's classroom where they felt as much loved by her as any of the other orphans. Hannah's children, the apple of her eye, were under the direct influence of the woman she hated more than any other, and there was nothing she could do about it.

Mary delighted in her task as teacher. Although many of the children were undernourished and stunted in their growth and so proved difficult to teach, some were bright and eager. But there were none so willing to learn as Ann, and none so naturally intelligent as her brother David. Both had received some schooling in England and so were much ahead of the other pupils, and Mary used them to instruct the younger children while, at the same time, giving them her special attention.

From the outset David was fascinated by Mary's abacus and begged to be allowed to use it. He had proved himself clever with numbers and could do much of the arithmetic Mary taught him mentally, not bothering with the slate on his lap. Ann, on the other hand, while competent with numbers, begged to be allowed to read. Finding books for an eight-year-old child was not an easy matter and the Reverend Thomas Smedley, still undecided about the merits of teaching the children God had intended to be the drones in the hives of life, did nothing to help the situation in the school.

Saving souls was clearly the major work of God and, he told himself, was as freely available to the poor as it was to the rich, to the clever as well as the stupid. In his infinite wisdom God made his salvation unstintingly available to all. But at this point God's universal design came to a halt. The qualities He gave to humans were dispensed, according to the needs of English society, which Smedley naturally accepted as being the closest to the divine intention.

To some God gave wisdom, for the wise are needed in some small proportion. Some He made clever, for these too are a necessary ingredient in the proportions of a just society. Others are possessed of natural skills to furnish the whole with artisans, teachers, clerks and shopkeepers, but most He made to be hewers of wood and drawers of water. They were the necessary human clay and had been allotted the largest and lowest space in the human family. By tampering with God's natural ordination Mary was attempting to change the balance of nature, and no good could possibly come of it. The saving of minds, Thomas Smedley concluded, was more likely to be the work of Satan than of a benign and loving God. The example he most often used to support his argument was that of the noble savage.

Mary took the midday meal with the preacher and his spinster sister. Elspeth, a quiet soul, was not able to counter her brother's aggressive nature and mostly kept her silence at the table. She was an excellent cook and took some care to see that Mary was well fed, always treating her with the utmost politeness though without venturing beyond the daily pleasantries.

Smedley more than made up for his sister's reticence. He possessed a viewpoint on all subjects except those which might interest a woman, and his opinions could almost certainly be counted upon to be of a negative persuasion. He used the dinner table as he might have done a pulpit, expounding on any subject he felt inclined to embrace without expecting argument or rebuttal from the two women who shared it with him.

The followers of John Wesley are of a naturally zealous disposition, the threat of fire and brimstone being the major part of their catechism. They hold that God's anger should be given precedence over His mercy and love, and agree that the fear of hellfire is the principal motivation for driving wicked people to salvation.

Thomas Smedley was well suited to this uncompromising faith, but his superiors nevertheless thought his nature too bitter to preach from an English pulpit, and so he had been sent to Van Diemen's Land where God's cause was secretly thought to be a hopeless one, except for the early salvation of its plague of illegitimate children.

Elspeth had accompanied him on his mission as housekeeper for, like Mary, she possessed a passion for children. She was much aggrieved by her brother's insistence that his charges be treated as creatures of little worth, with strict instructions that they be shown no outward sign of love. This cruel directive caused her to live in a clandestine way, loving the forlorn little creatures whenever she could clutch them unobserved to her bosom.

For a while Mary was willing to hold her tongue. She much enjoyed the food at Elspeth's table, which she took care to supply with fresh vegetables from the prison gardens so that she should not be at the mercy of the preacher's reluctant charity. She had been made to feel an uninvited guest from the very first meal when, after a prolonged and stony silence, the small, fat preacher suddenly threw down his napkin, slid back his chair and stormed from the room with the words, 'Vile claws!'

At the following midday meal Mary had come to the table to find a pair of white lace gloves placed between her knife and fork. For a moment she felt that her anger would cause her to explode. Her talons, grown in the prison, had been neatly cut to the perimeters of her fingers when she had come for her interview. But now she wished them long again so that she might rake the fleshy face of the preacher until the blood gushed from his rubicund cheeks to soak the napkin tied about his neck. As her anger abated she was overcome with humiliation. She fought to control her sobs, her face cast downwards and her poor, broken hands concealed upon her lap. A silent tear ran down her cheek and fell onto the gloves, placed so that the longest fingers appeared to be pointing accusingly at her.

'My dear Miss Abacus,' she heard Elspeth Smedley say in an unusually loud voice, 'I must apologise for my bad manners. I had quite forgotten to place gloves at the table for yesterday's luncheon. Can you possibly forgive me? It is all the fashion these days, but as Smedley and I eat mostly alone, I have grown careless of convention.'

Mary looked up slowly to be met by a smile from Elspeth who, she now saw, wore a pair of gloves identical to her own.

'I have made a brisket of beef with a tarragon sauce in the hope that you will forgive my appalling oversight.' Then Elspeth Smedley added lightly, 'The soup is made of the beautiful watercress you brought this morning from the rivulet. It is my favourite and I must thank you. Smedley does so much enjoy it too.'

It was the longest speech Mary had ever heard from the shy and naturally retiring Elspeth, and she felt sure that no person had ever addressed her with such kindness and compassion.

'Thank you, ma'am,' Mary murmured as she reached for the gloves in front of her.

'No, no, my dear, you must call me Elspeth, for you are as welcome at our table as any of our other friends.'

Though never in the least pleasant to her, the Reverend Thomas Smedley grew accustomed to Mary's presence at lunch. He placed little store in her opinions but, unlike his sister, Mary was not willing to listen in silence to his tirades or accept his pronouncements as though they were infallible. After a few weeks she was beginning to get results from several of the children in her class, and she was convinced that she could fill their small minds with a love of learning.

Smedley, though pretending to evince no interest in Mary's progress, would command her to debate him, often interrupting her, and when she made a point worthy of consideration he dismissed it with a flick of his wrist and the expostulation 'Bah!' On one occasion he had followed this with the words, 'They are nothing but savages to be likened to the black creatures that crawl like vermin among the hills.'

'We are but the creatures we are permitted to be, sir,' Mary protested. 'This is as true for the orphans as it is for the savage. Our nature is not formed within the womb but by what 'appens to us beyond it!'

'Ah! But you are quite wrong!' Smedley replied. 'The pig is happiest in its own mud! When rescued from his natural ways and habitat, the noble savage, no longer covered in the stench of fish oil but bathed and dressed in linen, is soon forlorn and woebegone. If you would have your Van Diemen's savage dine at the table of the governor, the food would prove unsuitable to his digestion, the linen chafing and uncomfortable to his skin, his posterior quickly wearied by the gilt chair and the custom of knife and fork and spoon likely to confound his primitive mind. How then by means of books and slate can you change this repulsive creature for the better? How indeed, hmm, Miss Abacus?'

'Sir, I know nothing of savages, it be the young minds of little 'uns of our own kind I seek to change. They are not by nature consigned to the pig sty, but are born the same and washed as clean o' the blood o' their birth as any noble child. If perchance they was placed in the nursery of a grand manor, there's none would know the difference and they would carry their proxy nobility as well as any Lord or Lady.'

'Oh, but you are quite wrong again, Miss Abacus! You have observed them in your own class, the close-set eyes, the sloping, beetle brows, the vacuous and slack-jawed visage with no dawn of comprehension seen to rise up into their dulled, indifferent eyes. These are not the substitute sons and daughters of the decent classes, they are already well branded to the bottom class, marked every bit as surely as the black skin of the aboriginal savage marks him to his sub-human species!'

It was true enough that several of the children in Mary's class had the precise appearance described by the Reverend Smedley and true, also, that not a flicker of comprehension seemed to show in their eyes when they were presented with an idea which required the smallest conjecture. But they sang and clapped with gusto and were much entertained with simple games and Mary, in many ways, loved them most of all.

'That ain't fair, sir!' she exclaimed hotly. 'I've worked in big houses in my time, and heard tell of others where wrong 'un's, idjits, are born to the gentry. King George himself, Farmer George, he had more than one loose screw rattlin' about in his royal noggin! You're quite right, there be some in me class won't take much to learnin' but most o' them make progress and will in time come to somethin'!'

'Ha! If we cannot save their souls in time, Miss Abacus, all they will come to is corruption and licence, drunkenness and thieving!' Thomas Smedley jabbed a fat finger at Mary. 'You will know that your school is not of my making. Should I have my way I would wish it gone in an instant! My work, Miss Abacus, is God's work, and when you interfere with God's natural laws and would think to change the clay from which each of us is formed, I can clearly enough see the devil's hand in it!'

'Sir, the devil has no monopoly on brains!' Mary replied, looking into her napkin and holding down her anger.

'Oh?' Thomas Smedley snorted, pointing at her again. 'Then is it the Lord God who sends a brothel keeper and a whore to my orphanage to teach His precious children?'

The three mornings Mary spent at the orphan school soon became four and then five. Mr Emmett would sometimes call around and watch as the children sang or recited a poem for his benefit. He had seen to it that blackboard, slates, chalk, paper, quills and blacking and even a few children's books were made available. There were never sufficient books, for Mary believed that reading was the basis for any education and would lead naturally to the desire to write, and created in a child the thirst for knowledge of every description.

She had even persuaded Mr Emmett to get the authorities to return her battered leather-bound copy of *Gulliver's Travels*. She used this to create in the breasts of her older children a sense of social justice, so that they might understand that it is the strong who manipulate the weak, and that bondage and poverty are not a natural state ordained by God, but imposed by those who enjoy wealth, privilege and power upon those who have no means to resist or overcome poverty and servitude.

In this way unknowingly perhaps, Mary began to teach the tenets of freedom upon which a community of convict slaves became the most egalitarian nation on earth. Mary and her class of fifty orphan children, together with one hundred and sixty thousand convicted thieves, whores, forgers, conmen, blasphemers, political dissenters, the diseased, illiterate, mentally handicapped flotsam and jetsam upon the sea of English and Irish life, formed the basis of this new nation. Undoubtedly this was the most unpropitious human raw material ever gathered in one place, yet it would be forged into a free and equal people who would never again tolerate a despotic regime or accept that any man's station is above that of any other.

In the matter of books for her pupils Mary enlisted the help of Elspeth Smedley, who rented books in large numbers from the Hobart Town Circulating Library. This institution was presided over by the stern-faced Mrs

Deane who, had she known their destination, would not have permitted the books to be released from her possession. Convicts were not allowed to rent books and the thought of orphans reading them, with their dirty little hands, would have caused a great fuss in the small community. As it was, Mrs Deane marvelled at Elspeth Smedley's ability to read so many volumes on every subject, and judged her quite the best-informed woman on the island. Privately she thought the parson's sister's reading was most eclectic, in some things juvenile to the greatest degree while her other tastes were distinctly scholarly. But she did not make the obvious connection that the books were being used in the orphanage. The very idea that the illegitimate brats of convicts and whores might be brought to learning was less believable than the notion that the moon was composed of green cheese.

The money for the books came, of course, from Mary's Potato Factory, and while Elspeth Smedley may herself have pondered the source of Mary's seemingly unlimited resources, she would not have dreamed of asking her for an explanation. Mary had encouraged Elspeth to become a teacher herself, and in this matter the gentle and retiring spinster sought to stand up to her bucolic older brother.

When confronted with Elspeth's request, Thomas Smedley ordered that she withdraw from the wicked influence of 'the Factory whore', as he had come to call Mary in private. He had long since cancelled Mary's salvation. She had clearly shown by her lack of humility and contrition, and by her willingness to argue with him on every conceivable subject, that her redemption had been nothing but a ruse to win his approval for her orphan school. He forbade Elspeth to enter Mary's class, or even to converse with her at the midday meal.

Elspeth had not disobeyed her brother's instructions. She found, however, that her extreme disappointment at his decision had entirely erased the numerous recipes she carried in her mind, save only for a recollection of how to boil potatoes.

For two weeks, morning, lunch and tea she served boiled potatoes and small beer until Thomas Smedley could stand it no longer, the demands of his stomach finally overcoming his principles. He had become quite pale and listless, and when the pangs of hunger and the desire for red meat could no longer be contained he had taken to walking down into Liverpool Street to take a meal at a chop house. He was a man who loved his food, and the boiled and fried mutton and badly prepared kangaroo flesh available as cheap fare in an eating house, though preferable to boiled potatoes, was not in the least to his liking. Elspeth was most grudgingly allowed to teach with Mary in the orphan school.

It was a decision which possessed the divine power to recall Elspeth's memory. That very night a splendid pot roast, garnished with tiny spring onions and a boat of rich gravy at its side, with a dish of rice and another of vegetables, was placed steaming upon the table, proving once again that principle is soon swamped by the gravy of greed.

David and Ann Solomon had not been to school since leaving England. An attempt had been made to enrol Ann in Mrs Bamber's boarding school for young ladies when Hannah had been assigned to the Newman family, but her application had been refused on the basis of breeding. The learning levels of both children were three years behind what might have been expected had they remained in England but the general intellectual fare served up at the orphanage was still not sufficient to occupy their minds. Mary had eventually allowed David to learn to work her abacus. Ann, too, had begged to be allowed to play with Mary's beads, insisting she also could make the numbers work. But Mary, sensing David's pride that he alone had been permitted to use her precious abacus, would not allow his sister the same privilege.

'Ann, you are our best reader and it be with books that you excel. David already knows the big numbers and can divide and multiply and add and subtract to make our very 'eads spin. Your turn will come when you be a little older and learn the bigger numbers.'

'It's not fair!' Ann protested, stamping her foot. 'I know a big number and I can write it too!' Whereupon she took up her slate and wrote the number 816.

'What number does that say, Ann?' Mary asked.

'Eight 'undred and sixteen, miss,' she exclaimed, then added triumphantly, 'See! I told you I can do big numbers!'

Mary took up the child's slate and, transposing the numbers, wrote 618 upon it. 'What is this number then?' she asked Ann. 'Say it in 'undreds again, like the last.'

The child stared without comprehension at the new number on her slate. 'It's not fair, I could learn it, I could so!' Ann began to sob, though more in anger at not getting her way, than in distress.

Mary, laughing, took Ann into her arms. 'Eight 'undred and sixteen be a lovely number, Ann. We will soon enough teach you others just as grand.'

Ann pulled away from Mary's embrace, her blue eyes large in her pinched little face as she pronounced,

'Anyway, our mum says it's the only big number we needs to know, and whatever should 'appen to 'er, we must never, never forget it!'

At this sudden recollection of her mother, Ann began to sniff and then to cry softly and although she was eight years old she was no bigger than a child of five or six and Mary took her once again onto her lap and this time she rocked her and kissed the centre parting of her lovely auburn hair and held her tight until she became calm.

Mary thought little more of the incident until the number 816 began to occur regularly in David's work on the abacus. He would often divide into it, subtract from it or find the various multiples of it.

'What be it with the number eight 'undred and sixteen, David?' Mary had finally asked. 'Were it perchance the number of your 'ouse in London?'

David flushed deeply and with a vigorous, though unconvincing, shake of his head replied, 'No, Miss, it be just a number. I didn't know as I were usin' it particular.'

But Mary noted that David Solomon never used the number again, while Ann continued to write it upon her slate when she appeared distracted. Later, when Ann had progressed and learned her multiples of ten and then of a hundred, the number 816 would still occur frequently in her arithmetic.

Though Mary had no time to ponder this childish conundrum she nonetheless tucked the number 816 away. She would not forget it, if only because her mind was so trained to numbers that no digit brought to her attention, for whatever purpose, was ever again forgotten.

Chapter Twenty-six

Ikey saw very little of Hobart Town upon his arrival back in Van Diemen's Land. He was taken directly to Richmond Gaol, some twenty miles out of town, where convicts were put to work upgrading the road to Colebrook. A huge penal settlement was being built to house the influx of convicts now that New South Wales was becoming a popular destination for free settlers from England.

'G'warn, get yer backs into it, yer miserable bastards!' Harris, the overseer of the road gang, liked to shout. 'Governor Arthur 'imself told me 'e needs a new place o' misery to 'ang ya and flog yer useless 'ides!'

In fact, Richmond Gaol served as much to hold the convicts building a road to Arthur's private property, Carrington, as for any other purpose. Governor Arthur abolished land grants to emancipists first, and then altogether, but had nonetheless awarded himself a great acreage, without the payment he demanded from everyone else. He then directed the ceaseless labour of convicts to be lavished upon it, equipping Carrington with a fine stone residence and outer building, fences and roads, all of which were the envy of the wealthiest free settler and worthy of any country estate in England. It was upon Arthur's own road near Richmond that Ikey found himself harnessed to a cart.

Much has been made of the Van Diemen's Land convict being made to pull the plough though, in truth, it was more as a cart horse than as an ox that he was customarily employed. The cart was as integral a part of the road gang as the pick-axe, shovel and wheelbarrow, and much the most onerous of the tasks allotted to a convict.

These carts, measuring six feet in length, two in depth and four and a half in width, were pulled by four men, as it was mistakenly calculated that this amount of human muscle is the equivalent to one well-conditioned cart horse. This might have been so if the men had been in excellent health and were the stature of a giant, six feet or more. But the prisoners were of an average English height, not much more than five feet and three inches and they were malnourished and scrawny. The four team members had leather collars which were attached by ropes and a hook to the cart. Near the extremity of the central harnessing pole were a pair of cross-bars which, when gripped, allowed for two men on either side of the pole to pull the cart. It was mandatory to fill the cart, usually with rocks and dirt, to the point of overflowing, which made it a herculean task to move.

Ikey had at first been given a pick-axe, a tool with which he was entirely unfamiliar. Besides, his confinement in chains on board ship had enfeebled him and his hands were as tender as an infant's. Despite being instructed by the more experienced lags to piss upon each hand to harden the surfaces of his palms, on Ikey's first day of labour his hands soon blistered. On the second day, the skin peeled away from the entire palm and even from between his fingers, and his fingernails were ripped off as a consequence of being made to labour with such a rough and heavy tool. But he was forced to labour for two more days until the handle of the pick was stained with his own blood, and particles of flesh remained upon it whenever he withdrew his hands. The pick itself was too large for even a robust man of his height, and Ikey was reduced to whimpering with each downward strike. Finally, an hour before sundown on the fourth day, he collapsed.

Several kicks of a more than tentative nature, administered by the overseer, Harris, failed to get Ikey to his feet. It was only when he was observed to cough blood that he was placed in a wheelbarrow after the day's work and several convicts, cursing him loudly, were made to take turns wheeling him back to Richmond Gaol.

That night the doctor was called to examine him. He thumped Ikey on the chest, and peeled back his eyes to peer at the jellied orb, whereupon he made him drop his breeches and, weighing his balls in his hand, commanded him to cough. Finally he squeezed Ikey's thigh and calf muscles. Standing up again he declared him fit to work.

'It be nothing but the softness of the voyage. This one will soon enough harden to labour. Put him back to work I say!' He seemed annoyed at being called out after supper for a matter so inconsequential and the superintendent felt compelled to apologise to him, explaining that Ikey was a prisoner of some renown or he would not have disturbed the good doctor.

Ikey groaned and held the lumps of raw flesh up for the surgeon to see. 'What about me hands?' he pleaded.

'Piss and spit soon fix them, my boy!' the doctor said, then turned to the superintendent. 'Tell the overseer to put this prisoner on carts – his legs be well muscled and strong enough by all accounts.'

Though the work on the carts was harder, each team being required to pull ten loads each of a mile every day, it suited Ikey better. Years of walking about the London rookeries at night had made his legs strong, and the strength of a prisoner's legs played the major function in pulling the brutal cart.

To add to the humiliation of the work, Harris thought it high jinks to place beside Ikey at the crossbar a black boy named Billygonequeer, who was captured as a lookout while other members of his Stoney Creek tribe were said to be raiding sheep. Billygonequeer had been in captivity three years when Ikey joined the road gang, and his major claim to fame was that he had received the most stripes to his back of any in their company. He would work as hard as any man at pulling the cart and no prisoner could fault him for not doing his share. But every few weeks, as though he sniffed something in the air, he grew most melancholy, would take no food, and refused to work by standing rigid in a single place. This was known to all in the road gang as 'Billy gone queer' and so the black boy had received this strange appendage to his name.

At night it was not customary to lock Billygonequeer in the cells. For if he should be placed in close confinement he would commence to shout all night so that no prisoner could sleep a wink. And so, summer and winter, with only a blanket to cover him for the coldest part of the year, he would be chained to a ring set into an outer wall which formed part of the courtyard of the gaol. Here he would sleep like an animal on the hard cobblestones.

But when Billygonequeer went queer, he would stand all night and look upwards at the stars and howl exactly like the Tasmanian tiger, the thylacine, a creature dog-like in appearance and extremely shy of humans. This beast, only seldom glimpsed in the outer camps and always in the depths of the forest where it would come to stand just beyond the edge of the firelight at night, was familiar to timber workers and road gangs for its dreadful howl. It was a hollow sound that came from inside, as though vibrating from deep within the chest, and was most disconcerting to the ear. Billygonequeer did not so much appear to make the sound as to *be* the sound. His eyes seemed to turn yellow and catch the light in the darkness, and his jaws unlocked and widened as the terrible creature cacophony came from him. They had tried to gag him once but this proved to no avail – the sound continued as though it emanated from his chest and sought no expulsion from his lips.

When morning came Billy still would not move and it was impossible to imagine that a man could stand so rigid and so long in one spot. If he should be knocked down by the overseer, as often happened, he would not cry out, but would get back to his feet and stand as before, impervious to pain.

Harris, despite having seen Billygonequeer go queer on numerous occasions, could not bring himself to accept his condition. He was a stickler for the rules and greatly afraid of the wrath of the authorities, and on each occasion he would cause Billy to be dragged before the district magistrate. Here Billy would stand before the beak, his dark eyes glazed over as though he were in some distant place of his imagining. Nor would he respond to questions, though his comprehension of English was said to be quite sufficient to this task. Finally, the magistrate, partly angered and bemused and in all parts impatient, would declare himself compelled to obey the law. He would hand down the most severe punishment for refusing to work, a sentence of one hundred lashes with the cat o' nine tails.

A month after Ikey had been put to the cart beside Billy, following the eating of their midday rations, Billy had suddenly turned his head in the direction of a breeze which had that very moment blown up and commenced to sigh high in the giant gum trees. He jumped to his feet and seemed to breathe deeply, pulling the air into his nostrils so that his broad nose flattened upon his face. In great agitation he began to tear his clothes from his slim body, as though some vicious biting insect were to be found within them. As each garment was removed he flung it into the bushes. Then he gave a great sigh and, naked as the day of his birth, stood rigid with his arms to his sides, the pale palms of his hands turned outward. His only movement was the distension and retraction of his nostrils as he pulled the wind into him, as though it were some invisible musk sent from heaven.

'Jaysus Christ! Billy's gone queer,' Seamus Calligan shouted. 'Sniffin' in the wind and that. I'll be damned if he'll not soon be standin' still as a bloody fence pole!'

Michael Mooney, Calligan's partner on the front cross-bar, cautioned Ikey not to catch the attention of Harris the overseer. 'Let him be a while, poor bugger will suffer enough soon as bloody Harris comes.'

'We'll not pull the cart with only the three of us,' Ikey ventured.

'We'll have to. Billygonequeer will not be comin' back these three weeks or more,' Mooney replied.

They left Billy standing and walked back to the cart. They were loading rock for gravel that day and the cart was almost too heavy for four men to pull. Now with only the three of them they were forced to lessen the load. Harris, seeing them pass with the load not extended beyond the rim of the cart, was soon alerted. Then he saw Ikey was alone at his cross-bar.

'Where's the nigger?' he shouted, using an expression he had picked up on an American whaling ship.

The three men brought the cart to a standstill. 'Billy's gone queer,' a reluctant Seamus replied.

Harris grinned. 'Oh 'e 'as now 'as 'e, that be most considerate o' the black bastard!' He turned and called another convict over to harness up beside Ikey. Then, rubbing his hands gleefully, he set off for the camp where the prisoners had taken their midday rations.

When the team returned for the evening muster they found Billy in the same spot as they'd left him. He was rigid as a well-rooted sapling, but with one eye half closed, and the blood from his nose caked upon his smooth ebony chest. His shoulders, too, were crimson caked, and it appeared as though the back of his head had been smashed with some sharp object. A great cloud of flies had settled about his shoulders and eyes, and swarmed about his wild black head. Billygonequeer did not appear to notice the presence of either the flies or the men standing around him.

The men did not ask how his injuries occurred. Those who had worked on the road gang for some time knew

Harris to be a coward and a bully, and when Billy went queer it was always an occasion for sadistic gratification on Harris's part.

Billy, still rigid, was wheeled back to Richmond, his thin legs, like two black poles, sticking out beyond the front lip of the wheel-barrow. No prisoner complained of the extra effort, even though each was himself exhausted from the day's toil. Ikey knew this was most peculiar. Compassion for another was not a part of the convict nature. To feel for another was to put oneself in danger. A singular and ruthless attention to one's own survival was paramount in all matters concerning the convict's life. Ikey understood these rules better than anyone, for he had always lived in accordance with them. Yet no one complained at the need for Billygonequeer's wheeled transportation back to Richmond Gaol.

Billy spent the night in the courtyard standing without the slightest movement, though once every few minutes he emitted the long, lonely howl of the forest dog creature.

Ikey found it impossible to sleep that night. He cursed himself quietly for his insomnia, and wondered how he could possibly feel disquiet and sorrow for the plight of a black savage. Ikey remembered only once before experiencing such a stirring of compassion, when he had impulsively given Abraham Reuban money and his Waterloo medal to give to Mary. Now he felt it again for his black partner, and felt ashamed that he should do so. Morning found him hollow-eyed and still despairing of Billy's plight. He tried all day to convince himself that such was not the case, but the feeling of deep, instinctive sorrow would not go away.

Ikey sensed that Billy was mourning, though how this

could have been brought about by a sudden shift of the wind on a day which seemed to Ikey like any other, was a mystery. But he was a Jew and he knew instinctively about loneliness and terror, and the evil golem that comes at times to molest and disturb the soul. The mischievous ghost of the past who comes to make a Jew feel guilty when, seemingly, with a shift of the winds of terror, those who would destroy him arrive, even when he has done nothing to deserve this fate. There is this eternal conundrum for every Jew who is *not* guilty but nevertheless feels guilty. Guilty of what? Guilty how? But guilty nonetheless.

For centuries the elders and the rabbis have questioned how it is that the victim should think himself to be guilty. How can a man feel guilty when it is his own blood, and the blood of his wife and children which has been spilled? Only the Jew knows how this can be done. But even a Jew does not know why he must be made to bear the shame of his own persecution.

Ikey could see in Billygonequeer the same mysterious forces, the same looming tragedy, the fear that a sudden change in the wind might bring with it a great destruction of his people. But he knew also that Billy's people had nowhere to go, no opportunity for a diaspora. No borders to steal across at night, no river to wade with forlorn bundles on their heads or mountain to scale with safety promised on the leeward side, no corrupt officials to bribe to gain a temporary haven. Billy's people had been placed at the ends of the earth. Now, with the coming of the white man, they would be pushed over its edge to oblivion, where only the ghosts of the eleven lost tribes of Israel dwell in the howling, mournful, swirling mists of eternity.

When Billy had gone queer and thrown off his clothes, Ikey had seen his back. The lines of scar tissue joined in a contorted lunar landscape of ridges and troughs, so that no single piece of clear black skin remained. Billy had been beaten so often that his back looked like a shiny, carelessly plaited garment of hide pitted with a dozen small craters of yellow pus.

They left Billygonequeer behind that day at Richmond Gaol in order that he might be taken before the district magistrate. A police magistrate alone could order only three dozen lashes and this, Harris felt, was insufficient to curb the black man's constant rebellion. When the men returned that night they found Billy in the courtyard still standing rigid, his yellow palms turned outward, chained to the ring set into the prison wall. Harris informed them jauntily that they would not muster as usual at dawn, but would be allowed to rest until nine of the clock, and thereafter would be required to march to the nearby courthouse where the triangle stood and where they would witness Billygonequeer's sentence of flogging – one hundred strokes of the cat. The men cheered, for a late rising was like a holiday.

'Be there a man among you who will volunteer to be the flagellator?' Harris asked.

'Where be Rufus Manning?' someone called.

'Gorn to Hobart to do a floggin'. There be twelve men called to the triangle there and only two to flog the livin' daylights out o' them,' Harris explained, then added, 'It's double rations for him what volunteers to flagellate the nigger!'

There was a murmur among the prisoners though none stepped forward. Harris watched them, his eyes seeming to fix on each man before travelling on. Billy-gonequeer stood rigidly behind him in chains. The over-seer saw the reluctance in each pair of eyes. 'Double rations and the 'arf day orf!' he now added.

The men shuffled and murmured among themselves. It was a prize each of them was much tempted to possess, and had it been any other man who was to be flogged, few would have hesitated. No man among them could remember when last he had felt his stomach contented. But they all felt differently about Billygone-queer, differently and afraid. Two flagellators who had whipped him in the past had died shortly afterwards, and were rumoured to have howled as they died, making the same dog-like noise as Billygonequeer. Afterwards the surgeon could find no cause of death, though there had been a look of great terror on their faces and both had torn at their guts until they drew deep furrows of blood. They did not for a moment believe that Manning had gone to Hobart. He had taken cover. Life on a road gang was not much to con-template, but to die howling like a dog with some great terror ripping the life out of you from within, and all for the sake of half a day's rest and a good tightener, was a more fearful prospect.

'You do it, Mr 'Arris!' one of the prisoners shouted. 'G'warn, you flog 'im, you flog Billygonequeer!'

Harris grew suddenly pale, and while he tried to laugh off the suggestion, the corners of his mouth seemed for a moment out of control. 'It's not me job,' he finally muttered.

'It's not ours neither!' several of the men volunteered and there was a knowing snigger among the prisoners.

Suddenly Billy's arm rose stiff as a ramrod and

pointed directly at Ikey, and from his throat came the howl. Harris turned to see the wild-eyed black pointing at Ikey's breast. Billy howled once more, then let his arm fall slowly to his side.

Ikey looked fearfully about him and then at the overseer and vigorously shook his head. 'Who, me? No, no, not me!' he said, taking a backwards step and bumping into the man behind him. 'Mercy be! I hates violence of any sort. Please, I begs you Mr Harris!' Ikey's eyes had grown wide with fear. 'No, no!' he repeated shaking his hand in front of his face. 'I cannot do it, I simply cannot, I should faint at the very prospect, I cannot abide the sight o' blood.' Ikey let out a sudden wail and fell to his knees at the overseer's feet. 'I begs you, no!' he sobbed.

The assembled prisoners were convulsed with laughter. Blood was such a common substance in their lives, they thought it hilarious that Ikey should declare his abhorrence to it. Before he had completed his prison sentence they knew he would see rivers of blood, until this substance would seem no more strange to him than the spittle on a man's tongue, or the beads of sweat gathered on his brow.

'Well now, you'll do nicely, it will be an excellent 'nitiation for ya, Ikey Solomon.' Harris smiled. 'Yer most fortunate, you are. You'll come to blood the easy way, not from the fresh opening of yer own Jew back, but upon the back o' the nigger!'

The gang mustered and was issued with their morning skilly and then marched by the three troopers who constantly guarded them to the nearby courthouse where the triangle stood.

The triangle, the dreaded flagellation post, was built

of strong scantlings, that is to say posts or purlins of about five inches in width. They were placed so as to form a space about ten feet square at the bottom, and secured by pins into the ground in a slanted manner so that they rose to meet at a point in the centre. Horizontal bars were fastened to these posts, each about two feet apart, and it was to these that the person to be flogged was secured. He faced inwards, his back outwards, with his ankles, knees and outstretched arms tightly bound to the bars. The victim of the triangle was stripped, either to the waist or, more often, naked, this so that the blood would not damage his clothes, which were government property. Eight or ten men could be fastened to a single triangle, and several flagellators employed to beat them. These were usually ticket of leave men, expressly appointed to the position, and many took great pride in their work. Prisoners could also be selected if they were sufficiently robust to lend some weight to the task.

Ikey did not fit the bill in the least. Puny, with narrow sloping shoulders and delicate arms, in his hands the cat o' nine appeared to be a most incongruous instrument. Ikey carried the whip of many tails awkwardly, as though it were repulsive to him, and the knotted ends of the cutting cord drooped to the ground at his feet. Ikey's limbs appeared to tremble of their own accord, and his knees shook violently. There was no doubt in the mind of those brought in to bear witness that Billygonequeer was in for a soft time, a mere tickle of the flesh, and this prospect immensely cheered those who watched.

'You will put yer back into it, ya hear, Solomon? Step up and lay the cat square an' 'ard or, I swear, you'll receive the same yerself!' Harris shouted. He reached out, grabbed the knotted whip from Ikey's reluctant fingers, and demonstrated how it should be used. The cords whistled through the air and landed with a single hard smack across the smooth wood of one of the triangle's posts. Ikey's eyes screwed up in horror, and he trembled more than ever.

Harris handed him the whip and turned to the doctor. 'We are ready to yer count, sir.'

The doctor nodded to Ikey to commence and Ikey, uttering a low moan, raised the whip and brought it down upon Billygonequeer's back. The blow was so ineffectual that it brought a sudden gale of laughter from the onlookers. One of the knots at the end of the cord must have entered a festering pit in Billy's back, for a thin trickle of blood ran from it. Ikey gave a soft moan and fainted dead away to the hilarious laughter of the prisoners.

The doctor examined Ikey then took smelling salts from his bag which revived him. But it was clear Ikey was not up to the task of flagellation. The doctor turned to Harris.

'We do not have a trooper who is corporal by rank among us. You will have to complete the flogging yourself.' There was a sudden and complete silence among the prisoners as they watched Harris.

'I am not inclined, sir. Can it not wait for Mr Manning? Some other day perhaps?'

'Nonsense, man! I have just seen how well you take to the task by the way you approached the whipping post. Get to it. I have but little time to waste in this tedious matter.'

'Sir, I shall lose respect among my men,' Harris tried again.

'Nay!' several prisoners shouted. 'That you will not! G'warn, Mr Harris, do the deed!'

'Be silent, you!' Harris snarled at the ranks, grateful to have a chance to vent his spleen.

'There you are, Harris, you have the full support of your men.' The doctor stooped and picked up the cat o' nine tails. 'Can't ask for more than that now, can you?' He handed the whip to Harris. 'Be a good person and do your duty in the name of the King.'

Harris seemed suddenly to lose all control and his face took on a fierce and desperate look. He lifted the whip and ran at Billygonequeer, and brought the cat down with all his might across the black man's back. He rained blow after blow on Billy, grunting and frothing at the mouth, so that long before he had completed the one hundred strokes he was exhausted and bowed down for want of energy. His hands were clasped upon his knees and his breath came in great gasps. Specks of flesh and blood splattered his blouse and face and hair.

'Why you are the consummate flagellator, Mr Harris. Taken to the art like a duck to water, eh?' the surgeon said calmly, then added, 'That be quite enough, cut the prisoner down.'

Throughout the terrible beating Billygonequeer did not once flinch or cry out. Nor did he register any expression when a trooper splashed his back with brine before cutting him from the triangle. He spat the leather mouthpiece out, strips of raw flesh hanging from his back, and stood rigid, eyes glazed, the yellow palms of his hands turned outwards. He then howled three times, the eerie call of the Tasmanian tiger dog, and the Irishmen among the prisoners were seen to cross themselves.

Billygonequeer was not placed in solitary confinement, as was the custom after a flogging, but chained once again to the wall in the courtyard. He stayed there for two weeks on bread and water until his back was sufficiently healed for him to return to the cart.

Each evening Ikey would go to the gaoler Mr Dodsworth and beg for liniment and clean rags, and he would clean out the wounds on Billy's back and to the back of his head, wincing and gagging as he cleared the maggots the flies had laid in the festering craters during the day. Billy had long since come out of his trance and he would smile as Ikey approached. Silently he'd allow Ikey to clean his wounds and rub the sulphur ointment into his back without flinching, though the pain must have been excruciating.

Ikey could not explain to himself this voluntary act of caring. He knew it to be completely contrary to his character and he was not aware of having undergone any change in his nature. In fact he seldom thought of Hannah and his children, and cared even less about their welfare. He would lie awake at night plotting to get Hannah's set of numbers for the safe, and told himself that, if ever he should succeed, he would escape his wife forever.

Occasionally, in a moment of sentimentality, he thought fondly of Mary, though he harboured no future ambitions for a reunion with her. He told himself he wished only for a future life as a rich man, a life far removed from any he had previously led, and he was determined not to bring any of the past into his future.

Though it may be said that every heart on earth is kindled to love, Ikey had so early in his life been denied affection that he was dulled to its prospect. He had never felt the singular need to love. He felt he had loved Mary, if only briefly, but he had no notion of what he might expect from such an emotion. He did not care if he himself were liked, for he had come to expect the opposite. Now that the sycophancy on which he depended as a rich man was no longer available to him, he fully expected that he would be greatly disliked. That he himself should be loved was not a thought which ever entered his head. And so Ikey's feelings for Billygonequeer were hard for him to understand, and filled him with apprehension.

Almost every day as he laboured at the cart he would decide to ignore the black man on his return to the prison that night. But he was never able to do so. Billygonequeer would smile at him, his gleaming white teeth filling his astonishing coal-black face, and Ikey, inwardly cursing himself for his foolishness, would be off to Mr Dodsworth for liniment and cloth.

Ikey, as was his natural manner, talked to Billygonequeer at great length. To this torrent of words Billy would sometimes grunt, or smile, adding little more than sounds and nods to this one-way dialogue. Occasionally Billy would clutch Ikey's hand or pat him on his face and say, 'Good pella, Ikey.' Then he might grin and repeat, 'Much, much, good pella, Ikey.' It was as though, by Ikey's mannerisms and the few words Billy had at his disposal, he could grasp what his companion was saying.

Sometimes Billygonequeer would hear a bird cry and say aloud its Aboriginal name until Ikey could pronounce it clearly. He'd gather fruit or nuts, or grub for roots, and always share what he found. Ikey got used to the fat white grubs Billy would find under the bark of fallen trees and found them delicious when roasted. Whenever they came upon wild honey they would feast on it secretly for days. In these ways Billy supplemented their prison diet with bush tucker, and there were some days on the road gang when the four men on the cart counted their stomachs more full than empty. It was a wondrous thing to see Billy's willingness to share everything he found, and the smallest wild morsel would be meticulously divided.

Ikey had spent his life in acquisition, sharing as little as possible, and keeping as much for himself as he could. It would be nice to think that Billygonequeer might have changed this aspect of his nature, that the primitive savage could teach Ikey the highest achievement of civilisation, the equitable sharing of the combined resources of any society.

Alas, this is not the lesson Ikey took from the black man. Instead he came to realise that it was this very characteristic which would lead to the ultimate demise of the Van Diemen's Land savage. The rapacious white tribe who were arriving in increasing numbers, not only as convicts but also as settlers, wanted to own everything they touched. They slashed and burned the wilderness so that they might graze their sheep and grow their corn. They erected fences around the land they now called their own and which henceforth they were prepared to defend with muskets and sometimes even their lives. They built church steeples and prison walls and homes of granite hewn from the virgin rock and timber cut from the umbrageous mountain forests. They possessed everything upon the island, the wild beasts that grazed upon its surface, the birds that flew over it, the fish that swam in its rushing river torrents and the barking seals resting in the quiet bays and secluded inlets. Everything they thought worthwhile was attached to the notion of ownership.

Against this urgent and anxious desire for appropriation stood a handful of savages who seldom even built a shelter against the weather. They dressed in a single kangaroo skin, and believed that all they could see and walk upon was owned by all who moved across the land, and yet by none. A people who did not comprehend that one person could own, or wish to own, more than any other.

Ikey understood at once that the Aboriginal tribes in Van Diemen's Land must surely perish because they lacked the two things that had made human progress possible, the existence of greed and the desire to possess property. Ikey understood acquisition as the only guarantee of his survival. He saw that Billygonequeer's people were doomed, for they had not learned this fundamental lesson. Without the need to own there is no need to compete and an uncompetitive society can only exist if it is allowed to develop in isolation. For Billy's people, the isolation had come to an end.

Ikey was aware that Billygonequeer probably did not understand what he was saying, but he said it nonetheless. He would talk as he cleaned Billy's wounds and rubbed salve into his back. 'You must become like us, you must learn our ways, your ways are over, my dear!' Ikey would repeat this over and over, but all he got from Billygonequeer was a big smile. A big white smile in a very black face and always the same response.

'You good pella, Ikey!'

It was not three weeks after Billygonequeer had taken his place again beside Ikey on the cart when Harris began to suffer stomach pains. He would be shouting at the prisoners, or simply walking along, when suddenly he would grab at his stomach, doubling over with pain as each spasm came to him.

The road gang did not need to be told that he was dying. 'Harris's gone queer,' they'd say gleefully among themselves. A month later the overseer was dead, and it was rumoured that all the same symptoms, self-laceration of the stomach and howling in the manner of Billygonequeer, were in attendance at his death bed. Furthermore, the coroner conducting the autopsy could find no fault with his stomach and intestines.

The gang was now working too far from Richmond Gaol to return at night so they proceeded from a new out station, a series of rough buildings erected beside the road. These were infested with lice and fleas, with the addition of other vermin when the weather grew colder. A new overseer, James Strutt, who had come out from Launceston, proved not too harsh by the standards of the day, dealing with trouble only when he found it.

It was from Strutt that Ikey first learned the true extent of the range war which was being waged against the island's native people. Strutt was a member of a part-time militia unit, formed independently of the government troopers, and he spoke with great enthusiasm of the tactics to be employed in the killing of blacks. He had been a member of the Black Line in October the previous year, and spoke disparagingly of the bumbling manner in which this manoeuvre had been conducted. The Black Line was a government sponsored operation intended to drive the Aboriginals out of the settled areas. The plan was to drive the blacks south and east towards East Bay Neck, through the Forestier Peninsula, and into the Tasman Peninsula, where it was proposed a permanent Aboriginal reserve would be set up.

The task force consisted of two thousand men, five hundred of these soldiers, seven hundred convicts and eight hundred free settlers and involved a thousand muskets and three hundred pairs of handcuffs. Three weeks later this avenging army returned having captured one old Aboriginal man and a young boy.

Strutt dismissed the operation as an example of how not to go about the task of eliminating the blacks. 'Government and soldier be not the way. It be a question of us agin them, free men agin savages and, by God, we'll settle it soon enough!' he'd boast.

The Church talked of the salvation of the noble savage. For its part, the government talked increasingly of saving these primitive creatures from extinction by rounding them all up and placing them on a suitable island, which was yet to be found, where they would be out of harm's way.

It was estimated that a thousand natives still existed of the original three thousand who were thought to be on the island when it had been declared a penal settlement. As it turned out, this calculation was incorrect. A white man's respiratory disease had struck the tribes and only a few hundred Aboriginals still existed on the land they had traditionally occupied.

But it should not be supposed that the Tasmanian native was without courage. With wooden spears against muskets they valiantly fought back and caused great consternation among the settlers. During the four-year period of martial law they killed eighty-nine

Europeans, while of the two hundred Aboriginals thought to be within the settled areas, fewer than fifty survived.

The government now believed that the natives might be persuaded to accept a safe haven. They appointed George Augustus Robinson, a religious zealot who spoke the main Aboriginal language, to peaceably round up what remained of the tribes for resettlement. In this task Robinson enlisted the help of an Aboriginal female, Truganini. She was his guide, and it was her influence which he hoped might persuade her people to capitulate, though the settlers thought the word 'guide' a very curious one for what they insisted was the true relationship between Robinson and the young and shapely Aboriginal woman.

If Church and State professed compassion for the Van Diemen's Land natives, the settlers held no such Christian or noble motives. They called openly for the elimination of the Tasmanian Aboriginal race and, in that duplicity so common to government, where a wink is as good as a nod, the authorities turned a blind eye as the settlers worked to bring that elimination about.

Governor Arthur issued a famous poster, which was nailed to trees in the wilderness, in which he showed the Aboriginals, by means of comic pictures, that there would be equal justice under British law. That a native killed by a white settler would see the culprit hanged as surely as if a black were to murder a white. Yet although hundreds of Aboriginal women and children were openly slaughtered, not a single European settler was ever hanged for the murder of a black.

Martial law was declared in 1828 which gave the military the right to apprehend or shoot on sight any

Aboriginal found in the settled areas. The military proved ineffective in this task, and roving parties of settlers were formed under the pretence of a militia such as the one to which Strutt belonged. A bounty was introduced for the capture of Aboriginals, five pounds being paid for every adult and two pounds for each child. It was open season, and though few natives were captured, many were murdered with as little concern for the consequences as if they were kangaroos or a flock of marauding cockatoos.

To the settlers, Robinson, 'the Black Shepherd', was a bad joke and Strutt would often expostulate, 'While that Abo fucker George Robinson be playing sheepdog we be playin' huntin' dog. Before he can muster them black bastards, they'll all be on the roll call for the dead. They's vermin, scum, they's not human like us, a single fly-blown sheep be worth five o' them and a good huntin' hound worth ten!'

Whereupon Strutt would tell with alacrity one of his numerous stories of the hunting trips undertaken to kill the blacks. The men in Ikey's road gang thought these stories a great entertainment. Two favourites were the tale of Paddy Hexagon, a stock-keeper who lived near Deloraine, who shot and killed nineteen Aboriginals with a swivel gun filled with nails, and another which the prisoners on the road gang called 'Stuffing Leaves'.

'G'warn then, Mr Strutt, tell us the one about the woman and the stuffin' o' leaves!' one of the prisoners asked one night when they'd moved from Richmond Gaol, and were accommodated at the out station in the bush.

They were sitting around a fire, Ikey seated next to the always silent Billygonequeer. Billy appeared not to listen to or even understand these horror stories. Instead he sat on his haunches with his back turned to the fire, and seemed more interested in the sound of the wind in the gum trees and the call of the frogs from a nearby stream.

This stream ran into a small wetland and Billygone-queer seemed to take an unusual interest in the frogs which resided there. Every once in a while he would cup his hands to his mouth and precisely imitate a call, though at a slightly deeper pitch. Whereupon all the frogs would grow suddenly silent. Then he would carry on in a froggy language as though he were delivering an address, pause, then deliver a single, though somewhat different note, and the frogs would continue their croaking chatter.

At first this was seen by the men as a great joke. But Billygonequeer would continue in earnest conversation in frog language until the gang got so used to his nightly routine of croaking and ribet-ribet-ing with nature that they took no more notice than if a loud belch or fart had taken place among one of their number.

'Oh aye, the woman with leaves, that be a most pleasin' hunt,' Strutt chuckled in reply. 'The women be the worst. They'll scratch your eyes out soon as look at you.' Strutt stroked his beard as though reviewing all the details of the tale before he began. 'There be three of us, Paddy Hexagon, Sam O'Leary and yours truly, and we's huntin' kangaroo in the Coal River area when we seen this gin who were pregnant like. "Oi!" we shouts, thinkin' her too fat to make a run for it, and five pound in the bounty bag if you please and very nice too! And if the child be near to born, another two for what's inside her belly.' He paused and the men laughed and one of them, a wit named Cristin Puding, known of course as 'Christmas Pudding', made a customary crack.

'That I needs to see! A government bounty man what pays two pound for what's not yet come outside to be properly skinned and cured!'

'Well we shouts again,' Strutt continued, casting a look of annoyance at Puding, for he did not wish him to steal even the smallest rumble of his thunder, or tiny scrap of the laughter yet to come. 'And she sets off, waddlin' like a duck and makin' for the shelter o' some trees not twenty yards away. She's movin' too, movin' fast for the fat black duck she's become.' This brought a laugh, for the gang had heard it often enough and were properly cued to respond.

'We sets off to get to her, but the grass 'tween her and us be high and she be into the trees. By the time we gets there she ain't nowhere to be seen. High 'n low we searches and we's about to give it away when we hears a cry up above. We looks up and there she be, up fifty feet or more in the branches of a gum tree, well disguised behind the leaves and all. How she gone and got up in her state I'm buggered if I knows. It were no easy climb.'

The road gang grew silent and even Billygonequeer ceased making his frog sounds.

'There she be, high up in the fork o' the tree and, by Jaysus, the child inside her is beginnin' to be borned! She's gruntin' somethin' awful, snuffin' and snoofin' like a fat sow and then it's a screamin' and a caterwaulin' as the head and shoulders come to sniff the world outside! "Here's sport for all!" Sam O'Leary, me mate, shouts. "We'll wait this one out!"'

'Wait this one out!' Cristin Puding shouted, turning to the others. 'Get it? Wait this one *out*!' But the other prisoners hushed him fast, anxious for the story to continue.

'Well, you'll not believe it,' Strutt continued, once again ignoring Puding, 'though I swear on me mother's grave it be true! Out come the bloody mess. The child's got the birth cord twisted round its neck and stranglin' him, only later it turns out to be a her, a little girl, and it's hangin' itself in the air, and the black gin's tryin' to hold onto the cord, but it's slippin' through her hands. "Five shilling to him what shoots it down first!" Paddy Hexagon shouts.'

Strutt stopped suddenly and rocked back on the log he'd sat on and then began to chuckle softly.

'Well you never seen such a loadin' and firin' and missin' and, all the time, the cord stretchin' longer and longer with the black woman holdin' on to it at her end and screamin' blue murder! Then Paddy takes a bead and fires and the little black bastard explodes like a ripe pumpkin! There be blood rainin' down on us! Jaysus! I can tell you, we was all a mess to behold. "Bastard! Bitch! Black whore!" O'Leary shouts at the gin screamin' and sobbin' up in the tree.' The foreman laughed again. 'His wife just made him a new shirt and now it be spoiled, soaked in Abo's blood! Paddy and me, we damn near carked we laughed so much!'

He paused, enjoying the eyes of all the men fixed upon him. ' "You'll pay fer this ya black bitch!" O'Leary shouts upwards at her, shakin' his fist. Then he takes a careful shot. Bullseye! He hits the gin in the stomach. But she don't come tumblin' down, instead she starts to pick leaves from the tree and stuff them in her gut, in the hole what O'Leary's musket's made. We all shoot, but she stays up, and each time a shot strikes home she spits at us and stuffs more leaves where the new holes be. There we all be. Us shootin' and her stuffin' gum leaves and screamin' and spittin', the baby lyin' broke on the ground. It were grand sport, but then I takes a shot and hits her in the head, dead between the eyes, and she come tumblin' down and falls plop, lifeless to the ground.'

The men around the overseer clapped and whistled. Only Ikey and Billygonequeer remained silent.

Ikey turned and spat into the dark, thankful that Billygonequeer would not have understood a word of the foreman's grisly tale. Then someone threw a branch on the embers, and the dry leaves crackled and flared up and in the wider circle of light cast by the fire Ikey saw that tears were flowing from Billy's dark eyes. Large silent tears which ran onto the point of his chin and splashed in tiny explosions of dust at his feet. The fire died back to normal, and in the dark Ikey reached out and touched Billy's shoulder and whispered softly.

'You *got* to learn to be like us, Billygonequeer!' Then he added, 'Not like them. Jesus no! Like a Jew. I'll teach you, my dear. You could be a black Jew. All you got to learn is, when you've got suffering you've got to add cunning. Suffering plus cunning equals survival! That be the arithmetic of a Jew's life!'

Billygonequeer turned slowly and looked directly at Ikey, sniffing and wiping the tears from his eyes with the back of his hand.

'You good pella, Ikey,' he said, his voice hoarse and barely above a whisper. Then, 'You gib me name, Ikey!'

Ikey looked momentarily puzzled. 'You've already

got a name, my dear. It ain't much, but it serves as good as most.'

Billygonequeer shook his head. 'Like Ikey. Name same like white pella.'

'Oh, you wants a proper name? Is that it, Billy?' He pointed to the men around the fire. 'Like them pella? Puding, Calligan, Mooney? Name like so?'

Billygonequeer nodded and smiled, his sad, teary face suddenly lighting up.

Ikey considered for a moment. After promising to turn Billygonequeer into a Jew he thought to give him a Jewish name, but then changed his mind. It would take too much explanation and might get Billygonequeer into even more trouble.

'William Lanney!' he said suddenly. It was the name of a carpenter mechanic who owed Ikey five pounds from a bet lost at ratting, a debt Ikey now knew he would never collect. 'Will-ee-am Lan-nee,' Ikey repeated slowly.

'Willeeamlanee!' Billygonequeer said in a musical tone as though it were the sound of a bird cry.

'No.' Ikey held up two fingers. 'Two words. William. Lanney.'

Billygonequeer was not only a dab hand at mastering frog calls, for he seemed now to grasp the pronunciation of his new name quite easily, 'William Lanney ... William Lanney,' he said, with tolerable accuracy.

Ikey laughed. 'Good pella, Mr William Lanney!'

Billygonequeer stretched out and touched Ikey's face as though he was memorising his features through the tips of his long, slender fingers. 'You good pella, Ikey! Much, much good, pella!' He tested his new name. 'William Lanney!'

It was time for the evening lock up. The prisoners were led to their huts, mustered, and then each was manacled to his bunk and all locked in for the night, except for Billygonequeer, who was manacled and chained to a large old blue gum to sleep the night in the open.

At dawn Ikey wakened as the javelin man, the trusted prisoner in charge, entered the hut and called over for the man to come and unlock his shackles so that he might go outside to take a piss.

Ikey walked out into the crisp dawn. Above him, where the early sunrise touched the top of the gum trees, he could hear the doves cooing. When he'd emptied his bladder Ikey strolled over to the tree where Billygonequeer had been chained for the night. Here he stopped in surprise. The shackles, still fixed in their locks, lay upon the ground, but Billygonequeer was missing.

Ikey stood for a moment not fully comprehending. He wondered if Billygonequeer might have already risen, though it was customary to unchain him last of all. Then he noticed that the manacles and shackles had not been opened, and that there were bloodstains on the inside surfaces.

Ikey felt a great ache grow such as he had not felt before. A deep heaviness which started somewhere in his chest, and rose up and filled his throat so that he was scarcely able to breathe. He could hear his heart beating in his ears, his head seemed for a moment to float, and he was close to fainting. He stood very still, and he could hear the burble of water flowing over rock, and the wash of the wind in the leaves above him. Ikey, the most solitary of men, now felt more completely alone than ever before.

571

'May Jehovah be with you, Billygonequeer,' Ikey said, the words hurting in his throat as he spoke to the chains which lay unopened in the beaten grass where his friend had last lain. Then he began to rock back and forth and at the same time to recite the Kaddish, the prayer for the dead. Hot tears rolled silently down his cheeks and disappeared into his scraggly beard as the words of the ancient prayer frosted in the cold morning air.

And may he walk continually in the land of life,
and may his soul rest in the bond of life.

Then he leaned against the smooth, cool bark of the gum tree and sobbed and sobbed. High above him in the silver gum trees he could hear the blue doves calling to their lost partners.

Chapter Twenty-seven

Imprisonment is intended to break the spirit, to render harmless those who are thought to be harmful. Such is the human condition that it will endure the brutal lash and the bread and water of society's pious outrage, but is finally broken by the relentless boredom of prison life. The blankness of time, the pointless repetition, the mindless routines undertaken in a bleak and purposeless landscape addles the brain and reduces a person to whimpering servility. Humans best survive when they are given purpose; a common enemy to defeat, revenge to wreak or a dream to cling to.

Mary survived her sentence because she had a dream. She saw her incarceration in the Female Factory as her apprenticeship out of the hell of her past. Henceforth, she determined that she would be judged by her competence and not doomed by the circumstances of her birth. Here, under the shadow of the great mountain, she would take her rightful place in life.

During the four grim years she spent at the Female Factory Mary knew that she had taken the first steps in her great good luck. The Potato Factory in the prison vegetable gardens had prospered and when she was granted her ticket of leave to live outside the prison she had accumulated the sum of five hundred pounds. Ann Gower also now possessed sufficient money, saved for her by Mary, to achieve an ambition she talked of a great deal, open a bawdy house on the waterfront area of Wapping.

The King's Orphan School had achieved exemplary results, with most of Mary's pupils numerate and literate and some beginning to show a most gratifying propensity for learning. So impressed was Mr Emmett, the chief clerk, that he persuaded Governor Arthur to offer Mary the position of headmistress. This independent position meant that she would no longer be under the baleful eye of the Reverend Smedley, and would be entitled to a small salary. Much to the dismay of Mary's sponsor, she had once again refused his generous offer.

'What ever shall we make of you, Mary Abacus? Will you never learn what is good for you? A more stubborn woman would be most difficult to find upon this island! If you were a man you would be quickly dismissed as a complete fool!'

Mary, who had the greatest respect for Mr Emmett, was sorry to be the cause of his disappointment. In the three years she had been teaching he had come to support her keenly and had seen to it that she was supplied with equipment from government stores, and that the Reverend Smedley did not unduly interfere with or undermine her work.

'Mr Emmett, sir, I thank you from the bottom o' me heart for the trust you have shown in me, but I must remind you, I am a teacher only for the lack o' someone more qualified. You gave me the position only because I believed the brats could take to learning.'

'I'll give you that, Mary, I'll give you that,' Mr Emmett repeated, somewhat mollified. 'You've proved us all wrong and a salutary lesson it has been, I agree.'

Mary smiled. 'You're very kind, Mr Emmett, but it be time for you to make a proper appointment. There be a widow, Mrs Emma Patterson, a free settler out from England, a Quaker I believe. She has excellent references and is well trained to her vocation. She has applied to us for a billet and she is much superior in her knowledge and methods to me or Miss Smedley.' Mary paused. 'You would do well to grant her the post in my stead.'

'Oh Mary, Mary, quite contrary, what shall we do with you?' Mr Emmett asked.

Mary grinned, thankful that he seemed reconciled to her decision. 'A reference, sir. I intend to apply for a clerking position, with some bookkeeping, just as you would have me do for the government, but in commerce. Will you grant it me?' She tilted her head and gave Emmett a most disarming smile. 'Please?'

The chief clerk tried his utmost to appear disapproving, but finally nodded his head. 'It will do you no good, my girl,' he said.

The position of headmistress of the orphan school was duly given to Mrs Patterson who, together with the patient and loving Elspeth Smedley, would ensure that the future for Mary's pupils was a bright one.

On the day before her ticket of leave was granted Mary took a tearful farewell from her orphans and cried all the way back to the Female Factory. She loved her children and had watched them grow and take pleasure in learning. Mary felt sure that some, at last, would have respectable lives. She wondered how she could possibly have given up her post, for the children loved her, gave her a purpose and had confirmed her as being a natural teacher. But deep in her heart she knew that teaching would not fulfil her ultimate ambition, that her skill with numbers and her abacus was meant for a different purpose.

With the Potato Factory, Mary had gained a further sense of business and was reminded again that the rules of supply and demand work best when they are predicated against the innate weakness of men. The brothel in Bell Alley and the supply of poteen from the Potato Factory both demonstrated this fundamental principle. To this end Ann Gower had begged that once they were free of the Female Factory they do more of the same. She also suggested they take the still with them so that they might continue in the trades that had been so lucrative for them in the prison vegetable gardens.

But Mary had resisted her friend's offer. She wanted no more of the criminal life, and was determined to be as free as the brilliant green parrots which had welcomed her to Van Diemen's Land. Freedom meant a great deal more to her than the opportunity to live a respectable existence in a new land, where old beliefs and habits were applied to circumstances which had greatly changed. She would use her freedom as though it were truly the gift of being born again to a new life. Mary's conviction that destiny had called her to something more than a life of drudgery had persisted, and she responded to it with a full heart and the unstinting application of her nimble mind. Her body had grown strong on a diet of fresh vegetables and from working in the open air, and she was ready to make whatever sacrifices were necessary.

Mary's ticket of leave included a probationary period of three years and then her sentence would be completed. She wished to use this time to learn a new trade, so she would be ready when she was permitted to go into business on her own. She would take a billet where she might learn the intricacies of trade, and her first task had been to purchase a copy of the *Colonial Times* so that she might peruse the advertisements for employment. The number of these which requested the need for a bookkeeper, eight in all, filled her heart with joy. But before she set about walking to each address she had a promise to keep to herself.

She had been escorted to the gates of the Female Factory by the keeper, Mr Drabble, not much past six in the morning. To Mary's surprise he had taken her hand.

'You have served your time, Mary Abacus, and I wish you well. It is my most earnest hope that you shall never return to this place.'

Mary smiled. 'Not as earnest as mine, Mr Drabble. You'll not see hide nor hair of us again!'

Mary had left without Ann Gower, who was to serve an extra week in solitary on bread and water for insubordination when drunk. Mary was somewhat relieved, for though she loved Ann she feared that she would never change, that she would always be, as the popular expression went, 'A nymph o' the pave', though such a description of Ann Gower would have been a gross underestimation of her rapidly growing size. A diet consisting largely of grog and potatoes had caused her to grow exceedingly gross, which Ann described to her customers as 'the luxury o' comfort on the ride', and she would have charged an extra sixpence if she could have gotten away with it. Mary had been reluctant to hand Ann the money she had saved on her behalf, though she told herself she could no longer be responsible for her friend. She had also given the still to her partner, to be secretly dismantled when Ann left the Factory. If Ann should show the minimum of good sense then she had the means to prosper well on the new waterfront area of Wapping.

Mary did not go directly into the town when she left the Female Factory. Carrying her bed roll, a clay pot, her abacus and a small cloth satchel, she climbed the hill immediately behind the Factory and headed towards the great mountain. Sometimes, on her way to the orphan school, she would divert into the tall trees growing on the slopes of Mount Wellington. Along a secret path of her own making she had discovered a small stream, though stream was too grand a word for the trickle of sweet, clear water which came from a large overhanging rock.

Mary now made her way to the secret rock set into the mountain side, which was flat at its top and made an ample ledge. She would sit on a carpet of moss surrounded by fern and look out beyond the shadow cast by the rock to where clumps of brilliant yellow wattle grew under the gum trees. The air around her was scented with blossom. Mountain blueberry, the berries ripe and brilliant, twisted and trailed over the smaller trees and shrubs, and every once in a while she would see a splash of wild fuchsia or a clump of pale pink and lilac early snowberries.

On hot summer days it was cool under the shelter of the rock, which was scarred with lichen and pocketed with moss. On mild winter days Mary would climb on top of the rock ledge and the sun would dapple through the leaves to warm her.

Mary imagined sleeping on this ledge so that she might see the stars at night. Slowly the desire grew in her and she would think upon this prospect as she lay in the stale dormitory filled with the tainted breath of forty other prisoners, a heaving, snoring body on either side of her. Finally she had determined that she was going to spend her first night of freedom on her secret rock under the stars.

Mary arrived at the rock no later than seven in the morning. She removed a clump of moss from deep within the recesses of the overhanging rock and carefully buried the clay pot. Inside it was the five hundred pounds she had saved. She replaced the moss and marked the spot with a handful of small pebbles which appeared to be resting naturally. Mary paused only to take a drink of water and wash her hands before leaving. With her she took her abacus and the small satchel in which she carried a pound in copper and silver and Mr Emmett's letter of recommendation. She walked further up the mountain slope, making a wide arc well away from her rock, until she found a woodcutter's path which led down to the precincts of Hobart Town.

She walked down Macquarie Street and into the centre of the town. Every inch of ground was taken up with some small business concern. Even the fronts of the houses and business establishments for some yards were taken up by traders with stalls and hastily erected sheds of canvas and hoarding. There were lollipop shops, oyster shops, barber shops and butcher stalls where flies hummed about the carcasses of lamb and kangaroo. Men and women shouted their wares at every approach with extravagant promises. 'Oyster the size of a plate!' one would shout. 'Fat lamb that weighs heavy to the pound!' cried a bloody-aproned butcher. 'Birds, song birds, what whistle hopera!' called a boy carrying a cage of yellow canaries.

At eight o'clock in the morning she was waiting at the doorway of the London & Overseas Insurance & Shipping Company, the first of the business concerns which had advertised for a bookkeeper clerk. Mary had arrived early, anxious to be the first if there should be a crowd of applicants. But she had no need to worry – Hobart Town had more billets for clerks than applicants to fill them.

By six o'clock that evening Mary had presented herself at each potential place of employ, dutifully proffering her letter of reference from Mr Emmett. Nothing had changed from her days in London. Mary was a woman, and a ticket of leave convict, and there had scarcely been a rejection of her services couched in even modestly polite language.

The first interview, which had taken place a few minutes after nine in the morning with the insurance and shipping company, had been no better or worse than the last. The manager, a tall, thin and exceedingly pompous chief clerk with the unprepossessing name of Archibald Pooley had looked askance at Mary, his eyes fixed on her mutilated hands. 'Be off with you, miss! I doubt that you could count to ten, but it would try my patience to test you even in this.'

'Please, sir, I have a reference.' Mary smiled brightly and proffered Mr Emmett's letter to the thin-lipped clerk.

He took the letter and held it up to the light. 'Ha! A forgery! No doubt about it!' He handed it back to Mary. 'Count yourself most fortunate that I do not have you arrested! Chief clerk of the colonial secretary's department, eh? You are not only forward but also most stupid. If this letter of reference had been from a lesser mortal than the inestimable Mr Emmett I might have believed in it.' Pooley wore an expression of utter disdain and now he tilted his head backwards as though assaulted by some odious smell. 'You reek of the Female Factory and you expect one to think you honest? Do you take me for a fool, miss?' He sniffed. Then his eyebrows shot heavenwards. 'Good God!' he exclaimed, pointing to Mary's abacus. 'What on earth is that?'

'Me abacus, sir. Please would you let me do a reckonin' for you, any calculation what is a part of your business?'

'Reckoning? On that contraption?' Pooley snorted. 'I sincerely trust you are not serious.'

Mary placed the abacus on a small table close to her and smiled.

'Any reckoning what pleases you, sir,' she said brightly, trying to hide her nervousness. 'As complicated as you wish.'

Pooley ignored Mary's request. 'That be a Chinee contraption, an abacus, is it not?'

'Yes, sir, and well able to do sums o' the most complicated nature,' Mary repeated.

'Not here it isn't!' Pooley said, alarmed. 'Beads for counting in my office? We do not count with beads here, just as we do not count with our fingers!' Then he brought his hands to his head. 'A woman *and* a convict who plays with beads thinks to clerk for me!'

He spoke this at the ceiling and seemed for a moment genuinely upset that Mary should think so low of him. 'Your kind are made to be washer women not book-keepers! Be gone, you have tried my patience long enough!'

As Mary left the scene of each not dissimilar rejection she could hear the words as they had reached her through the swirling, yellow mist of the London East India Docks:

Mary, Mary, Bloody Mary . . .
You're the monkey on our back!

She walked in some despair to the edge of Hobart Town and then, looking carefully lest she might be followed, veered into the shadows of a stand of tall trees that led to her rock. A chill autumn wind blew down from the mountain and the light was fading under the trees as she made her way to her secret sanctuary.

She had bought a small loaf of bread and a tiny jar of maple syrup. She'd not had anything to eat since her bowl of gruel at daybreak, her last meal at the Factory. Mary would have loved to stop at the orphanage, if only for a few moments, to regain her courage. She suddenly longed to have her children skipping around her anxious to be held and loved, she yearned to hold a child in her arms and feel its tender skin against her cheek. She knew she would also greatly miss Elspeth Smedley's midday meal which, despite the tedious presence of Thomas Smedley, had always caused her to feel less a prisoner and more like a civilised person. For the better part of an hour each day she could pretend to be normal. Now she was back to being dirt on the street. Although she had earned her

ticket of leave she was still regarded as convict scum and
she longed for the comfort of Elspeth's quiet voice. 'I fear
a little too much salt in the gravy, Mary. Will you forgive
my clumsiness?'

Elspeth had invited her to eat at the orphanage any
time she wished, but Mary knew that the resources of
the Reverend Smedley were meagre enough and that
Mrs Emma Patterson would now take her place at the
table. Besides, Mary told herself, she could no longer
return Elspeth's generosity. The bountiful supply of vegetables she had brought from the prison garden was no
longer available to her, and her pride would not allow
her to arrive empty-handed. Now, seated under the
rock where it was already dark, she devoured the loaf
which she had soaked in maple syrup. By the time she
was finished her hands and face were sticky but she
could not remember a treat more sumptuous. It was
Mary's first meal free of the shackles, and if it had been
a banquet set for a queen it could have not tasted better.
Mary washed, the icy mountain water leaving her poor,
twisted hands aching with the chill and her face devoid
of feeling, then climbed to the top of the rock to spread
her mattress roll and blanket.

Mary, who had spent many a dark night alone in
some foul corner of a London alley, had never before
slept open to the elements. Above her myriad stars
frosted the dark sky. Though she felt some trepidation
at so much open space, and though it was cold under
the thin blanket, she was stirred by a strange feeling of
happiness. She was free at last, born again under the
crystal stars of the great south land, a child of the green
parrots and the great mountain. Somewhere high up in
the trees she heard the call of a nightjar and before

she fell into an exhausted sleep she determined that in the morning she would once again visit Mr Emmett. She smiled to herself at the thought of the exasperation she would see on his small face, though she knew her benefactor was most fond of her.

As Mary had predicted, Mr Emmett at first professed himself annoyed at her return. 'Mary Abacus, you have twice rejected my charity and now you ask again. I repeat my offer. You may come to work in the government as a clerk. We have a great need for your skill at numbers and ability to write up a ledger, and I shall see that you are treated fairly.'

'Sir, please, I should learn nothing working for the government but the task o' working for the government. There be new settlers coming in greater numbers each year to make their homes on the island and I feel certain there will be abundant opportunity for trade. If I should learn an honest profession, it would be greatly to my advantage. I wants a man's work at clerking and I begs you to make enquiries on my behalf.'

'Mary, you are a woman!' Mr Emmett protested. 'It will be no easy matter to find you a position in any trade as a clerk.' Emmett looked at Mary steadily. 'You see, my dear, even though I trust you, few others would. They would think they take a double risk, both a woman *and* a convict, it is too much to ask of them. A woman and a convict put to the task of preparing their ledgers would be an abomination!'

Mary sighed. 'Will you not help me then?' She explained how she had been rejected at eight separate places the previous day.

The chief clerk looked at Mary without sympathy. 'Help you? How can I help you? I have tried everything

VAN DIEMEN'S LAND

I know to help you! You have rejected my offer to be a clerk with me and then another as a teacher! All that's left for your kind is scrubbing, working in the kitchen or as a washer woman!' He thought for a moment, then added, 'You cannot even work at a market garden as it is forbidden for you to own property.' Then, as if an idea had suddenly occurred to him, Mr Emmett brightened. 'Though perhaps you could rent it. There are plenty here who have property they are too idle to till, your skill with vegetables is well known and your fresh produce will find a ready sale in the markets.' He clapped his hands, delighted that he had solved Mary's problem. 'That's it! I shall make enquiries at once!'

Mary shook her head. 'I am truly grateful, sir, but I have worked as a kitchen maid, lady's maid, laundry maid, and in the Factory as a gardener.' She lifted her crippled hands. 'Me hands won't stand for it and nor will me head.' Mary looked pleadingly at the little man. 'I wants to learn a trade, Mr Emmett! Something to sell what people must have and what uses numbers and me own good sense!'

'And what of your sly grog, will that not profit you handsomely as a trade?' the chief clerk demanded suddenly.

Mary was greatly shocked and began to tremble violently. She was not aware that the chief clerk of the colonial secretary's department had known about the Potato Factory. Fortunately Mr Emmett did not thrust the barb further but waited for her to defend herself. Mary knew not to deny her guilt. Mr Emmett was not a cruel man and he did not listen to idle tittle-tattle. He would have been certain of his information before he sought to employ it against her.

585

'Sir, that were different,' she stammered. 'I were in the crime class and might as well be hung for a sheep as a lamb, there weren't nothing to lose.' Mary felt more in control of herself as she continued. 'It were good grog what didn't rot your guts like what's sold elsewhere, even in respectable taverns.'

'My dear, in Hobart Town there are no respectable taverns. Besides, if you had been caught, it might well have caused your sentence to be doubled!' Mr Emmett said sternly.

Mary looked appealingly at him. 'I owes you me life, sir. I don't think I could have endured without what you done for me at the orphan school. Now I owes you this too! For keeping stum! I thank you from the bottom o' me heart. Please, sir, I ain't never going back to the Female Factory. I don't want to start me new life as a mistress o' sly grog. I ain't so stupid as not to know that, sooner or later, I'd be caught and sent back to the Factory! I couldn't stand that, honest, I couldn't!'

Mr Emmett sighed. 'I'm most glad to hear that, Mary. I shall make enquiries, though I should not hold out any hopes if I were you.' He paused. 'Remember, I make no promises. You have seen for yourself how difficult it will be to persuade any business to take you on.' Then he added, shaking his head, 'You are a most stubborn woman, Mary Abacus. What will you do now? Have you a place to go?'

Mary remained silent and dropped her eyes.

'Well?'

Mary looked up slowly and smiled. She knew she could not remain camped under the rock. It snowed on the mountain in winter and she would freeze to death. Her green eyes rested on the chief clerk. 'I could tend your garden, sir, and sleep in your potting shed, if you was to give me rations.'

Emmett shook his head slowly. 'You take me to be too soft, Mary Abacus. Perhaps even an old fool to be used by a pretty woman. You refuse to be a market gardener, yet you would tend *my* garden?'

'Not soft, or a fool, Mr Emmett, but a person what's been wise and kind and most generous beyond anyone I've ever known.' There were tears in Mary's eyes as she said urgently, 'I shall repay your kindness, I swear. The time will come, I know it!' Mary blinked away her tears. 'It would only be a short while, sir. Until your enquiries prove fruitful, which I know they shall. All speak of you with great respect!'

Emmett looked doubtful and Mary hastily added, 'With the season changing, your roses need pruning and there be much clearing to be done so that your plants may catch the weaker winter sun, and your cold weather vegetables are not yet planted nor straw cut for the seed beds against the coming frost.'

'The potting shed?' Mr Emmett hesitated. 'It's not very big. I daresay we could find a corner for you in the servants' quarters.'

Mary laughed. The previous night spent under the stars had been cold but tolerable, and she had woken to a bright autumn morning with the raucous call of parakeets feeding on the nectar of the butter-coloured eucalypt blossom in the trees above her. Mary knew she had spent her last night with dirty snoring bodies squeezed hard against her sides.

But she hesitated, thinking that to object to this arrangement might cause Mr Emmett to decline her proposition altogether. Finally she found herself saying,

'Sir, I ain't got fancy notions about meself, but I ain't no servant ever no more! The potting shed be more than I'm used to. I have no wish to disturb your household. I have a blanket and mattress roll and will be glorious comfy.'

Mr Emmett looked at her in surprise but then a small smile played at the corners of his mouth. 'Very well, Mary, I shall tell cook to issue you with rations.'

Mary, of course, had sufficient money to live comfortably had she wished to siphon off only a small amount from the contents of the clay pot. She could have stayed in one of the numerous cheap boarding houses which took in ticket of leavers, though the idea did not occur to her. Comfort was not a consideration in her life, and the money she had made from the Potato Factory was to be used only to make a new life. Mary was determined she would have a profession. When she'd earned out her ticket of leave and was free, she would start on her own in business. She didn't much care what business except that it should cater for people's essential needs. She would not touch a penny of the five hundred pounds for any other purpose.

Mary could not light a fire in the tiny potting shed so she spread straw over the cold brick floor. At night she stuffed her clothes with newspaper and in this way remained tolerably warm. During the day she worked in Mr Emmett's garden. He would sometimes visit her when he returned home from work in the early evening, and twice he had brought her a glass of fruit punch flavoured with the heavenly taste of fresh apricots. Mary had scarcely wished to accept the delicious concoction for fear that it might corrupt her resolve.

Mr Emmett always came upon her in the same way.

As though to dispel any anticipation Mary might have at his approach, he would precede his arrival by shouting the selfsame words. 'Not much luck, my dear. If I may say so, no blasted luck at all!'

Mary would look up from where she was working and attempt a smile. 'I am much obliged to you, sir,' she would say, standing up at his approach and trying not to show her disappointment.

Mary took two hours each day to try to secure a position on her own, trudging into town if she should see an advertisement in the *Colonial Times*. This was the only money she spent, sixpence every week to purchase the newspaper. While there were vacant positions aplenty, none of those advertising for a clerk bookkeeper required a female bookkeeper who was a ticket of leave convict. Mr Emmett's letter was beginning to look weary at the folds and greasy at the edges, as though it too was possessed of a forlorn and hopeless disposition.

Mr Emmett tried again to get Mary to join him in the employ of the government but she would not surrender.

A month passed and Mr Emmett's garden was now well prepared for winter. Neat rows of winter cabbage and cauliflower seedlings filled their beds in the vegetable patch. The soil around the standard roses and young fruit trees had been dug around, aired and then bedded down with straw and the garden was now completely cleared of summer's dead leaf. Mary woke one chilly morning and went to the door of the potting shed. The grass outside was silver with hoar frost and, as was her habit each morning, she looked up at the great mountain. Snow had fallen during the night and had turned it into a veritable Christmas pudding. Above it an icy, cobalt sky stretched high and, though she could not see them, she could hear a flock of cockatoos in the trees near by.

'Please, mountain, let something happen today!' Mary appealed to the snow-covered monolith towering above her. 'The work be done in Mr Emmett's garden and I cannot accept no more charity.'

'Mary, Mary! Come here, girl!' She could hear Mr Emmett's excited voice before he reached her. It was just before sunset on the same day and Mary was planting lemon grass. 'Mary, where are you? It's good news at last!'

Mary stood up at Mr Emmett's approach.

'Good news, my dear!' he said a little breathlessly, flapping his arms as he came up to her. 'Mr Peter Degraves the sawmiller is building a brewery at the Cascades and he needs a clerk!'

Mary dropped the trowel she was holding and looked querulously at her benefactor. 'A woman, sir?'

'They'll take a chance on a woman ... on you!' Mr Emmett laughed, well pleased with himself.

'Have you told them I be ticket o' leave, sir?'

'Yes, yes, everything! Do not fret yourself, my dear. Mr Degraves has been in debtor's prison himself. He sees nothing to harm him in your past.' Mr Emmett grinned at Mary. 'I daresay those silly Chinese beads of yours will be just the very thing for counting bricks and timber eh?'

'A brewery is it? Will he keep me on when the building is complete?'

'If you serve him well, I don't see why not.'

Mary, unable to restrain herself, burst into tears and

Mr Emmett, no taller than she, even by an inch, stood beside her. He patted her clumsily on the back. 'Now, now, my dear, it isn't much, an outdoors job with winter almost here, among crude men loading drays, I doubt it will exercise your skills to any extent.'

'Gawd bless you, sir!' Mary whispered, her voice choked with relief.

'Tut, tut, you have little to thank me for, Mary Abacus. My garden is splendidly prepared for winter and I reward you with nothing but the smell of hops in your nostrils and the cussing of rough men in your ears. I think it a poor exchange indeed!'

'Thank you, sir, I will not forget this.'

'There is little for you to remember on my behalf, my dear,' Mr Emmett said gently. 'You are worthy of much, much more, Mary Abacus.'

The chief clerk of the colonial secretary's department was not to know that on the brisk autumn evening in late May 1831, he had watched a small woman with large green eyes, bright with recent tears, take the first tentative step in what would one day be a vast brewery empire that would stretch around the world. Mary Abacus had discovered the commodity men could not live without and yet was not condemned or forbidden by society.

The dream was in place, the new life begun, and Mary's great good luck had persisted. In the gathering darkness she could only just make out the frosted top of the mountain.

'Thank you!' Mary whispered, clasping Ikey's Waterloo medal tightly to her breast.

591

Chapter Twenty-eight

It is one of the great paradoxes in human migration that new beginnings often take with them old and often undesirable social customs. Those fleeing affliction or a hierarchical system for a new and free environment soon develop tyrannies and pecking orders of their own. Though in a penal colony one might expect a clear distinction between the convict and the free, the dichotomies of class in Van Diemen's Land were far more complicated and carefully graded. The relationship Mary enjoyed with Mr Emmett was all the more remarkable for this.

The first two great class distinctions were, of course, the free and the prisoner populations. This was a divide so wide that it was almost impossible to leap, even in exceptional circumstances. Mary had never been inside Mr Emmett's home, nor had she been introduced to his wife, Lucy. Occasionally they would meet in the garden, but Mary would stand with her head bowed and hands clasped in respectful silence while the grand lady passed by.

Lucy Emmett's pretty daughter, Millicent, had once stopped to talk with Mary, who was pruning and shaping the standard rose she had given Mr Emmett for his daughter's tenth birthday.

'Why! That's *my* rose!' Millicent exclaimed. 'I had quite forgotten it. Will you shape it well and make it beautiful again?'

'Yes, Miss Millicent, it will be perfect for the summer to come. It be robust enough and not much neglected.'

'Good! It was a present from Papa and grown just for me by a drunken wretch in the Female Factory!'

'Is that what your papa told you?' Mary asked softly.

'No, Mama told me that! Papa said there's good in everyone. But Mama said the women in the Female Factory were too low to be included in *everyone* and were long past being *good*.' Millicent tilted her head to one side. 'I think there is, don't you?'

'Is what, Miss Millicent?'

'Good in everyone.'

Mary gave a wry laugh. 'I've known some what could be in doubt and they didn't all come from the Female Factory neither.'

'Millicent! How *could* you! Come along *at once*!' Lucy Emmett's cry of alarm made her daughter jump.

'Coming, Mama!' Millicent called back. She cast a look of apprehension at Mary and fled without saying another word.

Mary could hear Lucy Emmett's high-pitched chiding for several minutes afterwards. Some time later Mr Emmett's wife entered the garden and passed by where Mary was weeding. At her approach Mary rose from her haunches with her hands clasped and head bowed. Some paces from where she stood Lucy Emmett halted as if to admire a late-blooming rose.

'You will be sent away at once should you venture

to talk to Miss Millicent again,' she hissed. She did not look directly at Mary and it was as though she were talking to the rose itself. Then she turned abruptly and left the garden.

Because Lucy Emmett's husband worked in the government, she was considered a 'true merino' by the free inhabitants of the colony – that is, they were among the first in point of social order. This circumstance was considered sufficient grounds for keeping aloof from the rest of the community. In fact it was considered degrading to associate with anyone who did not belong to her own *milieu*.

The government class were somewhat jeeringly known by the next order as the 'aristocracy'. This next, or second, order, more numerous and certainly wealthier and more influential in the colony, were the 'respectable' free inhabitants, the merchants, bankers, doctors, lawyers and clergymen who had no connection with the government above being required to pay its crippling taxes.

Below them came the free persons of low station, clerks and small tradesmen, butchers and bakers, who serviced the daily lives of the first-rate settlers. They had little chance of rising above their stations in life and were collectively possessed with an abiding anxiety that they might, through bankruptcy or some other misfortune, sink to the lowest but one level, that of the labouring class.

Below even the labourer was the emancipist, though this group was perhaps the most curious contradiction in the pecking order. Emancipists could, and often enough did, rise through the bottom ranks, past the labouring class and into the ranks of clerks and tradesmen.

The sons of emancipists, if educated in a profession and if they became immensely rich, could rise beyond even the third rank. Daughters had greater opportunities, if they were pretty and properly prepared. That is to say, if they attended the Polyglot Academy, where French, Italian and Spanish were taught by Ferrari's Comparative Method. They would also need to have been instructed by Monsieur Gilbert, a Professor of Dancing, before being considered sufficiently 'yeasted' to rise upwards.

No young woman, even if she was exceptionally beautiful and possessed the most elegant manners, could think to enter society without a comprehensive knowledge of the steps in all the new dances being practised in the salons of London and Paris.

Only then, and only if she should bring with her the added incentive of a great deal of money, was it possible to rise in due course to the ranks of a first rater. But even when the children of a successful emancipist achieved such Olympian heights, their flawed lineage remained and the whispers of the crinolined society matrons would continue for the next two generations.

The bottom station was, of course, the prisoner population and it included the ticket of leavers such as Mary. Between this class and all others, a strict line was drawn. In the presence of any free person in the community, prisoners were as if struck dumb. It was considered correct, even by the lowest of the free orders, to regard them as invisible, ghosts in canary-yellow jackets who laboured on the roads or at tasks beneath the dignity even of the labouring class. And, of course, if they were assigned as servants in a household, they were expected to exercise the minimum speech required to perform their daily duties.

Mr Emmett's courage and generosity of spirit can now be properly appreciated. He, a member of the first station, not only acknowledged the existence of Mary, a convict, but consistently helped her. Emmett was also something of a dreamer for supposing that Mary might be accepted by even the lowliest of government clerks had she taken up his offer to work in his department.

The marked contrast of Lucy Emmett's attitude towards Mary should not be drawn as an example of uncharitable behaviour. To speak to a prisoner, albeit a ticket of leaver, was beyond the imaginings of a pure merino woman, a nightmarish confrontation not to be contemplated even in the most unlikely social circumstances.

Thus, the likelihood of Mary securing a billet as a clerk in Hobart Town was very much in the order of impossible. Not only was she a woman, but such a position lay strictly within the precincts of the third class whereas she was condemned to work within the lowest of the low, the sixth class. It can only be supposed that, in bringing about Mary's appointment, Mr Emmett had favoured Peter Degraves with a government contract, or perhaps waived some building dispensation for the construction of his new brewery, or even invoked a Masonic rite in his position as Grand Master of Hobart's secret order of Free and Accepted Masons.

The gamble Peter Degraves took on Mary soon paid off. She was quick to learn, arrived early and worked late, and took no nonsense from the men, who eventually came to call her, with much admiration, Mother Mary of the Blessed Beads.

It was not only Mary's skill at bookkeeping that impressed her employers, but also her plain sense mixed

with some imagination. Mary was soon aware that pilfering on a building site by the labourers was costing the
owners a considerable amount each month, and that the
men regarded this scam as their natural right. She
requested an appointment with Peter Degraves at his
office higher up the slopes of the mountain, where he and
his brother-in-law owned the concession to cut the timber
right up to the rocky outcrop known as the organ pipes.

Degraves kept Mary waiting a considerable time
before he called her into his small, cluttered office. A
large cross-cut saw of the type used by convicts leaned
against one wall, its blade buckled into a gentle curve.
The room smelled of sawdust and the sap of new-cut
wood. Peter Degraves was a tall, fair, clean-shaven
man, not given to lard as were so many men in their
forties. He sat in his shirt sleeves with his waistcoat
unbuttoned and his clay-spattered boots resting upon a
battered-looking desk.

'Take a pew, Miss Abacus,' he said, indicating a small
upright wicker chair. 'What brings you to the sawmill?'

'Sir, I would speak to you about the site.'

'Ah! It goes well, Miss Abacus, the foreman says we
are ahead in time and I know our expenses are well
contained. You have done an excellent job.'

'Not as excellent as might be supposed,' Mary
answered.

Degraves looked surprised. 'Oh? Is there something I
ought to know about, Miss Abacus?'

'The pilfering, sir . . . on the site. It be considerable.'

Degraves shrugged. 'It was ever thus, Miss Abacus.
Petty crime within the labouring class is as common as
lice in an urchin's hair.' He spread his hands. 'We live,
after all, in a penal colony.'

'Mr Degraves, sir, I have an inventory and we are losing materials at the rate o' fifty pounds a week, two thousand seven hundred and four pounds a year. That be a considerable amount, would you not say?'

'Aye, it's a lot of money, but I've known worse in the sawmilling business.'

'We have one 'undred workmen on the site, each earns fourteen pounds a year in wages, that be . . .'

'Fourteen hundred pounds and, as you say, we are losing nearly double that! Just how would *you* prevent this, Miss Abacus?' Degraves asked in a somewhat patronising manner.

'The value o' the material what's nicked and sold in the taverns and on the sly be one-fifth o' the market value, no more'n ten pounds.'

'And just how do you know this?' Degraves asked, removing his feet from the desk. He pulled his chair closer and leaned forward, listening intently.

'I took various materials from the site and flogged them,' Mary replied calmly.

'You what? You stole from my site!'

'Not stole, sir, it all be written in the books. It were a test to see what the value o' the materials were on the sly.'

Degraves sat back and laughed. 'Why, that's damned clever! Ten pounds eh?' He paused then said, 'Well, that's the labouring class for you, not only dishonest but easily gulled and stupid to boot.'

'Let's give 'em the ten pounds, sir, or a little more, fifteen. That be three shillings per man per week extra in his pay packet, seven pounds two shillings and sixpence per year.'

'But, Miss Abacus,' Degraves protested, 'that's half again as much as they are paid now.'

'Sir, it ain't all the men what's stealing, most is family men as honest as the day. We make the money a weekly bonus, given a month in arrears and when we've determined no pilfering has taken place.'

'No pilfering?' Degraves laughed. 'Not a single nail or plank or brick or bag of mortar! I think you dream somewhat, Miss Abacus!'

'Well no, sir. I have allowed five pounds, that will be sufficient tolerance,' Mary said firmly.

'Twenty pounds and we save thirty, I'm most impressed! Do you think it can be made to work?'

'No, sir. It will not work with money,' Mary replied.

'Oh? How then?'

'In rations! A food chit issued to the labourer's wife what is worth three shillings a week. We pay the men on Saturdays and most of it be in the tavern keeper's hands by Sunday night with the brats starving at home for the rest o' the week. If there be the prospect o' three shillings worth o' rations from the company shop on a Monday, the family will eat that week.'

'Company shop? May I remind you, Miss Abacus, I am a sawmiller who is building a brewery, not a damned tradesman! Who will run this cornucopia of plenty?'

'I will, sir! There be enough money to pay the salary of a good shop assistant if we buy prudently and sell at shopkeepers' rates, and I will keep the books.'

'And will there be a further profit?' Degraves asked shrewdly.

'Yes, sir, to be used for the purchase of books for the orphanage school, as well as a Christmas party given to them by the brewery.'

Degraves laughed. 'Chits for workers' wives, company shops, books and Christmas parties for orphans, when will these fantasies end?' He grew suddenly stern. 'Miss Abacus, I am a practical man who has worked with rough men all my life. Mark my words, they will take your chit and steal as before. You cannot prevent a labouring man from stealing from his master.'

'You are perfectly right, sir. *You* cannot. *I* cannot. But his *wife* can! It's she who will be your policeman, she who will make her man deal with the thief what thinks to take advantage of all the other men by stealing from the site. Wives will make their husbands punish the guilty, for I guarantee she will let no villain take the bread out o' her little ones' mouths.'

Degraves leaned back into his chair. 'It be most clever, Miss Abacus, but I'm afraid it cannot be done. What of my reputation with my peers? Those who, like me, employ labour? They will not take kindly to the raising of a labourer's annual salary by more than fifty per cent! Let me tell you, there will be hell to pay!'

'Sir, heaven forbid! Raise in wages!' Mary appeared to be shocked at such a notion. 'It be a feeding scheme for the worker's family. The Church and the government will soon enough come out in support of you for such an act o' Christian charity!' Mary, afraid she might lose his support for fear of his peers, thought desperately. 'May I remind you that we have a large community o' Quakers what does not condone strong drink *and* there is them Temperance lot just started, the Van Diemen's Land Temperance Society. They's already kickin' up a fuss about the distilleries in the colony. But who will speak badly of a brewery what looks after workers' brats and cares about the education of orphans?'

Degraves smiled. There had already been several raised eyebrows in society concerning his intention to build a brewery. 'A model works, eh?' He frowned suddenly. 'Do you *really* think it will work, Miss Abacus?'

Mary knew she had won, and she was unable to conceal the excitement in her voice so she spoke quickly. 'Better than that, Mr Degraves, sir. We'll end up with the best and most honest workers in the colony on account o' the excellent family conditions what the boss o' the brewery Mr Peter Degraves has put into place!' She took a gulp of air and to this breathless sycophancy she added, 'Thank you, sir, I think it be most clever of you to think up such generous plans for those of us who is privileged to work for you!'

Degraves again looked surprised for a moment, then smiled. He was impressed. 'Why thank you, Miss Abacus, it's not a bad solution, even if I did not think of it myself.' His expression was whimsical when he added, 'You will, of course, let me know when I should reveal this brilliant new plan of mine to the men.'

'And to the *Colonial Times*, sir. The feeding scheme for workers' brats.'

Degraves nodded as he replaced his feet on the desk. 'Though I see little gain in helping the orphanage with the business of learning. These children are the illegitimate spawn of the island's scum and no good will come of it, I can assure you. Besides there is more ridicule in it than there be praise.'

'Sir, sometimes we may be allowed to take credit where no credit is due, and sometimes we deserve much more than we get. Besides, I were just like them poor little brats once.'

Degraves sighed and dismissed Mary with a backward wave of his hand. 'As you wish, Miss Abacus, I can see you do not surrender easily.'

Mary smiled and lowered her eyes to show her respect, though she laughed inwardly, thinking of the motto inscribed on her Waterloo medal. 'Thank you, sir, you have been most gracious,' she replied.

Degraves threw back his head and laughed. 'Prudent, Miss Abacus! Prudent to the tune of thirty pounds a week! I shall not think well of you if this turns out badly, and there will be little graciousness about my manner as I dismiss you from service.'

Mary continued to work for the brewery after its completion and by the time she had served out her ticket of leave she was intimate with every step in the process of making beer. She had been correct. Good men came from everywhere to seek employment at the new brewery where the practice of issuing ration chits had been continued and, as had also been the case on the work site, pilfering was reduced to insignificant proportions.

Written into the wrought-iron gate of the brewery were the words 'Happy workers make happy beer' and this motto also appeared on the labels of the bottled product. The beer they produced at the Cascades Brewery was of a light colour and very pure and, while there were a dozen other breweries in Hobart, none could match the quality of Peter Degraves' excellent light ale and pilsener-style beer. Such was its superiority that it quickly became popular all over the island and ships carrying the company's timber to New South Wales increasingly came also to carry barrels of Cascade beer to Sydney.

Mary soon realised that the difference in the beer was the quality of the malt they used and the pure mountain water. Peter Degraves had sited his mill near the confluence of the Hobart and the Guy Fawkes rivulets, damming them both to make a series of small lakes of pure mountain water. In addition to this he ran a pipe-line from Strickland Falls, about a mile further upstream, which was the source of the purest water of all. The crystal-clear waters fed from a spring which began near the summit of the great mountain, well above its winter snowline.

Strickland Falls was not far from Mary's secret rock and she was determined to own the land on which the rock stood and also have access to the water in the falls. In the third year of her employment at the brewery she marked out approximately ten acres which included her beloved rock, and which led down to the bank on the opposite side of the falls to the brewery pipeline.

In 1824 Governor Arthur had granted Peter Degraves two thousand acres on the side of the mountain for saw milling, and with a further grant taken together with several judicious purchases, he and his brother-in-law Hugh McIntosh now owned the entire side of Mount Wellington. Mary was resolute that she must somehow purchase these ten acres from Degraves and his ailing brother-in-law, though even if they should agree to sell it to her, she was still a ticket of leave convict and could not legally own property.

Once again Mary went to see Mr Emmett. They stood in his garden while she explained what she wanted.

'Mary, by all accounts you have done exceedingly well and Mr Degraves has often enough thanked me for recommending you to him. I daresay, if I can find a plausible reason for the purchase of this land, he may be friendly enough disposed to sell it, always supposing that he should receive a good price. But what possible reason could I have to purchase ten acres of useless land on the slopes of Mount Wellington?'

'You could tell him that you want some day to build a home and wish to secure a small part of the creek bank below the falls, sir.'

Mr Emmett shook his head. 'I have been to the falls but once. It is quite an expedition and, as I recall, they make a fearful racket. I should be the laughing stock of the free settlers and no one in their right mind would build among the trees so far from civilisation with the din of a waterfall drowning all conversation. Besides, I am known for the excellence of my garden and you know as well as I do that the soil under gum trees is leached of all its goodness and is infertile and not in the least suitable for the cultivation of an English garden.'

'A retreat, a place in nature to go to, sir?' Mary suggested a little lamely.

Mr Emmett ignored this remark. He was still taken up with the absurdity of the whole notion. 'Furthermore, the big trees in the area you speak of have already been cut. I would be buying a pig in a poke, half-grown trees and red gum scrub. People, who already count me odd, would think me gone quite mad! My wife would not be able to tolerate the shame of so foolish a decision.'

'Could you not do the transaction in secret, sir? Mr Degraves knows you not to be a fool and would not judge you one for this!' Mary brightened with a sudden thought. 'You could offer him a little more than what the land be worth and ask him to stay stum, I mean, remain silent. He is a man with a good eye for an extra shilling made and, as you say, he has already made his profit from the area we speaks of.'

Mr Emmett scratched the top of his head and looked vexed. 'Can you not wait, my dear? It is only a year before you obtain your freedom, and it is most unlikely that land so far from the town will prove any more attractive to a buyer in the meantime.'

Mary's eyes welled with tears. 'It be the rock, sir!' she suddenly announced.

Mr Emmett was unaffected by Mary's distress – he had seen Mary's tears before when she wanted something from him. 'The rock? What on earth are you talking about?'

Mary knuckled the tears from her large green eyes and sniffed. 'It be a rock on the mountain, a magic rock, I simply must own it!'

'A rock! Own a rock! Magic? You really do try my patience, Mary Abacus!' But she could see that Mr Emmett was curious and prepared to listen to her explanation.

With a fair degree of sniffing, Mary began, swearing Mr Emmett to secrecy for the silliness of it. She told him how she often went to the rock for comfort and how, when the blossom was out and the berries ripe, she would lie on the rock and watch the green parakeets feeding and squabbling in the trees and surrounding bush. 'Not parakeets,' Mr Emmett corrected, 'rosellas, my dear, green rosellas, they are native to this island.' Finally Mary told him how she had slept upon the rock under the stars the first night she had been released from the Female Factory.

This last pronouncement astonished Mr Emmett who, though a nature lover, had acquired a healthy respect for the Tasmanian wilderness. Mary's admission filled him with alarm. It was not uncommon for people who were inexperienced in the ways of the bush to be lost on the mountain slopes, some even perishing in a fall of rock or a sudden snowstorm. Besides the slopes were used by dangerous men who hid from the law during the day and crept down into the town at night.

It had already been noted that Mr Emmett was an unusual man and something of a dreamer, and now he listened attentively as though Mary's preposterous story made more sense to him than any logical reasons she might have. Finally, though cautioning her against the notion, he agreed to approach Peter Degraves and attempt to purchase the ten acres on the mountain on Mary's behalf.

Degraves drove a hard bargain, for despite their friendship, Emmett was a government man and no settler would wish to be bested by the government, even in a private transaction. He finally agreed to sell the title to the ten acres of light timber and scrub for forty pounds, a sum somewhat in advance of the current value of the land.

Mr Emmett had confided in him that as he grew older and the mountain became safer a small cottage in the woods seemed an attractive place for a retreat, where he might stay for short periods alone to read and write. Degraves, aware of the gossip to which such a peculiar notion might give rise in the society of the pure merinos, agreed to keep the land transaction secret and asked surprisingly few questions.

Mr Emmett handled the registration of the title deeds himself so that the purchase was not published in the *Government Gazette* until two years later, when it was transferred into the name of Mary Abacus, emancipist, resident, Mount Wellington Allotment No HT6784,

Hobart Town District, Van Diemen's Land. With the property came the rights to use the pathway created along the Cascade Brewery pipeline in perpetuity.

In digging up and breaking open her clay pot to give Mr Emmett the forty pounds, plus two more for stamp and registration duty, Mary had taken the first proprietorial step in her new life. The money made from the Potato Factory not only allowed her to acquire a small piece of her magic mountain, but with it came the purest commercial source of water for the brewing of beer available in the colony.

Mary determined that, when the time came, she would clear and use only what land she needed for a water mill, malt house and small brewery. Though this dream was well beyond the resources she ever seemed likely to acquire, she could see the brewery clearly in her imagination, the stone buildings sitting among the trees. The rest of the land would be left as nature intended, so that tree and bush would grow to splendid maturity, giving an abundance of blossom and fruit to attract the flocks of green parakeets Mr Emmett called rosellas.

Mary remained with the Cascade Brewery for another year after she had obtained her freedom. Peter Degraves was not concerned when he eventually heard that Mr Emmett had sold his land on the mountain to Mary. He had long since decided that Mary was rather strange and that she should wish to live alone on the mountain did not greatly surprise him. With the brewery's reputation established, he had turned to another grand adventure, building a theatre for the benefit of the citizens of the town, and he was also expanding into shipbuilding and flour milling.

Degraves was happy to know that Mary was the bookkeeper and accountant at the brewery as he had come to absolutely trust her financial judgement in all matters. But he did not estimate her above his own needs. And, if he thought about it at all, he would have expected Mary to regard her security of employment at the brewery as above the price of rubies, and consequently to show her gratitude in a lifetime of faithful and uncomplaining service to him.

He was greatly surprised, therefore, when in the spring of 1836 Mary resigned. The previous year, that is the year she had gained her freedom, had been a busy one for her. She had cleared the land for almost a quarter of an acre around as a fire break, leaving some of the tallest trees in place. With a fast-running stream fronting the clearing and the rush of water over rock, the leafy glade Mary had created for herself was to her mind as close as she was likely to get to heaven on earth.

In truth the mountain, while a paradise of nature, was a dangerous place for a lone woman. Fire was always a threat and could sweep through the forest without warning. The weather on the mountain was unpredictable; sudden mists could move down the slopes, closing in the mountain and making visibility impossible. As the felling of the tall timber increased, mud slides and falling rocks became commonplace during winter storms.

But it was from man that the greatest danger lay. The mountain was also home to desperate men, the dregs of the colony's society who were frequently on the run from the law. In the summer months they would sleep on the mountain during the day and creep back into town at night to rob and steal so that they might frequent the drinking dens, sly grog shops and brothels. There they were served with raw spirits made on the premises which often enough killed them and more usually sent them mad.

Those who could still walk when daylight came would drag themselves into the bush on the slopes of the mountains to sleep until nightfall when they would re-emerge. Though most were harmless enough, their brains addled with alcohol, pathetic, shambling creatures, some were dangerous. Mary could not hope to construct a hut on her property where she might safely live, even though she had taken the precaution of learning how to fire a pistol which she always carried in her bag when she visited her clearing among the trees.

Mary was tempted to call her idyllic surrounding by some romantic name gathered from a book or taken from her native England, but in the end she chose, for reasons of sentiment and luck, to call her brewery The Potato Factory.

Mary argued to herself that the poteen still had been the true start of her great good luck. It had earned her a reputation for a quality product. Most of the sly grog available in the drinking dens and brothels of Hobart Town was more likely to kill the customer than to send him on his way happily inebriated. Her experience at the Cascade Brewery had shown her once again that quality was of the utmost importance, and she was adamant that it would become the hallmark of everything she did. When the time came to build the second Potato Factory she would boast that her beer was made from the finest hops and malt available, and brewed from the purest mountain water in the world.

If the association with the humble potato was a peculiar inheritance for a beer of quality this did not occur to Mary. While she had a very tidy mind she was still a creature of intuition, and she did what felt right to her even when logic might suggest she do otherwise. Mary was wise enough to know that few things in this world are wrought by logic alone, and that where men are often shackled by its strict parameters, women can harness the power of their intuition to create both surprising and original results.

In her mind Mary saw the chiselled stone of her malt house and the larger building of the brewery beside it with its enormous brick chimney rising above the trees. She would sometimes stand beside the falls which thundered so loudly they drowned out all other sound, and within the silence created by this singular roar, she would conjure up the entire vision. Mary could plainly see the drays lined up around the loading dock, hear the shouts of the drivers to make the great Clydesdale horses move forward, their gleaming brasses jingling as they left the Potato Factory to take her barrels of ale and beer to tavern and dockside. She looked into the bubbling water which rushed over smooth stones at her feet and saw it passing through imaginary sluice gates and along some elevated fluming and into the buckets of a giant iron water wheel which would power the brewery machinery. And sometimes, when the dream was complete, she would smack her lips and, with the back of her hand, wipe imagined froth from her mouth as though she could truly taste the liquid amber of her own future creation.

This world is not short of dreamers, but to the dreamer in Mary was added a clever, practical and innovative mind which once committed would never surrender. All grand schemes, she told herself, may be broken down to small beginnings. Each step she took, no matter how tentative it might seem, would be linked to her grand design and would always be moving towards it, if only a fraction of an inch each time. This was a simple and perhaps naive philosophy based on perseverance, on knowing that the grandest tapestry begins with a single silken thread. And so the first thing Mary did upon leaving the Cascade Brewery was to apply for a licence to sell beer. And here, once again, she had prevailed on the long-suffering Mr Emmett to help her with the recommendations she needed to obtain it.

Mary decided that even though she lacked the resources to start her own brewery she had sufficient to rent a smallish building which had once been a corn mill at the mountain end of Collins Street and which backed directly onto the banks of the rivulet. She named it the Potato Factory and converted it into a home brewery. In the front room she created a shop where citizens could buy a bottle of beer to take home. She used a small rear room in the building as her sleeping chamber and paid one of the mechanics at the Cascade Brewery to construct a small lean-to kitchen at the back. The remainder of the space in the old mill was given over to making beer.

The malt and yeast Mary used were of the highest quality, and she bought her hops from a wholesale merchant who imported it from England, as the product grown in the Derwent Valley was not yet of the highest standard. She made a light beer with a clean taste which was much favoured by the better class of drinker among the labouring classes, tradesmen and the respectable poor, and she soon attracted the favourable attention of the Temperance Society. Temperance members agreed to abstain entirely from the use of distilled spirits, except for medicinal purposes, so the society actively encouraged the drinking of beer, though in the home and not in public houses where, in the boisterous company of fellow drinkers, they might enter into the numerous evils, both moral and physical, which follow the use of spirits.

Her beer did not have 'the wallop' to appeal to the majority of drinkers, but the Temperance movement was growing rapidly in numbers, and right from the outset Mary prospered. She soon put a product on the market which she labelled 'Temperance Ale', and in six months it had become her mainstay. Mary, if only in the smallest way, was up to her eyes in the beer business, and at the same time she was favoured by the authorities for the quality of her product and the prompt manner in which she paid her taxes. There were even those within the third class, the tradesmen, clerks and smaller merchants, who considered that some day she might be admitted into their lofty and hallowed ranks.

But if Mary's great good luck had well and truly begun, the opposite to it lay waiting at her doorstep. Hannah and, eighteen months later, Ikey, were released into the community as ticket of leave convicts.

Ikey barely survived his seven years until he received his ticket of leave. He had neither hate nor dreams but only greed to keep him from despair.

Money had never meant anything to Ikey except as

a means to an end. He played for the sake of the game – money was simply the barometer to show when he had won. He wasn't a gambler, for he figured his chances most carefully, weighing the odds to the most finite degree. Now, with seven years of penal servitude behind him, the game was no longer worth the candle. If he should return to his old life of crime and be caught again he knew he would certainly die, either in servitude or by means of the dreadful knotted loop.

Ikey told himself that, should he obtain the second half of the combination to the Whitechapel safe, he would retire to some far haven where he would live in peace and run a small tobacco business, with perhaps a little dabble here and a little negotiation there. But secretly he knew that he was a creature of London and captive to its crepuscular ways. He had disliked New York, and Rio even more, and judged the world outside England by these two unfortunate experiences. He knew that a return to crime in any significant way in Hobart Town would be both foolish and short-lived. Ikey was a marked man in the colony.

Three years on the road gang and two years thereafter as a brick maker in the penal settlement of Port Arthur, and another two returned to Richmond Gaol had been quite enough for him. His health had been destroyed in the damp road camps and in the brick pits. He had lost the courage for grand larceny, his bones ached with early rheumatism and his brain creaked for lack of wily purpose.

All that was left for Ikey was the determination to get from Hannah her half of the combination to the safe. He would lie in his cell at night and his heart would fibrillate with terror that he should not succeed in this. He knew that Hannah would have the support of her children when she received her ticket of leave, but that he might well be destitute, for he could not hope for mercy from his alienated family. But what Ikey feared most in all the world was not their rejection, or being forced into penury, but that people might see Ikey Solomon, Prince of Fences, had entirely lost his courage.

Chapter Twenty-nine

Hannah received her ticket of leave in early November 1835, with the proviso that she be restricted to the district of New Norfolk, a small country town on the banks of the Derwent River, some twenty-five miles upstream from Hobart Town. Her behaviour as a convict had proved troublesome for the authorities and they wished to remove her from the boisterous atmosphere and temptations of Hobart.

Hannah had objected strongly to this assignment as she was of a good mind to enter her old profession. Hobart was host to the American whaling ships during the season, as well as to sealers and convict transports, and to this itinerant population was added a large underclass of criminals and society's dregs well suited to Hannah's style of bawdy house.

She had pleaded her case to remain in Hobart because of her children, which was not an untruthful assertion. She asked for custody of Sarah and Mark from the orphanage, and begged that they might all be allowed to live with David and Ann, who now resided in the tiny cottage which had once been Ikey's tobacconist shop.

The chief magistrate finally agreed to a compromise. Ann was now fourteen and David sixteen and they were considered adults who no longer required the ministrations of a mother. But as Sarah had only just turned twelve and Mark was ten years old, they were allowed to accompany their mother to New Norfolk.

Being a practical woman Hannah soon enough adapted, taking up with a certain George Madden, an emancipist who had become a wealthy grain merchant, and also acted as a district constable.

Hannah was happy enough to swap bed for bread in preference to finding employment as a servant in the small town and Madden, who had a reputation as an energetic though often difficult man, also felt himself well served. He had gained the services of a skilful concubine in exchange for two children accustomed to life in an orphanage, who knew to stay well away from irascible adults.

Living with Madden allowed for a lazy life and Hannah was content to lord it over most of the locals as a grand lady on the arm of a wealthy and handsome man. That there was a good deal of gossip from the country folk regarding her lewd behaviour troubled her not at all. The people of New Norfolk were of no consequence to Hannah. They were emancipists who had served their sentences on Norfolk Island and later settled New Norfolk, and in the peculiar pecking order of the Van Diemen's Land convict, they were considered below the station of a main islander.

As for the few free settlers in the town, Hannah knew that no amount of airs and graces or playing at the *grande dame* could persuade them to include her in their society. So she made no attempt to enter it.

Besides, New Norfolk was only a temporary expedient forced upon her, and Madden a most convenient happen-stance. She dreamed of securing the fortune which lay waiting for her in the safe in Whitechapel and moving to Hobart Town, or perhaps even the mainland. There her wealth would soon secure good marriages for her two pretty daughters and sound careers for her two remaining sons.

Hannah also knew that sooner or later she would be confronted by the irksome presence of Ikey Solomon. But she comforted herself with the fact that he would need to serve at least seven years before he could expect his ticket of leave. This left her two years to contemplate her future, and to put into place several plans in order to defeat Ikey in that singular purpose which would preoccupy their lives the moment he was released.

Ikey must somehow be lulled into giving her his part of the combination. Hannah knew he would only do this if he felt completely confident about their shared future, and controlled their joint fortune. To accomplish the task of gaining Ikey's complete confidence, she needed to gather her family together and win back the affection of David and Ann, her two elder children. In particular David, who would play an important part in the plan to undermine her husband.

However, there was another reason why Hannah wished to regain the esteem and love of the two elder children still in Van Diemen's Land. She was determined to destroy any affection they might feel for Mary Abacus. Hannah was convinced that Mary had sought revenge for being transported. She felt certain that Ikey's scar-faced *goyem shiksa* whore had deliberately set out to steal the hearts and minds of her children, and turn them against their own flesh and blood.

Of course, this was entirely untrue. Mary was not even aware that Hannah had been the cause of her downfall. But no amount of persuasion would have convinced Hannah this was so. She had brooded on the matter too long, and what she had imagined in the dark recesses of her own vengeful mind had become an unshakable truth. Hannah had also concluded that Ikey and Mary were the collective cause of her demise, and it was a matter of personal honour to regain the love of David and Ann. She vowed to live long enough to punish Mary for plotting against her, and stealing her children's love.

Hannah intended to persuade David to win the complete trust of his father, while secretly maintaining his loyalty to her. After contriving a reconciliation with Ikey and convincing him that they should serve out their old age together, Hannah presumed David would logically be chosen to return to London, open the safe, and bring the contents back to Van Diemen's Land.

To this end Hannah needed David and his sister to settle in New Norfolk. She planned that they would take up a separate residence there so that when Ikey obtained his ticket of leave she would appear to leave Madden out of loyalty and affection for her real husband, and welcome Ikey back into the bosom of a loving and united family.

Hannah immediately set about cultivating the affection of her two elder children, who were frequently invited upriver to New Norfolk. This had not been a difficult thing to achieve. Ann had acted as a mother to young Mark and had always cared for her younger sister, and when Hannah had removed them from the orphanage Ann had been broken-hearted. She persuaded David that they should take the boat to New Norfolk and pay their respects to their mother, so that they might visit Sarah and Mark.

The first visit had been highly successful and was followed at regular intervals by others. Hannah was always sure to pay their two and sixpenny each-way ticket on the boat, and to furnish their return to Hobart with a handsome hamper, its crowning glory being a large fruit cake with sugar icing. She knew this to be a special favourite with David, who craved sweet things.

George Madden, too, seemed taken with Hannah's elder son. Hannah was pleasantly surprised when he offered David a position as a clerk in his grain business. Ann, most anxious to be close to her siblings, had pleaded with David to accept the offer. David, who was too bright for the dullards who were his superiors at the Hobart Water Works, and flattered by Madden's interest, accepted the position with alacrity. David rented the cottage in Liverpool Street, and brother and sister moved to New Norfolk.

Hannah had achieved her initial purpose with a minimum of fuss. There now remained plenty of time for her to win David's loyalty and affection before revealing her grand plan to sabotage Ikey.

But Ikey, as usual, was unpredictable, and he was released not five months after Hannah, rescued from servitude by a high-ranking government official who wished to remain anonymous. The official offered surety for Ikey and the government accepted his bond, whereupon Ikey left Port Arthur where he had served the past year of his sentence. He appealed to the reviewing magistrate to allow him to serve the first three years of his ticket of leave in New Norfolk.

'To live peaceably with my dear wife and children in New Norfolk, your honour. So that we may regain the lost years and grow old in love and kindness to each other.'

The magistrate who had signed Ikey's ticket of leave papers, a man known for his brusque manner, was quick to reply.

'There is much in your record of arrest of this kind of mawkish pronouncement, but very little demonstration of its successful consequence! I trust that on this occasion your high-blown rhetoric means more than the empty words of sentimental balderdash they have been in the past.'

For a moment Ikey's courage returned to him and he begged leave to make a statement. With an expression of deep hurt he offered the following pious testament.

'Your worship, I must beg to defend myself. My record will show that I escaped from custody in England to the safe and welcoming shores of America where no rules of extradition applied to send me back to England. Here I was immediately successful in matters of business but so missed the company of my dear wife and children that I risked all to walk back into the jaws of the English lion in order that we might be reunited.'

'A most fortunate circumstance for justice, but none-theless a very foolish decision,' the magistrate interrupted.

Ikey continued. 'A decision of the heart, your worship. A decision made by a husband and father who could not bear to be parted from his loving wife and six children. I have suffered much for what your worship calls my mawkish sentimentality, but I would do it again if it should put me even a mile nearer to my loved ones!'

'Methinks you might have made an excellent barrister, Mr Solomon,' the magistrate replied, then added, 'Neither fish, nor flesh, nor good red herring!' He looked sternly at the prisoner. 'Hear me well now, Isaac Solomon, I should advise you not to return to this court. My patience is well nigh worn through!'

The *Colonial Times* reported Ikey's little oration and many a tear was shed by every class of woman in the colony. Ikey's testament was held up as the epitome of a husband's love for his wife and children. Officers of the court were never popular, even with the free settlers, and the acerbic tongue of the reviewing magistrate served only to enhance the heroic nature of Ikey's charming speech. Despite his notoriety, there were those in the colony who would forever remain most kindly disposed to a man who could sacrifice his own freedom and welfare for the love of his family.

It was this same reportage in the *Colonial Times* that alerted Hannah to Ikey's imminent return. She scarcely had time to extricate herself and her two youngest children from the home of George Madden and take up residence with David and Ann before Ikey appeared on the doorstep.

Whatever may have happened to Ikey and Hannah in the six years they had been parted, their low regard for each other had changed little. After the initial euphoria of homecoming, much pretended by both, the curmudgeonly Ikey and the vociferous, sharp-tongued Hannah were soon back to their old ways.

621

Hannah denied Ikey her bed either as a place for rest or recreation. This did not unduly upset Ikey, whose libido had not increased any during his captivity. He was forced to sleep in a corner of their tiny bedroom on a narrow horsehair mattress not much better than the one he'd recently vacated in Port Arthur. When their relationship had settled back into their customary mutual dislike, Hannah had forced him from this space as well. Ikey's adenoidal snoring kept Hannah awake at night, so he was banished to a tiny compartment in the sloping roof where his nocturnal melodies had the advantage of rising heavenwards.

Several months went by, though there was not a day among them that was not fired with vitriol from one or both partners. Ikey had somewhere picked up the habit of drinking, without learning the knack of holding his drink. A mere tipple would send him home cantankerous, with the inevitable result of a dreadful fight with Hannah.

The four children kept their own counsel. They were reared as orphans and knew when to keep out of the way. Nevertheless, David and Ann did not take easily to Ikey treating them like children and, what's more, in a rude and imperious manner. Ikey failed to grasp this; as a child of eight he had been on the streets selling oranges and lemons and his father had beaten him severely if he held back a single penny earned. Now he demanded only that David give him a half portion of his salary. He expected Ann, who had obtained work as a shop assistant, to hand over her entire wage.

They found Ikey smelly and dirty and, as he seldom addressed them by their names, they had little reason to feel he cared for them. In fact, for the most part, he seemed to forget who they were, frequently referring to the nearest child as, 'You, c'mere!' The two younger children were terrified of him and fled at his approach.

Hannah had taken David aside when Ikey first arrived and carefully explained the reason why he should always appear to side with his father. David immediately understood the future advantage to him so he readily agreed. He capitulated to Ikey's demands for money, and dutifully took Ikey's side in his parents' frequent arguments.

But Ikey was not an easy friend to make, and he considered his son a fool to be exploited and humiliated. The young man's patience was growing increasingly thin. He had never liked Ikey, but now he found that he loathed him. David warned his mother that, whatever the reward, he could not take much more.

Hannah, aware that time was running out, decided to broach the subject of the Whitechapel safe with Ikey. She cooked him a mutton stew well flavoured with rosemary, and followed it with fresh curds. She then joined him at the kitchen table after he had pronounced the meal much to his liking.

'Ikey, it's six months we've been together.' Hannah smiled brightly and spread her hands. 'And,' she sighed, ' 'ere we still are!'

Ikey let out a loud burp. 'So?'

'Well, we should begin to, you know, make plans, don't you think?'

'Plan? What plans?'

'The safe?'

Ikey picked at his teeth with the sharp nail of his pinkie, retrieved a tiny morsel of meat, glanced at it briefly, then placed his finger back into his mouth and sucked the sliver from it. 'We can't do nothing until I have a full pardon, my dear. It would be too great a risk if we were to be seen to come into a great fortune while we are both still ticket o' leave lags.'

'We could send David to England. 'E could return with the money and purchase property on the stum and to yer instructions,' Hannah suggested.

'And just 'ow would we send 'im?' Ikey asked, a fair degree of sarcasm in his voice. Then he shrugged. 'We are penniless, my dear, stony broke and without a brass razoo!'

'The cottage in Hobart – we could sell it. That would be sufficient with some to spare.'

'And 'ow do we know we may trust him?' Ikey asked.

'But 'e's our son!' Hannah protested.

'So?'

' 'E's our own flesh and blood, and a fine young man what we should be proud to call our own!'

'Is that so, my dear? 'E were a boy when 'e went into the orphanage, and 'e came out a man. But what sort of man, eh? We don't know, we ain't been there to watch 'im grow. What sort of boys do you think come from orphanages then? I know boys well, very well! Let me tell you somethin' for nothin', boys what has been in an orphanage are good for bloody nothin' and not to be trusted under any circumstances.'

'David be a lovely boy, Ikey! 'Ard working and most clever with numbers!'

'I don't like 'im, too clever for 'is own good, and there is much of the weasel in 'im.' Ikey paused. 'It be 'is smile, all friendly like, but it comes with eyes 'ard as agate stones. Orphanage boys be all the same, dead sneaky and not to be trusted at all and under no circumstances whatsoever!'

'Well then, what about John or Moses?' Hannah asked. Her two sons in Sydney had always been a part of her contingency plan. 'They could leave from Sydney, nobody'd know, come back, invest the money like ya say they should, and when we gets our pardon it's happily ever after fer us, ain't that right, lovey?'

'Those two useless buggers!' Ikey exploded. 'Soon as we were nicked they scarpered, gorn, back to Sydney! No stickin' around to bring comfort, or to see if you or I could be assigned to them as servants. They simply sells up the shop,' Ikey thumped his chest several times, 'what *yours bloody truly* bought for 'em in Hobart and buggers off with the money, leaving us to fend for ourselves!'

'That's not fair, Ikey!' Hannah exclaimed. 'They tried to get me assigned, but the magistrate wouldn't 'ave no bar of it. John first, then Moses later, both tried.'

'Bullshit! They didn't try 'ard enough. What about me? They didn't try to get me assigned to them, did they? Not a letter, not a morsel o' concern these six years!'

'Ikey, you was road gang! You couldn't be assigned to nobody now could ya?'

'They could 'ave tried, anyway,' Ikey growled. 'They're no bloody good, spoilt by their mother they was! I wouldn't trust 'em further than I could blow me snot!'

'What then?' Hannah said exasperated. ' 'Ow are we gunna get the stuff out o' the peter if we can't trust our own kind to fetch it? You tell me.'

'I got a plan. You give me your set o' numbers and I'll take care of it,' Ikey said morosely, though suddenly his heart started to beat faster.

'What's ya take me for, *meshugannah* or summink?' Hannah asked, astonished. 'What plan? Let me hear yer plan, Ikey Solomon.'

'I can't tell you, it involves someone what has agreed to co-operate and what must remain a secret.'

'Secret, is it?' Hannah stood up abruptly from the table, her chair scooting off behind her. 'Some person what's secret? You've told some person what's secret 'bout the bloody safe, 'ave ya?' She paused, her nostrils dilating as her temper rose. But when she spoke again her voice, though menacing, remained even. 'It's 'er, ain't it?'

Ikey looked up at his wife in surprise. ' 'Er? What do you mean, 'er?'

'It's 'er, it's Mary bloody Abacus, ain't it!' Hannah leaned forward, pressing her palms down flat on the table, her shoulders hunched directly over the seated Ikey.

'Of course not! Whatever gave you such a peculiar notion, my dear?' Ikey tried to keep his voice calm, though Hannah's presence so near to him was unsettling.

Hannah's eyes narrowed and her face, now pulled into a furious expression, almost matched her flame-coloured hair.

'You bastard! Ya want me fuckin' numbers to give to that *goyim* slut, don't ya? That fuckin' dog's breath was gunna be the one to knap the ding!'

Hannah looked about her for something with which to strike Ikey, and he, sensing it was time to escape, fled from the room and out into the street.

'You bastard, you'll get nuffink from me, ya 'ear!' Hannah screamed after him, shaking her small fist at Ikey's rapidly diminishing back.

626

Ikey made for the nearest public house, ordered a double brandy and found a corner to himself. He had never been a drinking man and a double of brandy was usually more than enough to put him on his ear. But this time the liquor seemed to act in a benign way, bringing back into focus that glorious time when he was a leading member of London's criminal class. 'Practically the Lord Mayor o' thieves and villains. Prince o' Fences!' he mumbled pitifully to himself. It had a grand ring to it. Though now, on this miserable little island, it all seemed to be spun from the gossamer of an excitable imagination.

As the brandy worked its way through Ikey's bloodstream he began to imagine that it *had* been another life altogether. A primary existence, lived before this one of endless misery and despair, where his money had bought him respect and the royal title of thieves. Men had touched the brim of their cloth caps and mumbled a respectful greeting as he passed by or stood beside the ratting ring. Now he was reduced to human vermin, dirt, scum, the dregs of society, less even than the crud that clung to the hairy arses of the settlers who had the nerve to call themselves gentlemen.

And then the fiery liquid began to dance in his veins and Ikey cast his mind back seven years to when, in a flush of foolish sentiment, he had sent money and his Waterloo medal to Mary in Newgate. He'd all but forgotten Mary's existence, and Hannah's reminder had come as a shock. Occasionally, when he had first worked in the road gang, and especially when Billygonequeer had been with him, he would think of Mary with a sense of longing. But it was always in the past tense, as though she was dead, used up in his life. Ikey never thought that they might meet again, and after a while Mary had simply come closest to the words '*To my one and only blue dove,*' which were inscribed about the circle of roses surrounding two blue doves tattooed on his scrawny upper arm. The brandy in Ikey's blood settled into a mellow fluidity, and he grew sentimental, imagining what it might be like if he should find Mary again.

But at this point he made the fatal error of ordering a second glass of the fiery grape. The moment of sentimentality soon passed, and was replaced with an unreasoning rage. Stumbling home Ikey proceeded to yell violent obscenities until Hannah, David, Ann and Sarah collectively surrounded him. But after four years on a road gang cart, the former weakling was greatly increased in strength and each of them received several bony blows from Ikey's elbows before he was finally subdued.

Young Mark took off with great speed and shortly afterwards returned with George Madden who, acting in his capacity as a constable, arrested Ikey and locked him in the gaol house. Here Ikey shouted and screamed all night, cursing the perfidy of his family, with particular reference to the sexual prowess of 'the grand whore to whom I have the misfortune to be married'.

The police lock-up stood only a few yards from a public house. Ikey's boisterous remarks carried clearly into the street and quickly attracted the drinkers inside. Soon a fair crowd had gathered. By morning the small town of New Norfolk was agog with the whispered tales of Ikey's night in gaol. Ikey's family had finally had enough, and David caused him to be brought before the deputy police magistrate, where he was charged with drunkenness and violent conduct.

The case must have seemed clear enough to blind Freddy. But such is the nature of small towns, and so deep was the resentment held by the good burghers over Hannah's adultery with George Madden and, perhaps more precisely, her subsequent snooty behaviour towards all, that the charges were dismissed. The deputy police magistrate ruled that equal blame was attached to both parties. He warned both husband and wife that should such disorderly proceedings be repeated they would be returned to prison. Then, to the chagrin of some, and great amusement of most, he charged the assistant district constable, George Madden, to keep an eye on both husband and wife.

With the protection of George Madden, Hannah and David could do more or less as they wished and they lost no time in reducing Ikey to a most perilous state. He was unable to obtain work of any sort, though in this endeavour he did not seem to try very hard, and a word from the wealthy and influential Madden put a stop to any employer hiring him. David had also spread the word around that Ikey cheated at cribbage, which was true enough, so that there were none who would play with him, and this dried up Ikey's traditional source of drinking money.

Finally a desperate Ikey was provoked into prosecuting his wife. The deputy district magistrate, not at all pleased with the return of the miscreant couple to his court, to the delight of the townsfolk, brought in a verdict that the charge of disorderly conduct and the use of obscene language was proved. He ordered that Hannah be returned to the Female Factory for a period of three months.

After many such disputes, the authorities became

thoroughly disenchanted with 'The tribe of Solomon' as the chief probationary officer was wont to call Ikey's family. After some interdepartmental discussion, the authorities made one final ruling. The family should attempt a reconciliation in New Norfolk. But, if this should not come about, either husband or wife, but not both, must move to Hobart Town, with or without the remainder of the family. Having moved, they would not be permitted to return to New Norfolk until they received a conditional pardon. The authorities saw this as a clause so onerous that the quarrelsome couple would make every possible effort to reconcile their differences.

But, of course, no such thing happened. At first Hannah tried to persuade George Madden to move to Hobart, but he refused. He had obtained a five-year contract from Peter Degraves of the Cascade Brewery for the excellent barley grown in the area which would allow him to build his own mill. Hannah, faced with this logic, was forced to capitulate. Somehow she must force Ikey to move to Hobart, and in this endeavour she received the full co-operation of her family.

With no recourse to the law, Ikey was a doomed man. Hannah ordered him out of the house first thing each morning and he was not allowed to enter it again until curfew in the evening. His only sustenance was a small plate of boiled potatoes, and no member of the family would deign to talk to him.

Each day Ikey became more of the vagabond. His bald pate went unprotected from the sun and the unkempt hair either side of it now fell to his shoulders. Somewhere he had acquired a great coat which he tied about his waist with coarse string. This ragged garment served him in appearance as his splendid bespoke great coat had once served him in England. But whereas a glance at the greasy original would have revealed the quality of the wool and sound workmanship beneath the dirt, this equally dirty coat was poorly made and threadbare. Ikey's yellow London boots now became his prison shoes, scuffed and broken away at the toe.

Ikey Solomon, Prince of Fences, the most celebrated criminal of his time, was brought to his knees, not by the vicissitudes of a prisoner's life, but by the unforgiving judgements of his wife and children.

Hannah was now frequently seen in the company of George Madden, though she had not yet moved back into his spacious home. She waited until Ikey had reached a point of abject despair and then offered him an ultimatum; he must give her the combination and also sell the cottage in Hobart so that David might use the money to go to England to open the Whitechapel safe. But to this she added a new clause. Ikey would not receive half of their shared fortune, but only one-eighth.

Hannah had decided that the entire fortune was to be divided equally between the two of them and their six children. She knew that a one-eighth share of the contents of the safe was still sufficient for Ikey to live in comparative luxury for the remainder of his life in Van Diemen's Land. With seven-eighths of their combined fortune under her direct control, Hannah told herself she was willing to sacrifice an estimated fifty thousand pounds, 'for being well rid of the mangy bastard'.

If he did not agree to these conditions, Hannah told him, he could go to hell. She would live with George

Madden and wait for Ikey to die. Whereupon she would send her sons to England to remove the safe and bring it to Van Diemen's Land, where they would eventually find some way to open it. Ikey knew this threat to be idle, the safe having been fixed into a block of mortar too large to lift and, besides, it was fitted with a German combination lock of the same type used by the Bank of England, and no cracksman in Britain could ever hope to open it. But he was possessed of a morbid foreboding of his own death, and Hannah's willingness to wait until it occurred meant that he might die a pauper, a useless old lag, never able to enjoy the revenge of his wealth.

Ikey knew he should leave New Norfolk and move to Hobart. But he could not bring himself to do so for he lacked the necessary courage to cut himself off from his family. Ikey, the rich loner with a family for whom he cared not at all, was a far cry from Ikey, the poor loner with no future prospects, who lacked the internal fortitude and even the energy to begin again in the chancy business of crime.

Ikey tried to convince himself that Hobart was too small for a fence of his reputation, but he knew this to be only an excuse. His bones ached and the yellow teeth rattled in his head, and he saw death in every sunset. Ikey knew he would not survive another sentence. Fear gripped at his bowels and sucked the marrow of resolve from his bones, until it was better to get drunk than to think at all.

Sometimes, when the sun shone brightly and warmed his creaking bones, Ikey would consider his prospects in a more sober frame of mind. He could go kosher, that is to say, above board and respectable, a small businessman, perhaps a return to his tobacco shop. The sale of the cottage would supply the capital needed. But he knew in his heart that this was simply a quicker and quieter way to die.

Ikey loved the nocturnal life, the whispers and the knowing looks of criminal intrigue, the hard-eyed bargaining, the joy of a deal well struck and the satisfaction of a neatly laid-out ledger which marked in numbers the progress of his private war against those who would bring him undone. He thought of himself as the enemy, and expected to be taken seriously by the rich and mighty. He was the destructive element in a world carefully constructed to benefit the self-serving better classes. Ikey had beaten the law dozens of times in a system that thought nothing of hanging a boy for stealing twopence. And now the same system had beaten him, not with imprisonment, but by stealing his courage. Ikey knew that, without courage, there is no luck and no hope. He who dares, wins. For him to become a respectable small businessman on an island steeped in the blood and sorrow of the outrageous system against which he had always pitted his cunning and his wits would be the greatest defeat of all.

Ikey needed the fortune which lay in the Whitechapel safe to publicly proclaim the victory of his salvaged wealth. He knew he had been defeated. But the money he had stolen would at least allow him to flaunt his pyrrhic victory and so hide the immensity of that defeat, whereas meek respectability would forever emphasise his complete destruction.

This was the state of Ikey Solomon in October 1837 when he sat alone on the banks of the Derwent River watching a cormorant on a rock some distance off, its wet wings opened wide to the heat of the late morning sun.

'Mr Solomon?' The voice of a small boy came from behind him.

Ikey turned to see an urchin of about twelve standing a few feet to his left. The Ikey of old would have long since sensed the approach.

'Mr Ikey Solomon?' the boy repeated.

'You knows it's me, boy, so why does you ask?' Ikey said gruffly.

'I was told I must,' the boy replied.

'Told was you? And who might it be what told you?'

'I runs errands, sir,'

'Runs errands?' Ikey's voice changed to a more friendly tone. 'A working boy, a respectable boy, a boy what's not footloose and up to no good!' Ikey held a dirty hand out in the direction of the boy. 'Ah, I don't believe we 'as been introduced, my dear.'

'I knows who you is,' the urchin said, not taking Ikey's hand and seeing no reason to proffer his own or give Ikey his name.

'Ha! So you knows who I is. But you *asks* who I is. Is that not a curious thing to do? Askin' and knowin'?' Ikey returned his hand to his side.

'Them what give me the letter said I must ask first.'

Ikey's eyebrows arched in surprise. 'A letter! You 'as a letter for Ikey Solomon? I don't recall as I've 'ad a letter recently. Would you 'ave it in mind to tell me who gave you this precious letter?'

'Why?' the boy asked. Ikey immediately marked him as intelligent, a rare enough occurrence among the dull-brained urchins who roamed the streets of New Norfolk throwing stones at dogs and chickens.

'A very good question, my dear! An excellent and most perspicacious question! You see, my dear, there are some letters you will receive in life what are not to your advantage, a letter, for instance, what might contain a summons or a warrant. A letter is not always best opened or even received, if you takes my meaning.'

'I've never 'ad a letter,' the boy replied, unimpressed by this first cautionary lesson in life.

'That's a bloomin' shame, boy!'

'Not if you can't read, it ain't,' the urchin shot back.

What a waste of a boy! Ikey thought. How well this one would have done at the Academy of Light Fingers.

'Who? Who was it gave you the letter what I might take, or I might not? Being as I might be Mr Isaac Solomon, and yet I might decide not to be!'

'It come off a boat from 'Obart. The cap'n. 'E asks if I knows you and when I does 'e give me an 'apenny and . . .' the boy dug into the interior of his shirt and produced an envelope, '. . . 'e give me this 'ere letter.'

'What does it say on the envelope?' Ikey asked.

The boy shrugged. 'I already told you, I don't do no readin'.' He took two steps closer to the seated Ikey and proffered the envelope.

'Well that be another shame, boy, a bright lad like you what can't read? Tut, tut, must learn to read, boy. There are no prospects for a lad what can't read, no prospects whatsoever, and never to be 'eard of!' He glanced up at the urchin. 'Do you hear me, boy?'

'Don't you want your letter?' the urchin said and then added, 'I ain't no toff what needs to learn to read.'

Ikey still refrained from taking the letter. 'Can you count, boy?' It had been several days since he had sustained any sort of conversation, and the bright morning sun had ironed out some of his aches and pains, and it was like old times talking to the urchin standing beside him.

'Yessir, I can count real good.'

'Pennies in a shilling?'

'Twelve!' the boy snapped back.

'Shillings in a pound?'

'Twenty,' the boy said with alacrity, then added spontaneously, 'Four farving in a penny and two 'a'pennies, a guinea be a pound and one shillin' and I can count good to one 'undred and poss'bly even a thousand, but I ain't tried yet!'

'Bravo!' Ikey exclaimed and clapped in applause. 'Bravo! Methinks you should still learn to read, but you've got the right idea.' Ikey smiled at the boy. 'I'm sorry, lad, but I 'aven't got a ha'penny nor even a far-thing to give you for this splendid delivery of yours.' Ikey now finally took the letter from the boy's hand.

'That's orright, sir,' the boy replied. Then he cocked his head to one side and squinted down at Ikey. 'You ain't got even a farving, eh?' he asked somewhat incredulously.

Ikey shook his head, ashamed. 'Nothing, lad . . . I'm sorry. Next time I sees you I might 'ave one, or even a penny and you shall 'ave it!'

The boy dug into his trouser pocket and produced a sixpence which he rested on his thumb and forefinger and then flipped high into the air. The sunlight caught the bright silver coin as it spun, arched and descended and the boy slapped it onto the back of his hand and glanced down at it.

'It's 'eads! You lose!' he proclaimed happily. Then pocketing the coin he squinted at Ikey again. 'I suppose you is now gunna tell me you earned your present fortune 'cos you was so good at readin'?'

'Cheeky bugger!' Ikey shouted and made as if to rise. But the boy had already turned on his heels and was running up the steep bank of the river, his bare feet sending small pebbles and clods of red earth rolling into the water below. 'You'll go far, lad, that I'll vouch!' Ikey called after him, laughing.

'Cheer'o, mister,' the boy shouted back. 'See you in the library, then!'

Ikey looked down at the envelope in his hand. *Mr. Isaac Solomon Esq.*, was all it said, in an annoyingly familiar copperplate script. Ikey opened it very slowly, as though it might explode in his hands, and carefully unfolded the note. To his surprise it contained two one pound notes. He held each note in turn up to the sunlight to ascertain that they were genuine, then he began to read.

Hobart Town.
25th October 1837

Dear Mr Solomon,
    I have need of a good clerk who can keep an accurate ledger. If such a position should interest you, I urge you to come to Hobart and to make yourself known to the undersigned. I enclose the sum of two pounds to defray any expenses involved.
    I remain, yours sincerely,
    Mary Abacus. (Miss).
    The Potato Factory.

Chapter Thirty

Mary's first triumph in the brewing of beer did not come from the amber liquid itself, although it was conceded by most to be an excellent ale, crisp and clean to the taste and light on the stomach, but came instead from the label she placed on each bottle. As labels go it lacked any sign of the artistic but made up for this with words that caused the Temperance Society to recommend her product to all who had taken 'The Pledge'. Those of her customers who could read took great pleasure in the story on the label, and those who could not would soak the label off and have someone read it aloud so that they might share the exquisite feeling of righteousness it gave them.

Sold into Slavery

'**Tom Jones** is sold into slavery!' said a man to me the other day.

'Sold into slavery!' I cried. 'Is there anything like that now-a-days?'

'Indeed there is,' was the answer.

'Who bought him, pray?'

'Oh, it's a firm, and they own a good many slaves, and more shocking bad masters.'

'Can it be in these days? Who are they?' I asked.

'Well they have agents everywhere, who tell a pretty good story, and get hold of folk; but the name of the firm is Messrs. Rum, Gin & Spirits.'

I had heard of them, it is a firm of bad reputation, and yet how extensive are their dealings! What town has not felt their influence? Once in their clutches, it is about the hardest thing in the world to break away from them. You are sold and that is the end of it; sold to ruin sooner or later. I have seen people try to escape from them. Some, it is true, if they should take 'The Pledge', do escape to find the heavenly delights of Mary Abacus' most excellent and unadulterated Temperance Ale, sold at threepence half-penny a bottle, or threepence if the previous bottle be returned empty.

The Potato Factory.

Mary's Temperance Ale became such a success that the large Hobart breweries decided at once to bring out a version of their own. But here again Mary was not caught napping. With the help of Mr Emmett she had registered the names Temperance Ale and Temperance Beer, and also Pledge Ale and Pledge Beer, so that these names could be used exclusively by the Potato Factory.

This caused great annoyance among the beer barons, and they thought to take her to court for registering a name which they claimed was in common usage. But the advice of their various lawyers was to leave well alone.

The label also caused great annoyance to the local

importers of rum, gin, brandy and sweet Cape wine, as well as to the local manufacturers of the various ardent spirits available on the market. But the more they belly-ached, and shouted imprecations against Mary in the newspapers, the more popular her Temperance Ale became, not only among those customers who had signed the pledge and sworn off spirits, but also among those who liked a drop of the heavenly ambrosia as a matter of preference.

There was nothing the common people liked more than a poor, defenceless woman, only recently granted her conditional pardon, winning a point of law against the first raters, the whisky and beer barons, who grew rich on the pennies of the poor. To keep up demand, Mary was obliged to take on additional help. Soon she had three men working for her, as well as a girl of fifteen who came directly from the orphanage and who possessed the pretty name of Jessamy Hawkins.

Late one morning at the Potato Factory Jessamy came to Mary while she was testing the fermentation levels in the hop tanks.

'Mistress Mary, there be an old man what's called to see you.' The young maid looked concerned. 'I told him to go away, but he says he knows you, says he has a letter.' Then she added gratuitously, 'He's most smelly and has a shaggy beard and long hair, but is also bald and wears a coat what you might expect on an old lag what's a proper muck snipe, not ever to be redeemed.'

'Hush, Jessamy, do not speak like that, for all you know he could be a most loving father!'

'Gawd! I hope he's not mine!' Jessamy said, alarmed at the thought.

Mary laughed. 'Old lag what's a drunk, that description could fit half the bloomin' island. So, where be the letter, girl?'

'No, Mistress Mary, it weren't no letter what's *for* you! It were a letter he said he got *from* you. He says he comes because o' the letter you sent.'

Mary's heart started to pound. 'Dirty is he? And ragged?'

Jessamy nodded, brought her thumb and forefinger to her nose and pulled a horrid face.

'It's Ikey!' Mary said and her poor, crippled hands were suddenly all a-flutter, touching her hair, patting her apron, her hips, not quite knowing what they should do next. 'Bring my cotton gloves!' she commanded of Jessamy. Then she thought better of this. 'No, I'll get them, you take him into the bottle room and give him a glass of beer, tell him I'll be along presently.'

Mary removed her apron and ran her fingers through her hair, fluffing it as best she could in the absence of a mirror. Then she found a pair of clean cotton gloves and, with a feeling of some trepidation, entered the bottle shop.

Ikey crouched on a stool, clutching a glass of ale in both hands. He gasped as Mary entered, and his hands jerked upwards in alarm sending half the contents of the glass into his lap.

'Oh, Jesus! Oh, oh!' he exclaimed, looking down at the wet patch on his dirty coat and the mess at his feet. He wiped his hands on either side of the threadbare coat.

'Ikey? Ikey Solomon? It's you all right, Gawd help us!' Mary laughed, the spilt beer overcoming her nervousness. 'You always were a most nervous old bugger!'

Ikey grinned, which was not a pretty sight. Mary had forgotten how tiny he was, and he appeared to have lost several teeth and looked a great deal older than his fifty-two years. Jessamy was right, he stank to high heaven, even by the high standard of stink set by much of the local population.

'Nice to make your acquaintance again, my dear, news o' your remarkable success grows far and wide,' Ikey cackled. He looked around at the barrels of beer, and the racks of bottled ale stacked to the ceiling, as though weighing and valuing the contents to the last liquid ounce.

'Nonsense! News o' my remarkable success goes all the way down Liverpool Street and into Wapping, and not much further.'

'I is most proud of you, proud and honoured and most remarkably touched, my dear, and oh . . .' Ikey dug into the pocket of his coat and produced a pound. 'This be what's left o' the money you sent in your most kind letter, after the boat ticket and vittles eaten and five shillings paid for a week's board and lodging 'ere in town. That is, only until I can get back into my own 'ouse.'

'Change? You giving me change?' Mary looked incredulous. 'My goodness, we has reformed, hasn't we, then? Whatever could have come over you, Ikey Solomon?'

Ikey gave a phlegmy laugh and shook his head slowly. 'I admits, honesty ain't a habit what's come easy, Mary, my dear.' Mary saw that his back had become more hunched, though now he pulled himself as straight as he was able, wincing at a stab of rheumatism in his hip. Then he jerked at the ragged lapels of his coat and grinned, pushing his chin into the air.

'What you sees here, my dear, is a reformed man, honest as the day be long, reliable to the point o' stupidity and a ledger clerk what's to be praised for neatness, accuracy and the most amazing sagacity, experienced in all the ways o' gettin' what's owed to one quickly paid, and what one owes to others most tedious slow to be proceeded with!' He bowed slightly to Mary, bringing his broken shoes together. 'Isaac Solomon at your 'umble service, madam!'

'You'll need to sign the pledge and agree to take a bath once a month,' Mary said, unimpressed.

Ikey clutched at his chest. 'You knows I don't drink, least only most modest and circumspect, my dear! Bathe? Once a month?' His eyebrows shot up in alarm. 'Does you mean naked? No clothes? But, but ... that be like Port Arthur again! That be ridiculous and most onerous and unfair, and 'as nothing to do with clerking nor keeping ledgers fair and square!'

'Once a month, Ikey Solomon!' Mary repeated. Ikey could see from the tightness at the corners of her mouth that she meant it.

Ikey smiled unctuously. 'Tell you what I can do for you, my dear. I could wash me 'ands!' He held his hands up and spread his fingers wide. Mary observed them to be a far cry from clean. 'Not once a month, mind, but *every* time I works on the ledgers, once a day, even more, if you wishes! 'Ow about that, my dear?'

Mary shook her head and then folded her arms. 'Bathe once a month and take the pledge. I smoked you, Ikey, and I be most reliably informed that you has grown fond 'o the fiery grape!'

'Reliably informed, is it? That be most malicious

gossip and not to be trusted at all and in the least! A little brandy now and again to calm me nerves in the most unpleasant times experienced in New Norfolk, that were all it was, I swear it, my dear!'

'Well, then you will have no qualms about signing the pledge,' Mary replied calmly. 'You can drink beer here, and if you works well your nerves won't need no calming with the likes of us, Ikey Solomon.'

Ikey hung his head and sucked at his teeth, and seemed to be considering Mary's proposition. Finally, as though coming to a most regrettable decision, he shook his head slowly and in a forlorn voice said, 'Hot water, mind? In a room what's locked and no soap! Soap makes me skin itch somethin' awful!'

'Soap, but not prison soap,' Mary said, remembering well the harsh carbolic soap issued once a fortnight in the Female Factory which caused the skin to burn and itch for hours afterwards.

Ikey, of course, did not fit in well. He was not the sort to be put on a high stool with a green eyeshade to labour at ledgers while the sun shone brightly. Sunshine was a most abhorrent spectre for Ikey and had been one of the more difficult aspects of his imprisonment. Daylight was a time when Ikey's internal clock ran down, and Mary soon realised this.

After Ikey had bathed and signed the pledge, she had taken him to Thos Hopkins the tailor. Now everyone, even the most ignorant, knows that 'Thos' stands for Thomas at his christening, so that he was forced to spend his whole life explaining that his name was not Tom or Thomas but Thos. He was small and plump, somewhat irritable and a dreadful snob, but a very good bespoke tailor, and quite the most expensive in Hobart Town. He used only the best imported worsteds and demanded three fittings at the very least.

Thos Hopkins had recently signed the pledge and become a most enthusiastic user of Mary's Temperance Ale, to the point of half a dozen bottles taken most evenings. But he soon revealed that behind his snobbish façade lay an impecunious state of affairs, and he owed Mary nearly five pounds in credit. Were it not for the mounting debt he would not have permitted Ikey to enter his establishment.

Mary replaced Ikey's clothes, and had the bootmaker make him a pair of pigskin boots with long, narrow toes which served as yellow snouts in exactly the same manner as the pair he'd owned in England. The coat was made to Ikey's precise instructions. Half a hundred pockets appeared in the most peculiar places, so that the redoubtable Mr Hopkins eventually cried out at the very sight of Ikey entering his establishment. 'Bah! More pockets, I will not tolerate more pockets!'

Eventually the coat was completed and after seven years Ikey was back to something like his old self, which included a return to his nocturnal ways. He would appear at six of the evening at the Potato Factory, just as the other workers were departing, and work until midnight. At the stroke of twelve he would creep away, heading for Wapping and the docks to spend the night in the public houses, sly grog dens and brothels inhabited by sailors, whalers, drunks, thieves and the general riff-raff of Hobart Town.

Though Ikey was no longer in the crime business he could still be persuaded to pay out on a watch temporarily loaned and returned for a small commission added. This was merely the business of being an itinerant pawnbroker conveniently on the spot when a drunk or a sailor found himself without funds in the early hours of the morning. More importantly, Ikey now carried a large basket over his arm filled with various types, sizes, packets and prices of snuff, cigars and pipe baccy, and he moved from place to place selling his wares. If there was only a small profit to be made from this trade it did not overly concern Ikey because it gave him an excuse to spend the hours of the night at perambulation. Once again he was a creature of the dark hours.

This suited Mary perfectly, as in daylight hours Ikey proved a difficult proposition. He would argue with the men at the slightest provocation, and had an opinion about everything. What's more, he was a tiger when it came to debt.

A great many of Mary's customers came from the dock-side area of Wapping, the place in Hobart Town where the poor and the broken lived. Customers who required a drop of credit were a frequent and normal part of Mary's life. But Ikey, who had spent his life among the congregation of the unfortunate, had a very low opinion of the credit rating of the poor, and constantly grumbled and groused at the idea of giving them grog on the slate. Sometimes, when they came to the Potato Factory to beg a bottle or two for the night in advance of their weekly wages, he would soundly dress them down. A penny owed to Mary would irritate him until it was paid. While Mary found it difficult to argue with Ikey's diligence on her behalf, she knew how hard it was for many of her customers to stay on the pledge and not drink the raw spirit made by the sly grog merchants which would rot their stomachs, send them blind or even kill them.

Ikey had become more and more fidgety, often not appearing at the Potato Factory until mid-morning, and even then still bleary eyed. Finally, at about the time his new coat had acquired a suitably greasy patina, Mary tackled him as to the reason for his behaviour.

'It be the sunlight, my dear, seven years o' sunlight, too much o' the bright. Bright be always cruel, in the bright light the evil things done to a man is seen to be normal. I craves the dark. What a man does in the dark is his personal evil, what 'e does in the light 'e does in the name of truth, and that often be the most evil of all. People do not see clearly in the light, but they look carefully into the shadows. In the night I am a natural man, given to the feelings of honesty or deception, quite clear in the things I do, whether for good or for bad. In the light I am confused, for the most awful crimes are committed in the name of truth, and these always out loud, in the blazin' sunlight. It is a feeble notion that good is a thing of the light. Here, in the name of justice, property and ownership, poverty and starvation is considered a natural condition created for the advantage of those who rule, those who own the daylight. The poor and the miserable are thought to exist solely for the benefit of those who are born to the privilege.' Ikey paused after this tirade. He had surprised himself with his own eloquence. 'Ah, my dear, in the dark I can clearly see good and evil. Both can be separated like the white from the yolk. In the light I am blinded, stunned, eviscerated, rendered useless by the burning malevolence which blazes upon the earth with every sunrise.'

Mary had never heard Ikey talk like this, and she did not pretend to understand it all. She knew Ikey for what he was, a man possessed of cunning and greed, not given to the slightest charity. But now she became aware that Ikey had always exploited the rich and she could think of no instance where he had profited by robbing the poor. It was true that, as a fence, he had depended on the desperate poor to do his dirty work, but he had paid promptly and well for what they brought him. Even the brothel in Bell Alley had been for the gentry, where he caused the collective breeches of lawyers, magistrates, judges, barristers and bankers to be pulled down to mine the profit of their vanity, and milk their puny loins and their vainglorious attempts to recapture an imagined youth long since lost to rich food and port wine.

And so Ikey had returned to his old ways, and life at the Potato Factory continued without his avuncular interference, but with the advantage of his instinct for a bad debt approaching, and his sharp eye for any unscrupulous trader's attempt to bring Mary undone.

Mary spent the first hour with Ikey each evening before he started on the ledgers, and she served him the mutton stew and dish of fresh curds he loved. After he had wiped the foam from his beard, and in general declared the satisfaction of his stomach by the emission of various oleaginous noises, she would seek his counsel in those matters of immediate concern to her.

Their relationship was not in the least romantic, and Ikey would never again share Mary's bed. Mary had brought him back into her life because she earnestly believed his gift of the Waterloo medal was the reason for her good fortune in Van Diemen's Land. And it was Ikey who had given Mary her first chance at a decent life.

Mary never forgot a good deed or forgave a bad one,

and she repaid each with the appropriate gratitude or retribution. She had always lived in a hard world where no quarter was given; now she realised that an even harder one existed. She had discovered that those who possessed wealth and property were dedicated to two things: the enhancement of what they owned, and an absolute determination never to allow anyone below them to share in the spoils, using any means they could to dispossess them. Mary had not accepted this rich man's creed. She was determined that those who helped her would be rewarded with her loyalty whether they were king or beggarman, while those who sought to cheat her would eventually pay a bitter price.

Against his better judgment she had persuaded Mr Emmett to apply in his own name for Ikey's release and had, through the chief government clerk, secretly paid the bond and secured Ikey's early ticket of leave. In doing this Mary did not seek Ikey's gratitude, but was merely repaying a debt. In offering Ikey the position as her clerk Mary was not seeking to gloat at the reversal of their roles. She was simply keeping faith with her own personal creed.

It should not be imagined that Mary and Ikey formed an ideal couple. They quarrelled constantly. Ikey's imperious ways and scant regard for the proprieties of a relationship where he was the employee often left Mary furious. He was careless about her feelings and often disparaging of her opinions. But whereas the old Ikey may have caused her in a fit of temper to throw him onto the street, she soon discovered that the new Ikey was unable to make a decision. Mary came to see him as the devil's advocate, useful for his incisive mind but now without the courage of his convictions.

Mary was growing in prosperity and she soon had the money to construct a water-powered mill and malt house on her land at Strickland Falls on the slope of Mount Wellington. Although she was still a long way from owning her own brewery, she already sold her high-quality barley mash and malt to some of the smaller breweries, as well as using her superior ingredients to increase her own output.

To her now famous Temperance Ale she had added an excellent bitter, a dark, smooth, full-bodied beer with a nice creamy head when poured well from the bottle. It was rumoured that many of the island's nobs and pure merinos would send their servants to purchase her excellent bitter ale for their breakfast table. This new beer came in a distinctive green bottle and, in marked contrast to the verbosity of the Temperance Ale label, had an oval-shaped label which featured two green parakeets seated on a sprig of flowering red gum. In an arch above them was the name 'Bitter Rosella', which soon became known by all as 'Bitter Rosie', and in the curve below were the words 'The Potato Factory'. Underneath this ran the line which would one day become famous throughout the world: *'Brewed from the world's purest mountain water'*.

Chapter Thirty-one

In the general course of events, the meeting of an acquaintance sixteen thousand miles from where you had last known them would seem to be a miracle. But in the penal colonies of New South Wales or Van Diemen's Land, it was a very common experience. The under class of London, Manchester, Birmingham, Glasgow and Belfast were transported in their thousands. Men and women who had lived in the same dark, stinking courts and alleys, who had, as children, starved and played in the same cheerless streets, might run into one another in a tavern crowd in Hobart Town. An old accomplice might tap one on the shoulder and claim a drink and a hand-out, or simply an hour's gossip of people and places known in a past now much romanticised by time and absence.

Ikey came to expect a familiar yell across a crowded room from someone who recognised him from London or the provinces; though in truth, he was previously so well known by reputation that there were some who merely imagined a past association with him. It did not come as a total shock, therefore, when Ikey one night entered the Hobart Whale Fishery, a tavern frequented by whalers, and heard a high sweet voice raised above the noise of the crowd as it sung a pretty ditty. He had last heard that tune at the Pig 'n Spit, and knew at once that the voice belonged to Marybelle Firkin.

> *Fine Ladies and Gents*
> *come hear my sad tale*
> *The sun is long down and*
> *the moon has grown pale*
> *So drink up your rum*
> *and toss down your ale*
> *Come rest your tired heads*
> *on my pussy . . .*
> *come rest your tired heads*
> *on my pussy . . . cat's tail!*

Jack tars of every nation joined in the chorus so that the tavern shook with their boisterous singing.

> *Come rest your tired heads*
> *on my pussy . . .*
> *Come rest your tired heads*
> *on my pussy . . . cat's tail!*

Ikey listened as Marybelle Firkin now added a new verse to the song.

> *Whaleman, whaleman*
> *To Hobart you've come*
> *The hunt is now over*
> *the oil in the drum*
> *So lift up your tankards*
> *and drink to the whale*

Come rest your tired heads
on my pussy . . .
Come rest your tired heads
on my pussy . . . cat's tail!

The notorious tavern on the Old Wharf was crowded with whalemen returned from Antarctic waters with a successful season's catch behind them, and their canvas pockets bulging with silver American dollars, French francs and the King's pound.

The tars spent wildly at their first port of call in months, and the shopkeepers rubbed their hands in glee. But it was at the Hobart Whale Fishery where most of the money was spent. This was the tavern most favoured by the thirsty and randy jack tars, and it was here also that some of the more expensive of the town's whores gathered.

It was almost sunrise before Ikey was able to greet Marybelle Firkin, who loomed large, bigger than Ikey had ever imagined, holding a tankard of beer. Around her on the floor washed with stale beer and rum lay at least a dozen jack tars, quite oblivious to the coming day.

Marybelle Firkin, who now called herself Sperm Whale Sally, put down her tankard of Bitter Rosie and swept Ikey into her enormous arms, lifting him from the ground in the grandest of hugs, until he begged her for mercy.

'Oh Ikey, it is you!' she screamed with delight. Then she placed Ikey down and held him at arm's length. 'You 'aven't changed at all, lovey, 'andsome as ever!' She pointed to Ikey's bald head. 'No 'at! Where's your lovely 'at?'

653

Ikey touched the shiny top of his head as though he had only just noticed the absence of his broad-brimmed hat. 'It ain't kosher to wear a Jew's 'at here, my dear, and I have yet to find another I prefers.'

Ikey and Marybelle resumed their friendship, though in truth Sperm Whale Sally, as Marybelle now insisted she be called, had fallen on hard times. Though Ikey was largely, though indirectly, responsible for this, she bore him no malice. Her involvement on the morning of his notorious escape had brought her to the attention of the police, and the blind eye previously turned to the existence of the ratting den upstairs was now withdrawn. As a consequence the profits of the Pig 'n Spit had greatly decreased. With the closing down of the ratting ring, Thomas Tooth and George Betteridge had taken it into their minds to find another buyer for their Bank of England bill paper, no longer trusting Marybelle Firkin as their intermediary. When the two men were arrested they had named her to place bond for them, threatening to tell of her involvement if she did not acquiesce. At the plea of *Habeas Corpus*, the judge had set the bond very high and when this had been paid Marybelle Firkin found herself under suspicion and at the same time robbed of all of her available resources.

It was not long before she received a visit from a police sergeant whom she had regularly paid to overlook the existence of the ratting ring. Now, after first extorting a tidy bribe from her, he warned that she was about to be investigated by the City police over the matter of the bank paper.

Marybelle had left that same night under the assumed name of Sally Jones, taking the first available boat from Gravesend, which happened to be sailing on the morning tide for Van Diemen's Land. She had arrived in Hobart Town almost penniless, and had found that the only way she could maintain her voracious appetite was to join the ranks of the world's oldest profession. She had soon enough been christened Sperm Whale Sally by the jack tars who came off the whaling ships. She begged Ikey never to reveal her proper name, lest news of her presence in Hobart Town reach England.

'That be my story, Ikey,' Sperm Whale Sally concluded. 'Sad, but no sadder than most and not as sad as many a poor wretch.' She chuckled and placed her boot on the stomach of an unconscious tar under the table at her feet. 'It were pretty bad at first, ain't too much call for an 'arf crown Judy. I grow'd most skinny them first months. Not every whale man likes a four 'undred pound cuddle!' Sperm Whale Sally hooted with laughter. 'It's the 'Mericans what most favoured me, but they ain't always in port. But then, three year ago. I come up with this Blue Sally lark, and now I eats well with a bit to spare for when the whalin' ships be out to sea.' She nudged the man at her feet with the toe of her boot. 'I loves these whalemen, Ikey. They come in from the cruel, cold sea proper starvin' for a bit o' love and cuddlin'.' She started to positively wobble with laughter, 'and I 'as a lot of lovin' to give 'em if they got the stamina to win it!' She lifted her tankard of Bitter Rosie and swallowed half of it in one great gulp. 'Ikey Solomon, we goes back a long ways, it be most lovely to see you again!'

The Blue Sally Challenge was a grand contest known to the crew of every whaling ship that sailed the Pacific Ocean. The Blue Sally was treasured among whalemen above anything else they took to sea, and some of the more superstitious considered it a matter of life or death that the vessel they sailed in carried it flying from the topmast, even though it was nothing more than a modest piece of bunting, a white flag with the outline in blue of a sperm whale stitched upon it. It was common enough in whaling ports around the world for a ship's master or agent recruiting whalemen for the season to be asked two questions: the crewman's share of the catch and, 'Capt'n, do she sail under a Blue Sally?' So important had the flying of the Blue Sally become that a whaling ship sailing into a Pacific port without the blue and white bunting flying from her masthead was the subject of more than a little raucous innuendo as to the masculine nature of the men aboard her.

How this peculiar and unique contest first came about is a story best told by Sperm Whale Sally herself. She recounted it to Ikey early one morning when she was sufficiently sober, having eliminated that night's Blue Sally challenger with such a degree of ease that she was still happily tucking into a leg of pork alone at the challenge table, her opponent stretched out unconscious under it, both arms folded across his chest.

'As you knows, lovey, eatin' is me passion, and drinkin' is me Gawd given gift! So I decides to combine both in a grand competition. If them fuckers won't pay 'arf a crown for me body, they'll do so for me north and south, for me great cake 'ole.' Sperm Whale Sally laughed.

'I needs a story, whalemen being most superstitious and given to legends and the like. So I invents me own. It be a real beauty, lots of adventure and a grand opportunity for me voice, me bein' an actress an' all. I even invents a song what goes with it. That done the trick, the song, the sea shanty what o' course you've heard a hundred times or more.'

Sperm Whale Sally began to sing in the clear, sweet voice the whalemen loved.

> *Come gather around me, you jack tars and doxies*
> *I'll sing you the glorious whaleman's tale*
> *Let me tell you the story, of death and the glory*
> *of Rackham ... who rode on the tail of a Whale*
>
> *So take up your doxy and drink down your ale*
> *And dance a fine jig to a fine fishy tale*
> *We'll fly the Blue Sally wherever we sail*
> *and drink to the health o' the great sperm whale!*
>
> *It started at dawn on a bright Sabbath morning*
> *When Lord Nelson's body came 'ome pickled in rum*
> *Every jack tar mourned the great British sailor*
> *And drank to their hero as church bells were rung*
>
> *I be born to the sound o' the bells of St Paul's*
> *Where they buried the sealord all solemn and proper*
> *That very same day harpooner John Rackham*
> *Rode the tail of a whale around Davey Jones' locker*
>
> *The watch up the mainmast gave out a great shout,*
> *'A six pod to starboard all swimming in strong!'*
> *So they lowered a whale boat, harpoon gun and line*
> *Three cheers for the crew then the whale hunt was on*
>
> *John Rackham, he stood to his harpoon and line*
> *'Row the boat close, lads, 'til we see its great chest*

Steady she goes now, keep the bow straight
Or this great fearless fish will bring all to their rest!'

The boat's bow, on a crest, held still for a moment
Sufficient for Rackham to make good his aim
Then the harpoon flew screaming to carry the line
And buried its head in a great crimson stain

'Steady now, lads, let the fish make his dive
Then he'll turn for the top and the fight'll begin
Ship your oars, boys, take the ride as he runs
For the sperm has a courage that comes from within'

Ten fathoms down the fish turned from its dive
As the harpoon worked in, on the way to his heart
Then he spied the boat's belly directly above him
And he knew they'd pay for this terrible dart!

Fifty tons rose as the fish drove like thunder
Like a cork in a whirlpool the boat spun around
The jaws of the whale smashed through its planking
And the sharks made a meal o' the pieces they found!

John Rackham was saved as the fish drove him upwards
he found himself up on the nose of the whale
With a snort he was tossed sky high and then
backwards
and landed most neatly on the great creature's tail

'Let me live! Master Whale, I've a child to be born!
Spare my life and I promise to name it for you!'
'That's a fanciful tale,' cried the furious whale
'But how can I know what you say will be true?'

John Rackham he pondered then started to smile
'Not only its name, but its soul to you too!
And we'll make a white flag with your picture upon it
A great sperm whale emblazoned in blue!'

The great fish turned and swam straight to the ship
With a flick of his tail threw him safe in a sail
Then the deadly dart finally pierced his great heart
Now we fly the Blue Sally to honour the whale!

So take up your doxy and drink down your ale
And dance a fine jig to a fine fishy tale
We'll fly the Blue Sally wherever we sail
and drink to the health o' the great sperm whale!

Sperm Whale Sally started to laugh. 'It were the song and the story. Some likes the song and others the story. Whalemen loves to dance a jig and sing a shanty and they loves a good story too, and so I made 'em two o' the very best I could!'

Sperm Whale Sally always told the story with the utmost sincerity so that the whalemen, anxious for a new sea legend, wanted to believe it and many of them did. Sperm Whale Sally never told the story without singing the song about her dearest papa, whaleman John Rackham, and how he had been nearly killed and then saved by a great sperm whale while hunting in Antarctic waters on the same day that she had been born and Lord Nelson was brought back to England from Cape Trafalgar in Spain, his body pickled in rum to preserve it.

Though Sperm Whale Sally had been born a normal size baby, she immediately started to grow at an alarming rate, and she needed the breasts of four wet nurses to keep her satisfied. Her concerned mother took her to see a Romany woman who told her that she saw death and life in the form of a great fish. That the fish was her child's birth sign and it had stolen her spirit and exchanged it for its own, so she had a whale as a child, which would continue to grow, and nothing could stop her.

The gypsy prophesied that one day 'the child of the Great Fish' would return to the hunting grounds where the nearest of all fish were to be found. That her fish spirit, looking to find its natural home so that her own human spirit might return to her, would guide the hunters in their quest for the whale. But this only if there was one among them who could match the strength and endurance of the great female fish, and consummate this by entering her. This man would earn for his crew a talisman in the form of the fish flag. Those who flew it would be protected at sea and have bountiful luck in hunting the great sperm whale.

'Ah, Ikey, lovey! It were a feeble enough legend and a not very good song, both most contrived to begin with, but you know 'ow these things grow with a little bit added 'ere and a bit more there. The first season I were dead lucky, the ships o' Black Boss Cape Town and Tomahawk were the only two that 'ad earned a Blue Sally, though thank Gawd there were a great many others who tried and met with the greatest o' good luck. They took the biggest catches o' the season and not a jack tar among them were lost overboard or killed in a whale boat.'

Sperm Whale Sally laughed uproariously. 'That were all it took! When the *Sturmvogel* and the *Merryweather* come into port flyin' the Blue Sally, the legend were truly born. Suddenly I were the reincarnation o' the great fishy, the talisman, the good luck a whaleman takes to sea.' Sperm Whale Sally's great carcass wobbled again as she laughed. 'Blimey, it were on for one an' all!' She paused and wiped the sweat from her brow and sighed. 'Thank Gawd it ain't stopped since and I eats like a queen, and when the whalin' ships are in I earns sufficient to live well after they be gorn orf again to 'unt.'

The rules of the contest had formed over the years Sperm Whale Sally had been playing it, though, for all this, it remained much the same. The crew of a whaling ship would issue their challenge and nominate their man as challenger. They would pay their dues, half a crown per man on board the vessel, and the master would sign a statement that his crew, or the vessel itself, would meet the costs of the food and the drink consumed by Sperm Whale Sally and her challenger.

It was not unusual for a ship's master to be present at such a contest and it was often claimed that the Blue Sally meant so much to the crew of a whaling ship that some captains would advertise in their ports of origin for a crew member of sufficient size and drinking reputation to join, with an extra bonus promised if he should win a coveted Blue Sally for his vessel.

With the challenge formally made and payment guaranteed, the crew would choose pork or mutton, and the nature of the challenger's drink, this being a choice of rum, brandy, whisky or gin. Sperm Whale Sally's nomination was always ale. The rules required that her drink be matched with a strong spirit and that each contestant drink one kind of drink followed by the

661

other. Thus a pint of ale, followed by a tot of rum, was matched by both contestants drink for drink.

In addition, a roasted sheep or pig was placed on the table together with a barrel of ale and one of the challenger's nominated spirit. The publican, or the ship's master if he'd agreed to be present, would act as the meat carver, drink dispenser and master of the ceremony. His task was to pour the drinks openly so all might see they were not spiked to the disadvantage of the challenger. He would also carve equal amounts from the carcass and add the same number of roasted potatoes from a dish of one hundred equally sized.

Precisely two hours was allowed for the contest and if, after this time, the challenger was not 'under the table', that is to say unconscious, then he was led by Sperm Whale Sally to the beach some fifty yards from the Whale Fishery. This final ceremony was known as 'the Beaching of the Whale' where the victor was invited to mount and consummate his 'taking of the flag'.

Only in this way could a Blue Sally be won for a whaling ship and when the fleet was in, no night passed without a challenger. But when the fleet put back to sea there were very few 'who newly flew the Sally Blue', and many who swore they would return to try again.

There were also a few greatly envied ships who flew a 'Two Sally Blue', a flag which sported upon it two sperm whales, indicating successful challenges on two separate occasions.

And then there were the two vessels, the *Sturmvogel* and the *Merryweather*, who flew the 'True Blue', a Blue Sally which carried stitched against its white background three great sperm whales. Each one had been won by the ship by the two giant men, the negro, Black

Boss Cape Town, who claimed to come from a tribe deep in the African wilderness somewhere north of the Cape of Good Hope, and Tomahawk, the Red Indian, a Cheyenne from the American wilderness. Both men stood six feet and seven inches tall and could not walk frontways through the door of the Whale Fishery without touching the posts on either side.

In the manner of sailors there were some men, big men too, who when drunk enough would challenge the 'nigger' or the 'injun savage', but none were known who had remained on their feet beyond a blow delivered from the giant fist of either man. As winners of the True Blue they were occasioned the favours of Sperm Whale Sally without payment whenever they were in port. Although this had never occurred simultaneously, there was much speculation among whalemen as to what would be the consequence if this should happen, as everyone agreed, sooner or later, the two men must meet in combat.

The whaling season that year was a good one and the ships came into port, their holds fully loaded with whale oil and the promise of a big payout for the crews. The whole of Hobart Town prepared for the windfall of several hundred whalers let loose on the town with cash jingling in the pockets of their canvas ducks.

When the *Sturmvogel* came in on the morning tide and the *Merryweather* on the evening, both flying the True Blue, it was Pegleg Midnight who was the first to alert Sperm Whale Sally as she struggled to alight from a hired landau at ten o'clock of the night when her day began. Among much giggling and moaning she locked her great arms about the shoulders of the diminutive driver who, as she finally alighted, was momentarily obscured, smothered in a mountain of baby blue satin and pink flesh.

'Better stay home tonight, Sperm Whale Sally,' Pegleg shouted across to her.

'What, and starve to death!' Sperm Whale Sally called back. 'What be the matter, lovey?'

'Black Boss Cape Town and Tomahawk both be in town!' Pegleg said.

Sperm Whale Sally looked back at the landau. It took four men to load her but only one to set her down, so she shrugged. The two whaling vessels might be in for a fortnight or more, besides she hadn't been eating much all day, and had already been booked for a Blue Sally contest. And so she laughed and shrugged her shoulders. 'Ah well, may the best man win!' she said cheerily, then made her way slowly towards the Whale Fishery where a light supper of a roast leg of mutton and a dish of potatoes awaited her ravenous attention.

Pegleg Midnight, known by all to be a terrible gossip, was, surprisingly, not yet motherless drunk. Before the evening was an hour older he had caused word to be spread around all the dockside pubs, brothels, cock fights, sly grog shops and gaming dens, that Black Boss Cape Town and Tomahawk would square off at midnight, their prize the singular favours of the giant whore Sperm Whale Sally.

Chapter Thirty-two

Evening has a short stay in Hobart Town, a soft, still light that squeezes in between day and night as the great mountain sucks the last splash of sun into its rounded belly. Far below the wide river lies flat, like a sheet of tin, and the hills on its distant shore grow smoky and vague to the eye. Then night comes quicky, as though there should be a clap of thunder to accompany such wizardry.

It is as if the town sits in the hollow of a great hand which snaps its malicious fingers shut and crushes it into darkness. Voices grow still, dogs cease to bark and the wash of the incoming tide slaps hard and cold to the ear.

And then a silver glow rises across the river and comes to dance upon the fist of blackness and, as though cajoled by the light, the hand slowly opens to the candle of a rising moon. New stars pin themselves to the cold, high firmament and the night in Hobart Town is begun.

Such was the night when Tomahawk, the giant Red Indian, met Black Boss Cape Town in the Whale Fishery for the exclusive rights to the fair hand of Sperm Whale Sally.

Both men were legends in South Pacific and Antarctic waters, harpooners with a hundred and more kills to their name, and each had earned the True Blue which flew with pride from the masts of their ships.

Luck is a curious companion, it comes to those who believe they hold it, and is an elusive servant to those who doubt they possess it. The conviction that luck is your willing partner brings with it a sharper eye, a keener spirit, a willingness to take more chances, work harder, start earlier and work later. Luck bears the nostrils of success, for it can smell good fortune at a distance and leads those who possess it as surely to its source as a Sabbath roast does to the nose of a pious verger.

The men who sailed on the *Merryweather* and the *Sturmvogel* thought themselves blessed with good fortune and so their catches seemed blessed and a cut above the rest of the whaling fleet.

Moreover, the Americans on the *Merryweather* regarded their crew to be of an even higher status than the Danish ship, for it was rumoured that Sperm Whale Sally carried a tattoo on her enormous right breast which bore the name Tomahawk. It had alway been obvious to them that she favoured their man, and therefore their ship, above any other. Now, when they heard that this was not so, that the giant whore had issued a challenge to see who would win her favour, they had grown most indignant and then angry. They were convinced that their harpooner must teach Black Boss a lesson, and establish for all time their supremacy in the South Pacific.

On the *Sturmvogel* a similar dilemma existed. They knew about the tattoo, and reckoned how the Americans, known in Hobart Town as 'Jonathans', would think their man most especially favoured by Sperm Whale Sally.

They were first to arrive at the Whale Fishery, preceded by Pegleg Midnight who hobbled in on his dummy leg playing his fiddle at a furious pace so that almost all turned their heads. Pegleg continued to play until he reached the huge chair at the end of the challenge table and which was known as 'the Whale's Tail'. It was made of solid Tasmanian oak with the scene of John Rackham riding on the tail of a sperm whale, carved into its backrest. It was where Sperm Whale Sally always sat. Another identical chair, adorned with a carving of the Blue Sally, stood at the other end of the table and was known as 'the Flagging Chair', which was where the challenger sat. Pegleg Midnight brought his fiddle to a crescendo before abruptly stopping in the middle of the highest note.

'They be comin'', Black Boss Cape Town and the crew and master o' the *Sturmvogel*, and by all appearances they be most angry!' he shouted.

He had hardly completed this announcement when Black Boss Cape Town's giant body filled the doorway of the Whale Fishery. He stooped and pushed himself through the door, his shoulders touching either side of the door frame. Black Boss Cape Town walked over to where Sperm Whale Sally sat and upon his dark face was a most mischievous and charming grin. Then he stooped, and in a single movement picked her up and swung her around to face the astonished onlookers. Sperm Whale Sally squealed, but when she realised she was held securely her cries changed to delight. 'Goet, goet, much goet, Sperm Whale Sally!' the giant black man announced, and then swung her around again and deposited her neatly back into the chair.

Sperm Whale Sally, somewhat flustered and red in

the face, declared 'I guarantee 'e be a most pleasin' 'arpooner!' and wobbled with laughter. The tension was broken, and those who had come to witness the great bout were swept up in her merriment. Finally she jiggled to a halt and smiled sweetly at Black Boss Cape Town. 'Welcome, lovey, it be grand to see you safe returned! I trusts the True Blue flew true for you and that all your barrels be full o' the good oil?' She turned to the master of the *Sturmvogel*. 'Evenin', capt'n', then shouted towards the bar. 'Betsy, lovey, bring a double pint tankard o' Bitter Rosie for Mr Black Boss Cape Town, please, and a noggin o' best rum for the good capt'n!'

'We have come to fight!' Captain Jorgensen said suddenly in a raised voice. 'But also we must have a condition, if you please!'

Sperm Whale Sally looked up, shocked. 'Fight? What fight may that be then, capt'n?'

Jorgen Jorgensen drew back, momentarily nonplussed, having assumed everything to be settled, and that the idea of the fight had come from Sperm Whale Sally herself.

'You said, may the best man win!' Pegleg Midnight chipped in. 'Black Boss Cape Town 'ere come to fight the injun! They 'as to fight to see what ship lays the top claim to you, to the luck o' the great sperm whale!'

'Fight? For me?' Sperm Whale Sally drew herself against the back of the huge chair and brought both her hands to her breasts. 'There'll be no fights for me, lads!' She shook her head. 'Not on your bloomin' nelly!'

'We must fight!' Jorgensen repeated, banging his fist on the table.

Sperm Whale Sally looked up in alarm at the anger

in his voice. 'Whatever for, capt'n? You both flies the True Blue most proud!'

Captain Jorgensen was not used to explaining himself, and warily looked about the crowded room which had grown completely silent. He seemed conscious that what he was about to say might sound rather foolish. 'We want to have . . .' he paused and lightly tapped his heart with his forefinger. 'We fight for . . . your titty!'

'Huh?' Sperm Whale Sally's mouth fell open. A ripple of surprise came from the crowd and then silence as the onlookers waited for the response. She glanced down at her breasts, touching each with the tips of her fat fingers before looking up at Jorgensen. 'One or both?' she asked.

There was a howl of laughter from the crowd, but the master of the *Sturmvogel* was not amused.

'Starboard only!'

Sperm Whale Sally looked down at her right breast, then at the left one and then back up at the captain. 'So, what be wrong with me other titty?' she enquired mischievously, enjoying the captain's embarrassment and finding it difficult to restrain her laughter.

'Portside belong to Jonathan! *Sturmvogel* wants boarding rights on the starboard titty!' He turned and motioned to a jack tar who stood near to come forward. 'We'll fight the Jonathan injun and when Black Boss Cape Town beats him, Svensen here make a tattoo o' the *Sturmvogel* on your starboard titty.' He held out his hand to the jack tar and the man he'd called Svensen placed a small piece of paper in it. Captain Jorgen Jorgensen took three steps towards Sperm Whale Sally and handed her the paper. 'A picture o' the ship, most excellently drawn, Svensen will make a good artwork of it.'

Sperm Whale Sally looked at the picture of the Danish whaling ship and thought the pretty drawing would look most handsome on her breast. But she did not indicate this to the captain. Instead she slowly undid her bodice and peeled back the material covering the vast expanse of her left breast, stopping just short of the rosy sphere around her nipple. Resting high upon it was a crude tattoo of the head of an Indian chief and the single word, 'Tomahawk'.

Those in the crowd standing close enough to see the tattoo gasped. The rumour that she favoured the huge Indian was confirmed. Sperm Whale Sally seemed somewhat surprised herself at the presence of the tattoo, as if she had quite forgotten it existed.

And indeed she confirmed this, 'Blimey! I quite forgot it be there!' She covered the tattoo with her bodice and slowly did up the buttons. 'That be there since I were a young 'un, long before I come to Van Diemen's Land!' she said to Captain Jorgensen. 'That be there,' she began and then stopped suddenly, and looked up at Jorgen Jorgensen and added, 'I don't rightly remember . . .' her voice trailing off.

In fact she remembered it well. She'd been just fifteen years old, a young actress in a Drury Lane play named 'Trooper of the King', a story about the war against the American colonists. Cast as an Indian maiden, with no more than a walk-on part, she had become completely smitten with an actor playing the part of an Indian guide named Tomahawk. He had wined and dined her in the West End the night after the final performance. They caroused until the early hours and she had been too drunk to remember how or where she had been with him. All she recalled was waking up on a straw mattress in a cheap lodging house shortly before midday the following day to discover her erstwhile lover had departed and left his mark on her young breast in the form of a dark blue and very new tattoo.

'It 'as been there near all me life, capt'n! It ain't got nothin' to do with Mr Tomahawk the whaleman!' Sperm Whale Sally protested.

Jorgen Jorgensen shook his head, plainly not believing her. 'You been smoked, Sperm Whale Sally, we know it be there for the *Merryweather* and the injun savage.' He pointed at Sally's left breast. 'Portside be the *Merryweather* titty, now the starboard for Black Boss Cape Town and the *Sturmvogel*!'

'Three cheers for Black Boss Cape Town!' Pegleg shouted and the tavern resounded with three cheers for the giant black man who now stood with his arms folded, the front of his canvas shirt spread open to expose his immense barrel chest shiny with sweat.

'Oi! Remember me?' Sperm Whale Sally suddenly shouted. 'Ain't nobody gunna tattoo nothin' on me tits, you hear!'

There was a hushed silence and then someone shouted, 'Here they comes! The Jonathans are coming!'

All eyes turned to the doorway of the public house, though most could only see the crown of a top hat, because Captain Alexis 'Blackmouth' Perriman, who led the Americans, stood no more than five feet and three inches. Unlike Jorgen Jorgensen, who wore the clothes of a sailor coming ashore, a rough woollen suit of little style and most shabbily turned out, the captain of the *Merryweather* was dressed in a well-pressed top coat, clean linen, breeches, hose and well-shone buckled shoes. He was also clean shaven, but for a small tuft of dark beard stiffened with whale grease which grew at the point of his chin and was joined by a thin moustache which circled from either side of his top lip to meet the tuft. Within this hirsute oval stretched a small, thinly drawn mouth, downturned, so that it gave the impression of a vinegary disposition. He carried an ebony cane two-thirds as tall as himself with a whale bone carving of a sperm whale at its head, its eyes sparkling with what was claimed to be two blood red rubies.

Despite his appearance, he was a skipper who drove his men hard, was not himself backward in derring-do, and had a record as a whaling captain which was second to none. Following him were the crew of the *Merryweather*, mostly Jonathans, though there were several of the Irish among them. The last to enter the tavern was Tomahawk, the giant Red Indian. His hair was parted at the centre and had been braided in a single plait which fell five inches beyond his shoulders. He was as tall and as big around the shoulders as Black Boss Cape Town but did not possess a similar girth. Instead he tapered down to a slim waist, so that he gave the appearance of being the younger, stronger man.

Black Boss Cape Town carried three black stripes of a tribal cicatrisation down either cheek, and fitted into the stretched lobes of his ears were round discs the size of a silver dollar made of whale bone. In the centre of each was an inset of the outline of the sperm whale with its tail held high, carved of black horn.

Tomahawk wore no ornamentation save for his facial skin, which was completely tattooed with swirls and dots. Of the two savages he had the more fearsome appearance. Moreover, he did not smile as he walked over to the table to stand beside the master of the *Merryweather*. Tomahawk, dressed as a jack tar, folded his arms about his chest and looked directly ahead, as though he were there for the purposes of his own sweet repose, quite alone with his eyes inwardly cast.

Captain Perriman bowed his head slightly to Sperm Whale Sally and, turning, did the same to Captain Jorgen Jorgensen. 'Greetings captain,' he drawled.

Sperm Whale Sally smiled. 'Pleased to meetcha, capt'n!'

Jorgen Jorgensen went to extend his hand towards the American, but thought better of it and withdrew, then he nodded his head and grunted. 'Capt'n.'

Captain Perriman smiled thinly. 'Well, it be a fight then?' It was not so much a question as a statement. 'There should be rules,' he announced.

'Rules?' Jorgen Jorgensen looked puzzled. 'Whalemen do not fight to rules!'

'Aye, well, both are valuable men, captain. I feel sure you would not want your man killed nor even maimed, he be a harpooner be he not?'

Jorgensen pondered for a moment, and Sperm Whale Sally pushed herself up from her chair and pointed at the two captains. 'You listen to me, you pair o' right bastards!'

They both looked at her in surprise, as though they had quite forgotten she existed. 'What be it, woman?' Captain Perriman asked in an offhand and irritated voice.

'I already told you there ain't gunna be no fight and no one's gunna put a pitcher o' his ship on me tits!'

'But it is quite decided, Mistress Sally!' Jorgen Jorgensen replied, bemused by her sudden recalcitrance.

'Oh I see,' Captain Perriman said, smiling knowingly. He winked at the Danish captain and took his purse from his jacket and from it took a ten dollar American bill. Then he walked over to Sperm Whale Sally and threw it on the table in front of her.

Sperm Whale Sally looked at the bill. She might possibly have agreed to the tattoo for such a price but she wasn't going to be patronised by the supercilious Jonathan. Her voice was angry and aggressive. 'Now 'ang on a mo, capt'n! It ain't just the flamin' tattoo! It's me boys!' She pointed to Black Boss Cape Town and then to Tomahawk. 'They both o' them true blues, they both done what's needed, there ain't nothin' more they needs to do.' In a sudden impatient gesture she pushed the ten dollar bill away. 'You can stick yer Yankee money up yer tiny Jonathan arse!'

'My God, I do not believe my ears, a whore who turns down money?' Captain Perriman said, one eyebrow slightly arched.

'Well you 'eard of one now, Capt'n Blackmouth!'

Captain Jorgensen suddenly threw back his head and laughed. Then he took his purse from his jacket and added five English pounds to the American money. 'Be reasonable, Sally. You says you loves them both, but only one o' them be an owner of your titty!' He paused and spread his hands. 'Now that ain't fair!'

'Nobody owns me titty less they pays for it, and then it be only temporary!' Sperm Whale Sally said, eyeing the money on the table.

Jorgen Jorgensen pointed at his American counterpart. 'The *Merryweather* has got a titty permanent and the *Sturmvogel* ain't! If, as you says, they earned a True Blue the same, then we be entitled to one titty each. Now *that* be a fair proposition!'

'No!' Sperm Whale Sally shouted. 'And don't call me Sally, that be the privilege o' me friends!'

'Then will you cross it out?' Jorgen Jorgensen snapped back. He made an X in the air with his fingers. 'Svensen can put an X through that name, then the matter be finished and all's fair and square.'

Captain Perriman banged his ebony cane on the table and pointed to Sperm Whale Sally. 'Oh no you don't!' he cried. 'That tattoo on your portside titty belong to us and we ain't giving it up! No ma'am, not now, not never!' Then he turned and glared at the master of the *Sturmvogel*. 'We be rightfully the best ship, captain, and we aims to stay that way!'

The master of the *Sturmvogel* took out his wallet and threw it onto the pile in front of Sperm Whale Sally. 'You said it don't mean nothing, so now I'm paying you to cross it out!'

'Certainly!' Sperm Whale Sally said reaching over and picking up the ten English pounds, and leaving the American ten dollar bill on the table.

Captain Perriman went to his pocket and produced two more ten dollar bills and placed them on the table.

Jorgen Jorgensen matched him with another five pounds. 'Now we fight!' he said.

At that very moment Ikey arrived, pushing his way through the crowd, his basket bouncing on his arm. Sperm Whale Sally saw him coming and threw up her arms and shouted, 'Ikey Solomon, thank Gawd you come! I needs a spruiker what's gunna stop murder happenin'!'

675

Ikey looked about him and put his basket under the table. 'What's going on? There is nobody nowhere except here, my dear! The brothels are all closed, the cock fight's over early, all the other public houses be empty.' He pointed to the money on the table. 'Jesus! Who belongs to that?'

Sperm Whale Sally shook her head and quickly whispered the story to Ikey.

'Leave the details to me, my dear. I thinks we're going to be rich before this night be out!' Ikey said and then straightened up. 'It's me rheumatism, lift me up on the table please, my dear,' he requested.

Sperm Whale Sally rose slowly to her feet, and picked him up and placed him on the table.

'Ladies and gentlemen.' Ikey paused and grinned. 'That is if any here has the right to be called by either salutation!' This brought a laugh from the crowd and he waited for it to die down then paced the length of the table as though deep in thought. Finally he lifted his head and addressed the crowd.

'What we has here be a puzzlement and a problem, a bedevilment o' purpose and a contradiction o' temperament, what can be summed up and put together as a conundrum what is not easy to solve, my dears.' He spread out his hands and wiggled his long fingers as though they were groping for an invisible object. 'We got two tits! One what's snowy white and t'other what's got an Indian head and Tomahawk wrote all over it!' He paused to accept the laughter of the crowd. 'One what's occupied and one what's vacant! One what's rented and one what's seeking a tenant. And that be the conundrum!'

Ikey paused and pointed to Tomahawk, who seemed

676

not to have moved a muscle since he'd arrived. 'We have here this most honourable Red Indian gentleman by the name o' Mr Tomahawk! And . . .' he pointed to Black Boss Cape Town, 'the most worthy gentleman of African extraction by name o' Mr Black Boss Cape Town. Both is true blue and much loved by our very own Sperm Whale Sally!'

There was a cheer from the crowd at the mention of Sperm Whale Sally's name followed by some laughter at this amorous *ménage à trois*.

Ikey held his hand up for silence. 'Hands up them who wants to see these two lovely whalemen in a contest o' strength for the gaining o' tenancy to the two most beautiful and imposing and desirable areas o' mammary accommodation in the Pacific Ocean?'

There was a roar from the patrons and, seemingly, the hands of almost all the drinkers shot up. Ikey turned slightly and from the corner of his mouth whispered, 'Count the money, my dear.'

Sperm Whale Sally reached over and gathered up the money. She had long since counted it, but now she pretended to do so again.

'We have here some stiff what could be used as prize money if the two captains here agrees,' Ikey said. The crowd roared their approval and he turned to Jorgen Jorgensen and Blackmouth Perriman. 'What say you, gentlemen?'

They immediately agreed and Ikey turned to Sperm Whale Sally. 'What be the wager, my dear?'

'Fifteen pounds English, thirty Yankee dollars, lovey.' It was enough to feed her for several months and she was filled with consternation that Ikey might be giving it away as the wager.

The crowd gasped, it was a huge amount of money, more than double what a crew member received for a season of whaling. Ikey looked over the heads of the crowd until he saw Michael O'Flaherty. 'Publican! Your presence please!' he called.

Ikey turned and addressed both captains again. 'Michael O'Flaherty be as good a man as ever tapped a barrel of ale, gentlemen. Will you accept him to hold your money? If you do not agree to accept the rules o' the contest, then you shall have every penny back.'

Both captains nodded and O'Flaherty gathered up the money on the table. Ikey held his hand up until he had absolute silence.

'Ladies and gentlemen, as you knows Sperm Whale Sally will not tolerate violence.' He pointed to Tomahawk and Black Boss Cape Town. 'And no harm is to come to her true blue lads.' He paused so the full effect of his pronouncement could be heard. 'So, I now announces a grand contest of Indian arm wrestlin'!'

There was a groan from the crowd. Their minds were intent on the idea of a bloody fight between the two giant savages, and though a contest of arm wrestling would decide equally well who was the superior of the two, there is nothing like the taste of blood to excite a crowd.

Captain Perriman tapped his long stick on the table. 'And what about the money?' he demanded.

Ikey shrugged his shoulders and spread his hands. 'Why, my dear, the winner takes all!'

Sperm Whale Sally looked as though she might faint away and standing up shakily she slapped at Ikey's ankle. 'Oi! You gorn mad or somethin'?' she said in a loud whisper.

Ikey bent down so that only she could hear his reply. 'Trust me, my dear.' Then he straightened up and addressed the crowd. 'The winner o' the grand arm wrestlin' stakes all his winnings on the second grand contest o' the night!'

'Two contests?' Captain Jorgen Jorgensen asked. 'Why does not one decide?'

'Two grand arm wrestlin' contests!' Ikey replied, ignoring him. 'But first the rules and conditions! If Tomahawk should win then he will be given a chance to enter a second arm wrestlin' challenge, and if he should win this too, then the *Merryweather* tattoo stays!'

There was a roar of approval from the crowd. It meant that the Tomahawk tattoo would be truly earned in virtuous combat.

'If Black Boss Cape Town wins then we crosses out the tattoo and he may challenge again, and if he wins again then he will have a tattoo of the *Sturmvogel* placed upon the breast of Sperm Whale Sally!'

'And if each should win one contest?' Captain Perriman asked.

'That won't be possible, Captain,' Ikey said firmly. 'The second contest will be followed immediately after the first and will be against the wrestlin' arm o' Sperm Whale Sally!'

There was a moment of astonished silence, then the crowd burst into laughter at such an absurd idea. Ikey avoided looking at Sally so he did not see the look of utter dismay on her face. Had she been an integral part of some elaborate scam where she was required to act out her consternation in order to gull her mark, she could not possibly have performed better. She had trusted Ikey and he had caused her to lose a fortune.

Ikey turned to the two masters. 'Are you agreed, gentlemen?'

'That be most fair,' Captain Perriman, the first to recover from the surprise at this absurd idea, replied.

'Aye, it be right by us,' the master of the *Sturmvogel* said, still smiling at the idea of arm wrestling the giant whore.

'Mr O'Flaherty, will you please bring the stools and table for the contest?' Ikey asked. Then he announced to the crowd, 'Ladies and gentlemen, I shall be running a book, though only for your sporting interest, so that some o' the fine gentlemen here tonight might double their money!' He paused and took a breath, 'It's evens I offers on both contestants!'

What this meant, of course, was that Ikey could make no profit from the betting and this was thought most sporting by all, so there was considerable applause. 'One more detail, my dears!' Ikey shouted. 'I shall be offering twenty to one odds on Sperm Whale Sally, and two to one on whoever wins the first contest! As this contest will take place immediately after the first you should lay your bets for both now!'

There was a general guffaw. Had the odds even been two hundred to one placed on Sperm Whale Sally, only a fool would have ventured a shilling on the likelihood of her winning. But the chance of doubling their money on either Black Boss Cape Town or Tomahawk was a most attractive proposition. It is a testimony to greed that, in a room full of cut throats and thieves, no one paused to suspect Ikey's motives or ask how he would pay his bets if Sperm Whale Sally lost.

Meanwhile, Sperm Whale Sally was quite beside

herself. 'You'll not count me in on the betting, Ikey Solomon!' she said, her voice fraught with anxiety. 'I can't cover no losses.'

'Has I ever let you down in the past, my dear? Have you not profited gloriously in our mutual dealings?'

'Ha! That were before! But now I thinks you've gorn *meshugannah*! We've lost all that lovely money, now you's making barmy bets and I'm gunna end up with some bastard writin' all over me tits with a bloody needle!'

'Trust me, my dear, leave it all to your Uncle Ikey! At worst, maybe a little scratch on your titty. But there be a lot o' stiff to be won.' He paused and added, 'That reminds me, my dear, naturally we goes fifty-fifty with the winnings?'

'What bleedin' winnin's! You just gave the bloody money back to them two bastards!' She stabbed a finger in the direction of the ships' masters. 'You said winner takes all!'

'Only temporarily, my dear. Only for the Irishman to hold so everything looks kosher, above board, and exceedingly honest, and not to be doubted. In truth *our* winnings, my dear? Do you agree, fifty-fifty?'

'Jesus!' Sperm Whale Sally threw up her hands. 'Yes! Fifty-fifty o' fuck all! 'Elp your bleedin' self!' She looked as though she might cry. 'Ikey, how am I gunna arm wrestle one o' them monsters?'

'Now don't you fret, my dear, it be so easy it ain't even a proper scam worthy o' my intelligence!'

The table and stools were set in place for the contest, and the two giants made to take their seats. Michael O'Flaherty was given the role as the referee and the two masters were appointed as judges.

The rules of arm wrestling are universal and simple enough. The first man to push the back of the hand of his opponent to the table and hold it there for a count of three would be declared the winner. Ten minutes was allowed for the two contestants to tune up their muscles by building up a proper resistance against the arms of members of their own crew.

Ikey used the time to make book and as he expected, after each punter had bet on his favourite, he bet his winnings to continue on the winner of the first bout so that not a single bet was placed on Sperm Whale Sally.

Two glasses of fiery Cape brandy were brought and placed in front of Tomahawk and Black Boss Cape Town. Tomahawk had not uttered a word all evening and his silence, contrasted with the ebullient black man, had made him the favourite to win, the strength of silence being reckoned greater than the force of bombast.

Black Boss Cape Town lifted the brandy in his left hand, and bending his right arm showed his huge bicep to the crowd. 'We fight!' he said looking directly at Tomahawk and then threw back his head and tossed down the fiery drink in one gulp.

Tomahawk picked up his glass and for the very first time he looked at the huge black savage seated opposite him. 'You die, nigger!' he said and he too tossed down his brandy.

Black Boss Cape Town smiled and placed his glass down and reached out and patted Tomahawk on the top of his head. 'Goet boy!'

The Red Indian shot up from his stool and grabbed the throat of the huge black man. But Black Boss Cape Town had anticipated the move and his own hand moving from Tomahawk's head simultaneously clasped around the throat of the American savage. Then Tomahawk's left hand, still holding the brandy glass, slammed down on the edge of the table and in a flash the raw edge of the broken glass smashed into the face of his opponent. A huge crimson arc appeared under Black Boss Cape Town's eye as the jet black skin of his face opened up.

Black Boss Cape Town did not appear to flinch nor even lighten his grip on Tomahawk's throat, but his left fist swung around and smashed against the side of Tomahawk's face. A great hammer blow which felled the Red Indian. The big black pushed the table over and raised his boot to kick Tomahawk in the face when he was suddenly jerked backwards off his feet by a huge arm which gripped him about the neck in a wrestler's stranglehold. Thrown off balance, he could do nothing as Sperm Whale Sally's arm tightened about his throat.

'Now, now, there's a good gentleman, we'll have none o' that!' she hissed into his ear. She held Black Boss Cape Town in a lethal grip as the crew of the *Merryweather* hurried to pull the bewildered Tomahawk to his feet. Sperm Whale Sally increased her grip on Black Boss Cape Town and addressed the two startled captains. 'You will have your men arm wrestle or not at all, there will be no fights, do you understand, gentlemen?'

Black Boss Cape Town was near to fainting from the pressure she applied and should he have tried to regain his feet his neck would have snapped like a twig. Both captains nodded and Sperm Whale Sally spoke to her captive. 'Do you understand, Mr Black Boss Cape Town?'

An almost imperceptible sound came from the black man's throat. 'Bring me some sea sponges, Bridget!' she shouted towards the bar. 'And a bucket o' salt water!' She turned to Black Boss Cape Town. 'Sit down, lad, lemme fix your ugly gob!' Then Sperm Whale Sally released the huge harpooner from her deadly grip and pushed him into her whale's tail chair. 'Be there a doctor?' she shouted as she took a sponge from Bridget and applied pressure to the wound on Black Boss Cape Town's face.

It was not unusual for a member of the medical profession, either surgeon or dentist, to be present in a public house. And in a few moments, Surgeon Balthasar Tompkins stepped from the crowd and waddled towards where Sally sat. It was obvious he was somewhat the worse for wear and he rocked on his heels as he examined Black Boss Cape Town's face.

'Horsehair!' he bellowed. 'Horsehair and needle!'

In a few moments his young male assistant appeared carrying a bag and it was he who appeared to be doing all the work. But then he handed the needle and horsehair to the physician, who stitched the wound with surprising dexterity, neatly snipping each knot as he worked.

Throughout the procedure Black Boss Cape Town remained calm, only flinching slightly during the suturing. Finally the fat physician completed the task and Sperm Whale Sally wiped what remained of the blood from his face. It was a crude enough job, but it held well and there had not been sufficient blood loss for Black Boss Cape Town to have lost any of his strength.

At that moment Ikey's small frightened face appeared from under Sperm Whale Sally's Tasmanian oak table and, seeing all was well again, he emerged completely and assumed a nonchalant position.

'The bets are laid. The Indian arm wrestle contest be still on!' he shouted at Michael O'Flaherty. 'What say you, gentlemen?'

The crowd yelled their approval, and the two ships' masters glanced at each other and after a few moments nodded their consent. Ikey breathed a huge sigh of relief. He felt quite weak at the knees at the thought of losing the money.

The two men walked slowly back to the stools. 'To your positions, please,' O'Flaherty called. The Irishman held up a large red bandanna. 'Take the strain. Go!' he shouted, dropping the cloth.

The two men's arms stiffened as they took the strain, one then the other making his play. Pressure was slowly applied which would bend one arm close to the surface of the table while the onlookers screamed their encouragement to the man on whom they had placed their bet. Sweat fell from their faces and chests, and the linen of their coarse shirts was soaked through, but still there was no advantage to either. Sometimes they would rest in the centre, and then one would try a sudden lunge to catch the other by surprise. But while both came close to victory, neither could lay the other's hand down upon the table.

After forty minutes it was obvious that the strength was leaching from both men, though it appeared that Tomahawk was gradually gaining the advantage. The Red Indian was the younger man and, in the end, it seemed he would prove the stronger. The muscles on both their arms strained mightily, and at one point the biceps of Black Boss Cape Town started to cramp and he knew he must surely lose. The strain as he held his opponent's arm was so intense that the blood started to pump from between the sutures on his face and run down his cheek. Then, just as he felt his strength finally deserting him, the Red Indian's eyes suddenly filled with pain as he, too, was gripped by a violent muscle spasm and his huge biceps convulsed and his nose started to bleed copiously.

Still they held on, the Indian forcing the black man's hand almost to the table top, before it would be slowly lifted, each movement greatly taxing both wrestlers. The punters had taken to screaming with each turnabout as though, by their voices alone, they could add strength to the man they had backed.

Finally Tomahawk began to sense he had the black man's measure. The front of both their shirts was now drenched with blood as well as sweat. Beads of perspiration shone in the crinkly hair of Black Boss Cape Town, and the smooth dark hair of his opponent lay soaked against his coppery skin. Slowly, agonisingly slowly, Tomahawk worked his opponent's arm, forcing it towards the surface of the table. Black Boss Cape Town's hand was no more than an inch from the table when he spat into Tomahawk's face.

The shock was so great that the giant Red Indian lost control, and Black Boss forced his hand back to the upright position, and then over to the other side so that Tomahawk's hand was now only an inch from the table on the African's side.

Suddenly there rose in Tomahawk's throat a cry that seemed to come from deep within his belly as the black man's bloody spittle ran down his face. His eyes burned in his head as his hand rose and rose, pushing the negro's fist to the upright position and then slowly down, until, with a second great wail, he smashed the top of Black Boss Cape Town's hand onto the table. It was all over. Tomahawk had won the contest, though both men were too exhausted to lift their heads, and their arms lay limp and useless on the table.

Sperm Whale Sally moved across to where Tomahawk sat and gently raised his head. With a wet sea sponge she wiped his face clean. Then she did the same for Black Boss Cape Town, wiping the blood from his cheek. 'You both true blue, both my good lads!'

Ikey had somehow climbed back onto the table, and now he began to wave his hands and shout until the pandemonium ceased. 'I can't make no payment on the bets until the contest be complete!' Finally the crowd noise calmed down sufficiently for him to be heard. 'Tomahawk be the declared winner o' the first contest, now he must arm wrestle against Sperm Whale Sally!' He turned to the master of the *Sturmvogel*. 'Please captain, move your man!' Ikey pointed at the black man.

'Ikey! Whatever are you doing? These boys be exhausted,' Sperm Whale Sally shouted up at him.

'Yes, yes indeed, my dear, we must hurry, sit, sit, there is no time to waste!'

Sally suddenly realised what Ikey was up to, and as quickly as possible for someone her size, adjusted her massive bottom upon the vacated stool opposite Tomahawk.

'Will you get your hand up now, lad!' Michael O'Flaherty said to the exhausted and bewildered Red Indian.

Tomahawk raised his hand and Sperm Whale Sally

grabbed it and held it steady while both their elbows were pressed down on the table.

'Lady and gentleman, take your positions, please! May the best, er . . . contestant win.' O'Flaherty again held up the red bandanna. 'Take the strain. Go!'

Tomahawk had regained a surprising amount of strength in the few minutes he'd been allowed to rest and tried to force his opponent's hand down in one great effort. This was a big mistake. Sperm Whale Sally's hand dipped and then lowered almost to the surface of the table, but there it held, draining the Red Indian of all his remaining strength, then she forced it back to the upright position and started to push downwards. As publican of the Pig 'n Spit she had been required to stack and lift beer barrels on the full, and her fat was deceptive. She was very strong. What new strength Tomahawk had recovered was entirely spent on his first onslaught and not five minutes later Sperm Whale Sally slammed the back of the exhausted harpooner's hand onto the table.

It was a fitting ending. For generations whalers would tell the story of how the two greatest harpooners in the world had fought for the right to challenge the spirit of the great sperm whale. How after a great fight lasting several hours, between two of the strongest men in the world, the American Red Indian had won over the African giant. Then he pitted himself against the spirit of the great whale and was crushed in less than ten minutes. But the spirit of the great sperm whale would never desert them, nor any of the ships that flew the Blue Sally. But the greatest of the catch seemed always to go to the *Merryweather* and the *Sturmvogel*. Or so the legend goes.

It was all over. Ikey and Sperm Whale Sally had made a killing. Not only did they possess the money from both the *Merryweather* and the *Sturmvogel*, but they cleared nearly twenty pounds on the bets placed by the drinkers. Ikey could not remember when he had enjoyed himself as much, though he was a trifle disappointed when Sperm Whale Sally insisted that they buy drinks for the crews of both ships. Then to much shouting, joshing and general banter, Sperm Whale Sally bared her left titty and allowed Svensen, the tattoo artist from the *Sturmvogel*, to tattoo an X, cancelling the name Tomahawk.

'It be better this way, my lovies,' Sperm Whale Sally announced to the crew members who stood around her. 'Now you both be equal true blue! Both be equally blessed by the great good luck o' the spirit o' the sperm whale!' She paused, for she could see that the men from the *Merryweather* did not look altogether happy with this pronouncement and seemed reluctant to accept her blessing. 'One more thing be essential if we is to repair what happened tonight,' she announced solemnly. 'If you wishes to keep the luck o' the great sperm, you must do the spirit a final bidding.' She looked at Black Boss Cape Town and then at Tomahawk. 'You two must shake hands. Make peace the pair of you! You has broken your luck with your hatred and there is only one way to regain it. You must be friends.' She grinned and waited a moment and then said, 'As friends, together you must beach the whale tonight!'

There was a sudden howl of approval from both crews as the tension between them dissolved and they began to shake hands and drink to the health and happy hunting of both ships. Black Boss Cape Town extended his hand to Tomahawk, who took it and smiled, 'Good man!' he said. Black Boss Cape Town threw back his head and laughed. 'We fight!' he boomed happily, toasting the giant Red Indian.

Sperm Whale Sally took both giants by the hand and led them out of the Whale Fishery and into the dark towards the small beach that lay not fifty yards away.

The moon had climbed to its zenith, a bright silver coin suspended high above the great mountain. A million stars pricked a sky now closer to morning than to midnight. As Sperm Whale Sally sat upon the soft sand, a gentle wave washed into shore and she waited for the sound of it to retreat before she pointed to the giant African.

'Black Boss Cape Town, you be first and don't squeeze me left titty, it be most tender!' She laughed and then turned her head towards the Red Indian. 'You follow quick, Tomahawk. It must be done quick, the one after t'other, so the spirit o' the great sperm whale will reach you both in equal portion, and bring you the same great good luck in the next whalin' season!'

Sperm Whale Sally sighed and lifted her skirts above her gargantuan thighs. 'Jesus, I be starvin' hungry,' she thought as she fell on her back into the soft sand and watched the stars. 'The things a girl has to do to make a shillin'! I hope that bastard O'Flaherty ain't cancelled tonight's Blue Sally challenge, or I'll be obliged to eat both these bloody savages!' She guffawed inwardly at the notion as the shape of Black Boss Cape Town blotted out the moon. 'Oh Gawd, 'ere we goes again,' she thought. 'Lie back and think of a nice little pot roast, my girl!'

Chapter Thirty-three

The scam which Ikey perpetrated on the evening that Tomahawk and Black Boss Cape Town met became quite famous and was known among the local wags as the glorious night of 'Tit for Tat'. This incident had further enhanced the legend of Sperm Whale Sally and made the acquisition of a Blue Sally talisman even more desirable among the men of the whaling fleet. But it also served to benefit Ikey's own career. He was soon invited to become involved in the local gambling scene, in particular, in the sport of horse racing, which was just then becoming popular in the colony.

Ikey could now be seen at the horse races on a Saturday afternoon where he set up in a small way as an on-course bookmaker, but this did not curtail his nocturnal wandering. It was still his custom to perambulate from one waterfront dive to the next selling his tobacco, and he always finished up at the Whale Fishery to spend the last hour of each night in contented conversations with Sperm Whale Sally, happily recalling old times.

Ikey would sip at a glass of well-watered rum and Sperm Whale Sally would nurse her final quart pot of Bitter Rosie for the night. It was a time when Ikey felt almost like his old self, for Sperm Whale Sally never treated him any differently and did not seem to notice or care about his change in fortune. They were two old friends with a common past, content to be in each other's company, whether silent or merry, both calmed by the presence of the other after a loud and tiring night on the waterfront.

At the end of their hour together, around five of the clock in the morning, and with the help of four cellarmen from the Whale Fishery and Ikey's own puny contribution, which consisted mostly of meddlesome instructions, Sperm Whale Sally was lifted and manoeuvred and finally loaded into a waiting cart and transported by her driver Dick Smith to her rooms in Wapping scarcely half a mile away. Whereupon Ikey would make his way up the hill to the Potato Factory where, half an hour before sunrise, he would habitually take the first meal of the day with Mary.

Both Ikey and Sperm Whale Sally, the former as thin as a rake and plagued by rheumatism, and the other grown even larger than she had been on the night of the tit for tat scam some nine months previously, enjoyed rude good health by the standards of the day. They could be utterly relied upon to be a part of every Hobart night, but for Sunday, when the public houses were closed for the Sabbath.

Ikey therefore felt some concern when he arrived as usual at the Whale Fishery at four o'clock on the morning of the third Tuesday in November to find Sperm Whale Sally absent.

'Where be Mistress Sally?' Ikey asked a cellarman named Orkney, who was sweeping the spent sawdust from the floor. The Whale Fishery was almost empty, with only a handful of whalers still at the bar. Four drunken sailors sat slumped with their heads in their arms over various tables around the room, and two lay unconscious on the floor among the spew, piss and spilt ale. Orkney stopped sweeping and looked about the room.

'She be here earlier, guv, but be gorn a good hour since.'

'What, home?' Ikey queried in surprise.

'I expects not, guv, there were no cart.' He continued his sweeping, clearly having no more to add to the conversation.

Ikey walked over to the long bar where a weary Bridget was washing and stacking pewter tankards along the counter.

'Where be Mistress Sally, Bridget?' Ikey asked again.

The barmaid glanced over to Sperm Whale Sally's customary spot. 'Well I'll be blessed! She were there to be sure an' all, I seen 'er meself, I took 'er a quart pot o' bitter not a half hour since.' Bridget thought for a moment. 'Mind, she were off 'er grub tonight, I don't believe she ate more'n a couple o' legs o' mutton. Weren't no whaler gentleman eating neither, she paid for 'er victuals 'erself.' Noting the concerned look on Ikey's face, she smiled. 'Don't fret, Ikey love, she most probably just gorn outside to do a bit o' woman's business, if you knows what I mean.' Then she added, 'I seems to recall she said she 'ad a bit of a stomach ache an' all.'

Bridget took down a small pewter tankard, filled it to a third of its volume from a small casket of rum and then topped it almost to the brim with water. 'Here you are then, Ikey, your usual.' She smiled and in a comforting

693

voice added, 'Now you sit down, Ikey Solomon. Your friend Sally be back soon with no 'arm done I expects.'

Ikey sat in the flagging chair until Orkney had almost completed sweeping the large expanse of the floor. He pushed the foul sawdust into a large pile which blocked the doorway. This was a signal to anyone seeking a last drink before dawn that they were not welcome to enter. A good hour had elapsed since Ikey's arrival, which meant Sperm Whale Sally had been gone at the very least two hours by the cellarman's earlier reckoning.

'She must have gorn 'ome!' Bridget called over several times. Two of the barmaids who had been clearing up the kitchen had meanwhile been consulted, but both confessed they had not seen Sperm Whale Sally leave.

'It be half a mile to Wapping,' Ikey pointed out. 'She can't walk 'alf a mile home and it takes four people to lift her into a carriage, my dear.' Ikey was irritated at their apparent lack of concern. 'You would have seen her go if she'd been picked up by Dick Smith, besides, he always stops in for a pint before they leaves, don't he?'

Bridget was too tired to respond with any further sympathy and simply shrugged. 'She'll be back, I expects.' Ikey rose from the chair and, slinging his tobacco basket over his arm, asked Bridget for one of the lanterns which hung from the wall behind her.

'I'm going to take a look,' he announced.

'We'll be closing in half an hour,' Bridget said as she unhooked a lantern and handed it to Ikey. 'You be sure and bring it back, Ikey Solomon! Leave it at the back door. Mister O'Flaherty will dock me pay if it don't come back, 'e be most strict about not taking down no lamps from the wall!'

Ikey only grunted, upset that they did not share his concern for Sperm Whale Sally. He stepped gingerly through the pile of putrid sawdust at the door and walked out into the last vestiges of the night. It was half past four of the clock, with the sunrise less than an hour away.

The late spring night was cool, as it always is an hour before dawn, and a chill breeze blew in from the hills across the Derwent River. Ikey searched the dark corners and alleys along the waterfront, and checked under the hulls of two fishing boats pulled up onto a slip for scraping. Then he moved towards the small, dark beach where the doxies took sailors for 'sixpenny quick times' and which Sperm Whale Sally herself used for the consummation of a Blue Sally.

The beach was deserted. Ikey's boots squeaked as he trudged along the sand towards a wooden fisherman's jetty which ran some distance out into the river. Even when the tide was in, a small ramp built over a pipeline directly below the jetty provided a dry platform where drunks would sometimes take shelter from the rain. It was not a good place to sleep as the pipelines carried the entrails, fish heads and scales from a public fish market into the cove, and was notorious for the bravery of the rats who infested it at night when the tide was out. Many a sailor or hapless drunkard, falling into a stupor, had woken in the morning to find half an ear or nose missing, or his toes a gory, bloody mess where the rats had chewed through his leather boots.

Ikey stopped just short of the jetty and placed his basket on the sand. Then he climbed up onto the dark platform, which stank of rotting fish. The lantern cast only a small circle of light and he could hear the rats squeaking and see their darting black shadows as they scurried from the lighted perimeter back into the darkness.

Ikey was not repulsed by the stench or the rats. Rats were not only an integral part of the gaming ring, but an everyday occurrence in Ikey's life. In the rookeries of London rats and foul smells were a given, hardly to be remarked upon.

He moved deeper into the darkest part of the jetty so that the light from his lantern cast a wider glow. What he saw almost made his heart stop beating. A dozen rats sat on the giant shape of Sperm Whale Sally, who lay grotesquely huge and still upon the platform. Ikey let out a terrible moan, for he knew instantly that she was dead.

The rats scuttled away as Ikey plunged forward, missing his footing to land on his knees beside the giant shape of Sperm Whale Sally. Overcome with grief, he laid his head on Marybelle Firkin's cold breast and started to wail.

'Wake up!' he called desperately time and time again, shaking Sperm Whale Sally's massive shoulder. 'Wake up please, my dear!' Ikey sobbed wildly, the intensity of his grief totally unfamiliar to him. After a long while, he gradually became possessed of his wits again and he slowly recited the words of the Jewish prayer for the dead, even though he knew his friend was not of the Jewish faith.

Not since the departure of Billygonequeer had Ikey felt such a terrible loss and now he lay panting on the sand, too weak even to resolve to rise to his knees. People are people through other people; we constantly seek confirmation of our own existence by how we relate to others. In losing Sperm Whale Sally, Ikey was losing a part of both his present and his past. Only two people in his life had neither judged him nor made demands on him: Billygonequeer and Marybelle Firkin. They had accepted him for what he was and in doing so they had defined a softer, more vulnerable Ikey no one else knew. Both had given his life meaning beyond sheer greed and survival, and now both were gone. Ikey had lost more than two friends, he had lost himself; the Prince of Fences was finally dead.

Only Mary Abacus remained. Yet Mary, with her thriving business and her ambition, was growing more and more impatient with him. Ikey knew she now thought him an old man who argued too much and who had little of value to offer her.

The death of Marybelle Firkin filled Ikey with a terrible fear. He thought of himself dying, quite alone, with no one to mourn him and not even a minyan of ten good Jews to lay him properly to rest.

It was at this moment of his own extreme anxiety that he heard the mewling cry of an infant. At first he thought it to be the rats grown bold and moving closer, or some creature crying out in the night. But soon it came again, faint, muffled, but close at hand. Ikey rose unsteadily and held the lantern above the body of Sperm Whale Sally. One side of her bodice had been pulled away so that a great breast lay exposed. It was as if she had been in pain and had ripped at her bodice in some sudden agony. Above the surprisingly small areola of her pink nipple Ikey saw the tattoo of the Indian chief's head and the word Tomahawk crossed through with the blue X, which Svensen of the *Sturmvogel* had tattooed to cancel its potency as the symbol of the *Merryweather*.

Ikey now saw that her dress was soaked in blood, and that the pathetic whimpering sounds came from below her blood-stained skirt.

He quickly sought the hem of her skirt and petticoat and gingerly pulled them over her thighs. Something was moving beneath the sodden cloth and, expecting rats, he jerked the material upwards. What an astonished Ikey saw squirming between the gigantic thighs, were two newborn infants. He gasped, reeling back in shock, and it took a moment for him to recover sufficiently to take a closer look. The tiny bodies were sticky with blood, but he saw that one was the reddish white of any newborn child, while the other was black as the devil himself.

Ikey's heart commenced to beat rapidly, thumping in his chest as though it might jump entirely from his person, for he could see that both infants were alive, their tiny fists tightly clenched and their little legs kicking at the stinking air about them. Each was still attached to the umbilical cord, and from the black one's mouth popped tiny bubbles of spittle. Ikey reached inside his coat and pulled out a length of twine and a small knife he used for cutting plugs of tobacco for his customers. He cut the twine into two pieces about six inches long, tied off the umbilical cord at the base of each tiny navel aperture and then, some six inches higher, severed each of the bloody cords with the sharp blade. He had witnessed this procedure in a hundred netherkens in the rookeries of London where birth was often enough a public occurrence, and onlookers were charged a halfpenny for the privilege of attendance. But he was nevertheless surprised at how well he was coping with this startling emergency.

With this messy task completed, Ikey walked to the water's edge and washed the blood from his hands and from the blade of his knife, then retrieved the basket from where he had left it on the beach. He hastily emptied it by stuffing what remained of the contents into a dozen or so of the pockets in the lining of his coat.

The sun had started to rise and the body of Marybelle Firkin was now clearly visible in the dawn light. Ikey closed his friend's beautiful blue eyes. Then he removed the cloth which lined his tobacco basket, picked up each tiny infant and placed them carefully inside the basket.

The moment they were lifted the babies began to scream and Ikey panicked and swung the basket one way and then another as if it were a cradle. 'Shssh . . . shssh,' he repeated several times. But when the crying continued he placed the basket down on the sand and instantly a dozen or more flies settled on the babies, attracted by the blood which still covered them. He picked up the cloth and flapped it to set the flies to flight, then covered the basket. To his surprise, the crying stopped. Ikey hastily pulled the hems of Marybelle Firkin's bloody petticoat and skirt back down to her ankles, and covered her exposed breast with the torn bodice. Then, squinting into the early morning sun, he took up his basket and trudged heavily back along the beach towards the Whale Fishery.

It was completely light when Ikey passed the front door of the public house which was now firmly shut, the last of the drunks and drinkers having been evicted. Ikey walked around the back and left the lantern on the back doorstep. He checked the basket, lifting a corner of the cloth to see that both tiny infants seemed to have fallen asleep, and as quickly as his human burden allowed, made his way up the hill to the Potato Factory where he knew Mary Abacus would be long awake, grown impatient and somewhat cantankerous that he was late.

Ikey tried to picture Mary's surprise. She would, he knew, have cleaned the cold ashes from the hearth, set and lit a new fire and then taken the pot of oats which had been left to soak all night on the shelf above and hung it over the flames to boil. Small beer and a loaf of yesterday's bread would be waiting for him on the table, the meal they shared together every morning when he arrived back from what Mary called his 'caterwauling'. But today would be different and Ikey smiled to himself, not thinking for a moment that Mary might not take kindly to the gift of life he carried in the basket so innocently slung over his arm.

Ikey entered the gate to the Potato Factory and passed down the side of the old mill building to the rear where a small wooden annexe had been built. This contained an accounting office Ikey himself used in the evenings, Mary's bedroom, and the kitchen in which they ate, all facing onto a backyard piled high with beer casks, and which led directly down to the rivulet. The kitchen door was open, and he entered to see Mary stirring the pot of oatmeal porridge with a long-handled wooden spoon.

'Don't turn about, my dear, I have a surprise.'

'Humph! The best surprise you could give me, Ikey Solomon, would be to be on time!' Mary sniffed the air without looking up from the pot and brought her finger and thumb to her nose. 'And the next is to wash! Wherever you 'as been, you stinks worse than ever this morning!'

Ikey ignored her remarks and continued in a merry voice. 'A surprise what is a wish and a desire and a whole life of hopes and dreaming! A surprise what surpasses all other surprises and a delight you never thought you'd experience, my dear!' Ikey started to do a small jig in the doorway.

Mary was not accustomed to mirth from Ikey at such an early hour, and now turned at last towards him. 'Is you drunk, Ikey Solomon?' She placed her hands on her hips, still holding the porridge spoon. 'Surprise is it? No surprises if you please. Sit down and eat. I have a long busy day to begin, while you be soon snoring your head off!'

While she often talked in such a stern manner to Ikey, Mary's remonstrations were seldom intended to be hurtful. She looked forward to his presence first thing in the morning, for he often brought with him bits of juicy gossip passed on by the servants of the pure merinos and the uppercrust in Hobart Town society. Mary had little time to listen to gossip during the day and Ikey often brought her both merriment and useful information.

'Come and see, my dear, come and see what Ikey has brought for you!' The excitement was apparent in his voice as he took three paces towards Mary and then, like a magician at a country fair, whipped away the cloth from the top of his tobacco basket.

Mary reeled backwards, dropping the spoon, her hands clawing at her breasts. 'Oh Jesus! Oh Gawd! What 'ave you done?' she cried.

Ikey laughed and took another step towards her so that Mary now looked directly into the basket. 'This little one be Tommo!' he said, pointing to the tiny pink creature in the basket, then his long dirty index finger moved to the opposite end. 'And this big little 'un be Hawk! A black child to bring you luck and great good fortune, my dear!' Ikey turned and placed the basket on the table. 'What say you, Mary Abacus, my dear?'

The names of the two infants had come to him without any thought, though later he would congratulate himself at the clever notion of splitting the word tattooed on Marybelle Firkin's breast.

Mary was not naturally given to panic and now she again placed her poor broken hands on her hips and looked most sternly at Ikey. 'Ikey Solomon, I hopes you has a very, very good explanation!' she shouted. But while her expression was grim, her heart was beating fast as her mind raced to embrace the notion of keeping the two infants. 'Dear God, how could such a thing be possible?' she said inwardly, her thoughts a whirl of confusion and hope. 'Where? How? Whose be they?' she demanded of Ikey.

Ikey placed the basket on the table and calmly breaking a piece of bread off the stale loaf popped it into his mouth. 'Why, they's yours, my dear!' he said, beginning to chew. He explained to Mary what had occurred. 'Nobody knowed that Sperm Whale Sally were pregnant, my dear, it be possible that she herself did not know,' Ikey concluded.

'Ha! When they find her they'll know!' Mary replied, now somewhat recovered, then she added, 'What about the afterbirth?'

Ikey swallowed the crust he was chewing. Already the terrible private grief he felt at Marybelle Firkin's death was hidden completely from view. 'Rats, my dear, there be scores o' rats by the fish pipe. By now there will be precious little o' the birth bits left. They'll think she been gorn an' haemorrhaged, you know, internal like, and that be the cause o' her death. The coroner ain't going to look too close, she were a whore after all! Natural causes, my dear, that be what he'll say. With twice as much government money to be spent on a double-sized pauper's coffin he won't want no further complications or expenses!'

'She'll be buried proper, Ikey, in St David's burial ground. You'll see to that!' Mary instructed. She ran her hand across her flat stomach. 'But it don't solve nothing. How did I give birth to twins overnight when yesterday I weren't even pregnant?'

'Left on the doorstep, my dear,' Ikey said blandly. 'The men and young Jessamy, they'll stay stum, or even believe it if you say that be how it happened! Plenty o' whores don't want their newborn brats.' Ikey shrugged his thin shoulders. 'You are well known for your charity at the orphanage.' Ikey paused and looked directly at Mary, his scraggy right eyebrow slightly arched. 'O' course, my dear, if you don't want them two, I could always take them off to the foundling home and tell them there what happened this morning.'

Mary gasped. 'You'll do no such thing, Ikey Solomon! That be a death sentence – more newborn brats dies in the Foundlin' than lives to see their first week!' This was true. The first hour of almost every day saw Reverend Smedley officiating at the burial of foundling infants who had not survived their first few days at the home.

Mary had not taken her eyes off the two tiny babies and now she lifted the black one Ikey had named Hawk out of the basket and held him against her bosom.

Hawk's tiny mouth, feeling the skin of her neck against his lips, started to suck. That was all it took for Mary to fall utterly and completely in love. 'Give me t'other, Ikey,' she begged, her voice grown suddenly soft. Ikey plucked Tommo from the basket and laid him against her other breast where he too started to suck at the side of her neck. Mary knew, with a sudden, fierce happiness, that she would let no one take her new-found children from her.

Mary looked up at Ikey and tears gathered in her eyes. 'Thank you, Ikey,' she said tenderly. 'Thank you, my love.' Then Mary kissed the fine, matted hair on the infants' tiny heads and started to weep softly. She carried Tommo and Hawk into her bedroom, wrapped each of them in a blanket and placed them in the centre of her narrow bed. She told herself she must prepare hot water to wash away the blood, and tie down their little belly buttons with a strip of linen, then find two good wet nurses from the Female Factory. But for the moment all she could think to do as she looked down at the tiny creatures wrapped in the blanket was to clutch the Waterloo medal around her neck so tightly that the edges of the small medallion cut into the skin of her clenched fist. She turned to the window where the early sun touched the craggy top of the great mountain. 'Please,' she begged softly. 'Please let me keep them! Let them be mine forever!'

After a while she stopped crying and released her grasp on the medal. In the centre of her misshapen hand was a small cut where the edge of the medallion had punctured the skin, and from it oozed a bright drop of blood. Mary, not quite understanding what she was doing, dipped her forefinger into the blood and then returned to where the infants lay on the bed and touched the tip of her bloodied finger to their foreheads, first Tommo, then Hawk.

'You be my life's blood,' she cried. 'You be my everything, I shall never let you go!'

Chapter Thirty-four

For nearly four years Mary had been processing her own malt in her malthouse at Strickland Falls, crushing and preparing the barley mash using the power from the water mill she had constructed. At last she had the money to erect the first of her brewery buildings and to begin work on the chimney stack which would eventually be required. The chimney needed bricks and the skill of a master builder, so it could only be constructed a small section at a time as money became available. The other buildings were made of stone quarried on her own property. Mary's plan was that one day the quarry would become a small lake to store water for the brewery and lend further beauty to the woodland surroundings.

She still lacked the means to create a complete commercial brewery and it seemed unlikely that she would ever possess them. The steam turbines and huge fermenting vats and giant casks she required to compete against the likes of Peter Degraves' modern Cascade Brewery needed the kind of finance she could only hope to raise with a wealthy partner.

It was not a prosperous time in the colony. Several

of the smaller banks had collapsed and more than half of the free colonists were insolvent. The Bank of Van Diemen's Land would not readily invest in emancipists, particularly women, unless they had assets to secure the loan well in excess of the amount they wished to borrow. While there were private investors which a sharp lawyer might find in England, they usually demanded a controlling interest and Mary was determined that she would never allow anyone to threaten her independence.

The new buildings gave her the capacity to make much larger quantities of beer using the crystal-clear water that flowed from the falls. Furthermore, using time-honoured methods, she knew she would eventually own a small complete brewery which produced ale of a very high quality.

Though Mary was not considered a serious threat to any of the larger breweries, her Temperance Ale and Bitter Rosella had earned a reputation in the colony for their quality and some of the public houses not tied to the mainstream breweries now accepted Bitter Rosie by the barrel, which was a major boost to her production. In the past she had relied on supplying her beer in jugs brought by the purchaser, or in bottles. This had severely curtailed her output, for glass was a scarce commodity almost entirely imported from England.

However, it was through the production of bottled beer that Mary was to make her reputation. Ikey's nocturnal habits and excellent nose for gossip meant he was always the first to know what was contained in the manifest of any ship arriving into port. If there should be a consignment of bottles on board Mary instantly knew about it and purchased the lot before other merchants were any the wiser. She would also buy any bottles the ship used during the voyage, and many a ship's master knew her as Queen Bottle. In addition, any urchin who could lay his dirty little hands on a bottle knew it would fetch him a halfpenny at the Potato Factory.

Soon Mary had sufficient capital to order from England her first consignment of green quart beer bottles, which she used for her Temperance Ale, and so the Potato Factory became the first brewery to offer its product in sealed bottles to be consumed in the home. This meant that working folk, who could not afford to buy beer by the barrel, could purchase their beer not, as was the custom, by the jug, so that they had to hurry home in haste to keep the benefit of its good, creamy head, but in a sealed bottle to be enjoyed at their leisure.

The other brewers sneered at this nonsensical notion. They sold their beer in barrels to be consumed in public houses, and those who wished to take it home could bring their jugs to the ale house to be filled. They felt certain that quantities as small as a quart sold in expensive glass bottles would never catch on with the poor, who were the largest portion of the population who drank beer. They also thought Mary's Temperance Ale label another silly affectation as paper was relatively expensive, and a label on a bottle of three-penny beer was regarded as an outrageous waste.

Although Mary was prepared to take a lower profit for her beer by bottling and labelling it, she would not compromise on its quality. The people of Hobart Town, and those who lived further out in the country, immediately saw the benefits of what they called 'picnic beer', which could be transported in small quantities and drunk at leisure.

People soon realised that while they initially paid an extra halfpenny for the bottle, if they returned the empty for another full one they paid only the usual price of threepence for their beer. Furthermore, if they wished to surrender an empty bottle without buying an additional bottle of beer, Mary refunded the halfpenny they'd paid on the original deposit.

Soon Mary was selling all the beer she could make, and it was only the lack of glass bottles which prevented her from selling more. Thus Mary invented the concept of bottled beer with a paper label to indicate its quality and brand which would in time become commonplace on mainland Australia.

Six years had passed since Mary had been granted her unconditional pardon, and she now found herself welcomed into the society of tradesmen, clerks and the free settlers of smaller means who were collectively known as third raters. As an emancipist Mary rightfully belonged two social ranks further down the ladder. But her great business success, ardent support of the Temperance Society, stubborn courage against the beer barons and quiet manners, together with her charitable work for the orphanage, elevated her to the lofty heights of the third social position in the class ranking of the colony, this, despite the knowledge that she employed the odious Isaac Solomon, whom it was rumoured as common scandal had once been her paramour.

Any other woman of Mary's dubious background would have greatly cherished this unexpected promotion to the better classes. Hannah, for instance, would have made much of the opportunity. But Mary was far too busy to profit from the social advantages of her newly acquired status. This was just as well, for it was soon enough to be taken away from her.

Before long the rumours concerning Tommo and Hawk were spreading among the tattle-tongues of Hobart Town. The very idea that Mary, an unmarried woman, should take in as her own children these so-called twins, said to have been left on her doorstep, and the fact that one was obviously of aboriginal extraction, horrified the respectable classes. The infants had only been with Mary two months when she was summoned to see Mr Emmett at his offices.

She was ushered into his chambers by a clerk, who silently indicated the chair in front of a large desk and immediately left. Mr Emmett was working on some papers and did not look up at Mary, who was uncertain as to whether she should wait for permission to be seated. She thought this most unusual for they had been friends a long time and, besides, he was an unfailingly courteous man.

'Sit down please, Mary,' Mr Emmett said, still not looking up. He continued to write for a full minute, so that Mary could hear only the scratching of the goose-feather quill against the paper and the slow, measured tic-toc of the pendulum from a wall clock to the left of his desk.

Mary sat quietly in the chair with her hands folded in her lap. She was not accustomed to meeting Mr Emmett in this manner. She always accorded him the respect he deserved as a first rater and high official of the government, but their relationship over the years had become a warm and familiar one. Mary was also aware that he took secret pride in what she had achieved and he would visit the clearing on the mountain to watch each new construction. He had been very useful in the obtaining of various licences, and a positive stalwart in her fights with the beer barons and others who did not like to see an emancipist and, in particular, a woman succeed at what they felt was most decidedly the province of a man.

Finally, and to Mary's relief, Mr Emmett looked up and smiled. 'Good afternoon, sir,' she said also smiling. Mary was still a pretty, slender woman, and today she was wearing a neat dress and best bonnet of a russet colour which complemented her lovely green eyes.

'My dear Mary,' Mr Emmett began, 'it is always such a pleasure to see you, though perhaps today is a somewhat less pleasant occasion.'

'Oh?' Mary exclaimed. 'Is there something I has done wrong, sir?'

Mr Emmett spread his hands and leaned back slightly, both gestures intended to relax her. 'You have done so well, Mary, and there are many, even in the government, who think most highly of you. I am sure you know how I feel about your success. We are good friends, do you not agree?'

'I take it a great honour to be counted your friend, sir.'

Mr Emmett cleared his throat and now leaned slightly forward across the desk. 'Mary, you must listen to me. It is not right that you should take these children to be your own. They do not have the right blood and it will turn out badly for all concerned.'

'Tommo and Hawk?' Mary exclaimed in surprise.

'Yes! If that be their names, you must be rid of them!'

Mary had never before heard such a harsh, uncompromising tone in Mr Emmett's voice. 'But why, sir?' she pleaded. 'They just be orphans, there be hundreds like them.'

'They will destroy you! We cannot have it!'

'Destroy me? But I loves them like me own!' Mary cried.

Mr Emmett shook his head impatiently. 'Mary, I will not lie to you, they be of an inferior species and the Lord God would not have us to mix with them. You have seen how the aboriginal people of this island are. There can be no place for them in this society. I beg you to see reason. This child will destroy you and the other, though thought to be white, is, I am told, a twin and therefore of the same stock!'

'Mr Emmett, you must help me please. These are my children and I wish them to be given my name!'

Mr Emmett shook his head. 'You were always of a most stubborn nature, Mary Abacus, but this time I am right! You cannot keep them. Besides, in the matter of a name, it can only be that of their father.' Mr Emmett was not a cruel man, but now he paused and raised one eyebrow. 'And God alone knows who he might be! The children of a whore and a nigger are not to be given a decent English name.'

'If I adopt them they shall have mine, it be decent enough!' Mary said defiantly.

'Should you be married, yes, that might be possible, but you are a spinster woman and the law will not allow you to adopt them.' The chief clerk paused and looked at Mary, whom he could see was deeply distressed. 'Do not try, Mary, it will be to no avail and I would personally interfere in the matter!'

Mary stood up and moved to where Mr Emmett sat behind his desk. She knelt beside him and held him by the sleeve with both her hands. 'Please, Mr Emmett, they be my children. I loves them as though they were my very own flesh and blood. You *must* help me, I begs you!'

'Mary, do not distress yourself so! And please be seated,' Mr Emmett said sternly. 'We are not in my garden now or in the woods at Strickland Falls.' He pulled his arm away, forcing Mary to rise and return to her chair. 'I have consulted the attorney general on this matter. You simply must give up these children, Mary. You have technically conspired in their abduction and, while God knows it is as much a technical crime as real on this island with the mother dead and the father unknown, it is a crime nonetheless. The children are wards of the State and must be given over to the foundling home.'

Mary half rose in her chair. 'But ... but, they will die! I have seen what happens!'

'It is for the best, my dear. You will soon enough forget them.'

'And if I should find someone willing to adopt them?' Mary asked, a heartfelt sob escaping from her.

'What do you mean? Someone to adopt them, then give them over into your care?'

Mary nodded and sniffed. 'I loves them more than my life, sir.'

'Mary my dear, listen to me. They are scum! They will grow to be idiots! You have seen the vile offspring of harlots for yourself, the urchins in the streets in dirty rags, who grunt and snort like pigs, their minds not able to fully comprehend. These two of yours will be the same, even worse. They do not have the advantage of a full measure of English blood, but carry in their veins the instincts of the African savage, and God knows what else!'

713

'Sir, I were meself born o' the poorest class, the hopeless, the scum, as you calls it! I were myself a harlot! You have seen how in the orphanage we have brought children to learn, children what you said was hopeless, was scum, found bright and keen as any other. You said yourself you was wrong!'

'I am not wrong in this, Mary!' Mr Emmett said tersely. 'They were not black! Listen to me, please! There is more to this matter. The coroner thought not to make public his report of the results of the death of the prostitute known as Sperm Whale Sally, but it was his positive opinion that she died in childbirth. These are the two infants, the twins, born to her, are they not?'

Mary opened her mouth to reply and Mr Emmett lifted his index finger. 'Please do not lie to me, Mary. You and I have always spoken the truth.'

Mary sighed and looked directly at Mr Emmett, tears streaming down her cheeks. 'Ikey brought them home,' she said in a faltering voice.

'The morning the corpse was discovered?'

Mary nodded, biting her lower lip. Then she looked down at her hands, which were folded in her lap. Her shoulders shook as she sobbed.

'He stole them, Mary,' Mr Emmett said quietly. 'That is abduction. You helped in the kidnapping of two children and will be charged with complicity. If convicted you will both receive fourteen years!' He leaned back. 'For God's sake, woman, give them up now and nothing further will come of it!'

Mary felt the anger rising deep within her. On the streets of Hobart Town there were gangs of urchins in rags who were treated no better than stray dogs. It was so common to hear of street urchins of three and four years old found murdered having been brutally buggered, that the *Colonial Times* did not even make mention of it. These were the lost children of the island, so low in human reckoning that they barely existed in the minds of the general population. If they survived to the age of eight or nine they became hardened prostitutes, both male and female. Beyond the age of eleven, if they hadn't died of syphilis or some other infectious disease, most became drooling idiots or desperate criminals. Many were hanged before they reached fifteen years of age.

Newborn children, left by their destitute mothers on the steps of the foundling home, died more often than not and this was quietly condoned by the authorities. The King's orphanage could accommodate only a certain number, and was already thought to be a most onerous drain on the government coffers. Now the person Mary trusted more than any other in the world had turned against her, and was threatening her with prison for having saved two such children from certain death.

Mary knew that she was on her own again, that nothing had really changed. Her hand went to the Waterloo medal about her neck, and she held it tightly before looking up at Mr Emmett.

'You are wrong, sir! Ikey Solomon be their father!' Mary heard herself saying.

Mr Emmett's mouth fell open in astonishment. It was such a ludicrous assertion that he could not believe his ears. Several moments passed before he was able to speak. He shook his head in bewilderment.

'Mary Abacus, that is outrageous!' he cried. 'Ikey Solomon is a Jew!'

Mary looked directly into Mr Emmett's eyes. 'Hawk be a throwback, sir, on the maternal side.'

Mr Emmett remained quiet for a few moments and then he threw back his head and began to chuckle. Before long this had turned into genuine laughter. Eventually he stopped, removed his glasses and dabbed at his eyes with his handkerchief. 'And Ikey is the willing and happy father, is he?'

Mary could no longer restrain herself. 'I don't know, sir. I ain't told him yet!'

With this they both commenced to howl with laughter. Mr Emmett was now quite beside himself with mirth, and it took several minutes to regain his composure.

'Mary, I shall speak to the attorney general.' He looked most fondly at her. 'I fear you will suffer greatly in the choice you have made. The respectable class will not forgive you for this great indiscretion, my dear.'

'And you, sir?' Mary asked. 'Will you?'

Mr Emmett looked suddenly most awkward and picked up his quill and twirled it in his fingers. Without looking at Mary he declared, 'Me? Oh I am simply an old fool who is too easily led by the nose by a pretty young woman.'

Mary smiled, though her eyes filled again with tears. 'And if they be proved idjits, Mr Emmett, sir, they will be as equally loved as if they were the brightest o' brats!'

There is not much that can be said about the first few years of a child's life. They all seem to grow alarmingly quickly, and if they are loved and healthy they are usually of a pleasant enough disposition. They are a source of great pleasure as well as of moments of great anxiety when they suffer from the multitudinous childhood complaints every parent must of necessity endure. But the pleasure of infants is only known to those who are with them daily; to others, children only become interesting when they can think and ask questions.

Mary was a dedicated mother to Tommo and Hawk, and the two little boys returned her love with affection and trust. Sometimes, when she was busy at other tasks, the mere thought of them would overwhelm her and she would burst into tears of sheer joy for the love she felt for them. Mary was sure that life could bring her no greater moments of happiness than when the little boys were tugging at her skirts and demanding affection. Had she given birth to them she felt she could not have loved them any more deeply.

From the outset it became apparent that they would be quite differently sized. Tommo, considering his gigantic parents, was small boned and delicate in appearance, though not in the least sickly, and Hawk was large and seemed to grow bigger each day. As a baby Tommo seemed content with the single breast of his wet nurse, while Hawk would take all he could extract from his own and then greedily feed on the remaining breast of the woman who suckled his brother.

Jessamy Hawkins had grown into a pretty young lady, much sought after by young men. But she was of a sensible and independent mind, quick witted and with a laconic humour, and she doted on the two infants. She called Hawk 'Dark Thought', and Tommo 'After Thought'.

Tommo seemed the more adventurous of the twins.

He was always into some sort of mischief and, more often than not, Hawk would be the one caught with his fingers deep in the jam pot after being led there by Tommo. But Hawk questioned everything and, even as a small child, would not be put off by an incomplete answer.

Throughout their childhood they refused to be separated and Hawk sensed the need to protect the smaller Tommo against all-comers, dogs or other children who might want to harm him. Even if Mary grew angry with Tommo for some mischief and he fled from her, Hawk would stand in her way until, impatient and frustrated, she would slap him. The moment she did so, Hawk would stand firm and grin up at her. 'That's for Tommo, Mama!' he'd declare. 'He be punished now!'

Ikey, to his great surprise, confessed to being most fond of Mary's brats, but had nonetheless made Mary pay him ten pounds for each before he agreed to perjure himself by swearing he was their father. He protested that, as the world had never before heard of a black Jew, but with Hawk and Tommo given the name of Solomon, it was not appropriate that they be gentiles. Nevertheless, his conscience would be assuaged, he assured Mary, if she gave a donation of fifteen pounds to a fund created by Mr Louis Nathan to establish a synagogue for the four hundred and fifty Jews known to live in the colony. Ikey was getting older and increasingly he gave thought to his immortal soul. He thought it worthwhile to be in good standing within his faith. The remaining five pounds he wanted for an addition to Sperm Whale Sally's headstone.

Mary had paid for the burial of Marybelle Firkin, alias Sperm Whale Sally, who now rested among the respectable dead in St David's burial ground with both her names on her marble headstone, but she soon enough recouped the money.

Michael O'Flaherty, the proprietor of the Whale Fishery, had opened a fund for this purpose, and every whaleman who entered the port of Hobart in the year that followed had willingly given something towards Sperm Whale Sally's funeral expenses.

Sufficient money was raised to repay Mary and also to erect a handsome headstone made from expensive pure white marble imported from England. In fact, so grand was the headstone that it caused a furore among the church elders and the congregation, who felt it unbefitting that a whore should have a more impressive tombstone than the respectable and pious merchant John Rutkin who had been buried on the very same day.

There were even some who tried to insist that Sperm Whale Sally's grave be moved from consecrated ground, and there was talk of a petition to Governor Franklin, who had replaced Colonel Arthur.

But in the end the vicar, in a stirring sermon, pointed out that within his churchyard lay villains far greater than the giant whore, and that Mary Magdalene had herself been a scarlet women and had received the love and compassion of Jesus Christ. This had silenced the hotheads and, at the same time, caused a better quality of headstone to appear in the churchyard, the respectable classes not able to bear the shame of sealing their dead beneath a less imposing stone.

But despite the grandness of the memorial to Sperm Whale Sally, Ikey, in a rare display of sentiment, expressed his displeasure. He persuaded the stone mason who created the tombstone to procure a slab of rare bluestone and to carve from it the shape of a great sperm whale, and to inlay this onto the face of the existing white marble. Beneath this he caused to be engraved the words:

> So take up your doxy and drink your own ale
> And dance a fine jig to a fine fishy tale
> We'll fly the Blue Sally wherever we sail
> And drink to the health o' the great sperm whale!

It pleased Ikey greatly to know that the Blue Sally would forever fly above Sperm Whale Sally's grave and Mary was happy enough to meet the bill. Apart from Ikey's renewed religious scruples, she understood his sentimental desire to perpetuate in stone the spirit of the great sperm whale so that it might guard the grave of the mother of her two adopted sons.

And so yet another myth was born. At the beginning of the winter whaling season, for as long as men hunted the whale in the South Seas and came into port at Hobart Town, the captains and men of the great fully rigged brigantines and barques and the smaller local bay whalers would gather together at St David's church for a blessing of the whale fleet. After the blessing the ships' masters would pay for a barrel of rum to be consumed at the grave of Sperm Whale Sally. Each whaleman present would take a glass of rum and drink what became known as 'A Sally Salute', a tribute to the spirit of the great sperm whale. Then they would link arms, the Yankees and the British, Swedes, French, Portuguese and the islanders, and form a circle around the grave of sperm Whale Sally and sing the Blue Sally shanty.

This they sang with a great deal more gusto than the dreary rendition of The Sailor's Hymn they had earlier been required to render within the church. It was claimed that there were whalemen who spoke no English but who could sing this elegy to the whale perfectly, having learned it by rote from some old tar during the lonely nights at sea.

Mary nurtured only one great anxiety during the first two years of raising Tommo and Hawk, which sprang from the damning words of Mr Emmett. *'Mary my dear, listen to me. They be scum! They will grow to be idiots!'* She watched them intently in the cradle to see if their eyes followed her or whether they might be made to grab for some object she held or respond to some loving nonsensical sound she made to show a growing awareness. Her fears proved groundless. Tommo and Hawk cried and laughed, slept and ate and fell and walked and played like any other happy, healthy infants.

Mary left nothing to chance, though, and as soon as they could comprehend in the slightest she began reading to them. At four years old they could recite a host of nursery rhymes, the one closest to Mary's heart being Little Jack Horner, for it contained the two things she was most determined to give her children, good food and an education.

> *Little Jack Horner,*
> *Sat in the corner,*
> *Eating a Christmas pie;*
> *He put in his thumb,*
> *And pulled out a plum,*
> *And said, 'What a good boy am I!'*

He was feasting away,
And 'twas late in the day;
When his mother, who made it a rule
Her children should ever
Be learned and clever,
Came in to prepare him for school.

Mary was also determined that their morals should be of the strictest rectitude and they would be most severely punished should they not tell the truth. She had sent to England for a book with the rather long title, *The Good Child's Delight; or, the road to knowledge. In short, entertaining lessons of one or two syllables; Nursery morals; chiefly in monosyllables*. This she read to them so many times that Hawk, at the age of five, could recite the entire book. Others she bought from the Hobart Town Circulating Library, where she drove the stern-faced Mrs Deane quite mad with her requests for children's books. One of the boys' favourites, for they cried at each reading, was *The Happy Courtship, Merry Marriage, and Pic Nic Dinner, of Cock Robin, and Jenny Wren. To which is added, alas! the doleful death of the bridegroom.*

On their cots Mary constructed strings of wooden beads in the same configuration as an abacus, so that their earliest memories would be of the rattle and touch of the red and black beads in their tiny hands.

At five both children were well acquainted with the alphabet and could read well and write simple words upon their slates. Tommo was clever enough but would quickly become impatient, while Hawk seemed much more interested. At the age of seven, when Mary took them to Mrs Tibbett's primary school, an establishment which took the young children of the tradesmen rank, both Tommo and Hawk proved well in advance of other children in their class. Hawk was not only the largest child among his age group, he also stood out as the most intelligent.

Though children are not concerned with colour, their parents soon enough perceived the presence of Hawk and it did not take them long to complain about the black child. Mary was asked by Mrs Tibbett to remove Hawk and Tommo from the school.

It was a fight Mary knew she could not win, and she saw no point in venting her spleen on the hapless Mrs Tibbett, who seemed genuinely distressed that she was forced to make the demand. Besides, Mary felt that the school was holding back her children for the benefit of other children less well prepared.

So she determined that she would continue as she had begun and personally attend to the education of her two children. In this she had elicited Ikey's most reluctant assistance, particularly as she required that he teach them nothing in the way of dishonest practices. Ikey protested that he knew of no other way to teach an urchin, and that if he should be forbidden to teach Tommo and Hawk the gentle art of picking a pocket, or show them how to palm a card or otherwise cheat at cribbage, pick a simple lock, short change a customer, successfully enter a house though it be securely locked, or doctor a stolen watch, there was nothing contained in his lexicon of knowledge which he believed could be useful to them.

'You will teach them of human nature! They must grow up able to read a man or woman the way you do. How they stand or use their hands or smile or protest, how to know the fool from the villain and the good from the bad. Who to trust and who should be avoided. The manner o' the confidence man and the language o' the cheat and the liar. That is what I want them to know, Ikey Solomon!'

Ikey laughed. 'They are not Jews, my dear, they are not the raw material it has taken a thousand years and more to breed, so that this kind of wisdom is ingested without the need to think.'

'You must teach them, Ikey. Hawk most of all, for I fear greatly for him in this world where the dark people suffer even though they commit no crime, where the lowest wretch thinks himself superior to a black skin. You must teach Hawk to be a good reader of human nature.'

Ikey soon discovered that children with full bellies who are surrounded by love and attention make poor observers of human nature. Children learn the lessons in life by being thrown into life, and so he decided to take Hawk and Tommo to the races each Saturday. But first he taught them a new language. He found that both boys enjoyed the finger and hand actions which comprise the ancient silent language used among the traders in Petticoat Lane, Rosemary Lane, Whitechapel, Covent Garden and the other London markets. It is said that it is a language used by the Jews since the fall of the great temple of Solomon. That the Jews brought it to England in the Middle Ages and it became a language used in English prisons and had been brought to Port Arthur, where prisoners were not permitted to talk to each other. It was also most useful at the race track, where bookmakers talked to each other, setting the odds and laying of bets across the paddocks, and there it was commonly known as tic-tac.

Tommo and Hawk, like all young children, quickly

learned the rudiments of this language and it did not take long before they added some of their own unique signs and devices, which meant they could silently communicate to each other on any subject.

Ikey was delighted with their progress, and when they were seven he would take them to the races, where they would move from one on-course bookmaker to the other sending back the odds to Ikey so that he was seldom caught short or 'holding the bundle' as it is known in racing parlance. In exposing them to the myriad people to be found at the Hobart races he was able to begin teaching Tommo and Hawk the lessons Mary wanted them to learn. Ikey taught them how to look at a crowd and break it into its various components.

'If you knows what you're looking for in a crowd, my dear, then you can read it like a book.' He looked down at Hawk. 'A crowd be composed o' what, Mr Dark Thought?'

Hawk looked at Ikey with his big serious eyes. 'Folks?'

'Folks! That be a right and splendid answer, very clever indeed!'

'What sort o' folks, Mr After Thought?' he asked Tommo.

'Very ugly ones what stinks!' Tommo replied, waiting for the giggle to come from Hawk.

'Well, well, well and we are the pretty ones what smells perfect are we then?' Ikey said. 'I stinks meself and I am not very pretty I admits. So be the crowd all like me? Like Ikey Solomon?'

'All sorts of different folks,' Hawk replied for Tommo.

'Yes! With all sorts o' different needs and deeds,' Ikey

replied. 'Needs and deeds, that be what you have to learn, my dears. If you knows what folks needs, you can begin to understand their deeds.'

Ikey would patiently teach them how to spot the pickpocket, and to listen to the chatter of a tout, to notice the gestures and the patterns of speech of the confidence trickster, how to know when a man was a liar or a cheat. How body language was almost always the first way to judge a man.

'Then, when you've seen how he stands or sits or walks or uses his hands and his head, and he fits into a pattern, then, when you talks with him you listens with your stomachs, my dears.'

'Your stomach!' Tommo laughed. 'Be me belly button me new ear then?'

'That be most clever of you, Mister After Thought, most clever and to be remembered. "Let your belly button be your most important ear!"'

'Have you got a very big belly button then, Ikey?' Hawk asked. 'Big as your ear?'

'Huge, my dear!' Ikey slapped his pot belly. 'Nearly all be ear what's constantly listening.'

The two boys found this very funny. 'So what does you do with your ears on your head?' Hawk asked.

'Now that be another most clever question, Mister Dark Thought.' Ikey pulled at both his ears. 'These be your listening eyes.'

'Eyes can't listen!' both the boys shouted.

'Oh yes they can! If they be ears!' Ikey said solemnly.

'But ears can't see,' Hawk said emphatically.

'Oh yes they can! If they be eyes! Ears what is eyes and eyes what is ears is most important in the discovery o' human nature!'

'How?' they both chorused.

'Well, human speech be like pictures, only word pictures. When we speaks we paints a word picture what we wants others to see, but we only paints a part o' the picture what's in our heads. The other part, usually the most important part, we leaves behind, because it be the truth, the true picture. So your ears have to have eyes, so they can see how much o' the real picture what be in the head be contained in the words!'

'How then are eyes become ears?' Hawk asked.

'Well that be more complicated, but the way we moves our hands and heads, and folds our arms or opens them up, scratches our nose or puts our fingers over our lips, tugs our ear, twiddles our thumbs or fidgets, or puts one foot on the instep o' the other like Tommo be doing right now, that be what you calls the language o' the body. If you listen to the language o' the body with your eyes and sees the picture in the mind with your ears, you begins to get the drift o' the person, that is if you listens . . .'

'Through the ear in your belly?' Hawk shouted, delighted.

'Bravo! If he don't feel good in your stomach, then always trust it, my dears! Bad stomachs and bad men go well together!'

Tommo appeared to pay less attention to these lessons, but Hawk silently absorbed everything Ikey told him. Unlike his previous pupils in the Academy of Light Fingers, neither Tommo nor Hawk suffered from hunger and cold, homelessness or a lack of love. Privileged children only embrace the more difficult lessons in life when their survival is threatened and then it is often too late.

Both Mary's boys showed an early proficiency in numbers and constantly used the abacus, but once again it was Hawk who most quickly mastered the mysteries of calculation. By the time Ikey took them to the Saturday races Hawk carried his own small abacus and could calculate the odds in an instant and send them by sign language to his brother. Tommo would stand well outside the betting ring but where Ikey could glance up at him while he worked, and as he began to prosper as a bookmaker he came to rely increasingly on the two boys.

Mary spent as much time as she could spare with the boys tramping on the great mountain, and at Strickland Falls, and soon they knew the deeply wooded slopes and crags well enough to spend long hours exploring on their own. They hunted the shy opossum, who slept during the day in hollow tree trunks, and searched for birds' eggs, though Mary forbade them to gather the eggs or trap the rosellas and green parrots not yet able to fly, but which were sufficiently well feathered to sell in the markets.

Once, close to Strickland Falls, Hawk had his arm deep within the hole in a tree trunk looking for birds' eggs when he was bitten by a snake. Within a couple of minutes he had presented his puffed and swollen forefinger to Mary, who was fortunately working at the new buildings for the Potato Factory.

Mary lost no time and, consulting Dr Forster's *Book of Colonial Medicine*, she applied a tourniquet high up on Hawk's arm and sliced open the bite with a sharp knife, drawing a deep line down the flesh of his forefinger while ignoring his desperate yowling. Then she sucked the poison from the wound, spat it out, and

728

applied a liberal sprinkling of Condi's Crystals or, as it was called in the book, Permanganate of Potash. Though Hawk's hand remained swollen for a week, his forefinger recovered well, the scar from Mary's over-zealous cut being more damaging and permanent in its effect than the serpent's bite itself.

Mary was a strict mother who expected them to work. They gathered watercress and learned to tickle the mountain trout, and hunt for yabbies, the small freshwater crayfish abundant in the mountain streams, so that they would often bring home a bountiful supply. Sometimes they sold what they caught or gathered at the markets. They collected oysters off the rocks in the bay and set lobster traps, and both boys could swim like fish by the time they were five years old. At seven they were independent and spirited and in the rough and tumble of life in Hobart Town, where children of the poor grew up quickly and street urchins scavenged to stay alive, they mostly held their own. Though they would often enough come home to Mary torn, bleeding and beaten, robbed of the pennies or even a mighty sixpence they had earned.

Hawk's dark colour was almost always the problem, with the street urchins taking great delight in going after him. If Tommo and Hawk saw one of the gangs approaching and escape proved impossible, they ran until they found a wall and then, with their backs to it, would turn and fight their opponents. If they were not outnumbered they gave as much as they got and more. The street urchins learned to regard them with respect and to attack only in sizeable numbers, engaging the two boys just long enough to steal their catch, a brace of wood pigeons or several trout, a clutch of wild duck eggs or a couple of opossum.

Mary would patch them up, but offered little in the way of comfort. She loved her precious children so deeply that she often felt close to tears when they returned home with a black eye, bleeding nose or a thick lip. But she knew it was a hard world, and that they must learn to come to terms with it.

It was Ikey who finally gave them the key to a less eventful life. The two boys appeared at breakfast one morning, Tommo with both eyes shut and a swollen lip, and Hawk with one eye shut and a bruised and enlarged nose.

'Been in the wars, has we, then, my dears?' Ikey said.

'They've been fighting again,' Mary said, placing two bowls of porridge on the table. 'A couple o' proper hooligans, them two!'

'It were not our fault, Mama, it be the wild boys again!' Tommo said indignantly.

'You must run, don't fight them, just run,' Mary said emphatically. 'It's not cowardly to run, only prudent.'

'We had a bag of oysters what took two hours to collect,' Hawk protested. 'It were fourpence worth at least!'

'You can't run with a bag of oysters!' Tommo explained further.

'Well they got the oysters and you both got black eyes and fat lips and a bleeding nose, where's the sense to that?'

'We ain't scared, Mama,' Tommo said. 'Hawk hit three o' them terrible hard and I kicked one o' them in the shins so he went howling!'

'Of course, my dears, fisticuffs be all very well,' Ikey said, picking his teeth. 'But a much sharper sword would be your tongue!'

730

If the eyes of both boys had not been so well closed they would have rolled them in unison.

'They be idjits, Uncle Ikey. You can't try no reasoning on them, they not like us decent folks,' Tommo said.

'Don't you speak like that, Tommo Solomon!' Mary remonstrated. 'They be poor brats what's had no chance in life. They does the best they can to stay alive! They be just as decent as us given half a chance!'

'Talk to them, my dears, use your wits,' Ikey said. 'Wits be much more powerful than fists.' He rose from the table and stretched his arms above his shoulders. 'I'll be off, then. No lessons today, your Uncle Ikey's had a long, hard night.'

Later that morning the two boys were sitting on Mary's magic rock on the slopes of the mountain when Hawk turned to Tommo. 'What's you think Ikey be on about this morning?' he asked.

Tommo shrugged. 'It be Ikey stuff we be supposed to understand but can't.'

'I got an idea,' Hawk said.

Two days later the two boys found themselves accosted by five street urchins. They'd just returned from their lobster traps and their sack was bulging and bumping with six live lobsters they were hoping to sell to Mrs McKinney's fish shop for threepence.

Hawk looked at Tommo and the smaller boy nodded.

'Wotcha got?' the biggest of the urchins demanded.

Tommo and Hawk remained silent, and the snot-nose who had asked the original question made a grab for the bag in Hawk's hand.

'Careful,' Tommo shouted. 'They be magic lobsters what can curse you!'

The boy drew back confused. 'Wotcha mean?'

731

Hawk opened the bag, brought out a plump lobster and held it up above his head. The creature's claws and feelers waved wildly in the air.

'They can read your mind, them lobsters!'

The boys standing around jeered. 'That be fuckin' stoopid!' the first boy answered. 'Lobsters what can read me mind!'

Hawk pushed the live lobster into the face of the boy, who reeled back.

'Yeah, bullshit!' another of the urchins shouted. 'Ain't no lobsters what can do that!'

'Not your ordinary lobsters, that I admits, but these be special magic ones,' Tommo said quickly. 'It be the secret curse o' the people from Africa!'

'Who, him? The nigger?' the boy said, pointing to Hawk.

Hawk grinned. 'Black magic!' he said.

'Wanna see?' Tommo asked.

The urchins had now forgotten their original intention to rob Tommo and Hawk of the bag. 'Yeah!' they chorused.

'You brave enough to take the chance to be cursed by the great African lobster what swum all the way to visit us from the Cape o' Good Hope in Africa?' Tommo asked the eldest of the boys.

The urchin hesitated but then, seeing the others looking at him, said, 'It be stoopid! That be a fuckin' lobster like any uvver what's in the river.'

'G'warn, show us the magic!' the urchins challenged Tommo.

'Don't be cheeky!' Tommo said to the bunch of skinny boys standing around him. 'Or we'll curse the lot of you, not only him.' He scowled at the boy who had first accosted them and beckoned to the gang in a low voice. 'Come here where that African lobster creature can't hear what you is saying! Come right away all of you to that tree.' He pointed to a swamp oak about fifty feet away.

The urchins and their leader followed Tommo and stood beside the tree. 'Now I wants you each to whisper your name in me ear, one at a time, and then we'll ask the magic lobster to tell me brother what knows lobster language to tell us what your name be!' Tommo pointed to their original attacker. 'You what be double cursed already for saying it be a lobster what come from the river, you go first. Whisper your name in me ear with your back to the magic African lobster me brother's holding.'

Tommo knew the boy was known as Boxey, because his head was almost square. 'George,' Boxey whispered slyly into Tommo's ear, though loud enough for those gathered around to hear him. There was a giggle from the others at their leader's foxy trick.

Tommo stood facing Hawk fifty feet away and signalled him using the silent language. Hawk held the lobster up to his ear and appeared to listen. Then he shook his head and then the crustacean, and listened once more. Suddenly a big smile appeared on his face. 'The magic African lobster says the name given be George, but Boxey be the name what's real!' he shouted back at them.

The mouths of the urchins standing around Tommo fell open, and Boxey became very red in the face.

'You be careful, mate!' Tommo growled. 'Or you could be in real big trouble!'

Hawk suddenly held the lobster back to his ear. 'The

magic African lobster says if any boy gives him a wrong name again they be double cursed to drown at sea!' he shouted.

There was a further gasp of astonishment from the boys.

'You!' Tommo said, pointing to a skinny urchin who was dressed in rags with great holes showing through, 'Come and whisper your name.' The boy, even smaller than Tommo, looked up at him terrified. 'I dunno what's me real name, they calls me Minnow.' His eyes pleaded with Tommo. 'I don't wanna be cursed, please!'

'Yeah, well I'll do me best,' Tommo said. 'But I can't make no promise. Turn your back to the magic lobster so he can't see your lips,' he commanded sternly. The urchin, shaking all over, did as he was told.

Moments later Hawk called back, 'Minnow!'

Tommo turned to the leader of the gang. 'Boxey, you be real lucky this time! But be warned!' He turned to the other urchins. 'Anyone want to take a chance o' being cursed?' There were no further volunteers and so Tommo called over to Hawk, 'Put the lobster in the bag and come over!'

As Hawk approached the gang they started to back away from him. 'Don't run!' Tommo said. 'We got to lift the curse first!'

'What's you mean?' Boxey asked suspiciously, his voice slightly tremulous. 'You said we wasn't cursed if we be careful.' He seemed brighter than the others and suddenly asked, 'How come he's your brother and he be black?'

'That's what I means, we got to lift the curse!' Tommo replied.

'I were born same as him,' Hawk explained, pointing

to Tommo. 'Same's me brother, but I got cursed by the horrible African lobster and now I's black, see!'

'What you just seen here be black magic and folk's not s'posed to see black magic,' Tommo said. 'So me brother, what's turned black and is now the black magician what's forced to pass on the curse, will wave the lobster over your heads and then the curse be lifted. Now, if you please, a circle. Hold hands and make a circle. I'll tell you when to close your eyes!'

The boys formed into a circle holding hands with Hawk in the centre. Hawk lifted a lobster out of the bag and held it high above his head.

'Close your eyes tight now!' Tommo instructed. 'If you peeks you is cursed for life and you drowns all horrible out to sea but before that you turns black!'

Hawk started to recite:

> *Abracadabra, ho, ho, ho!*
> *Black as pitch, white as snow!*
> *Beware the black magician's curse*
> *Or things what's bad will soon be worse!*

Tommo waited for Hawk to place the lobster back into the bag. 'You can open your eyes, you be safe now,' Tommo instructed. 'Curse be lifted, but scarper quick and stay out of our way!' He then repeated Hawk's lines. 'Beware the black magician's curse, or things what's bad will soon be worse!'

'G'warn, clear off!' Hawk shouted, scowling fiercely. The urchins, terror etched on their dirty faces, turned and fled for their lives.

The two boys waited a few moments, most pleased with themselves. Then Hawk took up the wriggling bag of lobsters and they started to laugh. They continued laughing all the way up the hill to Mrs McKinney's fish shop.

'I reckons maybe Uncle Ikey be right,' Hawk said finally, then turned to Tommo and asked, 'Was you scared?'

'Yeah, shittin' meself!'

'Me too, but I reckon it's much better than getting your nose busted!'

'Blood' oath!' Tommo said happily.

Chapter Thirty-five

Towards the end of the seventh year of their lives, Tommo and Hawk disappeared on a perfectly calm winter's day somewhere on the slopes of Mount Wellington.

Hobart Town had wakened that morning to find that the first winter snow had fallen and crusted the summit of the great mountain. The day that followed was crisp, with winter sunshine bright and sharp as polished silver.

Mary had spent most of the day at the new Potato Factory buildings where the majority of her beer production was now taking place. The old mill was used increasingly as a bottle shop, managed by Jessamy Hawkins.

It was the daily custom of Tommo and Hawk to accompany Mary to the small cottage at Strickland Falls, which served both as an office and schoolroom, where she supervised their lessons.

However, on the day they disappeared the two boys had begged Mary to allow them to climb to the snowline. She had hesitated at first. It was a three-hour climb and the weather on the mountain had a habit of closing in even on a sunny day. But she had finally yielded to their beseeching, and at ten o'clock they took some bread and cheese and escaped their lessons to explore the snow at the summit before the warm sunshine should melt it.

Mary had cautioned them to be careful and to come home immediately wherever they were if the weather turned, and no later than an hour before sunset. Tommo and Hawk were as agile as mountain goats and had explored the mountain with Mary since they were toddlers. Furthermore, there was a log hut at the summit should the weather close in, and it contained a plentiful supply of wood left by the woodcutters who worked the slopes.

Despite the warm day it was always cold at the summit, and Mary had insisted they wear their opossum jackets which, though considered most unfashionable by the third raters, were much utilised by rural folk, shepherds, sealers, kangaroo hunters and woodcutters who worked the wilderness country. Mary had purchased these wonderfully soft and warm garments for the boys, and she kept them at the Potato Factory at Strickland Falls precisely because of the unpredictable moods of the mountain.

At four-thirty in the afternoon, an hour before sunset, like all mothers, Mary's ears were tuned for the home-coming calls of the two boys, although her expectation was pointless, because the roar of the falls would drown out the sounds of their approach. But they knew her routine, and her need to be back at the mill before the bells of St David's tolled for evensong.

Mary smiled to herself at the thought of the journey home with the two boys. It was the happiest part of the day for her, as she had them all to herself. She loved the walk through the woods and, as they approached the town, the smell of wood smoke and the sweep of the hazy hills across the great silver river spread below.

Tommo and Hawk would be scratched from crawling through brambles and so covered with dirt they might well need to be bathed even though it was not their tub night. Tommo would be running ahead and turning back and taking her hand, words tumbling out in fierce competition with Hawk to tell her of their grand adventure as they'd played in the first of the winter snow. Hawk would be carrying her basket, hopping and skipping beside her with his head full of serious questions or explanations of the things he'd seen.

They would arrive back at the old mill just as the working people of Hobart Town started to arrive to buy their beer to take home. It was a busy hour and Mary would help Jessamy with the customers until half past seven o'clock. Soon after, Ikey would arrive and Mary would make supper for them all. Then, when Ikey retired to work on the books, she would read to the boys. They seldom remained awake much beyond nine o'clock, when she locked up and washed her face and arms and retired to bed herself, but not before making Ikey a large mug of strong tea which he liked to take with milk and six teaspoons of caster sugar.

Though Mary worked exceedingly hard, she revelled in the calm of an ordered and uneventful life, and her ambition was in no way curtailed by the need to care for her boys. In fact they gave her a sense of purpose beyond the need to prove herself worthy in her own eyes, and on her own terms.

Even though Mr Emmett had been right and she had

been socially ostracised because of her dark-skinned son, Mary had never been concerned about social acceptance. During her earlier life, when she had been known as Egyptian Mary, she had witnessed sufficient of the behaviour of the male members of the first raters not to wish to adopt their affectations and manners, and she did not expect people of the tradesmen class would be any better.

Indeed, Mary's fights with the wealthy beer barons and spirit distillers of Hobart Town had been possible because she knew these rich and important men for what they were, and had not been cowed by their bullying. Moreover, her opinion of these pompous tyrants' wives, formed during her days as a chambermaid, was not greatly in advance of what she thought of their husbands.

Though she loved and respected Mr Emmett, Mary did not covet his lifestyle nor wish to be included in his milieu as a first rater, even if such a lofty ascent had been possible. She saw him for what he was, a rare example of a kind and compassionate human being who was independent of any class, and she hoped one day to emulate his example.

But for now Mary devoted herself to Tommo and Hawk. She was certain that her luck in this new land had a purpose, that she would create a foundation stone upon which her sons could build and that something worthwhile and wonderful would emerge. In her imagination Mary could clearly see the little brewery she would create in its perfect woodland setting, an inseparable part of her magic mountain. While she was not by nature capable of so pompous a thought, the Potato Factory would be her monument to the ability of the human spirit to survive and prosper against all odds.

Mary thought lovingly of her two boys and smiled to herself. She now possessed a destiny, a continuity in her new land. Tommo X Solomon and Hawk X Solomon would be the source of her second generation.

Mary chuckled to herself as she always did when she thought of the X in the boy's names. When Ikey had appeared somewhat sheepishly at the government offices and declared himself to be the father of Tommo and Hawk, he had registered his so-called offspring with an additional single X common to both names. The clerk who had presided over the registration had evinced not the slightest interest in enquiring what the X stood for, and had written out a certificate of birth exactly as Ikey had indicated.

Later, when Mary had demanded to know what the X stood for, Ikey shrugged his shoulders. 'It has to be there, it be a proper part o' their names, my dear, a grand initial, an ancient Hebrew sign,' he lied. In fact, the initial X was simply Ikey's mind working in its usual convoluted way. He told himself it represented the X which Svensen of the *Sturmvogel* had tattooed through the name Tomahawk on Sperm Whale Sally's breast to cancel the rights of the *Merryweather*. The additional justification was that he'd split the name Tomahawk in half to give each boy his name, but their names could be re-combined with the X to make a whole. Thus, Tommo X Hawk = Tomahawk = Twins. But in reality their names had simply been conjured up that first morning when he'd presented them in the basket to Mary and the X was just a feeble joke he'd thought of on the spur of the moment when he had gone to register the birth of the two boys.

However, Mary deduced her own explanation for the

singular initial. She, who was so very good at the business of numbers, concluded that the X is used as the unknown in mathematics, and that Tommo and Hawk were her two unknown factors. The letter X in calculations could be made to represent any number, and it was her duty to see that what it represented in her two sons was the sum of the very best she could do to make them men of whom she could be rightfully proud.

Mary smiled as she packed her basket in preparation for the boys' return. Then she bid the workmen goodnight, put on her warm coat, locked the cottage and walked over to the small bridge just below the falls, which she knew Tommo and Hawk must cross as they returned from the mountain.

Mary Abacus waited on the bridge and watched the water as it churned white at her feet. The thundering falls sent a fine mist into the air which created a rainbow in the late afternoon sunlight, and Mary could not imagine a more perfect moment. She was not to know that the magic mountain she loved so much had just swallowed up her precious children.

When the boys had not arrived by five o'clock she walked back to the office and found a lantern which had a good wick, and was well filled with the whale oil. Then she looked about and found half a loaf of bread, the remainder of the cheese she had given the boys and four apples. These she replaced in her basket together with several bandages and a bottle of iodine which she always kept on the premises. Then she took a small axe which hung behind the cottage door and this too she pushed, head first, into the basket. It was almost dark by the time Mary crossed the little bridge again, and set off along the path leading higher up the mountain.

There was only one path to the summit, though many hundreds of paths led from all over the mountain before converging on this main track, which was a forty-minute climb from the top. Mary determined that she would walk until the path which led from Strickland Falls intersected several others, a steady half-hour's walk up the mountain. The boys might have taken any of a dozen paths to arrive at this point, but she knew they must eventually turn into the one she now took for the journey home.

The trees became more dense as she climbed, and not more than twenty minutes after she had left it grew completely dark under the forest canopy. Mary stopped to light the lantern and then proceeded onwards. She had begun to call out, her voice echoing through the trees as she called their names.

Mary finally reached the intersection. It was getting cold so she gathered wood, a difficult task even with the help of the lantern, but she persisted until she had a large pile. She kept herself warm chopping the wood, stopping every minute or so to call out again. Finally she lit a fire and settled down to wait, hoping that if Tommo and Hawk were anywhere near they might smell the smoke or see the fire.

Though the night was cold it remained clear and no wind beyond the usual breeze stirred the tops of the trees. Mary told herself that this might not be the case at the summit, and Tommo and Hawk might have been caught in a change of weather and taken refuge in the hut. They were young, but it was unlikely they would do anything foolish. If the summit was suddenly to mist over they would know to stay put until morning. But in her heart Mary was terrified. She imagined a rock slide set in motion by the weight of the snow. She saw them venturing to the edge of a bluff, perhaps the mighty organ pipes, and the snow giving way and sending them crashing downwards nearly a thousand feet. She imagined any of a dozen incidents and all of them became vivid and concluded in her mind.

After two hours Mary knew that she would have to come down. Once again she lit the lantern, which she had put out to save the oil during her vigil by the fire. Wherever Tommo and Hawk were they could not descend in the dark, and she knew that no search party would set out to find them until first light. Mary set off down the path again and arrived at Strickland Falls nearly an hour later. She was scratched about and bleeding, for travelling a bush path at night is harrowing and her descent had been perilous. She had fallen on several occasions, though fortunately she had not lost the lantern. It took her another forty minutes to get back to the mill where Ikey and Jessamy were waiting, both of them terribly anxious. They'd already been up to Strickland Falls, and found it locked and had themselves not long been home.

Ikey had never seen Mary cry, but now she sat at the kitchen table and wept as she slowly spilled out the story. She blamed herself for letting the boys go, though Jessamy reminded her that they had roamed the slopes since they were four years old and the mountain was, in every sense, their own backyard.

At midnight Ikey left Jessamy asleep in an old armchair and Mary seated at the kitchen table with her head in her arms. Although she was tired and distraught almost beyond thinking, the ever-practical Mary had devised a rescue plan. She would make her appearance at Peter Degraves' saw mills at seven o'clock the following morning, when the timber cutters set off to work the slopes. But first she would call at the Degraves home and ask him for permission to pay his men a day's salary to send up a search party for Tommo and Hawk. They would set off from Strickland Falls so that if the children had spent the night safely in the hut on the summit they would be met along the path, not more than an hour and a half after first light. At this point the search would be over and the men, already on the mountain, could return to their work.

Mary was not foolish enough to suppose that this permission would be easily granted, for while her past employer was by the standards of the time a good man, he was tough and she knew he would expect her to pay for the value of the timber not produced while his men carried out the search. The loss of Tommo and Hawk would not be seen by him as a matter of great importance. Mary was of course, perfectly willing to meet his demands. The cost of a day's work of a hundred timber cutters would exhaust her available liquid resources, and possibly put her in debt to the brewer, but she cared not in the least about this.

Having resolved what to do at first light, she fell into a fitful sleep at the kitchen table only to be wakened an hour before dawn by Ikey.

'Come, my dear, I have brought help!' he said, shaking her gently by the shoulder.

Gathered in the street outside the Potato Factory were more than a hundred people. A more motley collection of the hopeless and forlorn would have been difficult to find anywhere in the South Seas. None among them would ever voluntarily have put one foot on the lowest slopes of the great mountain.

They were the drunks and whores, gamblers, pimps, touts, publicans' cellarmen, barmaids, whalemen and jack tars as well as other assorted human scrapings from the Hobart waterfront. Ann Gower, now the owner of a waterfront bawdy house, had taken a donkey cart and loaded herself upon it together with a large tea urn, so that she, too, might help.

Mary took one look at the crowd and knew Ikey must have finally gone senile. Though she perceived a handful of jack tars young enough to be useful, if the vast majority of this scraggy lot set foot upon the mountain, even on a cloudless summer day, few would return with every limb intact or even their lives, and most would be incapable of reaching the first tree line.

'Whatever has possessed you, Ikey Solomon?' Mary cried.

'My dear, I had thought to find some stout lads who might be persuaded to take on the search, but it is a great compliment to you that many felt that they should themselves come!'

After the initial shock, the sight of Ikey's caring volunteers lifted Mary's courage enormously. She thanked them for their generosity of spirit, but pointed out that the mountain was a dangerous and foreign place for most of them, and that they would more easily lose their own lives than help to find Tommo and Hawk.

She told them of her plan to use the timber cutters who worked the mountain slopes for Mr Peter Degraves' saw mills. If he should lend his support as she hoped he might, the mountain would be extensively searched before the day was out.

In fact, Mary knew that the mountain could not be thoroughly searched in a week or a month, and if

Tommo and Hawk had fallen down a precipice they might never be found.

'You have shown me a great honour,' Mary concluded, 'and I am most touched by your concern. I thank you from the bottom of me heart.'

People among the assembly shouted their encouragement and started to disperse when Ann Gower stood up in the cart. 'Oi!' she shouted, waving her arms to indicate that they should gather around. The crowd soon assembled about her, and waited for her to speak. 'You all knows who I is, and if ya don't, why not?' she bawled out. There was a ripple of laughter and she waited for it to die down. 'But Mary Abacus some 'ere knows only fer the decent beer she sells, but also knows 'er as a good woman. But she be more'n that, and I should know! Mary Abacus be the salt o' the earth, no better woman may be found on this island nor any ovver place I knows of!' Ann Gower paused and looked around her. 'Now we knows 'er brats what's lost ain't 'ers born, and we knows 'ow they come about. But that don't make no difference and even that one be black, that don't matter neiver! What do matter is that she loves 'em, and if we can't 'elp to find 'em because we not the sort to take to mountain climbin', we can pass the 'at around to pay for a few stout lads what knows the mountain and can make a search!'

She opened her handbag and took out ten shillings. 'Two shillin' be a good wage for a day for a timber cutter, so I now pays for five o' the buggers. Who's next?' Ann Gower pointed to Bridget from the Whale Fishery. 'Bridget O'Sullivan take orf ya bonnet and use it as an 'at, there's plenty 'ere what's mean as cat's piss, but they'll 'ave trouble denyin' a pretty girl like you!'

Very soon Bridget had collected a total of three pounds and sevenpence from the crowd. Ann Gower gave it to Mary, who knew well enough not to protest. It was a gesture of respect, and she accepted it for the generosity of spirit it represented.

Mary looked at the crowd with tears in her eyes. 'Thank you all,' she said simply. Turning to Ann Gower she smiled. 'You're a good woman, Ann Gower!'

Ann Gower drew back and looked askance at Mary. 'Don't ya go ruinin' me repitashin, Mary Abacus. I be a real bad woman, but a bloody good whore and ya knows it!' She turned to the crowd. 'C'mon, folks, it be sun-up soon, time to go 'ome to bed!'

Peter Degraves agreed readily to Mary's request but put only sixteen of his men to search the mountain, sensibly pointing out that the boys would only have covered a small section of the mountain to reach the summit and that sixteen men could cover this thoroughly. He accepted that she should pay them their daily wage though he did not ask her for compensation for the two days of sawmill profits he would lose because the men were taken away from their work.

'I'll write it off to good labour relations,' he laughed, Mary's earlier labour reforms at the Cascade Brewery had been maintained, and Degraves knew that he had been repaid a thousand times over by the loyalty and the honesty of the men who worked for him.

After two days the men had thoroughly searched the mountain and had not found the slightest sign of the two boys. Further searching was not practical. The mountain might hide their bodies for years if they had fallen down some deep ravine, but because it was assumed that Tommo and Hawk would have been in the area facing

Hobart Town and near the top of the mountain, this was where the search was focused. Eventually Mary conceded that nothing more could be done, though she personally spent the next two weeks alone on the mountain still desperately searching for her children.

Once she found a trap set for wood pigeon typical of the kind the boys might make, and on a thornberry bush adjacent to it she discovered a tiny tuft of opossum fur. Her heart started to beat furiously. After two days of calling out the boys' names her voice had ceased to function, and now she searched grimly and silently, entering small ravines and squeezing through rock formations terrified that at any moment she might come across the broken bodies of her sons. She was badly cut and scratched about and when she returned at night her clothes were often ripped to shreds. She ate little and her eyes became sunken, and her anguished silence made people begin to think she had gone mad.

Ikey and Jessamy Hawkins tried to comfort her, though they, too, were distraught, and the men who worked at the Potato Factory walked about in silent concern when she appeared.

It was during these two weeks on the mountain that Mary slowly became convinced that Tommo and Hawk had been abducted. At first she told herself this notion was absurd. Who would do such a thing and for what purpose? There could be no possible value in the kidnapping of two small boys. The beer barons and spirit manufacturers who had cause to dislike her were a possible explanation but, she knew, a poor one. They would not damage their own reputation with the public by so gratuitous a revenge. Wild men? This seemed more likely but, if so, they would by now have demanded a ransom.

Yet the feeling persisted and by the end of the fortnight, without any logical reason, other than that the
bodies of Tommo and Hawk had not been found, Mary
was certain that they had been abducted. She stopped
searching and started to evolve a plan.

For some months Mary had been working on a new
ale. She had tested it on a number of her customers,
who found it most pleasing to the palate. Mary now
had acceptance of her bottled beer throughout the
colony, and she was also shipping it to the new village
of Melbourne on the mainland. She now decided to call
her new beer Tomahawk. Upon the label she placed two
arms, a black and a white, gripped in the manner of
arm wrestling and directly under the inverted 'V' made
by the two arms was a picture of the head of a Red
Indian chief. Around the perimeter of the oval-shaped
label were the words: * *Pale Ale* * *The Potato Factory*
* *prop. Miss Mary Abacus* *

Directly under the Indian chief's head appeared the
words: *Fifty Pounds Reward*! and under this the injunc-
tion: (*see back*). At the back of the bottle Mary placed
a second label in the shape of a glass. It contained a
crude sketch of two small boys, one black and the other
white and the following words in the shape of a wine
glass.

KIDNAPPING!!
FIFTY POUNDS REWARD!
For information leading to
the recovery of the two boys
answering to the names of
Tommo & Hawk Solomon
and who are identified in

person by Miss Mary Abacus,
or Mr Ikey Solomon as same.
Tommo be small with blue
eyes and fair hair. Hawk be
black of skin and Negro
appearance. Both be 7
years old.
NO
QUESTIONS BE
ASKED OF PERSONS
ASSISTING IN RECOVERY!

Mary hoped that one of two things might happen. That someone might have seen Hawk, a black boy and therefore a curious sight, in the company of Tommo, a white one. Or that the kidnappers might attempt to claim the reward. It was, after all, a fortune, three times the yearly salary of a labourer or farm worker, and would also prove a tremendous incentive to a bounty hunter.

It did not take long for the disappearance of Tommo and Hawk to be known throughout the entire colony, and it was shortly afterwards that Ikey received a letter from his son David in New Norfolk asking him if he would come to the river town on a matter of extreme urgency. Ikey was glad of the excuse to go. Hannah had not contacted him in more than a year, and she had forbidden him to visit her. Her de facto George Madden had greatly prospered in the barley and hops business and Ikey, who was more and more conscious of his mortality, was terrified that she was prepared to wait until he was dead, whereupon she could claim the entire contents of the safe in Whitechapel and eventually find a way to open it.

David had been in contact with Ikey on two previous occasions. At other times he had sent Ann and then, on the last occasion, young Sarah was despatched to visit him with the excuse that they cared greatly about his welfare and wished to see him cared for. Sarah, who had little recollection of Ikey's perfidious nature, decided to remain with him and now shared the cottage in Elizabeth Street. This suited Ikey very well. His daughter made no demands on him, and she washed, cooked, and generally looked after his domestic affairs.

On each of his visits, David appeared to be warm and friendly and acted as though their stormy past had been entirely forgiven. There was much talk of blood being thicker than water, and the suggestion that an eventual reconciliation seemed quite possible with Hannah. It was obvious to Ikey that the boy had a good business head on his shoulders and had learned well the duplicity of effective persuasion.

However, he had soon enough perceived the motive behind the visits of his son and two daughters. David had by now been in the employ of George Madden for some years and there was talk of a partnership. Not long after she had arrived, Sarah let slip that the offer was far from generous, and was inspired by a great deal of nagging from Hannah. Apparently George Madden didn't wish to share with her son any part of his burgeoning empire, but wanted to keep peace with the formidable Hannah, so he had made the partnership offer on the proviso that four thousand pounds was paid. It was more than someone of David's means could ever possibly hope to raise, though it was still a fair offer for a partnership in such a prosperous business enterprise.

Ikey felt certain the urgent request that he should visit

New Norfolk was attached to the matter of the White-chapel safe, so he was much encouraged by David's note. That Hannah's avaricious hand would be in it somewhere he had no doubt.

Ikey was met by David at the New Norfolk wharf and taken to his lodgings, a small cottage which he occupied with Ann. She was at her place of work but had cooked a mutton stew and left fresh curds for Ikey's supper, the supposition being that he would not take the afternoon ferry but would stay overnight.

David offered Ikey brandy but he asked instead for tea. Since the death of Sperm Whale Sally he no longer drank at all and his preferred drink in the taverns at night was ginger beer.

David was dressed in a good suit of clothes such as might have been worn by any young man of prospects in a solid community such as New Norfolk. Predictably he misjudged Ikey by the fact that the coat Mary had bought for him eight years before was now ragged, and that his yellow pigskin boots, much soled and patched on the uppers, were well past their prime. David, while attempting to impress Ikey, had acquired the imperious tone of the successful grain merchant, and now spoke in a somewhat patronising manner to his father.

'The mater has put the affairs o' the family in my hands and it is time we talked,' he said to Ikey after he had placed a mug of tea before him.

'Oh yes, is your mother not well then?' Ikey asked, for he knew Hannah would never give over the reins to any of their sons unless she was on her death bed.

'In the very best o' health and much mellowed,' David said. Not waiting for a response, he continued, 'As I says, she has left things to me to clear up.'

'Things? What be these things, then?' Ikey asked.

'Well, I knows about the Whitechapel safe at home and I think we should resolve the matter, don't you?'

Ikey looked curiously across at his son. He had grown into a good-looking man, though already he was putting on weight, and the gold watch chain he wore looped over a pronounced paunch.

'Does you all know?' Ikey asked.

'No, only my mother and I, and o' course Moses and John in New South Wales.'

'Good, then your mother will agree to give me her half of the number and I shall arrange to have it opened and she shall have her share fifty-fifty, as was the original agreement!'

Ikey had long since come to the conclusion that he would give Hannah her half share. He now intended to remain in Van Diemen's Land, though not because he thought it a better place. He knew himself to be a broken man and he was forbidden to return to England. Should he move to another country, he would not have the energy to start again, or even to become accustomed to the life of a rich man in retirement.

While far from rich, he was no longer poor and life in Van Diemen's Land had taken a not disagreeable turn for him. He had grown happily accustomed to the presence of Tommo and Hawk as well as Mary in his life, and the disappearance of the two boys had both deeply shocked and saddened him. But he could never agree to receiving only one-eighth part of the Whitechapel fortune, as Hannah had proposed, nor could he bring himself to trust her with his part of the combination.

There was a prolonged silence between the two men

and then David finally cleared his throat. 'It be less than sensible to trust someone what's not a part o' the family, father. You have three sons, Moses and John in New South Wales and myself here. We are all business men and can be entrusted to do the task in a most sensible manner and at the same time get the most agreeable price in London for the merchandise.'

'Ha! Sensible for you will not, I daresay, turn out sensible for me, that I'll voucher!' Ikey said indignantly. 'Seven parts to you and one to me, that's what your mother thinks be sensible?' Ikey pointed to the gold chain draped across David's paunch. 'How much you pay for that fob?'

David looked down. 'Four pounds,' he replied, running his fingers along the chain.

'Ha! It not be worth a penny over two,' Ikey said. 'Sensible, is it? Negotiate a fair price, will you? Your lot wouldn't know a brass pisspot from the bloody holy grail, you wouldn't!'

'The holy what?' David asked.

'Nevermind, it ain't kosher anyway. Yes, fifty-fifty, but *you* gives me *your* half o' the combination or we ain't got no agreement, and that's telling you flat, my dear!' Ikey looked up into his son's face, expecting him to be intimidated.

Instead David smiled and said calmly, 'We can wait. You'll die soon, Ikey Solomon, but if you wants the money in your lifetime it's still only one-eighth to you and we gets your combination.'

At the mention of his death Ikey felt his innards tighten and then relax, and he thought, 'Oh Gawd, I'm gunna shit meself!' But he showed no outward sign of the dismay and was relieved when he felt his sphincter close and his bowels return to normal. 'Ha! I've smoked you, boy! I'll not die soon enough for you to buy the partnership you wants so badly with George Madden!'

David Solomon flushed, his face turning a deep crimson. He walked over to a drawer in the kitchen dresser and from it took a small package and handed it to Ikey.

'Open it, if you please!' David demanded.

The package was wrapped in brown paper and tied with string, the twine in a bow so that it came undone at a single tug. Ikey folded back the paper to find a second wrapping, this one composed of a scrap of white cloth. Ikey unfolded the cloth slowly, then gasped in horror and fainted dead away.

He recovered moments later to find David standing behind him shaking his shoulders vigorously. When he perceived Ikey to have come around he grabbed his ears and held his head tightly, so that he was forced to look directly in front of him and at the package which lay open on the table.

'That be your precious black child's forefinger!' David said. He released Ikey and came around to face him again. 'We got them both, Hawk and Tommo Solomon!' He had lost all pretence at politeness and shook his head and then spat on the floor. 'Jesus! How could you call them by our family name?'

Ikey looked directly down into his lap to avoid the sight of Hawk's severed finger. He was trembling violently and trying with little success to regain his composure. Ikey had seen much worse in his lifetime and there was no blood, the finger having long since been cut off. But the thought of it being Hawk's finger had shocked him more deeply than he could ever have imagined.

David took the parcel and in a most matter-of-fact manner rewrapped it and tied the string, then placed it back in front of Ikey. 'You have two days to give me your half o' the combination, Ikey Solomon, then we sends the second finger to Mary Abacus with a single instruction, a note what says '*Ask Ikey about this*'. If we don't hear from you in two more days, well, we'll send a third finger with the same note, then a fourth and then we'll start with a little white finger to match the black ones, does you get my drift, father?' David sneered.

'Mary knows nothing o' the safe and the numbers!' Ikey said at last, recovering his courage. 'But be warned, she has powerful friends in the government, she'll go directly to them and you'll be apprehended!'

David laughed. 'The whole bloody island knows about the kidnapped brats and the fifty pounds reward from the back o' her beer bottles. That were very clever, that was! But the finger could've come from anybody, we'll deny it come from us! The authorities well knows o' the quarrels between us. They'll not believe you, thinking it's spite. But *you'll* have to tell Mary what you knows,' David grinned, 'and you won't do that, will you, Ikey Solomon?' He took his watch from his pocket and clicked it open. 'It be half past three o'clock. The ferry for Hobart Town leaves at four o'clock.' David Solomon paused. 'Or perhaps you'd like to stay the night. Ann made you a mutton stew. Give us your answer in the morning?'

Ikey, shaking his head, rose from the table. 'I'll not be staying,' he said quietly, then he looked up at his son. 'I been a villain in my day. But I didn't do no harm what led to bloodshed, and them I stole from could always afford a little loss. I ain't saying what I done was right, but I've served my punishment and what's in that safe in England I've earned. Not one-eighth, but half and much more!' Ikey paused. 'But half will do, the other half be your mother's and she can share it any way she likes. But *you* didn't earn it, and let me tell you something for nothing, my boy! As for my name, the black Solomon and his brother make me proud of it for the first time in my life!'

David Solomon now shook with anger. 'What does ya mean, I hasn't earned it? You, ya bastard, you betrayed our mother so she were sent 'ere and Ann, Sarah, Mark and me, we were put in the bloody orphanage! We earned that money orright! Every fuckin' penny, ya miserable sod!' He stepped up to Ikey and tapped him on the chest. 'Two days, or ya gets the bloody boy what you're so fuckin' proud o' givin' yer name sent to Mary Abacus bit by fuckin' bit, and the white brat follows soon after!' David stepped back, the whites of his eyes showing, his hands now balled into a fist. He was breathing heavily and Ikey felt he was about to strike him, but for once he was not afraid.

Ikey shook his head. 'This was your mother's idea, wasn't it? It's not just the money, it be her revenge on Mary Abacus too, ain't that it?'

'She has a good right to it!' David said, dropping his hands to his side. 'That bitch tried to steal her husband and the affection o' her children!' He cleared his throat. 'You got two days, Ikey Solomon.' He picked the tiny parcel up and handed it to Ikey. 'Show this to your whore!' he shouted.

On the ferry home Ikey's mind was a whirl. David was right, he would not go to the authorities. With his record of family quarrels and vendettas they would never believe him and, besides, two urchins going missing was an everyday occurrence and hardly worth investigating. The mutilation he knew they would take more seriously, but it looked typically like the work of some desperate escaped convict or wild man, or even a sealer or kangaroo shooter who had heard about the reward. Moreover, it was a black hand. While they would not say so, Ikey knew they would attach much less importance to it than if it were white.

Having Hawk's finger in one of the pockets of his coat saddened Ikey most terribly. He could see Hawk's hands dancing in the air as he worked the silent language, his little black fingers so elegant and expressive. The thought that Hawk's dancing hands might soon be bloody stumps was almost more than he could bear. Yet Ikey could not bring himself to tell Mary of the money in the Whitechapel safe. He knew he must attempt to save the lives of Tommo and Hawk, but he was also convinced he would never see a penny of the money it had taken him a lifetime to earn if he gave Hannah his half of the combination. Ikey tried to convince himself that Mary would recover from the loss of her children. Even if she should never talk to him again, he was comfortable enough and sufficiently independent. 'Life goes on,' he repeated to himself several times. 'They were not really her children,' he told himself, though he knew Mary loved Tommo and Hawk as well as if they had been born her own. He, too, was greatly fond of the boys, but Ikey's entire life had been a matter of his own survival and the first rule was not to mourn the past but to move on. He refused, out of a lifetime of habit, to agonise over the matter. Although he might never bring himself to say so, Ikey knew himself to love Mary, but he saw no purpose in telling her about the safe in Whitechapel. He would need to invent something else to explain the package he carried. By the time the ferry had arrived back in Hobart Town, Ikey had cobbled together quite a different story.

The ferry had caught the outgoing tide on the lower reaches of the Derwent River and the trip back had taken slightly over two hours. It was just after half past six in the evening when Mary, helping Jessamy serve customers, saw Ikey arrive and motioned urgently for her to meet him at the rear of the mill.

She was already in the kitchen waiting, wiping her hands on her apron, when Ikey entered the doorway. It had been a month and two days since Tommo and Hawk disappeared. Mary ate almost nothing and was silent most of the time, talking only when she was required to do so and working until late into the night. The new Tomahawk beer had thankfully kept them all very busy, or they might not have been able to bear the thought of Mary's sorrow.

'What is it, Ikey?'

Ikey looked at Mary. 'Sit down, my dear.'

Mary saw the concern on his face. 'What is it?' she asked again and then pulled out a chair and sat down. 'It's bad, isn't it?'

Ikey nodded and drew himself up a chair, then told Mary the story of his visit to New Norfolk.

'So there it is, my dear, you get the boys back by signing the deeds to the Potato Factory over to David Solomon.'

Mary remained silent for almost a minute, then she looked up at Ikey, a terrible weariness showing in her beautiful green eyes. She nodded slowly and Ikey knew she would give up anything for her two boys. 'He were never a good lad, that David. Bright but of a mean spirit,' Mary said quietly, then she was silent again before adding a small voice, 'Show me.'

Ikey recoiled, his head jerking back. 'No, my dear, it will distress you!'

Mary looked up at him, her expression suddenly fierce. 'Show me! I want to see it for meself!'

Ikey removed the small parcel from the interior of his coat and placed it on the table in front of her. Mary's hands trembled as she picked at the bow and then removed the brown paper wrapping. Silent tears ran down her cheeks as she unfolded the grubby, white cloth so that she could barely see the finger. She started to weep, then to wail, choking at the same time, her head averted from the small dark object.

Ikey quickly rose from his chair to stand behind her and place his hands on her shoulders. 'Oh dear, oh dear! Oh my! Oh dear!' he babbled. He could think of nothing to say to comfort Mary.

After a while Mary reached into the pocket of her apron for a piece of rag, and wiped her eyes and blew her nose. Ikey reached over her to take up the parcel, but she saw his action and pushed his hand away. 'Leave it!' she commanded.

'But, my dear . . . '

Ikey stopped mid-sentence, for there was a surprised gasp from Mary and then she began to laugh, though in a hysterical manner, pointing at the finger.

'What is it, my dear?' Ikey cried, alarmed.

But Mary's hysterical laughter continued and finally Ikey slapped her hard. She stopped and looked at him wild-eyed. 'It's not Hawk's finger!' she cried, then wept again.

'What do you mean?' Ikey cried out. He repeated himself several times, 'What do you mean? What do you mean?' before Mary stopped crying. Now she took deep gulps of air to calm herself.

'Whatever can you mean?' Ikey repeated urgently.

'It be the right forefinger,' she said, pointing to the object before her. 'Hawk had a long scar down that finger where I cut and sucked it when he had the snake bite. A long, clean scar, not to be missed!'

Ikey remembered the incident well. 'Are you sure it be the right and not the left?' he said.

'Left were once broken in a fight, it mended a wee bit crooked,' Mary said emphatically. She glanced at the finger on the table and gave a small shudder. 'Besides, that finger be too small, much too small, that be the finger of an Aboriginal child!'

'You mean this be a scam?' Ikey cried in amazement. 'They's seen the beer label and cooked it all up!' Ikey whistled to himself. 'Jesus, I never thought that whore Hannah had that much imagination!'

Mary looked at Ikey and then said fiercely, 'That finger still come from a little brat! That be wicked and cruel enough beyond imagining.' She paused and pointed at Ikey. 'They could have taken the Potato Factory, they could have had the bloody lot, if only it would o' brought back me boys!' She burst into tears again and then shouted, 'Ikey, I swear, I dunno how and I dunno where, but Hannah's going to pay for this!'

Chapter Thirty-six

It was four months after his visit to New Norfolk when Ikey, in the course of his nightly peregrinations, sensed he was being followed. He changed direction, cutting down the lane past New Market and quickening his pace, thinking to slip into the Hope & Anchor, the tavern at the end of the lane facing onto the safety of Macquarie Street. But then he heard his name called softly in a voice he was never likely to forget.

'You good pella, Ikey!'

'Billygonequeer?' Ikey called back in surprise.

'No, no, William Lanney!' Billygonequeer said urgently as he came out of the darkness not five feet from where Ikey stood.

Ikey listened to the voice from the shadows, amazed that Billygonequeer could have been so close without his hearing him. The two men embraced and as Ikey's hands clasped around Billy's shoulders, he felt the raised scar tissue across his back through the coarse canvas shirt.

'Blimey, I thought you be dead!' Ikey exclaimed, beaming at Billygonequeer's dark face. 'What's happened to you then, my dear?'

Billygonequeer, who now spoke quite passable English, explained to Ikey that under the name William Lanney he had become a whaleman for Captain Kelly on one of the local whaling ships which worked the bays and channels during the winter season.

'Ikey, listen,' Billygonequeer said finally. 'I come about the black kid on the beer bottle.'

Ikey's heart missed a beat. 'What's you know about that, Billygonequeer?'

'William Lanney! You gimme the name y'self!' Billygonequeer cried urgently. 'I still on the lam, man!'

Ikey listened carefully as Billygonequeer told him what he knew. He had been down south at the whaling station at Recherche Bay where they had been boiling down the catch. They had thereafter sailed up the D'Entrecasteaux Channel, but opposite Huon Island had hit a squall and done some damage to the mizzen mast and so had taken shelter in the Huon River. The wind being fair, they had sailed upriver to Port Huon, and put ashore for some minor repairs. Here, Billy had gone for a walk along the riverbank some way from the settlement when, to his surprise, he had met seven Aboriginals, five of them half castes and two of full blood.

The full bloods explained they came from the upper reaches of the Kermandie River to the south-west, which stretched to the high mountain. They talked for some time and then told him that several days previously they had been out hunting rat kangaroo when they saw a wild man who rode a horse, behind which he caused a black boy to run. Curious, they had crept closer. The boy was tied about the neck with a rope which was attached to the saddle. The wild man passed close to where they hid and they could see that the boy was not an Aboriginal, but quite different in appearance to their own people. Billygonequeer concluded by saying that, nearly three weeks later, he had heard some of the whalemen talking about the fifty pounds reward posted on the beer bottles and he'd asked one of them to read it aloud. Hearing Ikey's name, he had decided to tell him what he knew. 'You good pella, Ikey!' he said, laughing at himself, for he now spoke much better English.

'What sort of country be it, these mountains?' Ikey asked at last.

Billygonequeer shook his head. 'You can't go there, boss!' he protested vehemently. 'It black fella place, wild men convict and some timber getter, very bad country.'

'Can you go with troopers?'

Billygonequeer sniffed. 'Troopers can't go this place, wild men kill!'

'Will I see you again?' Ikey asked.

'Hobart Town very dangerous for me,' Billygone-queer said. 'Three day,' he pointed to the ground, 'same time, I see you here.'

At breakfast the following morning Ikey told Mary what had transpired.

'It's Hawk!' Mary cried. 'Oh, Ikey, I know it's him!'

'There were no mention by the blacks of a sighting of Tommo, so it may not be, my dear,' Ikey cautioned. 'Besides it be wild country, only escaped convicts and timber getters, the roughest and most dangerous o' men, all outside the law and with a price on their 'eads. You won't be able to pay any cove sufficient so he be mad enough to go into those mountains!'

Mary looked at Ikey. 'I knows mountains, I been all over Mount Wellington. I knows the way o' the bush, I'll go meself!'

Ikey was too shocked at first to react, but finally regained his voice. 'You're mad, Mary Abacus, this be wild country such as you've never seen. No trooper will venture there for fear o' death. There be no roads, not even paths, it be virgin timber, grown so close and tall it be dark in daylight!'

'And how does you know all this?' Mary said sullenly.

'You forget, my dear, I was in a road gang. I knows the way of timber, only this be much worse – no man what's not bred to the mountains can live there. Even the timber getters be o' the worst sort, Irish and most o' them villains or in concert with the wild men. If a woman should venture there, even if she should not perish soon from the climate and hardship she must endure, she would soon enough be used in such a way that she would die of other causes, if you knows what I mean!'

'I knows what you mean, Ikey Solomon,' Mary said grimly. 'But no wild man's going to treat my boy like an animal!'

In Mary's eyes was the look Ikey had come to know well, and he realised nothing would dissuade her. He inwardly cursed himself for telling her about the sighting. After all, there was no way of knowing if it was Hawk, or even if the natives had told the truth.

'Perhaps we could muster some troopers at Southport? You could talk to Mr Emmett?'

'I got more chance on my own, Ikey. A woman on her own be the best bait to hook a wild man!'

766

'Shit no! No, Mary, I cannot have you do this!' Ikey cried. He'd presumed, if not troopers, that Mary would take some sort of armed escort on such a perilous journey.

'They've taken my boy and turned him into an animal and tied a rope around his neck! I tell you, I'd sooner die than not go after the bastard what done that to Hawk!'

'You will die, Mary!' Ikey said softly.

'Then I die trying, that's all!' Mary said angrily. 'It be better than living ashamed!'

'I'll come with you!' Ikey said, suddenly making up his mind.

Mary, astonished, looked at Ikey and smiled, then her eyes filled with tears. 'If you were to come we would most surely guarantee to perish,' she said tenderly. 'But I thanks you, Ikey Solomon, from the bottom o' me heart!'

Ikey had to admit to himself that he was secretly delighted with this reply, for he already regretted his decision.

'You will need to make sure your affairs are all in order, my dear,' he said sadly.

The next day Mary's enquiries revealed that, in three days, a small trading ketch, the *Isle of Erin*, would be leaving on the morning tide for Port Huon, and then on to the tiny new hamlet of Franklin. Mary booked passage, even though it was a cargo boat, and there were no cabins except the one which belonged to the captain. She was advised to bring her own oilskins as she would have to remain on deck throughout the two-day journey, the ship having to lay up at night against the sudden squalls which so often blew up along the D'Entrecasteaux Channel.

767

Ikey urged her to wait until he had spoken to Billy-gonequeer again, but there was no other boat for four days and Mary would not delay a moment longer. She knew that if news of her impending journey leaked out she would be forbidden by the authorities to travel into such wild country, so she settled her affairs and Ikey was sworn to secrecy. Mary told Jessamy Hawkins and the men at the Potato Factory at both the Old Mill and at Strickland Falls that she was going to do some trading with the small settlements along the Huon River. She instructed that they send a dray loaded with six dozen cases of Tomahawk and Temperance beer, and four fifty-gallon barrels of her strongest dark ale, to the Old Wharf where the *Isle of Erin* was docked.

On the third morning, just before sunrise, Mary left Hobart Town not sure that she would ever return. She looked up at the great mountain which had swallowed her two sons and said a quiet farewell, for she was now convinced that her mountain had not murdered Hawk and Tommo. She sat on the deck of the *Isle of Erin* on a case of Tomahawk beer, her umbrella spread open and her hand clasping the Waterloo medal. 'Bring me luck, and send the green parakeets to find my sons for me,' she begged the mountain. The summit of Mount Wellington was covered in cloud and a light drizzle fell. Though it was late spring, and the almond blossoms already out, there was mist on the river as the barque lofted sail and slipped into the ebb of the outgoing tide.

The voyage proved slow though uneventful. By the time they reached the channel the day had turned to bright sunshine and the small, clumsy and overloaded ketch seemed to make unnecessarily heavy work of a light breeze. At nightfall, they hove onto the leeward side of Huon Island under a near full moon.

Mary slept fitfully, for the night was cold. She had brought two blankets, one for herself and one for Hawk, or one for each of her children, as she hoped she'd find them both. Mary also wore her warm coat, this being the most she thought she could carry on her back when she set out on her journey into the mountains. The blankets and a supply of hard tack biscuit and dried meat, matches, sugar and tea made up the remainder of her burden, except for the small axe she'd carried up the mountain on the night Hawk and Tommo disappeared. It was heavy, but she knew she would need to take it along. The blankets she would roll up and place across the top of a canvas bag she had constructed, which was not unlike a child's school satchel, though somewhat bigger. Mary also carried fifty pounds in notes which were hidden in the brass cylinder of her prisoner's purse and deposited up her cunny. In her handbag she carried sufficient money for any expenses she might incur and as well a pearl-handled, pepperbox pistol.

The pistol had been presented to her by Ikey, who had bought it from Ann Gower. Ikey was most particular that it be light enough for a woman to handle yet carried four chambers, could be ready loaded, and deadly if fired at close range. Not being in the least accustomed to the workings of firearms he had diligently written down the instructions on how it should be loaded and Mary practised until she was certain how it was done. Though she had never before fired a pistol, she was confident that she was capable of using it should the occasion arise.

The *Isle of Erin* arrived in the tiny settlement of Port Huon by mid-afternoon of the second day. Mary's beer was loaded onto a bullock cart to be transported to the Kermandie River settlement, the driver happy to take a case of beer instead of payment, thinking himself much the better off with such a bargain. Mary sat beside the driver as they made slow progress into the small settlement.

The town seemed to be entirely constructed of bark and mud. The streets, if streets they could be called, were ruts where the unwary traveller might sink his boot half way to the knee in the wet.

The buildings were a testament to colonial ingenuity. A framework of wood was raised, and bark was peeled from green eucalypt in strips six feet long and two feet wide. The strips were flattened on level ground by poles laid across them and allowed to dry. When dry and stiff they made excellent walls, as well as serving, if lightly strutted, as doors and windows. Brown, warm-coated stringy bark provided the roof cladding. All that was then required was a slabbed chimney built above a base of stone, and lined a further four feet with stone topped with turf to protect the walls from fire. The flue, also of bark, was then carried up on a framework of poles to a suitable height above the ridgepole. From the chimney-breast up, the flue was boxed on all sides and experience taught just where to place the chimney to avoid down draughts. Thus everything was made locally and, if care was taken in the construction, a comfortable home could be built in a very short time.

The surrounding countryside rose steeply from the river and clearings for the small holdings around the settlement were a testament to sheer hard work. The natural growth which had to be removed before the soil could be tilled was a staggering five hundred tonnes per hectare. Ring-barked trees two hundred feet high stood like dead sentinels, while from their trunks huge strips of bark whispered and flapped in the wind. On the ground below cows grazed in paddocks sown with English grasses, coxfoot and white york, which provided fodder and hay for the winter. The rich virgin soil was deep-loamed and full of nutrients; at milking time, milch cows came in from the runs with full udders.

But despite this appearance of a tranquil farming community, the rising ground and huge trees made each acre taken from the forest a triumph over the forces of nature. The small community clung to the banks of the Kermandie River, and the wild country stretching towards the Hartz Mountains was not yet penetrated by settlers.

These forbidding parts of the interior were mostly occupied by isolated communities of itinerant timber getters, many of Irish origin, who lived further upriver and were said to be half wild and dangerous and unlikely to welcome strangers in their midst.

All male convicts who arrived in the colony would spend some time at hard labour producing timber and from that time on, any misdemeanour would result in a further stint on a timber gang. So, almost by definition, the worst offenders learned the most about the skill of the sawing pit, splitting logs and getting timber. In addition, the Irish, many of whom lacked the basic skills to work in towns, and being usually among the most intractable of convicts and also Roman Catholics in an overwhelmingly Protestant community, found timber getting was the only lawful skill they possessed upon emancipation. For many, isolation became their only way of avoiding trouble.

They seldom ventured with their families into the nearby towns and their children were wild things. They would score the timber, each with his individual mark and the number of his agent, and float it downriver. Every few weeks one of their kind might venture quietly into the small settlement and collect what was owing to them all. He might stop at the tavern for a few drinks, though he would usually buy what he needed of brandy and rum to take back into the forest, and leave with no more than a grunt to the publican.

It was claimed that should the law be foolish enough to wander into a timber camp, and if the timber getters should first see the law and the law not see them, then the law would be unlikely to see the sunset on the river again. It was a brave set of troopers or special constables who ventured out from the police station at Southport to patrol the small, scattered and isolated communities who lived in the dense, dark forests. And those who did travelled on horseback, so that they could more easily cover the ground or avoid a surprise attack.

Though these backwoodsmen would come out of the forest in winter to work at the Recherche Bay whaling stations during the peak season, they still kept to themselves, but should they drink, they turned into the very devil himself. The money they made during this period was spent in provisioning at the general store which they took back into the forests for the summer months.

As well, in the summer, escaped convicts and wild men roamed the mountain country. Food was relatively easy to get in the form of small animals and the easily captured native hen. In the winter they came nearer to the towns to raid the small farms and take a sheep or even a calf or pig, and if the property were not well guarded, or the owner away, to rape any women or children they would find. These were men outside the law and, like the timber getters, they lived lonely and brutal lives deep in the forests and mountains. They left the timber getters alone unless they should find one on his own, when they would murder him for his boots or axe or some other possession.

The bullock driver took Mary directly to the front of the tavern to avoid the mud. From the moment they entered the outskirts of the little town dozens of urchins, all with black mud caked up to their knees, had followed the cart and rudely yelled questions at Mary. But now they stood around shyly as she alighted and, first jumping a small mud pool, walked onto the verandah of the public house. It was the largest building in town, though it too was built of bark, but featured at one end a wall of stone containing a great high chimney which promised a hearth in the interior of splendid proportions.

Mary bid the driver wait and entered the tavern. At first, the smoke, smell and noise overwhelmed her senses. But when her eyes became accustomed to the dark she saw it to be a large rectangular room with a crowded bar running the full length of one side. The only natural light entering the room was from three small windows set up on the wall opposite the bar, this so that they should not be easily broken if a fight broke out.

The hearth at one end was as grand in size as it promised to be from the outside, but its tall chimney had nevertheless been badly designed. Smoke filled the room so that, with the addition of half a hundred pipes and cigars, it was far past the point of comfort for both the eyes and the nose. The low ceiling was long since blackened by the constant fumes and added to the dingy appearance of the place.

Several card tables occupied the centre of the room and wooden benches were placed against the outside walls, and all were occupied by human forms who, from the noxious smell they emitted, had not washed in a year. Men stood everywhere drinking beer and rum, while the players at the card tables with neat stacks of coins at their side must have found it difficult to communicate the least instruction in such an awful din. Mary observed that there were no women to be seen, not even a barmaid behind the counter.

As she walked in, there was an instant lull in the hubbub as the rough men standing and sitting everywhere appraised her. Eyes red from smoke and drinking followed her as she moved over to the bar, and two men leaning upon it stepped aside to let her in.

'Is there a publican?' Mary asked.

This, for some reason, caused the men within the room to explode with laughter.

'Aye!' said a voice as soon as the laughter had died down. It came from a door set into the centre of the wall behind the bar and, at the same instant, a big, burly man with a completely flat nose and eyes stretched to slits with puffed-up scar tissue made his appearance. As he came closer Mary saw that his ears, too, had the cauliflower appearance of a rough goer. She smiled nervously as he approached her and thought him ideally suited to his surroundings.

'You must forgive the men, not too many o' the fair sex do come in 'ere, miss,' he said, drying his hands on his dirty apron. 'Gin is it?'

'Ginger beer,' Mary said.

The publican looked somewhat embarrassed. 'Don't 'ave much call for ginger beer 'ere, miss.'

'Best rum, half and half and half a tot,' Mary pointed to a clay pitcher, 'if that be water.'

'Aye,' the publican said and took down a bottle of rum from the shelf behind him and poured a half measure into a glass, topping it with water from the jug.

Mary's call for best rum seemed to amuse the men and a second wave of laughter filled the room.

'Now, now, we'll have none o' that!' the publican called sharply, whereupon the laughter died down abruptly.

'Mary Abacus, from the Potato Factory, maybe you've heard o' my beer?' Mary announced to the publican, her voice firm, not betraying the nervousness she felt within.

'By Jesus, yes!' the publican exclaimed, plainly astonished. There was a murmur around the room and quite suddenly the mood changed. Mary sensed a new tone of respect from the drinkers.

'We don't get much o' yer stuff 'ere, Miss Abacus, though it be greatly liked when we does.' The publican stuck out his huge paw. 'Sam,' he said. 'Sam Goodhead.'

Mary fought back a smile at this inappropriate name. She said, 'I have some beer for sale. Would you be interested, Mr Goodhead?'

'Never get enough beer, miss. Always interested. Though o' course it depends on the price, don't it?'

Mary gave Sam Goodhead a description of the beer and told him the quantity and the price, which she'd set fairly low so that the beer would be seen as a bargain.

'I'll take the lot orf yer hands, Miss Abacus, 'appy to do business!'

'I shall need accommodation tonight. Does you have a safe room, Mr Goodhead?'

'Not 'ere I doesn't, but if you'd care to come 'ome to the missus, I daresay we can put some o' the brats together and find you a bed what's safe enough. We'd take it as a pleasure if you'd 'ave tea with us.'

The noise in the room gradually resumed its former level, though several men had left the tavern to inspect the beer on the bullock cart. When Sam Goodhead arrived with Mary the men were taunting the bullock driver, who now stood with his whip held aloft ready to strike at anyone who should attempt to lift a case of beer from the cart.

'Bring it 'round the back, mate,' the publican instructed. 'Two stout lads back there will 'elp you unload.' He turned to Mary. 'Them's well-coopered barrels if I say so meself,' he remarked.

'Keep them with my compliments, Mr Goodhead,' Mary said, then told the publican about the case of Tomahawk the bullock driver had taken as payment and that this should be deducted from the price and, further, that he should take a case of her new Tomahawk beer for his personal enjoyment with her compliments.

'We ain't 'ad this beer before, it be a new one then?' the publican said, shouldering a case of Tomahawk to take home with him. 'I shall look forward to it.'

Mrs Goodhead was an equal match for her husband in size and to Mary's keen eye looked somewhat knocked about in life herself, with one eye permanently closed and some scarring on her face. It was not the custom to enquire into the background of someone recently met, as most people in the colony had a similar and unfortunate story to tell. But after several of Mary's Tomahawk beers both her host and hostess became most loquacious, obviously maintaining a good head for liquor and, except for warming to the prospect of discussion, not otherwise disconcerted by it. Though they spoke briefly of their time as convicts in New South Wales, this was only to establish more quickly Sam's true past vocation, which was, Mary was not surprised to hear, that of a professional fighter. His wife, Esmeralda, had also been a fighter of some renown, originally in Bristol and later in the colony of New South Wales.

Sam had risen and shortly returned carrying an old poster which he handed to Mary. 'Read it aloud, please, Miss Abacus,' he said, laughing.

Mary held the poster up and began to read.

> *Sam Goodhead hereby challenges*
> *to fight any man in the colony for*
> *a prize of Five Pounds plus travel*
> *expenses and two gallons of beer.*
> *My wife Esmeralda shall fight any*
> *woman in the country, bar none;*
> *and for a prize of Two Pounds, travel*
> *expenses and a bottle of English Gin.*
> *My dog will fight any dog of 45 lb*
> *or less for two shillings, plus a juicy*

butcher's bone! My cock shall fight
any cock in the colony of any weight
for a shilling and a lb of good corn!

* * * * *

Apply, Mr Sam Goodhead,
Parramatta Post Office.

Both Sam and Esmeralda Goodhead laughed uproariously as Mary concluded.

'Aye, it does ya good to 'ave it read out loud. Though
we knows it orf by 'eart, we can't read neiver of us, so
it's good to 'ave it read by someone else once in a
while,' Sam declared happily.

This explained why the publican and his wife had not
broached the subject of the label on the Tomahawk
bottle, for they were by now on their sixth bottle.

Esmeralda finally rose and prepared supper, a meal of
roast beef with potatoes and swedes and a most delicious
pickled cabbage. She filled four plates for her children
and sent them outside to eat, and then brought three more
heaped helpings to the table where they had been drinking. It was a meal as good as any Mary had tasted, and
much more than she could eat. She excused herself after
having finished less than half the contents of the plate.

'Never you mind, love, the little 'uns'll polish that orf
soon enough, or Sam 'ere!' Esmeralda laughed.

After tea Sam produced a clay pipe, and when he had
it well stoked so that the room was fuggy with smoke,
Mary addressed him quietly.

'I has a proposition to put to you, Sam,' she said, for
they were now on Christian name terms.

'Put away, lass,' Sam Goodhead said, puffing contentedly on his pipe.

'It be in strictest confidence.'

Sam nodded. 'Aye, everythin' is. I'll not tell unless I can make a profit out of it,' he said with a wink.

'That be the point,' Mary said. 'If you stays stum, you makes a very big profit; if you talks, you owes me for the beer!'

'What's ya mean, lass?' Sam said, now most interested and leaning forward. Esmeralda, who was scouring a pot with her back to them, suddenly stopped scrubbing.

'I needs some advice and help, nothing more, 'cept I don't want any folks to know about it right off!'

'That's not so easy 'round 'ere.' Sam laughed. 'Scratch the 'ead of a pimple on yer arse and it's the talk o' the bleedin' town fer days. Your comin' 'ere today is already the news o' the month!'

'Year!' Esmeralda called.

'What is it then?' Sam Goodhead asked.

Mary told him that she needed someone who wouldn't talk about it to take her as far as it was possible to go up the Kermandie River and thereafter to give her, if possible, some directions which would take her to the high mountains. 'That's all, a boatman what will keep his gob shut and some directions possibly.'

Sam Goodhead whistled. 'And you'll give us what?'

'The whole consignment o' beer I brought,' Mary said.

Sam Goodhead sighed. 'I'm sorely tempted, lass.'

Esmeralda turned fom her pots. 'You'll do no such thing, Sam!' she shouted.

Sam Goodhead shrugged. 'If I did that, Mary, it be the same as killin' you. Ya can't take such a journey all alone. Ya can't even take a journey like that with a platoon o' troopers. I'm sorry, lass, it be suicide!'

Mary picked up an empty bottle of Tomahawk and read from the back label. Then she told them about the abduction of Tommo and Hawk and the news that Hawk, at least, had been captured by a wild man and had been seen by some Aboriginals in the region of the Hartz Mountains.

'Them blacks are a lyin', thievin' bunch. Most be now locked away, thank Gawd, but there still be a few 'round 'ere. Ya can't trust 'em though,' Sam said. His pipe had gone dead and he now set about scraping the spent tobacco from the top of the bowl and relighting what was left.

'Sam, I'm going anyway, all you can do is make it easier!' Mary cried.

Eventually she convinced Sam Goodhead that nothing would keep her from looking for Hawk.

'We've a lad works fer me at the pub, he 'as a boat and will keep 'is gob shut if I tells 'im,' the publican said. 'You'd best leave at first light, that way the town won't known yer gorn.' He puffed at his pipe. 'Though it won't take long before the bloody timber getters know!' He sighed. 'Gawd 'elp ya, Mary Abacus, yer a brave woman, and if I didn't know better, I'd say a very foolish one! If ya gets back alive I'll take yer beer as bonus. If ya doesn't, which be more than likely, we'll use the money fer a tombstone, though I'll vouch yer body won't be lyin' beneath it!'

Mary was surprised to see that Esmeralda was quietly weeping in the corner.

A heavy mist lay over the water as Mary stood on the shore waiting for a lad she knew only as Tom. She heard the slow splash of oars through the fog and soon

the outline of a small, flat-bottomed boat appeared
through the swirling vapour. Behind it was a second
boat, a smaller dinghy, attached by a rope to the boat
the boy was rowing. The boy shipped the oars and
Mary pulled the boat onto the shore and stepped into
it. The young lad standing midships took her canvas
bag and stowed it in the bow, and held his hand out to
steady her as she seated herself in the stern. Then,
without saying a word, he pushed the boat back into
deeper water, pulled it around with one oar until the
boat pointed upstream, and began to row.

The Kermandie was a slow-flowing river, but rowing
against the current with another skiff in tow was not
an easy matter, and every half hour Tom beached the
little boats and, his chest puffing violently, was forced
to rest. About nine of the clock the mist lifted and the
huge trees, which had appeared simply as shadowy out-
lines in the misted landscape, now showed clearly on
either shore. Mary found herself locked into a narrow
ribbon of water walled as surely and steeply by the
giant eucalypts as if the trees had been sheer cliffs of
solid rock. A flock of yellow-tailed black cockatoos flew
over at one point, their tinny screeching the only sound
they'd heard since leaving but for the lap of the oars in
the water and once the flap of a flock of chestnut teal
as they rose in alarm from the water. The sun was now
well up and Mary worked herself out of her coat. They
passed a black cormorant on a dead branch, its wings
spread to the new sun, and soon after a white-faced
heron stood on the shore, its long neck and sharp-
beaked head moving in slow jerks, made curious by the
slap of the oars. Though the trees on either side of the
river still looked cold and dark, the glare from the water

and the sun overhead made Mary feel uncomfortably hot. Tom's shirt was dark with sweat and his long, lank hair lay flat against his head. Mary saw beads of perspiration cutting thin streaks down his dirty neck.

The further they travelled the more dense the trees became. Giant prehistoric tree ferns, some of them forty feet high, grew at the water's edge, and occasionally they'd hear the splash of an unseen creature plop into the water from the riverbank. At one stage Mary, intimidated by her surroundings, whispered to Tom simply so that she might make some sort of human contact. But he held a finger to his lips. Once, about an hour out from the settlement, they heard the sound of an axe striking. Sharp, regular echoes seemed to bounce off the trees, though from somewhere much deeper into the forest. Mary was not sure whether the sound was frightening or comforting, but Tom shipped oars for a few moments and listened while the boat drifted backwards in the current. Then, Tom taking great care with his strokes, they moved on again.

After four hours with regular rests they came to a waterfall and Tom pulled the boats into shore.

'This be it, missus, we can't go further,' he shouted, his voice almost lost in the crash and tumble of water over rock.

Mary stepped onto the shore and Tom pulled the boat fully into the little pebbled beach, untied the smaller dinghy and dragged it also onto the safety of the riverbank. Then, straining mightily, he pulled the first dinghy into a clump of reeds and fern, piling the branches of dead trees over it until it was impossible to see. He placed three rocks close to each other, two together and one pointing to where the boat was hidden.

'I'll be back for the boat in ten days!' he shouted, pointing to the fern and reeds where it lay concealed.

Mary nodded and handed the lad a pound. He grinned, his work well rewarded. 'Thank 'ee, ma'am, Gawd bless 'ee now!' he shouted, touching the forelock of damp hair. Then he pushed the smaller dinghy back into the water. The tiny boat turned in the churning current at the foot of the falls, then the oars dug in and he steadied it, waved briefly and began to row away.

Mary watched as he disappeared around a bend in the river, rowing lazily in the firm current now driven faster by the falls. Then she rolled up her coat and strapped it with the blankets resting on top of her canvas bag, slipping her arms through its straps so that it sat firmly on her slim back. She stood for a moment and held the Waterloo medal in her hand, half praying that a pair of green rosellas might suddenly fly over as a sign, but nothing disturbed the bright blue cloudless sky overhead.

She had a map which Sam Goodhead had drawn, or perhaps obtained from elsewhere, and it showed a path leading directly from the waterfall in a direction due west. It took Mary some time to find the path, for it was much overgrown with bracken and fern. She soon stopped to take the axe from her pack, and her going was tediously slow. Though it was not past ten in the morning the forest was dark as though already deep into the afternoon, and as she travelled further into the giant trees she began to feel the weight of the journey on her mind.

For the first time Mary realised that she had no idea what she was doing or how she would find Hawk. Above her the trees towered two hundred feet into the

783

air and the wind in the high canopy gave off the sound of endless waves beating against a lonely shore. At noon she stopped beside a small stream, ate a little of her biscuit and drank from the mountain water. The straps of her canvas bag had cut into her shoulders, she was already badly scratched about the hands and face, and her bonnet was saturated with perspiration.

At nightfall Mary was still within the forest and the track had become almost impossible to find, so she halted beside a small stream some twenty yards distance from the path, marking several trees with the blade of the axe so that she might find her way back in the morning. She ate a little more of the hard biscuit and some dried meat, lit a small fire and boiled tea in her billy. The night became bitterly cold but Mary could not take the chance of going to sleep with a fire. She doused the fire, wrapped herself in both blankets and still wearing her coat she fell into a fitful sleep. She was exhausted, and the night sounds did not unduly disturb her for they were no different to those she had heard so often on her own mountain.

Mary woke up with the sun cutting through the misted trees and lay for a moment, all her senses suddenly alert for she could hear a most familiar sound. It was friendly to her ear until a moment later she realised where she was. She'd heard the sawing of Peter Degraves' timber cutters a thousand times on the mountain, a cross-cut saw being worked in a sawing pit. But now she realised it was coming from close by. Had she continued on another five minutes along the path the previous night, she would have stumbled right into a timber getters' camp.

She folded the blankets and packed her bag and, with

her heart beating fiercely, she drank from the stream and then regained the path. She crept along until she saw the camp ahead, four bark huts in a forest clearing. She could see several children playing and a pig tied to a stake and once a woman came out of one of the huts and yelled at the brats to come in and eat. And all through this Mary could hear the saw. Though she could not see the pit, she knew exactly what it would be like. The log would be placed longitudinally over the pit on wooden cross pieces, whereupon sawing lines would be drawn along it with chalk or charcoal. One man descended into the pit while the other stood on the log. The man in the pit pulled down to make the cutting stroke, the one above pulled the saw up clear of the wood and guided the cut along the line. It seemed such a normal and friendly occupation, and while she knew it was most strenuous work which built up bulging muscles if the body received sufficient nourishment, Mary had never before associated the sound with danger.

The path led directly to the clearing. Mary, hoping that the sound of the saw would cover her escape through the undergrowth, moved in a wide circle around the camp. She kept the sound of the saw in her ears so that she might find herself back on the path but on the other side of the timber getters' camp. Almost an hour later she regained the path with the sound of the cutting now well behind her.

But soon after Mary left the camp she had a sense of being watched. At first she told herself that her alarmed senses were a delayed reaction from having so nearly stumbled into the camp. But the feeling persisted and she could not be rid of it. Once she looked up to find a large, pitch-black, crow-like bird with burning ruby eyes looking at her. After the initial shock, she laughed quietly to herself. She was becoming frightened of shadows. At noon she stopped and moved off the path some distance and boiled a billy. She used only the driest, smallest twigs and built the fire against the trunk of a huge red gum so that any smoke she created would be sucked upwards against the trunk and dispersed unseen through the forest canopy.

It was then that she was attacked. From a hole in the tree she had disturbed a hive of wasps and they descended upon her in an angry storm. Mary had the presence of mind to grab her canvas bag and pluck the billy from the fire and run. She rushed headlong through the undergrowth, not caring about any sound she should make, the wasps stinging her furiously as she ran. She fell once and cut her arm and then got up and ran again until the wasps seemed no longer to torment her. Finally she stumbled to a halt and began to weep, her flesh covered in hundreds of stings so that she felt she could not possibly bear the pain.

She had stopped beside one of the numerous mossy banked streams that cut through the forest and in desperation threw down her canvas bag and ripped off her clothes. The wasps had penetrated through the material of her dress and her body and arms were covered in stings which hurt well beyond the lashes she had received on the *Destiny II*. Hysterical with the pain, Mary lay down naked in the stream. The icy water flowing over her body brought some relief, for her flesh soon grew numb. Her poor crippled hands were swollen to twice their normal size and her right hand was burned when she'd plucked the billy from the flames.

Though her bonnet had protected her head and she had no stings in her hair, her neck and face were badly stung and her lips were so swollen that she could not open her mouth.

Mary was soon chilled to the bone and was forced to rise from the stream and cover herself with the blankets. As soon as she warmed again the terrible pain returned and she seemed close to losing her senses. Her body had grown quite stiff as though it were paralysed and she could not move, though she was shuddering violently as if in great shock. Then she lost consciousness. Several times she seemed to see the crow with its ruby eyes and long, sharp beak, as though it were seeking to pluck out her eyes. Then a dog-like creature sat and watched her from a short distance, its green eyes sharp as lights in the night, and sometimes she caught flashes of a dark face hovering above her. She tried to scream but no sound came from her lips which seemed, in her delirium, to cover her entire face, enveloping her nose and puffing up her eyes.

How long she remained in this state Mary had not the least idea, but when she awoke it was morning, though whether of the next day or several days after, she could not tell. Her body and face were covered in a sticky balm, as though the wasp stings had themselves suppurated, but miraculously the pain was gone, and the swelling had abated and did not hurt to the touch. Mary washed in the stream until the sticky substance was removed from her body, hands and face and then she dressed, distressed to find that her garments were torn in several places from her flight through the undergrowth.

Mary ate, and boiled the billy for tea, for she found

herself very hungry. Then she packed her bag and prepared to leave, but suddenly she realised that she did
not know where the path lay. She moved around for
more than an hour without finding it and then knew
that she had become completely lost. Sam Goodhead
had cautioned her against leaving the track by more
than a few feet. 'Fer if ya become lost in the forest ya
will die as surely as if ya put a gun to yer own 'ead,'
he had warned.

It was then Mary heard the screech of the green
rosella, a sound she knew as well as the beat of her own
heart, the curious 'kussik-kussik' call repeated and then
a bell-like contact note; when alarmed, a shrill piping
sound. Rosellas do not fly in flocks in the spring but in
pairs, and now she heard them both as they chattered
somewhere to her left. Mary, ever superstitious and
with no better plan to follow, moved towards the
sound.

Mary had been three days in the forest, for though
she did not know it, she had lain all the next day and
the night that followed beside the stream in the delirium
caused from the wasp stings. Now, without questioning
the curious circumstances that the sound of the two
parrots never seemed far from her and that she never
seemed to approach nearer or to see them, she
responded to their call. Sometimes she would turn to
take an easier way through the undergrowth and she
would hear the shrill piping of alarm from the two
birds. After a while she learned to correct her course to
the sound of their calls.

Mary fervently believed that the great mountain had
answered her call for help. Even in her most prosaic
moments, Mary thought of the mountain as her friend

and lover, which was why she did not question the call of the two birds and the fact that they never left her.

Late on the afternoon of the fourth day she suddenly came across the track again and soon after broke out from the trees. She had been climbing steadily all day and now she found herself in a small valley above the tree line, a dent in a mountain which rose steeply upwards. It was as though a sharp line had been drawn where the mountain broke out of the apron of trees and into the coarse tussock grass of the high mountain country. The track now led upwards and seemed quite well worn, there being no forest growth to obscure it.

Mary walked along the track a short distance but then, in the fading light decided to retreat into the forest for the night. It was some minutes after she had returned and moved a safe distance from the track when she realised that the 'kussik-kussik' calls of the two rosellas were no longer with her.

She rose again at dawn, her body stiff and sore, and boiled the billy for tea. She ate sparingly, not knowing how much longer she would be in the wilderness and conscious that if she should find Hawk she would need to share her supplies with him.

However, by now her hope of finding her son was greatly diminished. The forest had left her in despair and even though she had come safely through it, she now saw that a wild man might hide effectively from a thousand troopers and not be found in a lifetime. Her only hope was the notion that the monster who had captured her son rode on horseback, and horses do not find fodder in the forest but need grassland. He would be forced to live or spend time near some sort of pasture, and this meant open ground.

Mary climbed steadily all morning. The mountains, she discovered, were punctured with small, sharp valleys like indented cones, many of them turned to small blue lakes with grassy walls too steep to climb down into. She would often stop for breath and far below her she could see the endless stretch of green forest turned blue in the distance, and the glinting, wide stretch of the Huon River twenty or more miles away. The mountain, despite the sun, grew cold as she rose higher, and a sharp, icy wind whipped her skin.

On her first night she found a small box canyon which was protected from the wind and made her camp. It was perhaps a foolish place to spend the night, for there was no place to retreat, but her hand throbbed painfully where it had been burned by the billy and Mary was too spent of effort to care. Her greatest concern was to escape the cutting wind. Besides, the mountain, but for rock and grass and bracken fern, was bare of any acceptable hiding place.

Mary woke with the crack of a rock striking near her head, her nostrils filled with the musty smell of horse sweat. She turned to look upwards and saw a horse and rider not fifteen paces from where she lay.

Mary now sat up with the blankets still clasped about her neck to form a protective tent about her body, groping for the pistol which she had placed fully loaded under a rock near her side the night before. The folds of the blanket concealed her free hand as she found it, though her swollen hand made it difficult to grip firmly the small pistol.

The man on the horse did not make a sound but simply stared down at her. He was dressed almost entirely in kangaroo and opossum skins but for a trooper's high-topped white cap much battered and entirely blackened. His filthy beard fell almost to his waist and his unkempt hair hung wild and knotted to his shoulders. What remained of his face was dark with dirt and criss-crossed with scars and his nose was squashed flat, like a pig's snout, and from it a stream of yellow snot ran into his matted beard. A red tongue flicked from the dark hair of his face as though he was tasting the air or testing the nature of the wind, savouring her body smell.

It was then that she saw Hawk. Or perhaps it wasn't, except that the skeleton attached to the rope which led from the back of the horse was black in colour. Mary gasped. 'Hawk!' she cried. The skeleton raised both its hands but did not speak and now Mary saw that it was her son. His hands worked slowly and Mary tried to follow. Hawk's hands simply spelled, 'Mama'.

'Hawk! Mama's come!' Mary shouted and then looking up at the monster on horseback she screamed, 'He's my boy, my precious boy, give me him!'

The creature looked backwards and jerked violently at the rope so that Hawk was thrown to his knees. Then he slowly dismounted and, undoing the rope from the saddle, pulled it, bringing Hawk back to his feet. He then dragged him over to a large boulder and tied him to it. Turning, he drove his fist into the child's face. Hawk made no sound as he fell.

At the sight of Hawk knocked to the ground from the vicious blow, Mary began to weep. 'You bastard! You fucking bastard!' she moaned, repeating the words over and over again in her terrible distress.

The man moved slowly to tie the reins of his horse to the point of a sharp rock. He knew he had Mary trapped. The bluff rose behind and on either side of her, and he himself blocked her only chance of escape.

Now he advanced slowly towards Mary, who rose to her feet as he approached. He was no more than four feet from her when she raised the pistol behind the blanket, but the wild man, perhaps sensing danger, suddenly lunged forward and threw her to the ground. The pistol fell from Mary's swollen hand on to her coat, which she had the previous night spread on the ground, so its falling made little noise. Mary landed on her back, the pistol digging painfully into her ribs.

The monster, now on top of her, panting violently, tore open the blankets which still half covered her, then ripped the top of her dress exposing her breasts. He was not a tall man but wide and powerfully strong, and he now spread one thick hand around Mary's throat to pin her down. With his free hand he began to tear the skirt from her body.

He was slobbering at the mouth, his tongue darting in and out. Then his arm rose above his shoulder and he smashed the side of her face with the back of his hand. Releasing his grip on her throat, he got to his knees and quickly pulled down his greasy hide trousers to show a huge, jerking erection. Parting Mary's legs roughly, he tried to force an entry.

Mary, almost unconscious from the blow, did not scream but fought to keep her wits about her and willingly allowed her legs to open. The monster was grunting and puffing as he tried to penetrate, but Mary's prisoner's purse prevented his penis from entering her. She felt his fingers grope at her and then with a grunt he withdrew the brass cylinder and threw it aside. Then he jammed himself between her legs, again trying to force his way into her. Mary felt the sharp pain as he entered and at the same moment she pulled the trigger of the pistol she held against his stomach. She pulled back the hammer and pulled the trigger a second time.

A look of complete and uncomprehending surprise appeared on the wild man's face and then he gripped his stomach with both hands. Mary set the hammer back and pulled a third time, this shot moving upwards and entering his heart, shortly followed by another. The creature jerked once and then his body slumped over her. Instantly he voided from both his natural apertures.

The sound of the four shots echoed and reverberated through the small canyon as Mary lay terrified under the fallen monster, his member still jerking within her.

Screaming, she pushed at the dead man and after a few frantic moments was able to climb out from under him. She was covered in blood and guts, shit and vomit, both her breasts stained crimson with his blood, which also soaked what remained of her dress and petticoat.

Mary did not even think to pause but ran towards Hawk, who had regained his feet and now cowered against the rock. She grabbed him and clasped him to her and howled as though she herself were some primitive creature and then, at last, she wept and wept, holding her son in her arms.

Chapter Thirty-seven

In years to come Hawk would grow into a man who stood six feet eight inches tall and weighed two hundred and eighty pounds with no lard upon him. People would whisper as he passed that he had once cheated the gallows. As proof they would point to the thick collar of scar tissue about his neck.

'The rope could not break his neck,' they'd whisper, 'but it took his voice.'

This last part was an appropriate enough explanation. Hawk had been dragged behind the wild man's horse and the constant pulling and falling had destroyed his vocal cords. He would never speak again. So that the full trauma of his experience might be truly appreciated, it should be added that during the six months he was enslaved he had been repeatedly sodomised.

On the return journey a most fortunate circumstance befell the terrified couple. The timber getters had found Mary's trail and set out to find who had intruded into their domain. They came upon Mary and Hawk making their way down the mountain on the wild man's horse not two hours after she had killed him. Mary was wearing her blood-stained overcoat to cover her nakedness, and

Hawk clutched one of the bloody blankets about his body.

Two of the timber getters continued up the mountain to inspect the corpse which Mary had covered with the remaining blanket, and the three others escorted Mary and Hawk safely down through the wilderness, allowing them to remain on the horse. The two men soon enough caught up with them and started to shout excitedly from some distance before they finally arrived.

'She's killed Mad Dog Mulray!' one of them cried. 'Shot 'im through the 'eart!' the other shouted so as not to be outdone by his partner. One of them carried over his shoulder a bundle made from the opossum skin coat the wild man had worn. The second one now wore a set of military pistols in his belt and was waving Mary's pepperbox pistol which, in her state of shock, she had entirely and most foolishly forgotten to retrieve.

There was much excitement among the three remaining men and the oldest, a man who had earlier most formally introduced himself to Mary as Hindmarsh, looked up at her admiringly. Then the lad threw the skin bundle to the ground and untied it. Inside was the severed head of the wild man.

Mary gasped, though she was too shocked to scream, or perhaps there was no screaming left in her. She instinctively grabbed Hawk and placed her hands over his eyes.

'You 'ave done us a great service, Mary Abacus,' Hindmarsh said at last. 'He were a divil, a monster creature, the anti-Christ hisself. He's murdered seven of our forest folk.' He touched the severed head with the toe of his boot and then turned to the lad who had placed it at his feet. 'Tie it up again, Saul.' Then he laughed.

'It will make a grand Christmas present on the gate post o' the police station in Southport!'

One of the young men now handed the prisoner's purse to Hindmarsh, who examined it briefly and then looked up at Mary.

'This be your'n miss?' he asked. It was obvious to Mary that he well knew the nature of the object he held in his hands.

Mary nodded. 'In it be fifty pounds, it were money offered for the recovery o' me son,' she explained. 'The reward like.' She placed her hand on Hawk's shoulder.

The men surrounding her were rough and ready and now they laughed and looked at each other, their expressions plainly bemused. 'The nigger be your son?' Hindmarsh asked surprised, looking first at Mary and then into Hawk's dark and frightened face.

'Yes, mine!' Mary cried fiercely.

Hawk jumped at the tone of Mary's voice and the blanket slipped to his shoulders and now Hindmarsh and the others saw where the flesh was cut half an inch into the boy's neck to expose the bones. In other parts it was festered and suppurating and slabs of pink scar tissue had been laid down from earlier rope burns. 'Jaysus, Mary Mother o' Gawd!' Hindmarsh said. Then he handed the brass cylinder back to Mary.

'This is not ours to own,' he said.

'I be happy to pay it all, if you'll escort us back to the river where we has a boat,' Mary said.

'Yes we knows about that,' Hindmarsh said. 'It were not very well hid.' He smiled. 'We'll be after takin' you anyways, miss, you'll not be payin' us for *that* privilege!' He pointed to the horse and then the pistols in the young man's belt. ''Orse and pistols, they be payment more'n enough.' He looked at the four younger men so that they might pay keener attention to what he was about to say. 'We owes you, Mary Abacus. You be a legend from now among the timber getters, accepted as one of our own kind and welcome to return at any time you wishes, even though I daresay you be a bloody Protestant!' He paused and then added with a grin, 'And so we won't be after makin' you a saint though you comes a bloody sight nearer than most I've 'eard o' what comes from Rome!'

Hawk spent long periods on his own on the mountain. It was as though he was eternally searching for Tommo, trying to recapture the essence of his brother. He soon regained the flesh on his bones and his neck healed well as young flesh does. Mary changed the label on the back of her Tomahawk beer to contain only Tommo's name and description, though all else remained.

Tomahawk Ale was now most famous in the colony and also in Melbourne and Sydney and it seemed almost the entire colony knew of the disappearance of Tommo. Mary never admitted it, but she secretly believed that Tommo was dead, though Hawk did not. Despite being repeatedly questioned in hand language by Ikey upon his return, Hawk could remember next to nothing of the kidnapping. The shock of the experience had completely erased his memory of the incident, but for the fact that they had not been captured by the wild man but by men who knew their names and had been most friendly.

Hawk continued with his studies and was seldom without a book in his hand. Always a serious child, he was now withdrawn and rarely smiled, though when he did, Mary would say, 'It's a smile that could brighten a dark room at midnight'. With the benefit of the hand language which Mary soon learned well, he was able to talk with her as well as Ikey and Jessamy, who had also learned the language. With others, provided they could read, he was able to write upon a slate which he carried on a string about his neck.

Ikey, fearing that Hawk's inability to talk might disadvantage him, spent more and more time with his adopted son. Hawk at ten was already working on the accounting books at the Potato Factory under Ikey's instructions. At thirteen he was most competent with a ledger and had developed a fair hand which Mary wished, when it matured, should be the most beautiful hand in the colony, and so she bought him the latest in handwriting manuals so that he might practise the perfection of his letters.

But Ikey feared that this was not enough and, without Mary's knowledge, he began to teach Hawk all the skills he knew. Hawk was too big in his frame to have ever been a pickpocket, but in all the other tricks of palming he became an expert. His large hands could conceal anything and there was not a card game he could not play or cheat at with great skill, though Ikey despaired of him for he would never cheat in a real game, but much preferred to win with his own wit and intellect. He taught Hawk how to 'christen' a watch, and how to recognise a forged banknote, of which there were a great many in circulation in Van Diemen's Land. Hawk also learned to lip read, even though his hearing was perfect. 'So you may read what a man says across a room or in a crowd,' Ikey explained. Conscious that he had been brought up by Mary to be honest in all his dealings, Hawk would sometimes ask Ikey why he should learn a certain skill.

'Bless you, my dear, it is not an honest world we live in and few can enjoy the luxury o' being entirely honest within it.' Ikey would cock his head to one side. 'Have you not noted that the expression most cherished by those who are rich is the term "the honest poor"? They take much time to extol this virtue in those who have nothing, whereas there is no expression in our language which talks o' "the honest rich"! Honesty, if it be truly earned, be, for the most part, the product o' poverty and occasionally, if it is practised by the rich, a characteristic of inherited wealth, though rare enough in even this circumstance!'

Ikey would warm to the subject. 'There is neither bread nor virtue in poverty but, because it be a necessity, for how else will the rich become rich if they do not have the poor to depend upon, it stands to reason that the rich must manufacture more poor if they are to grow more rich! The rich become rich by *taking* and the poor by *giving*. The rich take the labour o' the poor in return for a pittance calculated to make poor men near starve, so that they will fight each other for the privilege o' giving o' the labour the rich man depends upon!'

'But Mary be not like that, Ikey!' Hawk protested. 'There are none that starve who work at the Potato Factory!'

'Aye, Mary be different,' Ikey admitted. 'But you observe, she does not grow rich.'

'That be because she has no capital to buy the machinery she must have if she is to have a proper brewery!'

'Ha! Precisely and exactly and definitely and most certainly! My point precisely, my dear! If she should give the men less and not feed their brats ... If she should employ children for tuppence a day and not men for a shilling, she might soon have the capital to expand.'

'I should not wish her to do that!' Hawk replied, his hands working furiously. 'Her conscience and mine would not allow it!'

'Conscience?' Ikey said, surprised, one eyebrow raised. 'That be a luxury you be most fortunate to afford, my dear! That be the single greatest gift and also the worst advantage Mary has given you.'

'Why then must I learn of these ways of yours?' Hawk asked.

'You mean the ways o' perfidy?'

Hawk nodded his head.

'The perfidious man be the normal you will come across in life. Everyone you will meet in business will seek advantage over you, my dear. So you must learn to recognise the cheat and the liar and unless you know the manner of his scam, the method of his ways o' doing you down, you will be beaten. If you knows how a man should cheat at cribbage you will call him early. To know the scam is to make sure it does not happen to you.' Ikey laughed. 'Ah, my dear Hawk, you do not have the character to be a liar and a cheat!' Ikey paused. 'My only wish is that I teach you enough o' the perfidy o' mankind to prevent you from being a fool.'

'You wish me to be hard but fair in my dealings?' Hawk asked with his hands.

'Aye, but also to remember the first rule o' doing business, my dear!'

Hawk had a peculiar way of raising his left eyebrow when he wished Ikey to explain further.

'Always leave a little salt on the bread!' Ikey explained.

Hawk's eyebrow arched again and Ikey wondered how best he should answer him. He found Hawk's demeanour most strange, for at thirteen the boy had developed an acute sense of fairness and a natural dignity, and already the men who worked at the Potato Factory deferred to him willingly and took their instruction from him without the slightest hint of malice. These were rough men, born to the notion that the possessor of a black skin was the most inferior man who walked upon the earth's surface, yet they seemed to love the boy and eagerly sought his smile.

Though the kidnapping greatly saddened him, and his love for Tommo had left some part of him permanently distraught, Hawk retained no bitterness from the terrible experience with Mad Dog Mulray. The men who worked for Mary seemed to sense this and respected him accordingly.

Ikey had been pushed into the street from the moment he could crawl about in the courts and alleys of the rookery, and only a minority of the children who had crawled in the filth with him had survived childhood. As soon as he could run from authority he was sent out to scavenge and pilfer what he could from the streets. He had learned from the very beginning that the means of life were desperately scarce and that they went to the toughest. Cunning, quick responses to opportunity and danger, freedom from scruples and courage were the ingredients of survival. The costermonger with his fly weights made a living while the drudging bricklayer went under. The prostitute on the corner fed her children while those of the bloody-fingered woman who stitched gunny sacks starved to death. In a few fortunate minutes a gang of urchins could rob a badly loaded dray and earn more from the goods than their parents could earn in a week of labouring.

Ikey accepted the terms of this society where only the strong survived. But on the first day his father had pushed him onto the streets to trade with a tray of oranges and lemons he had been confronted with a new conundrum, a contradiction to all he instinctively knew in the game of survival. A rabbi had stopped the small boy and enquired as to the cost of a lemon.

'That'll be a ha'penny to you, rabbi,' Ikey had answered cheerily.

'Vun lemon is vun half penny? For twelve, how much?'

'Sixpence o' course!' Ikey replied cheekily. The reb was a foreigner and even if he was a rabbi he must be treated with a certain English disdain.

'Ja, so, let me see, I take only vun lemon for vun halfpenny, or thirteen for six pennies?'

'No, sir, rabbi, that be wrong! Them lemons be twelve for a sixpence!' Ikey corrected.

The rabbi sighed. 'So, tell me, my boy. You like to sell twelve lemons or vun lemon?'

'Twelve o' course, stands to reason, don't it?'

'Then ve negotiate! You know vot is negotiate?'

Ikey shook his head. 'Does it mean you be tryin' to get the better o' me, sir?'

'Very goet! You are a schmart boyski. But no, negotiate, it means I must vin and you also, you must vin!' The rabbi spread his hands. 'You sell more lemons and also, I get more lemons!' He smiled. 'You understand, ja?'

'But you gets one lemon what you 'asn't paid for!' Ikey said, indignant at the thought that the rabbi was trying to bamboozle him.

'Alvays you leave a little salt on the bread, my boy. Vun lemon costs vun half penny, twelve lemons cost six pennies, then vun lemon you give to me, that is not a lemon for buyink, that is a lemon for negotiatink, that is the little salt alvays you leave on the bread, so ven I vant lemons, I come back and you sell alvays more lemons to the rabbi, ja?'

'I tell you what, rabbi, 'ow's about twelve lemons and an orange for a sixpence, what say you?'

The rabbi laughed. 'Already you learnink goet to negotiate,' he said as he took the orange which cost a farthing and the dozen lemons and paid Ikey the sixpence.

'Always leave a little salt on the bread' had become an important lesson in Ikey's life. From the beginning he had always paid slightly above the going price for the stolen merchandise brought to him and it had played a significant part in earning him the title Prince of Fences. The rabbi had been correct, his 'customers' stayed loyal and always returned to him. Ikey had come to believe that 'leaving a little salt' was the reason for his good fortune and the source of his continued good luck. Ikey, like most villains, was a superstitious man who believed that luck is maintained through peculiar rituals and consistent behaviour.

And so Ikey explained the theory of a little salt on the bread to Hawk, who seemed to like this lesson more than most and made Ikey write it out on a slip of paper for him so that he might copy it into his diary. Ikey quickly wrote: *Remember, always leave a little salt on the bread.*

It was about this time that an event occurred which would change forever the lives of future generations of both families who carried the name Solomon.

Like most great changes there was very little to herald its coming, for it emerged out of a simple puzzle which Ikey, in a moment of mischief and amusement, had composed to bemuse Hawk, although, as with most things concerning Ikey Solomon, it contained a hidden agenda.

Ikey was becoming increasingly rheumatic and found his nightly sojourn around the Wapping and waterfront areas especially difficult. On some nights, out of weariness of step, he would remain too long in one place, and therefore be unable to complete his rounds on time or even to arrive at the Whale Fishery. More and more he relied on Hawk to help him at the races and afterwards he went straight to bed so that he could rise at midnight to do his rounds. He also became more preoccupied with death and was a regular and conscientious member of the new Hobart synagogue.

Ikey also realised that if Hannah and David and his two sons in New South Wales were determined to wait until his death so that they might claim the entire contents of the Whitechapel safe, he was left with a most peculiar dilemma: how to convey his combination number without telling either Mary or Hawk about the safe until he was certain he was on his death bed. It was still his greatest hope that Hannah and David would relent and agree to a fifty-fifty share of the safe and that Hannah would entrust the opening of the safe to his youngest son Mark and to Hawk, who would each separately hold a half of the combination.

Ikey had several times made this proposal only to have it rejected by Hannah and David. They insisted on the eight-part split and grew increasingly confident that they would soon be in possession of the entire contents as Sarah would often express her genuine concern at Ikey's frailty when she visited her family in New Norfolk.

Hannah knew also that Ikey could not openly leave his half of the treasure to Mary or her nigger brat in his will for fear that the authorities might confiscate it. Nor could he write his combination into it because, as his wife, she had the right to attend the reading of the will so that, even if Ikey told Mary or Hawk his combination number, without the addition of her own they could do nothing.

David had once suggested, if only to spite them, that Ikey on his death bed might go to the authorities about the Whitechapel safe, so that they received nothing. Hannah knew this to be impossible given Ikey's nature. And in this she was right. Even if Ikey had not wished to leave his share of the treasure to Mary and Hawk, he could never bring himself to allow the laws of England to triumph over him, even though he should be dead. Rather a thousand times the perfidious Hannah and her odious sons than the greedy coffers of England.

Ikey would have liked to tell Mary about the safe and its contents but he dared not do so for fear she would immediately know that the incident where David had presented him with the severed finger of an Aboriginal child had been brought about, not by his son's demand for Mary's brewery, but because of Ikey's reluctance to trust them with his half of the combination to the Whitechapel safe.

Though it was not possible to prove, Mary strongly believed that Hannah and David were more than mere scheming opportunists when they set up the finger scam. She was convinced they had genuinely attempted to kidnap Tommo and Hawk and their plan had gone disastrously wrong. Though Ikey did not admit it, he, too, had always felt that David knew a great deal more than he had said.

But if Ikey did not have the courage to face Mary's wrath, he knew that before he died he must confess his guilt and tell her of the reward he was to give her as penance. To this end Ikey taught Hawk how to value jewellery and as much as he could about the characteristics of each precious stone and how they should be inspected for purity. He purchased a set of gold scales and a testing kit and drilled Hawk in the weighing of gold and silver and in the testing of both to see if they were genuine and of what quality, though Hawk often declared himself puzzled that Ikey should wish him to be so interested. One day, while Ikey was explaining the valuation of diamonds and carefully drawing the various cuts of the stones, Hawk signalled that he was impatient with the lesson and wished it to end.

'Please, my dear, you *must* pay attention!' Ikey had said in something of a panic. 'There is a fortune waiting for you in this knowledge!'

'Why?' Hawk signalled, his face sullen. 'I shall be a brewer. What has the cut of diamonds got to do with the brewing of ale?'

'If you are to get the machinery you will need, and

806

own the land to grow your own hops as you must if you are to succeed, you will pay very close attention to what I say,' Ikey insisted.

Hawk was seldom impolite in his manners and though he knew Ikey to be a villain, he loved him, but now he had had enough. 'I grow weary of this stuff, Ikey. Mary says our great good fortune, our luck is in hard work and the making of good beer, that this is luck more than enough!'

Ikey looked at Hawk and then said quietly, 'Hawk, I shall give you a riddle and you *must* believe me, should you find the answer you may be halfway to owning a fortune which be a king's ransom!'

Hawk, who was very adroit at listening to his stomach, hearing with his eyes and seeing with his ears as Ikey had taught him, knew with absolute certainty that Ikey was no longer playing, or even attempting to teach him yet another tedious lesson. He indicated to Ikey that he was listening most carefully.

Ikey relaxed, regaining his composure. 'Ah, my dear, you 'ave done well, very well and exceedingly well and weller than most wells and better than most bests. I be most proud, you has the same affinity with numbers as Mary and perhaps you will become even better in time.' Ikey paused and appeared to be momentarily lost in thought, then he looked up at Hawk. 'Words can become numbers, just like the signs you now use to talk to me can become words. There are secret, silent numbers to be found in the most innocent words if you know how to decipher them. A code o' numbers to unlock a fortune!'

Hawk became immediately interested, for not only did he sense that Ikey had never been more serious, but that he was about to give him a riddle. There was nothing he loved more than solving one of his mentor's riddles. His eyebrow arched and his hands motioned Ikey to continue.

'Here is a riddle made to a poem to test you beyond all solving, my dear. But should you solve it, it be half o' the key to a great fortune.'

'And then shall I have the other half when I have solved this riddle?' Hawk asked wide-eyed.

Ikey shook his head. 'I cannot say, but without the answer to my riddle you have no hope. With it, there be a great chance that you will gain the fortune for Mary and yourself.'

'Will you give it to me then?' Hawk's hands shook with excitement as he made the words with his fingers.

Ikey cackled the way he had done when Hawk and Tommo were young and a new lesson was about to come from him, and he clapped his hands and rolled his eyes in secret congratulation at his own cleverness, just like old times, then he began to recite.

> *If perchance I should die*
> *And come to God's eternal rest*
> *Let me in plain pine coffin lie*
> *Hands clasped upon my breast.*

> *Let a minyan say kaddish for me*
> *in words ancient and profound*
> *In a chapel white, there safe it be*
> *'neath familiar English ground.*

> *On my flesh these words be writ:*
> *'To my one and only blue dove'*
> *To this cipher be one more to fit*
> *then add roses ringed to love.*

Hawk had never before been confronted with a riddle so elaborate or beautiful of rhyme and he fetched quill and paper and made Ikey write it down so that he knew every word was correct.

'Remember always,' Ikey chuckled as he read what he'd written, 'the answer is at arm's length and words can have two meanings!'

'Numbers from the words and words what has two meanings?' Hawk signalled, wanting to be sure he had it right.

'Aye, words what mean other things and numbers from words, if all is done properly you will be left with a three digit number! There be three more to come, six in all!' With this said, Ikey would co-operate no further.

Hawk worked for several weeks in what time he could spare on the riddle, but came no closer to solving it. Finally he had returned to Ikey, but he was evasive, other than to say, 'It be about London'.

This helped Hawk very little, for while Ikey had talked a great deal to the two boys about London when they'd been younger, he had only the knowledge of what he'd read about the great city and no more.

Finally, one evening when he and Mary were walking home from Strickland Falls after work, ashamed at his ineptitude, Hawk begged Mary to help him, telling her about the riddle and explaining what Ikey had said about it being half of a great treasure.

Hawk at fourteen was considered a grown man. He already towered above Mary and stood fully six feet. With his serious demeanour, many took him to be much older. He worked a full day with Mary at the Potato Factory and was reliable and hardworking, though

Mary sometimes wished he were not quite so serious-minded for a young lad.

Hawk handed her the slip of paper with the poem and Mary, who had much on her mind, read it somewhat cursorily and was unable to venture an opinion so she simply said, 'It be a nice poem, lovey.' Though in truth she thought it somewhat maudlin and typical of Ikey's increasing preoccupation with his own demise.

'What's a minyan and kaddish?' Hawk signalled.

'It's Jewish religion, a minyan be ten men what's got to be present when a Jew dies and kaddish, that be the prayer they says at the funeral,' Mary replied.

'Ikey said it be about London and a treasure, a treasure in London,' Hawk repeated and then asked with his hands, walking backwards so that Mary could plainly see his fingers, 'Did he ever say anything about a treasure to you?'

Mary shook her head. 'Careful, you'll fall,' she cautioned, then with Hawk once again at her side added, 'Ikey be very tight-fisted about money, tight-mouthed too, tight everything!' She laughed. 'He often stored stolen goods in all sorts o' places when he was prince o' all of London's fences.' Mary stopped, her head to one side and seemed to be thinking. 'Maybe it be the number of a house where he's got something stashed?' Then she added ruefully, 'Well, it ain't much use to him now. He can't go back to find it and he won't trust any o' his sons not to tell Hannah, so he might as well ...' She stopped suddenly in mid-sentence and pointed to Hawk and said softly, '... send you!'

Hawk looked startled at the idea. 'What do you mean?'

Mary did not answer for a moment, then she shrugged. 'I don't know, lovey, I'll think about it tonight. Make a copy o' this for me, will you?' She handed the poem back to Hawk.

Hawk nodded though he looked anxious. 'You'll tell me what you thinks, won't you? I be most anxious to be the one to work out the riddle.'

Mary laughed. 'Don't worry, lovey, it be more'n a mouthful, believe me. My stomach tells me Ikey be onto something what ain't no nursery rhyme.'

'A three digit number has to come out of all this,' Hawk said finally, folding the poem and placing it back in his pocket.

That night, after she had made Ikey his tea, Mary sat at the kitchen table with the poem and read it more carefully. The first incongruity which struck her were the words 'chapel white'. In the context of a Jewish funeral these seemed strangely Christian. Why would someone of the Jewish persuasion use them about his funeral?

'Chapel white?' she said aloud. She had passed the Duke Street synagogue a thousand times as a child and chapel to her was a word used by the Wesleyans and not at all appropriate to the ancient, gloomy building the Jews used as their church. Almost the moment she thought this the words transposed in her mind. 'White-chapel!' she exclaimed triumphantly, clicking her fingers. Mary's nimble mind now began to sniff at the words in quite a different way. Long after her usual time for bed she had isolated a group of words which could have a double meaning or be fitted together: *safe, beneath, familiar* and finally, *ground*. She was too tired to continue and finally went to bed.

The next morning after breakfast, when Ikey had left to totter down to his cottage in Elizabeth Street to sleep, she gave the words to Hawk.

'Work with these, there may be something,' she said explaining the link between the words 'chapel' and 'white', into the word Whitechapel. Several days passed and one morning Hawk came into Mary's office at Strickland Falls and gave her his brilliant smile. Then he started to signal, his fingers working frantically.

'The safe in Whitechapel containing Ikey's fortune is within the house beneath the ground!'

'Huh?' Mary said, taken aback. 'What you mean, lovey?'

Hawk handed Mary a piece of paper and Mary saw that it was written somewhat as an equation. But first he had transcribed the lines:

In a chapel white, there safe it be
'neath familiar English ground

Safe = Safety + Iron box. 'Neath = under. Familiar = family. English = London. Ground = soil + below surface.

Beneath these careful notations Hawk had written in his beautiful hand.

Translation: The treasure be in a safe below the ground in the family home in Whitechapel.

'Good boy!' Mary beamed, delighted with her son's tenacity and careful analysis. But then she added, 'That be the second verse, what of the first and the third?'

Hawk signalled that he was convinced that the first verse was meant to deflect any suspicion of a hidden meaning and meant exactly what it said. Then he frowned. 'Last verse be most difficult, Mama.'

Mary set aside her barley mash register, a ledger in which she kept the temperature of the barley mash as it came out of the crusher. 'Here, let me see that poem again?' she asked.

Hawk produced the poem and Mary read the first and the last verse. She agreed that with the first verse Ikey had meant to mislead by the very fact that there was no ambiguity within it. But the last verse sounded very strange and she read it aloud.

> *On my flesh these words be writ:*
> *'To my one and only blue dove'*
> *To this cipher be one more to fit*
> *then add roses ringed to love.*

Mary pointed to the word 'cipher'. 'This verse is where the numbers be,' then added, 'but what numbers? Why does we need numbers?'

Hawk smiled and Mary was delighted at his sudden lightness of mood. 'Like the safe you bought, Mama, they be a combination!' he signalled.

'Oh my Gawd!' Mary cried. 'You're right, you're dead right!' Her heart started to beat so loudly that she could hear the thumping of it in her throat. 'If we can get the numbers from the verse then we've got the combination to the safe, the fortune!'

Hawk shook his head slowly.

'What you mean?' Mary cried, disappointment written on her face.

Hawk's fingers spoke. 'Half, we got half the combination.'

'Half?'

'Ikey said the poem only be half, three digits. Six is what's needed.'

Mary had in the past often wondered about Ikey's persistence with his family, for whom, with the exception of Sarah and perhaps Ann, she knew he had a general dislike, as well as a great loathing for Hannah and in recent years David. His periodical visits to New Norfolk, taken with their history with the Newmans and the debacle when he had come out of Port Arthur, had never made any sense. Ikey was a loner by nature and his pretence at being a diligent and caring family man had never convinced Mary in the least. She had often urged him, for his own peace of mind, to cut his ties completely, but he had always made the same reply: 'We have unfinished business, my dear.'

Now Mary knew what it was. Hannah had one half of the combination to the safe in their home in White-chapel and would not part with it.

Mary urged Hawk to keep trying to isolate the numbers as she herself would, but admitted, 'Alas, I doesn't know nothing useful about the last verse, save that it should lead to three numbers, but if we should somehow find them then you must not tell Ikey!'

Mary realised that if she had half of the combination she had the means to avenge herself on Hannah Solomon. But she simply told Hawk of the probability that Hannah possessed the second set of numbers. Hawk looked disappointed. 'It don't matter, lovey. We will find a way. Trust Mama! It be most terrible important you stay stum! Ikey must not know, we tell him nothing, all right?'

Hawk nodded, his fingers working fast and his face took on a look of determination. 'I shall solve it or die!'

Mary grabbed him and kissed him. 'Life is too precious that you should die for money, lovey. If you has to die, then die for love!'

'Like you was prepared to do for me?' Hawk's fingers spoke and his eyes were serious.

Tears rolled down Mary's cheeks. 'You and Tommo, gladly,' she whispered.

'Mama, we shall find Tommo too!' Hawk's fingers said. 'And I shall never tell Ikey if we should find the numbers.'

Mary and Hawk became obsessed with solving the riddle of the last verse and were hardly able to wait for Ikey to go to his ledgers before they began each evening.

The third line in the last verse, 'To this cipher be one more to fit', seemed at first obvious to Mary. The second set of numbers, Hannah's set, were the *one more to fit*, which would give them the total combination. Hawk agreed that this might be so, but then logically the numbers must come from the first two lines in the last verse and, in particular, from the second line, 'To my one and only blue dove', as the first line of the last verse was simply a location of some sort and the final line, 'then add roses ringed to love', was an addition to whatever discovery or number they would make in the second line.

On my flesh these words be writ: = **location**
'To my one and only blue dove' = **key to numbers**
To this cipher be one more to fit = **Hannah's combination**
then add roses ringed to love = **additional information.**

815

It did not take them long to realise that the line 'On my flesh these words be writ' must represent a tattoo worn by Ikey, and while Mary had slept with Ikey perhaps a dozen times while they were joint owners of Egyptian Mary's she did not remember any such tattoo. However, she admitted to herself that the dreaded deed took place in the dark and that he might quite possibly have obtained the tattoo while a convict in Van Diemen's Land, in which case she would know nothing about it.

However, this did not overly concern them, they simply assumed that the words were written on Ikey's flesh, as all the other information made sense, and worked on the second line for the numbers they were now convinced it contained.

Both Mary and Hawk were practised in leaps of logic and exceedingly good at numbers, and they soon worked out a logical way of converting the line 'To my one and only blue dove' into numbers. They took each letter and equated it with its number in the alphabet, for example the letter $A = 1$, $B = 2$, $Z = 26$, and so on. They gave each letter in the line its appropriate number and the total came to 276. If they reduced this number down to the next lowest it became $2 + 7 + 6 = 15$ and if they reduced this further, it became $1 + 5 = 6$. As they already knew the final result must have three digits the combination number could only be 276.

But they were both too logical of mind to believe this, for it made the final line 'then add roses ringed to love' redundant to the solution. Both knew Ikey's mind was too tidy for this and he would not simply add a gratuitous line to complete the rhyme. The final line must be one of great importance to the whole.

816

But they could go no further and after a few more weeks were forced to abandon their efforts, almost convincing themselves that the number must be 276. Finally Mary capitulated and gave Hawk permission to ask Ikey if the number was 276. Though she insisted he tell Ikey that he had reached this conclusion on his own, and if Ikey asked if she was involved to deny it. This way, Mary concluded, Ikey would tell the truth.

It was now six months since Ikey had posed the riddle and he was most impressed when Hawk told him he had solved it.

'I hope you are right, my dear!' Ikey said.

Hawk was ready to listen to his stomach, hear with his eyes and see with his ears. He handed Ikey a piece of paper with the numbers 276 written on it and Ikey laughed and shook his head slowly. 'No, my dear, you are quite wrong!'

Hawk, close to tears from frustration, bowed his head in bewilderment.

'I told you, the answer be at arm's length,' Ikey said, smiling. But again he would say no more.

At about this time a misfortune struck Mary, for she could not obtain sufficient hops from local sources to meet her needs and she was forced to buy expensive imported hops from Kent. This meant she must put up her beer prices, which was very much to her disadvantage, for times were still hard in the colony and competition most keen.

At first Mary believed it was the local brewers trying to make things difficult for her, but eventually she discovered it was yet another of Hannah's tricks. During this period when the supply of local hops had dried up, even though the season had been a good one, Ikey made yet another visit to New Norfolk and was depressed for days after his return. Mary then discovered that George Madden had cornered the entire market for the distribution of hops in the colony and it was he who would not sell to her. Mary was quick enough to realise that this decision was yet another pressure from Hannah for Ikey's half of the combination. Mary confronted Ikey with the reason for his visit and he admitted that this was what had happened, but again avoided the issue of the combination and explained that Hannah was still avenging herself on Mary for stealing the affection of her children and the love of her husband. Though he conceded that, under the circumstances, this was a somewhat bizarre explanation, he insisted it was true.

Mary, who was never easily beaten, determined that she would rent land and grow her own hops. She made the decision to use what few assets she had to send Hawk to England, to the county of Kent, so he could learn the most superior method of growing hops and return with all the varieties of seed he could obtain. She had only the money to pay his fare but if, when he returned, she could rent land with an agreement to buy it one day, she would never again be compromised by the likes of George Madden. Hawk was nearly fifteen years old and Mary had no hesitation in placing her trust in him, though she had a second reason for sending him to England.

Hawk still carried an absolute conviction in his heart that Tommo was alive.

'If Tommo were dead, Mama, I should know!' he would insist, and as he grew older the certainty that his brother was alive became even stronger. On several occasions he had 'spoken' to Mary about going to find him. Hawk now stood well over six feet and was enormously strong, and Mary knew that he was old enough to leave her. This single determination, to find his brother, was more powerful than anything else in his life. Hawk was all Mary had and loved and she thought that by sending him over to England for two years she would delay losing him.

Mary also had a plan which she revealed to Hawk on the morning of his departure. She handed him a brass key, a duplicate of one she had found some years before in Ikey's overcoat, which she knew to be the key to Ikey's Whitechapel home. She urged Hawk to use it to enter the house.

'We must determine whether a safe exists beneath the floor,' Mary said.

Hawk sighed and then signalled, 'But, Mama, we have come to a dead end, what is the use? We do not know Ikey's numbers, and if we did, it is only half the combination.'

Mary touched him on the sleeve. 'Ikey is not a young man and I believe he will give me his part of the combination if he thinks he is going to die. If there be a treasure he will do anything so as to avoid Hannah having it all, that much I know for certain.' She suddenly paused and announced dramatically, 'And I has the second half!' Mary relished the look of amazement which appeared on Hawk's face. 'That's right, I knows Hannah's combination, Ann give it to me when she were a little 'un in the orphanage! David Solomon were always writing it on his slate and working with it on the abacus. Ann told me it were a number their mother give them what they must never, never forget in case she should die! The number eight hundred and sixteen!'

Hawk signalled the numbers, '816?'

Mary nodded. 'Just you make sure there be a safe in that house, lovey.'

Ikey was terribly distraught at the news of Hawk's departure to England, for he was convinced he would not live long enough to see Hawk again.

Hawk was able to comfort him a little by promising to spend his last day helping Ikey at the Saturday races, even though he would rather have climbed the mountain and spent time with Mary. Hawk was by now doing most of the work at the races and he knew Ikey could not manage without him. This would be Ikey's last day as a bookmaker. Poor Ikey had given up his nocturnal wandering, unable to manage the walking. The races were his only remaining pleasure.

Hawk would take a sad memory away with him of this last day with Ikey. Late in the afternoon, while Hawk's back was turned, a drunken punter accosted Ikey, accusing him of cheating, and knocked him to the ground. Hawk arrived moments later and picked the drunk off Ikey's prostrate and squealing body, giving the man a cuff across the side of the head which sent him spinning to the ground. Hawk picked up the sobbing Ikey. The shoulder of his ancient coat and also the sleeve of his shirt had been torn in the struggle so that his thin white arm hung bare. It was then that Hawk saw the tattoo. It was of two blue doves surrounded by a garland of red roses, and in a ribbon across the top of the circle of roses was the legend, *To my one and only blue dove.*

Hawk took scant notice of this at the time, being more concerned for Ikey's welfare. Later, when he thought about it, he simply concluded that their guess had been correct and Ikey wore a tattoo with words from the poem. He told Mary of his findings and they congratulated each other on their perspicacity, but otherwise decided the information was of no additional help.

With Hawk away, Ikey seemed to fade and in the next year he progressively became an old man much dependent on his daughter Sarah, and on Mary, who was increasingly under pressure as local hops were being denied her and imported stock was not always available.

Ikey decided to relent, and acknowledged that one-eighth of his fortune was still sufficient to buy a large tract of land and give Mary the financial independence she desperately needed if she were to survive. He felt it was time to settle his moral debts before he died and though he was deeply humiliated that Hannah and David Solomon had finally beaten him, Ikey's love for Mary was such that he was prepared to compromise. But he decided not to tell Mary until he had the one-eighth portion safely deposited in her bank account.

Ikey proposed that one of Hannah's sons, he preferred it to be Mark, should take a ship to England with her combination to the safe, while he would instruct Hawk by letter of his combination and the whereabouts of the safe.

Hannah was adamant that David go. It delighted her to think that he was to be pitted against a fifteen-year-old nigger mute, and she felt sure David would not allow Hawk to win even an eighth of the value of the treasure. But she insisted that David leave immediately, that was in two days' time, when the *Midas*, a convict ship, was leaving Hobart bound for London.

Hannah's reason for this was so that Ikey's letter to Hawk could not arrive in London before David and thus allow Hawk to get to the safe first and have it removed, or worse, attempt to open it. Ikey argued that the safe could not be opened without the combination, even if it were given over to the Bank of England. Its removal would involve the demolition of a wall of the house and, as the safe was set in concrete, it would require a very large dock crane and a gang of men to lift it out of the ground. Nevertheless, Hannah was resolute that Ikey's letter must go on the same ship as David Solomon so that the two could meet and visit the Whitechapel house on the same day and simultaneously open the safe.

Ikey smelt a rat and thought David would bribe the captain to give him Ikey's letter, so he did not entrust it to the captain but gave it instead to the ship's chaplain whom he swore to secrecy and added further to the man of God's integrity with a nice little stipend for his ministry.

Chapter Thirty-eight

On a day of persistent drizzle, with swirling clouds obscuring the top of the great mountain, the *Midas* sailed from the river port bound for London. On board was Mr David Solomon, who had been carefully drilled in the description of each item in the safe and the value of the gem stones. Though Hannah was not as expert as Ikey in this she had a keen eye for appraisal and knew each precious stone individually. Also in his luggage was a set of scales for weighing gold and a new pistol of American design.

The voyage home to England was uneventful and the *Midas* berthed at Gravesend, where David immediately sent a letter by courier to Hawk at the hop farm where he worked asking him to come to London at once to meet him on board the *Midas*. On the same day Hawk received a message from the ship's chaplain that a letter awaited him from Mr Ikey Solomon which he was instructed to hand over to him personally on board.

When Hawk opened the letter Ikey was already dead. He had passed away not two weeks previously. His funeral had been a mixed affair, one of the first few to take place in the Hobart synagogue which had been open for five years. One hundred and eighty of the male Jews in Hobart Town attended Ikey's funeral and filled the tiny synagogue to overflowing. As well, standing outside, was a crowd which the polite society of Hobart found most undesirable. Publicans and whores, touts, con men, cock fight proprietors, sly grog merchants and most of the racing fraternity of Hobart Town stood outside the little synagogue.

The minyan of ten good men consisted of Hobart's most prominent Jews: Philip Levy, Samuel Moses, Jacob Frankel, Abraham Reuban, Judah Solomon, Isaac Feldman, Edward Magnus, Abraham Wolff, Isaac Marks and Philip Phillips. Ikey was buried in the Jewish cemetery according to the ancient rites and beliefs of his own people and though Mark and Moses attended, as only men are allowed to attend an orthodox funeral, Sarah stood outside the cemetery with Mary and both wept, while Hannah stood apart with Ann, dry-eyed and triumphant.

What transpired between Hawk and David is best revealed in the account David Solomon gave to his mother on his return to Van Diemen's Land. He told how the *dumb nigger* nodded in agreement when he asked if Ikey's letter contained his half of the combination to the Whitechapel safe. Then he proposed they both inspect and test the safe to ensure it had not been tampered with, and then remain present to observe while each worked his part of the combination. Finally, that the coin in the form of gold sovereigns be divided with one in eight going to Hawk, while the gold and silver ingots be weighed and that Hawk should receive one-eighth part of the total weight of each. The gem stones would be divided into lots of eight and then they would toss a coin to see who would have the first pick from each lot. To all this the *schwarzer* had silently agreed.

David then told of how they had set out in a carriage to the house in Whitechapel in the company of the shipwright from the *Midas* and his bag of tools. The shipwright had removed the heavy planking from the front door and then left. It was a miserably cold February day when the two men, each carrying a bull's eye lamp, entered the house, which had stood empty for over twenty years.

They moved along the dusty hallway, brushing aside cobwebs and going straight to the scullery, for both had a location plan, Hawk from Ikey and David from Hannah. David opened the closely fitted scullery door with a key given to him by his mother which had hung about her neck as long as he could remember.

The room contained no windows and the air within it was most stale, though surprisingly free of dust. While Hawk Solomon held the bull's eye lamp, David read the instructions which triggered the false nails in the floorboards, and carefully lifted each board until the door of the huge safe beneath was clearly exposed. David stooped down and tested the handle of the safe, giving it a firm pull. It was obviously locked. He rose and allowed Hawk to do the same.

David confessed that at this point his heart was pounding and his face must have shown his excitement, though he couldn't speak for the nigger, 'it being dark an' all'. His hands shook as he tried to hold the torch steady for Hawk as the black boy's numbers were the first part of the combination. Hawk had dialled quickly, his huge hands graceful to the touch and the numbers

690 appeared and then a distinct click sounded. Then Hawk rose and placed his torch on a shelf so that the room was dimly lit and then held David's torch directed at the wheels of the combination lock. David, his hands trembling, dialled 816 whereupon there was another click. For a moment all that could be heard was their rapid breathing, Hawk's steady and David's coming fast as though he were short of breath. Hawk tapped David on the shoulder and indicated that he should be the one to open the safe. David pulled, but nothing happened, the door remained shut.

'Oh Jesus!' David exclaimed.

Hawk pushed him aside and handed him back his bull's eye lamp, then he took the handle in both hands and pulled the safe open in a single jerk.

David would tell Hannah how he was not sure what might meet his eyes, perhaps small boxes and rotting canvas bags spilling over with gold and silver and precious jewels. But what they both witnessed was an empty safe, except for a single envelope sealed with red wax. It was addressed to 'The Solomon Family'.

Hawk, in his 'telling' of the same story to Mary, told how David was the first to react, dropping the lamp and commencing to hop from one foot to the other, wailing and moaning and tearing at his hair, while Hawk stood silent, his head bent, one hand covering his face though he continued to follow David by looking through his fingers.

Hawk told how he finally went down on one knee and reached into the empty safe to retrieve the envelope which he handed to David, whose hands were shaking so that he could barely break open the seal. Hawk had noticed a slight bulge in the envelope and now David removed from it a man's gold signet ring heavily crusted with diamonds and rubies. Then he withdrew the note and attempted to open its careful folds, but his fist had tightened around the ring and his remaining hand was shaking too violently to do so.

David, sobbing, handed the note to Hawk.

'Read it! Fer Chrissakes, read it!' he screamed at Hawk, forgetting that Hawk was a mute. Hawk slowly opened the note and held it up to David to read, without looking at it. In Ikey's handwriting were the words:

Remember, always leave a little salt on the bread.

'What can it mean?' David sobbed. 'Whatever can it mean?' Then he fell on his knees. 'We are done for! My family is destroyed!' he wailed. 'Ikey Solomon has beaten us all hands up!'

Later that evening, Hawk wrote a letter to Mary.

My Ever Dear Mama,

Today I have met David Solomon, the son of Mistress Hannah Solomon of New Norfolk, whom I know to be Ikey's estranged wife. With him we have visited the premises of Ikey's old residence in Petticoat Lane, Whitechapel, on an errand entrusted to me by Ikey in a letter received this day of which he tells me you are unaware and in which he begs me now to acquaint you of the contents, as he is not sure that he will remain alive in the many months for it to arrive in England. Ikey is ever the pessimist and I expect he is as well as ever.

However, I am happy to inform you that the letter instructed me to go with Master David Solomon, recently embarked from the ship, Midas, to the house in Whitechapel where Master Solomon had been acquainted by his mother as to the whereabouts of a certain safe hidden beneath the scullery floor.

Included in Ikey's letter was the combination number which I was to use upon the safe. Whereupon Master David, also bearing a number given to him by Mistress Solomon, would add his to make the complete combination, the two numbers to effect the opening of the safe.

Ikey's letter further instructed me to take a one-eighth share of the contents of the safe and then to return to Van Diemen's Land where I was to bring this portion to you. Though none of this is to be known by you. Alas, I cannot conceal it from you and I have not given Ikey my word that I would not tell you first in a letter, as he wishes me simply to arrive home as a surprise.

Ikey's letter also included the deeds of the house and instructed that I should sell the property and also return the money to you keeping a ten percentum for myself for expenses while I remain in England. A most generous offer which I shall accept with gratitude.

Alas, I regret to inform you that the safe when opened was empty, that is, save for a sealed envelope. When opened it contained an envelope addressed in printed writing to The Solomon Family, the note within contained only these words in Ikey's handwriting:

'Always remember to leave a little salt on the bread.'

You will recall it is a saying much favoured by Ikey.

And now to business which I trust will always remain only between you and I, dear Mama.

You will remember the two lines in the riddle poem:

'To this cipher be one more to fit
&
then add roses ringed to love'

By much speculation it came to me some months ago that 'To this cipher' meant not Hannah's part of the combination but only one number, and not three. The lowest number when the number 276 is finally reduced is $2 + 7 + 6 = 15$ and $1 + 5 = 6$. I took the number for the line 'To my one and only blue dove' to be six.

Then again, by working some weeks in my spare time on the conundrum I came one evening to the notion that the ring of roses seen surrounding Ikey's tattoo was in the shape of a zero, the cipher '0'. I now had two numbers, six and zero. But it was the final one which took me near to despair, until some weeks ago I chanced to read the final line in a different manner, 'then add roses ringed ... to love'. The third number was, I concluded, contained in the reduction to a single number of the sum of the numbers made of the word, love!

These I soon worked out, which you will see from

using the alphabet code are: 12 + 15 + 22 + 5 = 54. When reduced to the lowest possible number, that is 4 + 5 = 9. The third number was nine.

I now had three numbers, 6, 0, 9, and the final line tells me clearly that the ring of roses (the '0') is added to the word 'love' so the zero, I surmised, must come after the number nine.

I am pleased to inform you that I concluded the number must be 690. Using the numbers you had given me as being the combination held by Mistress Hannah, I had a sequence complete of 690816. This proved sufficient to open the safe some four weeks before I received Ikey's letter of instruction when David Solomon and I met on board.

I must inform you that Mr David Solomon has taken ship to return home with the sad news of the missing contents to the safe. This letter will be despatched in the care of the captain of the same vessel, the Mermaid, bound for Hobart. You should expect great unexplained lamentation from Ikey and even perchance some effect to his heart, so you must tell him immediately! You should also anticipate considerable wrath should you meet up with Mistress Hannah, or she come upon Ikey. For with him Master David carries the note from Ikey and a magnificent gold signet ring encrusted with diamonds and rubies, so that Ikey could be true to the message written on the note. I feel sure Ikey will be most pleased at the notion.

I am therefore delighted, my dear Mama, to acquaint you with the news that you are now a woman of most considerable means. The value of the gold and silver in sovereigns and in the form of ingots, and there be a great many precious stones besides, is in the region of one hundred thousand pounds. If you wish you shall have the land in the entire Huon Valley for the cultivation of hops.

I am now exceedingly happy to inform you that I have learned all we will need to know on the tilling, sowing, netting and havesting of hops and have, with my own hands, worked every part of the growing and harvesting process. I have also acquired fifty bags of the finest quality seed.

I now most eagerly and impatiently await your instructions to come home as I must set out upon my search for my brother Tommo.

I remain, your humble, loving and obedient son, Hawk X Solomon.

P.S. I caution you to burn this letter at the conclusion of your having read it. I will include a bank draft for the value of Ikey's house made out in your name, to the Bank of Van Diemen's Land, though I shall find the ten percentum commission most useful. I shall bring you a new Sunday bonnet, some bright ribbon, which I do not suppose you will affect, a winter coat, two of the splendid crinoline gowns so popular with our young Queen Victoria and several pairs of good stout, English boots. H.X.S.

Hawk's letter crossed with one from Mary.

My darling Hawk,
I thank God every day that he has given you to me. Though I confess I also thank the great

mountain as often. My news is both wonderful and sad; Ikey has passed away, though peacefully in his sleep. I wish you to come home at once. This letter is extremely short for there is a ship which leaves for England within the hour.

And now! Our Tommo is back!

This morning at eight of the clock there was a knock at the door and a boy in rags who looked not much more than eleven years old, skinny and of a dirty appearance stood as I opened it. His hair was fair and his eyes a most beautiful blue.

'Mama, I am home, will you take me back?' he asked.

I love you, Hawk Solomon, and we are all together again, Mary, Tommo and Hawk!

Your loving mother,

Mary Abacus.

ALSO BY
BRYCE COURTENAY

THE POWER OF ONE

First with your head and then with your heart...

So says Hoppie Groenewald, boxing champion, to a seven-year-old boy who dreams of being the welterweight champion of the world. For the young Peekay, it is a piece of advice he will carry with him throughout his life.

Born in a South Africa divided by racism and hatred, this one small boy will come to lead all the tribes of Africa. Through enduring friendships with Hymie and Gideon, Peekay gains the strength he needs to win out. And in a final conflict with his childhood enemy, the Judge, Peekay will fight to the death for justice...

Bryce Courtenay's classic bestseller is a story of the triumph of the human spirit – a spellbinding tale for all ages

Tandia

Tandia was overwrought, sitting in the front row of the boxing ring, before the fight began between the man she loved the most and the man she hated the most in the world.

Tandia is a child of all Africa: half Indian, half African, beautiful and intelligent, she is only sixteen when she is first brutalised by the police. Her fear of the white man leads her to join the black resistance movement, where she trains as a terrorist.

Joining her in the fight for justice is the one white man Tandia can trust, the welterweight champion of the world, Peekay. Now the man she loves most must fight their common enemy in order to save both their lives.

A compelling story of good and evil from Australia's most popular storyteller, Bryce Courtenay

APRIL FOOL'S DAY

In the end, love is more important than everything and it will conquer and overcome anything. Or that's how Damon saw it, anyway. Damon wanted a book that talked a lot about love.

Damon Courtenay died on the morning of *April Fool's Day*. In this tribute to his son, Bryce Courtenay lays bare the suffering behind this young man's life. Damon's story is one of lifelong struggle, his love for Celeste, the compassion of a family, and a fight to the end for integrity.

A testimony to the power of love, *April Fool's Day* is also about understanding: how when we confront our worst, we can become our best.

A powerful account of life and death from one of Australia's best authors

The Australian Trilogy

The Potato Factory

Ikey Solomon and his partner in crime, Mary Abacus, make the harsh journey from thriving nineteenth-century London to the convict settlement of Van Diemen's Land. In the back-streets and dives of Hobart Town, Mary builds The Potato Factory, where she plans a new future. But her ambitions are threatened by Ikey's wife, Hannah, her old enemy. As each woman sets out to destroy the other, the families are brought to the edge of disaster.

Tommo & Hawk

Brutally kidnapped and separated in childhood, Tommo and Hawk are reunited in Hobart Town. Together they escape their troubled pasts and set off on a journey into manhood. From whale hunting in the Pacific to the Maori wars in New Zealand, from the Rocks in Sydney to the miners' riots at the goldfields, Tommo and Hawk must learn each other's strengths and weaknesses in order to survive.

Solomon's Song

When Mary Abacus dies, she leaves her business empire in the hands of the warring Solomon family. Hawk Solomon is determined to bring together both sides of the tribe – but it is the new generation who must fight to change the future. Solomons are pitted against Solomons as the families are locked in a bitter struggle that crosses battlefields and continents to reach a powerful conclusion.

WHITETHORN

From Bryce Courtenay comes *Whitethorn* a novel of Africa. The time is 1939: White South Africa is a deeply divided nation with many of the Afrikaner people fanatically opposed to the English.

The world is on the brink of war with South Africa electing to fight for the Allied cause against Germany. Six year old Tom Fitzsaxby finds himself in the Boys Farm, an orphanage in a small remote town in the high mountains, where the Afrikaners side fanatically with Hitler's Germany.

Tom's English name alone proves sufficient for him to be racially ostracised. And so begins some of life's tougher lessons for the small, lonely boy.

Like the whitethorn, one of Africa's most enduring plants, Tom learns how to survive in the harsh climate of racial hatred. Then a terrible event sets him on a journey to ensure that justice is done. On the way, his most unexpected discovery is love.

SYLVIA

'*I am Sylvia Honeyeater; I think myself born around 1196, and this is the story of my life. I am cursed by folk as an optimist and a dreamer, which is a dangerous combination . . .*'

From master storyteller Bryce Courtenay comes the colourful epic of Sylvia Honeyeater, a peasant born in the late 12th century into a Europe torn by religious intolerance. With a singing voice that can literally charm the birds out of the trees, and an acute and questioning mind that refuses to accept unreasoned beliefs, Sylvia leaves her birthplace to embark on a pilgrimage. Together with a band of larger-than-life characters, she sets out to form a Children's Crusade, who plan to travel to the Holy Land.

From a bawdy life as an entertainer in a whorehouse to an austere and frequently cruel existence in a nunnery, she fights to be true to her destiny. In an age when signs and portents were eagerly sought as indications of blessedness, Sylvia finds herself either cast as an instrument of Satan or adored as a miracle-worker. And her mysterious birthmark causes much confusion: can this peasant maid indeed be a chosen messenger?

This is storytelling at its very best. *Sylvia* is a tale of adversity and triumph, of adventure and crusades, and of a beautiful and gifted woman.

THE PERSIMMON TREE

In the heartwood of the sacred persimmon tree is ebony, the hardest, most beautiful of all woods. This is a symbol of life, a heartwood that will outlast everything man can make, a core within that, come what may, cannot be broken and represents our inner strength and divine spirit.

It is 1942 in the Dutch East Indies, and Nick Duncan is a young Australian butterfly collector in search of a single exotic butterfly. With invading Japanese forces coming closer by the day, Nick falls in love with the beguiling Anna Van Heerden.

Yet their time together is brief, as both are forced into separate, dangerous escapes. They plan to reunite and marry in Australia but it is several years before their paths cross again, scarred forever by the dark events of a long, cruel war.

Set against the dramatic backdrop of the Pacific during the Second World War, Bryce Courtenay gives us a story of love and friendship born of war, and the power of each in survival.